t of Dysart

W

KIDNAPPED

KIDNAPPED

BEING MEMOIRS OF THE ADVENTURES OF DAVID BALFOUR IN THE YEAR 1751

HOW HE WAS KIDNAPPED AND CAST AWAY; HIS SUFFERINGS IN A DESERT ISLE; HIS JOURNEY IN THE WILD HIGHLANDS; HIS ACQUAINTANCE WITH ALAN BRECK STEWART AND OTHER NOTORIOUS HIGHLAND JACOBITES; WITH ALL THAT HE SUFFERED AT THE HANDS OF HIS UNCLE, EBENEZER BALFOUR OF SHAWS, FALSELY SO CALLED

WRITTEN BY HIMSELF

AND NOW SET FORTH BY

ROBERT LOUIS STEVENSON

ILLUSTRATED BY

N. C. WYETH

Canadian representatives: General Publishing Co., Ltd.,
30 Lesmill Road, Don Mills, Ontario M3B 2T6.

International representatives: Worldwide Media Services, Inc.,
115 East Twenty-third Street, New York, New York 10010.

9 8 7 6 5 4 3 2 1

Digit on the right indicates the number of this printing.

Library of Congress Cataloging-in-Publication Number 89–43033

ISBN 0–89471–780–4 (cloth)

Published by Courage Books,
an imprint of Running Press Book Publishers,
125 South Twenty-second Street, Philadelphia, Pennsylvania 19103.

DEDICATION

My Dear Charles Baxter:

If you ever read this tale, you will likely ask yourself more questions than I should care to answer: as for instance how the Appin murder has come to fall in the year 1751, how the Torran rocks have crept so near to Earraid, or why the printed trial is silent as to all that touches David Balfour. These are nuts beyond my ability to crack. But if you tried me on the point of Alan's guilt or innocence, I think I could defend the reading of the text. To this day you will find the tradition of Appin clear in Alan's favour. If you inquire, you may even hear that the descendants of "the other man" who fired the shot are in the country to this day. But that other man's name, inquire as you please, you shall not hear; for the Highlander values a secret for itself and for the congenial exercise of keeping it. I might go on for long to justify one point and own another indefensible; it is more honest to confess at once how little I am touched by the desire of accuracy. This is no furniture for the scholar's library, but a book for the winter evening school-room when the tasks are over and the hour for bed draws near; and honest Alan, who was a grim old fire-eater in his day, has in this new avatar no more desperate purpose than to steal some young gentleman's attention from his Ovid, carry him awhile into the Highlands and the last century, and pack him to bed with some engaging images to mingle with his dreams.

As for you, my dear Charles, I do not even ask you to like this tale. But perhaps when he is older, your son will; he may then be pleased to find his father's name on the fly-leaf; and in the meanwhile it pleases me to set it there, in memory of many days that were happy and some (now perhaps as pleasant to remember) that were sad. If it is strange for me to look back from a distance both in time and space on these bygone adventures of our youth, it must be stranger for you who thread the same

DEDICATION

streets — who may to-morrow open the door of the old Speculative, where we begin to rank with Scott and Robert Emmet and the beloved and inglorious Macbean — or may pass the corner of the close where that great society, the L. J. R., held its meetings and drank its beer, sitting in the seats of Burns and his companions. I think I see you, moving there by plain daylight, beholding with your natural eyes those places that have now become for your companion a part of the scenery of dreams. How, in the intervals of present business, the past must echo in your memory! Let it not echo often without some kind thoughts of your friend,

R. L. S.

SKERRYVORE,
 BOURNEMOUTH.

CONTENTS

CONTENTS

ILLUSTRATIONS

ILLUSTRATIONS

KIDNAPPED

CHAPTER I

I SET OFF UPON MY JOURNEY TO THE HOUSE
OF SHAWS

I WILL begin the story of my adventures with a certain morning early in the month of June, the year of grace 1751, when I took the key for the last time out of the door of my father's house. The sun began to shine upon the summit of the hills as I went down the road; and by the time I had come as far as the manse, the blackbirds were whistling in the garden lilacs, and the mist that hung around the valley in the time of the dawn was beginning to arise and die away.

Mr. Campbell, the minister of Essendean, was waiting for me by the garden gate, good man! He asked me if I had breakfasted; and hearing that I lacked for nothing, he took my hand in both of his and clapped it kindly under his arm.

"Well, Davie, lad," said he, "I will go with you as far as the ford, to set you on the way."

And we began to walk forward in silence.

"Are ye sorry to leave Essendean?" said he, after awhile.

"Why, sir," said I, "if I knew where I was going, or what was likely to become of me, I would tell you candidly.

KIDNAPPED

Essendean is a good place indeed, and I have been very happy there; but then I have never been anywhere else. My father and mother, since they are both dead, I shall be no nearer to in Essendean than in the Kingdom of Hungary; and, to speak truth, if I thought I had a chance to better myself where I was going I would go with a good will."

"Ay?" said Mr. Campbell. "Very well, Davie. Then it behoves me to tell your fortune; or so far as I may. When your mother was gone, and your father (the worthy, Christian man) began to sicken for his end, he gave me in charge a certain letter, which he said was your inheritance. 'So soon,' says he, 'as I am gone, and the house is redd up and the gear disposed of' (all which, Davie, hath been done), 'give my boy this letter into his hand, and start him off to the house of Shaws, not far from Cramond. That is the place I came from,' he said, 'and it's where it befits that my boy should return. He is a steady lad,' your father said, 'and a canny goer; and I doubt not he will come safe, and be well liked where he goes.' "

"The house of Shaws!" I cried. "What had my poor father to do with the house of Shaws?"

"Nay," said Mr. Campbell, "who can tell that for a surety? But the name of that family, Davie, boy, is the name you bear — Balfours of Shaws: an ancient, honest, reputable house, peradventure in these latter days decayed. Your father, too, was a man of learning as befitted his position; no man more plausibly conducted school; nor had he the manner or the speech of a common dominie; but (as ye will yourself remember) I took aye a pleasure to have him

[4]

to the manse to meet the gentry; and those of my own house, Campbell of Kilrennet, Campbell of Dunswire, Campbell of Minch, and others, all well-kenned gentlemen had pleasure in his society. Lastly, to put all the elements of this affair before you, here is the testamentary letter itself, super-scrived by the own hand of our departed brother."

He gave me the letter, which was addressed in these words: "To the hands of Ebenezer Balfour, Esquire, of Shaws, in his house of Shaws, these will be delivered by my son, David Balfour." My heart was beating hard at this great prospect now suddenly opening before a lad of seven-teen years of age, the son of a poor country dominie in the Forest of Ettrick.

"Mr. Campbell," I stammered, "and if you were in my shoes, would you go?"

"Of a surety," said the minister, "that would I, and with-out pause. A pretty lad like you should get to Cramond (which is near in by Edinburgh) in two days of walk. If the worst came to the worst, and your high relations (as I can-not but suppose them to be somewhat of your blood) should put you to the door, ye can but walk the two days back again and risp at the manse door. But I would rather hope that ye shall be well received, as your poor father forecast for you, and for anything that I ken come to be a great man in time. And here, Davie, laddie," he resumed, "it lies near upon my conscience to improve this parting, and set you on the right guard against the dangers of the world."

Here he cast about for a comfortable seat, lighted on a big boulder under a birch by the trackside, sat down upon it with a very long, serious upper lip, and the sun now shining in upon us between two peaks, put his pocket-handkerchief over his cocked hat to shelter him. There, then, with up-lifted forefinger, he first put me on my guard against a con-siderable number of heresies, to which I had no temptation, and urged upon me to be instant in my prayers and reading of the Bible. That done, he drew a picture of the great house that I was bound to, and how I should conduct myself with its inhabitants.

"Be soople, Davie, in things immaterial," said he. "Bear ye this in mind, that, though gentle born, ye have had a country rearing. Dinnae shame us, Davie, dinnae shame us! In yon great, muckle house, with all these domestics, upper and under, show yourself as nice, as circumspect, as quick at the conception, and as slow of speech as any. As for the laird — remember he's the laird; I say no more: honour to whom honour. It's a pleasure to obey a laird; or should be, to the young."

"Well, sir," said I, "it may be; and I'll promise you I'll try to make it so."

"Why, very well said," replied Mr. Campbell, heartily. "And now to come to the material, or (to make a quibble) to the immaterial. I have here a little packet which con-tains four things." He tugged it, as he spoke, and with some great difficulty, from the skirt pocket of his coat. "Of these four things, the first is your legal due: the little pickle money for your father's books and plenishing, which I have bought (as I have explained from the first) in the design of re-selling at a profit to the incoming dominie. The other

KIDNAPPED

THE ADVENTURES OF DAVID BALFOUR
ROBERT LOUIS STEVENSON

Illustrated By
N. C. WYETH

N.C. Wyeth created this color title page illustration for an earlier edition of Kidnapped.

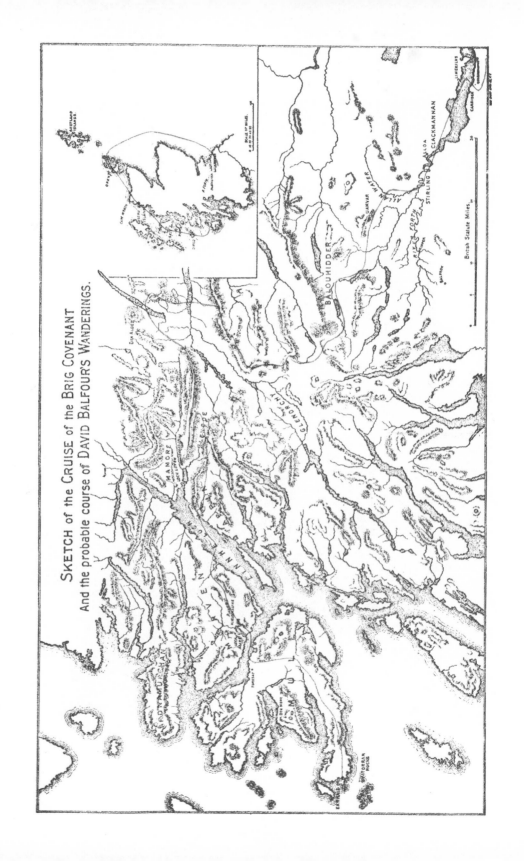

Sketch of the Cruise of the Brig Covenant
And the probable course of David Balfour's Wanderings.

THE SIEGE OF THE ROUND-HOUSE

It came all of a sudden when it did, with a rush of feet and a roar, and then a shout from Alan (page 83)

THE TORRENT IN THE VALLEY OF GLENCOE

I had scarce time to measure the distance or to understand the peril before
I had followed him, and he had caught and stopped me (page 178)

three are gifties that Mrs. Campbell and myself would be
blithe of your acceptance. The first, which is round, will
likely please ye best at the first off-go; but, O Davie, laddie,
it 's but a drop of water in the sea; it 'll help you but a step,
and vanish like the morning. The second, which is flat and
square and written upon, will stand by you through life, like
a good staff for the road, and a good pillow to your head in
sickness. And as for the last, which is cubical, that 'll see
you, it 's my prayerful wish, into a better land."

With that he got upon his feet, took off his hat, and
prayed a little while aloud, and in affecting terms, for a young
man setting out into the world; then suddenly took me in
his arms and embraced me very hard; then held me at arm's
length, looking at me with his face all working with sorrow;
and then whipped about, and crying good-bye to me, set
off backward by the way that we had come at a sort of
jogging run. It might have been laughable to another; but
I was in no mind to laugh. I watched him as long as he was
in sight; and he never stopped hurrying, nor once looked
back. Then it came in upon my mind that this was all his
sorrow at my departure; and my conscience smote me hard
and fast, because I, for my part, was overjoyed to get away
out of that quiet country-side, and go to a great, busy house,
among rich and respected gentlefolk of my own name and
blood.

"Davie, Davie," I thought, "was ever seen such black
ingratitude? Can you forget old favours and old friends at
the mere whistle of a name? Fie, fie; think shame!"

And I sat down on the boulder the good man had just

left, and opened the parcel to see the nature of my gifts. That which he had called cubical, I had never had much doubt of; sure enough it was a little Bible, to carry in a plaid-neuk. That which he had called round, I found to be a shilling piece; and the third, which was to help me so wonderfully both in health and sickness all the days of my life, was a little piece of coarse yellow paper, written upon thus in red ink:

"To Make Lilly of the Valley Water.—Take the flowers of lilly of the valley and distil them in sack, and drink a spoonful or two as there is occasion. It restores speech to those that have the dumb palsey. It is good against the Gout; it comforts the heart and strengthens the memory; and the flowers, put into a Glasse, close stopt, and set into ane hill of ants for a month, then take it out, and you will find a liquor which comes from the flowers, which keep in a vial; it is good, ill or well, and whether man or woman."

And then, in the minister's own hand, was added:

"Likewise for sprains, rub in; and for the cholic, a great spoonful in the hour."

To be sure, I laughed over this; but it was rather tremulous laughter; and I was glad to get my bundle on my staff's end and set out over the ford and up the hill upon the farther side; till, just as I came on the green drove-road running wide through the heather, I took my last look of Kirk Essendean, the trees about the manse, and the big rowans in the kirkyard where my father and my mother lay.

CHAPTER II

I COME TO MY JOURNEY'S END

O N the forenoon of the second day, coming to the top of a hill, I saw all the country fall away before me down to the sea; and in the midst of this descent, on a long ridge, the city of Edinburgh smoking like a kiln. There was a flag upon the castle, and ships moving or lying anchored in the firth; both of which, for as far away as they were, I could distinguish clearly; and both brought my country heart into my mouth.

Presently after, I came by a house where a shepherd lived, and got a rough direction for the neighbourhood of Cramond; and so, from one to another, worked my way to the westward of the capital by Colinton, till I came out upon the Glasgow road. And there, to my great pleasure and wonder, I beheld a regiment marching to the fifes, every foot in time; an old red-faced general on a grey horse at the one end, and at the other the company of Grenadiers, with their Pope's-hats. The pride of life seemed to mount into my brain at the sight of the red coats and the hearing of that merry music.

A little farther on, and I was told I was in Cramond parish, and began to substitute in my inquiries the name of the house of Shaws. It was a word that seemed to surprise those of whom I sought my way. At first I thought the plainness of my appearance, in my country habit, and that all dusty from the road, consorted ill with the greatness of the place to which I was bound. But after two, or maybe three, had given me the same look and the same answer, I began to take it in my head there was something strange about the Shaws itself.

The better to set this fear at rest, I changed the form of my inquiries; and spying an honest fellow coming along a lane on the shaft of his cart, I asked him if he had ever heard tell of a house they called the house of Shaws.

He stopped his cart and looked at me, like the others.

"Ay," said he. "What for?"

"It 's a great house?" I asked.

"Doubtless," says he. "The house is a big, muckle house."

"Ay," said I, "but the folk that are in it?"

"Folk?" cried he. "Are ye daft? There 's nae folk there — to call folk."

"What?" say I; "not Mr. Ebenezer?"

"Ou, ay," says the man; "there 's the laird, to be sure, if it 's him you 're wanting. What 'll like be your business, mannie?"

"I was led to think that I would get a situation," I said, looking as modest as I could.

"What?" cries the carter, in so sharp a note that his very horse started; and then, "Well, mannie," he added, "it 's nane of my affairs; but ye seem a decent-spoken lad;

and if ye'll take a word from me, ye'll keep clear of the Shaws."

The next person I came across was a dapper little man in a beautiful white wig, whom I saw to be a barber on his rounds; and knowing well that barbers were great gossips, I asked him plainly what sort of a man was Mr. Balfour of the Shaws.

"Hoot, hoot, hoot," said the barber, "nae kind of a man, nae kind of a man at all"; and began to ask me very shrewdly what my business was; but I was more than a match for him at that, and he went on to his next customer no wiser than he came.

I cannot well describe the blow this dealt to my illusions. The more indistinct the accusations were, the less I liked them, for they left the wider field to fancy. What kind of a great house was this, that all the parish should start and stare to be asked the way to it? or what sort of a gentleman, that his ill-fame should be thus current on the wayside? If an hour's walking would have brought me back to Essendean, I had left my adventure then and there, and returned to Mr. Campbell's. But when I had come so far a way already, mere shame would not suffer me to desist till I had put the matter to the touch of proof; I was bound, out of mere self-respect, to carry it through; and little as I liked the sound of what I heard, and slow as I began to travel, I still kept asking my way and still kept advancing.

It was drawing on to sundown when I met a stout, dark, sour-looking woman coming trudging down a hill; and she, when I had put my usual question, turned sharp about, ac-

companied me back to the summit she had just left, and
pointed to a great bulk of building standing very bare upon
a green in the bottom of the next valley. The country was
pleasant round about, running in low hills, pleasantly watered
and wooded, and the crops, to my eyes, wonderfully good;
but the house itself appeared to be a kind of ruin; no road
led up to it; no smoke arose from any of the chimneys; nor
was there any semblance of a garden. My heart sank.
"That!" I cried.

The woman's face lit up with a malignant anger. "That
is the house of Shaws!" she cried. "Blood built it; blood
stopped the building of it; blood shall bring it down. See
here!" she cried again — "I spit upon the ground, and crack
my thumb at it! Black be its fall! If ye see the laird, tell
him what ye hear; tell him this makes the twelve hunner and
nineteen time that Jennet Clouston has called down the curse
on him and his house, byre and stable, man, guest, and master,
wife, miss, or bairn — black, black be their fall!"

And the woman, whose voice had risen to a kind of
eldritch sing-song, turned with a skip, and was gone. I
stood where she left me, with my hair on end. In those
days folk still believed in witches and trembled at a curse;
and this one, falling so pat, like a wayside omen, to arrest
me ere I carried out my purpose, took the pith out of my
legs.

I sat me down and stared at the house of Shaws. The
more I looked, the pleasanter that country-side appeared;
being all set with hawthorn bushes full of flowers; the fields
dotted with sheep; a fine flight of rooks in the sky; and

every sign of a kind soil and climate; and yet the barrack in the midst of it went sore against my fancy.

Country folk went by from the fields as I sat there on the side of the ditch, but I lacked the spirit to give them a good-e'en. At last the sun went down, and then, right up against the yellow sky, I saw a scroll of smoke go mounting, not much thicker, as it seemed to me, than the smoke of a candle; but still there it was, and meant a fire, and warmth, and cookery, and some living inhabitant that must have lit it; and this comforted my heart.

So I set forward by a little faint track in the grass that led in my direction. It was very faint indeed to be the only way to a place of habitation; yet I saw no other. Presently it brought me to stone uprights, with an unroofed lodge beside them, and coats of arms upon the top. A main entrance it was plainly meant to be, but never finished; instead of gates of wrought iron, a pair of hurdles were tied across with a straw rope; and as there were no park walls, nor any sign of avenue, the track that I was following passed on the right hand of the pillars, and went wandering on toward the house.

The nearer I got to that, the drearier it appeared. It seemed like the one wing of a house that had never been finished. What should have been the inner end stood open on the upper floors, and showed against the sky with steps and stairs of uncompleted masonry. Many of the windows were unglazed, and bats flew in and out like doves out of a dove-cote.

The night had begun to fall as I got close; and in three of the lower windows, which were very high up and narrow, and well barred, the changing light of a little fire began to glimmer.

Was this the palace I had been coming to? Was it within these walls that I was to seek new friends and begin great fortunes? Why, in my father's house on Essen-Waterside, the fire and the bright lights would show a mile away, and the door open to a beggar's knock!

I came forward cautiously, and giving ear as I came, heard some one rattling with dishes, and a little dry, eager cough that came in fits; but there was no sound of speech, and not a dog barked.

The door, as well as I could see it in the dim light, was a great piece of wood all studded with nails; and I lifted my hand with a faint heart under my jacket, and knocked once. Then I stood and waited. The house had fallen into a dead silence; a whole minute passed away, and nothing stirred but the bats overhead. I knocked again, and hearkened again. By this time my ears had grown so accustomed to the quiet, that I could hear the ticking of the clock inside as it slowly counted out the seconds; but whoever was in that house kept deadly still, and must have held his breath.

I was in two minds whether to run away; but anger got the upper hand, and I began instead to rain kicks and buffets on the door, and to shout out aloud for Mr. Balfour. I was in full career, when I heard the cough right overhead, and jumping back and looking up, beheld a man's head in a tall nightcap, and the bell mouth of a blunderbuss, at one of the first-storey windows.

"It's loaded," said a voice.

I COME TO MY JOURNEY'S END

"I have come here with a letter," I said, "to Mr. Ebenezer Balfour of Shaws. Is he here?"

"From whom is it?" asked the man with the blunderbuss.

"That is neither here nor there," said I, for I was growing very wroth.

"Well," was the reply, "ye can put it down upon the doorstep, and be off with ye."

"I will do no such thing," I cried. "I will deliver it into Mr. Balfour's hands, as it was meant I should. It is a letter of introduction."

"A what?" cried the voice, sharply.

I repeated what I had said.

"Who are ye, yourself?" was the next question, after a considerable pause.

"I am not ashamed of my name," said I. "They call me David Balfour."

At that, I made sure the man started, for I heard the blunderbuss rattle on the window-sill; and it was after quite a long pause, and with a curious change of voice, that the next question followed:

"Is your father dead?"

I was so much surprised at this, that I could find no voice to answer, but stood staring.

"Ay," the man resumed, "he 'll be dead, no doubt; and that 'll be what brings ye chapping to my door." Another pause, and then defiantly, "Well, man," he said, "I 'll let ye in"; and he disappeared from the window.

CHAPTER III

I MAKE ACQUAINTANCE OF MY UNCLE

PRESENTLY there came a great rattling of chains and bolts, and the door was cautiously opened and shut to again behind me as soon as I had passed.

"Go into the kitchen and touch naething," said the voice; and while the person of the house set himself to replacing the defences of the door, I groped my way forward and entered the kitchen.

The fire had burned up fairly bright, and showed me the barest room I think I ever put my eyes on. Half-a-dozen dishes stood upon the shelves; the table was laid for supper with a bowl of porridge, a horn spoon, and a cup of small beer. Besides what I have named, there was not another thing in that great, stone-vaulted, empty chamber but lock-fast chests arranged along the wall and a corner cupboard with a padlock.

As soon as the last chain was up, the man rejoined me. He was a mean, stooping, narrow-shouldered, clay-faced creature; and his age might have been anything between fifty and seventy. His nightcap was of flannel, and so was the nightgown that he wore, instead of coat and waistcoat, over his ragged shirt. He was long unshaved; but what most distressed and even daunted me, he would neither take his eyes away from me nor look me fairly in the face. What he was, whether by trade or birth, was more than I could fathom; but he seemed most like an old, uprofitable serving-man, who should have been left in charge of that big house upon board wages.

"Are ye sharp-set?" he asked, glancing at about the level of my knee. "Ye can eat that drop parritch?"

I said I feared it was his own supper.

"O," said he, "I can do fine wanting it. I 'll take the ale, though, for it slockens[1] my cough." He drank the cup about half out, still keeping an eye upon me as he drank; and then suddenly held out his hand. "Let 's see the letter," said he.

I told him the letter was for Mr. Balfour; not for him.

"And who do ye think I am?" says he. "Give me Alexander's letter!"

"You know my father's name?"

"It would be strange if I didnae," he returned, "for he was my born brother; and little as ye seem to like either me or my house, or my good parritch, I 'm your born uncle, Davie, my man, and you my born nephew. So give us the letter, and sit down and fill your kyte."

If I had been some years younger, what with shame, weariness, and disappointment, I believe I had burst into tears. As it was, I could find no words, neither black nor white, but handed him the letter, and sat down to the porridge with as little appetite for meat as ever a young man had.

[1] Moistens.

Meanwhile, my uncle, stooping over the fire, turned the letter over and over in his hands.

"Do ye ken what's in it?" he asked, suddenly.

"You see for yourself, sir," said I, "that the seal has not been broken."

"Ay," said he, "but what brought you here?"

"To give the letter," said I.

"No," says he, cunningly, "but ye 'll have had some hopes, nae doubt?"

"I confess, sir," said I, "when I was told that I had kins-folk well-to-do, I did indeed indulge the hope that they might help me in my life. But I am no beggar; I look for no favours at your hands, and I want none that are not freely given. For as poor as I appear, I have friends of my own that will be blithe to help me."

"Hoot-toot!" said Uncle Ebenezer, "dinnae fly up in the snuff at me. We 'll agree fine yet. And, Davie, my man, if you're done with that bit parritch, I could just take a sup of it myself. Ay," he continued, as soon as he had ousted me from the stool and spoon, "they 're fine, halesome food — they 're grand food, parritch." He murmured a little grace to himself and fell to. "Your father was very fond of his meat, I mind; he was a hearty, if not a great eater; but as for me, I could never do mair than pyke at food." He took a pull at the small beer, which probably reminded him of hospitable duties, for his next speech ran thus: "If ye 're dry ye 'll find water behind the door."

To this I returned no answer, standing stiffly on my two feet, and looking down upon my uncle with a mighty angry heart. He, on his part, continued to eat like a man under some pressure of time, and to throw out little darting glances now at my shoes and now at my home-spun stockings. Once only, when he had ventured to look a little higher, our eyes met; and no thief taken with a hand in a man's pocket could have shown more lively signals of distress. This set me in a muse, whether his timidity arose from too long a disuse of any human company; and whether perhaps, upon a little trial, it might pass off, and my uncle change into an altogether different man. From this I was awakened by his sharp voice.

"Your father's been long dead?" he asked.

"Three weeks, sir," said I.

"He was a secret man, Alexander — a secret, silent man," he continued. "He never said muckle when he was young. He'll never have spoken muckle of me?"

"I never knew, sir, till you told it me yourself, that he had any brother."

"Dear me, dear me!" said Ebenezer. "Nor yet of Shaws, I dare say?"

"Not so much as the name, sir," said I.

"To think o' that!" said he. "A strange nature of a man!" For all that, he seemed singularly satisfied, but whether with himself, or me, or with this conduct of my father's, was more than I could read. Certainly, however, he seemed to be outgrowing that distaste, or ill-will, that he had conceived at first against my person; for presently he jumped up, came across the room behind me, and hit me a smack upon the shoulder. "We'll agree fine yet!" he cried.

"I'm just as glad I let you in. And now come awa' to your bed."

To my surprise, he lit no lamp or candle, but set forth into the dark passage, groped his way, breathing deeply, up a flight of steps, and paused before a door, which he unlocked. I was close upon his heels, having stumbled after him as best I might; and then he bade me go in, for that was my chamber. I did as he bid, but paused after a few steps, and begged a light to go to bed with.

"Hoot-toot!" said Uncle Ebenezer, "there's a fine moon."

"Neither moon nor star, sir, and pit-mirk," [1] said I. "I cannae see the bed."

"Hoot-toot, hoot-toot!" said he. "Lights in a house is a thing I dinnae agree with. I'm unco feared of fires. Good night to ye, Davie, my man." And before I had time to add a further protest, he pulled the door to, and I heard him lock me in from the outside.

I did not know whether to laugh or cry. The room was as cold as a well, and the bed, when I had found my way to it, as damp as a peat-hag; but by good fortune I had caught up my bundle and my plaid, and rolling myself in the latter, I lay down upon the floor under lee of the big bedstead, and fell speedily asleep.

With the first peep of day I opened my eyes, to find myself in a great chamber, hung with stamped leather, furnished with fine embroidered furniture, and lit by three fair windows. Ten years ago, or perhaps twenty, it must have been as pleasant a room to lie down or to awake in as a man could

---

[1] Dark as the pit.

wish; but damp, dirt, disuse, and the mice and spiders had done their worst since then. Many of the window-panes, besides, were broken; and indeed this was so common a feature in that house, that I believe my uncle must at some time have stood a siege from his indignant neighbours — perhaps with Jennet Clouston at their head.

Meanwhile the sun was shining outside; and being very cold in that miserable room, I knocked and shouted till my gaoler came and let me out. He carried me to the back of the house, where was a draw-well, and told me to "wash my face there, if I wanted"; and when that was done, I made the best of my own way back to the kitchen, where he had lit the fire and was making the porridge. The table was laid with two bowls and two horn spoons, but the same single measure of small beer. Perhaps my eye rested on this particular with some surprise, and perhaps my uncle observed it; for he spoke up as if in answer to my thought, asking me if I would like to drink ale — for so he called it.

I told him such was my habit, but not to put himself about.

"Na, na," said he; "I 'll deny you nothing in reason."

He fetched another cup from the shelf; and then, to my great surprise, instead of drawing more beer, he poured an accurate half from one cup to the other. There was a kind of nobleness in this that took my breath away; if my uncle was certainly a miser, he was one of that thorough breed that goes near to make the vice respectable.

When we had made an end of our meal, my uncle Ebenezer unlocked a drawer, and drew out of it a clay pipe and a lump of tobacco, from which he cut one fill before he locked it up again. Then he sat down in the sun at one of the windows and silently smoked. From time to time his eyes came coasting round to me, and he shot out one of his questions. Once it was, "And your mother?" and when I had told him that she, too, was dead, "Ay, she was a bonnie lassie!" Then, after another long pause, "Whae were these friends o' yours?"

I told him they were different gentlemen of the name of Campbell; though, indeed, there was only one, and that the minister, that had ever taken the least note of me; but I began to think my uncle made too light of my position, and finding myself all alone with him, I did not wish him to suppose me helpless.

He seemed to turn this over in his mind; and then, "Davie, my man," said he, "ye 've come to the right bit when ye came to your uncle Ebenezer. I 've a great notion of the family, and I mean to do the right by you; but while I 'm taking a bit think to mysel' of what 's the best thing to put you to — whether the law, or the meenistry, or maybe the army, whilk is what boys are fondest of — I wouldnae like the Balfours to be humbled before a wheen Hieland Campbells, and I 'll ask you to keep your tongue within your teeth. Nae letters; nae messages; no kind of word to onybody; or else — there 's my door."

"Uncle Ebenezer," said I, "I 've no manner of reason to suppose you mean anything but well by me. For all that, I would have you to know that I have a pride of my own. It was by no will of mine that I came seeking you; and if you show me your door again, I'll take you at the word."

He seemed grievously put out. "Hoots-toots," said he, "ca' cannie, man — ca' cannie! Bide a day or two. I'm nae warlock, to find a fortune for you in the bottom of a parritch bowl; but just you give me a day or two, and say naething to naebody, and as sure as sure, I'll do the right by you."

"Very well," said I, "enough said. If you want to help me, there's no doubt but I'll be glad of it, and none but I'll be grateful."

It seemed to me (too soon, I dare say) that I was getting the upper hand of my uncle; and I began next to say that I must have the bed and bedclothes aired and put to sun-dry; for nothing would make me sleep in such a pickle.

"Is this my house or yours?" said he, in his keen voice, and then all of a sudden broke off. "Na, na," said he, "I didnae mean that. What's mine is yours, Davie, my man, and what's yours is mine. Blood's thicker than water; and there's naebody but you and me that ought the name." And then on he rambled about the family, and its ancient greatness, and his father that began to enlarge the house, and himself that stopped the building as a sinful waste; and this put it in my head to give him Jennet Clouston's message.

"The limmer!" he cried. "Twelve hunner and fifteen — that's every day since I had the limmer rompit![1] Dod, David, I'll have her roasted on red peats before I'm by with it! A witch — a proclaimed witch! I'll aff and see the session clerk."

[1] Sold up.

And with that he opened a chest, and got out a very old and well-preserved blue coat and waistcoat, and a good enough beaver hat, both without lace. These he threw on any way, and taking a staff from the cupboard, locked all up again, and was for setting out, when a thought arrested him.

"I cannae leave you by yoursel' in the house," said he. "I 'll have to lock you out."

The blood came to my face. "If you lock me out," I said, "it 'll be the last you 'll see of me in friendship."

He turned very pale, and sucked his mouth in. "This is no the way," he said, looking wickedly at a corner of the floor — "this is no the way to win my favour, David."

"Sir," says I, "with a proper reverence for your age and our common blood, I do not value your favour at a boddle's purchase. I was brought up to have a good conceit of myself; and if you were all the uncle, and all the family, I had in the world ten times over, I would n't buy your liking at such prices."

Uncle Ebenezer went and looked out of the window for awhile. I could see him all trembling and twitching, like a man with palsy. But when he turned round, he had a smile upon his face.

"Well, well," said he, "we must bear and forbear. I 'll no go; that 's all that 's to be said of it."

"Uncle Ebenezer," I said, "I can make nothing out of this. You use me like a thief; you hate to have me in this house; you let me see it, every word and every minute: it 's not possible that you can like me; and as for me, I 've spoken to you as I never thought to speak to any man. Why do

you seek to keep me, then? Let me gang back — let me gang
back to the friends I have, and that like me!"

"Na, na; na, na," he said, very earnestly. "I like you
fine; we 'll agree fine yet; and for the honour of the house I
couldnae let you leave the way ye came. Bide here quiet,
there 's a good lad; just you bide here quiet a bittie, and ye 'll
find that we agree."

"Well, sir," said I, after I had thought the matter out in
silence, "I 'll stay awhile. It 's more just I should be helped
by my own blood than strangers; and if we don't agree, I 'll
do my best it shall be through no fault of mine."

CHAPTER IV

I RUN A GREAT DANGER IN THE HOUSE OF SHAWS

FOR a day that was begun so ill, the day passed fairly well. We had the porridge cold again at noon, and hot porridge at night; porridge and small beer was my uncle's diet. He spoke but little, and that in the same way as before, shooting a question at me after a long silence; and when I sought to lead him to talk about my future, slipped out of it again. In a room next door to the kitchen, where he suffered me to go, I found a great number of books, both Latin and English, in which I took great pleasure all the afternoon. Indeed, the time passed so lightly in this good company, that I began to be almost reconciled to my residence at Shaws; and nothing but the sight of my uncle, and his eyes playing hide-and-seek with mine, revived the force of my distrust.

One thing I discovered, which put me in some doubt. This was an entry on the fly-leaf of a chap-book (one of Patrick Walker's) plainly written by my father's hand and thus conceived: "To my brother Ebenezer on his fifth birth-day." Now, what puzzled me was this: That, as my father was of course the younger brother, he must either have

made some strange error, or he must have wri͓
was yet five, an excellent, clear, manly hand of

I tried to get this out of my head; but th͔
down many interesting authors, old and new, hist͔
and story-book, this notion of my father's hand
stuck to me; and when at length I went back into the ͔͔chen,
and sat down once more to porridge and small beer, the first
thing I said to Uncle Ebenezer was to ask him if my father
had not been very quick at his book.

"Alexander? No him!" was the reply. "I was far
quicker mysel'; I was a clever chappie when I was young.
Why, I could read as soon as he could."

This puzzled me yet more; and a thought coming into my
head, I asked if he and my father had been twins.

He jumped upon his stool, and the horn spoon fell out of
his hand upon the floor. "What gars ye ask that?" he said,
and he caught me by the breast of the jacket, and looked
this time straight into my eyes: his own were little and light,
and bright like a bird's, blinking and winking strangely.

"What do you mean?" I asked, very calmly, for I was
far stronger than he, and not easily frightened. "Take your
hand from my jacket. This is no way to behave."

My uncle seemed to make a great effort upon himself.
"Dod, man, David," he said, "ye shouldnae speak to me
about your father. That's where the mistake is." He sat
awhile and shook, blinking in his plate. "He was all the
brother that ever I had," he added, but with no heart in his
voice; and then he caught up his spoon and fell to supper
again, but still shaking.

KIDNAPPED

Now this last passage, this laying of hands upon my person and sudden profession of love for my dead father, went so clean beyond my comprehension that it put me into both fear and hope. On the one hand, I began to think my uncle was perhaps insane and might be dangerous; on the other, there came up into my mind (quite unbidden by me and even discouraged) a story like some ballad I had heard folk singing, of a poor lad that was a rightful heir and a wicked kinsman that tried to keep him from his own. For why should my uncle play a part with a relative that came, almost a beggar, to his door, unless in his heart he had some cause to fear him?

With this notion, all unacknowledged, but nevertheless getting firmly settled in my head, I now began to imitate his covert looks; so that we sat at table like a cat and a mouse, each stealthily observing the other. Not another word had he to say to me, black or white, but was busy turning something secretly over in his mind; and the longer we sat and the more I looked at him, the more certain I became that the something was unfriendly to myself.

When he had cleared the platter, he got out a single pipeful of tobacco, just as in the morning, turned round a stool into the chimney corner, and sat awhile smoking, with his back to me.

"Davie," he said, at length, "I've been thinking"; then he paused, and said it again. "There's a wee bit siller that I half promised ye before ye were born," he continued; "promised it to your father. O, naething legal, ye understand; just gentlemen daffing at their wine. Well, I keepit that bit money separate — it was a great expense, but a promise is a promise — and it has grown by now to be a matter of just precisely — just exactly" — and here he paused and stumbled — "of just exactly forty pounds!" This last he rapped out with a sidelong glance over his shoulder; and the next moment added, almost with a scream, "Scots!"

The pound Scots being the same thing as an English shilling, the difference made by this second thought was considerable; I could see, besides, that the whole story was a lie, invented with some end which it puzzled me to guess; and I made no attempt to conceal the tone of raillery in which I answered —

"O, think again, sir! Pounds sterling, I believe!"

"That's what I said," returned my uncle: "pounds sterling! And if you'll step out-by to the door a minute, just to see what kind of a night it is, I'll get it out to ye and call ye in again."

I did his will, smiling to myself in my contempt that he should think I was so easily to be deceived. It was a dark night, with a few stars low down; and as I stood just outside the door, I heard a hollow moaning of wind far off among the hills. I said to myself there was something thundery and changeful in the weather, and little knew of what a vast importance that should prove to me before the evening passed.

When I was called in again, my uncle counted out into my hand seven and thirty golden guinea pieces; the rest was in his hand, in small gold and silver; but his heart failed him there, and he crammed the change into his pocket.

"There," said he, "that 'll show you! I 'm a queer man, and strange wi' strangers; but my word is my bond, and there 's the proof of it."

Now, my uncle seemed so miserly that I was struck dumb by this sudden generosity, and could find no words in which to thank him.

"No a word!" said he. "Nae thanks; I want nae thanks. I do my duty; I 'm no saying that everybody would have done it; but for my part (though I 'm a careful body, too) it 's a pleasure to me to do the right by my brother's son; and it 's a pleasure to me to think that now we 'll agree as such near friends should."

I spoke him in return as handsomely as I was able; but all the while I was wondering what would come next, and why he had parted with his precious guineas; for as to the reason he had given, a baby would have refused it.

Presently he looked towards me sideways.

"And see here," says he, "tit for tat."

I told him I was ready to prove my gratitude in any reasonable degree, and then waited, looking for some monstrous demand. And yet, when at last he plucked up courage to speak, it was only to tell me (very properly, as I thought) that he was growing old and a little broken, and that he would expect me to help him with the house and the bit garden.

I answered, and expressed my readiness to serve.

"Well," he said, "let 's begin." He pulled out of his pocket a rusty key. "There," says he, "there 's the key of the stair-tower at the far end of the house. Ye can only win into it from the outside, for that part of the house is no finished. Gang ye in there, and up the stairs, and bring me down the chest that's at the top. There's papers in 't," he added.

"Can I have a light, sir?" said I.

"Na," said he, very cunningly. "Nae lights in my house."

"Very well, sir," said I. "Are the stairs good?"

"They're grand," said he; and then, as I was going: "Keep to the wall," he added; "there's nae bannisters. But the stairs are grand underfoot."

Out I went into the night. The wind was still moaning in the distance, though never a breath of it came near the house of Shaws. It had fallen blacker than ever; and I was glad to feel along the wall, till I came the length of the stair-tower door at the far end of the unfinished wing. I had got the key into the keyhole and had just turned it, when all upon a sudden, without sound of wind or thunder, the whole sky lighted up with wild fire and went black again. I had to put my hand over my eyes to get back to the colour of the darkness; and indeed I was already half blinded when I stepped into the tower.

It was so dark inside, it seemed a body could scarce breathe; but I pushed out with foot and hand, and presently struck the wall with the one, and the lowermost round of the stair with the other. The wall, by the touch, was of fine hewn stone; the steps too, though somewhat steep and narrow, were of polished masonwork, and regular and solid underfoot. Minding my uncle's word about the bannisters,

KIDNAPPED

I kept close to the tower side, and felt my way in the pitch darkness with a beating heart.

The house of Shaws stood some five full storeys high, not counting lofts. Well, as I advanced, it seemed to me the stair grew airier and a thought more lightsome; and I was wondering what might be the cause of this change, when a second blink of the summer lightning came and went. If I did not cry out, it was because fear had me by the throat; and if I did not fall, it was more by Heaven's mercy than my own strength. It was not only that the flash shone in on every side through breaches in the wall, so that I seemed to be clambering aloft upon an open scaffold, but the same passing brightness showed me the steps were of unequal length, and that one of my feet rested that moment within two inches of the well.

This was the grand stair! I thought; and with the thought, a gust of a kind of angry courage came into my heart. My uncle had sent me here, certainly to run great risks, perhaps to die. I swore I would settle that "perhaps," if I should break my neck for it; got me down upon my hands and knees; and as slowly as a snail, feeling before me every inch, and testing the solidity of every stone, I continued to ascend the stair. The darkness, by contrast with the flash, appeared to have redoubled; nor was that all, for my ears were now troubled and my mind confounded by a great stir of bats in the top part of the tower, and the foul beasts, flying downwards, sometimes beat about my face and body.

The tower, I should have said, was square; and in every corner the step was made of a great stone of a different shape, to join the flights. Well, I had come close to one of these turns, when, feeling forward as usual, my hand slipped upon an edge and found nothing but emptiness beyond it. The stair had been carried no higher; to set a stranger mounting it in the darkness was to send him straight to his death; and (although, thanks to the lightning and my own precautions, I was safe enough) the mere thought of the peril in which I might have stood, and the dreadful height I might have fallen from, brought out the sweat upon my body and relaxed my joints.

But I knew what I wanted now, and turned and groped my way down again, with a wonderful anger in my heart. About half-way down, the wind sprang up in a clap and shook the tower, and died again; the rain followed; and before I had reached the ground level it fell in buckets. I put out my head into the storm, and looked along towards the kitchen. The door, which I had shut behind me when I left, now stood open, and shed a little glimmer of light; and I thought I could see a figure standing in the rain, quite still, like a man hearkening. And then there came a blinding flash, which showed me my uncle plainly, just where I had fancied him to stand; and hard upon the heels of it, a great tow-row of thunder.

Now, whether my uncle thought the crash to be the sound of my fall, or whether he heard in it God's voice denouncing murder, I will leave you to guess. Certain it is, at least, that he was seized on by a kind of panic fear, and that he ran into the house and left the door open behind him. I followed as softly as I could, and, coming unheard into the kitchen, stood and watched him.

KIDNAPPED

He had found time to open the corner cupboard and bring out a great case bottle of aqua vitæ, and now sat with his back towards me at the table. Ever and again he would be seized with a fit of deadly shuddering and groan aloud, and carrying the bottle to his lips, drink down the raw spirits by the mouthful.

I stepped forward, came close behind him where he sat, and suddenly clapping my two hands down upon his shoulders — "Ah!" cried I.

My uncle gave a kind of broken cry like a sheep's bleat, flung up his arms, and tumbled to the floor like a dead man. I was somewhat shocked at this; but I had myself to look to first of all, and did not hesitate to let him lie as he had fallen. The keys were hanging in the cupboard; and it was my design to furnish myself with arms before my uncle should come again to his senses and the power of devising evil. In the cupboard were a few bottles, some apparently of medicine; a great many bills and other papers, which I should willingly enough have rummaged, had I had the time; and a few necessaries that were nothing to my purpose. Thence I turned to the chests. The first was full of meal; the second of moneybags and papers tied into sheaves; in the third, with many other things (and these for the most part clothes) I found a rusty, ugly-looking Highland dirk without the scabbard. This, then, I concealed inside my waistcoat, and turned to my uncle.

He lay as he had fallen, all huddled, with one knee up and one arm sprawling abroad; his face had a strange colour of blue, and he seemed to have ceased breathing. Fear came on me that he was dead; then I got water and dashed it in his face; and with that he seemed to come a little to himself, working his mouth and fluttering his eyelids. At last he looked up and saw me, and there came into his eyes a terror that was not of this world.

"Come, come," said I; "sit up."

"Are ye alive?" he sobbed. "O man, are ye alive?"

"That am I," said I. "Small thanks to you!"

He had begun to seek for his breath with deep sighs. "The blue phial," said he — "in the aumry — the blue phial." His breath came slower still.

I ran to the cupboard, and, sure enough, found there a blue phial of medicine, with the dose written on it on a paper, and this I administered to him with what speed I might.

"It's the trouble," said he, reviving a little; "I have a trouble, Davie. It's the heart."

I set him on a chair and looked at him. It is true I felt some pity for a man that looked so sick, but I was full besides of righteous anger; and I numbered over before him the points on which I wanted explanation: why he lied to me at every word; why he feared that I should leave him; why he disliked it to be hinted that he and my father were twins — "Is that because it is true?" I asked; why he had given me money to which I was convinced I had no claim; and, last of all, why he had tried to kill me. He heard me all through in silence; and then, in a broken voice, begged me to let him go to bed.

"I'll tell ye the morn," he said; "as sure as death I will."

And so weak was he that I could do nothing but consent.

KIDNAPPED

I locked him into his room, however, and pocketed the key; and then returning to the kitchen, made up such a blaze as had not shone there for many a long year, and wrapping myself in my plaid, lay down upon the chests and fell asleep.

CHAPTER V

I GO TO THE QUEEN'S FERRY

MUCH rain fell in the night; and the next morning there blew a bitter wintry wind out of the north-west, driving scattered clouds. For all that, and before the sun began to peep or the last of the stars had vanished, I made my way to the side of the burn, and had a plunge in a deep whirling pool. All aglow from my bath, I sat down once more beside the fire, which I replenished, and began gravely to consider my position.

There was now no doubt about my uncle's enmity; there was no doubt I carried my life in my hand, and he would leave no stone unturned that he might compass my destruction. But I was young and spirited, and like most lads that have been country-bred, I had a great opinion of my shrewdness. I had come to his door no better than a beggar and little more than a child; he had met me with treachery and violence; it would be a fine consummation to take the upper hand, and drive him like a herd of sheep.

I sat there nursing my knee and smiling at the fire; and I saw myself in fancy smell out his secrets one after another, and grow to be that man's king and ruler. The warlock of Essendean, they say, had made a mirror in which men could

[37]

read the future; it must have been of other stuff than burning coal, for in all the shapes and pictures that I sat and gazed at, there was never a ship, never a seaman with a hairy cap, never a big bludgeon for my silly head, or the least sign of all those tribulations that were ripe to fall on me.

Presently, all swollen with conceit, I went up-stairs and gave my prisoner his liberty. He gave me good-morning civilly; and I gave the same to him, smiling down upon him from the heights of my sufficiency. Soon we were set to breakfast, as it might have been the day before.

"Well, sir," said I, with a jeering tone: "have you nothing more to say to me?" And then, as he made no articulate reply: "It will be time, I think, to understand each other," I continued. "You took me for a country Johnnie Raw, with no more mother-wit or courage than a porridge-stick. I took you for a good man, or no worse than others at the least. It seems we were both wrong. What cause you have to fear me, to cheat me, and to attempt my life —— "

He murmured something about a jest, and that he liked a bit of fun; and then, seeing me smile, changed his tone, and assured me he would make all clear as soon as we had breakfasted. I saw by his face that he had no lie ready for me, though he was hard at work preparing one; and I think I was about to tell him so, when we were interrupted by a knocking at the door.

Bidding my uncle sit where he was, I went to open it, and found on the doorstep a half-grown boy in sea-clothes. He had no sooner seen me than he began to dance some steps of the sea-hornpipe (which I had never before heard of, far less seen), snapping his fingers in the air and footing it right cleverly. For all that, he was blue with the cold; and there was something in his face, a look between tears and laughter, that was highly pathetic and consisted ill with this gaiety of manner.

"What cheer, mate?" says he, with a cracked voice.

I asked him soberly to name his pleasure.

"O pleasure!" says he; and then began to sing:

> "For it's my delight, of a shiny night,
> In the season of the year."

"Well," said I, "if you have no business at all, I will even be so unmannerly as to shut you out."

"Stay, brother!" he cried. "Have you no fun about you? or do you want to get me thrashed? I 've brought a letter from old Heasyoasy to Mr. Belflower." He showed me a letter as he spoke. "And I say, mate," he added, "I 'm mortal hungry."

"Well," said I, "come into the house, and you shall have a bite if I go empty for it."

With that I brought him in and set him down to my own place, where he fell-to greedily on the remains of breakfast, winking to me between whiles, and making many faces, which I think the poor soul considered manly. Meanwhile, my uncle had read the letter and sat thinking; then, suddenly, he got to his feet with a great air of liveliness, and pulled me apart into the farthest corner of the room.

"Read that," said he, and put the letter in my hand.

Here it is, lying before me as I write:

KIDNAPPED

"The Hawes Inn, at the Queen's Ferry.

"Sir, — I lie here with my hawser up and down, and send my cabin-boy to informe. If you have any further commands for over-seas, to-day will be the last occasion, as the wind will serve us well out of the firth. I will not seek to deny that I have had crosses with your doer,[1] Mr. Rankeillor; of which, if not speedily redd up, you may looke to see some losses follow. I have drawn a bill upon you, as per margin, and am, sir, your most obedt., humble servant,

"ELIAS HOSEASON."

"You see, Davie," resumed my uncle, as soon as he saw that I had done, "I have a venture with this man Hoseason, the captain of a trading brig, the *Covenant,* of Dysart. Now, if you and me was to walk over with yon lad, I could see the captain at the Hawes, or maybe on board the *Covenant* if there was papers to be signed; and so far from a loss of time, we can jog on to the lawyer, Mr. Rankeillor's. After a' that's come and gone, ye would be swier[2] to believe me upon my naked word; but ye 'll believe Rankeillor. He's factor to half the gentry in these parts; an auld man, forby, highly respeckit, and he kenned your father."

I stood awhile and thought. I was going to some place of shipping, which was doubtless populous, and where my uncle durst attempt no violence, and, indeed, even the society of the cabin-boy so far protected me. Once there, I believed I could force on the visit to the lawyer, even if my uncle were now insincere in proposing it; and, perhaps, in the bottom of my heart, I wished a nearer view of the sea and ships. You are to remember I had lived all my life in the inland hills, and just two days before had my first sight

[1] Agent.   [2] Unwilling.

of the firth lying like a blue floor, and the sailed ships moving on the face of it, no bigger than toys. One thing with another, I made up my mind.

"Very well," says I, "let us go to the Ferry."

My uncle got into his hat and coat, and buckled an old rusty cutlass on; and then we trod the fire out, locked the door and set forth upon our walk.

The wind, being in that cold quarter the north-west, blew nearly in our faces as we went. It was the month of June; the grass was all white with daisies, and the trees with blossom; but, to judge by our blue nails and aching wrists, the time might have been winter and the whiteness a December frost.

Uncle Ebenezer trudged in the ditch, jogging from side to side like an old ploughman coming home from work. He never said a word the whole way; and I was thrown for talk on the cabin-boy. He told me his name was Ransome, and that he had followed the sea since he was nine, but could not say how old he was, as he had lost his reckoning. He showed me tattoo marks, baring his breast in the teeth of the wind and in spite of my remonstrances, for I thought it was enough to kill him; he swore horribly whenever he remembered, but more like a silly schoolboy than a man; and boasted of many wild and bad things that he had done: stealthy thefts, false accusations, ay, and even murder; but all with such a dearth of likelihood in the details, and such a weak and crazy swagger in the delivery, as disposed me rather to pity than to believe him.

I asked him of the brig (which he declared was the finest ship that sailed) and of Captain Hoseason, in whose praises he was equally loud. Heasyoasy (for so he still named the skipper) was a man, by his account, that minded for nothing either in heaven or earth; one that, as people said, would "crack on all sail into the day of judgment"; rough, fierce, unscrupulous, and brutal; and all this my poor cabin-boy had taught himself to admire as something seamanlike and manly. He would only admit one flaw in his idol. "He ain't no seaman," he admitted. "That's Mr. Shuan that navigates the brig; he's the finest seaman in the trade, only for drink; and I tell you I believe it! Why, look 'ere"; and turning down his stocking he showed me a great, raw, red wound that made my blood run cold. "He done that — Mr. Shuan done it," he said, with an air of pride.

"What!" I cried, "do you take such savage usage at his hands? Why, you are no slave, to be so handled!"

"No," said the poor moon-calf, changing his tune at once, "and so he'll find. See 'ere," and he showed me a great case-knife, which he told me was stolen. "O," says he, "let me see him try; I dare him to; I'll do for him! O, he ain't the first!" And he confirmed it with a poor, silly, ugly oath.

I have never felt such pity for any one in this wide world as I felt for that half-witted creature, and it began to come over me that the brig *Covenant* (for all her pious name) was little better than a hell upon the seas.

"Have you no friends?" said I.

He said he had a father in some English seaport, I forget which. "He was a fine man, too," he said, "but he's dead."

I GO TO THE QUEEN'S FERRY

"In Heaven's name," cried I, "can you find no reputable life on shore?"

"O, no," says he, winking and looking very sly, "they would put me to a trade. I know a trick worth two of that, I do!"

I asked him what trade could be so dreadful as the one he followed, where he ran the continual peril of his life, not alone from wind and sea, but by the horrid cruelty of those who were his masters. He said it was very true; and then began to praise the life, and tell what a pleasure it was to get on shore with money in his pocket, and spend it like a man, and buy apples, and swagger, and surprise what he called stick-in-the-mud boys. "And then it's not all as bad as that," says he; "there's worse off than me: there's the twenty-pounders. O, laws! you should see them taking on. Why, I've seen a man as old as you, I dessay" — (to him I seemed old) — "ah, and he had a beard, too — well, and as soon as we cleared out of the river, and he had the drug out of his head — my! how he cried and carried on! I made a fine fool of him, I tell you! And then there's little uns, too: oh, little by me! I tell you, I keep them in order. When we carry little uns, I have a rope's end of my own to wollop 'em." And so he ran on, until it came in on me what he meant by twenty-pounders were those unhappy criminals who were sent over-seas to slavery in North America, or the still more unhappy innocents who were kidnapped or trepanned (as the word went) for private interest or vengeance.

Just then we came to the top of the hill, and looked down on the Ferry and the Hope. The Firth of Forth (as is very well known) narrows at this point to the width of a good-sized river, which makes a convenient ferry going north, and turns the upper reach into a landlocked haven for all manner of ships. Right in the midst of the narrows lies an islet with some ruins; on the south shore they have built a pier for the service of the Ferry; and at the end of the pier, on the other side of the road, and backed against a pretty garden of holly-trees and hawthorns, I could see the building which they called the Hawes Inn.

The town of Queensferry lies farther west, and the neighbourhood of the inn looked pretty lonely at that time of day, for the boat had just gone north with passengers. A skiff, however, lay beside the pier, with some seamen sleeping on the thwarts; this, as Ransome told me, was the brig's boat waiting for the captain; and about half a mile off, and all alone in the anchorage, he showed me the *Covenant* herself. There was a sea-going bustle on board; yards were swinging into place; and as the wind blew from that quarter, I could hear the song of the sailors as they pulled upon the ropes. After all I had listened to upon the way, I looked at that ship with an extreme abhorrence; and from the bottom of my heart I pitied all poor souls that were condemned to sail in her.

We had all three pulled up on the brow of the hill; and now I marched across the road and addressed my uncle: "I think it right to tell you, sir," says I, "there's nothing that will bring me on board that *Covenant*."

He seemed to waken from a dream. "Eh?" he said. "What's that?"

I told him over again.

"Well, well," he said, "we'll have to please ye, I suppose. But what are we standing here for? It's perishing cold; and if I'm no mistaken, they're busking the *Covenant* for sea."

CHAPTER VI

WHAT BEFELL AT THE QUEEN'S FERRY

AS soon as we came to the inn, Ransome led us up the stair to a small room, with a bed in it, and heated like an oven by a great fire of coal. At a table hard by the chimney, a tall, dark, sober-looking man sat writing. In spite of the heat of the room, he wore a thick sea-jacket, buttoned to the neck, and a tall hairy cap drawn down over his ears; yet I never saw any man, not even a judge upon the bench, look cooler, or more studious and self-possessed, than this ship-captain.

He got to his feet at once, and coming forward, offered his large hand to Ebenezer. "I am proud to see you, Mr. Balfour," said he, in a fine deep voice, "and glad that ye are here in time. The wind's fair, and the tide upon the turn; we'll see the old coal-bucket burning on the Isle of May before to-night."

"Captain Hoseason," returned my uncle, "you keep your room unco hot."

"It's a habit I have, Mr. Balfour," said the skipper. "I'm a cold-rife man by my nature; I have a cold blood, sir. There's neither fur, nor flannel — no, sir, nor hot rum, will warm up what they call the temperature. Sir, it's the same with most men that have been carbonadoed, as they call it, in the tropic seas."

"Well, well, captain," replied my uncle, "we must all be the way we 're made."

But it chanced that this fancy of the captain's had a great share in my misfortunes. For though I had promised myself not to let my kinsman out of sight, I was both so impatient for a nearer look of the sea, and so sickened by the closeness of the room, that when he told me to "run down-stairs and play myself awhile," I was fool enough to take him at his word.

Away I went, therefore, leaving the two men sitting down to a bottle and a great mass of papers; and crossing the road in front of the inn, walked down upon the beach. With the wind in that quarter, only little wavelets, not much bigger than I had seen upon a lake, beat upon the shore. But the weeds were new to me — some green, some brown and long, and some with little bladders that crackled between my fingers. Even so far up the firth, the smell of the sea-water was exceedingly salt and stirring; the *Covenant,* besides, was beginning to shake out her sails, which hung upon the yards in clusters; and the spirit of all that I beheld put me in thoughts of far voyages and foreign places.

I looked, too, at the seamen with the skiff — big brown fellows, some in shirts, some with jackets, some with coloured handkerchiefs about their throats, one with a brace of pistols stuck into his pockets, two or three with knotty bludgeons, and all with their case-knives. I passed the time of day with one that looked less desperate than his fellows, and asked him of the sailing of the brig. He said they would get under way as soon as the ebb set, and expressed his gladness to be out of a port where there were no taverns and fiddlers; but all with such horrifying oaths, that I made haste to get away from him.

This threw me back on Ransome, who seemed the least wicked of that gang, and who soon came out of the inn and ran to me, crying for a bowl of punch. I told him I would give him no such thing, for neither he nor I was of an age for such indulgences. "But a glass of ale you may have, and welcome," said I. He mopped and mowed at me, and called me names; but he was glad to get the ale, for all that; and presently we were set down at a table in the front room of the inn, and both eating and drinking with a good appetite.

Here it occurred to me that, as the landlord was a man of that county, I might do well to make a friend of him. I offered him a share, as was much the custom in those days; but he was far too great a man to sit with such poor customers as Ransome and myself, and he was leaving the room, when I called him back to ask if he knew Mr. Rankeillor.

"Hoot, ay," says he, "and a very honest man. And, O, by-the-by," says he, "was it you that came in with Ebenezer?" And when I had told him yes, "Ye 'll be no friend of his?" he asked, meaning, in the Scottish way, that I would be no relative.

I hold him no, none.

"I thought not," said he, "and yet ye have a kind of gliff [1] of Mr. Alexander."

[1] Look.

WHAT BEFELL AT THE QUEEN'S FERRY

I said it seemed that Ebenezer was ill-seen in the country.

"Nae doubt," said the landlord. "He's a wicked auld man, and there's many would like to see him girning in the tow:[1] Jennet Clouston and mony mair that he has harried out of house and hame. And yet he was ance a fine young fellow, too. But that was before the sough[2] gaed abroad about Mr. Alexander; that was like the death of him."

"And what was it?" I asked.

"Ou, just that he had killed him," said the landlord. "Did ye never hear that?"

"And what would he kill him for?" said I.

"And what for, but just to get the place," said he.

"The place?" said I. "The Shaws?"

"Nae other place that I ken," said he.

"Ay, man?" said I. "Is that so? Was my — was Alexander the eldest son?"

"'Deed was he," said the landlord. "What else would he have killed him for?"

And with that he went away, as he had been impatient to do from the beginning.

Of course, I had guessed it a long while ago; but it is one thing to guess, another to know; and I sat stunned with my good fortune, and could scarce grow to believe that the same poor lad who had trudged in the dust from Ettrick Forest not two days ago, was now one of the rich of the earth, and had a house and broad lands, and might mount his horse to-morrow. All these pleasant things, and a thousand others, crowded into my mind, as I sat staring before me out of the

[1] Rope.   [2] Report.

[49]

inn window, and paying no heed to what I saw; only I remember that my eye lighted on Captain Hoseason down on
the pier among his seamen, and speaking with some authority. And presently he came marching back towards the
house, with no mark of a sailor's clumsiness, but carrying his
fine, tall figure with a manly bearing, and still with the same
sober, grave expression on his face. I wondered if it was
possible that Ransome's stories could be true, and half dis-
believed them; they fitted so ill with the man's looks. But,
indeed, he was neither so good as I supposed him, nor quite
so bad as Ransome did; for, in fact, he was two men, and left
the better one behind as soon as he set foot on board his vessel.

The next thing, I heard my uncle calling me, and found
the pair in the road together. It was the captain who addressed me, and that with an air (very flattering to a young
lad) of grave equality.

"Sir," said he, "Mr. Balfour tells me great things of
you; and for my own part, I like your looks. I wish I was
for longer here, that we might make the better friends; but
we 'll make the most of what we have. Ye shall come on
board my brig for half an hour, till the ebb sets, and drink
a bowl with me."

Now, I longed to see the inside of a ship more than words
can tell; but I was not going to put myself in jeopardy, and
I told him my uncle and I had an appointment with a lawyer.

"Ay, ay," said he, "he passed me word of that. But, ye
see, the boat 'll set ye ashore at the town pier, and that 's
but a penny stonecast from Rankeillor's house." And here
he suddenly leaned down and whispered in my ear: "Take

care of the old tod;[1] he means mischief. Come aboard till I can get a word with ye." And then, passing his arm through mine, he continued aloud, as he set off towards his boat: "But, come, what can I bring ye from the Carolinas? Any friend of Mr. Balfour's can command. A roll of tobacco? Indian feather-work? a skin of a wild beast? a stone pipe? the mocking-bird that mews for all the world like a cat? the cardinal bird that is as red as blood? — take your pick and say your pleasure."

By this time we were at the boat-side, and he was handing me in. I did not dream of hanging back; I thought (the poor fool!) that I had found a good friend and helper, and I was rejoiced to see the ship. As soon as we were all set in our places, the boat was thrust off from the pier and began to move over the waters; and what with my pleasure in this new movement and my surprise at our low position, and the appearance of the shores, and the growing bigness of the brig as we drew near to it, I could hardly understand what the captain said, and must have answered him at random.

As soon as we were alongside (where I sat fairly gaping at the ship's height, the strong humming of the tide against its sides, and the pleasant cries of the seamen at their work), Hoseason, declaring that he and I must be the first aboard, ordered a tackle to be sent down from the main-yard. In this I was whipped into the air and set down again on the deck, where the captain stood ready waiting for me, and instantly slipped back his arm under mine. There I stood some while, a little dizzy with the unsteadiness of all around

[1] Fox.

me, perhaps a little afraid, and yet vastly pleased with these strange sights; the captain meanwhile pointing out the strangest, and telling me their names and uses.

"But where is my uncle?" said I suddenly.

"Ay," said Hoseason, with a sudden grimness, "that's the point."

I felt I was lost. With all my strength, I plucked myself clear of him and ran to the bulwarks. Sure enough, there was the boat pulling for the town, with my uncle sitting in the stern. I gave a piercing cry — "Help, help! Murder!" — so that both sides of the anchorage rang with it, and my uncle turned round where he was sitting, and showed me a face full of cruelty and terror.

It was the last I saw. Already strong hands had been plucking me back from the ship's side; and now a thunderbolt seemed to strike me; I saw a great flash of fire, and fell senseless.

CHAPTER VII

I GO TO SEA IN THE BRIG "COVENANT"
OF DYSART

I CAME to myself in darkness, in great pain, bound hand and foot, and deafened by many unfamiliar noises. There sounded in my ears a roaring of water as of a huge mill-dam, the thrashing of heavy sprays, the thundering of the sails, and the shrill cries of seamen. The whole world now heaved giddily up, and now rushed giddily downward; and so sick and hurt was I in body, and my mind so much confounded, that it took me a long while, chasing my thoughts up and down, and ever stunned again by a fresh stab of pain, to realise that I must be lying somewhere bound in the belly of that unlucky ship, and that the wind must have strengthened to a gale. With the clear perception of my plight, there fell upon me a blackness of despair, a horror of remorse at my own folly, and a passion of anger at my uncle, that once more bereft me of my senses.

When I returned again to life, the same uproar, the same confused and violent movements, shook and deafened me; and presently, to my other pains and distresses, there was added the sickness of an unused landsman on the sea. In that time of my adventurous youth, I suffered many hardships; but none that was so crushing to my mind and body, or lit by so few hopes, as these first hours aboard the brig.

I heard a gun fire, and supposed the storm had proved too strong for us, and we were firing signals of distress. The thought of deliverance, even by death in the deep sea, was welcome to me. Yet it was no such matter; but (as I was afterwards told) a common habit of the captain's, which I here set down to show that even the worst man may have his kindlier side. We were then passing, it appeared, within some miles of Dysart, where the brig was built, and where old Mrs. Hoseason, the captain's mother, had come some years before to live; and whether outward or inward bound, the *Covenant* was never suffered to go by that place by day, without a gun fired and colours shown.

I had no measure of time; day and night were alike in that ill-smelling cavern of the ship's bowels where I lay; and the misery of my situation drew out the hours to double. How long, therefore, I lay waiting to hear the ship split upon some rock, or to feel her reel head foremast into the depths of the sea, I have not the means of computation. But sleep at length stole from me the consciousness of sorrow.

I was awakened by the light of a hand-lantern shining in my face. A small man of about thirty, with green eyes and a tangle of fair hair, stood looking down at me.

"Well," said he, "how goes it?"

I answered by a sob; and my visitor then felt my pulse and temples, and set himself to wash and dress the wound upon my scalp.

I GO TO SEA IN THE BRIG "COVENANT"

"Ay," said he, "a sore dunt.[1] What, man? Cheer up! The world's no done; you've made a bad start of it, but you'll make a better. Have you had any meat?"

I said I could not look at it: and thereupon he gave me some brandy and water in a tin pannikin, and left me once more to myself.

The next time he came to see me, I was lying betwixt sleep and waking, my eyes wide open in the darkness, the sickness quite departed, but succeeded by a horrid giddiness and swimming that was almost worse to bear. I ached, besides, in every limb, and the cords that bound me seemed to be of fire. The smell of the hole in which I lay seemed to have become a part of me; and during the long interval since his last visit I had suffered tortures of fear, now from the scurrying of the ship's rats, that sometimes pattered on my very face, and now from the dismal imaginings that haunt the bed of fever.

The glimmer of the lantern, as a trap opened, shone in like the heaven's sunlight; and though it only showed me the strong, dark beams of the ship that was my prison, I could have cried aloud for gladness. The man with the green eyes was the first to descend the ladder, and I noticed that he came somewhat unsteadily. He was followed by the captain. Neither said a word; but the first set to and examined me, and dressed my wound as before, while Hoseason looked me in my face with an odd, black look.

"Now, sir, you see for yourself," said the first: "a high fever. no appetite, no light, no meat: you see for yourself what that means."

[1] Stroke.

[55]

"I am no conjurer, Mr. Riach," said the captain.

"Give me leave, sir," said Riach; "you 've a good head upon your shoulders, and a good Scotch tongue to ask with; but I will leave you no manner of excuse; I want that boy taken out of this hole and put in the forecastle."

"What ye may want, sir, is a matter of concern to nobody but yoursel'," returned the captain; "but I can tell ye that which is to be. Here he is; here he shall bide."

"Admitting that you have been paid in a proportion," said the other, "I will crave leave humbly to say that I have not. Paid I am, and none too much, to be the second officer of this old tub, and you ken very well if I do my best to earn it. But I was paid for nothing more."

"If ye could hold back your hand from the tin-pan, Mr. Riach, I would have no complaint to make of ye," returned the skipper; "and instead of asking riddles, I make bold to say that ye would keep your breath to cool your porridge. We 'll be required on deck," he added, in a sharper note, and set one foot upon the ladder.

But Mr. Riach caught him by the sleeve.

"Admitting that you have been paid to do a murder —" he began.

Hoseason turned upon him with a flash.

"What 's that?" he cried. "What kind of talk is that?"

"It seems it is the talk that you can understand," said Mr. Riach, looking him steadily in the face.

"Mr. Riach, I have sailed with ye three cruises," replied the captain. "In all that time, sir, ye should have learned to know me: I 'm a stiff man, and a dour man; but for what ye say the now — fie, fie! — it comes from a bad heart and a black conscience. If ye say the lad will die ——"

"Ay, will he!" said Mr. Riach.

"Well, sir, is not that enough?" said Hoseason. "Flit him where ye please!"

Thereupon the captain ascended the ladder; and I, who had lain silent throughout this strange conversation, beheld Mr. Riach turn after him and bow as low as to his knees in what was plainly a spirit of derision. Even in my then state of sickness, I perceived two things: that the mate was touched with liquor, as the captain hinted, and that (drunk or sober) he was like to prove a valuable friend.

Five minutes afterwards my bonds were cut, I was hoisted on a man's back, carried up to the forecastle, and laid in a bunk on some sea-blankets; where the first thing that I did was to lose my senses.

It was a blessed thing indeed to open my eyes again upon the daylight, and to find myself in the society of men. The forecastle was a roomy place enough, set all about with berths, in which the men of the watch below were seated smoking, or lying down asleep. The day being calm and the wind fair, the scuttle was open, and not only the good daylight, but from time to time (as the ship rolled) a dusty beam of sunlight shone in, and dazzled and delighted me. I had no sooner moved, moreover, than one of the men brought me a drink of something healing which Mr. Riach had prepared, and bade me lie still and I should soon be well again. There were no bones broken, he explained: "A clour[1] on

[1] Blow.

the head was naething. Man," said he, "it was me that gave it ye!"

Here I lay for the space of many days a close prisoner, and not only got my health again, but came to know my companions. They were a rough lot indeed, as sailors mostly are: being men rooted out of all the kindly parts of life, and condemned to toss together on the rough seas, with masters no less cruel. There were some among them that had sailed with the pirates and seen things it would be a shame even to speak of; some were men that had run from the king's ships, and went with a halter round their necks, of which they made no secret; and all, as the saying goes, were "at a word and a blow" with their best friends. Yet I had not been many days shut up with them before I began to be ashamed of my first judgment, when I had drawn away from them at the Ferry pier, as though they had been unclean beasts. No class of man is altogether bad, but each has its own faults and virtues; and these shipmates of mine were no exception to the rule. Rough they were, sure enough; and bad, I suppose; but they had many virtues. They were kind when it occurred to them, simple even beyond the simplicity of a country lad like me, and had some glimmerings of honesty.

There was one man, of maybe forty, that would sit on my berthside for hours and tell me of his wife and child. He was a fisher that had lost his boat, and thus been driven to the deep-sea voyaging. Well, it is years ago now: but I have never forgotten him. His wife (who was "young by him," as he often told me) waited in vain to see her man return; he would never again make the fire for her in the morning, nor yet keep the bairn when she was sick. Indeed, many of these poor fellows (as the event proved) were upon their last cruise; the deep seas and cannibal fish received them; and it is a thankless business to speak ill of the dead.

Among other good deeds that they did, they returned my money, which had been shared among them; and though it was about a third short, I was very glad to get it, and hoped great good from it in the land I was going to. The ship was bound for the Carolinas; and you must not suppose that I was going to that place merely as an exile. The trade was even then much depressed; since that, and with the rebellion of the colonies and the formation of the United States, it has, of course, come to an end; but in those days of my youth, white men were still sold into slavery on the plantations, and that was the destiny to which my wicked uncle had condemned me.

The cabin-boy Ransome (from whom I had first heard of these atrocities) came in at times from the round-house, where he berthed and served, now nursing a bruised limb in silent agony, now raving against the cruelty of Mr. Shuan. It made my heart bleed; but the men had a great respect for the chief mate, who was, as they said, "the only seaman of the whole jing-bang, and none such a bad man when he was sober." Indeed, I found there was a strange peculiarity about our two mates: that Mr. Riach was sullen, unkind, and harsh when he was sober, and Mr. Shuan would not hurt a fly except when he was drinking. I asked about the captain; but I was told drink made no difference upon that man of iron.

KIDNAPPED

I did my best in the small time allowed me to make something like a man, or rather I should say something like a boy, of the poor creature, Ransome. But his mind was scarce truly human. He could remember nothing of the time before he came to sea; only that his father had made clocks, and had a starling in the parlour which could whistle "The North Countrie"; all else had been blotted out in these years of hardship and cruelties. He had a strange notion of the dry land, picked up from sailor's stories: that it was a place where lads were put to some kind of slavery called a trade, and where apprentices were continually lashed and clapped into foul prisons. In a town, he thought every second person a decoy, and every third house a place in which seamen would be drugged and murdered. To be sure, I would tell him how kindly I had myself been used upon that dry land he was so much afraid of, and how well fed and carefully taught both by my friends and my parents: and if he had been recently hurt, he would weep bitterly and swear to run away; but if he was in his usual crackbrain humour, or (still more) if he had had a glass of spirits in the round-house, he would deride the notion.

It was Mr. Riach (Heaven forgive him!) who gave the boy drink; and it was, doubtless, kindly meant; but besides that it was ruin to his health, it was the pitifullest thing in life to see this unhappy, unfriended creature staggering, and dancing, and talking he knew not what. Some of the men laughed, but not all; others would grow as black as thunder (thinking, perhaps, of their own childhood or their own children) and bid him stop that nonsense, and think what he was doing. As for me, I felt ashamed to look at him, and the poor child still comes about me in my dreams.

All this time, you should know, the *Covenant* was meeting continual head-winds and tumbling up and down against head-seas, so that the scuttle was almost constantly shut, and the forecastle lighted only by a swinging lantern on a beam. There was constant labour for all hands; the sails had to be made and shortened every hour; the strain told on the men's temper; there was a growl of quarrelling all day long from berth to berth; and as I was never allowed to set my foot on deck, you can picture to yourselves how weary of my life I grew to be, and how impatient for a change.

And a change I was to get, as you shall hear; but I must first tell of a conversation I had with Mr. Riach, which put a little heart in me to bear my troubles. Getting him in a favourable stage of drink (for indeed he never looked near me when he was sober), I pledged him to secrecy, and told him my whole story.

He declared it was like a ballad; that he would do his best to help me; that I should have paper, pen, and ink, and write one line to Mr. Campbell and another to Mr. Rankeillor; and that if I had told the truth, ten to one he would be able (with their help) to pull me through and set me in my rights.

"And in the meantime," says he, "keep your heart up. You 're not the only one, I 'll tell you that. There 's many a man hoeing tobacco over-seas that should be mounting his horse at his own door at home; many and many! And life is all a variorum, at the best. Look at me: I 'm a laird's son and more than half a doctor, and here I am, man-Jack to Hoseason!"

I thought it would be civil to ask him for his story.

He whistled loud.

"Never had one," said he. "I like fun, that's all." And he skipped out of the forecastle.

CHAPTER VIII

THE ROUND–HOUSE

ONE night, about eleven o'clock, a man of Mr. Riach's watch (which was on deck) came below for his jacket; and instantly there began to go a whisper about the forecastle that "Shuan had done for him at last." There was no need of a name; we all knew who was meant; but we had scarce time to get the idea rightly in our heads, far less to speak of it, when the scuttle was again flung open, and Captain Hoseason came down the ladder. He looked sharply round the bunks in the tossing light of the lantern; and then, walking straight up to me, he addressed me, to my surprise, in tones of kindness.

"My man," said he, "we want ye to serve in the round-house. You and Ransome are to change berths. Run away aft with ye."

Even as he spoke, two seamen appeared in the scuttle, carrying Ransome in their arms; and the ship at that moment giving a great sheer into the sea, and the lantern swinging, the light fell direct on the boy's face. It was as white as wax, and had a look upon it like a dreadful smile. The blood in me ran cold, and I drew in my breath as if I had been struck.

KIDNAPPED

"Run away aft; run away aft with ye!" cried Hoseason.

And at that I brushed by the sailors and the boy (who neither spoke nor moved), and ran up the ladder on deck.

The brig was sheering swiftly and giddily through a long, cresting swell. She was on the starboard tack, and on the left hand, under the arched foot of the foresail, I could see the sunset still quite bright. This, at such an hour of the night, surprised me greatly; but I was too ignorant to draw the true conclusion — that we were going north-about round Scotland, and were now on the high sea between the Orkney and Shetland Islands, having avoided the dangerous currents of the Pentland Firth. For my part, who had been so long shut in the dark and knew nothing of head-winds, I thought we might be half-way or more across the Atlantic. And indeed (beyond that I wondered a little at the lateness of the sunset light) I gave no heed to it, and pushed on across the decks, running between the seas, catching at ropes, and only saved from going overboard by one of the hands on deck, who had been always kind to me.

The round-house, for which I was bound, and where I was now to sleep and serve, stood some six feet above the decks, and considering the size of the brig, was of good dimensions. Inside were a fixed table and bench, and two berths, one for the captain and the other for the two mates, turn and turn about. It was all fitted with lockers from top to bottom, so as to stow away the officers' belongings and a part of the ship's stores; there was a second store-room underneath, which you entered by a hatchway in the middle of the deck; indeed, all the best of the meat and drink and the whole of the powder were collected in this place; and all the firearms, except the two pieces of brass ordnance, were set in a rack in the aftermost wall of the round-house. The most of the cutlasses were in another place.

A small window with a shutter on each side, and a sky-light in the roof, gave it light by day; and after dark there was a lamp always burning. It was burning when I entered, not brightly, but enough to show Mr. Shuan sitting at the table, with the brandy bottle and a tin pannikin in front of him. He was a tall man, strongly made and very black; and he stared before him on the table like one stupid.

He took no notice of my coming in; nor did he move when the captain followed and leant on the berth beside me, look-ing darkly at the mate. I stood in great fear of Hoseason, and had my reasons for it; but something told me I need not be afraid of him just then; and I whispered in his ear: "How is he?" He shook his head like one that does not know and does not wish to think, and his face was very stern.

Presently Mr. Riach came in. He gave the captain a glance that meant the boy was dead as plain as speaking, and took his place like the rest of us; so that we all three stood without a word, staring down at Mr. Shuan, and Mr. Shuan (on his side) sat without a word, looking hard upon the table.

All of a sudden he put out his hand to take the bottle; and at that Mr. Riach started forward and caught it away from him, rather by surprise than violence, crying out, with an oath, that there had been too much of this work alto-gether, and that a judgment would fall upon the ship. And as he spoke (the weather sliding-doors standing open) he tossed the bottle into the sea.

Mr. Shuan was on his feet in a trice; he still looked dazed, but he meant murder, ay, and would have done it, for the second time that night, had not the captain stepped in between him and his victim.

"Sit down!" roars the captain. "Ye sot and swine, do ye know what ye've done? Ye've murdered the boy!"

Mr. Shuan seemed to understand; for he sat down again, and put his hand to his brow.

"Well," he said, "he brought me a dirty pannikin!"

At that word, the captain and I and Mr. Riach all looked at each other for a second with a kind of frightened look; and then Hoseason walked up to his chief officer, took him by the shoulder, led him across to his bunk, and bade him lie down and go to sleep, as you might speak to a bad child. The murderer cried a little, but he took off his sea-boots and obeyed.

"Ah!" cried Mr. Riach, with a dreadful voice, "ye should have interfered long syne. It's too late now."

"Mr. Riach," said the captain, "this night's work must never be kennt in Dysart. The boy went overboard, sir; that's what the story is; and I would give five pounds out of my pocket it was true!" He turned to the table. "What made ye throw the good bottle away?" he added. "There was nae sense in that, sir. Here, David, draw me another. They're in the bottom locker"; and he tossed me a key. "Ye'll need a glass yourself, sir," he added to Riach. "Yon was an ugly thing to see."

THE ROUND–HOUSE

So the pair sat down and hob-a-nobbed; and while they did so, the murderer, who had been lying and whimpering in his berth, raised himself upon his elbow and looked at them and at me.

That was the first night of my new duties; and in the course of the next day I had got well into the run of them. I had to serve at the meals, which the captain took at regular hours, sitting down with the officer who was off duty; all the day through I would be running with a dram to one or other of my three masters; and at night I slept on a blanket thrown on the deck boards at the aftermost end of the round-house, and right in the draught of the two doors. It was a hard and a cold bed; nor was I suffered to sleep without interruption; for some one would be always coming in from deck to get a dram, and when a fresh watch was to be set, two and sometimes all three would sit down and brew a bowl together. How they kept their health, I know not, any more than how I kept my own.

And yet in other ways it was an easy service. There was no cloth to lay; the meals were either of oatmeal porridge or salt junk, except twice a week, when there was duff; and though I was clumsy enough and (not being firm on my sea-legs) sometimes fell with what I was bringing them, both Mr. Riach and the captain were singularly patient. I could not but fancy they were making up lee-way with their consciences, and that they would scarce have been so good with me if they had not been worse with Ransome.

As for Mr. Shuan, the drink or his crime, or the two together, had certainly troubled his mind. I cannot say I ever saw him in his proper wits. He never grew used to my being there, stared at me continually (sometimes, I could have thought, with terror), and more than once drew back from my hand when I was serving him. I was pretty sure from the first that he had no clear mind of what he had done, and on my second day in the round-house I had the proof of it. We were alone, and he had been staring at me a long time, when all at once, up he got, as pale as death, and came close up to me, to my great terror. But I had no cause to be afraid of him.

"You were not here before?" he asked.

"No, sir," said I.

"There was another boy?" he asked again; and when I had answered him, "Ah!" says he, "I thought that," and went and sat down, without another word, except to call for brandy.

You may think it strange, but for all the horror I had, I was still sorry for him. He was a married man, with a wife in Leith; but whether or no he had a family, I have now forgotten; I hope not.

Altogether it was no very hard life for the time it lasted, which (as you are to hear) was not long. I was as well fed as the best of them; even their pickles, which were the great dainty, I was allowed my share of; and had I liked I might have been drunk from morning to night, like Mr. Shuan. I had company, too, and good company of its sort. Mr. Riach, who had been to the college, spoke to me like a friend when he was not sulking, and told me many curious things, and some that were informing; and even the captain, though he kept me at the stick's end the most part of the time, would sometimes unbuckle a bit, and tell me of the fine countries he had visited.

The shadow of poor Ransome, to be sure, lay on all four of us, and on me and Mr. Shuan in particular, most heavily. And then I had another trouble of my own. Here I was, doing dirty work for three men that I looked down upon, and one of whom, at least, should have hung upon a gallows; that was for the present; and as for the future, I could only see myself slaving alongside of negroes in the tobacco fields. Mr. Riach, perhaps from caution, would never suffer me to say another word about my story; the captain, whom I tried to approach, rebuffed me like a dog and would not hear a word; and as the days came and went, my heart sank lower and lower, till I was even glad of the work which kept me from thinking.

CHAPTER IX

THE MAN WITH THE BELT OF GOLD

MORE than a week went by, in which the ill-luck that had hitherto pursued the *Covenant* upon this voyage grew yet more strongly marked. Some days she made a little way; others, she was driven actually back. At last we were beaten so far to the south that we tossed and tacked to and fro the whole of the ninth day, within sight of Cape Wrath and the wild, rocky coast on either hand of it. There followed on that a council of the officers, and some decision which I did not rightly understand, seeing only the result: that we had made a fair wind of a foul one and were running south.

The tenth afternoon there was a falling swell and a thick, wet, white fog that hid one end of the brig from the other. All afternoon, when I went on deck, I saw men and officers listening hard over the bulwarks — "for breakers," they said; and though I did not so much as understand the word, I felt danger in the air, and was excited.

Maybe about ten at night, I was serving Mr. Riach and the captain at their supper, when the ship struck something with a great sound, and we heard voices singing out. My two masters leaped to their feet.

THE MAN WITH THE BELT OF GOLD

"She's struck!" said Mr. Riach.

"No, sir," said the captain. "We've only run a boat down."

And they hurried out.

The captain was in the right of it. We had run down a boat in the fog, and she had parted in the midst and gone to the bottom with all her crew but one. This man (as I heard afterwards) had been sitting in the stern as a passenger, while the rest were on the benches rowing. At the moment of the blow, the stern had been thrown into the air, and the man (having his hands free, and for all he was encumbered with a frieze overcoat that came below his knees) had leaped up and caught hold of the brig's bowsprit. It showed he had luck and much agility and unusual strength, that he should have thus saved himself from such a pass. And yet, when the captain brought him into the round-house, and I set eyes on him for the first time, he looked as cool as I did.

He was smallish in stature, but well set and as nimble as a goat; his face was of a good open expression, but sunburnt very dark, and heavily freckled and pitted with the small-pox; his eyes were unusually light and had a kind of dancing madness in them, that was both engaging and alarming; and when he took off his great-coat, he laid a pair of fine silver-mounted pistols on the table, and I saw that he was belted with a great sword. His manners, besides, were elegant, and he pledged the captain handsomely. Altogether I thought of him, at the first sight, that here was a man I would rather call my friend than my enemy.

The captain, too, was taking his observations, but rather

of the man's clothes than his person. And to be sure, as soon as he had taken off the great-coat, he showed forth mighty fine for the round-house of a merchant brig: having a hat with feathers, a red waistcoat, breeches of black plush, and a blue coat with silver buttons and handsome silver lace; costly clothes, though somewhat spoiled with the fog and being slept in.

"I 'm vexed, sir, about the boat," says the captain.

"There are some pretty men gone to the bottom," said the stranger, "that I would rather see on the dry land again than half a score of boats."

"Friends of yours?" said Hoseason.

"You have none such friends in your country," was the reply. "They would have died for me like dogs."

"Well, sir," said the captain, still watching him, "there are more men in the world than boats to put them in."

"And that 's true, too," cried the other, "and ye seem to be a gentleman of great penetration."

"I have been in France, sir," says the captain, so that it was plain he meant more by the words than showed upon the face of them.

"Well, sir," says the other, "and so has many a pretty man, for the matter of that."

"No doubt, sir," says the captain, "and fine coats."

"Oho!" says the stranger, "is that how the wind sets?" And he laid his hand quickly on his pistols.

"Don't be hasty," said the captain. "Don't do a mischief before ye see the need of it. Ye 've a French soldier's coat upon your back and a Scotch tongue in your head, to be sure; but so has many an honest fellow in these days, and I dare say none the worse of it."

"So?" said the gentleman in the fine coat: "are ye of the honest party?" (meaning, Was he a Jacobite? for each side, in these sort of civil broils, takes the name of honesty for its own).

"Why, sir," replied the captain, "I am a true-blue Protestant, and I thank God for it." (It was the first word of any religion I had ever heard from him, but I learnt afterwards he was a great church-goer while on shore.) "But, for all that," says he, "I can be sorry to see another man with his back to the wall."

"Can ye so, indeed?" asked the Jacobite. "Well, sir, to be quite plain with ye, I am one of those honest gentlemen that were in trouble about the years forty-five and six; and (to be still quite plain with ye) if I got into the hands of any of the red-coated gentry, it's like it would go hard with me. Now, sir, I was for France; and there was a French ship cruising here to pick me up; but she gave us the go-by in the fog — as I wish from the heart that ye had done yoursel'! And the best that I can say is this: If ye can set me ashore where I was going, I have that upon me will reward you highly for your trouble."

"In France?" says the captain. "No, sir; that I cannot do. But where ye come from — we might talk of that."

And then, unhappily, he observed me standing in my corner, and packed me off to the galley to get supper for the gentleman. I lost no time, I promise you; and when I came back into the round-house, I found the gentleman had taken a money-belt from about his waist, and poured out a guinea or two upon the table. The captain was looking at the guineas, and then at the belt, and then at the gentleman's face; and I thought he seemed excited.

"Half of it," he cried, "and I 'm your man!"

The other swept back the guineas into the belt, and put it on again under his waistcoat. "I have told ye, sir," said he, "that not one doit of it belongs to me. It belongs to my chieftain," and here he touched his hat, " and while I would be but a silly messenger to grudge some of it that the rest might come safe, I should show myself a hound indeed if I bought my own carcase any too dear. Thirty guineas on the sea-side, or sixty if ye set me on the Linnhe Loch. Take it, if ye will; if not, ye can do your worst."

"Ay," said Hoseason. "And if I give ye over to the soldiers?"

"Ye would make a fool's bargain," said the other. "My chief, let me tell you, sir, is forfeited, like every honest man in Scotland. His estate is in the hands of the man they call King George; and it is his officers that collect the rents, or try to collect them. But for the honour of Scotland, the poor tenant bodies take a thought upon their chief lying in exile; and this money is a part of that very rent for which King George is looking. Now, sir, ye seem to me to be a man that understands things: bring this money within the reach of Government, and how much of it 'll come to you?"

"Little enough, to be sure," said Hoseason; and then, "if they knew," he added, drily. "But I think, if I was to try, that I could hold my tongue about it."

THE MAN WITH THE BELT OF GOLD

"Ah, but I 'll begowk[1] ye there!" cried the gentleman. "Play me false, and I 'll play you cunning. If a hand is laid upon me, they shall ken what money it is."

"Well," returned the captain, "what must be must. Sixty guineas, and done. Here 's my hand upon it."

"And here 's mine," said the other.

And thereupon the captain went out (rather hurriedly, I thought), and left me alone in the round-house with the stranger.

At that period (so soon after the forty-five) there were many exiled gentlemen coming back at the peril of their lives, either to see their friends or to collect a little money; and as for the Highland chiefs that had been forfeited, it was a common matter of talk how their tenants would stint themselves to send them money, and their clansmen out-face the soldiery to get it in, and run the gauntlet of our great navy to carry it across. All this I had, of course, heard tell of; and now I had a man under my eyes whose life was forfeit on all these counts and upon one more, for he was not only a rebel and a smuggler of rents, but had taken service with King Louis of France. And as if all this were not enough, he had a belt full of golden guineas round his loins. Whatever my opinions, I could not look on such a man without a lively interest.

"And so you 're a Jacobite?" said I, as I set meat before him.

"Ay," said he, beginning to eat. "And you, by your long face, should be a Whig?"[2]

---

[1] Befool.

[2] Whig or Whigamore was the cant name for those who were loyal to King George.

"Betwixt and between," said I, not to annoy him; for indeed I was as good a Whig as Mr. Campbell could make me.

"And that's naething," said he. "But I'm saying, Mr. Betwixt-and-Between," he added, "this bottle of yours is dry; and it's hard if I'm to pay sixty guineas and be grudged a dram upon the back of it."

"I'll go and ask for the key," said I, and stepped on deck.

The fog was as close as ever, but the swell almost down. They had laid the brig to, not knowing precisely where they were, and the wind (what little there was of it) not serving well for their true course. Some of the hands were still hearkening for breakers; but the captain and the two officers were in the waist with their heads together. It struck me (I don't know why) that they were after no good; and the first word I heard, as I drew softly near, more than confirmed me.

It was Mr. Riach, crying out as if upon a sudden thought:

"Couldn't we wile him out of the round-house?"

"He's better where he is," returned Hoseason; "he hasn't room to use his sword."

"Well, that's true," said Riach; "but he's hard to come at."

"Hut!" said Hoseason. "We can get the man in talk, one upon each side, and pin him by the two arms; or if that'll not hold, sir, we can make a run by both the doors and get him under hand before he has the time to draw."

At this hearing, I was seized with both fear and anger

at these treacherous, greedy, bloody men that I sailed with. My first mind was to run away; my second was bolder.

"Captain," said I, "the gentleman is seeking a dram, and the bottle's out. Will you give me the key?"

They all started and turned about.

"Why, here's our chance to get the firearms!" Riach cried; and then to me: "Hark ye, David," he said, "do ye ken where the pistols are?"

"Ay, ay," put in Hoseason. "David kens; David's a good lad. Ye see, David my man, yon wild Hielandman is a danger to the ship, besides being a rank foe to King George, God bless him!"

I had never been so be-Davided since I came on board; but I said Yes, as if all I heard were quite natural.

"The trouble is," resumed the captain, "that all our fire-locks, great and little, are in the round-house under this man's nose; likewise the powder. Now, if I, or one of the officers, was to go in and take them, he would fall to thinking. But a lad like you, David, might snap up a horn and a pistol or two without remark. And if ye can do it cleverly, I'll bear it in mind when it'll be good for you to have friends; and that's when we come to Carolina."

Here Mr. Riach whispered him a little.

"Very right, sir," said the captain; and then to myself: "And see here, David, yon man has a beltful of gold, and I give you my word that you shall have your fingers in it."

I told him I would do as he wished, though indeed I had scarce breath to speak with; and upon that he gave me the key of the spirit locker, and I began to go slowly back to the round-house. What was I to do? They were dogs and thieves; they had stolen me from my own country; they had killed poor Ransome; and was I to hold the candle to another murder? But then, upon the other hand, there was the fear of death very plain before me; for what could a boy and a man, if they were as brave as lions, against a whole ship's company?

I was still arguing it back and forth, and getting no great clearness, when I came into the round-house and saw the Jacobite eating his supper under the lamp; and at that my mind was made up all in a moment. I have no credit by it; it was by no choice of mine, but as if by compulsion, that I walked right up to the table and put my hand on his shoulder.

"Do ye want to be killed?" said I.

He sprang to his feet, and looked a question at me as clear as if he had spoken.

"O!" cried I, "they're all murderers here; it's a ship full of them! They've murdered a boy already. Now it's you."

"Ay, ay," said he; "but they haven't got me yet." And then looking at me curiously, "Will ye stand with me?"

"That will I!" said I. "I am no thief, nor yet murderer. I'll stand by you."

"Why, then," said he, "what's your name?"

"David Balfour," said I; and then, thinking that a man with so fine a coat must like fine people, I added for the first time, "of Shaws."

It never occurred to him to doubt me, for a Highlander is used to see great gentlefolk in great poverty; but as he had no estate of his own, my words nettled a very childish vanity he had.

"My name is Stewart," he said, drawing himself up. "Alan Breck, they call me. A king's name is good enough for me, though I bear it plain and have the name of no farm-midden to clap to the hind-end of it."

And having administered this rebuke, as though it were something of a chief importance, he turned to examine our defences.

The round-house was built very strong, to support the breaching of the seas. Of its five apertures, only the sky-light and the two doors were large enough for the passage of a man. The doors, besides, could be drawn close: they were of stout oak, and ran in grooves, and were fitted with hooks to keep them either shut or open, as the need arose. The one that was already shut I secured in this fashion; but when I was proceeding to slide to the other, Alan stopped me.

"David," said he — "for I cannae bring to mind the name of your landed estate, and so will make so bold as to call you David — that door, being open, is the best part of my defences."

"It would be yet better shut," says I.

"Not so, David," says he. "Ye see, I have but one face; but so long as that door is open and my face to it, the best part of my enemies will be in front of me, where I would aye wish to find them."

Then he gave me from the rack a cutlass (of which there were a few besides the firearms), choosing it with great care, shaking his head and saying he had never in all his life seen poorer weapons; and next he set me down to the table with a powder-horn, a bag of bullets and all the pistols, which he bade me charge.

"And that will be better work, let me tell you," said he, "for a gentleman of decent birth, than scraping plates and raxing[1] drams to a wheen tarry sailors."

Thereupon he stood up in the midst with his face to the door, and drawing his great sword, made trial of the room he had to wield it in.

"I must stick to the point," he said, shaking his head; "and that's a pity, too. It doesn't set my genius, which is all for the upper guard. And now," said he, "do you keep on charging the pistols, and give heed to me."

I told him I would listen closely. My chest was tight, my mouth dry, the light dark to my eyes; the thought of the numbers that were soon to leap in upon us kept my heart in a flutter; and the sea, which I heard washing round the brig, and where I thought my dead body would be cast ere morning, ran in my mind strangely.

"First of all," said he, "how many are against us?"

I reckoned them up; and such was the hurry of my mind, I had to cast the numbers twice. "Fifteen," said I.

Alan whistled. "Well," said he, "that can't be cured. And now follow me. It is my part to keep this door, where I look for the main battle. In that, ye have no hand. And mind and dinnae fire to this side unless they get me down; for I would rather have ten foes in front of me than one friend like you cracking pistols at my back."

[1] Reaching.

I told him, indeed I was no great shot.

"And that's very bravely said," he cried, in a great admiration of my candour. "There's many a pretty gentleman that wouldnae dare to say it."

"But then, sir," said I, "there is the door behind you, which they may perhaps break in."

"Ay," said he, "and that is a part of your work. No sooner the pistols charged, than ye must climb up into yon bed where ye're handy at the window; and if they lift hand against the door, ye're to shoot. But that's not all. Let's make a bit of a soldier of ye, David. What else have ye to guard?"

"There's the skylight," said I. "But indeed, Mr. Stewart, I would need to have eyes upon both sides to keep the two of them; for when my face is at the one, my back is to the other."

"And that's very true," said Alan. "But have ye no ears to your head?"

"To be sure!" cried I. "I must hear the bursting of the glass!"

"Ye have some rudiments of sense," said Alan, grimly.

CHAPTER X

THE SIEGE OF THE ROUND–HOUSE

BUT now our time of truce was come to an end. Those on deck had waited for my coming till they grew impatient; and scarce had Alan spoken, when the captain showed face in the open door.

"Stand!" cried Alan, and pointed his sword at him.

The captain stood, indeed; but he neither winced nor drew back a foot.

"A naked sword?" says he. "This is a strange return for hospitality."

"Do ye see me?" said Alan. "I am come of kings; I bear a king's name. My badge is the oak. Do ye see my sword? It has slashed the heads off mair Whigamores than you have toes upon your feet. Call up your vermin to your back, sir, and fall on! The sooner the clash begins, the sooner ye 'll taste this steel throughout your vitals."

The captain said nothing to Alan, but he looked over at me with an ugly look. "David," said he, "I 'll mind this"; and the sound of his voice went through me with a jar.

Next moment he was gone.

"And now," said Alan, "let your hand keep your head, for the grip is coming."

THE SIEGE OF THE ROUND-HOUSE

Alan drew a dirk, which he held in his left hand in case they should run in under his sword. I, on my part, clambered up into the berth with an armful of pistols and something of a heavy heart, and set open the window where I was to watch. It was a small part of the deck that I could overlook, but enough for our purpose. The sea had gone down, and the wind was steady and kept the sails quiet; so that there was a great stillness in the ship, in which I made sure I heard the sound of muttering voices. A little after, and there came a clash of steel upon the deck, by which I knew they were dealing out the cutlasses and one had been let fall; and after that, silence again.

I do not know if I was what you call afraid; but my heart beat like a bird's, both quick and little; and there was a dimness came before my eyes which I continually rubbed away, and which continually returned. As for hope, I had none; but only a darkness of despair and a sort of anger against all the world that made me long to sell my life as dear as I was able. I tried to pray, I remember, but that same hurry of my mind, like a man running, would not suffer me to think upon the words; and my chief wish was to have the thing begin and be done with it.

It came all of a sudden when it did, with a rush of feet and a roar, and then a shout from Alan, and a sound of blows and some one crying out as if hurt. I looked back over my shoulder, and saw Mr. Shuan in the doorway, crossing blades with Alan.

"That's him that killed the boy!" I cried.

"Look to your window!" said Alan; and as I turned back

to my place, I saw him pass his sword through the mate's body.

It was none to soon for me to look to my own part; for my head was scarce back at the window, before five men, carrying a spare yard for a battering-ram, ran past me and took post to drive the door in. I had never fired with a pistol in my life, and not often with a gun; far less against a fellow-creature. But it was now or ever; and just as they swang the yard, I cried out: "Take that!" and shot into their midst.

I must have hit one of them, for he sang out and gave back a step, and the rest stopped as if a little disconcerted. Before they had time to recover, I sent another ball over their heads; and at my third shot (which went as wide as the second) the whole party threw down the yard and ran for it.

Then I looked round again into the deck-house. The whole place was full of the smoke of my own firing, just as my ears seemed to be burst with the noise of the shots. But there was Alan, standing as before; only now his sword was running blood to the hilt, and himself so swelled with triumph and fallen into so fine an attitude, that he looked to be invincible. Right before him on the floor was Mr. Shuan, on his hands and knees; the blood was pouring from his mouth, and he was sinking slowly lower, with a terrible, white face; and just as I looked, some of those from behind caught hold of him by the heels and dragged him bodily out of the round-house. I believe he died as they were doing it.

"There's one of your Whigs for ye!" cried Alan; and then turning to me, he asked if I had done much execution.

THE SIEGE OF THE ROUND-HOUSE

I told him I had winged one, and thought it was the captain.

"And I 've settled two," says he. "No, there 's not enough blood let; they 'll be back again. To your watch, David. This was but a dram before meat."

I settled back to my place, re-charging the three pistols I had fired, and keeping watch with both eye and ear.

Our enemies were disputing not far off upon the deck, and that so loudly that I could hear a word or two above the washing of the seas.

"It was Shuan bauchled[1] it," I heard one say.

And another answered him with a "Wheesht, man! He 's paid the piper."

After that the voices fell again into the same muttering as before. Only now, one person spoke most of the time, as though laying down a plan, and first one and then another answered him briefly, like men taking orders. By this, I made sure they were coming on again, and told Alan.

"It 's what we have to pray for," said he. "Unless we can give them a good distaste of us, and done with it, there 'll be nae sleep for either you or me. But this time, mind, they 'll be in earnest."

By this, my pistols were ready, and there was nothing to do but listen and wait. While the brush lasted, I had not the time to think if I was frighted; but now, when all was still again, my mind ran upon nothing else. The thought of the sharp swords and the cold steel was strong in me; and presently, when I began to hear stealthy steps and a brush-

[1] Bungled.

[85]

ing of men's clothes against the round-house wall, and knew
they were taking their places in the dark, I could have found
it in my mind to cry out aloud.

All this was upon Alan's side; and I had begun to think
my share of the fight was at an end, when I heard some one
drop softly on the roof above me.

Then there came a single call on the sea-pipe, and that
was the signal. A knot of them made one rush of it, cutlass
in hand, against the door; and at the same moment, the glass
of the skylight was dashed in a thousand pieces, and a man
leaped through and landed on the floor. Before he got his
feet, I had clapped a pistol to his back, and might have shot
him, too; only at the touch of him (and him alive) my whole
flesh misgave me, and I could no more pull the trigger than
I could have flown.

He had dropped his cutlass as he jumped, and when he
felt the pistol, whipped straight round and laid hold of me,
roaring out an oath; and at that either my courage came
again, or I grew so much afraid as came to the same thing;
for I gave a shriek and shot him in the midst of the body.
He gave the most horrible, ugly groan and fell to the floor.
The foot of a second fellow, whose legs were dangling through
the skylight, struck me at the same time upon the head; and
at that I snatched another pistol and shot this one through
the thigh, so that he slipped through and tumbled in a lump
on his companion's body. There was no talk of missing,
any more than there was time to aim; I clapped the muzzle
to the very place and fired.

I might have stood and stared at them for long, but I

heard Alan shout as if for help, and that brought me to my senses.

He had kept the door so long; but one of the seamen, while he was engaged with others, had run in under his guard and caught him about the body. Alan was dirking him with his left hand, but the fellow clung like a leech. Another had broken in and had his cutlass raised. The door was thronged with their faces. I thought we were lost, and catching up my cutlass, fell on them in flank.

But I had not time to be of help. The wrestler dropped at last; and Alan, leaping back to get his distance, ran upon the others like a bull, roaring as he went. They broke before him like water, turning, and running, and falling one against another in their haste. The sword in his hands flashed like quicksilver into the huddle of our fleeing enemies; and at every flash there came the scream of a man hurt. I was still thinking we were lost, when lo! they were all gone, and Alan was driving them along the deck as a sheep-dog chases sheep.

Yet he was no sooner out than he was back again, being as cautious as he was brave; and meanwhile the seamen continued running and crying out as if he was still behind them; and we heard them tumble one upon another into the forecastle, and clap-to the hatch upon the top.

The round-house was like a shambles; three were dead inside, another lay in his death agony across the threshold; and there were Alan and I victorious and unhurt.

He came up to me with open arms. "Come to my arms!" he cried, and embraced and kissed me hard upon both cheeks.

KIDNAPPED

"David," said he, "I love you like a brother. And O, man," he cried in a kind of ecstasy, "am I no a bonny fighter?"

Thereupon he turned to the four enemies, passed his sword clean through each of them, and tumbled them out of doors one after the other. As he did so, he kept humming and singing and whistling to himself, like a man trying to recall an air; only what *he* was trying was to make one. All the while, the flush was in his face, and his eyes were as bright as a five-year-old child's with a new toy. And presently he sat down upon the table, sword in hand; the air that he was making all the time began to run a little clearer, and then clearer still; and then out he burst with a great voice into a Gaelic song.

I have translated it here, not in verse (of which I have no skill) but at least in the king's English. He sang it often afterwards. and the thing became popular; so that I have heard it, and had it explained to me, many's the time.

> "This is the song of the sword of Alan;
> The smith made it,
> The fire set it;
> Now it shines in the hand of Alan Breck.
>
> "Their eyes were many and bright,
> Swift were they to behold,
> Many the hands they guided:
> The sword was alone.
>
> "The dun deer troop over the hill,
> They are many, the hill is one;
> The dun deer vanish,
> The hill remains.

THE SIEGE OF THE ROUND-HOUSE

"Come to me from the hills of heather,
Come from the isles of the sea.
O far-beholding eagles,
Here is your meat."

Now this song which he made (both words and music) in the hour of our victory, is something less than just to me, who stood beside him in the tussle. Mr. Shuan and five more were either killed outright or thoroughly disabled; but of these, two fell by my hand, the two that came by the skylight. Four more were hurt, and of that number, one (and he not the least important) got his hurt from me. So that, altogether, I did my fair share both of the killing and the wounding, and might have claimed a place in Alan's verses. But poets have to think upon their rhymes; and in good prose talk, Alan always did me more than justice.

In the meanwhile, I was innocent of any wrong being done me. For not only I knew no word of the Gaelic; but what with the long suspense of the waiting, and the scurry and strain of our two spirits of fighting, and more than all, the horror I had of some of my own share in it, the thing was no sooner over than I was glad to stagger to a seat. There was that tightness on my chest that I could hardly breathe; the thought of the two men I had shot sat upon me like a nightmare; and all upon a sudden, and before I had a guess of what was coming, I began to sob and cry like any child.

Alan clapped my shoulder, and said I was a brave lad and wanted nothing but a sleep.

"I'll take the first watch," said he. "Ye've done well

by me, David, first and last; and I wouldn't lose you for all
Appin — no, nor for Breadalbane."

So I made up my bed on the floor; and he took the first
spell, pistol in hand and sword on knee, three hours by the
captain's watch upon the wall. Then he roused me up, and
I took my turn of three hours; before the end of which it
was broad day, and a very quiet morning, with a smooth,
rolling sea that tossed the ship and made the blood run to
and fro on the round-house floor, and a heavy rain that
drummed upon the roof. All my watch there was nothing
stirring; and by the banging of the helm, I knew they had
even no one at the tiller. Indeed (as I learned afterwards)
there were so many of them hurt or dead, and the rest in so
ill a temper, that Mr. Riach and the captain had to take
turn and turn like Alan and me, or the brig might have gone
ashore and nobody the wiser. It was a mercy the night had
fallen so still, for the wind had gone down as soon as the rain
began. Even as it was, I judged by the wailing of a great
number of gulls that went crying and fishing round the ship,
that she must have drifted pretty near the coast or one of
the islands of the Hebrides; and at last, looking out of the
door of the round-house, I saw the great stone hills of Skye
on the right hand, and, a little more astern, the strange isle
of Rum.

CHAPTER XI

THE CAPTAIN KNUCKLES UNDER

ALAN and I sat down to breakfast about six of the clock. The floor was covered with broken glass and in a horrid mess of blood, which took away my hunger. In all other ways we were in a situation not only agreeable but merry; having ousted the officers from their own cabin, and having at command all the drink in the ship — both wine and spirits — and all the dainty part of what was eatable, such as the pickles and the fine sort of bread. This, of itself, was enough to set us in good humour, but the richest part of it was this, that the two thirstiest men that ever came out of Scotland (Mr. Shuan being dead) were now shut in the fore-part of the ship and condemned to what they hated most — cold water.

"And depend upon it," Alan said, "we shall hear more of them ere long. Ye may keep a man from the fighting, but never from his bottle."

We made good company for each other. Alan, indeed, expressed himself most lovingly; and taking a knife from the table, cut me off one of the silver buttons from his coat.

"I had them," says he, "from my father, Duncan Stewart; and now give ye one of them to be a keepsake for last night's work. And wherever ye go and show that button, the friends of Alan Breck will come around you."

He said this as if he had been Charlemagne, and commanded armies; and indeed, much as I admired his courage, I was always in danger of smiling at his vanity: in danger, I say, for had I not kept my countenance, I would be afraid to think what a quarrel might have followed.

As soon as we were through with our meal he rummaged in the captain's locker till he found a clothes-brush; and then taking off his coat, began to visit his suit and brush away the stains, with such care and labour as I supposed to have been only usual with women. To be sure, he had no other; and, besides (as he said), it belonged to a king and so behoved to be royally looked after.

For all that, when I saw what care he took to pluck out the threads where the button had been cut away, I put a higher value on his gift.

He was still so engaged when we were hailed by Mr. Riach from the deck, asking for a parley; and I, climbing through the skylight and sitting on the edge of it, pistol in hand and with a bold front, though inwardly in fear of broken glass, hailed him back again and bade him speak out. He came to the edge of the round-house, and stood on a coil of rope, so that his chin was on a level with the roof; and we looked at each other awhile in silence. Mr. Riach, as I do not think he had been very forward in the battle, so he had got off with nothing worse than a blow upon the cheek: but he looked out of heart and very weary, having been all night afoot, either standing watch or doctoring the wounded.

THE CAPTAIN KNUCKLES UNDER

"This is a bad job," said he at last, shaking his head.

"It was none of our choosing," said I.

"The captain," says he, "would like to speak with your friend. They might speak at the window."

"And how do we know what treachery he means?" cried I.

"He means none, David," returned Mr. Riach, "and if he did, I 'll tell ye the honest truth, we couldnae get the men to follow."

"Is that so?" said I.

"I 'll tell ye more than that," said he. "It 's not only the men; it 's me. I 'm frich'ened, Davie." And he smiled across at me. "No," he continued, "what we want is to be shut of him."

Thereupon I consulted with Alan, and the parley was agreed to and parole given upon either side; but this was not the whole of Mr. Riach's business, and he now begged me for a dram with such instancy and such reminders of his former kindness, that at last I handed him a pannikin with about a gill of brandy. He drank a part, and then carried the rest down upon the deck, to share it (I suppose) with his superior.

A little after, the captain came (as was agreed) to one of the windows, and stood there in the rain, with his arm in a sling, and looking stern and pale, and so old that my heart smote me for having fired upon him.

Alan at once held a pistol in his face.

"Put that thing up!" said the captain. "Have I not passed my word, sir? or do ye seek to affront me?"

"Captain," says Alan, "I doubt your word is a breakable. Last night ye haggled and argle-bargled like an apple-wife;

and then passed me your word, and gave me your hand to back it; and ye ken very well what was the upshot. Be damned to your word!" says he.

"Well, well, sir," said the captain, "ye 'll get little good by swearing." (And truly that was a fault of which the captain was quite free.) "But we have other things to speak," he continued, bitterly. "Ye 've made a sore hash of my brig; I haven't hands enough left to work her; and my first officer (whom I could ill spare) has got your sword throughout his vitals, and passed without speech. There is nothing left me, sir, but to put back into the port of Glasgow after hands; and there (by your leave) ye will find them that are better able to talk to you."

"Ay?" said Alan; "and faith, I 'll have a talk with them mysel'! Unless there 's naebody speaks English in that town, I have a bonny tale for them. Fifteen tarry sailors upon the one side, and a man and a halfling boy upon the other! O, man, it 's peetiful!"

Hoseason flushed red.

"No," continued Alan, "that 'll no do. Ye 'll just have to set me ashore as we agreed."

"Ay," said Hoseason, "but my first officer is dead — ye ken best how. There 's none of the rest of us acquaint with this coast, sir; and it 's one very dangerous to ships."

"I give ye your choice," says Alan. "Set me on dry ground in Appin, or Ardgour, or in Morven, or Arisaig, or Morar; or, in brief, where ye please, within thirty miles of my own country; except in a country of the Campbells. That 's a broad target. If ye miss that, ye must be as feckless at the sailoring as I have found ye at the fighting. Why, my poor country people in their bit cobles[1] pass from island to island in all weathers, ay, and by night too, for the matter of that."

"A coble 's not a ship, sir," said the captain. "It has nae draught of water."

"Well, then, to Glasgow if ye list!" says Alan. "We 'll have the laugh of ye at the least."

"My mind runs little upon laughing," said the captain. "But all this will cost money, sir."

"Well, sir," says Alan, "I am nae weathercock. Thirty guineas, if ye land me on the sea-side; and sixty, if ye put me in the Linnhe Loch."

"But see, sir, where we lie, we are but a few hours' sail from Ardnamurchan," said Hoseason. "Give me sixty, and I 'll set ye there."

"And I 'm to wear my brogues and run jeopardy of the red-coats to please you?" cries Alan. "No, sir; if ye want sixty guineas earn them, and set me in my own country."

"It 's to risk the brig, sir," said the captain, "and your own lives along with her."

"Take it or want it," says Alan.

"Could ye pilot us at all?" asked the captain, who was frowning to himself.

"Well, it 's doubtful," said Alan. "I 'm more of a fighting man (as ye have seen for yoursel') than a sailor-man. But I have been often enough picked up and set down upon this coast, and should ken something of the lie of it."

[1] Coble: a small boat used in fishing.

The captain shook his head, still frowning.

"If I had lost less money on this unchancy cruise," says he, "I would see you in a rope's end before I risked my brig, sir. But be it as ye will. As soon as I get a slant of wind (and there's some coming, or I'm the more mistaken) I'll put it in hand. But there's one thing more. We may meet in with a king's ship and she may lay us aboard, sir, with no blame of mine: they keep the cruisers thick upon this coast, ye ken who for. Now, sir, if that was to befall, ye might leave the money."

"Captain," says Alan, "if ye see a pennant, it shall be your part to run away. And now, as I hear you're a little short of brandy in the fore-part, I'll offer ye a change: a bottle of brandy against two buckets of water."

That was the last clause of the treaty, and was duly executed on both sides; so that Alan and I could at last wash out the round-house and be quit of the memorials of those whom we had slain, and the captain and Mr. Riach could be happy again in their own way, the name of which was drink.

CHAPTER XII

I HEAR OF THE "RED FOX"

BEFORE we had done cleaning out the round-house, a breeze sprang up from a little to the east of north. This blew off the rain and brought out the sun.

And here I must explain; and the reader would do well to look at a map. On the day when the fog fell and we ran down Alan's boat, we had been running through the Little Minch. At dawn after the battle, we lay becalmed to the east of the Isle of Canna or between that and Isle Eriska in the chain of the Long Island. Now to get from here to the Linnhe Loch, the straight course was through the narrows of the Sound of Mull. But the captain had no chart; he was afraid to trust his brig so deep among the islands; and the wind serving well, he preferred to go by west of Tiree and come up under the southern coast of the great Isle of Mull.

All day the breeze held in the same point, and rather freshened than died down; and towards afternoon, a swell began to set in from around the outer Hebrides. Our course, to go round about the inner isles, was to the west of south, so that at first we had this swell upon our beam, and were much rolled about. But after nightfall, when we had turned the end of Tiree and began to head more to the east, the sea came right astern.

KIDNAPPED

Meanwhile, the early part of the day, before the swell came up, was very pleasant; sailing, as we were, in a bright sunshine and with many mountainous islands upon different sides. Alan and I sat in the round-house with the doors open on each side (the wind being straight astern), and smoked a pipe or two of the captain's fine tobacco. It was at this time we heard each other's stories, which was the more important to me, as I gained some knowledge of that wild Highland country on which I was soon to land. In those days, so close on the back of the great rebellion, it was needful a man should know what he was doing when he went upon the heather.

It was I that showed the example, telling him all my misfortune; which he heard with great good-nature. Only, when I came to mention that good friend of mine, Mr. Campbell the minister, Alan fired up and cried out that he hated all that were of that name.

"Why," said I, "he is a man you should be proud to give your hand to."

"I know nothing I would help a Campbell to," says he, "unless it was a leaden bullet. I would hunt all of that name like blackcocks. If I lay dying, I would crawl upon my knees to my chamber window for a shot at one."

"Why, Alan," I cried, "what ails ye at the Campbells?"

"Well," says he, "ye ken very well that I am an Appin Stewart, and the Campbells have long harried and wasted those of my name; ay, and got lands of us by treachery — but never with the sword," he cried loudly, and with the word brought down his fist upon the table. But I paid the less attention to this, for I knew it was usually said by those who have the underhand. "There's more than that," he continued, "and all in the same story: lying words, lying papers, tricks fit for a peddler, and the show of what's legal over all, to make a man the more angry."

"You that are so wasteful of your buttons," said I, "I can hardly think you would be a good judge of business."

"Ah!" says he, falling again to smiling, "I got my wastefulness from the same man I got the buttons from; and that was my poor father, Duncan Stewart, grace be to him! He was the prettiest man of his kindred; and the best swordsman in the Hielands, David, and that is the same as to say, in all the world, I should ken, for it was him that taught me. He was in the Black Watch, when first it was mustered; and, like other gentlemen privates, had a gillie at his back to carry his firelock for him on the march. Well, the King, it appears, was wishful to see Hieland swordsmanship; and my father and three more were chosen out and sent to London town, to let him see it at the best. So they were had into the palace and showed the whole art of the sword for two hours at a stretch, before King George and Queen Carline, and the Butcher Cumberland, and many more of whom I havenae mind. And when they were through, the King (for all he was a rank usurper) spoke them fair and gave each man three guineas in his hand. Now, as they were going out of the palace and showed the whole art of the sword for two hours my father, as he was perhaps the first private Hieland gentleman that had ever gone by that door, it was right he should give the poor porter a proper notion of their quality. So he gives the King's three guineas into the man's hand, as if it was his common custom; the three others that came behind him did the same; and there they were on the street, never a penny better for their pains. Some say it was one, that was the first to fee the King's porter; and some say it was another; but the truth of it is, that it was Duncan Stewart, as I am willing to prove with either sword or pistol. And that was the father that I had, God rest him!"

"I think he was not the man to leave you rich," said I.

"And that's true," said Alan. "He left me my breeks to cover me, and little besides. And that was how I came to enlist, which was a black spot upon my character at the best of times, and would still be a sore job for me if I fell among the red-coats."

"What," cried I, "were you in the English army?"

"That was I," said Alan. "But I deserted to the right side at Preston Pans — and that's some comfort."

I could scarcely share this view: holding desertion under arms for an unpardonable fault in honour. But for all I was so young, I was wiser than say my thought. "Dear, dear," says I, "the punishment is death."

"Ay," said he, "if they got their hands on me, it would be a short shrift and a lang tow for Alan! But I have the King of France's commission in my pocket, which would aye be some protection."

"I misdoubt it much," said I.

"I have doubts mysel'," said Alan drily.

"And, good heaven, man," cried I, "you that are a condemned rebel, and a deserter, and a man of the French King's

— what tempts ye back into this country? It's a braving of Providence."

"Tut!" says Alan, "I have been back every year since forty-six!"

"And what brings ye, man?" cried I.

"Well, ye see, I weary for my friends and country," said he. "France is a braw place, nae doubt; but I weary for the heather and the deer. And then I have bit things that I attend to. Whiles I pick up a few lads to serve the King of France: recruits, ye see; and that's aye a little money. But the heart of the matter is the business of my chief, Ardshiel."

"I thought they called your chief Appin," said I.

"Ay, but Ardshiel is the captain of the clan," said he, which scarcely cleared my mind. "Ye see, David, he that was all his life so great a man, and come of the blood and bearing the name of kings, is now brought down to live in a French town like a poor and private person. He that had four hundred swords at his whistle, I have seen, with these eyes of mine, buying butter in the market-place, and taking it home in a kale-leaf. This is not only a pain but a disgrace to us of his family and clan. There are the bairns forby, the children and the hope of Appin, that must be learned their letters and how to hold a sword, in that far country. Now, the tenants of Appin have to pay a rent to King George; but their hearts are staunch, they are true to their chief; and what with love and a bit of pressure, and maybe a threat or two, the poor folk scrape up a second rent for Ardshiel. Well, David, I'm the hand that carries it." And he struck the belt around his body, so that the guineas rang.

"Do they pay both?" cried I.

"Ay, David, both," says he.

"What! two rents?" I repeated.

"Ay, David," said he. "I told a different tale to yon captain man; but this is the truth of it. And it's wonderful to me how little pressure is needed. But that's the handiwork of my good kinsman and my father's friend, James of the Glens: James Stewart, that is: Ardshiel's half-brother. He it is that gets the money in, and does the management."

This was the first time I heard the name of that James Stewart, who was afterwards so famous at the time of his hanging. But I took little heed at the moment, for all my mind was occupied with the generosity of these poor Highlanders.

"I call it noble," I cried. "I'm a Whig, or little better; but I call it noble."

"Ay," said he, "ye're a Whig, but ye're a gentleman; and that's what does it. Now, if ye were one of the cursed race of Campbell, ye would gnash your teeth to hear tell of it. If ye were the Red Fox . . ." And at that name, his teeth shut together, and he ceased speaking. I have seen many a grim face, but never a grimmer than Alan's when he had named the Red Fox.

"And who is the Red Fox?" I asked, daunted, but still curious.

"Who is he?" cried Alan. "Well, and I'll tell you that. When the men of the clans were broken at Culloden and the good cause went down, and the horses rode over the fetlocks in the best blood of the north, Ardshiel had to flee like a poor deer upon the mountains — he and his lady and his bairns.

MR. CAMPBELL, THE MINISTER OF ESSENDEAN

With that he prayed a little while aloud, and in affecting terms, for a young man setting out into the world (page 7)

MR. BALFOUR, OF THE HOUSE OF SHAWS

What he was, whether by trade or birth, was more than I could fathom (page 17)

AT QUEEN'S FERRY

And the spirit of all that I beheld put me in thoughts of far voyages and foreign places (page 47)

THE BRIG "COVENANT" IN A FOG

All afternoon, when I went on deck, I saw men and officers listening hard over the bulwarks (page 70)

A sair job we had of it before we got him shipped; and while he still lay in the heather, the English rogues, that couldnae come at his life, were striking at his rights. They stripped him of his powers; they stripped him of his lands; they plucked the weapons from the hands of his clansmen, that had borne arms for thirty centuries; ay, and the very clothes off their backs — so that it 's now a sin to wear a tartan plaid, and a man may be cast into a gaol if he has but a kilt about his legs. One thing they couldnae kill. That was the love the clansmen bore their chief. These guineas are the proof of it. And now, in there steps a man, a Campbell, red-headed Colin of Glenure —"

"Is that him you call the Red Fox?" said I.

"Will ye bring me his brush?" cries Alan, fiercely. "Ay, that 's the man. In he steps, and gets papers from King George, to be so-called King's factor on the lands of Appin. And at first he sings small, and is hail-fellow-well-met with Sheamus — that 's James of the Glens, my chieftain's agent. But by-and-by, that came to his ears that I have just told you; how the poor commons of Appin, the farmers and the crofters and the boumen, were wringing their very plaids to get a second rent, and send it over-seas for Ardshiel and his poor bairns. What was it ye called it, when I told ye?"

"I called it noble, Alan," said I.

"And you little better than a common Whig!" cries Alan. "But when it came to Colin Roy, the black Campbell blood in him ran wild. He sat gnashing his teeth at the wine table. What! should a Stewart get a bite of bread, and him not be able to prevent it? Ah! Red Fox, if ever I hold you at a gun's end, the Lord have pity upon ye!" (Alan stopped to swallow down his anger.) "Well, David, what does he do? He declares all the farms to let. And, thinks he, in his black heart, 'I 'll soon get other tenants that 'll overbid these Stewarts, and Maccolls, and Macrobs' (for these are all names in my clan, David), 'and then,' thinks he, 'Ardshiel will have to hold his bonnet on a French roadside.' "

"Well," said I, "what followed?"

Alan laid down his pipe, which he had long since suffered to go out, and set his two hands upon his knees.

"Ay," said he, "ye 'll never guess that! For these same Stewarts, and Maccolls, and Macrobs (that had two rents to pay, one to King George by stark force, and one to Ardshiel by natural kindness) offered him a better price than any Campbell in all broad Scotland; and far he sent seeking them — as far as to the sides of Clyde and the dross of Edinburgh — seeking, and fleeching, and begging them to come, where there was a Stewart to be starved and a red-headed hound of a Campbell to be pleasured!"

"Well, Alan," said I, "that is a strange story, and a fine one, too. And Whig as I may be, I am glad the man was beaten."

"Him beaten?" echoed Alan. "It 's little ye ken of Campbells, and less of the Red Fox. Him beaten? No: nor will be, till his blood 's on the hillside! But if the day comes, David man, that I can find time and leisure for a bit of hunting, there grows not enough heather in all Scotland to hide him from my vengeance!"

"Man Alan," said I, "ye are neither very wise nor very

Christian to blow off so many words of anger. They will do the man ye call the Fox no harm, and yourself no good. Tell me your tale plainly out. What did he next?"

"And that's a good observe, David," said Alan. "Troth and indeed, they will do him no harm; the more's the pity! And barring that about Christianity (of which my opinion is quite otherwise, or I would be nae Christian), I am much of your mind."

"Opinion here or opinion there," said I, "it's a kent thing that Christianity forbids revenge."

"Ay," said he, "it's well seen it was a Campbell taught ye! It would be a convenient world for them and their sort, if there was no such a thing as a lad and a gun behind a heather bush! But that's nothing to the point. This is what he did."

"Ay," said I, "come to that."

"Well, David," said he, "since he couldnae be rid of the loyal commons by fair means, he swore he would be rid of them by foul. Ardshiel was to starve: that was the thing he aimed at. And since them that fed him in his exile would-nae be brought out — right or wrong, he would drive them out. Therefore he sent for lawyers, and papers, and red-coats to stand at his back. And the kindly folk of that country must all pack and tramp, every father's son out of his father's house, and out of the place where he was bred and fed, and played when he was a callant. And who are to succeed them? Bare-leggit beggars! King George is to whistle for his rents; he maun dow with less; he can spread his butter thinner: what cares Red Colin? If he can hurt Ardshiel, he has his wish; if he can pluck the meat from my chieftain's table, and the bit toys out of his children's hands, he will gang hame singing to Glenure!"

"Let me have a word," said I. "Be sure, if they take less rents, be sure Government has a finger in the pie. It's not this Campbell's fault, man — it's his orders. And if ye killed this Colin to-morrow, what better would ye be? There would be another factor in his shoes, as fast as spur can drive."

"Ye're a good lad in a fight," said Alan; "but, man! ye have Whig blood in ye!"

He spoke kindly enough, but there was so much anger under his contempt that I thought it was wise to change the conversation. I expressed my wonder how, with the Highlands covered with troops, and guarded like a city in a siege, a man in his situation could come and go without arrest.

"It's easier than ye would think," said Alan. "A bare hillside (ye see) is like all one road; if there's a sentry at one place, ye just go by another. And then the heather's a great help. And everywhere there are friends' houses and friends' byres and haystacks. And besides, when folk talk of a country covered with troops, it's but a kind of a byword at the best. A soldier covers nae mair of it than his boot-soles. I have fished a water with a sentry on the other side of the brae, and killed a fine trout; and I have sat in a heather bush within six feet of another, and learned a real bonny tune from his whistling. This was it," said he, and whistled me the air.

"And then, besides," he continued, "it's no sae bad now as it was in forty-six. The Hielands are what they call pacified. Small wonder, with never a gun or a sword left from Cantyre to Cape Wrath, but what tenty[1] folk have hidden in their thatch! But what I would like to ken, David, is just how long? Not long, ye would think, with men like Ardshiel in exile and men like the Red Fox sitting birling the wine and oppressing the poor at home. But it's a kittle thing to decide what folk'll bear, and what they will not. Or why would Red Colin be riding his horse all over my poor country of Appin, and never a pretty lad to put a bullet in him?"

And with this Alan fell into a muse, and for a long time sat very sad and silent.

I will add the rest of what I have to say about my friend, that he was skilled in all kinds of music, but principally pipe-music; was a well-considered poet in his own tongue; had read several books both in French and English; was a dead shot, a good angler, and an excellent fencer with the small sword as well as with his own particular weapon. For his faults, they were on his face, and I now knew them all. But the worst of them, his childish propensity to take offence and to pick quarrels, he greatly laid aside in my case, out of regard for the battle of the round-house. But whether it was because I had done well myself, or because I had been a witness of his own much greater prowess, is more than I can tell. For though he had a great taste for courage in other men, yet he admired it most in Alan Breck.

[1] Careful.

CHAPTER XIII

THE LOSS OF THE BRIG

IT was already late at night, and as dark as it ever would be at that season of the year (and that is to say, it was still pretty bright), when Hoseason clapped his hand into the round-house door.

"Here," said he, "come out and see if ye can pilot."

"Is this one of your tricks?" asked Alan.

"Do I look like tricks?" cries the captain. "I have other things to think of — my brig's in danger!"

By the concerned look of his face, and, above all, by the sharp tones in which he spoke of his brig, it was plain to both of us he was in deadly earnest; and so Alan and I, with no great fear of treachery, stepped on deck.

The sky was clear; it blew hard, and was bitter cold; a great deal of daylight lingered; and the moon, which was nearly full, shone brightly. The brig was close hauled, so as to round the southwest corner of the Island of Mull, the hills of which (and Ben More above them all, with a wisp of mist upon the top of it) lay full upon the larboard bow. Though it was no good point of sailing for the *Covenant,* she tore through the seas at a great rate, pitching and straining, and pursued by the westerly swell.

THE LOSS OF THE BRIG

Altogether it was no such ill night to keep the seas in; and I had begun to wonder what it was that sat so heavily upon the captain, when the brig rising suddenly on the top of a high swell, he pointed and cried to us to look. Away on the lee bow, a thing like a fountain rose out of the moonlit sea, and immediately after we heard a low sound of roaring.

"What do ye call that?" asked the captain, gloomily.

"The sea breaking on a reef," said Alan. "And now ye ken where it is; and what better would ye have?"

"Ay," said Hoseason, "if it was the only one."

And sure enough, just as he spoke there came a second fountain farther to the south.

"There!" said Hoseason. "Ye see for yourself. If I had kent of these reefs, if I had had a chart, or if Shuan had been spared, it's not sixty guineas, no, nor six hundred, would have made me risk my brig in sic a stoneyard! But you, sir, that was to pilot us, have ye never a word?"

"I'm thinking," said Alan, "these'll be what they call the Torran Rocks."

"Are there many of them?" says the captain.

"Truly, sir, I am nae pilot," said Alan; "but it sticks in my mind there are ten miles of them."

Mr. Riach and the captain looked at each other.

"There's a way through them, I suppose?" said the captain.

"Doubtless," said Alan, "but where? But it somehow runs in my mind once more that it is clearer under the land."

"So?" said Hoseason. "We'll have to haul our wind then, Mr. Riach; we'll have to come as near in about the

end of Mull as we can take her, sir; and even then we 'll have
the land to kep the wind off us, and that stoneyard on our
lee. Well, we 're in for it now, and may as well crack on.''

With that he gave an order to the steersman, and sent
Riach to the foretop. There were only five men on deck,
counting the officers; these being all that were fit (or, at least,
both fit and willing) for their work. So, as I say, it fell to
Mr. Riach to go aloft, and he sat there looking out and hailing the deck with news of all he saw.

"The sea to the south is thick," he cried; and then, after
a while, "it does seem clearer in by the land."

"Well, sir," said Hoseason to Alan, "we 'll try your way
of it. But I think I might as well trust to a blind fiddler.
Pray God you 're right."

"Pray God I am!" says Alan to me. "But where did I
hear it? Well, well, it will be as it must."

As we got nearer to the turn of the land the reefs began
to be sown here and there on our very path; and Mr. Riach
sometimes cried down to us to change the course. Sometimes,
indeed, none too soon; for one reef was so close on the brig's
weather board that when a sea burst upon it the lighter
sprays fell upon her deck and wetted us like rain.

The brightness of the night showed us these perils as
clearly as by day, which was, perhaps, the more alarming.
It showed me, too, the face of the captain as he stood by the
steersman, now on one foot, now on the other, and sometimes blowing in his hands, but still listening and looking
and as steady as steel. Neither he nor Mr. Riach had shown
well in the fighting; but I saw they were brave in their own

trade, and admired them all the more because I found Alan very white.

"Ochone, David," says he, "this is no the kind of death I fancy!"

"What, Alan!" I cried, "you're not afraid?"

"No," said he, wetting his lips, "but you'll allow, yourself, it's a cold ending."

By this time, now and then sheering to one side or the other to avoid a reef, but still hugging the wind and the land, we had got round Iona and begun to come alongside Mull. The tide at the tail of the land ran very strong, and threw the brig about. Two hands were put to the helm, and Hoseason himself would sometimes lend a help; and it was strange to see three strong men throw their weight upon the tiller, and it (like a living thing) struggle against and drive them back. This would have been the greater danger had not the sea been for some while free of obstacles. Mr. Riach, besides, announced from the top that he saw clear water ahead.

"Ye were right," said Hoseason to Alan. "Ye have saved the brig, sir; I'll mind that when we come to clear accounts." And I believe he not only meant what he said, but would have done it; so high a place did the *Covenant* hold in his affections.

But this is matter only for conjecture, things having gone otherwise than he forecast.

"Keep her away a point," sings out Mr. Riach. "Reef to windward!"

And just at the same time the tide caught the brig, and threw the wind out of her sails. She came round into the wind like a top, and the next moment struck the reef with such a dunch as threw us all flat upon the deck, and came near to shake Mr. Riach from his place upon the mast.

I was on my feet in a minute. The reef on which we had struck was close in under the southwest end of Mull, off a little isle they call Earraid, which lay low and black upon the larboard. Sometimes the swell broke clean over us; sometimes it only ground the poor brig upon the reef, so that we could hear her beat herself to pieces; and what with the great noise of the sails, and the singing of the wind, and the flying of the spray in the moonlight, and the sense of danger, I think my head must have been partly turned, for I could scarcely understand the things I saw.

Presently I observed Mr. Riach and the seamen busy round the skiff, and, still in the same blank, ran over to assist them; and as soon as I set my hand to work, my mind came clear again. It was no very easy task, for the skiff lay amid-ships and was full of hamper, and the breaking of the heavier seas continually forced us to give over and hold on; but we all wrought like horses while we could.

Meanwhile such of the wounded as could move came clambering out of the fore-scuttle and began to help; while the rest that lay helpless in their bunks harrowed me with screaming and begging to be saved.

The captain took no part. It seemed he was struck stupid. He stood holding by the shrouds, talking to himself and groaning out aloud whenever the ship hammered on the rock. His brig was like wife and child to him; he had looked on, day by day, at the mishandling of poor Ransome; but when it came to the brig, he seemed to suffer along with her.

All the time of our working at the boat, I remember only one other thing: that I asked Alan, looking across at the shore, what country it was; and he answered, it was the worst possible for him, for it was a land of the Campbells.

We had one of the wounded men told off to keep a watch upon the seas and cry us warning. Well, we had the boat about ready to be launched, when this man sang out pretty shrill: "For God's sake, hold on!" We knew by his tone that it was something more than ordinary; and sure enough, there followed a sea so huge that it lifted the brig right up and canted her over on her beam. Whether the cry came too late, or my hold was too weak, I know not; but at the sudden tilting of the ship I was cast clean over the bulwarks into the sea.

I went down, and drank my fill, and then came up, and got a blink of the moon, and then down again. They say a man sinks a third time for good. I cannot be made like other folk, then; for I would not like to write how often I went down, or how often I came up again. All the while, I was being hurled along, and beaten upon and choked, and then swallowed whole; and the thing was so distracting to my wits, that I was neither sorry nor afraid.

Presently, I found I was holding to a spar, which helped me somewhat. And then all of a sudden I was in quiet water, and began to come to myself.

It was the spare yard I had got hold of, and I was amazed to see how far I had travelled from the brig. I hailed her, indeed; but it was plain she was already out of cry. She was still holding together; but whether or not they had yet launched the boat, I was too far off and too low down to see.

While I was hailing the brig, I spied a tract of water lying between us where no great waves came, but which yet boiled white all over and bristled in the moon with rings and bubbles. Sometimes the whole tract swung to one side, like the tail of a live serpent; sometimes, for a glimpse, it would all disappear and then boil up again. What it was I had no guess, which for the time increased my fear of it; but I now know it must have been the roost or tide race, which had carried me away so fast and tumbled me about so cruelly, and at last, as if tired of that play, had flung out me and the spare yard upon its landward margin.

I now lay quite becalmed, and began to feel that a man can die of cold as well as of drowning. The shores of Earraid were close in; I could see in the moonlight the dots of heather and the sparkling of the mica in the rocks.

"Well," thought I to myself, "if I cannot get as far as that, it 's strange!"

I had no skill of swimming, Essen Water being small in our neighborhood; but when I laid hold upon the yard with both arms, and kicked out with both feet, I soon begun to find that I was moving. Hard work it was, and mortally slow; but in about an hour of kicking and splashing, I had got well in between the points of a sandy bay surrounded by low hills.

The sea was here quite quiet; there was no sound of any surf; the moon shone clear; and I thought in my heart I had never seen a place so desert and desolate. But it was dry land; and when at last it grew so shallow that I could leave the yard and wade ashore upon my feet, I cannot tell if I was more tired or more grateful. Both, at least, I was: tired as I never was before that night; and grateful to God as I trust I have been often, though never with more cause.

CHAPTER XIV

THE ISLET

WITH my stepping ashore I began the most unhappy part of my adventures. It was half-past twelve in the morning, and though the wind was broken by the land, it was a cold night. I dared not sit down (for I thought I should have frozen), but took off my shoes and walked to and fro upon the sand, bare-foot, and beating my breast with infinite weariness. There was no sound of man or cattle; not a cock crew, though it was about the hour of their first waking; only the surf broke outside in the distance, which put me in mind of my perils and those of my friend. To walk by the sea at that hour of the morning, and in a place so desert-like and lonesome, struck me with a kind of fear.

As soon as the day began to break I put on my shoes and climbed a hill — the ruggedest scramble I ever undertook — falling, the whole way, between big blocks of granite, or leaping from one to another. When I got to the top the dawn was come. There was no sign of the brig, which must have lifted from the reef and sunk. The boat, too, was nowhere to be seen. There was never a sail upon the ocean; and in what I could see of the land was neither house nor man.

THE ISLET

I was afraid to think what had befallen my shipmates, and afraid to look longer at so empty a scene. What with my wet clothes and weariness, and my belly that now began to ache with hunger, I had enough to trouble me without that. So I set off eastward along the south coast, hoping to find a house where I might warm myself, and perhaps get news of those I had lost. And at the worst, I considered the sun would soon rise and dry my clothes.

After a little, my way was stopped by a creek or inlet of the sea, which seemed to run pretty deep into the land; and as I had no means to get across, I must needs change my direction to go about the end of it. It was still the roughest kind of walking; indeed the whole, not only of Earraid, but of the neighboring part of Mull (which they call the Ross) is nothing but a jumble of granite rocks with heather in among. At first the creek kept narrowing as I had looked to see; but presently to my surprise it began to widen out again. At this I scratched my head, but had still no notion of the truth: until at last I came to a rising ground, and it burst upon me all in a moment that I was cast upon a little barren isle, and cut off on every side by the salt seas.

Instead of the sun rising to dry me, it came on to rain, with a thick mist; so that my case was lamentable.

I stood in the rain, and shivered, and wondered what to do, till it occurred to me that perhaps the creek was fordable. Back I went to the narrowest point and waded in. But not three yards from shore, I plumped in head over ears; and if ever I was heard of more, it was rather by God's grace than my own prudence. I was no wetter (for that could hardly be), but I was all the colder for this mishap; and having lost another hope was the more unhappy.

And now, all at once, the yard came in my head. What had carried me through the roost would surely serve me to cross this little quiet creek in safety. With that I set off, undaunted, across the top of the isle, to fetch and carry it back. It was a weary tramp in all ways, and if hope had not buoyed me up, I must have cast myself down and given up. Whether with the sea salt, or because I was growing fevered, I was distressed with thirst, and had to stop, as I went, and drink the peaty water out of the hags.

I came to the bay at last, more dead than alive; and at the first glance, I thought the yard was something farther out than when I left it. In I went, for the third time, into the sea. The sand was smooth and firm, and shelved gradually down, so that I could wade out till the water was almost to my neck and the little waves splashed into my face. But at that depth my feet began to leave me, and I durst venture in no farther. As for the yard, I saw it bobbing very quietly some twenty feet beyond.

I had borne up well until this last disappointment; but at that I came ashore, and flung myself down upon the sands and wept.

The time I spent upon the island is still so horrible a thought to me, that I must pass it lightly over. In all the books I have read of people cast away, they had either their pockets full of tools, or a chest of things would be thrown upon the beach along with them, as if on purpose. My case was very different. I had nothing in my pockets but money and

THE ISLET

Alan's silver button; and being inland bred, I was as much short of knowledge as of means.

I knew indeed that shell-fish were counted good to eat; and among the rocks of the isle I found a great plenty of limpets, which at first I could scarcely strike from their places, not knowing quickness to be needful. There were, besides, some of the little shells that we call buckies; I think periwinkle is the English name. Of these two I made my whole diet, devouring them cold and raw as I found them; and so hungry was I, that at first they seemed to me delicious.

Perhaps they were out of season, or perhaps there was something wrong in the sea about my island. But at least I had no sooner eaten my first meal than I was seized with giddiness and retching, and lay for a long time no better than dead. A second trial of the same food (indeed I had no other) did better with me, and revived my strength. But as long as I was on the island, I never knew what to expect when I had eaten; sometimes all was well, and sometimes I was thrown into a miserable sickness; nor could I ever distinguish what particular fish it was that hurt me.

All day it streamed rain; the island ran like a sop, there was no dry spot to be found; and when I lay down that night, between two boulders that made a kind of roof, my feet were in a bog.

The second day I crossed the island to all sides. There was no one part of it better than another; it was all desolate and rocky; nothing living on it but game birds which I lacked the means to kill, and the gulls which haunted the outlying rocks in a prodigious number. But the creek, or strait, that cut off the isle from the main-land of the Ross, opened out on the north into a bay, and the bay again opened into the Sound of Iona; and it was the neighbourhood of this place that I chose to be my home; though if I had thought upon the very name of home in such a spot, I must have burst out weeping.

I had good reasons for my choice. There was in this part of the isle a little hut of a house like a pig's hut, where fishers used to sleep when they came there upon their business; but the turf roof of it had fallen entirely in; so that the hut was of no use to me, and gave me less shelter than my rocks. What was more important, the shell-fish on which I lived grew there in great plenty; when the tide was out I could gather a peck at a time and this was doubtless a convenience. But the other reason went deeper. I had become in no way used to the horrid solitude of the isle, but still looked round me on all sides (like a man that was hunted), between fear and hope that I might see some human creature coming. Now, from a little up the hillside over the bay, I could catch a sight of the great, ancient church and the roofs of the people's houses in Iona. And on the other hand, over the low country of the Ross, I saw smoke go up, morning and evening, as if from a homestead in a hollow of the land.

I used to watch this smoke, when I was wet and cold, and had my head half turned with loneliness; and think of the fireside and the company, till my heart burned. It was the same with the roofs of Iona. Altogether, this sight I had of men's homes and comfortable lives, although it put a point on my own sufferings, yet it kept hope alive, and helped me to eat my raw shell-fish (which had soon grown to be a disgust), and saved me from the sense of horror I had whenever I was quite alone with dead rocks, and fowls, and the rain, and the cold sea.

I say it kept hope alive; and indeed it seemed impossible that I should be left to die on the shores of my own country, and within view of a church-tower and the smoke of men's houses. But the second day passed; and though as long as the light lasted I kept a bright look-out for boats on the Sound or men passing on the Ross, no help came near me. It still rained, and I turned in to sleep, as wet as ever, and with a cruel sore throat, but a little comforted, perhaps, by having said good-night to my next neighbours, the people of Iona.

Charles the Second declared a man could stay outdoors more days in the year in the climate of England than in any other. This was very like a king, with a palace at his back and changes of dry clothes. But he must have had better luck on his flight from Worcester than I had on that miserable isle. It was the height of the summer; yet it rained for more than twenty-four hours, and did not clear until the afternoon of the third day.

This was the day of incidents. In the morning I saw a red-deer, a buck with a fine spread of antlers, standing in the rain on the top of the island; but he had scarce seen me rise from under my rock, before he trotted off upon the other side. I supposed he must have swum the strait; though what should bring any creature to Earraid, was more than I could fancy.

KIDNAPPED

A little after, as I was jumping about after my limpets, I was startled by a guinea-piece, which fell upon a rock in front of me and glanced off into the sea. When the sailors gave me my money again, they kept back not only about a third of the whole sum, but my father's leather purse; so that from that day out, I carried my gold loose in a pocket with a button. I now saw there must be a hole, and clapped my hand to the place in a great hurry. But this was to lock the stable door after the steed was stolen. I had left the shore at Queensferry with near on fifty pounds; now I found no more than two guinea-pieces and a silver shilling.

It is true I picked up a third guinea a little after, where it lay shining on a piece of turf. That made a fortune of three pounds and four shillings, English money, for a lad, the rightful heir of an estate, and now starving on an isle at the extreme end of the wild Highlands.

This state of my affairs dashed me still further; and indeed my plight on that third morning was truly pitiful. My clothes were beginning to rot; my stockings in particular were quite worn through, so that my shanks went naked; my hands had grown quite soft with the continual soaking; my throat was very sore, my strength had much abated, and my heart so turned against the horrid stuff I was condemned to eat, that the very sight of it came near to sicken me.

And yet the worst was not yet come.

There is a pretty high rock on the northwest of Earraid, which (because it had a flat top and overlooked the Sound) I was much in the habit of frequenting; not that ever I stayed in one place, save when asleep, my misery giving me no rest. Indeed, I wore myself down with continual and aimless goings and comings in the rain.

As soon, however, as the sun came out, I lay down on the top of that rock to dry myself. The comfort of the sunshine is a thing I cannot tell. It set me thinking hopefully of my deliverance, of which I had begun to despair; and I scanned the sea and the Ross with a fresh interest. On the south of my rock, a part of the island jutted out and hid the open ocean, so that a boat could thus come quite near me upon that side, and I be none the wiser.

Well, all of a sudden, a coble with a brown sail and a pair of fishers aboard of it, came flying round that corner of the isle, bound for Iona. I shouted out, and then fell on my knees on the rock and reached up my hands and prayed to them. They were near enough to hear — I could even see the colour of their hair; and there was no doubt but they observed me, for they cried out in their Gaelic tongue, and laughed. But the boat never turned aside, and flew on, right before my eyes, for Iona.

I could not believe such wickedness, and ran along the shore from rock to rock, crying on them piteously; even after they were out of reach of my voice, I still cried and waved to them; and when they were quite gone, I thought my heart would have burst. All the time of my troubles I wept only twice. Once, when I could not reach the yard, and now, the second time, when these fishers turned a deaf ear to my cries. But this time I wept and roared like a wicked child, tearing up the turf with my nails, and grinding my face in the earth. If a wish would kill men, those two fishers would never have seen morning, and I should likely have died upon my island.

When I was a little over my anger, I must eat again, but with such loathing of the mess as I could now scarce control. Sure enough, I should have done as well to fast, for my fishes poisoned me again. I had all my first pains; my throat was so sore I could scarce swallow; I had a fit of strong shuddering, which clucked my teeth together; and there came on me that dreadful sense of illness, which we have no name for either in Scotch or English. I thought I should have died, and made my peace with God, forgiving all men, even my uncle and the fishers; and as soon as I had thus made up my mind to the worst, clearness came upon me; I observed the night was falling dry; my clothes were dried a good deal; truly, I was in a better case than ever before, since I had landed on the isle; and so I got to sleep at last, with a thought of gratitude.

The next day (which was the fourth of this horrible life of mine) I found my bodily strength run very low. But the sun shone, the air was sweet, and what I managed to eat of the shell-fish agreed well with me and revived my courage.

I was scarce back on my rock (where I went always the first thing after I had eaten) before I observed a boat coming down the Sound, and with her head, as I thought, in my direction.

I began at once to hope and fear exceedingly; for I thought these men might have thought better of their cruelty and be coming back to my assistance. But another disappointment, such as yesterday's, was more than I could bear. I turned my back, accordingly, upon the sea, and did not look again till I had counted many hundreds. The boat was still heading for the island. The next time I counted the full thousand, as slowly as I could, my heart beating so as to hurt me. And then it was out of all question. She was coming straight to Earraid!

I could no longer hold myself back, but ran to the seaside and out, from one rock to another, as far as I could go. It is a marvel I was not drowned; for when I was brought to a stand at last, my legs shook under me, and my mouth was so dry, I must wet it with the sea-water before I was able to shout.

All this time the boat was coming on; and now I was able to perceive it was the same boat and the same two men as yesterday. This I knew by their hair, which the one had of a bright yellow and the other black. But now there was a third man along with them, who looked to be of a better class.

As soon as they were come within easy speech, they let down their sail and lay quiet. In spite of my supplications, they drew no nearer in, and what frightened me most of all, the new man tee-hee'd with laughter as he talked and looked at me.

Then he stood up in the boat and addressed me a long while, speaking fast and with many wavings of his hand. I told him I had no Gaelic; and at this he became very angry, and I began to suspect he thought he was talking English. Listening very close, I caught the word "whateffer" several times; but all the rest was Gaelic and might have been Greek and Hebrew for me.

KIDNAPPED

"Whatever," said I, to show him I had caught a word.

"Yes, yes — yes, yes," says he, and then he looked at the other men, as much as to say, "I told you I spoke English," and began again as hard as ever in the Gaelic.

This time I picked out another word, "tide." Then I had a flash of hope. I remembered he was always waving his hand towards the mainland of the Ross.

"Do you mean when the tide is out — ?" I cried, and could not finish.

"Yes, yes," said he. "Tide."

At that I turned tail upon their boat (where my adviser had once more begun to tee-hee with laughter), leaped back the way I had come, from one stone to another, and set off running across the isle as I had never done before. In about half an hour I came out upon the shores of the creek; and, sure enough, it was shrunk into a little trickle of water, through which I dashed, not above my knees, and landed with a shout on the main island.

A sea-bred boy would not have stayed a day on Earraid; which is only what they call a tidal islet, and except in the bottom of the neaps, can be entered and left twice in every twenty-four hours, either dry-shod, or at the most by wading. Even I, who had the tide going out and in before me in the bay, and even watched for the ebbs, the better to get my shell-fish — even I (I say) if I had sat down to think, instead of raging at my fate, must have soon guessed the secret, and got free. It was no wonder the fishers had not understood me. The wonder was rather that they had ever guessed my pitiful illusion, and taken the trouble to come back. I had starved with cold and hunger on that island for close upon one hundred hours. But for the fishers, I might have left my bones there, in pure folly. And even as it was, I had paid for it pretty dear, not only in past sufferings, but in my present case; being clothed like a beggar-man, scarce able to walk, and in great pain of my sore throat.

I have seen wicked men and fools, a great many of both; and I believe they both get paid in the end; but the fools first.

CHAPTER XV

THE LAD WITH THE SILVER BUTTON: THROUGH THE ISLE OF MULL

THE Ross of Mull, which I had now got upon, was rugged and trackless, like the isle I had just left; being all bog, and brier, and big stone. There may be roads for them that know that country well; but for my part I had no better guide than my own nose, and no other landmark than Ben More.

I aimed as well as I could for the smoke I had seen so often from the island; and with all my great weariness and the difficulty of the way came upon the house in the bottom of a little hollow about five or six at night. It was low and longish, roofed with turf and built of unmortared stones; and on a mound in front of it, an old gentleman sat smoking his pipe in the sun.

With what little English he had, he gave me to understand that my shipmates had got safe ashore, and had broken bread in that very house on the day after.

"Was there one," I asked, "dressed like a gentleman?"

He said they all wore rough great-coats; but to be sure, the first of them, the one that came alone, wore breeches and stockings, while the rest had sailors' trousers.

THROUGH THE ISLE OF MULL

"Ah," said I, "and he would have a feathered hat?"

He told me, no, that he was bareheaded like myself.

At first I thought Alan might have lost his hat; and then the rain came in my mind, and I judged it more likely he had it out of harm's way under his great-coat. This set me smiling, partly because my friend was safe, partly to think of his vanity in dress.

And then the old gentleman clapped his hand to his brow, and cried out that I must be the lad with the silver button.

"Why, yes!" said I, in some wonder.

"Well, then," said the old gentleman, "I have a word for you, that you are to follow your friend to his country, by Torosay."

He then asked me how I had fared, and I told him my tale. A south-country man would certainly have laughed; but this old gentleman (I call him so because of his manners, for his clothes were dropping off his back) heard me all through with nothing but gravity and pity. When I had done, he took me by the hand, led me into his hut (it was no better) and presented me before his wife, as if she had been the Queen and I a duke.

The good woman set oat-bread before me and a cold grouse, patting my shoulder and smiling to me all the time, for she had no English; and the old gentleman (not to be behind) brewed me a strong punch out of their country spirit. All the while I was eating, and after that when I was drinking the punch, I could scarce come to believe in my good fortune; and the house, though it was thick with the peat-smoke and as full of holes as a colander, seemed like a palace.

KIDNAPPED

The punch threw me in a strong sweat and a deep slumber; the good people let me lie; and it was near noon of the next day before I took the road, my throat already easier and my spirits quite restored by good fare and good news. The old gentleman, although I pressed him hard, would take no money, and gave me an old bonnet for my head; though I am free to own I was no sooner out of view of the house than I very jealously washed this gift of his in a wayside fountain.

Thought I to myself: "If these are the wild Highlanders, I could wish my own folk wilder."

I not only started late, but I must have wandered nearly half the time. True, I met plenty of people, grubbing in little miserable fields that would not keep a cat, or herding little kine about the bigness of asses. The Highland dress being forbidden by law since the rebellion, and the people condemned to the Lowland habit, which they much disliked, it was strange to see the variety of their array. Some went bare, only for a hanging cloak or great-coat, and carried their trousers on their backs like a useless burthen: some had made an imitation of the tartan with little parti-coloured stripes patched together like an old wife's quilt; others, again, still wore the Highland philabeg, but by putting a few stitches between the legs transformed it into a pair of trousers like a Dutchman's. All those makeshifts were condemned and punished, for the law was harshly applied, in hopes to break up the clan spirit; but in that out-of-the-way, sea-bound isle, there were few to make remarks and fewer to tell tales.

They seemed in great poverty; which was no doubt natural, now that rapine was put down, and the chiefs kept no longer an open house; and the roads (even such a wandering, country by-track as the one I followed) were infested with beggars. And here again I marked a difference from my own part of the country. For our Lowland beggars — even the gownsmen themselves, who beg by patent — had a louting, flattering way with them, and if you gave them a plack and asked change, would very civilly return you a boddle. But these Highland beggars stood on their dignity, asked alms only to buy snuff (by their account) and would give no change.

To be sure, this was no concern of mine, except in so far as it entertained me by the way. What was much more to the purpose, few had any English, and these few (unless they were of the brotherhood of beggars) not very anxious to place it at my service. I knew Torosay to be my destination, and repeated the name to them and pointed; but instead of simply pointing in reply, they would give me a screed of Gaelic that set me foolish; so it was small wonder if I went out of my road as often as I stayed in it.

At last, about eight at night, and already very weary, I came to a lone house, where I asked admittance, and was refused, until I bethought me of the power of money in so poor a country, and held up one of my guineas in my finger and thumb. Thereupon, the man of the house, who had hitherto pretended to have no English, and driven me from his door by signals, suddenly began to speak as clearly as was needful, and agreed for five shillings to give me a night's lodging and guide me the next day to Torosay.

I slept uneasily that night, fearing I should be robbed; but I might have spared myself the pain; for my host was no robber, only miserably poor and a great cheat. He was not alone in his poverty; for the next morning, we must go five miles about to the house of what he called a rich man to have one of my guineas changed. This was perhaps a rich man for Mull; he would have scarce been thought so in the south; for it took all he had — the whole house was turned upside down, and a neighbour brought under contribution, before he could scrape together twenty shillings in silver. The odd shilling he kept for himself, protesting he could ill afford to have so great a sum of money lying "locked up." For all that he was very courteous and well spoken, made us both sit down with his family to dinner, and brewed punch in a fine china bowl, over which my rascal guide grew so merry that he refused to start.

I was for getting angry, and appealed to the rich man (Hector Maclean was his name), who had been a witness to our bargain and to my payment of the five shillings. But Maclean had taken his share of the punch, and vowed that no gentleman should leave his table after the bowl was brewed; so there was nothing for it but to sit and hear Jacobite toasts and Gaelic songs, till all were tipsy and staggered off to the bed or the barn for their night's rest.

Next day (the fourth of my travels) we were up before five upon the clock; but my rascal guide got to the bottle at once, and it was three hours before I had him clear of the house, and then (as you shall hear) only for a worse disappointment.

As long as we went down a heathery valley that lay before Mr. Maclean's house, all went well; only my guide looked constantly over his shoulder, and when I asked him the cause, only grinned at me. No sooner, however, had we crossed the back of a hill, and got out of sight of the house windows, than he told me Torosay lay right in front, and that a hill-top (which he pointed out) was my best landmark.

"I care very little for that," said I, "since you are going with me."

The impudent cheat answered me in the Gaelic that he had no English.

"My fine fellow," I said, "I know very well your English comes and goes. Tell me what will bring it back? Is it more money you wish?"

"Five shillings, mair," said he, "and hersel' will bring ye there."

I reflected awhile and then offered him two, which he accepted greedily, and insisted on having in his hands at once — "for luck," as he said, but I think it was rather for my misfortune.

The two shillings carried him not quite as many miles; at the end of whch distance; he sat down upon the wayside and took off his brogues from his feet, like a man about to rest.

I was now red-hot. 'Ha!" said I, "have you no more English?"

He said impudently, "No."

At that I boiled over, and lifted my hand to strike him; and he, drawing a knife from his rags, squatted back and grinned at me like a wildcat. At that, forgetting everything but my anger, I ran in upon him, put aside his knife with my left, and struck him in the mouth with the right. I was a strong lad and very angry, and he but a little man; and he went down before me heavily. By good luck, his knife flew out of his hand as he fell.

I picked up both that and his brogues, wished him a good morning, and set off upon my way, leaving him barefoot and disarmed. I chuckled to myself as I went, being sure I was done with that rogue, for a variety of reasons. First, he knew he could have no more of my money; next, the brogues were worth in that country only a few pence; and, lastly, the knife, which was really a dagger, it was against the law for him to carry.

In about half an hour of walk, I overtook a great, ragged man, moving pretty fast but feeling before him with a staff. He was quite blind, and told me he was a catechist, which should have put me at my ease. But his face went against me; it seemed dark and dangerous and secret; and presently, as we began to go on alongside, I saw the steel butt of a pistol sticking from under the flap of his coat-pocket. To carry such a thing meant a fine of fifteen pounds sterling upon a first offence, and transportation to the colonies upon a second. Nor could I quite see why a religious teacher should go armed, or what a blind man could be doing with a pistol.

I told him about my guide, for I was proud of what I had done, and my vanity for once got the heels of my prudence. At the mention of the five shillings he cried out so loud that I made up my mind I should say nothing of the other two, and was glad he could not see my blushes.

"Was it too much?" I asked, a little faltering.

THE WRECK OF THE "COVENANT"

It was the spare yard I had got hold of, and I was amazed to see how far I had travelled from the brig (page 113)

ON THE ISLAND OF EARRAID

But the second day passed; and as long as the light lasted I kept a bright look-out for boats on the Sound or men passing on the Ross (page 121)

THE BLIND BEGGAR ON THE ISLE OF MULL

In about half an hour of walk, I overtook a great, ragged man, moving pretty fast but feeling before him with a staff (page 134)

THE MURDERER OF ROY CAMPBELL OF GLENURE

At that the murderer gave a little, quick look over his shoulder, and began to run (page 154)

"Too much!" cries he. "Why, I will guide you to Torosay myself for a dram of brandy. And give you the great pleasure of my company (me that is a man of some learning) in the bargain."

I said I did not see how a blind man could be a guide; but at that he laughed aloud, and said his stick was eyes enough for an eagle.

"In the Isle of Mull, at least," says he, "where I know every stone and heather-bush by mark of head. See, now," he said, striking right and left, as if to make sure, "down there a burn is running; and at the head of it there stands a bit of a small hill with a stone cocked upon the top of that; and it's hard at the foot of the hill, that the way runs by to Torosay; and the way here, being for droves, is plainly trodden, and will show grassy through the heather."

I had to own he was right in every feature, and told my wonder.

"Ha!" says he, "that's nothing. Would ye believe me now, that before the Act came out, and when there were weepons in this country, I could shoot? Ay, could I!" cries he, and then with a leer: "If ye had such a thing as a pistol here to try with, I would show ye how it's done."

I told him I had nothing of the sort, and gave him a wider berth. If he had known, his pistol stuck at that time quite plainly out of his pocket, and I could see the sun twinkle on the steel of the butt. But by the better luck for me, he knew nothing, thought all was covered, and lied on in the dark.

He then began to question me cunningly, where I came

from, whether I was rich, whether I could change a five-shilling piece for him (which he declared he had that moment in his sporran), and all the time he kept edging up to me and I avoiding him. We were now upon a sort of green cattle-track which crossed the hills towards Torosay, and we kept changing sides upon that like dancers in a reel. I had so plainly the upper-hand that my spirits rose, and indeed I took a pleasure in this game of blindman's buff; but the catechist grew angrier and angrier, and at last began to swear in Gaelic and to strike for my legs with his staff.

Then I told him that, sure enough, I had a pistol in my pocket as well as he, and if he did not strike across the hill due south I would even blow his brains out.

He became at once very polite, and after trying to soften me for some time, but quite in vain, he cursed me once more in Gaelic and took himself off. I watched him striding along, through bog and brier, tapping with his stick, until he turned the end of a hill and disappeared in the next hollow. Then I struck on again for Torosay, much better pleased to be alone than to travel with that man of learning. This was an unlucky day; and these two, of whom I had just rid myself, one after the other, were the two worst men I met with in the Highlands.

At Torosay, on the Sound of Mull and looking over to the mainland of Morven, there was an inn with an innkeeper, who was a Maclean, it appeared, of a very high family; for to keep an inn is thought even more genteel in the Highlands than it is with us, perhaps as partaking of hospitality, or perhaps because the trade is idle and drunken. He spoke good

English, and finding me to be something of a scholar, tried me first in French, where he easily beat me, and then in the Latin, in which I don't know which of us did best. This pleasant rivalry put us at once upon friendly terms; and I sat up and drank punch with him (or to be more correct, sat up and watched him drink it), until he was so tipsy that he wept upon my shoulder.

I tried him, as if by accident, with a sight of Alan's button; but it was plain he had never seen or heard of it. Indeed, he bore some grudge against the family and friends of Ardshiel, and before he was drunk he read me a lampoon, in very good Latin, but with a very ill meaning, which he had made in elegiac verses upon a person of that house.

When I told him of my catechist, he shook his head, and said I was lucky to have got clear off. "That is a very dangerous man," he said; "Duncan Mackiegh is his name; he can shoot by the ear at several yards, and has been often accused of highway robberies, and once of murder."

"The cream of it is," says I, "that he called himself a catechist."

"And why should he not?" says he, "when that is what he is. It was Maclean of Duart gave it to him because he was blind. But perhaps it was a peety," says my host, "for he is always on the road, going from one place to another to hear the young folk say their religion; and, doubtless, that is a great temptation to the poor man."

At last, when my landlord could drink no more, he showed me to a bed, and I lay down in very good spirits; having travelled the greater part of that big and crooked Island of

Mull, from Earraid to Torosay, fifty miles as the crow flies, and (with my wanderings) much nearer a hundred, in four days and with little fatigue. Indeed I was by far in better heart and health of body at the end of that long tramp than I had been at the beginning.

CHAPTER XVI

THE LAD WITH THE SILVER BUTTON: ACROSS MORVEN

THERE is a regular ferry from Torosay to Kinlochaline on the mainland. Both shores of the Sound are in the country of the strong clan of the Macleans, and the people that passed the ferry with me were almost all of that clan. The skipper of the boat, on the other hand, was called Neil Roy Macrob; and since Macrob was one of the names of Alan's clansmen, and Alan himself had sent me to that ferry, I was eager to come to private speech of Neil Roy.

In the crowded boat this was of course impossible, and the passage was a very slow affair. There was no wind, and as the boat was wretchedly equipped, we could pull but two oars on one side, and one on the other. The men gave way, however, with a good will, the passengers taking spells to help them, and the whole company giving the time in Gaelic boat-songs. And what with the songs, and the sea-air, and the good-nature and spirit of all concerned, and the bright weather, the passage was a pretty thing to have seen.

But there was one melancholy part. In the mouth of Loch Aline we found a great sea-going ship at anchor; and this I supposed at first to be one of the King's cruisers which were kept along that coast, both summer and winter, to prevent communication with the French. As we got a little nearer, it became plain she was a ship of merchandise; and what still more puzzled me, not only her decks, but the sea-beach also, were quite black with people, and skiffs were continually plying to and fro between them. Yet nearer, and there began to come to our ears a great sound of mourning, the people on board and those on the shore crying and lamenting one to another so as to pierce the heart.

Then I understood this was an emigrant ship bound for the American colonies.

We put the ferry-boat alongside, and the exiles leaned over the bulwarks, weeping and reaching out their hands to my fellow-passengers, among whom they counted some near friends. How long this might have gone on I do not know, for they seemed to have no sense of time: but at last the captain of the ship, who seemed near beside himself (and no great wonder) in the midst of this crying and confusion, came to the side and begged us to depart.

Thereupon Neil sheered off; and the chief singer in our boat struck into a melancholy air, which was presently taken up both by the emigrants and their friends upon the beach, so that it sounded from all sides like a lament for the dying. I saw the tears run down the cheeks of the men and women in the boat, even as they bent at the oars; and the circumstances and the music of the song (which is one called "Lochaber no more") were highly affecting even to myself.

At Kinlochaline I got Neil Roy upon one side on the beach, and said I made sure he was one of Appin's men.

ACROSS MORVEN

"And what for no?" said he.

"I am seeking somebody," said I; "and it comes in my mind that you will have news of him. Alan Breck Stewart is his name." And very foolishly, instead of showing him the button, I sought to pass a shilling in his hand.

At this he drew back. "I am very much affronted," he said; "and this is not the way that one shentleman should behave to another at all. The man you ask for is in France; but if he was in my sporran," says he, "and your belly full of shillings, I would not hurt a hair upon his body."

I saw I had gone the wrong way to work, and without wasting time upon apologies, showed him the button lying in the hollow of my palm.

"Aweel, aweel," said Neil; "and I think ye might have begun with that end of the stick, whatever! But if ye are the lad with the silver button, all is well, and I have the word to see that ye come safe. But if ye will pardon me to speak plainly," says he, "there is a name that you should never take into your mouth, and that is the name of Alan Breck; and there is a thing that ye would never do, and that is to offer your dirty money to a Hieland shentleman."

It was not very easy to apologise; for I could scarce tell him (what was the truth) that I had never dreamed he would set up to be a gentleman until he told me so. Neil on his part had no wish to prolong his dealings with me, only to fulfil his orders and be done with it; and he made haste to give me my route. This was to lie the night in Kinlochaline in the public inn; to cross Morven the next day to Ardgour, and lie the night in the house of one John of the Claymore, who was warned that I might come; the third day, to be set across one loch at Corran and another at Balachulish, and then ask my way to the house of James of the Glens, at Aucharn in Duror of Appin. There was a good deal of ferrying, as you hear; the sea in all this part running deep into the mountains and winding about their roots. It makes the country strong to hold and difficult to travel, but full of prodigious wild and dreadful prospects.

I had some other advice from Neil: to speak with no one by the way, to avoid Whigs, Campbells, and the "red-soldiers"; to leave the road and lie in a bush if I saw any of the latter coming, "for it was never chancy to meet in with them"; and in brief, to conduct myself like a robber or a Jacobite agent, as perhaps Neil thought me.

The inn at Kinlochaline was the most beggarly vile place that ever pigs were styed in, full of smoke, vermin, and silent Highlanders. I was not only discontented with my lodging, but with myself for my mismanagement of Neil, and thought I could hardly be worse off. But very wrongly, as I was soon to see; for I had not been half an hour at the inn (standing in the door most of the time, to ease my eyes from the peat smoke) when a thunderstorm came close by, the springs broke in a little hill on which the inn stood, and one end of the house became a running water. Places of public entertainment were bad enough all over Scotland in those days; yet it was a wonder to myself, when I had to go from the fireside to the bed in which I slept, wading over the shoes.

Early in my next day's journey I overtook a little, stout, solemn man, walking very slowly with his toes turned out, sometimes reading in a book and sometimes marking the place with his finger, and dressed decently and plainly in something of a clerical style.

This I found to be another catechist, but of a different order from the blind man of Mull: being indeed one of those sent out by the Edinburgh Society for Propagating Christian Knowledge, to evangelise the more savage places of the Highlands. His name was Henderland; he spoke with the broad south-country tongue, which I was beginning to weary for the sound of; and besides common countryship, we soon found we had a more particular bond of interest. For my good friend, the minister of Essendean, had translated into the Gaelic in his by-time a number of hymns and pious books which Henderland used in his work, and held in great esteem. Indeed, it was one of these he was carrying and reading when we met.

We fell in company at once, our ways lying together as far as to Kingairloch. As we went, he stopped and spoke with all the wayfarers and workers that we met or passed; and though of course I could not tell what they discoursed about, yet I judged Mr. Henderland must be well liked in the countryside, for I observed many of them to bring out their mulls and share a pinch of snuff with him.

I told him as far in my affairs as I judged wise; as far, that is, as they were none of Alan's; and gave Balachulish as the place I was travelling to, to meet a friend; for I thought Aucharn, or even Duror, would be too particular, and might put him on the scent.

On his part, he told me much of his work and the people

he worked among, the hiding priests and Jacobites, the Dis-
arming Act, the dress, and many other curiosities of the time
and place. He seemed moderate; blaming Parliament in
several points, and especially because they had framed the
Act more severely against those who wore the dress than
against those who carried weapons.

This moderation put it in my mind to question him of the
Red Fox and the Appin tenants; questions which, I thought,
would seem natural enough in the mouth of one travelling
to that country.

He said it was a bad business. "It's wonderful," said he,
"'where the tenants find the money, for their life is mere
starvation. (Ye don't carry such a thing as snuff, do ye, Mr.
Balfour? No. Well, I'm better wanting it.) But these
tenants (as I was saying) are doubtless partly driven to it.
James Stewart in Duror (that's him they call James of the
Glens) is half-brother to Ardshiel, the captain of the clan;
and he is a man much looked up to, and drives very hard.
And then there's one they call Alan Breck ——"

"Ah!" I cried, "what of him?"

"What of the wind that bloweth where it listeth?" said
Henderland. "He's here and awa; here to-day and gone to-
morrow: a fair heather-cat. He might be glowering at the
two of us out of yon whin-bush, and I wouldnae wonder!
Ye'll no carry such a thing as snuff, will ye?"

I told him no, and that he had asked the same thing more
than once.

"It's highly possible," said he, sighing. "But it seems
strange ye shouldnae carry it. However, as I was saying,

this Alan Breck is a bold, desperate customer, and well kent to be James' right hand. His life is forfeit already; he would boggle at naething; and maybe, if a tenant-body was to hang back he would get a dirk in his wame."

"You make a poor story of it all, Mr. Henderland," said I. "If it is all fear upon both sides, I care to hear no more of it."

"Na," said Mr. Henderland, "but there's love too, and self-denial that should put the like of you and me to shame. There's something fine about it; no perhaps Christian, but humanly fine. Even Alan Breck, by all that I hear, is a chield to be respected. There's many a lying sneck-draw sits close in kirk in our own part of the country, and stands well in the world's eye, and maybe is a far worse man, Mr. Balfour, than yon misguided shedder of man's blood. Ay, ay, we might take a lesson by them. — Ye'll perhaps think I've been too long in the Hielands?" he added, smiling to me.

I told him not at all; that I had seen much to admire among the Highlanders; and if he came to that, Mr. Campbell himself was a Highlander.

"Ay," said he, "that's true. It's a fine blood."

"And what is the King's agent about?" I asked.

"Colin Campbell?" says Henderland. "Putting his head in a bees' byke!"

"He is to turn the tenants out by force, I hear?" said I.

"Yes," says he, "but the business has gone back and forth, as folk say. First, James of the Glens rode to Edinburgh, and got some lawyer (a Stewart, nae doubt — they all hing together like bats in a steeple) and had the proceedings stayed. And then Colin Campbell cam' in again, and had the upper-hand before the Barons of Exchequer. And now they tell me the first of the tenants are to flit to-morrow. It's to begin at Duror under James's very windows, which doesnae seem wise by my humble way of it."

"Do you think they'll fight?" I asked.

"Well," says Henderland, "they're disarmed — or supposed to be — for there's still a good deal of cold iron lying by in quiet places. And then Colin Campbell has the sogers coming. But for all that, if I was his lady wife, I wouldnae be well pleased till I got him home again. They're queer customers, the Appin Stewarts."

I asked if they were worse than their neighbours.

"No they," said he. "And that's the worst part of it. For if Colin Roy can get his business done in Appin, he has it all to begin again in the next country, which they call Mamore, and which is one of the countries of the Camerons. He's King's Factor upon both, and from both he has to drive out the tenants; and indeed, Mr. Balfour (to be open with ye), it's my belief that if he escapes the one lot, he'll get his death by the other."

So we continued talking and walking the great part of the day; until at last, Mr. Henderland, after expressing his delight in my company, and satisfaction at meeting with a friend of Mr. Campbell's ("whom," says he, "I will make bold to call that sweet singer of our covenanted Zion"), proposed that I should make a short stage, and lie the night in his house a little beyond Kingairloch. To say truth, I was overjoyed; for I had no great desire for John of the Claymore, and since my double misadventure, first with the guide and next with the gentleman skipper, I stood in some fear of any Highland stranger. Accordingly we shook hands upon the bargain, and came in the afternoon to a small house, standing alone by the shore of the Linnhe Loch. The sun was already gone from the desert mountains of Ardgour upon the hither side, but shone on those of Appin on the farther; the loch lay as still as a lake, only the gulls were crying round the sides of it; and the whole place seemed solemn and uncouth.

We had no sooner come to the door of Mr. Henderland's dwelling, than to my great surprise (for I was now used to the politeness of Highlanders) he burst rudely past me, dashed into the room, caught up a jar and a small horn-spoon, and began ladling snuff into his nose in most excessive quantities. Then he had a hearty fit of sneezing, and looked round upon me with a rather silly smile.

"It's a vow I took," says he. "I took a vow upon me that I wouldnae carry it. Doubtless it's a great privation; but when I think upon the martyrs, not only to the Scottish Covenant but to other points of Christianity, I think shame to mind it."

As soon as we had eaten (and porridge and whey was the best of the good man's diet) he took a grave face and said he had a duty to perform by Mr. Campbell, and that was to inquire into my state of mind towards God. I was inclined to smile at him since the business of the snuff; but he had not spoken long before he brought the tears into my eyes. There are two things that men should never weary of, goodness and humility; we get none too much of them in this rough world among cold, proud people; but Mr. Henderland had their very speech upon his tongue. And though I was a good deal puffed up with my adventures and with having come off, as the saying is, with flying colours; yet he soon had me on my knees beside a simple, poor old man, and both proud and glad to be there.

Before we went to bed he offered me sixpence to help me on my way, out of a scanty store he kept in the turf wall of his house; at which excess of goodness I knew not what to do. But at last he was so earnest with me that I thought it the more mannerly part to let him have his way, and so left him poorer than myself.

CHAPTER XVII

THE DEATH OF THE RED FOX

THE next day Mr. Henderland found for me a man who had a boat of his own and was to cross the Linnhe Loch that afternoon into Appin, fishing. Him he prevailed on to take me, for he was one of his flock; and in this way I saved a long day's travel and the price of the two public ferries I must otherwise have passed.

It was near noon before we set out; a dark day with clouds, and the sun shining upon little patches. The sea was here very deep and still, and had scarce a wave upon it; so that I must put the water to my lips before I could believe it to be truly salt. The mountains on either side were high, rough and barren, very black and gloomy in the shadow of the clouds, but all silver-laced with little watercourses where the sun shone upon them. It seemed a hard country, this of Appin, for people to care as much about as Alan did.

There was but one thing to mention. A little after we had started, the sun shone upon a little moving clump of scarlet close in along the water-side to the north. It was much of the same red as soldiers' coats; every now and then, too, there came little sparks and lightnings, as though the sun had struck upon bright steel.

KIDNAPPED

I asked my boatman what it should be, and he answered he supposed it was some of the red soldiers coming from Fort William into Appin, against the poor tenantry of the country. Well, it was a sad sight to me; and whether it was because of my thoughts of Alan, or from something prophetic in my bosom, although this was but the second time I had seen King George's troops, I had no good will to them.

At last we came so near the point of land at the entering in of Loch Leven that I begged to be set on shore. My boatman (who was an honest fellow and mindful of his promise to the catechist) would fain have carried me on to Balachulish; but as this was to take me farther from my secret destination, I insisted, and was set on shore at last under the wood of Lettermore (or Lettervore, for I have heard it both ways) in Alan's country of Appin.

This was a wood of birches, growing on a steep, craggy side of a mountain that overhung the loch. It had many openings and ferny howes; and a road or bridle track ran north and south through the midst of it, by the edge of which, where was a spring, I sat down to eat some oat-bread of Mr. Henderland's and think upon my situation.

Here I was not only troubled by a cloud of stinging midges, but far more by the doubts of my mind. What I ought to do, why I was going to join myself with an outlaw and a would-be murderer like Alan, whether I should not be acting more like a man of sense to tramp back to the south country direct, by my own guidance and at my own charges, and what Mr. Campbell or even Mr. Henderland would think of me if they should ever learn my folly and presumption: these were the doubts that now began to come in on me stronger than ever.

As I was so sitting and thinking, a sound of men and horses came to me through the wood; and presently after, at a turning of the road, I saw four travellers come into view. The way was in this part so rough and narrow that they came single and led their horses by the reins. The first was a great, red-headed gentleman, of an imperious and flushed face, who carried his hat in his hand and fanned himself, for he was in a breathing heat. The second, by his decent black garb and white wig, I correctly took to be a lawyer. The third was a servant, and wore some part of his clothes in tartan, which showed that his master was of a Highland family, and either an outlaw or else in singular good odour with the Government, since the wearing of tartan was against the Act. If I had been better versed in these things, I would have known the tartan to be of the Argyle (or Campbell, colours. This servant had a good-sized portmanteau strapped on his horse, and a net of lemons (to brew punch with) hanging at the saddle-bow; as was often enough the custom with luxurious travellers in that part of the country.

As for the fourth, who brought up the tail, I had seen his like before, and knew him at once to be a sheriff's officer.

I had no sooner seen these people coming than I made up my mind (for no reason that I can tell) to go through with my adventure; and when the first came alongside of me, I rose up from the bracken and asked him the way to Aucharn.

He stopped and looked at me, as I thought, a little oddly; and then, turning to the lawyer, "Mungo," said he, "there 's many a man would think this more of a warning than two pyats. Here am I on my road to Duror on the job ye ken; and here is a young lad starts up out of the bracken, and speers if I am on the way to Aucharn."

"Glenure," said the other, "this is an ill subject for jesting."

These two had now drawn close up and were gazing at me, while the two followers had halted about a stone-cast in the rear.

"And what seek ye in Aucharn?" said Colin Roy Campbell of Glenure, him they called the Red Fox; for he it was that I had stopped.

"The man that lives there," said I.

"James of the Glens," says Glenure, musingly; and then to the lawyer: "Is he gathering his people, think ye?"

"Anyway," says the lawyer, "we shall do better to bide where we are, and let the soldiers rally us."

"If you are concerned for me," said I, "I am neither of his people nor yours, but an honest subject of King George, owing no man and fearing no man."

"Why, very well said," replies the Factor. "But if I may make so bold as ask, what does this honest man so far from his country? and why does he come seeking the brother of Ardshiel? I have power here, I must tell you. I am King's Factor upon several of these estates, and have twelve files of soldiers at my back."

"I have heard a waif word in the country," said I, a little nettled, "that you were a hard man to drive."

He still kept looking at me, as if in doubt.

THE DEATH OF THE RED FOX

"Well," said he, at last, "your tongue is bold; but I am no unfriend to plainness. If ye had asked me the way to the door of James Stewart on any other day but this, I would have set ye right and bidden ye God speed. But to-day — eh, Mungo?" And he turned again to look at the lawyer.

But just as he turned there came the shot of a firelock from higher up the hill; and with the very sound of it Glenure fell upon the road.

"O, I am dead!" he cried, several times over.

The lawyer had caught him up and held him in his arms, the servant standing over and clasping his hands. And now the wounded man looked from one to another with scared eyes, and there was a change in his voice, that went to the heart.

"Take care of yourselves," says he. "I am dead."

He tried to open his clothes as if to look for the wound, but his fingers slipped on the buttons. With that he gave a great sigh, his head rolled on his shoulder, and he passed away.

The lawyer said never a word, but his face was as sharp as a pen and as white as the dead man's; the servant broke out into a great noise of crying and weeping, like a child; and I, on my side, stood staring at them in a kind of horror. The sheriff's officer had run back at the first sound of the shot, to hasten the coming of the soldiers.

At last the lawyer laid down the dead man in his blood upon the road and got to his own feet with a kind of stagger.

I believe it was his movement that brought me to my

senses; for he had no sooner done so than I began to scramble up the hill, crying out, "The murderer! the murderer!"

So little a time had elapsed, that when I got to the top of the first steepness, and could see some part of the open mountain, the murderer was still moving away at no great distance. He was a big man, in a black coat, with metal buttons, and carried a long fowling-piece.

"Here!" I cried. "I see him!"

At that the murderer gave a little, quick look over his shoulder, and began to run. The next moment he was lost in a fringe of birches; then he came out again on the upper side, where I could see him climbing like a jackanapes, for that part was again very steep, and then dipped behind a shoulder, and I saw him no more.

All this time I had been running on my side, and had got a good way up, when a voice cried upon me to stand.

I was at the edge of the upper wood, and so now, when I halted and looked back, I saw all the open part of the hill below me.

The lawyer and the sheriff's officer were standing just above the road, crying and waving on me to come back; and on their left, the red-coats, musket in hand, were beginning to struggle singly out of the lower wood.

"Why should I come back?" I cried. "Come you on!"

"Ten pounds if ye take that lad!" cried the lawyer. "He's an accomplice. He was posted here to hold us in talk."

At that word (which I could hear quite plainly, though it was to the soldiers and not to me that he was crying it) my heart came in my mouth with quite a new kind of terror. Indeed, it is one thing to stand the danger of your life, and quite another to run the peril of both life and character. The thing, besides, had come so suddenly, like thunder out of a clear sky, that I was all amazed and helpless.

The soldiers began to spread, some of them to run, and others to put up their pieces and cover me; and still I stood.

"Jouk¹ in here among the trees," said a voice close by.

Indeed, I scarce knew what I was doing, but I obeyed; and as I did so, I heard the firelocks bang and the balls whistle in the birches.

Just inside the shelter of the trees I found Alan Breck standing, with a fishing-rod. He gave me no salutation; indeed it was no time for civilities; only "Come!" says he, and set off running along the side of the mountain towards Balachulish; and I, like a sheep, to follow him.

Now we ran among the birches; now stooping behind low humps upon the mountain-side; now crawling on all-fours among the heather. The pace was deadly: my heart seemed bursting against my ribs; and I had neither time to think nor breath to speak with. Only I remember seeing with wonder, that Alan every now and then would straighten himself to his full height and look back; and every time he did so, there came a great far-away cheering and crying of the soldiers.

Quarter of an hour later, Alan stopped, clapped down flat in the heather, and turned to me.

"Now," said he, "it's earnest. Do as I do, for your life."

¹ Duck.

And at the same speed, but now with infinitely more precaution, we traced back again across the mountain-side by
the same way that we had come, only perhaps higher; till
at last Alan threw himself down in the upper wood of Lettermore, where I had found him at the first, and lay, with his
face in the bracken, panting like a dog.

My own sides so ached, my head so swam, my tongue so
hung out of my mouth with heat and dryness, that I lay beside him like one dead.

CHAPTER XVIII

I TALK WITH ALAN IN THE WOOD OF LETTERMORE

ALAN was the first to come round. He rose, went to the border of the wood, peered out a little, and then returned and sat down.

"Well," said he, "yon was a hot burst, David."

I said nothing, nor so much as lifted my face. I had seen murder done, and a great, ruddy, jovial gentleman struck out of life in a moment; the pity of that sight was still sore within me, and yet that was but a part of my concern. Here was murder done upon the man Alan hated; here was Alan skulking in the trees and running from the troops; and whether his was the hand that fired or only the head that ordered, signified but little. By my way of it, my only friend in that wild country was blood-guilty in the first degree; I held him in horror; I could not look upon his face; I would have rather lain alone in the rain on my cold isle, than in that warm wood beside a murderer.

"Are ye still wearied?" he asked again.

"No," said I, still with my face in the bracken; "no, I am not wearied now, and I can speak. You and me must twine." [1] I said. "I liked you very well, Alan, but your ways

[1] Part.

are not mine, and they 're not God's: and the short and the long of it is just that we must twine."

"I will hardly twine from ye, David, without some kind of reason for the same," said Alan, mighty gravely. "If ye ken anything against my reputation, it 's the least thing that ye should do, for old acquaintance' sake, to let me hear the name of it; and if ye have only taken a distaste to my society, it will be proper for me to judge if I 'm insulted."

"Alan," said I, "what is the sense of this? Ye ken very well yon Campbell-man lies in his blood upon the road."

He was silent for a little; then says he, "Did ever ye hear tell of the story of the Man and the Good People?" — by which he meant the fairies.

"No," said I, "nor do I want to hear it."

"With your permission, Mr. Balfour, I will tell it you, whatever," says Alan. "The man, ye should ken, was cast upon a rock in the sea, where it appears the Good People were in use to come and rest as they went through to Ireland. The name of this rock is called the Skerryvore, and it 's not far from where we suffered shipwreck. Well, it seems the man cried so sore, if he could just see his little bairn before he died! that at last the king of the Good People took peety upon him, and sent one flying that brought back the bairn in a poke[1] and laid it down beside the man where he lay sleeping. So when the man woke, there was a poke beside him and something into the inside of it that moved. Well, it seems he was one of these gentry that think aye the worst of things; and for greater security, he stuck his dirk through-

[1] Bag.

out that poke before he opened it, and there was his bairn dead. I am thinking to myself, Mr. Balfour, that you and the man are very much alike."

"Do you mean you had no hand in it?" cried I, sitting up.

"I will tell you first of all, Mr. Balfour of Shaws, as one friend to another," said Alan, "that if I were going to kill a gentleman, it would not be in my own country, to bring trouble on my clan; and I would not go wanting sword and gun, and with a long fishing-rod upon my back."

"Well," said I, "that's true!"

"And now," continued Alan, taking out his dirk and laying his hand upon it in a certain manner, "I swear upon the Holy Iron I had neither art nor part, act nor thought in it."

"I thank God for that!" cried I, and offered him my hand.

He did not appear to see it.

"And here is a great deal of work about a Campbell!" said he. "They are not so scarce, that I ken!"

"At least," said I, "you cannot justly blame me, for you know very well what you told me in the brig. But the temptation and the act are different, I thank God again for that. We may all be tempted; but to take a life in cold blood, Alan!" And I could say no more for the moment. "And do you know who did it?" I added. "Do you know that man in the black coat?"

"I have nae clear mind about his coat," said Alan cunningly; "but it sticks in my head that it was blue."

"Blue or black, did ye know him?" said I.

"I couldnae just conscientiously swear to him," says Alan. "He gaed very close by me, to be sure, but it's a strange thing that I should just have been tying my brogues."

"Can you swear that you don't know him, Alan?" I cried, half angered, half in a mind to laugh at his evasions.

"Not yet," says he; "but I've a grand memory for forgetting, David."

"And yet there was one thing I saw clearly," said I; "and that was, that you exposed yourself and me to draw the soldiers."

"It's very likely," said Alan; "and so would any gentleman. You and me were innocent of that transaction."

"The better reason, since we were falsely suspected, that we should get clear," I cried. "The innocent should surely come before the guilty."

"Why, David," said he, "the innocent have aye a chance to get assoiled in court; but for the lad that shot the bullet, I think the best place for him will be the heather. Them that havenae dipped their hands in any little difficulty, should be very mindful of the case of them that have. And that is the good Christianity. For if it was the other way round about, and the lad whom I couldnae just clearly see had been in our shoes, and we in his (as might very well have been), I think we would be a good deal obliged to him oursel's if he would draw the soldiers."

When it came to this, I gave Alan up. But he looked so innocent all the time, and was in such clear good faith in what he said, and so ready to sacrifice himself for what he deemed his duty, that my mouth was closed. Mr. Henderland's words came back to me: that we ourselves might take a lesson by these wild Highlanders. Well, here I had taken mine. Alan's morals were all tail-first; but he was ready to give his life for them, such as they were.

"Alan," said I, "I'll not say it's the good Christianity as I understand it, but it's good enough. And here I offer ye my hand for the second time."

Whereupon he gave me both of his, saying surely I had cast a spell upon him, for he could forgive me anything. Then he grew very grave, and said we had not much time to throw away, but must both flee that country: he, because he was a deserter, and the whole of Appin would now be searched like a chamber, and every one obliged to give a good account of himself; and I, because I was certainly involved in the murder.

"O!" says I, willing to give him a little lesson, "I have no fear of the justice of my country."

"As if this was your country!" said he. "Or as if ye would be tried here, in a country of Stewarts!"

"It's all Scotland," said I.

"Man, I whiles wonder at ye," said Alan. "This is a Campbell that's been killed. Well, it'll be tried in Inverara, the Campbells' head place; with fifteen Campbells in the jury-box and the biggest Campbell of all (and that's the Duke) sitting cocking on the bench. Justice, David? The same justice, by all the world, as Glenure found awhile ago at the roadside."

This frightened me a little, I confess, and would have frightened me more if I had known how nearly exact were Alan's predictions; indeed it was but in one point that he exaggerated, there being but eleven Campbells on the jury; though as the other four were equally in the Duke's dependence, it mattered less than might appear. Still, I cried out that he was unjust to the Duke of Argyle, who (for all he was a Whig) was yet a wise and honest nobleman.

"Hoot!" said Alan, "the man's a Whig, nae doubt; but I would never deny he was a good chieftain to his clan. And what would the clan think if there was a Campbell shot, and naebody hanged, and their own chief the Justice General? But I have often observed," says Alan, "that you Low-country bodies have no clear idea of what's right and wrong."

At this I did at last laugh out aloud, when to my surprise, Alan joined in, and laughed as merrily as myself.

"Na, na," said he, "we're in the Hielands, David; and when I tell ye to run, take my word and run. Nae doubt it's a hard thing to skulk and starve in the heather, but it's harder yet to lie shackled in a red-coat prison."

I asked him whither we should flee; and as he told me "to the Lowlands," I was a little better inclined to go with him; for, indeed, I was growing impatient to get back and have the upper-hand of my uncle. Besides, Alan made so sure there would be no question of justice in the matter, that I began to be afraid he might be right. Of all deaths, I would truly like least to die by the gallows; and the picture of that uncanny instrument came into my head with extraordinary clearness (as I had once seen it engraved at the top of a pedlar's ballad) and took away my appetite for courts of justice.

"I'll chance it, Alan," said I. "I'll go with you."

"But mind you," said Alan, "it's no small thing. Ye

maun lie bare and hard, and brook many an empty belly. Your bed shall be the moorcock's, and your life shall be like the hunted deer's, and ye shall sleep with your hand upon your weapons. Ay, man, ye shall taigle many a weary foot, or we get clear! I tell ye this at the start, for it 's a life that I ken well. But if ye ask what other chance ye have, I answer: Nane. Either take to the heather with me, or else hang."

"And that 's a choice very easily made," said I; and we shook hands upon it.

"And now let 's take another keek at the red-coats," says Alan, and he led me to the northeastern fringe of the wood.

Looking out between the trees, we could see a great side of mountain, running down exceeding steep into the waters of the loch. It was a rough part, all hanging stone, and heather, and big scrogs of birchwood; and away at the far end towards Balachulish, little wee red soldiers were dipping up and down over hill and howe, and growing smaller every minute. There was no cheering now, for I think they had other uses for what breath was left them; but they still stuck to the trail, and doubtless thought that we were close in front of them.

Alan watched them, smiling to himself.

"Ay," said he, "they 'll be gey weary before they 've got to the end of that employ! And so you and me, David, can sit down and eat a bite, and breathe a bit longer, and take a dram from my bottle. Then we 'll strike for Aucharn, the house of my kinsman, James of the Glens, where I must get my clothes, and my arms, and money to carry us along; and then, David, we'll cry 'Forth, Fortune!' and take a cast among the heather."

So we sat again and ate and drank, in a place whence we could see the sun going down into a field of great, wild, and houseless mountains, such as I was now condemned to wander in with my companion. Partly as we so sat, and partly afterwards, on the way to Aucharn, each of us narrated his adventures; and I shall here set down so much of Alan's as seems either curious or needful.

It appears he ran to the bulwarks as soon as the wave was passed; saw me, and lost me, and saw me again, as I tumbled in the roost; and at last had one glimpse of me clinging on the yard. It was this that put him in some hope I would maybe get to land after all, and made him leave those clues and messages which had brought me (for my sins) to that unlucky country of Appin.

In the meanwhile, those still on the brig had got the skiff launched, and one or two were on board of her already, when there came a second wave greater than the first, and heaved the brig out of her place, and would certainly have sent her to the bottom, had she not struck and caught on some projection on the reef. When she had struck first, it had been bows-on, so that the stern had hitherto been lowest. But now her stern was thrown in the air, and the bows plunged under the sea; and with that, the water began to pour into the fore-scuttle like the pouring of a mill-dam.

It took the colour out of Alan's face, even to tell what followed. For there were still two men lying impotent in their bunks; and these, seeing the water pour in and thinking the ship had foundered, began to cry out aloud, and that with such harrowing cries that all who were on deck tumbled one after another into the skiff and fell to their oars. They were not two hundred yards away, when there came a third great sea; and at that the brig lifted clean over the reef; her canvas filled for a moment, and she seemed to sail in chase of them, but settling all the while; and presently she drew down and down, as if a hand was drawing her; and the sea closed over the *Covenant* of Dysart.

Never a word they spoke as they pulled ashore, being stunned with the horror of that screaming; but they had scarce set foot upon the beach when Hoseason woke up, as if out of a muse, and bade them lay hands upon Alan. They hung back indeed, having little taste for the employment; but Hoseason was like a fiend, crying that Alan was alone, that he had a great sum about him, that he had been the means of losing the brig and drowning all their comrades, and that here was both revenge and wealth upon a single cast. It was seven against one; in that part of the shore there was no rock that Alan could set his back to; and the sailors began to spread out and come behind him.

"And then," said Alan, "the little man with the red head — I havenae mind of the name that he is called."

"Riach," said I.

"Ay," said Alan, "Riach! Well, it was him that took up the clubs for me, asked the men if they werenae feared of a judgment, and, says he, 'Dod, I'll put my back to the Hielandman's mysel'.' That's none such an entirely bad little man, yon little man with the red head," said Alan. "He has some spunks of decency."

"Well," said I, "he was kind to me in his way."

"And so he was to Alan," said he; "and by my troth, I found his way a very good one! But ye see, David, the loss of the ship and the cries of these poor lads sat very ill upon the man; and I 'm thinking that would be the cause of it."

"Well, I would think so," says I; "for he was as keen as any of the rest at the beginning. But how did Hoseason take it?"

"It sticks in my mind that he would take it very ill," says Alan. "But the little man cried to me to run, and indeed I thought it was a good observe, and ran. The last that I saw they were all in a knot upon the beach, like folk that were not agreeing very well together."

"What do you mean by that?" said I.

"Well, the fists were going," said Alan; "and I saw one man go down like a pair of breeks. But I thought it would be better no to wait. Ye see there 's a strip of Campbells in that end of Mull, which is no good company for a gentleman like me. If it hadnae been for that I would have waited and looked for ye mysel', let alone giving a hand to the little man." (It was droll how Alan dwelt on Mr. Riach's stature, for, to say the truth, the one was not much smaller than the other.) "So," says he, continuing, "I set my best foot forward, and whenever I met in with any one I cried out there was a wreck ashore. Man, they didnae stop to fash with me! Ye should have seen them linking for the beach! And when they got there they found they had had the pleasure of a

run, which is aye good for a Campbell. I 'm thinking it
was a judgment on the clan that the brig went down in
the lump and didnae break. But it was a very unlucky
thing for you, that same; for if any wreck had come ashore
they would have hunted high and low, and would soon have
found ye."

CHAPTER XIX

THE HOUSE OF FEAR

NIGHT fell as we were walking, and the clouds, which had broken up in the afternoon, settled in and thickened, so that it fell, for the season of the year, extremely dark. The way we went was over rough mountain-sides; and though Alan pushed on with an assured manner, I could by no means see how he directed himself.

At last, about half-past ten of the clock, we came to the top of a brae, and saw lights below us. It seemed a house door stood open and let out a beam of fire and candle-light; and all round the house and steading five or six persons were moving hurriedly about, each carrying a lighted brand.

"James must have tint his wits," said Alan. "If this was the soldiers instead of you and me, he would be in a bonny mess. But I dare say he 'll have a sentry on the road, and he would ken well enough no soldiers would find the way that we came."

Hereupon he whistled three times, in a particular manner. It was strange to see how, at the first sound of it, all the moving torches came to a stand, as if the bearers were affrighted; and how, at the third, the bustle began again as before.

THE HOUSE OF FEAR

Having thus set folks' minds at rest, we came down the brae, and were met at the yard gate (for this place was like a well-doing farm) by a tall, handsome man of more than fifty, who cried out to Alan in the Gaelic.

"James Stewart," said Alan, "I will ask ye to speak in Scotch, for here is a young gentleman with me that has nane of the other. This is him," he added, putting his arm through mine, "a young gentleman of the Lowlands, and a laird in his country too, but I am thinking it will be the better for his health if we give his name the go-by."

James of the Glens turned to me for a moment, and greeted me courteously enough; the next he had turned to Alan.

"This has been a dreadful accident," he cried. "It will bring trouble on the country." And he wrung his hands.

"Hoots!" said Alan, "ye must take the sour with the sweet, man. Colin Roy is dead, and be thankful for that!"

"Ay," said James, "and by my troth, I wish he was alive again! It's all very fine to blow and boast beforehand; but now it's done, Alan; and who's to bear the wyte[1] of it? The accident fell out in Appin — mind ye that, Alan; it's Appin that must pay; and I am a man that has a family."

While this was going on I looked about me at the servants. Some were on ladders, digging in the thatch of the house or the farm buildings, from which they brought out guns, swords, and different weapons of war; others carried them away; and by the sound of mattock blows from somewhere farther down the brae, I suppose they buried them. Though they were all so busy, there prevailed no kind of

[1] Blame.

order in their efforts; men struggled together for the same gun and ran into each other with their burning torches; and James was continually turning about from his talk with Alan, to cry out orders which were apparently never understood. The faces in the torchlight were like those of people overborne with hurry and panic; and though none spoke above his breath, their speech sounded both anxious and angry.

It was about this time that a lassie came out of the house carrying a pack or bundle; and it has often made me smile to think how Alan's instinct awoke at the mere sight of it.

"What's that the lassie has?" he asked.

"We're just setting the house in order, Alan," said James, in his frightened and somewhat fawning way. "They'll search Appin with candles, and we must have all things straight. We're digging the bit guns and swords into the moss, ye see; and these, I am thinking, will be your ain French clothes. We'll be to bury them, I believe."

"Bury my French clothes!" cried Alan. "Troth, no!" And he laid hold upon the packet and retired into the barn to shift himself, recommending me in the meanwhile to his kinsman.

James carried me accordingly into the kitchen, and sat down with me at table, smiling and talking at first in a very hospitable manner. But presently the gloom returned upon him; he sat frowning and biting his fingers; only remembered me from time to time; and then gave me but a word or two and a poor smile, and back into his private terrors. His wife sat by the fire and wept, with her face in her hands; his eldest son was crouched upon the floor, running over a great mass of papers and now and again setting one alight and burning it to the bitter end; all the while a servant lass with a red face was rummaging about the room, in a blind hurry of fear, and whimpering as she went; and every now and again one of the men would thrust in his face from the yard, and cry for orders.

At last James could keep his seat no longer, and begged my permission to be so unmannerly as walk about. "I am but poor company altogether, sir," says he, "but I can think of nothing but this dreadful accident, and the trouble it is like to bring upon quite innocent persons."

A little after he observed his son burning a paper which he thought should have been kept; and at that his excitement burst out so that it was painful to witness. He struck the lad repeatedly.

"Are you gone gyte?"[1] he cried. "Do you wish to hang your father?" and forgetful of my presence, carried on at him a long time together in the Gaelic, the young man answering nothing; only the wife, at the name of hanging, throwing her apron over her face and sobbing out louder than before.

This was all wretched for a stranger like myself to hear and see; and I was right glad when Alan returned, looking like himself in his fine French clothes, though (to be sure) they were now grown almost too battered and withered to deserve the name of fine. I was then taken out in my turn by another of the sons, and given that change of clothing of which I had stood so long in need, and a pair of Highland

[1] Mad.

[171]

brogues made of deer-leather, rather strange at first, but after a little practice very easy to the feet.

By the time I came back Alan must have told his story; for it seemed understood that I was to fly with him, and they were all busy upon our equipment. They gave us each a sword and pistols, though I professed my inability to use the former; and with these, and some ammunition, a bag of oat-meal, an iron pan, and a bottle of right French brandy, we were ready for the heather. Money, indeed, was lacking. I had about two guineas left; Alan's belt having been de-spatched by another hand, that trusty messenger had no more than seventeen-pence to his whole fortune; and as for James, it appears he had brought himself so low with journeys to Edinburgh and legal expenses on behalf of the tenants, that he could only scrape together three-and-five-pence-halfpenny, the most of it in coppers.

"This 'll no do," said Alan.

"Ye must find a safe bit somewhere near by," said James, "and get word sent to me. Ye see, ye 'll have to get this business prettily off, Alan. This is no time to be stayed for a guinea or two. They 're sure to get wind of ye, sure to seek ye, and by my way of it, sure to lay on ye the wyte of this day's accident. If it falls on you, it falls on me that am your near kinsman and harboured ye while ye were in the country. And if it comes on me—" he paused, and bit his fingers, with a white face. "It would be a painful thing for our friends if I was to hang," said he.

"It would be an ill day for Appin," says Alan.

"It 's a day that sticks in my throat," said James. "O

man, man, man — man Alan! you and me have spoken like two fools!" he cried, striking his hand upon the wall so that the house rang again.

"Well, and that's true, too," said Alan; "and my friend from the Lowlands here" (nodding at me) "gave me a good word upon that head, if I would only have listened to him."

"But see here," said James, returning to his former manner, "if they lay me by the heels, Alan, it's then that you'll be needing the money. For with all that I have said and that you have said, it will look very black against the two of us; do ye mark that? Well, follow me out, and ye'll see that I'll have to get a paper out against ye mysel'; I'll have to offer a reward for ye; ay, will I! It's a sore thing to do between such near friends; but if I get the dirdum[1] of this dreadful accident, I'll have to fend for myself, man. Do ye see that?"

He spoke with a pleading earnestness, taking Alan by the breast of the coat.

"Ay," said Alan, "I see that."

"And ye'll have to be clear of the country, Alan — ay, and clear of Scotland — you and your friend from the Lowlands, too. For I'll have to paper your friend from the Lowlands. Ye see that, Alan — say that ye see that!"

I thought Alan flushed a bit. "This is unco hard on me that brought him here, James," said he, throwing his head back. "It's like making me a traitor!"

"Now, Alan, man!" cried James. "Look things in the face! He'll be papered anyway; Mungo Campbell'll be sure

---

[1] Blame.

to paper him; what matters if I paper him too? And then, Alan, I am a man that has a family." And then, after a little paise on both sides, "And, Alan, it 'll be a jury of Campbells," said he.

"There 's one thing," said Alan, musingly, "that naebody kens his name."

"Nor yet they shallnae, Alan! There 's my hand on that," cried James, for all the world as if he had really known my name and was foregoing some advantage. "But just the habit he was in, and what he looked like, and his age, and the like? I couldnae well do less."

"I wonder at your father's son," cried Alan, sternly. "Would ye sell the lad with a gift? Would ye change his clothes and then betray him?"

"No, no, Alan," said James. "No, no: the habit he took off — the habit Mungo saw him in." But I thought he seemed crestfallen; indeed, he was clutching at every straw, and all the time, I dare say, saw the faces of his hereditary foes on the bench, and in the jury-box, and the gallows in the background.

"Well, sir," says Alan, turning to me, "what say ye to that? Ye are here under the safeguard of my honour; and it 's my part to see nothing done but what shall please you."

"I have but one word to say," said I; "for to all this dispute I am a perfect stranger. But the plain common-sense is to set the blame where it belongs, and that is on the man who fired the shot. Paper him, as ye call it, set the hunt on him; and let honest, innocent folk show their faces in safety." But at this both Alan and James cried out in horror; bidding me hold my tongue, for that was not to be thought of; and asking me what the Camerons would think? (which confirmed me, it must have been a Cameron from Mamore that did the act) and if I did not see that the lad might be caught? "Ye havenae surely thought of that?" said they, with such innocent earnestness, that my hands dropped at my side and I despaired of argument.

"Very well, then," said I, "paper me, if you please, paper Alan, paper King George! We're all three innocent, and that seems to be what's wanted. But at least, sir," said I to James, recovering from my little fit of annoyance, "I am Alan's friend, and if I can be helpful to friends of his, I will not stumble at the risk."

I thought it best to put a fair face on my consent, for I saw Alan troubled; and, besides (thinks I to myself), as soon as my back is turned, they will paper me, as they call it, whether I consent or not. But in this I saw I was wrong; for I had no sooner said the words, than Mrs. Stewart leaped out of her chair, came running over to us, and wept first upon my neck and then on Alan's, blessing God for our goodness to her family.

"As for you, Alan, it was no more than your bounden duty," she said. "But for this lad that has come here and seen us at our worst, and seen the goodman fleeching like a suitor, him that by rights should give his commands like any king — as for you, my lad," she says, "my heart is wae not to have your name, but I have your face; and as long as my heart beats under my bosom, I will keep it, and think of it, and bless it." And with that she kissed me, and burst once more into such sobbing, that I stood abashed.

"Hoot, hoot," said Alan, looking mighty silly. "The day comes unco soon in this month of July; and to-morrow there'll be a fine to-do in Appin, a fine riding of dragoons, and crying of 'Cruachan!'[1] and running of red-coats; and it behoves you and me to the sooner be gone."

Thereupon we said farewell, and set out again, bending somewhat eastwards, in a fine mild dark night, and over much the same broken country as before.

[1] The rallying-word of the Campbells.

CHAPTER XX

THE FLIGHT IN THE HEATHER: THE ROCKS

SOMETIMES we walked, sometimes ran; and as it drew on to morning, walked ever the less and ran the more. Though, upon its face, that country appeared to be a desert, yet there were huts and houses of the people, of which we must have passed more than twenty, hidden in quiet places of the hills. When we came to one of these, Alan would leave me in the way, and go himself and rap upon the side of the house and speak awhile at the window with some sleeper awakened. This was to pass the news; which, in that country, was so much of a duty that Alan must pause to attend to it even while fleeing for his life; and so well attended to by others, that in more than half of the houses where we called they had heard already of the murder. In the others, as well as I could make out (standing back at a distance and hearing a strange tongue), the news was received with more of consternation than surprise.

For all our hurry, day began to come in while we were still far from any shelter. It found us in a prodigious valley, strewn with rocks and where ran a foaming river. Wild mountains stood around it; there grew there neither grass nor trees; and I have sometimes thought since then, that it may have been the valley called Glencoe, where the massacre was in the time of King William. But for the details of our itinerary, I am all to seek; our way lying now by short cuts, now by great detours; our pace being so hurried, our time of journeying usually by night; and the names of such places as I asked and heard being in the Gaelic tongue and the more easily forgotten.

The first peep of morning, then, showed us this horrible place, and I could see Alan knit his brow.

"This is no fit place for you and me," he said. "This is a place they 're bound to watch."

And with that he ran harder than ever down to the water-side, in a part where the river was split in two among three rocks. It went through with a horrid thundering that made my belly quake; and there hung over the lynn a little mist of spray. Alan looked neither to the right nor to the left, but jumped clean upon the middle rock and fell there on his hands and knees to check himself, for that rock was small and he might have pitched over on the far side. I had scarce time to measure the distance or to understand the peril before I had followed him, and he had caught and stopped me.

So there we stood, side by side upon a small rock slippery with spray, a far broader leap in front of us, and the river dinning upon all sides. When I saw where I was, there came on me a deadly sickness of fear, and I put my hand over my eyes. Alan took me and shook me; I saw he was speaking, but the roaring of the falls and the trouble of my mind prevented me from hearing; only I saw his face was red with anger, and that he stamped upon the rock. The same look showed me the water raging by, and the mist hanging in the air: and with that I covered my eyes again and shuddered.

The next minute Alan had set the brandy bottle to my lips, and forced me to drink about a gill, which sent the blood into my head again. Then, putting his hands to his mouth, and his mouth to my ear, he shouted, "Hang or drown!" and turning his back upon me, leaped over the farther branch of the stream, and landed safe.

I was now alone upon the rock, which gave me the more room; the brandy was singing in my ears; I had this good example fresh before me, and just wit enough to see that if I did not leap at once, I should never leap at all. I bent low on my knees and flung myself forth, with that kind of anger of despair that has sometimes stood me in stead of courage. Sure enough, it was but my hands that reached the full length; these slipped, caught again, slipped again; and I was sliddering back into the lynn, when Alan seized me, first by the hair, then by the collar, and with a great strain dragged me into safety.

Never a word he said, but set off running again for his life, and I must stagger to my feet and run after him. I had been weary before, but now I was sick and bruised, and partly drunken with the brandy; I kept stumbling as I ran, I had a stitch that came near to overmaster me; and when at last Alan paused under a great rock that stood there among a number of others, it was none too soon for David Balfour.

A great rock I have said; but by rights it was two rocks leaning together at the top, both some twenty feet high, and at the first sight inaccessible. Even Alan (though you may

say he had as good as four hands) failed twice in an attempt
to climb them; and it was only at the third trial, and then by
standing on my shoulders and leaping up with such force
as I thought must have broken my collar-bone, that he secured a lodgment. Once there, he let down his leathern girdle;
and with the aid of that and a pair of shallow footholds in
the rock, I scrambled up beside him.

Then I saw why we had come there; for the two rocks,
being both somewhat hollow on the top and sloping one to
the other, made a kind of dish or saucer, where as many as
three or four men might have lain hidden.

All this while Alan had not said a word, and had run and
climbed with such a savage, silent frenzy of hurry, that I knew
that he was in mortal fear of some miscarriage. Even now
we were on the rock he said nothing, nor so much as relaxed
the frowning look upon his face; but clapped flat down, and
keeping only one eye above the edge of our place of shelter
scouted all round the compass. The dawn had come quite
clear; we could see the stony sides of the valley, and its bottom,
which was bestrewed with rocks, and the river, which went
from one side to another, and made white falls; but nowhere
the smoke of a house, nor any living creature but some eagles
screaming round a cliff.

Then at last Alan smiled.

"Ay," said he, "now we have a chance"; and then looking at me with some amusement. "Ye 're no very gleg[1] at
the jumping," said he.

At this I suppose I coloured with mortification, for he

[1] Brisk.

added at once: "Hoots: small blame to ye! To be feared of a thing and yet to do it, is what makes the prettiest kind of a man. And then there was water there, and water's a thing that dauntons even me. No, no," said Alan, "it's no you that's to blame, it's me."

I asked him why.

"Why," said he, "I have proved myself a gomeral this night. For first time of all I take a wrong road, and that in my own country of Appin; so that the day has caught us where we should never have been; and thanks to that, we lie here in some danger and mair discomfort. And next (which is the worst of the two, for a man that has been so much among the heather as myself) I have come wanting a water-bottle, and here we lie for a long summer's day with naething but neat spirit. Ye may think that a small matter; but before it comes night, David, ye'll give me news of it."

I was anxious to redeem my character, and offered, if he would pour out the brandy, to run down and fill the bottle at the river.

"I wouldnae waste the good spirit either," says he. "It's been a good friend to you this night; or in my poor opinion, ye would still be cocking on yon stone. And what's mair," says he, "ye may have observed (you that's a man of so much penetration) that Alan Breck Stewart was perhaps walking quicker than his ordinar'."

"You!" I cried, "you were running fit to burst."

"Was I so?" said he. "Well, then, ye may depend upon it, there was nae time to be lost. And now here is enough said; gang you to your sleep, lad, and I'll watch."

Accordingly, I lay down to sleep; a little peaty earth had drifted in between the top of the two rocks, and some bracken grew there, to be a bed to me; the last thing I heard was still the crying of the eagles.

I dare say it would be nine in the morning when I was roughly awakened, and found Alan's hand pressed upon my mouth.

"Wheesht!" he whispered. "Ye were snoring."

"Well," said I, surprised at his anxious and dark face, "and why not?"

He peered over the edge of the rock, and signed to me to do the like.

It was now high day, cloudless, and very hot. The valley was as clear as in a picture. About half a mile up the water was a camp of red-coats; a big fire blazed in their midst, at which some were cooking; and near by, on the top of a rock about as high as ours, there stood a sentry, with the sun sparkling on his arms. All the way down along the river-side were posted other sentries; here near together, there widelier scattered; some planted like the first, on places of command, some on the ground level and marching and counter-marching, so as to meet half-way. Higher up the glen, where the ground was more open, the chain of posts was continued by horse-soldiers, whom we could see in the distance riding to and fro. Lower down, the infantry continued; but as the stream was suddenly swelled by the confluence of a considerable burn, they were more widely set, and only watched the fords and stepping-stones.

I took but one look at them, and ducked again into my

place. It was strange indeed to see this valley, which had lain so solitary in the hour of dawn, bristling with arms and dotted with the red coats and breeches.

"Ye see," said Alan, "this was what I was afraid of, Davie: that they would watch the burnside. They began to come in about two hours ago, and, man! but ye 're a grand hand at the sleeping! We 're in a narrow place. If they get up the sides of the hill, they could easy spy us with a glass; but if they 'll only keep in the foot of the valley, we 'll do yet. The posts are thinner down the water; and, come night, we 'll try our hand at getting by them."

"And what are we to do till night?" I asked.

"Lie here," says he, "and birstle."

That one good Scotch word, "birstle," was indeed the most of the story of the day that we had now to pass. You are to remember that we lay on the bare top of a rock, like scones upon a girdle; the sun beat upon us cruelly; the rock grew so heated, a man could scarce endure the touch of it; and the little patch of earth and fern, which kept cooler, was only large enough for one at a time. We took turn about to lie on the naked rock, which was indeed like the position of that saint that was martyred on a gridiron; and it ran in my mind how strange it was, that in the same climate and at only a few days' distance, I should have suffered so cruelly, first from cold upon my island and now from heat upon this rock.

All the while we had no water, only raw brandy for a drink, which was worse than nothing; but we kept the bottle as cool as we could, burying it in the earth, and got some relief by bathing our breasts and temples.

[183]

KIDNAPPED

The soldiers kept stirring all day in the bottom of the valley, now changing guard, now in patrolling parties hunting among the rocks. These lay round in so great a number, that to look for men among them was like looking for a needle in a bottle of hay; and being so hopeless a task, it was gone about with the less care. Yet we could see the soldiers pike their bayonets among the heather, which sent a cold thrill into my vitals; and they would sometimes hang about our rock, so that we scarce dared to breathe.

It was in this way that I first heard the right English speech; one fellow as he went by actually clapping his hand upon the sunny face of the rock on which we lay, and plucking it off again with an oath. "I tell you it's 'ot," says he; and I was amazed at the clipping tones and the odd sing-song in which he spoke, and no less at that strange trick of dropping out the letter "h." To be sure, I had heard Ransome; but he had taken his ways from all sorts of people, and spoke so imperfectly at the best, that I set down the most of it to childishness. My surprise was all the greater to hear that manner of speaking in the mouth of a grown man; and indeed I have never grown used to it; nor yet altogether with the English grammar, as perhaps a very critical eye might here and there spy out even in these memoirs.

The tediousness and pain of these hours upon the rock grew only the greater as the day went on; the rock getting still the hotter and the sun fiercer. There were giddiness, and sickness, and sharp pangs like rheumatism, to be supported. I minded then, and have often minded since, on the lines in our Scotch psalm: —

THE FLIGHT IN THE HEATHER

"The moon by night thee shall not smite,
Nor yet the sun by day;"

and indeed it was only by God's blessing that we were neither of us sun-smitten.

At last, about two, it was beyond men's bearing, and there was now temptation to resist, as well as pain to thole. For the sun being now got a little into the west, there came a patch of shade on the east side of our rock, which was the side sheltered from the soldiers.

"As well one death as another," said Alan, and slipped over the edge and dropped on the ground on the shadowy side.

I followed him at once, and instantly fell all my length, so weak was I and so giddy with that long exposure. Here, then, we lay for an hour or two, aching from head to foot, as weak as water, and lying quite naked to the eye of any soldier who should have strolled that way. None came, however, all passing by on the other side; so that our rock continued to be our shield even in this new position.

Presently we began again to get a little strength; and as the soldiers were now lying closer along the river-side, Alan proposed that we should try a start. I was by this time afraid of but one thing in the world; and that was to be set back upon the rock; anything else was welcome to me; so we got ourselves at once in marching order, and began to slip from rock to rock one after the other, now crawling flat on our bellies in the shade, now making a run for it, heart in mouth.

The soldiers, having searched this side of the valley after a fashion, and being perhaps somewhat sleepy with the sul-

[185]

triness of the afternoon, had now laid by much of their vigilance, and stood dozing at their posts or only kept a look-out along the banks of the river; so that in this way, keeping down the valley and at the same time towards the mountains, we drew steadily away from their neighbourhood. But the business was the most wearing I had ever taken part in. A man had need of a hundred eyes in every part of him, to keep concealed in that uneven country and within cry of so many and scattered sentries. When we must pass an open place, quickness was not all, but a swift judgment not only of the lie on the whole country, but of the solidity of every stone on which we must set foot; for the afternoon was now fallen so breathless that the rolling of a pebble sounded abroad like a pistol shot, and would start the echo calling among the hills and cliffs.

By sundown we had made some distance, even by our slow rate of progress, though to be sure the sentry on the rock was still plainly in our view. But now we came on something that put all fears out of season; and that was a deep rushing burn, that tore down, in that part, to join the glen river. At the sight of this we cast ourselves on the ground and plunged head and shoulders in the water; and I cannot tell which was the more pleasant, the great shock as the cool stream went over us, or the greed with which we drank of it.

We lay there (for the banks hid us), drank again and again, bathed our chests, let our wrists trail in the running water till they ached with the chill; and at last, being wonderfully renewed, we got out the meal-bag and made drammach in the iron pan. This, though it is but cold water mingled with oatmeal, yet makes a good enough dish for a hungry man; and where there are no means of making fire, or (as in our case) good reason for not making one, it is the chief stand-by of those who have taken to the heather.

As soon as the shadow of the night had fallen, we set forth again, at first with the same caution, but presently with more boldness, standing our full height and stepping out at a good pace of walking. The way was very intricate, lying up the steep sides of mountains and along the brows of cliffs; clouds had come in with the sunset, and the night was dark and cool; so that I walked without much fatigue, but in continual fear of falling and rolling down the mountains, and with no guess at our direction.

The moon rose at last and found us still on the road; it was in its last quarter, and was long beset with clouds; but after awhile shone out and showed me many dark heads of mountains, and was reflected far underneath us on the narrow arm of a sea-loch.

At this sight we both paused: I struck with wonder to find myself so high and walking (as it seemed to me) upon clouds; Alan to make sure of his direction.

Seemingly he was well pleased, and he must certainly have judged us out of ear-shot of all our enemies; for throughout the rest of our night-march he beguiled the way with whistling of many tunes, warlike, merry, plaintive; reel tunes that made the foot go faster; tunes of my own south country that made me fain to be home from my adventures; and all these, on the great, dark, desert mountains, making company upon the way.

CHAPTER XXI

THE FLIGHT IN THE HEATHER:
THE HEUGH OF CORRYNAKIEGH

EARLY as day comes in the beginning of July, it was still dark when we reached our destination, a cleft in the head of a great mountain, with a water running through the midst, and upon the one hand a shallow cave in a rock. Birches grew there in a thin, pretty wood, which a little farther on was changed into a wood of pines. The burn was full of trout; the wood of cushat-doves; on the open side of the mountain beyond, whaups would be always whistling, and cuckoos were plentiful. From the mouth of the cleft we looked down upon a part of Mamore, and on the sea-loch that divides that country from Appin; and this from so great a height as made it my continual wonder and pleasure to sit and behold them.

The name of the cleft was the Heugh of Corrynakiegh; and although from its height and being so near upon the sea, it was often beset with clouds, yet it was on the whole a pleasant place, and the five days we lived in it went happily.

We slept in the cave, making our bed of heather bushes which we cut for that purpose, and covering ourselves with Alan's great-coat. There was a low concealed place, in a turning of the glen, where we were so bold as to make fire: so that we could warm ourselves when the clouds set in, and cook hot porridge, and grill the little trouts that we caught with our hands under the stones and overhanging banks of the burn. This was indeed our chief pleasure and business; and not only to save our meal against worse times, but with a rivalry that much amused us, we spent a great part of our days at the water-side, stripped to the waist and groping about or (as they say) guddling for these fish. The largest we got might have been a quarter of a pound; but they were of good flesh and flavour, and when broiled upon the coals, lacked only a little salt to be delicious.

In any by-time Alan must teach me to use my sword, for my ignorance had much distressed him; and I think besides, as I had sometimes the upper-hand of him in the fishing, he was not sorry to turn to an exercise where he had so much the upper hand of me. He made it somewhat more of a pain than need have been, for he stormed at me all through the lessons in a very violent manner of scolding, and would push me so close that I made sure he must run me through the body. I was often tempted to turn tail, but held my ground for all that, and got some profit of my lessons; if it was but to stand on guard with an assured countenance, which is often all that is required. So, though I could never in the least please my master, I was not altogether displeased with myself.

In the meanwhile, you are not to suppose that we neglected our chief business, which was to get away.

"It will be many a long day," Alan said to me on our

first morning, "before the red-coats think upon seeking Corrynakiegh; so now we must get word sent to James, and he must find the siller for us."

"And how shall we send that word?" says I. "We are here in a desert place, which yet we dare not leave; and unless ye get the fowls of the air to be your messengers, I see not what we shall be able to do."

"Ay?" said Alan. "Ye're a man of small contrivance, David."

Thereupon he fell in a muse, looking in the embers of the fire; and presently, getting a piece of wood, he fashioned it in a cross, the four ends of which he blackened on the coals. Then he looked at me a little shyly.

"Could ye lend me my button?" says he. "It seems a strange thing to ask a gift again, but I own I am laith to cut another."

I gave him the button; whereupon he strung it on a strip of his great-coat which he had used to bind the cross; and tying in a little sprig of birch and another of fir, he looked upon his work with satisfaction.

"Now," said he, "there is a little clachan" (what is called a hamlet in the English) "not very far from Corrynakiegh, and it has the name of Koalisnacoan. There there are living many friends of mine whom I could trust with my life, and some that I am no just so sure of. Ye see, David, there will be money set upon our heads; James himsel' is to set money on them; and as for the Campbells, they would never spare siller where there was a Stewart to be hurt. If it was otherwise, I would go down to Koalisnacoan whatever, and trust my life into these people's hands as lightly as I would trust another with my glove."

"But being so?" said I.

"Being so," said he, "I would as lief they didnae see me. There's bad folk everywhere, and what's far worse, weak ones. So when it comes dark again, I will steal down into that clachan, and set this that I have been making in the window of a good friend of mine, John Breck Maccoll, a bouman[1] of Appin's."

"With all my heart," says I; "and if he finds it, what is he to think?"

"Well, says Alan, "I wish he was a man of more penetration, for by my troth I am afraid he will make little enough of it! But this is what I have in my mind. This cross is something in the nature of the crosstarrie, or fiery cross, which is the signal of gathering in our clans; yet he will know well enough the clan is not to rise, for there it is standing in his window, and no word with it. So he will say to himsel', *The clan is not to rise, but there is something.* Then he will see my button, and that was Duncan Stewart's. And then he will say to himsel', *The son of Duncan is in the heather, and has need of me.*"

"Well," said I, "it may be. But even supposing so, there is a good deal of heather between here and the Forth."

"And that is a very true word," says Alan. "But then John Breck will see the sprig of birch and the sprig of pine; and he will say to himsel' (if he is a man of any penetration

[1] A bouman is a tenant who takes stock from the landlord and shares with him the increase.

at all, which I misdoubt), *Alan will be lying in a wood which is both of pines and birches.* Then he will think to himsel', *That is not so very rife hereabout;* and then he will come and give us a look up in Corrynakiegh. And if he does not, David, the devil may fly away with him, for what I care; for he will not be worth the salt to his porridge."

"Eh, man," said I, drolling with him a little, "you 're very ingenious! But would it not be simpler for you to write him a few words in black and white?"

"And that is an excellent observe, Mr. Balfour of Shaws," says Alan, drolling with me; "and it would certainly be much simpler for me to write to him, but it would be a sore job for John Breck to read it. He would have to go to the school for two-three years; and it 's possible we might be wearied waiting on him."

So that night Alan carried down his fiery cross and set it in the bouman's window. He was troubled when he came back; for the dogs had barked and the folk run out from their houses; and he thought he had heard a clatter of arms and seen a red-coat come to one of the doors. On all accounts we lay the next day in the borders of the wood and kept a close look-out, so that if it was John Breck that came we might be ready to guide him, and if it was the red-coats we should have time to get away.

About noon a man was to be spied, straggling up the open side of the mountain in the sun, and looking round him as he came, from under his hand. No sooner had Alan seen him than he whistled; the man turned and came a little towards us: then Alan would give another "peep!" and the man would come still nearer; and so by the sound of whistling, he was guided to the spot where we lay.

He was a ragged, wild, bearded man, about forty, grossly disfigured with the small-pox, and looked both dull and savage. Although his English was very bad and broken, yet Alan (according to his very handsome use, whenever I was by) would suffer him to speak no Gaelic. Perhaps the strange language made him appear more backward than he really was; but I thought he had little good-will to serve us, and what he had was the child of terror.

Alan would have had him carry a message to James; but the bouman would hear of no message. "She was forget it," he said in his screaming voice; and would either have a letter or wash his hands of us.

I thought Alan would be gravelled at that, for we lacked the means of writing in that desert. But he was a man of more resources than I knew; searched the wood until he found the quill of a cushat-dove, which he shaped into a pen; made himself a kind of ink with gunpowder from his horn and water from the running stream; and tearing a corner from his French military commission (which he carried in his pocket, like a talisman to keep him from the gallows), he sat down and wrote as follows:

"DEAR KINSMAN, — Please send the money by the bearer to the place he kens of.

"Your affectionate cousin,

"A. S."

This he intrusted to the bouman, who promised to make what manner of speed he best could, and carried it off with him down the hill.

KIDNAPPED

He was three full days gone, but about five in the evening of the third, we heard a whistling in the wood, which Alan answered; and presently the bouman came up the water-side, looking for us, right and left. He seemed less sulky than before, and indeed he was no doubt well pleased to have got to the end of such a dangerous commission.

He gave us the news of the country; that it was alive with red-coats; that arms were being found, and poor folk brought in trouble daily; and that James and some of his servants were already clapped in prison at Fort William, under strong suspicion of complicity. It seemed it was noised on all sides that Alan Breck had fired the shot; and there was a bill issued for both him and me, with one hundred pounds reward.

This was all as bad as could be; and the little note the bouman had carried us from Mrs. Stewart was of a miserable sadness. In it she besought Alan not let himself be captured, assuring him, if he fell in the hands of the troops, both he and James were no better than dead men. The money she had sent was all that she could beg or borrow, and she prayed heaven we could be doing with it. Lastly, she said, she enclosed us one of the bills in which we were described.

This we looked upon with great curiosity and not a little fear, partly as a man may look in a mirror, partly as he might look into the barrel of an enemy's gun to judge if it be truly aimed. Alan was advertised as "a small, pock-marked, active man of thirty-five or thereby, dressed in a feathered hat, a French side-coat of blue with silver buttons, and lace a great deal tarnished, a red waistcoat and breeches of black shag"; and I as "a tall strong lad of about eighteen, wearing an old blue coat, very ragged, an old Highland bonnet, a long homespun waistcoat, blue breeches; his legs bare, low-country shoes, wanting the toes; speaks like a Lowlander, and has no beard."

Alan was well enough pleased to see his finery so fully remembered and set down; only when he came to the word tarnish, he looked upon his lace like one a little mortified. As for myself, I thought I cut a miserable figure in the bill; and yet was well enough pleased, too, for since I had changed these rags, the description had ceased to be a danger and become a source of safety.

"Alan," said I, "you should change your clothes."

"Na, troth!" said Alan, "I have nae others. A fine sight I would be, if I went back to France in a bonnet!"

This put a second reflection in my mind: that if I were to separate from Alan and his tell-tale clothes I should be safe against arrest, and might go openly about my business. Nor was this all; for suppose I was arrested when I was alone, there was little against me; but suppose I was taken in company with the reputed murderer, my case would begin to be grave. For generosity's sake I dare not speak my mind upon this head; but I thought of it none the less.

I thought of it all the more, too, when the bouman brought out a green purse with four guineas in gold, and the best part of another in small change. True, it was more than I had. But then Alan, with less than five guineas, had to get as far as France; I, with my less than two, not beyond Queensferry; so that taking things in their proportion, Alan's society was not only a peril to my life, but a burden on my purse.

But there was no thought of the sort in the honest head of my companion. He believed he was serving, helping, and protecting me. And what could I do but hold my peace, and chafe, and take my chance of it?

"It's little enough," said Alan, putting the purse in his pocket, "but it'll do my business. And now, John Breck, if ye will hand me over my button, this gentleman and me will be for taking the road."

But the bouman, after feeling about in a hairy purse that hung in front of him in the Highland manner (though he wore otherwise the Lowland habit, with sea-trousers), began to roll his eyes strangely, and at last said, "Her nainsel will loss it," meaning he thought he had lost it.

"What!" cried Alan, "you will lose my button, that was my father's before me? Now I will tell you what is in my mind, John Breck: it is in my mind this is the worst day's work that ever ye did since ye was born."

And as Alan spoke, he set his hands on his knees and looked at the bouman with a smiling mouth, and that dancing light in his eyes that meant mischief to his enemies.

Perhaps the bouman was honest enough; perhaps he had meant to cheat and then, finding himself alone with two of us in a desert place, cast back to honesty as being safer; at least, and all at once, he seemed to find that button and handed it to Alan.

"Well, and it is a good thing for the honour of the Maccolls," said Alan, and then to me: "Here is my button back again, and I thank you for parting with it, which is of a piece with all your friendships to me." Then he took the warmest parting of the bouman. "For," says he, "ye have done very well by me, and set your neck at a venture, and I will always give you the name of a good man."

Lastly, the bouman took himself off by one way; and Alan and I (getting our chattels together) struck into another to resume our flight.

CHAPTER XXII

THE FLIGHT IN THE HEATHER: THE MOOR

SOME seven hours' incessant, hard travelling brought us early in the morning to the end of a range of mountains. In front of us there lay a piece of low, broken, desert land, which we must now cross. The sun was not long up, and shone straight in our eyes; a little, thin mist went up from the face of the moorland like a smoke; so that (as Alan said) there might have been twenty squadron of dragoons there and we none the wiser.

We sat down, therefore, in a howe of the hillside till the mist should have risen, and made ourselves a dish of drammach, and held a council of war.

"David," said Alan, "this is the kittle bit. Shall we lie here till it comes night, or shall we risk it, and stave on ahead?"

"Well," said I, "I am tired indeed, but I could walk as far again, if that was all."

"Ay, but it isnae," said Alan, "nor yet the half. This is how we stand: Appin's fair death to us. To the south it's all Campbells, and no to be thought of. To the north; well, there's no muckle to be gained by going north; neither for you, that wants to get to Queensferry, nor yet for me, that wants to get to France. Well, then, we'll can strike east."

THE FLIGHT IN THE HEATHER

"East be it!" says I, quite cheerily; but I was thinking, in to myself: "O, man, if you would only take one point of the compass and let me take any other, it would be the best for both of us."

"Well, then, east, ye see, we have the muirs," said Alan. "Once there, David, it's mere pitch-and-toss. Out on yon bald, naked, flat place, where can a body turn to? Let the red-coats come over a hill, they can spy you miles away; and the sorrow's in their horses' heels, they would soon ride you down. It's no good place, David; and I'm free to say, it's worse by daylight than by dark."

"Alan," said I, "hear my way of it. Appin's death for us; we have none too much money, nor yet meal; the longer they seek, the nearer they may guess where we are; it's all a risk; and I give my word to go ahead until we drop."

Alan was delighted. "There are whiles," said he, "when ye are altogether too canny and Whiggish to be company for a gentleman like me; but there come other whiles when ye show yoursel' a mettle spark; and it's then, David, that I love ye like a brother."

The mist rose and died away, and showed us that country lying as waste as the sea; only the moorfowl and the pewees crying upon it, and far over to the east, a herd of deer, moving like dots. Much of it was red with heather; much of the rest broken up with bogs and hags and peaty pools; some had been burnt black in a heath fire; and in another place there was quite a forest of dead firs, standing like skeletons. A wearier-looking desert man never saw; but at least it was clear of troops, which was our point.

KIDNAPPED

We went down accordingly into the waste, and began to make our toilsome and devious travel towards the eastern verge. There were the tops of mountains all round (you are to remember) from whence we might be spied at any moment; so it behoved us to keep in the hollow parts of the moor, and when these turned aside from our direction to move upon its naked face with infinite care. Sometimes, for half an hour together, we must crawl from one heather bush to another, as hunters do when they are hard upon the deer. It was a clear day again, with a blazing sun; the water in the brandy bottle was soon gone; and altogether, if I had guessed what it would be to crawl half the time upon my belly and to walk much of the rest stooping nearly to the knees, I should certainly have held back from such a killing enterprise.

Toiling and resting and toiling again, we wore away the morning; and about noon lay down in a thick bush of heather to sleep. Alan took the first watch; and it seemed to me I had scarce closed my eyes before I was shaken up to take the second. We had no clock to go by; and Alan stuck a sprig of heath in the ground to serve instead; so that as soon as the shadow of the bush should fall so far to the east, I might know to rouse him. But I was by this time so weary that I could have slept twelve hours at a stretch; I had the taste of sleep in my throat; my joints slept even when my mind was waking; the hot smell of the heather, and the drone of the wild bees, were like possets to me; and every now and again I would give a jump and find I had been dozing.

The last time I woke I seemed to come back from farther away, and thought the sun had taken a great start in the heavens. I looked at the sprig of heath, and at that I could have cried aloud: for I saw I had betrayed my trust. My head was nearly turned with fear and shame; and at what I saw, when I looked out around me on the moor, my heart was like dying in my body. For sure enough, a body of horse-soldiers had come down during my sleep, and were drawing near to us from the south-east, spread out in the shape of a fan and riding their horses to and fro in the deep parts of the heather.

When I waked Alan, he glanced first at the soldiers, then at the mark and the position of the sun, and knitted his brows with a sudden, quick look, both ugly and anxious, which was all the reproach I had of him.

"What are we to do now?" I asked.

"We'll have to play at being hares," said he. "Do ye see yon mountain?" pointing to one on the north-eastern sky.

"Ay," said I.

"Well, then," says he, "let us strike for that. Its name is Ben Alder; it is a wild, desert mountain full of hills and hollows, and if we can win to it before the morn, we may do yet."

"But, Alan," cried I, "that will take us across the very coming of the soldiers!"

"I ken that fine," said he; "but if we are driven back on Appin, we are two dead men. So now, David man, be brisk!"

With that he began to run forward on his hands and knees with an incredible quickness, as though it were his natural way of going. All the time, too, he kept winding in and out in the lower parts of the moorland where we were the best concealed. Some of these had been burned or at least scathed with fire; and there rose in our faces (which were close to the ground) a blinding, choking dust as fine as smoke. The water was long out; and this posture of running on the hands and knees brings an overmastering weakness and weariness, so that the joints ache and the wrists faint under your weight.

Now and then, indeed, where was a big bush of heather, we lay awhile, and panted, and putting aside the leaves, looked back at the dragoons. They had not spied us, for they held straight on; a half-troop, I think, covering about two miles of ground, and beating it mighty thoroughly as they went. I had awakened just in time; a little later, and we must have fled in front of them, instead of escaping on one side. Even as it was, the least misfortune might betray us; and now and again, when a grouse rose out of the heather with a clap of wings, we lay as still as the dead and were afraid to breathe.

The aching and faintness of my body, the labouring of my heart, the soreness of my hands, and the smarting of my throat and eyes in the continual smoke of dust and ashes, had soon grown to be so unbearable that I would gladly have given up. Nothing but the fear of Alan lent me enough of a false kind of courage to continue. As for himself (and you are to bear in mind that he was cumbered with a great-coat) he had first turned crimson, but as time went on the redness began to be mingled with patches of white; his breath cried and whistled as it came; and his voice, when he whispered his observations in my ear during our halts, sounded like nothing human. Yet he seemed in no way dashed in spirits, nor did he at all abate in his activity; so that I was driven to marvel at the man's endurance.

At length, in the first gloaming of the night, we heard a trumpet sound, and looking back from among the heather, saw the troop beginning to collect. A little after, they had built a fire and camped for the night, about the middle of the waste.

At this I begged and besought that we might lie down and sleep.

"There shall be no sleep the night!" said Alan. "From now on, these weary dragoons of yours will keep the crown of the muirland, and none will get out of Appin but winged fowls. We got through in the nick of time, and shall we jeopard what we 've gained? Na, na, when the day comes, it shall find you and me in a fast place on Ben Alder."

"Alan," I said, "it 's not the want of will: it 's the strength that I want. If I could, I would; but as sure as I 'm alive I cannot."

"Very well, then," said Alan. "I 'll carry ye."

I looked to see if he were jesting; but no, the little man was in dead earnest; and the sight of so much resolution shamed me.

"Lead away!" said I. "I 'll follow."

He gave me one look as much as to say, "Well done, David!" and off he set again at his top speed.

It grew cooler and even a little darker (but not much) with the coming of the night. The sky was cloudless; it was still early in July, and pretty far north; in the darkest part of that night, you would have needed pretty good eyes to read, but for all that, I have often seen it darker in a winter mid-day. Heavy dew fell and drenched the moor like rain; and this refreshed me for a while. When we stopped to breathe, and I had time to see all about me, the clearness and sweetness of the night, the shapes of the hills like things asleep, and the fire dwindling away behind us, like a bright spot in the midst of the moor, anger would come upon me in a clap that I must still drag myself in agony and eat the dust like a worm.

By what I have read in books, I think few that have held a pen were ever really wearied, or they would write of it more strongly. I had no care of my life, neither past nor future, and I scarce remembered there was such a lad as David Balfour; I did not think of myself, but just of each fresh step which I was sure would be my last, with despair — and of Alan, who was the cause of it, with hatred. Alan was in the right trade as a soldier; this is the officer's part to make men continue to do things, they know not wherefore, and when, if the choice was offered, they would lie down where they were and be killed. And I dare say I would have made a good enough private; for in these last hours it never occurred to me that I had any choice but just to obey as long as I was able, and die obeying.

Day began to come in, after years, I thought; and by that time we were past the greatest danger, and could walk upon our feet like men, instead of crawling like brutes. But, dear heart have mercy! what a pair we must have made, going double like old grandfathers, stumbling like babes, and as white as dead folk. Never a word passed between us; each set his mouth and kept his eyes in front of him, and lifted up his foot and set it down again, like people lifting weights at a country play;[1] all the while, with the moorfowl crying "peep!" in the heather, and the light coming slowly clearer in the east.

I say Alan did as I did. Not that ever I looked at him, for I had enough ado to keep my feet; but because it is plain he must have been as stupid with weariness as myself, and looked as little where we were going, or we should not have walked into an ambush like blind men.

It fell in this way. We were going down a heathery brae, Alan leading and I following a pace or two behind, like a fiddler and his wife; when upon a sudden the heather gave a rustle, three or four ragged men leaped out, and the next moment we were lying on our backs, each with a dirk at his throat.

I don't think I cared; the pain of this rough handling was quite swallowed up by the pains of which I was already full; and I was too glad to have stopped walking to mind about a dirk. I lay looking up in the face of the man that held me; and I mind his face was black with the sun, and his eyes very light, but I was not afraid of him. I heard Alan and another whispering in the Gaelic; and what they said was all one to me.

Then the dirks were put up, our weapons were taken away, and we were set face to face, sitting in the heather.

[1] Village fair.

KIDNAPPED

"They are Cluny's men," said Alan. "We couldnae have fallen better. We're just to bide here with these, which are his out-sentries, till they can get word to the chief of my arrival."

Now Cluny Macpherson, the chief of the clan Vourich, had been one of the leaders of the great rebellion six years before; there was a price on his life; and I had supposed him long ago in France, with the rest of the heads of that desperate party. Even tired as I was, the surprise of what I heard half wakened me.

"What," I cried, "is Cluny still here?"

"Ay, is he so!" said Alan. "Still in his own country and kept by his own clan. King George can do no more."

I think I would have asked farther, but Alan gave me the put-off. "I am rather wearied," he said, "and I would like fine to get a sleep." And without more words, he rolled on his face in a deep heather bush, and seemed to sleep at once.

There was no such thing possible for me. You have heard grasshoppers whirring in the grass in the summer time? Well, I had no sooner closed my eyes, than my body, and above all my head, belly, and wrists, seemed to be filled with whirring grasshoppers; and I must open my eyes again at once, and tumble and toss, and sit up and lie down; and look at the sky which dazzled me, or at Cluny's wild and dirty sentries, peering out over the top of the brae and chattering to each other in the Gaelic.

That was all the rest I had, until the messenger returned; when, as it appeared that Cluny would be glad to receive us, we must get once more upon our feet and set forward. Alan was in excellent good spirits, much refreshed by his sleep, very hungry, and looking pleasantly forward to a dram and a dish of hot collops, of which, it seems, the messenger had brought him word. For my part, it made me sick to hear of eating. I had been dead-heavy before, and now I felt a kind of dreadful lightness, which would not suffer me to walk. I drifted like a gossamer; the ground seemed to me a cloud, the hills a feather-weight, the air to have a current, like a running burn, which carried me to and fro. With all that, a sort of horror of despair sat on my mind, so that I could have wept at my own helplessness.

I saw Alan knitting his brows at me, and supposed it was in anger; and that gave me a pang of light-headed fear, like what a child may have. I remember, too, that I was smiling, and could not stop smiling, hard as I tried; for I thought it was out of place at such a time. But my good companion had nothing in his mind but kindness; and the next moment, two of the gillies had me by the arms, and I began to be carried forward with great swiftness (or so it appeared to me, although I dare say it was slowly enough in truth), through a labyrinth of dreary glens and hollows and into the heart of that dismal mountain of Ben Alder.

CHAPTER XXIII

CLUNY'S CAGE

WE came at last to the foot of an exceeding steep wood, which scrambled up a craggy hillside, and was crowned by a naked precipice.

"It's here," said one of the guides, and we struck up hill.

The trees clung upon the slope, like sailors on the shrouds of a ship, and their trunks were like the rounds of a ladder, by which we mounted.

Quite at the top, and just before the rocky face of the cliff sprang above the foliage, we found that strange house which was known in the country as "Cluny's Cage." The trunks of several trees had been wattled across, the intervals strengthened with stakes, and the ground behind this barricade levelled up with earth to make the floor. A tree, which grew out from the hillside, was the living centre-beam of the roof. The walls were of wattle and covered with moss. The whole house had something of an egg shape; and it half hung, half stood in that steep, hillside thicket, like a wasp's nest in a green hawthorn.

Within, it was large enough to shelter five or six persons with some comfort. A projection of the cliff had been cunningly employed to be the fireplace; and the smoke rising against the face of the rock, and being not dissimilar in colour, readily escaped notice from below.

This was but one of Cluny's hiding-places; he had caves, besides, and underground chambers in several parts of his country; and following the reports of his scouts, he moved from one to another as the soldiers drew near or moved away. By this manner of living, and thanks to the affection of his clan, he had not only stayed all this time in safety, while so many others had fled or been taken and slain: but stayed four or five years longer, and only went to France at last by the express command of his master. There he soon died; and it is strange to reflect that he may have regretted his Cage upon Ben Alder.

When we came to the door he was seated by his rock chimney, watching a gillie about some cookery. He was mighty plainly habited, with a knitted nightcap drawn over his ears, and smoked a foul cutty pipe. For all that he had the manners of a king, and it was quite a sight to see him rise out of his place to welcome us.

"Well, Mr. Stewart, come awa', sir!" said he, "and bring in your friend that as yet I dinna ken the name of."

"And how is yourself, Cluny?" said Alan. "I hope ye do brawly, sir. And I am proud to see ye, and to present to ye my friend the Laird of Shaws, Mr. David Balfour."

Alan never referred to my estate without a touch of a sneer, when we were alone; but with strangers, he rang the words out like a herald.

"Step in by, the both of ye, gentlemen," says Cluny. "I make ye welcome to my house, which is a queer, rude place for certain, but one where I have entertained a royal personage, Mr. Stewart — ye doubtless ken the personage I have in my eye. We 'll take a dram for luck, and as soon as this handless man of mine has the collops ready, we 'll dine and take a hand at the cartes as gentlemen should. My life is a bit driegh," says he, pouring out the brandy; "I see little company, and sit and twirl my thumbs, and mind upon a great day that is gone by, and weary for another great day that we all hope will be upon the road. And so here 's a toast to ye: The Restoration!"

Thereupon we all touched glasses and drank. I am sure I wished no ill to King George; and if he had been there himself in proper person, it 's like he would have done as I did. No sooner had I taken out the dram than I felt hugely better, and could look on and listen, still a little misty perhaps, but no longer with the same groundless horror and distress of mind.

It was certainly a strange place, and we had a strange host. In his long hiding, Cluny had grown to have all manner of precise habits, like those of an old maid. He had a particular place, where no one else must sit; the Cage was arranged in a particular way, which none must disturb; cookery was one of his chief fancies, and even while he was greeting us in, he kept an eye to the collops.

It appears he sometimes visited or received visits from his wife and one or two of his nearest friends, under the cover of night; but for the more part lived quite alone, and communicated only with his sentinels and the gillies that waited on him in the Cage. The first thing in the morning, one of them, who was a barber, came and shaved him, and gave him the news of the country, of which he was immoderately greedy. There was no end to his questions; he put them as earnestly as a child; and at some of the answers, laughed out of all bounds of reason, and would break out again laughing at the mere memory, hours after the barber was gone.

To be sure, there might have been a purpose in his questions; for though he was thus sequestered, and like the other landed gentlemen of Scotland, stripped by the late Act of Parliament of legal powers, he still exercised a patriarchal justice in his clan. Disputes were brought to him in his hiding-hole to be decided; and the men of his country, who would have snapped their fingers at the Court of Session, laid aside revenge and paid down money at the bare word of this forfeited and hunted outlaw. When he was angered, which was often enough, he gave his commands and breathed threats of punishment like any king; and his gillies trembled and crouched away from him like children before a hasty father. With each of them, as he entered, he ceremoniously shook hands, both parties touching their bonnets at the same time in a military manner. Altogether, I had a fair chance to see some of the inner workings of a Highland clan; and this with a proscribed, fugitive chief; his country conquered; the troops riding upon all sides in quest of him, sometimes within a mile of where he lay; and when the least of the ragged fellows, whom he rated and threatened, could have made a fortune by betraying him.

On that first day, as soon as the collops were ready, Cluny gave them with his own hand a squeeze of a lemon (for he was well supplied with luxuries) and bade us draw in to our meal.

"They," said he, meaning the collops, "are such as I gave his Royal Highness in this very house; bating the lemon juice, for at that time we were glad to get the meat and never fashed for kitchen.[1] Indeed, there were mair dragoons than lemons in my country in the year forty-six."

I do not know if the collops were truly very good, but my heart rose against the sight of them, and I could eat but little. All the while Cluny entertained us with stories of Prince Charlie's stay in the Cage, giving us the very words of the speakers, and rising from his place to show us where they stood. By these, I gathered the Prince was a gracious, spirited boy, like the son of a race of polite kings, but not so wise as Solomon. I gathered, too, that while he was in the Cage, he was often drunk; so the fault that has since, by all accounts, made such a wreck of him, had even then begun to show itself.

We were no sooner done eating than Cluny brought out an old, thumbed, greasy pack of cards, such as you may find in a mean inn; and his eyes brightened in his face as he proposed that we should fall to playing.

Now this was one of the things I had been brought up to eschew like disgrace; it being held by my father neither the part of a Christian nor yet of a gentleman to set his own livelihood and fish for that of others, on the cast of painted pasteboard. To be sure, I might have pleaded my fatigue, which was excuse enough; but I thought it behoved that I

[1] Condiment.

should bear a testimony. I must have got very red in the face, but I spoke steadily, and told them I had no call to be a judge of others, but for my own part, it was a matter in which I had no clearness.

Cluny stopped mingling the cards. "What in deil's name is this?" says he. "What kind of Whiggish, canting talk is this, for the house of Cluny Macpherson?"

"I will put my hand in the fire for Mr. Balfour," says Alan. "He is an honest and a mettle gentleman, and I would have ye bear in mind who says it. I bear a king's name," says he, cocking his hat; "and I and any that I call friend are company for the best. But the gentleman is tired, and should sleep; if he has no mind to the cartes, it will never hinder you and me. And I 'm fit and willing, sir, to play ye any game that ye can name."

"Sir," says Cluny, "in this poor house of mine I would have you to ken that any gentleman may follow his pleasure. If your friend would like to stand on his head, he is welcome. And if either he, or you, or any other man, is not preceesely satisfied, I will be proud to step outside with him."

I had no will that these two friends should cut their throats for my sake.

"Sir," said I, "I am very wearied, as Alan says; and what 's more, as you are a man that likely has sons of your own, I may tell you it was a promise to my father."

"Say nae mair, say nae mair," said Cluny, and pointed me to a bed of heather in a corner of the Cage. For all that he was displeased enough, looked at me askance, and grumbled when he looked. And indeed it must be owned that both my scruples and the words in which I declared them, smacked somewhat of the Covenanter, and were little in their place among wild Highland Jacobites.

What with the brandy and the venison, a strange heaviness had come over me; and I had scarce lain down upon the bed before I fell into a kind of trance, in which I continued almost the whole time of our stay in the Cage. Sometimes I was broad awake and understood what passed; sometimes I only heard voices, or men snoring, like the voice of a silly river; and the plaids upon the wall dwindled down and swelled out again, like firelight shadows on the roof. I must sometimes have spoken or cried out, for I remember I was now and then amazed at being answered; yet I was conscious of no particular nightmare, only of a general, black, abiding horror — a horror of the place I was in, and the bed I lay in, and the plaids on the wall, and the voices, and the fire, and myself.

The barber-gillie, who was a doctor too, was called in to prescribe for me; but as he spoke in the Gaelic, I understood not a word of his opinion, and was too sick even to ask for a translation. I knew well enough I was ill, and that was all I cared about.

I paid little heed while I lay in this poor pass. But Alan and Cluny were most of the time at the cards, and I am clear that Alan must have begun by winning; for I remember sitting up, and seeing them hard at it, and a great glittering pile of as much as sixty or a hundred guineas on the table. It looked strange enough, to see all this wealth in a nest upon a cliff-side, wattled about growing trees. And even then, I thought it seemed deep water for Alan to be riding, who had no better battle-horse than a green purse and a matter of five pounds.

The luck, it seems, changed on the second day. About noon I was awakened as usual for dinner, and as usual refused to eat, and was given a dram with some bitter infusion which the barber had prescribed. The sun was shining in at the open door of the Cage, and this dazzled and offended me. Cluny sat at the table, biting the pack of cards. Alan had stooped over the bed, and had his face close to my eyes; to which, troubled as they were with the fever, it seemed of the most shocking business.

He asked me for a loan of my money.

"What for?" said I.

"O, just for a loan," said he.

"But why?" I repeated. "I don't see."

"Hut, David!" said Alan, "ye wouldnae grudge me a loan?"

I would, though, if I had had my senses! But all I thought of then was to get his face away, and I handed him my money.

On the morning of the third day, when we had been forty-eight hours in the Cage, I awoke with a great relief of spirits, very weak and weary indeed, but seeing things of the right size and with their honest, everyday appearance. I had a mind to eat, moreover, rose from bed of my own movement, and as soon as we had breakfasted, stepped to the entry of the Cage and sat down outside in the top of the wood. It was a grey day with a cool, mild air: and I sat in a dream all morning, only disturbed by the passing by of Cluny's scouts and servants coming with provisions and reports; for as the coast was at that time clear, you might almost say he held court openly.

When I returned, he and Alan had laid the cards aside, and were questioning a gillie; and the chief turned about and spoke to me in the Gaelic.

"I have no Gaelic, sir," said I.

Now since the card question, everything I said or did had the power of annoying Cluny. "Your name has more sense than yourself, then," said he angrily; "for it's good Gaelic. But the point is this. My scout reports all clear in the south, and the question is, have ye the strength to go?"

I saw cards on the table, but no gold; only a heap of little written papers, and these all on Cluny's side. Alan, besides, had an odd look, like a man not very well content; and I began to have a strong misgiving.

"I do not know if I am as well as I should be," said I, looking at Alan; "but the little money we have has a long way to carry us."

Alan took his under-lip into his mouth, and looked upon the ground.

"David," says he at last, "I've lost it; there's the naked truth."

"My money too?" said I.

"Your money too," says Alan, with a groan. "Ye shouldnae have given it me. I'm daft when I get to the cartes."

"Hoot-toot! hoot-toot!" said Cluny. "It was all daffing; it's all nonsense. Of course you'll have your money back again, and the double of it, if ye 'll make so free with me. It would be a singular thing for me to keep it. It's not to be supposed that I would be any hindrance to gentlemen in your situation; that would be a singular thing!" cries he, and began to pull gold out of his pocket with a mighty red face.

Alan said nothing, only looked on the ground.

"Will you step to the door with me, sir?" said I.

Cluny said he would be very glad, and followed me readily enough, but he looked flustered and put out.

"And now, sir," says I, "I· must first acknowledge your generosity."

"Nonsensical nonsense!" cries Cluny. "Where 's the generosity? This is just a most unfortunate affair; but what would ye have me do — boxed up in this bee-skep of a cage of mine — but just set my friends to the cartes, when I can get them? And if they lose, of course, it 's not to be supposed —" And here he came to a pause.

"Yes," said I, "if you lose, you give them back their money; and if they win, they carry away yours in their pouches! I have said before that I grant your generosity; but to me, sir, it 's a very painful thing to be placed in this position."

There was a little silence, in which Cluny seemed always as if he was about to speak, but said nothing. All the time he grew redder and redder in the face.

"I am a young man," said I, "and I ask your advice. Advise me as you would your son. My friend fairly lost his money, after having fairly gained a far greater sum of yours; can I accept it back again? Would that be the right part for me to play? Whatever I do, you can see for yourself it must be hard upon a man of any pride."

"It's rather hard on me, too, Mr. Balfour," said Cluny, "and ye give me very much the look of a man that has entrapped poor people to their hurt. I wouldnae have my friends come to any house of mine to accept affronts; no," he cried, with a sudden heat of anger, "nor yet to give them!"

"And so you see, sir," said I, "there is something to be said upon my side; and this gambling is a very poor employ for gentlefolks. But I am still waiting your opinion."

I am sure if ever Cluny hated any man it was David Balfour. He looked me all over with a warlike eye, and I saw the challenge at his lips. But either my youth disarmed him, or perhaps his own sense of justice. Certainly it was a mortifying matter for all concerned, and not least Cluny; the more credit that he took it as he did.

"Mr. Balfour," said he, "I think you are too nice and covenanting, but for all that you have the spirit of a very pretty gentleman. Upon my honest word, ye may take this money — it's what I would tell my son — and here's my hand along with it!"

CHAPTER XXIV

THE FLIGHT IN THE HEATHER:
THE QUARREL

ALAN and I were put across Loch Errocht under cloud of night, and went down its eastern shore to another hiding-place near the head of Loch Rannoch, whither we were led by one of the gillies from the Cage. This fellow carried all our luggage and Alan's great-coat in the bargain, trotting along under the burthen, far less than the half of which used to weigh me to the ground, like a stout hill pony with a feather; yet he was a man that, in plain contest, I could have broken on my knee.

Doubtless it was a great relief to walk disencumbered; and perhaps without that relief, and the consequent sense of liberty and lightness, I could not have walked at all. I was but new risen from a bed of sickness; and there was nothing in the state of our affairs to hearten me for much exertion; travelling, as we did, over the most dismal deserts in Scotland, under a cloudy heaven, and with divided hearts among the travellers.

For long, we said nothing; marching alongside or one behind the other, each with a set countenance: I, angry and proud, and drawing what strength I had from these two violent and sinful feelings; Alan, angry and ashamed, ashamed that he had lost my money, angry that I should take it so ill.

KIDNAPPED

The thought of a separation ran always the stronger in my mind; and the more I approved of it, the more ashamed I grew of my approval. It would be a fine, handsome, generous thing, indeed, for Alan to turn round and say to me: "Go, I am in the most danger, and my company only increases yours." But for me to turn to the friend who certainly loved me, and say to him: "You are in great danger, I am in but little; your friendship is a burden; go, take your risks and bear your hardships alone —" no, that was impossible; and even to think of it privily to myself, made my cheeks to burn.

And yet Alan had behaved like a child, and (what is worse) a treacherous child. Wheedling my money from me while I lay half-conscious was scarce better than theft; and yet here he was trudging by my side, without a penny to his name, and by what I could see, quite blithe to sponge upon the money he had driven me to beg. True, I was ready to share it with him; but it made me rage to see him count upon my readiness.

These were the two things uppermost in my mind; and I could open my mouth upon neither without black ungenerosity. So I did the next worst, and said nothing, nor so much as looked once at my companion, save with the tail of my eye.

At last, upon the other side of Loch Errocht, going over a smooth, rushy place, where the walking was easy, he could bear it no longer, and came close to me.

"David," says he, "this is no way for two friends to take a small accident. I have to say that I 'm sorry; and so that 's said. And now if you have anything, ye 'd better say it."

THE FLIGHT IN THE HEATHER

"O," says I, "I have nothing."

He seemed disconcerted; at which I was meanly pleased.

"No," said he, with rather a trembling voice, "but when I say I was to blame?"

"Why, of course, ye were to blame," said I, coolly; "and you will bear me out that I have never reproached you."

"Never," says he; "but ye ken very well that ye 've done worse. Are we to part? Ye said so once before. Are ye to say it again? There 's hills and heather enough between here and the two seas, David; and I will own I 'm no very keen to stay where I 'm no wanted."

This pierced me like a sword, and seemed to lay bare my private disloyalty.

"Alan Breck!" I cried; and then: "Do you think I am one to turn my back on you in your chief need? You dursn't say it to my face. My whole conduct 's there to give the lie to it. It 's true, I fell asleep upon the muir; but that was from weariness, and you do wrong to cast it up to me ——"

"Which is what I never did," said Alan.

"But aside from that," I continued, "what have I done that you should even me to dogs by such a supposition? I never yet failed a friend, and it 's not likely I 'll begin with you. There are things between us that I can never forget, even if you can."

"I will only say this to ye, David," said Alan, very quietly, "that I have long been owing ye my life, and now I owe ye money. Ye should try to make that burden light for me."

This ought to have touched me, and in a manner it did, but the wrong manner. I felt I was behaving badly; and was now not only angry with Alan, but angry with myself in the bargain; and it made me the more cruel.

"You asked me to speak," said I. "Well, then, I will. You own yourself that you have done me a disservice; I have had to swallow an affront: I have never reproached you, I never named the thing till you did. And now you blame me," cried I, "because I cannæ laugh and sing as if I was glad to be affronted. The next thing will be that I 'm to go down upon my knees and thank you for it! Ye should think more of others, Alan Breck. If ye thought more of others, ye would perhaps speak less about yourself; and when a friend that likes you very well has passed over an offence without a word, you would be blithe to let it lie, instead of making it a stick to break his back with. By your own way of it, it was you that was to blame; then it shouldnae be you to seek the quarrel."

"Aweel," said Alan, "say nae mair."

And we fell back into our former silence; and came to our journey's end, and supped, and lay down to sleep, without another word.

The gillie put us across Loch Rannoch in the dusk of the next day, and gave us his opinion as to our best route. This was to get us up at once into the tops of the mountains: to go round by a circuit, turning the heads of Glen Lyon, Glen Lochay, and Glen Dochart, and come down upon the lowlands by Kippen and the upper waters of the Forth. Alan was little pleased with a route which led us through the country of his blood-foes, the Glenorchy Campbells. He objected that by turning to the east, we should come almost at once among the Athole Stewarts, a race of his own name and lineage, although following a different chief, and come besides by a far easier and swifter way to the place whither we were bound. But the gillie, who was indeed the chief man of Cluny's scouts, had good reasons to give him on all hands, naming the force of troops in every district, and alleging finally (as well as I could understand) that we should nowhere be so little troubled as in a country of the Campbells.

Alan gave way at last, but with only half a heart. "It's one of the dowiest countries in Scotland," said he. "There's naething there that I ken, but heath, and crows, and Campbells. But I see that ye're a man of some penetration; and be it as ye please!"

We set forth accordingly by this itinerary; and for the best part of three nights travelled on eerie mountains and among the well-heads of wild rivers; often buried in mist, almost continually blown and rained upon, and not once cheered by any glimpse of sunshine. By day, we lay and slept in the drenching heather; by night, incessantly clambered upon break-neck hills and among rude crags. We often wandered; we were often so involved in fog, that we must lie quiet till it lightened. A fire was never to be thought of. Our only food was drammach and a portion of cold meat that we had carried from the Cage; and as for drink, Heaven knows we had no want of water.

This was a dreadful time, rendered the more dreadful by the gloom of the weather and the country. I was never warm; my teeth chattered in my head; I was troubled with a very sore throat, such as I had on the isle; I had a painful stitch in my side, which never left me; and when I slept in my wet bed, with the rain beating above and the mud oozing below me, it was to live over again in fancy the worst part of my adventures — to see the tower of Shaws lit by lightning, Ransome carried below·on the men's backs, Shuan dying on the round-house floor, or Colin Campbell grasping at the bosom of his coat. From such broken slumbers, I would be aroused in the gloaming, to sit up in the same puddle where I had slept, and sup cold drammach; the rain driving sharp in my face or running down my back in icy trickles; the mist enfolding us like as in a gloomy chamber — or, perhaps, if the wind blew, falling suddenly apart and showing us the gulf of some dark valley where the streams were crying aloud.

The sound of an infinite number of rivers came up from all round. In this steady rain the springs of the mountain were broken up; every glen gushed water like a cistern; every stream was in high spate, and had filled and overflowed its channel. During our night tramps, it was solemn to hear the voice of them below in the valleys, now booming like thunder, now with an angry cry. I could well understand the story of the Water Kelpie, that demon of the streams, who is fabled to keep wailing and roaring at the ford until the coming of the doomed traveller. Alan I saw believed it, or half believed it; and when the cry of the river rose more than usually sharp, I was little surprised (though, of course, I would still be shocked) to see him cross himself in the manner of the Catholics.

During all these horrid wanderings we had no familiarity, scarcely even that of speech. The truth is that I was sickening for my grave, which is my best excuse. But besides that I was of an unforgiving disposition from my birth, slow to take offence, slower to forget it, and now incensed both against my companion and myself. For the best part of two days he was unweariedly kind; silent, indeed, but always ready to help, and always hoping (as I could very well see) that my displeasure would blow by. For the same length of time I stayed in myself, nursing my anger, roughly refusing his services, and passing him over with my eyes as if he had been a bush or a stone.

The second night, or rather the peep of the third day, found us upon a very open hill, so that we could not follow our usual plan and lie down immediately to eat and sleep. Before we had reached a place of shelter, the grey had come pretty clear, for though it still rained, the clouds ran higher; and Alan, looking in my face, showed some marks of concern.

"Ye had better let me take your pack," said he, for perhaps the ninth time since we had parted from the scout beside Loch Rannoch.

"I do very well, I thank you," said I, as cold as ice.

Alan flushed darkly. "I 'll not offer it again," he said. "I 'm not a patient man, David."

"I never said you were," said I, which was exactly the rude, silly speech of a boy of ten.

Alan made no answer at the time, but his conduct answered for him. Henceforth, it is to be thought, he quite forgave himself for the affair at Cluny's; cocked his hat again, walked jauntily, whistled airs, and looked at me upon one side with a provoking smile.

KIDNAPPED

The third night we were to pass through the western end of the country of Balquhidder. It came clear and cold, with a touch in the air like frost, and a northerly wind that blew the clouds away and made the stars bright. The streams were full, of course, and still made a great noise among the hills; but I observed that Alan thought no more upon the Kelpie, and was in high good spirits. As for me, the change of weather came too late; I had lain in the mire so long that (as the Bible has it) my very clothes "abhorred me"; I was dead weary, deadly sick and full of pains and shiverings; the chill of the wind went through me, and the sound of it confused my ears. In this poor state I had to bear from my companion something in the nature of a persecution. He spoke a good deal, and never without a taunt. "Whig" was the best name he had to give me. "Here," he would say, "here's a dub for ye to jump, my Whiggie! I ken you're a fine jumper!" And so on; all the time with a gibing voice and face.

I knew it was my own doing, and no one else's; but I was too miserable to repent. I felt I could drag myself but little farther; pretty soon, I must lie down and die on these wet mountains like a sheep or a fox, and my bones must whiten there like the bones of a beast. My head was light perhaps; but I began to love the prospect, I began to glory in the thought of such a death, alone in the desert, with the wild eagles besieging my last moments. Alan would repent then, I thought; he would remember, when I was dead, how much he owed me, and the remembrance would be torture. So I went like a sick, silly, and bad-hearted schoolboy, feeding my anger against a fellow-man, when I would have been better on my knees, crying on God for mercy. And at each of Alan's taunts, I hugged myself. "Ah!" thinks I to myself, "I have a better taunt in readiness; when I lie down and die, you will feel it like a buffet in your face; ah, what a revenge! ah, how you will regret your ingratitude and cruelty!"

All the while, I was growing worse and worse. Once I had fallen, my leg simply doubling under me, and this had struck Alan for the moment; but I was afoot so briskly, and set off again with such a natural manner, that he soon forgot the incident. Flushes of heat went over me, and then spasms of shuddering. The stitch in my side was hardly bearable. At last I began to feel that I could trail myself no farther: and with that, there came on me all at once the wish to have it out with Alan, let my anger blaze, and be done with my life in a more sudden manner. He had just called me "Whig." I stopped.

"Mr. Stewart," said I, in a voice that quivered like a fiddle-string, "you are older than I am, and should know your manners. Do you think it either very wise or very witty to cast my politics in my teeth? I thought, where folk differed, it was the part of gentlemen to differ civilly; and if I did not, I may tell you I could find a better taunt than some of yours."

Alan had stopped opposite to me, his hat cocked, his hands in his breeches pockets, his head a little on one side. He listened, smiling evilly, as I could see by the starlight; and when I had done he began to whistle a Jacobite air. It was the air made in mockery of General Cope's defeat at Preston Pans:

"Hey, Johnnie Cope, are ye waukin' yet?
And are your drums a-beatin' yet?"

And it came in my mind that Alan, on the day of that battle, had been engaged upon the royal side.

"Why do ye take that air, Mr. Stewart?" said I. "Is that to remind me you have been beaten on both sides?"

The air stopped on Alan's lips. "David!" said he.

"But it's time these manners ceased," I continued; "and I mean you shall henceforth speak civilly of my King and my good friends the Campbells."

"I am a Stewart —" began Alan.

"O!" says I, "I ken ye bear a king's name. But you are to remember, since I have been in the Highlands, I have seen a good many of those that bear it; and the best I can say of them is this, that they would be none the worse of washing."

"Do you know that you insult me?" said Alan, very low.

"I am sorry for that," said I, "for I am not done; and if you distaste the sermon, I doubt the pirliecue[1] will please you as little. You have been chased in the field by the grown men of my party; it seems a poor kind of pleasure to out-face a boy. Both the Campbells and the Whigs have beaten you; you have run before them like a hare. It behoves you to speak of them as of your betters."

Alan stood quite still, the tails of his great-coat clapping behind him in the wind.

"This is a pity," he said at last. "There are things said that cannot be passed over."

[1] A second sermon.

THE FLIGHT IN THE HEATHER

"I never asked you to," said I. "I am as ready as yourself."

"Ready?" said he.

"Ready," I repeated. "I am no blower and boaster like some that I could name. Come on!" And drawing my sword, I fell on guard as Alan himself had taught me.

"David!" he cried. "Are ye daft? I cannae draw upon ye, David. It's fair murder."

"That was your look-out when you insulted me," said I.

"It's the truth!" cried Alan, and he stood for a moment, wringing his mouth in his hand like a man in sore perplexity. "It's the bare truth," he said, and drew his sword. But before I could touch his blade with mine, he had thrown it from him and fallen to the ground. "Na, na," he kept saying, "na, na — I cannae, I cannae."

At this the last of my anger oozed all out of me; and I found myself only sick, and sorry, and blank, and wondering at myself. I would have given the world to take back what I had said; but a word once spoken, who can recapture it? I minded me of all Alan's kindness and courage in the past, how he had helped and cheered and borne with me in our evil days; and then recalled my own insults, and saw that I had lost for ever that doughty friend. At the same time, the sickness that hung upon me seemed to redouble, and the pang in my side was like a sword for sharpness. I thought I must have swooned where I stood.

This it was that gave me a thought. No apology could blot out what I had said; it was needless to think of one, none could cover the offence; but where an apology was vain, a mere cry for help might bring Alan back to my side. I put my pride away from me. "Alan!" I said; "if ye cannae help me, I must just die here."

He started up sitting, and looked at me.

"It's true," said I. "I'm by with it. O, let me get into the bield of a house — I'll can die there easier." I had no need to pretend; whether I chose or not, I spoke in a weeping voice that would have melted a heart of stone.

"Can ye walk?" asked Alan.

"No," said I, "not without help. This last hour my legs have been fainting under me; I've a stitch in my side like a red-hot iron; I cannae breathe right. If I die, ye'll can forgive me, Alan? In my heart, I liked ye fine — even when I was the angriest."

"Wheesht, wheesht!" cried Alan. "Dinna say that! David man, ye ken —" He shut his mouth upon a sob. "Let me get my arm about ye," he continued; "that's the way! Now lean upon me hard. Gude kens where there's a house! We're in Balwhidder, too; there should be no want of houses, no, nor friends' houses here. Do ye gang easier so, Davie?"

"Ay," said I, "I can be doing this way"; and I pressed his arm with my hand.

Again he came near sobbing. "Davie," said he, "I'm no a right man at all; I have neither sense nor kindness; I could nae remember ye were just a bairn, I couldnae see ye were dying on your feet; Davie, ye'll have to try and forgive me."

"O man, let's say no more about it!" said I. "We're

AT THE CARDS IN CLUNY'S CAGE

But Alan and Cluny were most of the time at the cards (page 214)

TWO PIPERS IN BALQUHIDDER

All night long the brose was going and the pipes changing hands (page 240)

MR. RANKEILLOR, THE LAWYER

Here he sat down, and bade me be seated (page 258)

THE PARTING

For we both knew without a word said that we had come to where our ways parted (page 288)

neither one of us to mend the other — that 's the truth! We must just bear and forbear, man Alan. O, but my stitch is sore! Is there nae house?"

"I 'll find a house to ye, David," he said, stoutly. "We 'll follow down the burn, where there 's bound to be houses. My poor man, will ye no be better on my back?"

"O, Alan," says I, "and me a good twelve inches taller?"

"Ye 're no such a thing," cried Alan, with a start. "There may be a trifling matter of an inch or two; I 'm no saying I 'm just exactly what ye would call a tall man, whatever; and I dare say," he added, his voice tailing off in a laughable manner, "now when I come to think of it, I dare say ye 'll be just about right. Ay, it 'll be a foot, or near hand; or may be even mair!"

It was sweet and laughable to hear Alan eat his words up in the fear of some fresh quarrel. I could have laughed, had not my stitch caught me so hard; but if I had laughed, I think I must have wept too.

"Alan," cried I, "what makes ye so good to me? What makes ye care for such a thankless fellow?"

"'Deed, and I don't know," said Alan. "For just precisely what I thought I liked about ye, was that ye never quarrelled — and now I like ye better!"

CHAPTER XXV

IN BALQUHIDDER

AT the door of the first house we came to, Alan knocked, which was no very safe enterprise in such a part of the Highlands as the Braes of Balquhidder. No great clan held rule there; it was filled and disputed by small septs, and broken remnants, and what they call "chiefless folk," driven into the wild country about the springs of Forth and Teith by the advance of the Campbells. Here were Stewarts and Maclarens, which came to the same thing, for the Maclarens followed Alan's chief in war, and made but one clan with Appin. Here, too, were many of that old, proscribed, nameless, red-handed clan of the Macgregors. They had always been ill-considered, and now worse than ever, having credit with no side or party in the whole country of Scotland. Their chief, Macgregor of Macgregor, was in exile; the more immediate leader of that part of them about Balquhidder, James More, Rob Roy's eldest son, lay waiting his trial in Edinburgh Castle; they were in ill-blood with Highlander and Lowlander, with the Grahames, the Maclarens, and the Stewarts; and Alan, who took up the quarrel of any friend, however distant, was extremely wishful to avoid them.

IN BALQUHIDDER

Chance served us very well; for it was a household of Maclarens that we found, where Alan was not only welcome for his name's sake but known by reputation. Here then I was got to bed without delay, and a doctor fetched, who found me in a sorry plight. But whether because he was a very good doctor, or I a very young, strong man, I lay bedridden for no more than a week, and before a month I was able to take the road again with a good heart.

All this time Alan would not leave me though I often pressed him, and indeed his foolhardiness in staying was a common subject of outcry with the two or three friends that were let into the secret. He hid by day in a hole of the braes under a little wood; and at night, when the coast was clear, would come into the house to visit me. I need not say if I was pleased to see him; Mrs. Maclaren, our hostess, thought nothing good enough for such a guest; and as Duncan Dhu (which was the name of our host) had a pair of pipes in his house, and was much of a lover of music, this time of my recovery was quite a festival, and we commonly turned night into day.

The soldiers let us be; although once a party of two companies and some dragoons went by in the bottom of the valley, where I could see them through the window as I lay in bed. What was much more astonishing, no magistrate came near me, and there was no question put of whence I came or whither I was going; and in that time of excitement, I was as free of all inquiry as though I had lain in a desert. Yet my presence was known before I left to all the people in Balquhidder and the adjacent parts; many coming about the house on visits and these (after the custom of the country) spreading the news among their neighbours. The bills, too, had now been printed. There was one pinned near the foot of my bed, where I could read my own not very flattering portrait and, in larger characters, the amount of the blood money that had been set upon my life. Duncan Dhu and the rest that knew that I had come there in Alan's company, could have entertained no doubt of who I was; and many others must have had their guess. For though I had changed my clothes, I could not change my age or person; and Lowland boys of eighteen were not so rife in these parts of the world, and above all about that time, that they could fail to put one thing with another, and connect me with the bill. So it was, at least. Other folk keep a secret among two or three near friends, and somehow it leaks out; but among these clansmen, it is told to a whole countryside, and they will keep it for a century.

There was but one thing happened worth narrating; and that is the visit I had of Robin Oig, one of the sons of the notorious Rob Roy. He was sought upon all sides on a charge of carrying a young woman from Balfron and marrying her (as was alleged) by force; yet he stepped about Balquhidder like a gentleman in his own walled policy. It was he who had shot James Maclaren at the plough stilts, a quarrel never satisfied; yet he walked into the house of his blood enemies as a rider[1] might into a public inn.

Duncan had time to pass me word of who it was; and we looked at one another in concern. You should under-

[1] Commercial traveller.

stand, it was then close upon the time of Alan's coming; the two were little likely to agree; and yet if we sent word or sought to make a signal, it was sure to arouse suspicion in a man under so dark a cloud as the Macgregor.

He came in with a great show of civility, but like a man among inferiors; took off his bonnet to Mrs. Maclaren, but clapped it on his head again to speak to Duncan; and having thus set himself (as he would have thought) in a proper light, came to my bedside and bowed.

"I am given to know, sir," says he, "that your name is Balfour."

"They call me David Balfour," said I, "at your service."

"I would give ye my name in return, sir," he replied, "but it's one somewhat blown upon of late days; and it'll perhaps suffice if I tell ye that I am own brother to James More Drummond or Macgregor, of whom ye will scarce have failed to hear."

"No, sir," said I, a little alarmed; "nor yet of your father, Macgregor-Campbell." And I sat up and bowed in bed; for I thought best to compliment him, in case he was proud of having had an outlaw to his father.

He bowed in return. "But what I am come to say, sir," he went on, "is this. In the year '45, my brother raised a part of the 'Gregara,' and marched six companies to strike a stroke for the good side; and the surgeon that marched with our clan and cured my brother's leg when it was broken in the brush at Preston Pans, was a gentleman of the same name precisely as yourself. He was brother to Balfour of Baith; and if you are in any reasonable degree of nearness one of that gentleman's kin, I have come to put myself and my people at your command."

You are to remember that I knew no more of my descent than any cadger's dog; my uncle, to be sure, had prated of some of our high connections, but nothing to the present purpose; and there was nothing left me but that bitter disgrace of owning that I could not tell.

Robin told me shortly he was sorry he had put himself about, turned his back upon me without a sign of salutation, and as he went towards the door, I could hear him telling Duncan that I was "only some kinless loon that didn't know his own father." Angry as I was at these words, and ashamed of my own ignorance, I could scarce keep from smiling that a man who was under the lash of the law (and was indeed hanged some three years later) should be so nice as to the descent of his acquaintances.

Just in the door, he met Alan coming in; and the two drew back and looked at each other like strange dogs. They were neither of them big men, but they seemed fairly to swell out with pride. Each wore a sword, and by a movement of his haunch, thrust clear the hilt of it, so that it might be the more readily grasped and the blade drawn.

"Mr. Stewart, I am thinking," says Robin.

"Troth, Mr. Macgregor, it's not a name to be ashamed of," answered Alan.

"I did not know ye were in my country, sir," says Robin.

"It sticks in my mind that I am in the country of my friends the Maclarens," says Alan.

"That's a kittle point," returned the other. "There

may be two words to say to that. But I think I will have heard that you are a man of your sword?"

"Unless ye were born deaf, Mr. Mcgregor, ye will have heard a good deal more than that," says Alan. "I am not the only man that can draw steel in Appin; and when my kinsman and captain, Ardshiel, had a talk with a gentleman of your name, not so many years back, I could never hear that the Macgregor had the best of it."

"Do ye mean my father, sir?" says Robin.

"Well, I wouldnae wonder," said Alan. "The gentleman I have in my mind had the ill-taste to clap Campbell to his name."

"My father was an old man," returned Robin. "The match was unequal. You and me would make a better pair, sir."

"I was thinking that," said Alan.

I was half out of bed, and Duncan had been hanging at the elbow of these fighting cocks, ready to intervene upon the least occasion. But when that word was uttered, it was a case of now or never; and Duncan, with something of a white face to be sure, thrust himself between.

"Gentlemen," said he, "I will have been thinking of a very different matter, whateffer. Here are my pipes, and here are you two gentlemen who are baith acclaimed pipers. It's an auld dispute which one of ye's the best. Here will be a braw chance to settle it."

"Why, sir," said Alan, still addressing Robin, from whom indeed he had not so much as shifted his eyes, nor yet Robin from him, "why, sir," says Alan, "I think I will have heard some sough[1] of the sort. Have ye music, as folk say? Are ye a bit of a piper?"

"I can pipe like a Macrimmon!" cries Robin.

"And that is a very bold word," quoth Alan.

"I have made bolder words good before now," returned Robin, "and that against better adversaries."

"It is easy to try that," says Alan.

Duncan Dhu made haste to bring out the pair of pipes that was his principal possession, and to set before his guests a mutton-ham and a bottle of that drink which they call Athole brose, and which is made of old whiskey, strained honey and sweet cream, slowly beaten together in the right order and proportion. The two enemies were still on the very breach of a quarrel; but down they sat, one upon each side of the peat fire, with a mighty show of politeness. Maclaren pressed them to taste his mutton-ham and "the wife's brose," reminding them the wife was out of Athole and had a name far and wide for her skill in that confection. But Robin put aside these hospitalities as bad for the breath.

"I would have ye to remark, sir," said Alan, "that I havenae broken bread for near upon ten hours, which will be worse for the breath than any brose in Scotland."

"I will take no advantages, Mr. Stewart," replied Robin. "Eat and drink; I'll follow you."

Each ate a small portion of the ham and drank a glass of the brose to Mrs. Maclaren; and then after a great number of civilities, Robin took the pipes and played a little spring in a very ranting manner.

[1] Rumour.

"Ay, ye can blow," said Alan; and taking the instrument from his rival, he first played the same spring in a manner identical with Robin's; and then wandered into variations, which, as he went on, he decorated with a perfect flight of grace-notes, such as pipers love, and call the "warblers."

I had been pleased with Robin's playing; Alan's ravished me.

"That's no very bad, Mr. Stewart," said the rival, "but ye show a poor device in your warblers."

"Me!" cried Alan, the blood starting to his face. "I give ye the lie."

"Do ye own yourself beaten at the pipes, then," said Robin, "that ye seek to change them for the sword?"

"And that's very well said, Mr. Macgregor," returned Alan; "and in the meantime" (laying a strong accent on the word), "I take back the lie. I appeal to Duncan."

"Indeed, ye need appeal to naebody," said Robin. "Ye're a far better judge than any Maclaren in Balquhidder: for it's a God's truth that you're a very creditable piper for a Stewart. Hand me the pipes."

Alan did as he asked; and Robin proceeded to imitate and correct some part of Alan's variations, which it seemed that he remembered perfectly.

"Ay, ye have music," said Alan, gloomily.

"And now be the judge yourself, Mr. Stewart," said Robin; and taking up the variations from the beginning, he worked them throughout to so new a purpose, with such ingenuity and sentiment, and with so odd a fancy and so quick a knack in the grace-notes, that I was amazed to hear him.

As for Alan, his face grew dark and hot, and he sat and gnawed his fingers, like a man under some deep affront. "Enough!" he cried. "Ye can blow the pipes — make the most of that." And he made as if to rise.

But Robin only held out his hand as if to ask for silence, and struck into the slow measure of a pibroch. It was a fine piece of music in itself, and nobly played; but it seems, besides, it was a piece peculiar to the Appin Stewarts and a chief favourite with Alan. The first notes were scarce out, before there came a change in his face; when the time quickened, he seemed to grow restless in his seat; and long before that piece was at an end, the last signs of his anger died from him, and he had no thought but for the music.

"Robin Oig," he said, when it was done, "ye are a great piper. I am not fit to blow in the same kingdom with ye. Body of me! ye have mair music in your sporran than I have in my head! And though it still sticks in my mind that I could maybe show ye another of it with the cold steel, I warn ye beforehand — it 'll no be fair! It would go against my heart to haggle a man that can blow the pipes as you can!"

Thereupon that quarrel was made up; all night long the brose was going and the pipes changing hands; and the day had come pretty bright, and the three men were none the better for what they had been taking, before Robin as much as thought upon the road.

CHAPTER XXVI

END OF THE FLIGHT: WE PASS THE FORTH

THE month, as I have said, was not yet out, but it was already far through August, and beautiful warm weather, with every sign of an early and great harvest, when I was pronounced able for my journey. Our money was now run to so low an ebb that we must think first of all on speed; for if we came not soon to Mr. Rankeillor's, or if when we came there he should fail to help me, we must surely starve. In Alan's view, besides, the hunt must have now greatly slackened; and the line of the Forth and even Stirling Bridge, which is the main pass over that river, would be watched with little interest.

"It's a chief principle in military affairs," said he, "to go where ye are least expected. Forth is our trouble; ye ken the saying, 'Forth bridles the wild Hielandman.' Well, if we seek to creep round about the head of that river and come down by Kippen or Balfron, it's just precisely there that they'll be looking to lay hands on us. But if we stave on straight to the auld Brig of Stirling, I'll lay my sword they let us pass unchallenged."

The first night, accordingly, we pushed to the house of a Maclaren in Strathire, a friend of Duncan's, where we slept the twenty-first of the month, and whence we set forth again about the fall of night to make another easy stage. The twenty-second we lay in a heather bush on the hillside in Uam Var, within view of a herd of deer, the happiest ten hours of sleep in a fine, breathing sunshine and one bone-dry ground, that I have ever tasted. That night we struck Allan Water, and followed it down; and coming to the edge of the hills saw the whole Carse of Stirling underfoot, as flat as a pancake, with the town and castle on a hill in the midst of it, and the moon shining on the Links of Forth.

"Now," said Alan, "I kenna if ye care, but ye 're in your own land again. We passed the Hieland Line in the first hour; and now if we could but pass yon crooked water, we might cast our bonnets in the air."

In Allan Water, near by where it falls into the Forth, we found a little sandy islet, overgrown with burdock, butterbur and the like low plants, that would just cover us if we lay flat. Here it was we made our camp, within plain view of Stirling Castle, whence we could hear the drums beat as some part of the garrison paraded. Shearers worked all day in the field on one side of the river, and we could hear the stones going on the hooks and the voices and even the words of the men talking. It behoved to lie close and keep silent. But the sand of the little isle was sun-warm, the green plants gave us shelter for our heads, we had food and drink in plenty; and to crown all, we were within sight of safety.

As soon as the shearers quit their work and the dusk began to fall, we waded ashore and struck for the Bridge of Stirling, keeping to the fields and under the field fences.

The bridge is close under the castle hill, an old, high,

narrow bridge with pinnacles along the parapet; and you may conceive with how much interest I looked upon it, not only as a place famous in history, but as the very doors of salvation to Alan and myself. The moon was not yet up when we came there; a few lights shone along the front of the fortress, and lower down a few lighted windows in the town; but it was all mighty still, and there seemed to be no guard upon the passage.

I was for pushing straight across; but Alan was more wary.

"It looks unco quiet," said he; "but for all that we 'll lie down here cannily behind a dyke, and make sure."

So we lay for about a quarter of an hour, whiles whispering, whiles lying still and hearing nothing earthly but the washing of the water on the piers. At last there came by an old, hobbling woman with a crutch stick; who first stopped a little, close to where we lay, and bemoaned herself and the long way she had travelled; and then set forth again up the steep spring of the bridge. The woman was so little, and the night still so dark, that we soon lost sight of her; only heard the sound of her steps, and her stick, and a cough that she had by fits, draw slowly farther away.

"She 's bound to be across now," I whispered.

"Na," said Alan, "her foot still sounds boss[1] upon the bridge."

And just then — "Who goes?" cried a voice, and we heard the butt of a musket rattle on the stones. I must suppose the sentry had been sleeping, so that had we tried,

---

[1] Hollow.

we might have passed unseen; but he was awake now, and the chance forfeited.

"This 'll never do," said Alan. "This 'll never, never do for us, David."

And without another word, he began to crawl away through the fields; and a little after, being well out of eye-shot, got to his feet again, and struck along a road that led to the eastward. I could not conceive what he was doing; and indeed I was so sharply cut by the disappointment, that I was little likely to be pleased with anything. A moment back and I had seen myself knocking at Mr. Rankeillor's door to claim my inheritance, like a hero in a ballad; and here was I back again, a wandering, hunted blackguard, on the wrong side of Forth.

"Well?" said I.

"Well," said Alan, "what would ye have? They 're none such fools as I took them for. We have still the Forth to pass, Davie — weary fall the rains that fed and the hillsides that guided it!"

"And why go east?" said I.

"Ou, just upon the chance!" said he. "If we cannae pass the river, we 'll have to see what we can do for the firth."

"There are fords upon the river, and none upon the firth," said I.

"To be sure there are fords, and a bridge forbye," quoth Alan; "and of what service, when they are watched?"

"Well," said I, "but a river can be swum."

"By them that have the skill of it," returned he; "but

I have yet to hear that either you or me is much of a hand at that exercise; and for my own part: I swim like a stone."

"I 'm not up to you in talking back, Alan," I said; "but I can see we 're making bad worse. If it 's hard to pass a river, it stands to reason it must be worse to pass a sea."

"But there 's such a thing as a boat," says Alan, "or I 'm the more deceived."

"Ay, and such a thing as money," says I. "But for us that have neither one or other, they might just as well not have been invented."

"Ye think so?" said Alan.

"I do that," said I.

"David," says he, "ye 're a man of small invention and less faith. But let me set my wits upon the hone, and if I cannae beg, borrow, nor yet steal a boat, I 'll make one!"

"I think I see ye!" said I. "And what 's more than all that: if ye pass a bridge, it can tell no tales; but if we pass the firth, there 's the boat on the wrong side — somebody must have brought it — the country-side will all be in a bizz ——"

"Man!" cried Alan, "if I make a boat, I 'll make a body to take it back again! So deave me with no more of your nonsense, but walk (for that 's what you 've got to do) — and let Alan think for ye."

All night, then, we walked through the north side of the Carse under the high line of the Ochil mountains; and by Alloa and Clackmannan and Culross, all of which we avoided; and about ten in the morning, mighty hungry and tired, came to the little clachan of Limekilns. This is a place that sits near in by the water-side, and looks across the Hope to the town of the Queensferry. Smoke went up from both of these, and from other villages and farms upon all hands. The fields were being reaped; two ships lay anchored, and boats were coming and going on the Hope. It was altogether a right pleasant sight to me; and I could not take my fill of gazing at these comfortable, green, cultivated hills and the busy people both of the field and sea.

For all that, there was Mr. Rankeillor's house on the south shore, where I had no doubt wealth awaited me; and here was I upon the north, clad in poor enough attire of an outlandish fashion, with three silver shillings left to me of all my fortune, a price set upon my head, and an outlawed man for my sole company.

"Oh, Alan!" said I, "to think of it! Over there, there's all that heart could want waiting me; and the birds go over, and the boats go over — all that please can go, but just me only! O, man, but it's a heart-break!"

In Limekilns we entered a small change-house, which we only knew to be a public by the wand over the door, and bought some bread and cheese from a good-looking lass that was the servant. This we carried with us in a bundle, meaning to sit and eat it in a bush of wood on the sea-shore, that we saw some third part of a mile in front. As we went, I kept looking across the water and sighing to myself; and though I took no heed of it, Alan had fallen into a muse. At last he stopped in the way.

"Did ye take heed of the lass we bought this of?" says he, tapping on the bread and cheese.

"To be sure," said I, "and a bonny lass she was."

"Ye thought that?" cries he. "Man, David, that's good news."

"In the name of all that's wonderful, why so?" says I. "What good can that do?"

"Well," said Alan, with one of his droll looks, "I was rather in hopes it would maybe get us that boat."

"If it were the other way about, it would be liker it," said I.

"That's all that you ken, ye see," said Alan. "I don't want the lass to fall in love with ye, I want her to be sorry for ye, David; to which end there is no manner of need that she should take you for a beauty. Let me see" (looking me curiously over). "I wish ye were a wee thing paler; but apart from that ye'll do fine for my purpose — ye have a fine, hang-dog, rag-and-tatter, clappermaclaw kind of a look to ye, as if ye had stolen the coat from a potato-bogle. Come; right about, and back to the change-house for that boat of ours."

I followed him, laughing.

"David Balfour," said he, "ye're a very funny gentleman by your way of it, and this is a very funny employ for ye, no doubt. For all that, if ye have any affection for my neck (to say nothing of your own) ye will perhaps be kind enough to take this matter responsibly. I am going to do a bit of play-acting, the bottom ground of which is just exactly as serious as the gallows for the pair of us. So bear it, if ye please, in mind, and conduct yourself according."

"Well, well," said I, "have it as you will."

KIDNAPPED

As we got near the clachan, he made me take his arm
and hang upon it like one almost helpless with weariness;
and by the time he pushed open the change-house door, he
seemed to be half carrying me. The maid appeared surprised (as well she might be) at our speedy return; but Alan
had no words to spare for her in explanation, helped me to
a chair, called for a tass of brandy with which he fed me
in little sips, and then breaking up the bread and cheese
helped me to eat it like a nursery-lass; the whole with that
grave, concerned, affectionate countenance, that might have
imposed upon a judge. It was small wonder if the maid
were taken with the picture we presented, of a poor, sick,
overwrought lad and his most tender comrade. She drew
quite near, and stood leaning with her back on the next
table.

"What's like wrong with him?" said she at last.

Alan turned upon her, to my great wonder, with a kind
of fury. "Wrong?" cries he. "He's walked more hundreds of miles than he has hairs upon his chin, and slept
oftener in wet heather than dry sheets. Wrong, quo' she!
Wrong enough, I would think! Wrong, indeed!" and he
kept grumbling to himself as he fed me, like a man ill-pleased.

"He's young for the like of that," said the maid.

"Ower young," said Alan, with his back to her.

"He would be better riding," says she.

"And where could I get a horse to him?" cried Alan,
turning on her with the same appearance of fury. "Would
ye have me steal?"

I thought this roughness would have sent her off in

dudgeon, as indeed it closed her mouth for the time. But my companion knew very well what he was doing; and for as simple as he was in some things of life, had a great fund of roguishness in such affairs as these.

"Ye deednae tell me," she said at last — "ye 're gentry."

"Well," said Alan, softened a little (I believe against his will) by this artless comment, "and suppose we were? Did ever you hear that gentrice put money in folk's pockets?"

She sighed at this, as if she were herself some disinherited great lady. "No," says she, "that 's true indeed."

I was all this while chafing at the part I played, and sitting tongue-tied between shame and merriment; but somehow at this I could hold in no longer, and bade Alan let me be, for I was better already. My voice stuck in my throat, for I ever hated to take part in lies; but my very embarrassment helped on the plot, for the lass no doubt set down my husky voice to sickness and fatigue.

"Has he nae friends?" said she, in a tearful voice.

"That has he so!" cried Alan, "if we could but win to them! — friends and rich friends, beds to lie in, food to eat, doctors to see to him — and here he must tramp in the dubs and sleep in the heather like a beggarman."

"And why that?" says the lass.

"My dear," said Alan, "I cannae very safely say; but I 'll tell you what l 'll do instead," says he, "I 'll whistle ye a bit tune." And with that he leaned pretty far over the table, and in a mere breath of a whistle, but with a wonderful pretty sentiment, gave her a few bars of "Charlie is my darling."

"Wheesht," says she, and looked over her shoulder to the door.

"That's it," said Alan.

"And him so young!" cries the lass.

"He's old enough to —— " and Alan struck his forefinger on the back part of his neck, meaning that I was old enough to lose my head.

"It would be a black shame," she cried, flushing high.

"It's what will be, though," said Alan, "unless we manage the better."

At this the lass turned and ran out of that part of the house, leaving us alone together, Alan in high good humour at the furthering of his schemes, and I in bitter dudgeon at being called a Jacobite and treated like a child.

"Alan," I cried, "I can stand no more of this."

"Ye'll have to sit it then, Davie," said he. "For if ye upset the pot now, ye may scrape your own life out of the fire, but Alan Breck is a dead man."

This was so true that I could only groan; and even my groan served Alan's purpose, for it was overheard by the lass as she came flying in again with a dish of white puddings and a bottle of strong ale.

"Poor lamb!" says she, and had no sooner set the meat before us, than she touched me on the shoulder with a little friendly touch, as much as to bid me cheer up. Then she told us to fall to, and there would be no more to pay; for the inn was her own, or at least her father's, and he was gone for the day to Pittencrieff. We waited for no second bidding, for bread and cheese is but cold comfort and the puddings smelt excellently well; and while we sat and ate, she took up that same place by the next table, looking on, and thinking and frowning to herself, and drawing the string of her apron through her hand.

"I 'm thinking ye have rather a long tongue," she said at last to Alan.

"Ay," said Alan; "but ye see I ken the folk I speak to."

"I would never betray ye," said she, "if ye mean that."

"No," said he, "ye 're not that kind. But I 'll tell ye what ye would do, ye would help."

"I couldnae," said she, shaking her head. "Na, I couldnae."

"No," said he, "but if ye could?"

She answered him nothing.

"Look here, my lass," said Alan, "there are boats in the Kingdom of Fife, for I saw two (no less) upon the beach, as I came in by your town's end. Now if we could have the use of a boat to pass under cloud of night into Lothian, and some secret, decent kind of a man to bring that boat back again and keep his counsel, there would be two souls saved — mine to all likelihood — his to a dead surety. If we lack that boat, we have but three shillings left in this wide world; and where to go, and how to do, and what other place there is for us except the chains. of a gibbet — I give you my naked word, I kenna! Shall we go wanting, lassie? Are ye to lie in your warm bed and think upon us, when the wind gowls in the chimney and the rain tirls on the roof? Are ye to eat your meat by the cheeks of a red fire, and think upon this poor sick lad of mine, biting his finger ends on a blae muir for cauld and hunger? Sick or sound, he must aye be moving; with the death grapple at his throat he must aye be trailing in the rain on the long roads; and when he gants his last on a rickle of cauld stanes, there will be nae friends near him but only me and God."

At this appeal, I could see the lass was in great trouble of mind, being tempted to help us, and yet in some fear she might be helping malefactors; and so now I determined to step in myself and to allay her scruples with a portion of the truth.

"Did ever you hear," said I, "of Mr. Rankeillor of the Ferry?"

"Rankeillor the writer?" said she. "I daur say that!"

"Well," said I, "it's to his door that I am bound, so you may judge by that if I am an ill-doer; and I will tell you more, that though I am indeed, by a dreadful error, in some peril of my life, King George has no truer friend in all Scotland than myself."

Her face cleared up mightily at this, although Alan's darkened.

"That's more than I would ask," said she. "Mr. Rankeillor is a kennt man." And she bade us finish our meat, get clear of the clachan as soon as might be, and lie close in the bit wood on the sea-beach. "And ye can trust me," says she, "I'll find some means to put you over."

At this we waited for no more, but shook hands with her upon the bargain, made short work of the puddings, and set forth again from Limekilns as far as to the wood. It was a small piece of perhaps a score of elders and hawthorns and

a few young ashes, not thick enough to veil us from passers-
by upon the road or beach. Here we must lie, however,
making the best of the brave warm weather and the good
hopes we now had of a deliverance, and planning more particularly what remained for us to do.

We had but one trouble all day; when a strolling piper
came and sat in the same wood with us; a red-nosed, blear-
eyed, drunken dog, with a great bottle of whiskey in his
pocket, and a long story of wrongs that had been done him
by all sorts of persons, from the Lord President of the Court
of Session, who had denied him justice, down to the Bailies
of Inverkeithing who had given him more of it than he de-
sired. It was impossible but he should conceive some suspicion of two men lying all day concealed in a thicket and
having no business to allege. As long as he stayed there he
kept us in hot water with prying questions; and after he was
gone, as he was a man not very likely to hold his tongue,
we were in the greater impatience to be gone ourselves.

The day came to an end with the same brightness; the
night fell quiet and clear; lights came out in houses and
hamlets and then, one after another, began to be put out;
but it was past eleven, and we were long since strangely
tortured with anxieties, before we heard the grinding of
oars upon the rowing-pins. At that, we looked out and
saw the lass herself coming rowing to us in a boat. She
had trusted no one with our affairs, not even her sweetheart,
if she had one; but as soon as her father was asleep, had
left the house by a window, stolen a neighbour's boat, and
come to our assistance single-handed.

[253]

KIDNAPPED

I was abashed how to find expression for my thanks; but she was no less abashed at the thought of hearing them; begged us to lose no time and to hold our peace, saying (very properly) that the heart of our matter was in haste and silence; and so, what with one thing and another, she had set us on the Lothian shore not far from Carriden, had shaken hands with us, and was out again at sea and rowing for Limekilns, before there was one word said either of her service or our gratitude.

Even after she was gone, we had nothing to say, as indeed nothing was enough for such a kindness. Only Alan stood a great while upon the shore shaking his head.

"It is a very fine lass," he said at last. "David, it is a very fine lass." And a matter of an hour later, as we were lying in a den on the sea-shore and I had been already dozing, he broke out again in commendations of her character. For my part, I could say nothing, she was so simple a creature that my heart smote me both with remorse and fear: remorse because we had traded upon her ignorance; and fear lest we should have anyway involved her in the dangers of our situation.

CHAPTER XXVII

I COME TO MR. RANKEILLOR

THE next day it was agreed that Alan should fend for himself till sunset; but as soon as it began to grow dark, he should lie in the fields by the roadside near to Newhalls, and stir for naught until he heard me whistling. At first I proposed I should give him for a signal the "Bonnie House of Airlie," which was a favourite of mine; but he objected that as the piece was very commonly known, any ploughman might whistle it by accident; and taught me instead a little fragment of a Highland air, which has run in my head from that day to this, and will likely run in my head when I lie dying. Every time it comes to me, it takes me off to that last day of my uncertainty, with Alan sitting up in the bottom of the den, whistling and beating the measure with a finger, and the grey of the dawn coming on his face.

I was in the long street of Queensferry before the sun was up. It was a fairly built burgh, the houses of good stone, many slated; the town-hall not so fine, I thought, as that of Peebles, nor yet the street so noble; but take it altogether, it put me to shame for my foul tatters.

As the morning went on, and the fires began to be kin-

dled, and the windows to open, and the people to appear out
of the houses, my concern and despondency grew ever the
blacker. I saw now that I had no grounds to stand upon;
and no clear proof of my rights, nor so much as of my own
identity. If it was all a bubble, I was indeed sorely cheated
and left in a sore pass. Even if things were as I conceived,
it would in all likelihood take time to establish my conten-
tions; and what time had I to spare with less than three
shillings in my pocket, and a condemned, hunted man upon
my hands to ship out of the country? Truly, if my hope
broke with me, it might come to the gallows yet for both of
us. And as I continued to walk up and down, and saw
people looking askance at me upon the street or out of windows, and nudging or speaking one to another with smiles,
I began to take a fresh apprehension: that it might be no
easy matter even to come to speech of the lawyer, far less
to convince him of my story.

For the life of me I could not muster up the courage to
address any of these reputable burghers; I thought shame
even to speak with them in such a pickle of rags and dirt;
and if I had asked for the house of such a man as Mr. Rankeillor, I suppose they would have burst out laughing in
my face. So I went up and down, and through the street,
and down to the harbour-side, like a dog that has lost its
master, with a strange gnawing in my inwards, and every
now and then a movement of despair. It grew to be high
day at last, perhaps nine in the forenoon; and I was worn
with these wanderings, and chanced to have stopped in front
of a very good house on the landward side, a house with

I COME TO MR. RANKEILLOR

beautiful, clear glass windows, flowering knots upon the sills, the walls new-harled[1] and a chase-dog sitting yawning on the step like one that was at home. Well, I was even envying this dumb brute, when the door fell open and there issued forth a shrewd, ruddy, kindly, consequential man in a well-powdered wig and spectacles. I was in such a plight that no one set eyes on me once, but he looked at me again; and this gentleman, as it proved, was so much struck with my poor appearance that he came straight up to me and asked me what I did.

I told him I was come to the Queensferry on business, and taking heart of grace, asked him to direct me to the house of Mr. Rankeillor.

"Why," said he, "that is his house that I have just come out of; and for a rather singular chance, I am that very man."

"Then, sir," said I, "I have to beg the favour of an interview."

"I do not know your name," said he, "nor yet your face."

"My name is David Balfour," said I.

"David Balfour?" he repeated, in rather a high tone, like one surprised. "And where have you come from, Mr. David Balfour?" he asked, looking me pretty drily in the face.

"I have come from a great many strange places, sir," said I; "but I think it would be as well to tell you where and how in a more private manner."

He seemed to muse awhile, holding his lip in his hand,

[1] Newly rough-cast.

and looking now at me and now upon the causeway of the street.

"Yes," says he, "that will be the best, no doubt." And he led me back with him into his house, cried out to some one whom I could not see that he would be engaged all morning, and brought me into a little dusty chamber full of books and documents. Here he sat down, and bade me be seated; though I thought he looked a little ruefully from his clean chair to my muddy rags. "And now," says he, "if you have any business, pray be brief and come swiftly to the point. *Nec gemino bellum Trojanum orditur ab ovo —* do you understand that?" says he, with a keen look.

"I will even do as Horace says, sir," I answered, smiling, "and carry you *in medias res.*" He nodded as if he was well pleased, and indeed his scrap of Latin had been set to test me. For all that, and though I was somewhat encouraged, the blood came in my face when I added: "I have reason to believe myself some rights on the estate of Shaws."

He got a paper book out of a drawer and set it before him open. "Well?" said he.

But I had shot my bolt and sat speechless.

"Come, come, Mr. Balfour," said he, "you must continue. Where were you born?"

"In Essendean, sir," said I, "the year 1733, the 12th of March."

He seemed to follow this statement in his paper book; but what that meant I knew not. "Your father and mother?" said he.

"My father was Alexander Balfour, schoolmaster of that

place," said I, "and my mother Grace Pitarrow; I think her people were from Angus."

"Have you any papers proving your identity?" asked Mr. Rankeillor.

"No, sir," said I, "but they are in the hands of Mr. Campbell, the minister, and could be readily produced. Mr. Campbell, too, would give me his word; and for that matter, I do not think my uncle would deny me."

"Meaning Mr. Ebenezer Balfour?" says he.

"The same," said I.

"Whom you have seen?" he asked.

"By whom I was received into his own house," I answered.

"Did you ever meet a man of the name of Hoseason?" asked Mr. Rankeillor.

"I did so, sir, for my sins," said I; "for it was by his means and the procurement of my uncle, that I was kidnapped within sight of this town, carried to sea, suffered shipwreck and a hundred other hardships, and stand before you to-day in this poor accoutrement."

"You say you were shipwrecked," said Rankeillor; "where was that?"

"Off the south end of the Isle of Mull," said I. "The name of the isle on which I was cast up is the Island Earraid."

"Ah!" says he, smiling, "you are deeper than me in the geography. But so far, I may tell you, this agrees pretty exactly with other informations that I hold. But you say you were kidnapped; in what sense?"

KIDNAPPED

"In the plain meaning of the word, sir," said I. "I was on my way to your house, when I was trepanned on board the brig, cruelly struck down, thrown below, and knew no more of anything till we were far at sea. I was destined for the plantations; a fate that, in God's providence, I have escaped."

"'The brig was lost on June the 27th," says he, looking in his book, "and we are now at August the 24th. Here is a considerable hiatus, Mr. Balfour, of near upon two months. It has already caused a vast amount of trouble to your friends; and I own I shall not be very well contented until it is set right."

"Indeed, sir," said I, "these months are very easily filled up; but yet before I told my story, I would be glad to know that I was talking to a friend."

"This is to argue in a circle," said the lawyer. "I cannot be convinced till I have heard you. I cannot be your friend till I am properly informed. If you were more trustful, it would better befit your time of life. And you know, Mr. Balfour, we have a proverb in the country that evil-doers are aye evil-dreaders."

"You are not to forget, sir," said I, "that I have already suffered by my trustfulness; and was shipped off to be a slave by the very man that (if I rightly understand) is your employer?"

All this while I had been gaining ground with Mr. Rankeillor, and in proportion as I gained ground, gaining confidence. But at this sally, which I made with something of a smile myself, he fairly laughed aloud.

I COME TO MR. RANKEILLOR

"No, no," said he, "it is not so bad as that. *Fui, non sum.* I *was* indeed your uncle's man of business; but while you (*imberbis juvenis custode remoto*) were gallivanting in the west, a good deal of water has run under the bridges; and if your ears did not sing, it was not for lack of being talked about. On the very day of your sea disaster, Mr. Campbell stalked into my office, demanding you from all the winds. I had never heard of your existence; but I had known your father; and from matters in my competence (to be touched upon hereafter) I was disposed to fear the worst. Mr. Ebenezer admitted having seen you; declared (what seemed improbable) that he had given you considerable sums; and that you had started for the continent of Europe, intending to fulfil your education, which was probable and praiseworthy. Interrogated how you had come to send no word to Mr. Campbell, he deponed that you had expressed a great desire to break with your past life. Further interrogated where you now were, protested ignorance, but believed you were in Leyden. That is a close sum of his replies. I am not exactly sure that any one believed him," continued Mr. Rankeillor with a smile; "and in particular he so much disrelished some expressions of mine that (in a word) he showed me to the door. We were then at a full stand; for whatever shrewd suspicions we might entertain, we had no shadow of probation. In the very article, comes Captain Hoseason with the story of your drowning; whereupon all fell through; with no consequences but concern to Mr. Campbell, injury to my pocket, and another blot upon your uncle's character, which could very ill afford it. And now, Mr. Balfour," said he, "you understand the whole process of these matters, and can judge for yourself to what extent I may be trusted."

Indeed he was more pedantic than I can represent him, and placed more scraps of Latin in his speech; but it was all uttered with a fine geniality of eye and manner which went far to conquer my distrust. Moreover, I could see he now treated me as if I was myself beyond a doubt; so that first point of my identity seemed fully granted.

"Sir," said I, "if I tell you my story, I must commit a friend's life to your discretion. Pass me your word it shall be sacred; and for what touches myself, I will ask no better guarantee than just your face."

He passed me his word very seriously. "But," said he, "these are rather alarming prolocutions; and if there are in your story any little jostles to the law, I would beg you to bear in mind that I am a lawyer, and pass lightly."

Thereupon I told him my story from the first, he listening with his spectacles thrust up and his eyes closed, so that I sometimes feared he was asleep. But no such matter! he heard every word (as I found afterward) with such quickness of hearing and precision of memory as often surprised me. Even strange outlandish Gaelic names, heard for that time only, he remembered and would remind me of, years after. Yet when I called Alan Breck in full, we had an odd scene. The name of Alan had of course rung through Scotland, with the news of the Appin murder and the offer of the reward; and it had no sooner escaped me than the lawyer moved in his seat and opened his eyes.

I COME TO MR. RANKEILLOR

"I would name no unnecessary names, Mr. Balfour," said he; "above all of Highlanders, many of whom are obnoxious to the law."

"Well, it might have been better not," said I, "but since I have let it slip, I may as well continue."

"Not at all," said Mr. Rankeillor. "I am somewhat dull of hearing, as you may have remarked; and I am far from sure I caught the name exactly. We will call your friend, if you please, Mr. Thomson — that there may be no reflections. And in future, I would take some such way with any Highlander that you may have to mention — dead or alive."

By this, I saw he must have heard the name all too clearly, and had already guessed I might be coming to the murder. If he chose to play this part of ignorance, it was no matter of mine; so I smiled, said it was no very Highland-sounding name, and consented. Through all the rest of my story Alan was Mr. Thomson; which amused me the more, as it was a piece of policy after his own heart. James Stewart, in like manner, was mentioned under the style of Mr. Thomson's kinsman; Colin Campbell passed as a Mr. Glen; and to Cluny, when I came to that part of my tale, I gave the name of "Mr. Jameson, a Highland chief." It was truly the most open farce, and I wondered that the lawyer should care to keep it up; but, after all, it was quite in the taste of that age, when there were two parties in the state, and quiet persons, with no very high opinions of their own, sought out every cranny to avoid offence to either.

"Well, well," said the lawyer, when I had quite done,

"this is a great epic, a great Odyssey of yours. You must tell it, sir, in a sound Latinity when your scholarship is riper; or in English if you please, though for my part I prefer the stronger tongue. You have rolled much; *quæ regio in terris* — what parish in Scotland (to make a homely translation) has not been filled with your wanderings? You have shown, besides, a singular aptitude for getting into false positions; and, yes, upon the whole, for behaving well in them. This Mr. Thomson seems to me a gentleman of some choice qualities, though perhaps a trifle bloody-minded. It would please me none the worse, if (with all his merits) he were soused in the North Sea, for the man, Mr. David, is a sore embarrassment. But you are doubtless quite right to adhere to him; indubitably, he adhered to you. It comes — we may say — he was your true companion; nor less *paribus curis vestigia figit,* for I dare say you would both take an orra thought upon the gallows. Well, well, these days are fortunately by; and I think (speaking humanly) that you are near the end of your troubles."

As he thus moralised on my adventures, he looked upon me with so much humour and benignity that I could scarce contain my satisfaction. I had been so long wandering with lawless people, and making my bed upon the hills and under the bare sky, that to sit once more in a clean, covered house, and to talk amicably with a gentleman in broadcloth, seemed mighty elevations. Even as I thought so, my eye fell on my unseemly tatters, and I was once more plunged in confusion. But the lawyer saw and understood me. He rose, called over the stair to lay another plate, for Mr. Balfour would stay to dinner, and led me into a bedroom in the upper part of the house. Here he set before me water and soap, and a comb; and laid out some clothes that belonged to his son; and here, with another apposite tag, he left me to my toilet.

CHAPTER XXVIII

I GO IN QUEST OF MY INHERITANCE

I MADE what change I could in my appearance; and blithe was I to look in the glass and find the beggarman a thing of the past, and David Balfour come to life again. And yet I was ashamed of the change too, and, above all, of the borrowed clothes. When I had done, Mr. Rankeillor caught me on the stair, made me his compliments, and had me again into the cabinet.

"Sit ye down, Mr. David," said he, "and now that you are looking a little more like yourself, let me see if I can find you any news. You will be wondering, no doubt, about your father and your uncle? To be sure it is a singular tale; and the explanation is one that I blush to have to offer you. For," says he, really with embarrassment, "the matter hinges on a love affair."

"Truly," said I, "I cannot very well join that notion with my uncle."

"But your uncle, Mr. David, was not always old," replied the lawyer, "and what may perhaps surprise you more, not always ugly. He had a fine, gallant air; people stood in their doors to look after him, as he went by upon a mettle horse. I have seen it with these eyes, and I ingenuously

[266]

confess, not altogether without envy; for I was a plain lad myself and a plain man's son; and in those days it was a case of *Odi te, qui bellus es, Sabelle.*"

"It sounds like a dream," said I.

"Ay, ay," said the lawyer, "that is how it is with youth and age. Nor was that all, but he had a spirit of his own that seemed to promise great things in the future. In 1715, what must he do but run away to join the rebels? It was your father that pursued him, found him in a ditch, and brough him back *multum gementem;* to the mirth of the whole country. However, *majora canamus* — the two lads fell in love, and that with the same lady. Mr. Ebenezer, who was the admired and the beloved, and the spoiled one, made, no doubt, mighty certain of the victory; and when he found he had deceived himself, screamed like a peacock. The whole country heard of it; now he lay sick at home, with his silly family standing round the bed in tears; now he rode from public-house to public-house, and shouted his sorrows into the lug of Tom, Dick, and Harry. Your father, Mr. David, was a kind gentleman; but he was weak, dolefully weak; took all this folly with a long countenance; and one day — by your leave! — resigned the lady. She was no such fool, however; it's from her you must inherit your excellent good sense; and she refused to be bandied from one to another. Both got upon their knees to her; and the upshot of the matter for that while was that she showed both of them the door. That was in August; dear me! the same year I came from college. The scene must have been highly farcical."

KIDNAPPED

I thought myself it was a silly business, but I could not forget my father had a hand in it. "Surely, sir, it had some note of tragedy," said I.

"Why, no, sir, not at all," returned the lawyer. "For tragedy implies some ponderable matter in dispute, some *dignus vindice nodus;* and this piece of work was all about the petulance of a young ass that had been spoiled, and wanted nothing so much as to be tied up and soundly belted. However, that was not your father's view; and the end of it was, that from concession to concession on your father's part, and from one height to another of squalling, sentimental selfishness upon your uncle's, they came at last to drive a sort of bargain, from whose ill results you have recently been smarting. The one man took the lady, the other the estate. Now, Mr. David, they talk a great deal of charity and generosity; but in this disputable state of life, I often think the happiest consequences seem to flow when a gentleman consults his lawyer, and takes all the law allows him. Anyhow, this piece of Quixotry on your father's part, as it was unjust in itself, has brought forth a monstrous family of injustices. Your father and mother lived and died poor folk; you were poorly reared; and in the meanwhile, what a time it has been for the tenants on the estate of Shaws! And I might add (if it was a matter I cared much about) what a time for Mr. Ebenezer!"

"And yet that is certainly the strangest part of all," said I, "that a man's nature should thus change."

"True," said Mr. Rankeillor. "And yet I imagine it was natural enough. He could not think that he had played

[268]

a handsome part. Those who knew the story gave him the cold shoulder; those who knew it not, seeing one brother disappear, and the other succeed in the estate, raised a cry of murder; so that upon all sides he found himself evited. Money was all he got by his bargain; well, he came to think the more of money. He was selfish when he was young, he is selfish now that he is old; and the latter end of all these pretty manners and fine feelings you have seen for yourself."

"Well, sir," said I, "and in all this, what is my position?"

"The estate is yours beyond a doubt," replied the lawyer. "It matters nothing what your father signed, you are the heir of entail. But your uncle is a man to fight the indefensible; and it would be likely your identity that he would call in question. A lawsuit is always expensive, and a family lawsuit always scandalous; besides which, if any of your doings with your friend Mr. Thomson were to come out, we might find that we had burned our fingers. The kidnapping, to be sure, would be a court card upon our side, if we could only prove it. But it may be difficult to prove; and my advice (upon the whole) is to make a very easy bargain with your uncle, perhaps even leaving him at Shaws where he has taken root for a quarter of a century, and contenting yourself in the meanwhile with a fair provision."

I told him I was very willing to be easy, and that to carry family concerns before the public was a step from which I was naturally much averse. In the meantime (thinking to myself) I began to see the outlines of that scheme on which we afterwards acted.

KIDNAPPED

"The great affair," I asked, "is to bring home to him the kidnapping?"

"Surely," said Mr. Rankeillor, "and if possible, out of court. For mark you here, Mr. David: we could no doubt find some men of the *Covenant* who would swear to your reclusion; but once they were in the box, we could no longer check their testimony, and some word of your friend Mr. Thomson must certainly crop out. Which (from what you have let fall) I cannot think to be desirable."

"Well, sir," said I, "here is my way of it." And I opened my plot to him.

"But this would seem to involve my meeting the man Thomson?" says he, when I had done.

"I think so, indeed, sir," said I.

"Dear doctor!" cries he, rubbing his brow. "Dear doctor! No, Mr. David, I am afraid your scheme is inadmissible. I say nothing against your friend, Mr. Thomson: I know nothing against him; and if I did — mark this, Mr. David! — it would be my duty to lay hands on him. Now I put it to you: is it wise to meet? He may have matters to his charge. He may not have told you all. His name may not be even Thomson!" cries the lawyer, twinkling; "for some of these fellows will pick up names by the roadside as another would gather haws."

"You must be the judge, sir," said I.

But it was clear my plan had taken hold upon his fancy, for he kept musing to himself till we were called to dinner and the company of Mrs. Rankeillor; and that lady had scarce left us again to ourselves and a bottle of wine, ere he was back harping on my proposal. When and where was I to meet my friend Mr. Thomson; was I sure of Mr. T.'s discretion; supposing we could catch the old fox tripping, would I consent to such and such a term of an agreement — these and the like questions he kept asking at long intervals, while he thoughtfully rolled his wine upon his tongue. When I had answered all of them, seemingly to his contentment, he fell into a still deeper muse, even the claret being now forgotten. Then he got a sheet of paper and a pencil, and set to work writing and weighing every word, and at last touched a bell and had his clerk into the chamber.

"Torrance," he said, "I must have this written out fair against to-night; and when it is done, you will be so kind as put on your hat and be ready to come along with this gentleman and me, for you will probably be wanted as a witness."

"What, sir," cried I, as soon as the clerk was gone, "are you to venture it?"

"Why, so it would appear," says he, filling his glass. "But let us speak no more of business. The very sight of Torrance brings in my head a little droll matter of some years ago, when I had made a tryst with the poor oaf at the cross of Edinburgh. Each had gone his proper errand; and when it came four o'clock, Torrance had been taking a glass and did not know his master, and I, who had forgot my spectacles, was so blind without them, that I give you my word I did not know my own clerk." And thereupon he laughed heartily.

KIDNAPPED

I said it was an odd chance, and smiled out of politeness; but what held me all the afternoon in wonder, he kept returning and dwelling on this story, and telling it again with fresh details and laughter; so that I began at last to be quite put out of countenance and feel ashamed for my friend's folly.

Towards the time I had appointed with Alan, we set out from the house, Mr. Rankeillor and I arm in arm, and Torrance following behind with the deed in his pocket and a covered basket in his hand. All through the town, the lawyer was bowing right and left, and continually being buttonholed by gentlemen on matters of burgh or private business; and I could see he was one greatly looked up to in the county. At last we were clear of the houses, and began to go along the side of the haven and towards the Hawes Inn and the Ferry pier, the scene of my misfortune. I could not look upon the place without emotion, recalling how many that had been there with me that day were now no more: Ransome taken, I could hope, from the evil to come; Shuan passed where I dared not follow him; and the poor souls that had gone down with the brig in her last plunge. All these, and the brig herself, I had outlived, and come through these hardships and fearful perils without scath. My only thought should have been of gratitude; and yet I could not behold the place without sorrow for others and a chill of recollected fear.

I was so thinking when, upon a sudden, Mr. Rankeillor cried out, clapped his hand to his pockets, and began to laugh.

I GO IN QUEST OF MY INHERITANCE

"Why," he cries, "if this be not a farcical adventure! After all that I said, I have forgot my glasses!"

At that, of course, I understood the purpose of his anecdote, and knew that if he had left his spectacles at home, it had been done on purpose, so that he might have the benefit of Alan's help without the awkwardness of recognising him. And indeed it was well thought upon; for now (suppose things to go the very worst) how could Rankeillor swear to my friend's identity, or how be made to bear damaging evidence against myself? For all that, he had been a long while of finding out his want, and had spoken to and recognised a good few persons as we came through the town; and I had little doubt myself that he saw reasonably well.

As soon as we were past the Hawes (where I recognised the landlord smoking his pipe in the door, and was amazed to see him look no older) Mr. Rankeillor changed the order of march, walking behind with Torrance and sending me forward in the manner of a scout. I went up the hill, whistling from time to time my Gaelic air; and at length I had the pleasure to hear it answered and to see Alan rise from behind a bush. He was somewhat dashed in spirits, having passed a long day alone skulking in the county, and made but a poor meal in an alehouse near Dundas. But at the mere sight of my clothes, he began to brighten up; and as soon as I had told him in what a forward state our matters were and the part I looked to him to play in what remained, he sprang into a new man.

"And that is a very good notion of yours," says he; "and

I dare to say that you could lay your hands upon no better man to put it through than Alan Breck. It is not a thing (mark ye) that any one could do, but takes a gentleman of penetration. But it sticks in my head your lawyerman will be somewhat wearying to see me," says Alan.

Accordingly I cried and waved on Mr. Rankeillor, who came up alone and was presented to my friend, Mr. Thomson.

"Mr. Thomson, I am pleased to meet you," said he. "But I have forgotten my glasses; and our friend, Mr. David here" (clapping me on the shoulder), "will tell you that I am little better than blind, and that you must not be surprised if I pass you by to-morrow."

This he said, thinking that Alan would be pleased; but the Highlandman's vanity was ready to startle at a less matter than that.

"Why, sir," says he, stiffly, "I would say it mattered the less as we are met here for a particular end, to see justice done by Mr. Balfour; and by what I can see, not very likely to have much else in common. But I accept your apology, which was a very proper one to make."

"And that is more than I could look for, Mr. Thomson," said Rankeillor, heartily. "And now as you and I are the chief actors in this enterprise, I think we should come into a nice agreement; to which end, I propose that you should lend me your arm, for (what with the dusk and the want of my glasses) I am not very clear as to the path; and as for you, Mr. David, you will find Torrance a pleasant kind of body to speak with. Only let me remind you, it's quite needless he should hear more of your adventures or those of — ahem — Mr. Thomson."

Accordingly these two went on ahead in very close talk, and Torrance and I brought up the rear.

Night was quite come when we came in view of the house of Shaws. Ten had been gone some time; it was dark and mild, with a pleasant, rustling wind in the south-west that covered the sound of our approach; and as we drew near we saw no glimmer of light in any portion of the building. It seemed my uncle was already in bed, which was indeed the best thing for our arrangements. We made our last whispered consultations some fifty yards away; and then the lawyer and Torrance and I crept quietly up and crouched down beside the corner of the house; and as soon as we were in our places, Alan strode to the door without concealment and began to knock.

CHAPTER XXIX

I COME INTO MY KINGDOM

FOR some time Alan volleyed upon the door, and his knocking only roused the echoes of the house and neighbourhood. At last, however, I could hear the noise of a window gently thrust up, and knew that my uncle had come to his observatory. By what light there was, he would see Alan standing, like a dark shadow, on the steps; the three witnesses were hidden quite out of his view; so that there was nothing to alarm an honest man in his own house. For all that, he studied his visitor awhile in silence, and when he spoke his voice had a quaver of misgiving.

"What's this?" says he. "This is nae kind of time of night for decent folk; and I hae nae trokings[1] wi' nighthawks. What brings ye here? I have a blunderbush."

"Is that yoursel', Mr. Balfour?" returned Alan, stepping back and looking up into the darkness. "Have a care of that blunderbuss; they're nasty things to burst."

"What brings ye here? and whae are ye?" says my uncle, angrily.

"I have no manner of inclination to rowt out my name to the country-side," said Alan; "but what brings me here is another story, being more of your affair than mine; and

[1] Dealings.

[276]

if ye 're sure it 's what ye would like, I 'll set it to a tune and sing it to you."

"And what is 't?" asked my uncle.

"David," says Alan.

"What was that?" cried by uncle, in a mighty changed voice.

"Shall I give ye the rest of the name, then?" said Alan.

There was a pause; and then, "I 'm thinking I 'll better let ye in," says my uncle, doubtfully.

"I dare say that," said Alan; "but the point is, Would I go? Now I will tell you what I am thinking. I am thinking that it is here upon this doorstep that we must confer upon this business; and it shall be here or nowhere at all whatever; for I would have you to understand that I am as stiffnecked as yoursel', and a gentleman of better family."

This change of note disconcerted Ebenezer; he was a little while digesting it, and then says he, "Weel, weel, what must be must," and shut the window. But it took him a long time to get down-stairs, and a still longer to undo the fastenings, repenting (I dare say) and taken with fresh claps of fear at every second step and every bolt and bar. At last, however, we heard the creak of the hinges, and it seems my uncle slipped gingerly out and (seeing that Alan had stepped back a pace or two) sat him down on the top door-step with the blunderbuss ready in his hands.

"And now," says he, "mind I have my blunderbush, and if ye take a step nearer ye 're as good as deid."

"And a very civil speech," says Alan, "to be sure."

"Na," says my uncle, "but this is no a very chancy kind

of a proceeding, and I 'm bound to be prepared. And now that we understand each other, ye 'll can name your business."

"Why," says Alan, "you that are a man of so much understanding, will doubtless have perceived that I am a Hieland gentleman. My name has nae business in my story; but the county of my friends is no very far from the Isle of Mull, of which ye will have heard. It seems there was a ship lost in those parts; and the next day a gentleman of my family was seeking wreck-wood for his fire along the sands, when he came upon a lad that was half drowned. Well, he brought him to; and he and some other gentleman took and clapped him in an auld, ruined castle, where from that day to this he has been a great expense to my friends. My friends are a wee wild-like, and not so particular about the law as some that I could name; and finding that the lad owned some decent folk, and was your born nephew, Mr. Balfour, they asked me to give ye a bit call and confer upon the matter. And I may tell ye at the off-go, unless we can agree upon some terms, ye are little likely to set eyes upon him. For my friends," added Alan, simply, "are no very well off."

My uncle cleared his throat. "I 'm no very caring," says he. "He wasnae a good lad at the best of it, and I 've nae call to interfere."

"Ay, ay," said Alan, "I see what ye would be at: pretending ye don't care, to make the ransom smaller."

"Na," said my uncle, "it 's the mere truth. I take nae manner of interest in the lad, and I 'll pay nae ransom, and ye can make a kirk and a mill of him for what I care."

I COME INTO MY KINGDOM

"Hoot, sir," says Alan. "Blood's thicker than water, in the deil's name! Ye cannae desert your brother's son for the fair shame of it; and if ye did, and it came to be kennt, ye wouldnae be very popular in your country-side, or I'm the more deceived."

"I'm no just very popular the way it is," returned Ebenezer; "and I dinnae see how it would come to be kennt. No by me, onyway; nor yet by you or your friends. So that's idle talk, my buckie," says he.

"Then it'll have to be David that tells it," said Alan.

"How that?" says my uncle, sharply.

"Ou, just this way," says Alan. "My friends would doubtless keep your nephew as long as there was any likelihood of siller to be made of it, but if there was nane, I am clearly of opinion they would let him gang where he pleased, and be damned to him!"

"Ay, but I'm no very caring about that either," said my uncle. "I wouldnae be muckle made up with that."

"I was thinking that," said Alan.

"And what for why?" asked Ebenezer.

"Why, Mr. Balfour," replied Alan, "by all that I could hear, there were two ways of it: either ye liked David and would pay to get him back; or else ye had very good reasons for not wanting him, and would pay for us to keep him. It seems it's not the first; well then, it's the second; and blythe am I to ken it, for it should be a pretty penny in my pocket and the pockets of my friends."

"I dinnae follow ye there," said my uncle.

"No?" said Alan. "Well, see here: you dinnae want

the lad back; well, what do ye want done with him, and how much will ye pay?"

My uncle made no answer, but shifted uneasily on his seat.

"Come, sir," cried Alan. "I would have you to ken that I am a gentleman; I bear a king's name; I am nae rider to kick my shanks at your hall door. Either give me an answer in civility, and that out of hand; or by the top of Glencoe, I will ram three feet of iron through your vitals."

"Eh, man," cried my uncle, scrambling to his feet, "give me a meenit! What's like wrong with ye? I'm just a plain man and nae dancing master; and I'm trying to be as ceevil at it's morally possible. As for that wild talk, it's fair disrepitable. Vitals, says you! And where would I be with my blunderbush?" he snarled.

"Powder and your auld hands are but as the snail to the swallow against the bright steel in the hands of Alan," said the other. "Before your jottering finger could find the trigger, the hilt would dirl on your breast-bane."

"Eh, man, whae's denying it?" said my uncle. "Pit it as ye please, hae't your ain way; I'll do naething to cross ye. Just tell me what like ye'll be wanting, and ye'll see that we'll can agree fine."

"Troth, sir," said Alan, "I ask for nothing but plain dealing. In two words: do ye want the lad killed or kept?"

"O, sirs!" cried Ebenezer. "O, sirs, me! that's no kind of language!"

"Killed or kept!" repeated Alan.

I COME INTO MY KINGDOM

"O, keepit, keepit!" wailed my uncle. "We'll have nae bloodshed, if you please."

"Well," says Alan, "as ye please; that'll be the dearer."

"The dearer?" cries Ebenezer. "Would ye fyle your hands wi' crime?"

"Hoot!" said Alan, "they're baith crime, whatever! And the killing's easier, and quicker, and surer. Keeping the lad'll be a fashious[1] job, a fashious, kittle business."

"I'll have him keepit, though," returned my uncle. "I never had naething to do with onything morally wrong; and I'm no gaun to begin to pleasure a wild Hielandman."

"Ye're unco scrupulous," sneered Alan.

"I'm a man o' principle," said Ebenezer, simply; "and if I have to pay for it, I'll have to pay for it. And besides," says he, "ye forget the lad's my brother's son."

"Well, well," said Alan, "and now about the price. It's no very easy for me to set a name upon it; I would first have to ken some small matters. I would have to ken, for instance, what ye gave Hoseason at the first go-off?"

"Hoseason?" cries my uncle, struck aback. "What for?"

"For kidnapping David," says Alan.

"It's a lee, it's a black lee!" cried my uncle. "He was never kidnapped. He leed in his throat that tauld ye that. Kidnapped? He never was!"

"That's no fault of mine nor yet of yours," said Alan; "nor yet of Hoseason's, if he's a man that can be trusted."

"What do ye mean?" cried Ebenezer. "Did Hoseason tell ye?"

[1] Troublesome.

[281]

"Why, ye donnered auld runt, how else would I ken?" cried Alan. "Hoseason and me are partners; we gang shares; so ye can see for yoursel' what good ye can do leeing. And I must plainly say ye drove a fool's bargain when ye let a man like the sailor-man so far forward in your private matters. But that's past praying for; and ye must lie on your bed the way ye made it. And the point in hand is just this: what did ye pay him?"

"Has he tauld ye himsel'?" asked my uncle.

"That's my concern," said Alan.

"Weel," said my uncle, "I dinnae care what he said, he leed, and the solemn God's truth is this, that I gave him twenty pound. But I'll be perfec'ly honest with ye: for by that, he was to have the selling of the lad in Caroliny, whilk would be as muckle mair, but no from my pocket, ye see."

"Thank you, Mr. Thomson. That will do excellently well," said the lawyer, stepping forward; and then mighty civilly, "Good-evening, Mr. Balfour," said he.

And, "Good-evening, Uncle Ebenezer," said I.

And, "It's a braw nicht, Mr. Balfour," added Torrance.

Never a word said my uncle, neither black nor white; but just sat where he was on the top doorstep and stared upon us like a man turned to stone. Alan filched away his blunderbuss; and the lawyer, taking him by the arm, plucked him up from the doorstep, led him into the kitchen, whither we all followed, and set him down in a chair beside the hearth, where the fire was out and only a rushlight burning.

There we all looked upon him for a while, exulting greatly

in our success, but yet with a sort of pity for the man's shame.

"Come, come, Mr. Ebenezer," said the lawyer, "you must not be down-hearted, for I promise you we shall make easy terms. In the meanwhile give us the cellar key, and Torrance shall draw us a bottle of your father's wine in honour of the event." Then, turning to me and taking me by the hand, "Mr. David," says he, "I wish you all joy in your good fortune, which I believe to be deserved." And then to Alan, with a spice of drollery, "Mr. Thomson, I pay you my compliment; it was most artfully conducted; but in one point you somewhat outran my comprehension. Do I understand your name to be James? or Charles? or is it George, perhaps?"

"And why should it be any of the three, sir?" quoth Alan, drawing himself up, like one who smelt an offence.

"Only, sir, that you mentioned a king's name," replied Rankeillor; "and as there has never yet been a King Thomson, or his fame at least has never come my way, I judged you must refer to that you had in baptism."

This was just the stab that Alan would feel keenest, and I am free to confess he took it very ill. Not a word would he answer, but stepped off to the far end of the kitchen, and sat down and sulked; and it was not till I stepped after him, and gave him my hand, and thanked him by title as the chief spring of my success, that he began to smile a bit, and was at last prevailed upon to join our party.

By that time we had the fire lighted, and a bottle of wine uncorked; a good supper came out of the basket, to which Torrance and I and Alan set ourselves down; while the lawyer and my uncle passed into the next chamber to consult. They stayed there closeted about an hour; at the end of which period they had come to a good understanding, and my uncle and I set our hands to the agreement in a formal manner. By the terms of this, my uncle bound himself to satisfy Rankeillor as to his intromissions, and to pay me two clear thirds of the yearly income of Shaws.

So the beggar in the ballad had come home; and when I lay down that night on the kitchen chests, I was a man of means and had a name in the country. Alan and Torrance and Rankeillor slept and snored on their hard beds; but for me who had lain out under heaven and upon dirt and stones, so many days and nights, and often with an empty belly, and in fear of death, this good change in my case unmanned me more than any of the former evil ones; and I lay till dawn, looking at the fire on the roof and planning the future.

CHAPTER XXX

GOOD–BYE

SO far as I was concerned myself, I had come to port; but I had still Alan, to whom I was so much beholden, on my hands; and I felt besides a heavy charge in the matter of the murder and James of the Glens. On both these heads I unbosomed to Rankeillor the next morning, walking to and fro about six of the clock before the house of Shaws, and with nothing in view but the fields and woods that had been my ancestors' and were now mine. Even as I spoke on these grave subjects, my eye would take a glad bit of a run over the prospect, and my heart jump with pride.

About my clear duty to my friend, the lawyer had no doubt. I must help him out of the county at whatever risk; but in the case of James, he was of a different mind.

"Mr. Thomson," says he, "is one thing, Mr. Thomson's kinsman quite another. I know little of the facts, but I gather that a great noble (whom we will call, if you like, the D. of A.)[1] has some concern and is even supposed to feel some animosity in the matter. The D. of A. is doubtless an excellent nobleman; but, Mr. David, *timeo qui nocuere deos.*

[1] The Duke of Argyle.

If you interfere to balk his vengeance, you should remember there is one way to shut your testimony out; and that is to put you in the dock. There, you would be in the same pickle as Mr. Thomson's kinsman. You will object that you are innocent; well, but so is he. And to be tried for your life before a Highland jury, on a Highland quarrel and with a Highland judge upon the bench, would be a brief transition to the gallows."

Now I had made all these reasonings before and found no very good reply to them; so I put on all the simplicity I could. "In that case, sir," said I, "I would just have to be hanged — would I not?"

"My dear boy," cries he, "go in God's name, and do what you think is right. It is a poor thought that at my time of life I should be advising you to choose the safe and shameful; and I take it back with an apology. Go and do your duty; and be hanged, if you must, like a gentleman. There are worse things in the world than to be hanged."

"Not many, sir," said I, smiling.

"Why, yes, sir," he cried, "very many. And it would be ten times better for your uncle (to go no farther afield) if he were hanging decently upon a gibbet."

Thereupon he turned into the house (still in a great fervour of mind, so that I saw I had pleased him heartily) and there he wrote me two letters, making his comments on them as he wrote.

"This," says he, "is to my bankers, the British Linen Company, placing a credit to your name. Consult Mr. Thomson, he will know of ways; and you, with this credit, can supply the means. I trust you will be a good husband of your money; but in the affair of a friend like Mr. Thomson, I would be even prodigal. Then for his kinsman, there is no better way than that you should seek the Advocate, tell him your tale, and offer testimony; whether he may take it or not, is quite another matter, and will turn on the D. of A. Now, that you may reach the Lord Advocate well recommended, I give you here a letter to a namesake of your own, the learned Mr. Balfour of Pilrig, a man whom I esteem. It will look better that you should be presented by one of your own name; and the laird of Pilrig is much looked up to in the Faculty and stands well with Lord Advocate Grant. I would not trouble him, if I were you, with any particulars; and (do you know?) I think it would be needless to refer to Mr. Thomson. Form yourself upon the laird, he is a good model; when you deal with the Advocate, be discreet; and in all these matters, may the Lord guide you, Mr. David!"

Thereupon he took his farewell, and set out with Torrance for the Ferry, while Alan and I turned our faces for the city of Edinburgh. As we went by the footpath and beside the gateposts and the unfinished lodge, we kept looking back at the house of my fathers. It stood there, bare and great and smokeless, like a place not lived in; only in one of the top windows, there was the peak of a nightcap bobbing up and down and back and forward, like the head of a rabbit from a burrow. I had little welcome when I came, and less kindness while I stayed; but at least I was watched as I went away.

[287]

KIDNAPPED

Alan and I went slowly forward upon our way, having little heart either to walk or speak. The same thought was uppermost in both, that we were near the time of our parting; and remembrance of all the bygone days sat upon us sorely. We talked indeed of what should be done; and it was resolved that Alan should keep to the county, biding now here, now there, but coming once in the day to a particular place where I might be able to communicate with him, either in my own person or by messenger. In the meanwhile, I was to seek out a lawyer, who was an Appin Stewart, and a man therefore to be wholly trusted; and it should be his part to find a ship and to arrange for Alan's safe embarkation. No sooner was this business done, than the words seemed to leave us; and though I would seek to jest with Alan under the name of Mr. Thomson, and he with me on my new clothes and my estate, you could feel very well that we were nearer tears than laughter.

We came the by-way over the hill of Corstorphine; and when we got near to the place called Rest-and-be-Thankful, and looked down on Corstorphine bogs and over to the city and the castle on the hill, we both stopped, for we both knew without a word said that we had come to where our ways parted. Here he repeated to me once again what had been agreed upon between us: the address of the lawyer, the daily hour at which Alan might be found, and the signals that were to be made by any that came seeking him. Then I gave what money I had (a guinea or two of Rankeillor's) so that he should not starve in the meanwhile; and then we stood a space, and looked over at Edinburgh in silence.

GOOD–BYE

"Well, good-bye," said Alan, and held out his left hand.

"Good-bye," said I, and gave the hand a little grasp, and went off down hill.

Neither one of us looked the other in the face, nor so long as he was in my view did I take one back glance at the friend I was leaving. But as I went on my way to the city, I felt so lost and lonesome, that I could have found it in my heart to sit down by the dyke, and cry and weep like any baby.

It was coming near noon when I passed in by the West Kirk and the Grassmarket into the streets of the capital. The huge height of the buildings, running up to ten and fifteen storeys, the narrow arched entries that continually vomited passengers, the wares of the merchants in their windows, the hubbub and endless stir, the foul smells and the fine clothes, and a hundred other particulars too small to mention, struck me into a kind of stupor of surprise, so that I let the crowd carry me to and fro; and yet all the time what I was thinking of was Alan at Rest-and-be-Thankful; and all the time (although you would think I would not choose but to be delighted with these braws and novelties) there was a cold gnawing in my inside like a remorse for something wrong.

The hand of Providence brought me in my drifting to the very doors of the British Linen Company's bank.

The Covena

America and Americans

VOLUME I: FROM EXPLORATION TO RECONSTRUCTION

America and Americans

VOLUME I: FROM EXPLORATION TO RECONSTRUCTION

HERBERT J. BASS
Professor of History • Temple University

GEORGE A. BILLIAS
Professor of History • Clark University

EMMA JONES LAPSANSKY
Assistant Professor of History • Temple University

SILVER BURDETT COMPANY
MORRISTOWN, NEW JERSEY
GLENVIEW, ILLINOIS   PALO ALTO
DALLAS   ATLANTA

ACKNOWLEDGMENTS

Page 4: Excerpt from "The New Immigrants: Still the Promised Land." Reprinted by permission from *TIME, The Weekly Newsmagazine;* Copyright Time Inc. 1976. Page 64: Excerpt from *White over Black: American Attitudes Toward the Negro, 1550-1812* by Winthrop D. Jordan. Reprinted by permission of The University of North Carolina Press and the Institute of Early American History and Culture. Page 110: Excerpt from *The American Historical Review,* January 1926, p. 231, by Charles M. Andrews. Reprinted by permission. Page 172: Excerpt from "The American Revolution and the World" by Gordon Wood from *Brown Alumni Monthly,* July-August 1976, p. 26. © Gordon Wood. Reprinted by permission. Page 316: George W. Pierson, *The Moving American* (New York: Alfred A. Knopf, 1973), pp. 7-8. Page 317: "Daniel Boone" from *A Book of Americans* by Rosemary and Stephen Vincent Benét. Copyright 1933 by Rosemary and Stephen Vincent Benét. Copyright renewed © 1961 by Rosemary Carr Benét. Reprinted by permission of Brandt & Brandt Literary Agents, Inc. Page 320: Excerpts from *Westward Expansion: A History of the American Frontier* by Ray A. Billington. Copyright 1974 Macmillan Publishing Co., Inc. Reprinted by permission.

CREDITS

Maps: Lothar Roth
Graphs and Charts: John D. Firestone Associates
Unit Openers: Stefan Martin
Silhouettes: Herman Vestal

All presidential portraits are from the United States Bureau of Engraving and Printing unless otherwise indicated.

Chapter 1 2: © Harald Sund. 5: Rare Book Division, New York Public Library, Astor, Lenox and Tilden Foundations. 6: *t.l.* Ron Toelke; *t.r., b.l., b.r.* Culver Pictures; *b.m.* The Bettmann Archive. 9: Bibliothèque Nationale. 13: Tiroler Landesmuseum Ferdinandeum, Innsbruck. 14: No credit. 15: Alan Band Associates, courtesy of the Victoria and Albert Museum, London.
Chapter 2 18: Abby Aldrich Rockefeller Folk Art Collection. 20: Virginia State Library. 21: Brown Brothers. 22: National Park Service, Jamestown. 24, 27: Culver Pictures. 31: The New-York Historical Society. 33: No credit.
Chapter 3 38: New York State Historical Association, Cooperstown. 40: Rare Book Division, New York Public Library, Astor, Lenox and Tilden Foundations. 42: Detail, Enoch Pratt Free Library. 45: William L. Clements Library, University of Michigan. 47, 50: Culver Pictures. 53: Massachusetts Charitable Mechanics Association, on loan to Science Museum of Boston.
Chapter 4 56: Courtesy of The Henry Francis du Pont Winterthur Museum. 59: National Portrait Gallery, Smithsonian Institution. 60: Courtesy of the American Museum of Natural History. 62: Brown Brothers. 63, 65: Culver Pictures. 67: The Bettmann Archive. 69: John Work Garrett Library of Johns Hopkins University. 72: Peabody Museum of Salem, photo by Mark Sexton. 74: Culver Pictures.
Great Americans 78: Civico Museo Giovo, Como, Italy. 80, 82: Rare Book Division, New York Public Library, Astor, Lenox and Tilden Foundations. 83: Courtesy of the Edward E. Ayer Collection, The Newberry Library, Chicago. 85: United States Postal Service. 87: No credit. 89: The John Carter Brown Library, Brown University. 93: South Carolina Department of Parks, Recreation and Tourism. 95: Charleston Library Society. 97: Museum of Early Southern Decorative Arts. 98: Courtesy of The Henry Francis du Pont Winterthur Museum. 99: Culver Pictures. 101: Historical Society of Pennsylvania.
Chapter 5 106: Detail, The New-York Historical Society. 109: Historical Society of Pennsylvania. 113: *l.* Emmet Collection, Manuscripts and Archives Division, New York Public Library, Astor, Lenox and Tilden Foundations. 115: Detail, Massachusetts Historical Society. 116: The Bettmann Archive. 118: Rhode Island Historical Society. 121: United States Postal Service. 123: Reproduced through the courtesy of the Virginia Historical Society.
Chapter 6 129: Courtesy Fort Ticonderoga Museum. 130: Culver Pictures. 133: American Antiquarian Society. 143: Library of Congress. 144: Mike Godfrey for Silver Burdett.
Chapter 7 146: Anne S.K. Brown Military Collection. 149: The Bettmann Archive. 150: Culver Pictures; except *b.m.* The New-York Historical Society. 152: United States Postal Service. 158: Brown Brothers. 159: New York Public Library Picture Collection.
Chapter 8 164, 166: Historical Society of Pennsylvania. 171: Bibliothèque Nationale. 172: Culver Pictures. 174: From *History of Hungary,* picture by Stephan Pekary, Cserlpfalvi.
Great Americans 179: *t.* Library of Congress; *b.* Washington-Custis-Lee Collection, Washington and Lee University. 181: Library of Congress. 186: Culver Pictures. 189: Valentine Museum, Richmond. 190, 191: Massachusetts Historical Society. 193: George Dow, courtesy U.S. Department of the Interior, National Park Service. Adams National Historic Site, Quincy, Massachusetts. 194: Library of Congress. 196: Thomas Jefferson Memorial Foundation. 197: Courtesy T. Jefferson Coolidge. 198: Smithsonian Institution. 201: Rare Book Division, New York Public Library, Astor, Lenox and Tilden Foundations.
Chapter 9 204: Independence National Historical Park. 206: Culver Pictures. 211: The Bettmann Archive. 212: The New-York Historical Society. 214: Stokes Collection, New York Public Library. 216: Culver Pictures. 218: The New-York Historical Society. 219: United States Department of the Treasury.
Chapter 10 248: Collection of L.L. Bean. Trenton. 253: New York City Art Commission. 254: Stokes Collection, New York Public Library. 257: Giraudon, courtesy Musée Carnavalet. 261: Courtesy Pennsylvania Academy of Fine Arts. 262: Culver Pictures. 263: Library of Congress. 264: New York State Historical Association.
Chapter 11 266: Louisiana State Museum. 268: Mariners Museum, Newport News. 272: Filson Club. 273: United States Supreme Court. 274: Amon Carter Museum. 276: The Bettmann Archive. 277: Library of Congress. 278: Anne S.K. Brown Military Collection. 280: The New-York Historical Society. 283: Culver Pictures. 285: *l.* Culver Pictures; *m.* Library of Congress.
Great Americans 296: Charles Strickland Collection. 298: Courtesy Boston Athenaeum. 300: G. Ahrens/Shostal Associates. 301: Stokes Collection, New York Public Library. 303: John Ross Robertson Collection, Metropolitan Toronto Library, photo by Brian Boyle. 304: Library of Congress. 306: Royal Ontario Museum. 307: Culver Pictures. 308: National Collection of Fine Arts, Smithsonian Institution, Gift of Sulgrave Institution of the United States and Great Britain.
Chapter 12 314: The New-York Historical Society. 317: Missouri Historical Society. 321: Culver Pictures. 325: The New-York Historical Society. 328: Munson-Williams-Proctor Museum, Utica. 330: Library of Congress. 331: Culver Pictures.
Chapter 13 334: J.N. Bartfield Galleries. 340, 341: Culver Pictures. 345: The Bettmann Archive. 349: Library of Congress. 351: The New-York Historical Society. 352: Culver Pictures. 353: *l., m.* Culver Pictures.
Chapter 14 362: I.N. Phelps Stokes Collection, New York Public Library. 364: Courtesy Connecticut State Library. 367, 368: Culver Pictures. 369: The Bettmann Archive. 371: Print Collection, New York Public Library. 372: The Bettmann Archive.
Chapter 15 376: © Harald Sund. 378: Northern Natural Gas Company Collection, Joslyn Art Museum, Omaha, Nebraska. 385: Photo used by permission of Curator's Division, Historical Department of The Church of Jesus Christ of Latter-Day Saints.
Great Americans 394: *l.* Brown Brothers; *m.* Library of Congress; *r.* Culver Pictures. 395: Smithsonian Institution. 396: Courtesy of the Boston Art Commission. 397: The Bettmann Archive. 401: Culver Pictures. 403: New York State Historical Association. 405, 406: Culver Pictures. 410: D.C. Clarke/Bruce Coleman. 413: © Russ Kinne/Photo Researchers, Inc. 414: National Library of Medicine, Bethesda, Maryland. 415: National Portrait Gallery.
Chapter 16 423, 424: Culver Pictures. 426, 430: The Bettmann Archive. 433: National Portrait Gallery.
Chapter 17 439: Hirschl and Adler Galleries. 440: St. John Fisher College. 442: The Bettmann Archive. 444: Louisiana State Museum. 447: Courtesy Kenneth Newman, Old Print Shop, New York City. 450: Culver Pictures. 453: Kansas Historical Society. 457: Culver Pictures.
Chapter 18 460: Anne S.K. Brown Military Collection. 463: Library of Congress. 464: Culver Pictures. 467: *l.* The Bettmann Archive; *r.* Cook Collection, Valentine Museum. 462: The Bettmann Archive. 468: © Bradley Smith/Photo Researchers, Inc. 471: Culver Pictures. 473: *t.l.* Library of Congress; *t.r.* The Bettmann Archive; *b.l., b.r.* Culver Pictures.
Chapter 19 476: Library of Congress. 478: Culver Pictures. ;479: *l.* Library of Congress; *m., r.* Culver Pictures. 480: Anne S.K. Brown Military Collection. 483, 485, 487, 488: Culver Pictures. 493: The New-York Historical Society. 494, 496: Culver Pictures.
Great Americans 506: *t.* Library of Congress. *b.* The Meserve Collection. 507: The Bettmann Archive. 509: Illinois State Historical Society. 511: Culver Pictures. 513: San Jacinto Museum of History Association. 514, 516: Library of Congress. 518: Sophia Smith Collection, Smith College. 521: National Portrait Gallery. 523, 525: Culver Pictures. 527: Detail, The Rockefeller Collection. 529: Steve Thompson/Uniphoto. 531: Courtesy P.T. Barnum Museum, photo by Corbit Studio. 533: Courtesy of The Collection of Philip Sills, photo by Paulus Leeser for Silver Burdett.

CONTENTS

Unit **3**

Americans and Limited Government   205

THE MAKING OF A NATION

Unit **4**

Americans: A People on the Move   313

EXPANSION, DEMOCRACY, AND INDUSTRIALISM

Unit 5

Americans: Freedom and Equality
419

A NATION DIVIDED

Maps, Charts, Tables, and Special-Interest Materials

Unit 1

Americans and Opportunity

THE COLONIAL PERIOD

THE PROMISE OF AMERICA

IN THE YEAR 1516, an Englishman named Sir Thomas More wrote a book called *Utopia.* The book was about a society that Sir Thomas created in his imagination. His Utopians lived amidst plenty. Everyone had an opportunity to live a good and happy life. They enjoyed liberty and freedom of thought. They were considerate of each other's rights and were careful not to offend one another's beliefs. A peace-loving people, they went to war only in self-defense. Ever since More wrote this book, the words *Utopia* and *utopian* have come to mean perfect or ideal.

Since Utopia was a product of Sir Thomas More's imagination, he was free to place it anywhere on earth. The spot he chose was an imaginary island off the American coast. Europeans had learned of America's existence a few years earlier through the voyages of Christopher Columbus. They saw it as an untouched wilderness, a place where one could start afresh, free from injustices of the Old World lands. To Sir Thomas More, America was the natural setting for his perfect society.

Two hundred sixty-six years later, in 1782, a French immigrant to America, Michel Guillaume Jean de Crèvecoeur, wrote a volume of essays called *Letters from an American Farmer.* Crèvecoeur and his American-born wife had settled on a farm in Orange County, New York. In one essay Crèvecoeur explained how America changed immigrants. We have changed a few words and shortened his paragraph to make his meaning clearer.

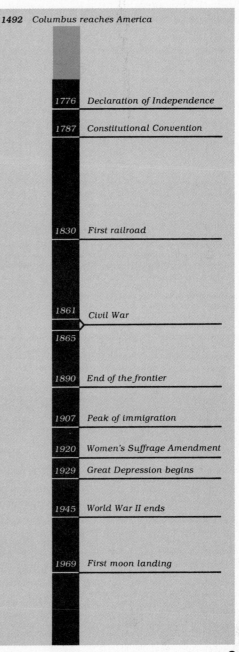

1492	Columbus reaches America
1776	Declaration of Independence
1787	Constitutional Convention
1830	First railroad
1861	Civil War
1865	
1890	End of the frontier
1907	Peak of immigration
1920	Women's Suffrage Amendment
1929	Great Depression begins
1945	World War II ends
1969	First moon landing

In this great American asylum, the poor of Europe have by some means met together. Can wretches who wander about, who work and starve, call England or any other kingdom their country? No! But in America, everything makes them new people; new laws, a new mode of living, a new social system. In Europe they were as so many useless plants, . . . they withered, and were mowed down by want, hunger, and war; but now in America they have taken roots and flourished.

In 1976, almost two hundred years after Crèvecoeur, Bit Chuen Wu, a twenty-three-year-old Chinese immigrant, became part owner of a small restaurant in Palo Alto, California. After several weeks in his new business, Wu looked back on his life in America.

Since I am in America, I have time only for work, just go home and watch TV, then go to sleep. I am too tired to read newspaper. I have no time to meet girls. I do the kitchen work. I wait on tables. But it is o.k. In Hong Kong I never get a chance to save money and become my own boss. It is very good to be your own boss. You get the profits.

A Country Where Everything Was Possible

The writings and remarks of Sir Thomas More, Crèvecoeur, and Bit Chuen Wu span more than four and a half centuries. Still, a common theme runs through them. It is the idea of America as a land of opportunity. Opportunity did not mean the same to all three. Reread the words of Crèvecoeur and Bit Chuen Wu, for instance. You will quickly see what some of the differences are. But whether their interest was in peace, plenty, and freedom, or a place where broken men and women could start again, or a land where one could become one's own boss, all three of these people saw America as the country where everything was possible.

For nearly four hundred years, people the world over have seen these same opportunities in America. Goethe, the great German poet, summed it up: *Amerika, du hast besser,* "America, you have it better." More than forty million people over the years have been led by that belief to leave their native lands for America. Probably most people in the world still share Goethe's view.

To most Americans today it is clear that not everyone has shared in this opportunity equally. Too often minorities have not. Nor have the poor. Yet it is also true that many millions, including members of racial and religious minorities, have found in America a chance to be what they wanted to be. They have found opportunities to make of themselves and their lives what they can.

The idea of America as a land of opportunity continues to have a strong hold on our minds today. In 1976—200 years after this country was born—a group of college freshmen were asked to rank the traits they thought were most clearly American. The majority placed Opportunity near the top of their lists.

America's abundance. How did it happen that America came to be so identified with the idea of opportunity? The place to start looking for the answer to this question is in the very beginnings of our history. For the idea of America as a land of opportunity, as More's *Utopia* suggests, is as old as America itself.

4

That idea in turn was connected with America's abundance—its rich soil, thick forests, and large deposits of metals and minerals.

From the time Europeans first became aware of the New World, they thought of it as the land of plenty. Read, for example, one of Columbus's first reports of the New World. In it he is describing the island of Hispaniola in the Caribbean Sea. Columbus believed he had landed in Asia, on islands then known as the Indies (today the East Indies). That is why he called the people Indians. Note how the picture of a land of plenty runs through Columbus's report.

In this drawing from a French book of 1584, Christopher Columbus holds an astrolabe, a navigational device for measuring the angle between the horizon and the stars or planets.

> This island and all the others are very fertile. . . . Its lands are filled with trees of a thousand kinds. . . . there are very large tracts of cultivable lands, and there is honey, and there are birds of many kinds, and fruits in great diversity. In the interior are mines of metals, and the population is without number.

Columbus's voyage. Christopher Columbus, an Italian by birth, was sailing under the flag of Spain when he sighted land in the Western Hemisphere on October 12, 1492. At that time, Spain and a number of other European nations were seeking new trade routes to the Indies. There they could get beautiful silks, shining jewels, and such spices as pepper and cloves.

Trade with the Far East at that time was slow, dangerous, and costly. The trade routes between Europe and Eastern Asia ran for hundreds of miles—across deserts and through mountain passes—in regions where bandits lay in wait. For these varied reasons, Europeans dreamed of finding a water route to the Far East. A water route would increase trade and bring riches to the nation that discovered it.

Columbus had long believed he could reach the Far East by sailing west from Europe. After many years he had finally persuaded the King and Queen of Spain to back him with ships and money. Columbus did not know, of course, that a great land mass blocked his way. The stories of earlier seafarers going to the Western Hemisphere had been lost or forgotten (see page 8).

SOME EXPLORERS OF AMERICA

Francisco de Coronado, was a Spanish noblemen who explored the American Southwest in 1540 and 1541. Searching for gold, he led his expedition as far east as Kansas. His men were the first Europeans to see the Grand Canyon.

Juan Ponce de León, a Spaniard, landed in 1513 in what is now Florida. There he sought in vain for a legendary spring called the Fountain of Youth. He conquered the island of Puerto Rico and served as its governor.

Henry Hudson, an English sea captain, made four voyages to America between 1607 and 1611. He explored the river and the bay that now carry his name, but he failed to find what he was seeking—a northern sea route to Asia.

John Cabot, an Italian sea captain sailing under the flag of England, reached the coast of North America in 1497, probably in what is now eastern Canada. His voyage gave England its claim to the mainland of North America.

Robert Sieur de La Salle of France became a fur trader in Canada. In 1682 he explored the Mississippi to its mouth and claimed the entire region for France. On a later expedition, he was assassinated by one of his own men.

Gold, glory, and God. Columbus made four voyages to the New World, but he never realized what he had done. He died thinking he had found an all-water route to the islands of the Far East.

Only slowly did the truth dawn on Europeans. As it did, America captured their imagination. Every European country that could do so hurried to claim part of the New World. John Cabot, an Italian captain like Columbus, explored the northeastern part of North America for England. John Verrazano and Jacques Cartier sailed along the eastern coast of North America and claimed it for the King of France. Spanish adventurers pushed into Central and South America. And Pedro Cabral took possession of what we now call Brazil for Portugal.

The explorers who followed Columbus, and the kings and queens who sent them forth, were all motivated by the same three things. They sought, first of all, gold. By custom, the king would receive one fifth of all gold found, but the explorers could keep the rest. They also hoped to bring glory to their country and king. And, in that deeply religious age, they wanted to carry the Christian religion to other peoples in the world. Gold, glory, and God, then, inspired the search for new lands.

Columbus himself well illustrates the point. He hoped to find gold—recall his reference to "mines of metals" in his report about Hispaniola. He also hoped to find an all-water route to Asia, a deed that would bring glory to him personally and to the King and Queen of Spain. And he wanted to convert the Indians to Christianity. Columbus sometimes signed his name *Christo Ferens*, "Christ

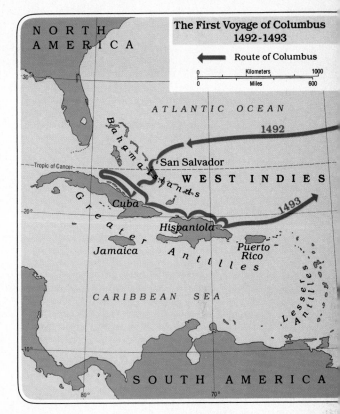

What chain of islands of the West Indies did Columbus first sight? What major islands did he sail along? Did he sight the coast of what is today the United States?

Bearer," showing his desire to carry the name of Christ to non-Christian peoples. In fact, he even planned to use part of the riches he might find to pay for a new Christian crusade to the Holy Land.

Explorers and conquerers. Spain was the nation that followed up Columbus's voyages most quickly. During the 1500s the Spanish explorers expanded their

Who Discovered America?

When the discovery of America is mentioned, most people think of Columbus and the date 1492. The fact is that men and women reached America long before Columbus. The first discoverers of America were the people we know as Indians. They came from Siberia, across what is now the Bering Strait, into North America at least 25,000 years ago.

Can we say that Columbus was the first *European* to touch American

shores? Once again, others came before him. A Norse explorer named Leif Ericson reached the North American coast around the year 1000. Sailing west from Greenland, Ericson and his companions landed on a shore they called Vinland. This may have been Newfoundland.

Still other people from the Eastern Hemisphere may have reached America long before Columbus. Claims have been made that Celts, Carthaginians, and Phoenicians explored North America as early as 800 B.C. It is known that French fishermen sailed to the waters off Newfoundland at an early date and dried their catch on shore. In the ninth century, Scandinavians occupied Iceland and drove out Irish colonists living there. These Irish wanderers were bold and skillful sailors in their skin-covered boats. Might the Irish, then, have been the first to reach America?

Scholars have put forth still different ideas about the early comers to America. Some think Africans reached the New World in very early times. And it is believed by some that an inscription found in Brazil shows that a boatload of Jews or Phoenicians sailed to America from the Red Sea as early as the sixth century B.C. Several archaeologists have argued that Japanese fishing boats, Chinese junks, and Polynesian outrigger canoes brought people across the Pacific to America in the distant past.

If some—or all—of these peoples did reach America before 1492, why does Columbus's name loom so large in American history? The answer is that it was Columbus's rediscovery of America—after earlier voyages had been forgotten—that resulted in lasting contact with the rest of the world.

It took many hundreds of years for people to advance along the migration routes shown below.

Arrival of the First Americans

⬅ Migration routes

Kilometers 2000
Miles 1500

ASIA

Bering Strait

Alaska

Arctic Circle

NORTH AMERICA

ATLANTIC OCEAN

Tropic of Cancer

SOUTH AMERICA

PACIFIC OCEAN

claims to the lands in and around the Caribbean Sea and the Gulf of Mexico. Those claims included most of what are today the southern and western parts of the United States.

Ponce de León, De Soto, and Coronado explored lands extending from Florida to the Grand Canyon in Arizona. In 1565 in Florida the Spaniards founded St. Augustine. It is today the oldest city in the United States.

The Spaniards' main attention, however, centered on lands farther to the south. There they discovered two rich Indian civilizations—those of the Aztecs of Mexico and the Incas of Peru. The Spanish invaders were led by Cortes in Mexico and by Pizarro in Peru. Using guns and horses, they overcame the Indians. They seized the Indians' gold and silver and forced them to dig for more in the mines. The treasure taken from the Aztecs and Incas made Spain in the 1500s the richest nation in the world.

In the race to discover and claim new lands, Portugal was next to Spain. A nation of great sailors and navigators, Portugal claimed Brazil in South America and created a vast empire in Asia and Africa.

In the late 1500s and 1600s, other European countries plunged into the race for colonies. Because the Spaniards were already well established in South and Central America, the latecomers centered their attention on North America. The French founded several settlements in eastern Canada, beginning in 1608. Holland, following up the voyages of Henry Hudson on the river that now bears his name, founded a colony in North America. It was called New Netherland. The colony's main settlement,

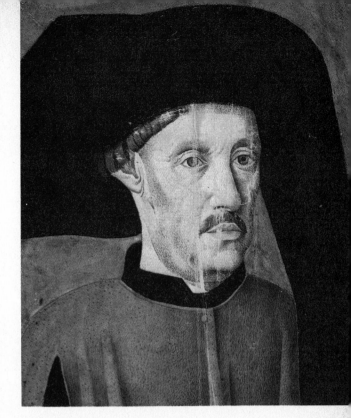

Prince Henry of Portugal enlisted the aid of scholars, mapmakers, and sea captains to advance the study of geography and navigation. His efforts ushered in the Age of Exploration.

named New Amsterdam, was founded in 1624 where New York City stands today. And a small group of Swedes and Finns founded a colony, New Sweden, on the Delaware River.

CHECKUP

1. In what respects did the feelings of Sir Thomas More, Crèvecoeur, and Bit Chuen Wu about America differ? How were their feelings alike?
2. What was Columbus seeking when he sighted land in the Western Hemisphere?
3. What parts of the New World did Spain explore and lay claim to? Where did other European countries make claims?

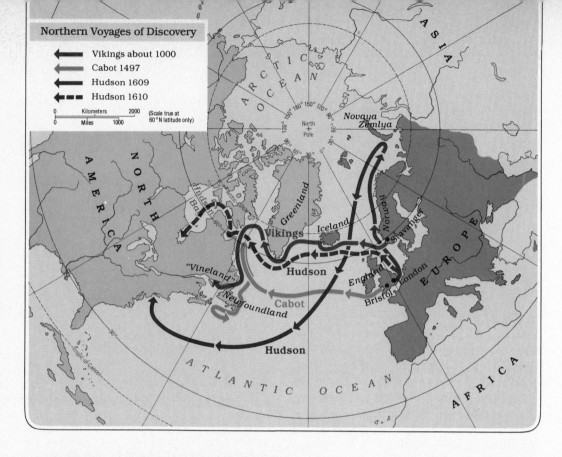

Northern Voyages of Discovery

→ Vikings about 1000
→ Cabot 1497
→ Hudson 1609
→ Hudson 1610

Kilometers 0 — 2000
Miles 0 — 1000
(Scale true at 60°N latitude only)

ARCTIC OCEAN

North Pole

ASIA

Novaya Zemlya

NORTH AMERICA

Hudson Bay

Greenland

Iceland

Vikings

Norway

Stavanger

EUROPE

"Vineland"

Hudson

Neufoundland

Cabot

England

London

Bristol

Hudson

ATLANTIC OCEAN

AFRICA

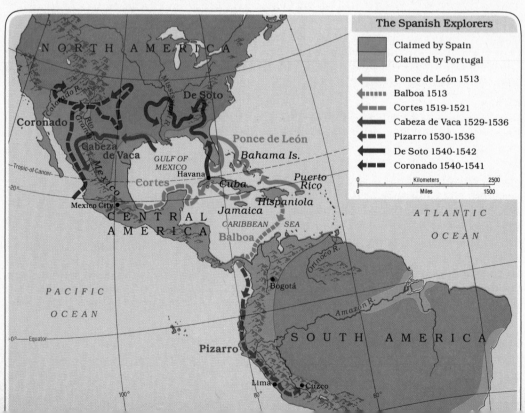

The Spanish Explorers

■ Claimed by Spain
■ Claimed by Portugal

→ Ponce de León 1513
→ Balboa 1513
→ Cortes 1519–1521
→ Cabeza de Vaca 1529–1536
→ Pizarro 1530–1536
→ De Soto 1540–1542
→ Coronado 1540–1541

Kilometers 0 — 2500
Miles 0 — 1500

NORTH AMERICA

Colorado R.

De Soto

Coronado

Rio Grande

Mississippi R.

Cabeza de Vaca

Mexico

GULF OF MEXICO

Cortes

Havana

Ponce de León

Bahama Is.

Cuba

Puerto Rico

Mexico City

CENTRAL AMERICA

Jamaica

Hispaniola

CARIBBEAN SEA

Balboa

Tropic of Cancer

20°

ATLANTIC OCEAN

PACIFIC OCEAN

Bogotá

Orinoco R.

Amazon R.

SOUTH AMERICA

Pizarro

Equator 0°

Lima

Cuzco

100°

80°

60°

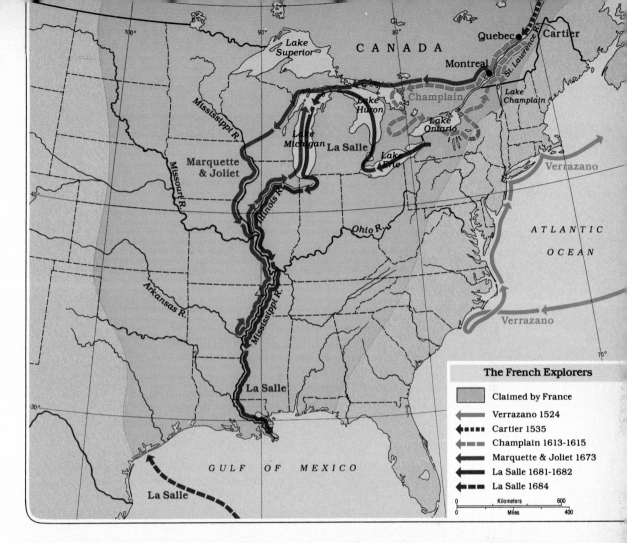

The French Explorers

	Claimed by France
→(grey arrow)	Verrazano 1524
◄•••••	Cartier 1535
◄ - - - (grey dashed)	Champlain 1613-1615
◄━━━	Marquette & Joliet 1673
◄━━━	La Salle 1681-1682
◄ ■ ■ ■	La Salle 1684

Kilometers 0 — 600
Miles 0 — 400

(Upper left) The first European explorers of the northeastern coast of North America are believed to have been the Vikings. The remains of a Viking settlement have been unearthed in northern Newfoundland. John Cabot and Henry Hudson, both sailing under the English flag, also explored this northern coastline. England's claims to North America were based on the exploration of Cabot.

(Lower left) During the first half of the sixteenth century, Spanish explorers ranged through New World lands from Kansas to Peru. Of those whose routes are shown on this map, Cabeza de Vaca may have had the most amazing journey. Shipwrecked off the Texas coast, he and a few companions wandered for eight years through the countryside of northern Mexico before reaching a Spanish settlement.

(Above) The French centered their exploration efforts on the St. Lawrence River, the Great Lakes, and the Mississippi River. However, Verrazano, an Italian sailing under the French flag, explored the Atlantic coast from Massachusetts to the Carolinas. Verrazano is believed to have been the first European to sail into the waters of New York Bay.

England and the Race for Colonies

It was England, one of the last nations to enter the race for colonies, that was to leave the greatest mark on North America. During the middle part of the sixteenth century, while Spain was gobbling up much of South and Central America, England was tied up with religious and political quarrels at home. But with the reign of Queen Elizabeth, from 1558 to 1603, many of these problems were settled.

An expanding trade. During these years, trade brought prosperity to England. English merchants enjoyed a growing trade in wool with European countries across the English Channel. They also reached out for trade with distant lands. The expense and risk of such trade in those days was too great for any one person. But English merchants came up with an idea for pooling their money and sharing the risks. This idea was the *joint stock company.*

Merchants would buy "shares," or "stock," in the company at so much per share. If there was a loss—for example, if a company's ship sank—the merchants would lose what they had put in, but no more. Profits would be divided according to the number of shares each person held. By the late 1500s, English merchants were using the joint stock company to promote trade with places as far away as Russia and India.

Reasons for colonizing. As England became more prosperous, a number of persons became interested in founding colonies. Through their writings, they tried to convince others that colonies would be a good thing for England. One of these writers was a clergyman named Richard Hakluyt. Earlier we summed up the motives of European explorers and rulers in three words—God, gold, and glory. When you read the following piece written by Hakluyt, try to find the sentences in which he appeals to each of these motives. To do this you will need two additional facts. First, England was a Protestant country and the deadly enemy of Catholic Spain. Second, once a year King Philip of Spain sent a fleet to carry gold and silver from the New World to Spain. We have changed some words in order to make Hakluyt's meaning clearer.

> Planting an English colony would keep the Spanish from taking all of America. From America, England could get trees for masts and such naval supplies as pitch, hemp, and tar. With the best ship builders in the world and with an ample supply of brave young men, presently unemployed, to man its vessels, how easy will it be for our navy to keep the Spanish navy from making its yearly voyage to Spain with gold and silver. Planting a colony in America would also promote the Protestant religion. Too, it would provide a place where the many unemployed in England could grow up under better conditions than at present.

Another Englishman who wrote in favor of colonizing in America was Sir George Peckham. In fact, Peckham invested money in a company that tried to plant a colony in Newfoundland as early as 1583. He gave these reasons why England should encourage the founding of colonies in America.

> . . . it is well known that all [Indians] . . . take [great] delight in any garment no matter how simple. . . . What a market

After the great Spanish fleet, called the Armada, was routed by the English in 1588, England became a major power in the race for colonies in the New World.

for our English clothes will result from this, and what a great benefit to all those engaged in making and selling clothes.

Our country will be generally benefitted, moreover, because a great many unemployed who are . . . burdens [in England] will be put to work in America. . . .

And then Peckham sums up (again, words have been changed slightly):

Then shall Her Majesty's empire be enlarged. Idleness will be banished from the country, depressed towns will be revived, many poor and needy persons will be helped and the Indians taught to know Christ.

Which of the arguments that Hakluyt used do you find repeated by Peckham? What new reasons for colonizing does Peckham add?

Attracting investors. Queen Elizabeth could not afford to finance colonies as did the King of Spain. Instead, she made contracts with private individuals and companies to plant colonies for England. What possible gains attracted them to risk their money in such chancy ventures? Again, we can turn to Sir George Peckham for part of the answer. In the same pamphlet from which we quoted above, Peckham addresses a paragraph to the persons he is trying to interest in investing:

Now, to the merchants who are disposed to support worthy projects I will say . . . that in that part of America are found the most wholesome and best climate, the most fertile soil, and all those products for which

13

we now have to make dangerous voyages to Barbary, Spain, Portugal, France, Italy, Moscovy, and Eastland.

What does Peckham think will attract merchants to invest in colonies? Add to these the hope of finding gold and silver, and you can see why some men might risk their money to found a colony.

Several Englishmen, including Sir Walter Raleigh and Sir George Peckham, did try to found colonies in North America before 1600. All of them failed, and lost small fortunes in the attempts. Their experiences showed that colonizing was too expensive for individuals, or even for small groups. When the English finally succeeded in planting a colony in Virginia, it was through a joint stock company.

Attracting settlers. One can understand why kings and queens, adventurers and investors, might want colonies in the New World. But why should the ordinary people of England want to leave home to live there?

A part of the answer is in the writings of Richard Hakluyt and Sir George Peckham that you read earlier. What is the economic condition that they describe at that time in England? If you cannot recall, turn to pages 12 and 13 and reread what they wrote.

The condition that Hakluyt and Peckham describe was connected with the wool trade you read about earlier. As the demand for wool increased, England's large landowners saw that they could make more money by raising sheep on their land than by renting the land out in small lots to farm families, as they had been doing. The changeover from farming to sheep raising was called the

enclosure movement, because the owners *enclosed*, or fenced in, their fields. Thousands who had formerly farmed were thrown off the land by the enclosure movement. They roamed the roads looking for work. People in this condition might well be interested in trying for a new life in the New World—especially if it was all that Peckham said it was.

An advertisement of the Virginia Company of London gives some further clues as to why common people might

In the early 1600s, a variety of books and leaflets were printed in England to attract settlers to Virginia. The opening page of one such book is shown below.

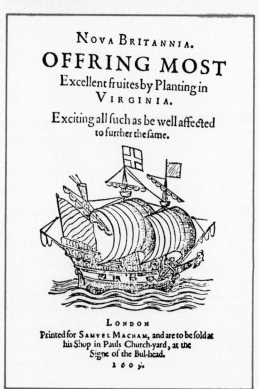

In the early seventeenth century, the changeover from farming to sheepraising on the large estates of England forced many farm families off the land and encouraged emigration to America.

decide to become colonists. The Virginia Company was a joint stock company formed by a small group of merchants and gentlemen in London. In 1606, James I, the new King of England, gave the company a *charter,* or contract, to found a colony in America.

Following is one of the leaflets that the company handed out on the streets in several English cities. As you read it, ask yourself these questions: To whom is this advertisement addressed? What attractions does it offer one to become a colonist?

This notice is published to announce the expedition to all workmen of whatever occupation—blacksmiths, carpenters, barrelmakers, ship builders, wood workers, and all work with any kind of metal, brickmakers, architects, bakers, weavers, shoemakers, sawers of lumber, spinners of wool, and all others, both men and women, of any occupation—who wish to join this voyage for colonizing the country. . . . They will be listed as investors in this voyage to Virginia, where they will have houses to live in, vegetable gardens and orchards, and food and clothing provided by the Company. Besides, they will receive a share in all the products and profits that may result from their labor, each in proportion; and they will also receive a share of the land that is to be divided, for themselves and their heirs forever.

The importance of land. You may have noted one theme that runs through nearly all the writings aimed at interesting investors, "gentlemen," and ordinary people in the New World. Write as they may about riches and precious metals, all of them sooner or later come to the idea of land—abundant land.

To understand why that theme would have such an appeal, you need to understand the importance of land in the England of that day. Land was the greatest source of wealth and income in sixteenth- and seventeenth-century England. It was also the yardstick by which one's importance was measured. Generally speaking, the more land one owned, the more important one was. That is why rich merchants bought large landed estates. Owning a large amount of land marked one as a member of the upper class. Since family land was usually inherited by the oldest son, younger sons had to look elsewhere for land of their own. Even at the bottom of the social ladder, land was important. Independent, small farmers who owned land had a higher standing and more rights than those who farmed on rented land.

Between 1540 and 1640, England's population doubled. In a country where land was so important, there simply was not enough of it to go around. And being scarce, land became all the more costly.

Something for everyone. Thus America offered something for everyone. For rulers and adventurers, gold and glory; for merchants, markets and raw materials; for the deeply religious, an opportunity to spread Christianity; and for all alike, land. By the early 1600s, England was ready to enter the race to found colonies in the New World.

CHECKUP

1. Why was the joint stock company effective in promoting England's trade?
2. What arguments were put forth by those who favored the planting of English colonies in the New World?
3. Why might people in England want to leave their homeland and become colonists in America?

Key Facts from Chapter 1

1. Those who have come to America from earliest times onward have seen it as a land of opportunity.
2. The picture of America as a land of opportunity is closely related to its abundance of natural resources, especially land.
3. The first discoverers of America were the people that Columbus called Indians.
4. Columbus's voyage in 1492 was important because it ushered in an era of New World exploration and colonization.
5. The three-fold aim of the European explorers of America was to find gold, to win glory, and to spread the Christian religion.

★ REVIEWING THE CHAPTER ★

People, Places, and Events

Review Questions

1. In what ways did each of the following people see America as a land of opportunity: Sir Thomas More, Crèvecoeur, and Bit Chuen Wu? *Pp. 3–4*

2. What three natural resources contributed to the idea of America as a land of plenty? *P. 5*

3. Why were Europeans interested in finding new trade routes to the Far East? *P. 5*

4. How did Spain become the world's richest nation in the 1500s? *P. 9*

5. Which nations established claims on North America? *P. 9*

6. List five reasons why England became interested in founding colonies in the New World. *Pp. 12–13*

7. Why might the ordinary English person, especially the farmer, have been willing to leave England and settle in the New World? *Pp. 14–16*

Chapter Test

Complete each sentence by writing the correct answer on a separate piece of paper.

1. Sir Thomas More located Utopia (off the coast of America, on the lost continent of Atlantis).

2. For hundreds of years, America has been identified with the idea of (hard times, opportunity).

3. European merchants dreamed of finding a (land, water) route to the Far East.

4. The motives that led Europeans to explore the New World can be summed up as (gold, glory, and God; liberty, equality, and fraternity).

5. Spanish claims in the New World include most of what are today the (southern and western, northern and eastern) parts of the United States.

6. Most of North America was eventually claimed by explorers from (France and England, Norway and Italy).

7. In order to share the financial risks of founding a colony, English merchants organized (royal companies, joint stock companies).

8. The enclosure movement encouraged many English (farmers, factory workers) to move to the New World.

9. In order to establish a new settlement, the English colonists needed a (letter, charter) from the English ruler.

10. In sixteenth- and seventeenth-century England, a person's importance was measured by his or her ownership of (ships, land).

THE ENGLISH COLONIES

IN LATE DECEMBER 1606, three ships with 120 men and boys set sail from England for America. Four months later the ships entered Chesapeake Bay, and the passengers put ashore on a swampy peninsula a few miles up the James River. So was founded Jamestown, England's first permanent colony in the New World.

The Jamestown Colony

The leader of the Jamestown colony was called a governor, but he was really more like a manager in charge of a business. He took his orders from the investors back in England. And they left no doubt, from the very first orders, that his job was to produce a profit. The governor was to divide the settlers into three groups of 40 each. The first group was to build a storehouse for food and a fort to protect against Indian attack. The second would grow food. The third group of settlers would get on with the business of making a profit for the London investors. They were to explore the rivers, looking for the dreamed-of water route to the Far East. And when they came upon a spot where it was felt there might be minerals, half of them were to dig for gold.

To help in this effort, the Virginia Company sent over two goldsmiths, two refiners, and several jewelers. They came in the second shipload of settlers, arriving on New Year's Day, 1608. At the same time, the colony's settlers were supposed to enter into trade with the Indians for furs and food.

Hard times. The first several years of the Virginia colony went badly. The death rate was very high, mainly because of sickness and disease. Sixteen of the original 120 had died aboard ship. Of the remaining 104, 51 died before the second group arrived. The death rate among the second group was equally high.

Further, the colony failed to raise enough food to feed itself. There were several reasons for this. One was that the men wasted time chasing after gold, which they never found, rather than raising food crops. Another reason was that over half of the first group of settlers and a third of the second were "gentlemen." People in the "gentlemen" class did not work with their hands in England, and they clearly didn't plan to do so in Virginia.

Still another reason for the food shortage had to do with the ownership of land. The advertisement had read, "They will also receive a share of land that is divided, for themselves and their heirs forever." But in Virginia the settlers learned that this would not happen for many years. In the meantime, the company owned all the land. Since everyone was fed from the common storehouse, regardless of how much or how little he worked, there developed an attitude of "let the other fellow do it."

In 1608 Captain John Smith became the leader of the governing group. He knew that the colony could not keep depending on investors in London for food. Instead of foolishly hunting for gold, Virginians would have to cut

19

Captain John Smith not only provided leadership at Jamestown but also explored the coast of the region which he named *New England*.

trees, clear fields, and till the soil. That meant everyone. Smith ordered: "He that will not work shall not eat."

But in 1609 Smith returned to England. The following winter was the worst time yet for the colony. Food ran out, and settlers fell victim to illness. Of the 600 men who had come to Virginia from England, there were but 60 alive by the spring of 1610. These survivors were preparing to give up and leave for England when a fleet arrived with supplies and new settlers.

Land and tobacco. During the next few years two important developments changed the future of the Virginia colony. One concerned land. Beginning in 1614 the company allotted three acres (1.2 ha) practically rent free to those who had lived in the colony for seven years. Except for a small amount of corn that settlers had to give to the warehouse, whatever food was grown on the land remained theirs. By 1616 a majority of the colonists were living on land that they could call their own.

In a history of the Virginia colony that Captain John Smith wrote in 1624, he describes what followed:

> When our people were fed out of the common store, and labored jointly together, glad was he who could slip [away] from his labor, or [sleep] over his task . . . the most honest among them would hardly [work] so much . . . in a week, as now for themselves they will do in a day.

The second important development had to do with Virginia's economy. The London investors had hoped that Virginia could produce something that could be sold at a profit. During the first few years of the settlement, the company had sent over gold refiners, glassblowers, winemakers, and silk growers. Their efforts had been for nothing.

What finally saved the colony was not gold or wine or silk, but a humble weed—tobacco. Virginia Indians had long grown a bitter-tasting type of tobacco. In 1612 John Rolfe, one of the colonists, experimented with seeds of a milder tobacco, grown in the West Indies. Virginia's climate and soil turned out to be ideal for this new crop. In England smoking had become something of a craze about 30 years earlier, and tobacco brought high prices. Within a few years everyone in the colony was raising it on every available piece of land—even in the streets of Jamestown.

By 1619 England was receiving over 40,000 pounds (18,000 kg) of tobacco every year from Virginia, more than from any other place in the world. Ten years later, Virginia sent thirty times as much. Virginia at last had a crop that could bring it prosperity.

The headright system. The crying need now was for laborers to raise the tobacco. The Virginia Company tried many ways to get people to America. It sent over orphaned children. It tried to attract people who were willing to work for the company on the same terms as earlier settlers. It advertised for women who wished to find husbands—until then only a few already married women had come to Virginia.

There was one magnet, however, that could draw people to the New World more than any other. That was the opportunity to own land. The company had taken one step in that direction in 1614. In 1618 it went all the way with the *headright system.* A gift of land, usually 50 to 100 acres (20 to 40 ha), was given to any person in England

THE METRIC SYSTEM

In the text at the top of page 20, you will see the words "three acres (1.2 ha)." This means that 1.2 ha, or hectares, is about the same as three acres. A hectare is a unit of measure in the metric system.

The metric system for measuring area, distance, weight, capacity, and temperature is in use in all major countries except the United States. Plans are being made to "go metric" here also.

To prepare you for this change, both U.S. and metric measurements are given in this book. Each U.S. measurement in this book is followed by the metric measurement that is about equal to it. Acres are changed to hectares (ha), inches to centimeters (cm), feet or yards to meters (m), miles to kilometers (km), pounds to kilograms (kg), quarts to liters (l), and degrees Fahrenheit (°F) to degrees Celsius (°C).

The first task of the English colonists at Jamestown in 1607 was to build shelters and a fort.

Jamestown, the first permanent English settlement in America, was located on swampy ground beside the James River in Virginia. Inside the stockade, at left, were a church, storehouse, and dwellings.

who would move to Virginia. Instead of having to work for the company for seven years, a landless Englishman could become an instant landowner. A settler could get another 50 acres (20 ha) free by paying the transportation of some other person to Virginia. *Indentured servants*—persons who agreed to work for a number of years for whoever would pay their passage to America— would also get a headright of 50 free acres at the end of their term of service.

Fifty acres! This was more land than many an Englishman dared dream of owning in a lifetime. With this change in land policy, the stream of settlers grew rapidly. The headright system enabled many to acquire huge estates by paying the fare of other persons, perhaps indentured servants, to the colony. And servants were willing to come because they could look forward to the time when they, too, might own land in Virginia.

In the years from 1619 to 1624, 4,500 settlers came to Virginia, and the colony was safely established.

A promise fulfilled. Thus for many of the Virginia colonists, the promise of opportunity in America was fulfilled. Near the end of his history of Virginia, Captain John Smith explains the appeal of America in these words:

What man who is poor . . . can desire more contentment than to walk over and plant the land he has obtained by risking his life? . . . Here nature and liberty give us freely that which we lack or have to pay dearly for in England. What pleasure can be greater than to grow tired from . . . planting vines, fruits, or vegetables, from working their own mines, fields, gardens, orchards, buildings, ships, and other works?

22

Two final notes on the Virginia colony. First, in 1619 a new and unexpected supply of labor arrived in Virginia. A Dutch ship carrying a cargo of twenty black Africans landed in Jamestown. Thus began one of the most tragic chapters in American history. You will read about what followed later in this unit.

Second, while Virginia settlers became prosperous, the Virginia Company never did. Once colonists owned their own land, profits from tobacco growing went mostly to them. What little the company received was made on selling the crop in England for the planters. In 1624 King James took over the colony, thus ending the company's role.

CHECKUP

1. Why did things go badly for the Jamestown colony in its first years?
2. What two developments changed the colony's future for the better?
3. Describe the headright system. What effect did it have on Virginia's growth?

The New England Colonies

To a number of English people, America represented an opportunity of quite a different kind. This was the opportunity to worship God as they chose.

During the Protestant Reformation, in the 1500s, King Henry VIII broke away from the Roman Catholic church and established the Church of England, placing himself at its head. His action left the English people divided for more than a century.

The majority of the English accepted the Church of England, or the Anglican church, as it was called. On one side of them stood those who remained Roman Catholics and refused to recognize the Anglican church as the new national faith. On the other side were the Protestants who wanted the Anglican church to move much further away from the Roman Catholic church. Faced with dissent on both sides, English monarchs persecuted both Catholics and extreme Protestants.

The Puritans. The more extreme English Protestants were called Puritans, because they wanted to "purify" the Anglican church by removing all Catholic influences. Thus they wanted to do away with priests' robes and most rituals. They felt there should be no religious statues, stained-glass windows, and music during services. Such things, the Puritans said, came between the people and their worship of God. They also thought that each local congregation should govern itself, and so wished to do away with bishops, a holdover from Catholicism.

Most Puritans had no wish to leave the Anglican church. A small minority, however, saw no hope of reforming the church from within and left it. These Separatists formed their own congregations and proceeded to hold their own religious services.

King James I, who came to power in 1603, did not take kindly to the Puritans, whether Separatists or not. As king, remember, James was not only the ruler of England but also the head of the Anglican church. To defy the church was also to defy him. James therefore ordered the Puritans to get in line or he would "harry [drive] them out of the land." When the Puritans refused, James was as good as his word.

The Pilgrims. Fearing arrest, a small band of Separatists, later known as Pilgrims, fled to Holland in 1609. There they had complete religious freedom and they prospered. The Pilgrims worried, however, lest their children take on Dutch ways and forget their English heritage. After ten years, therefore, they decided to leave Holland for America.

One of their leaders got permission to plant a colony on the territory of the Virginia Company. A group of London merchants financed them. The Pilgrims planned to set up a trading post and fishing settlement. All the capital and profits were to be placed in a common pool for seven years, by which time they hoped to pay off their debt to their London backers.

On September 16, 1620, the *Mayflower*, a leaky vessel of 180 tons (160 t), left England bound for America. Of the 101 passengers aboard, there were 35 Pilgrims from Holland and 52 other Separatists from England. Many of those who were not Pilgrims were going to America more for the opportunity to get land or work there than for religious reasons.

The Plymouth colony. Blown off course, the *Mayflower* arrived at Cape Cod, outside the territory of the Virginia Company, in early November. Nevertheless,

After a voyage of 64 days, the Pilgrims landed on Cape Cod in November 1620. They came ashore, sent out an exploring party, heated water and washed clothes, and then sailed on to the site of Plymouth.

the Pilgrims decided to settle at what is now Plymouth, Massachusetts.

Through the harsh winter that followed, the Pilgrims struggled to keep their tiny colony alive. The first year was as desperate as that in Jamestown. By spring, 44 people had died. Only after several hard years did the Plymouth colony establish itself. Discouraged by the colony's inability to make a profit, the London backers stopped sending supplies in 1624. Three years later the partnership between the merchants and Pilgrims ended, and the colony was on its own.

Plymouth grew slowly. By 1648 it had managed to pay off its debt to the London merchants, but it never really prospered. In 1691 it was absorbed by its larger neighbor, the Massachusetts Bay Colony. Still, Plymouth was the first colony to realize the opportunity that America gave to those seeking religious freedom. Its example influenced thousands of later settlers.

Massachusetts Bay Colony. One group of non-Separatist Puritans and their leader, a lawyer named John Winthrop, watched the Pilgrim experiment with great interest. When it became clear that the new king, Charles I, would reintroduce certain Catholic practices, these Puritans also decided to move to America. There they would be able to lead Christian lives according to the rules of conduct in the Bible. Their community would be a model of godliness. It would, they were sure, win the admiration and imitation of all England.

In 1629 these Puritans formed a joint stock company, called the Massachusetts Bay Company, and elected Win-

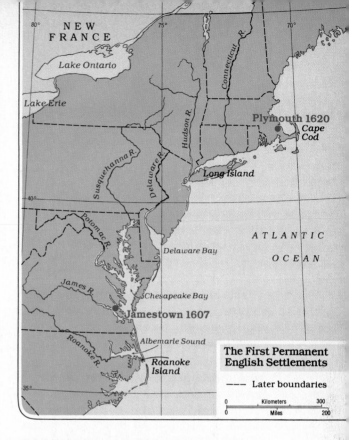

The First Permanent English Settlements

------ Later boundaries

The first permanent English settlements were at Jamestown and Plymouth, but other English settlements had been attempted earlier. One was at Roanoke Island where, in 1587, a colony of about 150 people was set up. When a ship put in there in 1590, the settlers had disappeared. No one knows what happened to the Lost Colony.

throp governor. During the next six months, 1,000 men, women, and children left to take up life in the wilderness of New England.

The question of motive. What you have read so far would lead you to conclude that John Winthrop had a simple, single motive in going to America. Yet Winthrop may have had another reason. He had several sons, and in England it was common practice for a father to give his sons half his property when they came of age, usually at twenty-one. Three of

25

Winthrop's sons had recently come of age. In his journal, Winthrop remarks that he has given away half of his estate to his sons and could no longer live as well as he had before. He asks (again, wording has been changed to make his meaning clearer):

> Why, then, should I continue to stay in England (where an acre of land costs as much as a hundred acres in America) at a time when that whole rich continent lies unused?

What may have been Winthrop's other motive for going to America? Which motive do you think was more important, this one or the religious motive?

Why did it happen? The last question points up a major problem we always face in understanding both the past and present. The hardest thing to know is not *what* happened but *why* it happened; not *what* people did but *why* they did it. In other words, the causes of events and the motives of people are the most difficult things to know for certain.

Sometimes we can be fairly sure that several motives were, or are, present. But then it is difficult to be sure which was the most important. Earlier in this unit you read that the explorers were motivated by God, gold, and glory. True enough. But which of these three was most important in their minds? Would any one of them have been motive enough to explore if the other two had been absent? And if so, would the same motive have been the most important one for each of the explorers? In trying to answer such questions, we must not assume too quickly that what would be the most important to us was, or is, most important to others. That is especially true when we are dealing with the motives of people of an earlier age or a different culture.

At times, we can be fairly confident that we understand people's motives. The motives of the 35 Pilgrims who left Holland for America, for example, are quite clear. More often, we are left with uncertainty.

Which motive was the most important in leading John Winthrop and his fellow Puritans to come to America? Most probably it was the religious one. But would Winthrop and others have come to America even if the religious motive had not been present? That we can never know for sure. The entry in Winthrop's journal makes it clear that he had mixed motives, and this was true in the case of many other settlers.

The Puritan settlements. Winthrop's group spent its first winter in the Massachusetts Bay Colony in a settlement called Salem. In 1630 they founded Boston, which became the colony's capital. Soon they started other communities nearby.

Although founded as a trading company, the Massachusetts Bay Colony quickly changed into a self-governing commonwealth. Laws were based on the Bible and Puritan belief. All members were required to attend church. The clergy and the elected officials were to be obeyed without question, for it was believed they held their authority from God. This was a tight community of true believers. Strangers were not welcome, nor was disagreement allowed.

Massachusetts grew rapidly. Between 1633 and 1643, about 20,000 persons came. Did all of them come for religious reasons? It is true that religious persecution in England had become worse during this time. But only about 4,000 of those who came were members of Puritan churches in England. That suggests that a good many of the 20,000 were drawn to America at least partly by the same kinds of opportunity that drew settlers to Jamestown—the chance for land and jobs and the hope of improving their lives.

Rhode Island. The strictness of the Massachusetts Puritan leaders led to the founding of the colony of Rhode Island. Roger Williams was a young minister in Massachusetts Bay. Winthrop and others thought his religious ideas were dangerous. Williams believed, among other things, that the government should have no authority over the people in matters of religion. He also argued that the land on which the Bay Colony was located still belonged to the Indians, since the English settlers had never purchased it from them.

Fearing that such ideas might lead to a revolt against their authority, the Puritan leaders brought Williams to trial. They convicted him and ordered him banished in 1635. Warned by friends that he was going to be shipped back to England, Williams fled into Indian country. For fourteen weeks he lived in the wintry wilderness, kept alive by the Narragansett Indians who gave him food and shelter. In the spring of 1636, Williams started his own settlement at Providence.

Two years later, the Puritan leaders ordered out Anne Hutchinson, another dissenter. Anne Hutchinson had been

Anne Hutchinson, whose religious views were not acceptable to the Puritan rulers of Massachusetts Bay, was brought to trial, found guilty, and forced to leave the colony for Rhode Island.

holding meetings in her home to discuss church sermons. She soon began to preach that people would find God's guidance through an inner light rather than from the sermons of a minister. Such ideas were too much for the Puritan clergy. They also criticized Anne for stepping out of her "proper" place as an obedient Puritan wife and mother and doing things that only men should do. Hutchinson was tried, found guilty, and driven from the colony. She settled in

27

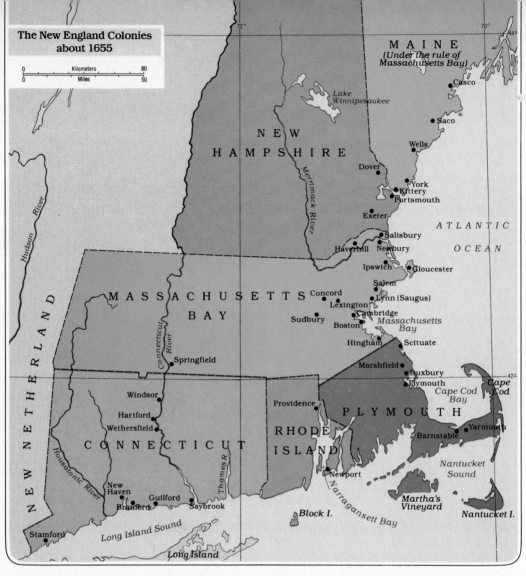

The New England Colonies about 1655

Kilometers 0 — 80
Miles 0 — 50

MAINE
(Under the rule of Massachusetts Bay)

Casco

Lake Winnipesaukee

Saco

NEW
HAMPSHIRE

Wells

Dover

York
Kittery
Portsmouth

Exeter

ATLANTIC

OCEAN

Salisbury

Haverhill Newbury

Ipswich Gloucester

Salem

Concord
Lexington Lynn (Saugus)

MASSACHUSETTS
BAY

Cambridge
Sudbury Boston

Massachusetts
Bay

Hingham Scituate

Springfield

Marshfield Duxbury
Plymouth

Cape Cod
Bay

Cape
Cod

Windsor

Providence

PLYMOUTH

Hartford

Wethersfield

RHODE
ISLAND

Barnstable Yarmouth

CONNECTICUT

Nantucket
Sound

New
Haven

Guilford

Branford Saybrook

Newport

Martha's
Vineyard

Block I.

Nantucket I.

Stamford

Long Island Sound

Long Island

Hudson River

NEW NETHERLAND

Connecticut River

Housatonic River

Thames R.

Narragansett Bay

Merrimack River

The Great Migration of the 1630s saw more than 20,000 people emigrate to New England. Numerous settlements were made. On the map note the boundary between Massachusetts Bay and Plymouth colonies. It was in effect until 1690, when Plymouth became a part of Massachusetts Bay Colony.

Narragansett, not far from Providence. Later, other religious dissenters founded communities in the area.

In 1663 the King of England combined all of these settlements into the colony of Rhode Island. The colony's charter guaranteed religious freedom to all.

Connecticut, New Hampshire, and Maine. Three other New England colonies were formed under quite different circumstances. In 1635 and 1636, whole congregations left Massachusetts for the rich Connecticut Valley. Unlike Williams and Hutchinson, these people had no quarrel with religious leaders in

Massachusetts. They simply were seeking better farmlands.

One congregation, led by the Reverend Thomas Hooker, set up several communities along the Connecticut River. Another Massachusetts group, headed by John Davenport and Theophilus Eaton, started a colony in New Haven. In 1662 Connecticut received a royal charter that set up a government for all settlements in that region.

Other colonists from Massachusetts Bay moved to the north. A number of small fishing villages and fur trading posts already existed there. Massachusetts claimed all this territory, but in 1679 the residents in one part of it got their own charter from the king. They founded the colony of New Hampshire. The other area, known as the Province of Maine, was to remain a part of Massachusetts until 1820.

CHECKUP

1. Why was the Plymouth colony founded?
2. How did the Pilgrims and the Puritans differ? How were they alike?
3. Who were the first colonists in Rhode Island and Connecticut? Why did they move there from Massachusetts?

The Middle and Southern Colonies

In 1624 Captain John Smith, in his history of Virginia, gave the following advice to those who wished to plant colonies in America. Again we have changed the wording slightly:

Do not rely too much on renting, dividing, or selling lands for your own profit. And do not impose too much on ordinary settlers, either by requiring them to pay too much

of their produce into your common storehouse or by any heavy tax for the sake of your immediate profit. But give every man as much land as he can farm freely without limitation, paying you half his produce or upon some other terms. And at the end of five or six years let him have twenty, thirty, or forty, or a hundred acres for every acre he has cultivated, for himself and his heirs forever. . . .

In such a colony a servant who will work can within four or five years live as well there as his master did here in England. For where so much land lies unused in America, a man would be mad to start by buying or renting or paying very much for it.

Smith understood that without the labor of ordinary people, no colony could succeed. He also understood that the promise of free land, more than anything else would bring these people to America.

The wisdom of Smith is clear to us today. Oddly, later colonial promoters did not follow his lead at first. They each had their own goals and their own ideas of how to succeed. Some wanted to keep most of the land for themselves and rule like a king over those who worked it. In the end, however, most of them had to return to John Smith's blueprint for success.

Maryland. The founding of Maryland is a case in point. Sir George Calvert, a wealthy friend of the king, wanted a colony of his own. Owning a colony could bring wealth and status, but Calvert also had another reason. A recent convert to Catholicism, he sought a haven for his fellow Catholics, who were still being persecuted in England.

In 1632 King Charles I gave Calvert a large area of land, naming it Maryland in

In 1752, Baltimore was a fishing and farming village of 100 people. Its name came from the title of Maryland's founders, George and Cecilius Calvert, the first and second Lord Baltimore.

honor of his queen. Calvert would rule and do with the land as he wished. George Calvert died that year, and the grant of land was given to his son Cecilius Calvert, who carried out his father's plan.

That plan was to divide the land into a few great estates, called *baronies.* Each owner would bring over peasants to live under his rule and work the land. Calvert's profits would come from an annual fee, called a *quitrent,* that the land-holders would pay him.

The plan never worked. Calvert did give out a number of large estates, but the owners found it hard to attract people to work them. And for good reason. Why should one go to Maryland

to live as a peasant on someone else's land when Virginia offered free land under the headright system?

To attract more settlers, Calvert adopted the same idea of giving free land to those who paid their own way over. A husband and wife were promised 100 acres (40 ha) each, with 100 acres more for each servant they brought, and 50 acres (20 ha) for each child under six-teen. To anyone who brought over five men between the ages of sixteen and fifty, Calvert gave 2,000 acres (800 ha).

Calvert soon had to give up on his dream of making Maryland a haven for Catholics. Landowners wanted workers too much to be fussy about their religion. They accepted Protestants as well as

30

Catholics. Soon Protestants outnumbered Catholics in the colony.

The two groups quarreled bitterly. To put an end to this trouble, Calvert urged the legislature to pass the Toleration Act in 1649. This law was hardly tolerant by today's standards. It granted religious freedom to all Christians, but atheists, Jews, and other non-Christians who entered Maryland could be put to death. Even with these restrictions, the act was an important step toward greater religious liberty.

With these changes, Maryland began to grow. In many ways it was like Virginia. It was a land of many small farmers and an increasing number of large plantations. And as in Virginia, the major crop was tobacco.

The Carolinas. The story of the Carolina colony was similar to that of Maryland. In 1663 King Charles II gave a large tract of land to eight of his supporters. Like Cecilius Calvert, these men had grand ideas of setting up great estates and running their colony entirely for their own profit. In their plan, they and their descendants would own the land forever and rule its inhabitants.

The Carolina proprietors, like Calvert in Maryland, very quickly had to adopt the advice that John Smith had given forty years earlier. To attract settlers, they offered a headright of 100 acres (40 ha) for each settler, with additional land for each servant who was brought over.

Carolina gradually developed into two separate parts that were quite different from one another. The southern part was a land of large plantations, worked mostly by slave labor. Rice was the main *pay crop* — that is, the crop to sell. The northern region was settled mostly by small farmers. They raised tobacco, and, for the most part, they worked their own land without the use of slaves. Their trade was mainly with Virginia. In 1729, the two sections were split into the separate colonies of South Carolina and North Carolina.

New York. You will recall that New York was originally the Dutch colony of New Netherland. Britain seized it in 1664 in a war with Holland. The English king, Charles II, gave his brother, the Duke of York, the former Dutch colony as well as everything else between Maryland and Canada—excepting Pennsylvania—that had not already been given away. The Duke was to be the absolute ruler and

In its style of architecture and in its general appearance, the city of New York reminded visitors in colonial times that, until 1664, it had been New Amsterdam, a Dutch settlement.

owner of New York. He could set up any kind of government he wanted. He could keep, sell, or rent the unoccupied lands.

A large group of non-English Europeans, mostly Dutch, were already living in New York when the English took it over. Wisely, the Duke put a governor in charge with orders to treat the conquered Dutch with "humanity and gentleness." He did not try to force upon them any change in language, religion, or customs. The colony was large enough for all.

To build up the English population, the governor gave large amounts of land on Long Island to friends. They in return sold the land in small pieces at low prices. New York did not adopt the headright system, and this colony grew more slowly than several of those that did.

New Jersey. One of the first things the Duke of York did when he got his huge land grant was to give a large slice of it to two friends, Lord John Berkeley and Sir George Carteret. That piece, lying between the Hudson and Delaware rivers, became New Jersey. The old colony of New Sweden, as well as settlements of Dutch, Finns, and English, already existed in this area.

Berkeley and Carteret advertised in England for settlers. They also gave part of their land to other proprietors. But like New York, New Jersey grew slowly.

Pennsylvania. The colonizer who best understood the appeal of America to ordinary people was William Penn. Penn was a member of a religious group called the Society of Friends, also known as the Quakers. Penn longed for a place where this much-persecuted group could follow its ways in peace. King Charles II owed a large sum of money to Penn's father. When the father died, Penn persuaded the King in 1681 to pay off the debt with land in America. He called it Pennsylvania, meaning "Penn's woods."

Penn intended his colony to be both a religious haven and a good business. He invited all persons who wanted religious freedom to come. This meant not only Quakers in England but all other groups who were being persecuted in Europe. The colony would govern itself, and there would be complete political and religious freedom.

These promises and a description of the fine soil and climate Penn put into a pamphlet he called *Some Account of the Province of Pennsylvania.* Shrewdly, Penn translated the pamphlet into French, Dutch, and German and distributed it widely in Europe. He aimed his appeal to those who might buy or rent land as well as to those who would come as servants. Each newcomer who paid the way over would receive 50 acres (20 ha) free. One could buy larger lots very cheaply—5,000 acres (2,000 ha) for just 100 pounds. Small plots could be rented for as little as a penny an acre. Indentured servants were promised 50 acres on completion of their service.

How did Penn expect to make his colony profitable? Francis Pastorius, who was a German minister, led one of the early groups that settled in Pennsylvania. In a report home, he explained:

Our Governor, William Penn, intends to establish and encourage the growing and manufactory of woolens; to introduce the cultivation of the vine, for which this country is peculiarly adapted, so that our Company had better send us a quantity of

Sidelights on History

Indentured Servants

What would you do if you wanted to come to America from England to settle and did not have the money to pay the passage? You would have done what thousands of settlers like Robert, below, did: you would sign on as an indentured servant. This meant signing a contract, or an indenture, promising to work for a number of years to repay the passage money. Here is a copy of Robert's indenture, in 1619.

> The said Robert does hereby [contract] faithfully to serve the said Sir William, Richard, George and John for three years from the day of his landing [in] Virginia, there to be employed in the lawful and reasonable works and labors . . . and to be obedient to such governors . . . as they shall from time to time appoint and set over him. In consideration thereof, the said Sir William, Richard, George and John do covenant to transport him . . . with all convenient speed into the said land of Virginia at their costs and charges . . . and to maintain him with [food and clothing] . . . and in the end of the said term to make him a free man . . . and to grant said Robert thirty acres of land.

During Robert's three-year term of service, he was not a free man. He could work only for his masters or anyone they asked him to work for. Robert was not free to leave the place where he was employed, nor could he marry without the consent of his masters. In return for his labor, as noted, his masters were to pay his transportation to Virginia and to provide him with food and clothing.

After Robert had served his three years, he would become a free man and would be released from his contract. He would be given what were known as "freedom dues"—in this case, 30 acres (12 ha)—to allow him to set himself up as an independent farmer.

Both men and women came over as indentured servants. Some found their masters treated them kindly; others were treated cruelly. But whether the treatment was kind or cruel, many persons like Robert took this opportunity to get to America.

In exchange for passage to America, many Europeans bound themselves to labor for a definite period, often three to five years. They often served as farm workers, especially in the Middle Colonies.

The Quakers, shown here at one of their meetings, were among Pennsylvania's first settlers.

wine-barrels and vats of various sorts, also all kinds of farming and gardening implements. . . .

The land that Pastorius bought lay north of Philadelphia. Others bought land farther west, and Pennsylvania prospered.

Delaware. The history of Delaware is closely connected with that of Pennsylvania. The colony had passed through the hands of the Swedes and Dutch before the English took it over along with New York in 1664. In 1682 Delaware was granted to William Penn along with Pennsylvania. For the next 22 years, the two colonies had the same governor and legislature. After 1704, Delaware was allowed its own legislature.

Most of the settlers were small farmers, who worked their land without either indentured servants or slaves. A policy of religious toleration helped the small colony to grow rapidly.

Georgia. Georgia was the last of the thirteen colonies to be settled. Although the main reasons for its founding were different from those for all the other colonies, Georgia illustrates the idea of America as opportunity as much as they.

In England in the 1700s, persons who could not pay their debts were put in jail. They stayed there until family or friends paid those debts or until they somehow worked their way out. Many never did, and died in jail.

James Oglethorpe, an English reformer and soldier, was moved by their condition. One of his own close friends had died in debtor's prison. Oglethorpe came up with the idea of a colony where such prisoners could get a new start in life. He also pointed out to the king that the colony might serve as a military barrier against the Spanish, who then owned Florida. In 1732 the King gave Oglethorpe and twenty trustees a charter. The following year, the first group of settlers arrived in Georgia, the colony that gave the unfortunate a second chance.

During its first 20 years, Georgia grew slowly. Few were attracted to a colony where they might have to face military attacks by the Spanish as well as malaria. While everyone was given 50 acres (20 ha) free and tools, no one was allowed to own more. Slavery was also prohibited. Contrary to Oglethorpe's plans, the majority of early settlers were neither debtors nor English. A large number came from Austria, Switzerland, and Germany.

After 1752, slavery was allowed, and settlers were permitted to acquire more than 50 acres. This gave rise to plantations, on which were grown rice and indigo, a plant from which was made a blue dye for coloring cloth. But by 1760 Georgia's population was still only 9,000, a third of whom were slaves. It remained the smallest of the thirteen colonies as measured by population.

A babble of languages. Until about 1700, although there were pockets of non-English people here and there, colonial society was mainly English. England was the main source of immigration, and English was spoken nearly everywhere.

Beginning in the 1700s, that sameness ended. The New England colonies remained mainly English all through the colonial period. But by 1776, in the colonies from New York south, half the population was non-English. Germans, Scots, Scotch-Irish, Swiss, Africans, and French had come streaming into America, many as indentured servants. Soon a babble of languages was heard up and down the land.

For most of these people, as for the English, America meant opportunity and free or cheap land. But for many, it was not simply a wish to do something better that led them to emigrate from the Old World. It was the desperate need to leave something worse.

We know this because of the years in which each group of immigrants arrived. Immigrants came to America in a series of waves between 1700 and 1776. Each wave came at a time of serious problems for that group in its homeland. Sometimes the problems were economic, like famine. Sometimes there was political persecution, and sometimes religious. Often several of these problems occurred at once.

The Scotch-Irish. An example of a people beset by several problems was the Scotch-Irish. These people were Scots whom the British king moved to northern Ireland to keep down the restless Irish in the early 1600s. The Scotch-

Irish were Presbyterians in religion. They soon felt discriminated against by the Anglican church. English landlords also caused resentment by raising the rents. On the heels of this came crop failures in 1716 and 1717. In the next fifty years, 250,000 Scotch-Irish left for America. Most of them settled in the middle and southern colonies.

The story was similar in other lands. Skilled workers left Switzerland for America when unemployment struck in the early 1730s. From France came the Huguenots—Protestants persecuted in a Catholic land. From Ireland came Catholics—persecuted by their Protestant English rulers. And from the many German provinces came thousands who were fleeing religious persecution, frequent wars, and hard times.

The stamp of England. Little more than a hundred years after its first shaky settlement at Jamestown, the English firmly controlled the Atlantic coast of North America from Canada to Georgia. They also owned sugar-rich islands in the Caribbean Sea. Even though the population had come from many lands, the stamp of England was on most of North America. English was the language of the government and of two thirds of the people. Settlers lived under the laws of England, and of local governments, modeled on England's. They used goods bought from England, and they accepted English institutions.

This did not mean, however, that life in the colonies was no different from life in England. Most colonists had originally planned to reproduce their European ways of life in the New World setting, and to some extent, they succeeded. But the special conditions in America brought about changes from the beginning. In the next chapter, you will look at a few of those changes.

CHECKUP

1. What thing did the founders of the colonies soon find was most important in attracting settlers?
2. How did Calvert, Penn, and Oglethorpe differ in their approaches to setting up colonies?
3. How did the Old World backgrounds of settlers in the middle and southern colonies differ from the backgrounds of those in the New England colonies?

Key Facts from Chapter 2

1. The first permanent English colony in America was established at Jamestown, Virginia, in 1607.
2. The desire to worship in their own way and to own land were among the reasons why Europeans settled in America in colonial times.
3. The Maryland Toleration Act of 1649 was, despite limitations, an important step toward religious liberty.
4. Until about 1700, colonial society was mostly English; after that time, there were increasing numbers of other nationalities.

★ REVIEWING THE CHAPTER ★

People, Places, and Events

Jamestown *P. 19*

John Smith *P. 19*

Mayflower *P. 24*

Plymouth colony *P. 24*

Massachusetts Bay Colony *P. 25*

John Winthrop *P. 25*

Roger Williams *P. 27*

Anne Hutchinson *P. 27*

Sir George Calvert *P. 29*

Toleration Act, 1649 *P. 31*

Lord John Berkeley *P. 32*

Sir George Carteret *P. 32*

William Penn *P. 32*

James Oglethorpe *P. 35*

Review Questions

1. Explain why early Jamestown seemed destined to fail. Why didn't it fail? *P. 19*

2. Who were the Puritans? What was the difference between a Puritan and a Separatist? *P. 23*

3. Which two settlements united to become the colony of Massachusetts? Explain how Massachusetts was governed. *Pp. 25–26*

4. Why did Calvert have to give up his dream of making Maryland a refuge for Catholics? *Pp. 30–31*

5. How did the economic growth of the Carolina colony cause it to develop into two separate parts? *P. 31*

6. Why was William Penn so successful in founding Pennsylvania? *P. 32*

7. How does the founding of Georgia illustrate the idea of America as a land of opportunity? *P. 34*

8. Why did people from countries other than England settle in the English colonies? *P. 35*

Chapter Test

Complete the chart on the English colonies by filling in each blank space with the correct answer. Write your answers on a separate piece of paper.

Name of colony	Founder or leader	Reason for settlement
1. _____	John Smith	Profit
2. _____	Pilgrims	Religious freedom
3. Massachusetts Bay	_____	Religious freedom
4. Rhode Island	_____	Religious freedom
5. Maryland	Calvert	_____
6. _____	Duke of York	Profit
7. New Jersey	_____	Profit
8. Pennsylvania	William Penn	_____
9. _____	William Penn	Religious freedom, profit
10. Georgia	_____	Refuge for debtors

REALIZING THE PROMISE

IN VIRGINIA, land free and labor scarce
In England, land scarce and labor plenty

So went two lines of an English poem of 1647. Those two lines explain much about colonial America. You have already seen the connection between them and the decision of thousands to leave England for America. And you will remember how they are related to both indentured service and slavery. In this chapter you will see how these two lines also help explain many other things— religion and government in the English colonies, the shape of the colonial economy, the position of workers, and the position of women.

Religion and Government

The seventeenth and eighteenth centuries were an age of strong religious beliefs and intolerance. Even those who sought religious freedom for themselves were very quick to deny it to others. You will recall how the Puritans of Massachusetts dealt with dissenters, such as Roger Williams and Anne Hutchinson. They also persecuted Quakers, and even condemned them to death for not following Puritan laws. Needless to say, Catholics and Jews were few in Massachusetts for many years.

Freedom of religion. But the future did not belong to intolerant people like the Puritans. It belonged instead to people like Roger Williams and William Penn who practiced freedom of religion in their colonies.

Religious toleration did not come all at once in America. It grew gradually, and even by the time of the American Revolution it was not complete. Toleration gained for two reasons. One was that people like Penn sincerely believed in religious freedom and promoted it. The second was the ever important fact of labor shortage in America. Colonizers quickly discovered that a promise of religious freedom increased their chances of attracting settlers. You will recall that when Catholic landowners in Maryland needed people to work the land, they gladly settled for Protestant farmers. Three years after the founding of Carolina, the proprietors included the following as the first point in their advertisement for settlers: "Full and free liberty of conscience is granted to all, so that no man is to be molested or questioned concerning matters of religious concern." The owners of New Jersey also assured everyone of freedom of conscience.

Thus in several colonies there were people of many religions. A traveler to Philadelphia in the eighteenth century was surprised at the number of different religions he found in the tavern where he stayed. At his table sat "Roman Catholics, Church men, Presbyterians, Quakers, Newlightmen, Methodists, Seventh Day men, Moravians, Anabaptists, and one Jew." In New York City in the 1750s, one observer counted two Anglican churches, two Lutheran, and one Quaker meetinghouse. A similar distribution existed in the neighboring colony of New Jersey.

Puritanism

John Winthrop, governor of Massachusetts Bay, symbolized the spirit of Puritanism that resulted in New England's successful settlement. Like most Puritans, he came to America to practice his own idea of a "Godly life." What Winthrop hoped to do was to establish a much more perfect Christian community than England had ever known. If the Puritans of New England succeeded, then, Winthrop believed, the inhabitants of Old England would follow their example. For this reason he wrote, just before landing in Massachusetts in 1630, that his colony would be "as a City set on a Hill, the eyes of all people . . . upon us."

What Winthrop and the other Puritans did in Massachusetts influenced all of American history. As one great scholar wrote, "Without some understanding of Puritanism . . . there is no understanding of America." When the descendants of New England settlers migrated westward, they carried Puritan attitudes with them clear across the continent.

What were these Puritan traits, and how have they influenced America? The Puritans believed first of all in the idea of a mission in history. Just as the Puritans believed Massachusetts should become a "City set on a Hill," so most Americans have believed their country has some larger role to play in human history and that it should set an exam-

ple for other nations. Puritans believed deeply in religion and morality. Many historians feel that America's religious history and moral attitudes as a people are connected to what happened in early New England. The Puritans had a great respect for learning. The American emphasis on education, scholars feel, can be traced back to these seventeenth-century origins. In their business life, the Puritans believed in hard work, constant activity, and thrift. Many Americans in the nineteenth and twentieth centuries have shared a belief in these same values. Finally, the Puritans believed in constitutionalism and limited government—ideals that Americans have cherished.

Thus, America's cultural heritage and national character may be said to have their roots in the Puritan tradition of John Winthrop and other founders of New England.

The *New England Primer*, reflecting Puritan values, was long used in American schools.

The Great Awakening. In the 1730s and 1740s, a series of great religious revivals swept the colonies. Called the Great Awakening, the revivals split many Protestant churches in two. The religious meetings attracted thousands of people from the lower classes of society. One effect was to spread democratic ideas in religion.

All of this does not mean that religious toleration was complete. You will recall that the Toleration Act of 1649 in Maryland was not extremely tolerant. In many colonies, Catholics and Jews could not hold office, and often could not vote. In some, however, such barriers were dropped in practice. Even with the restrictions that remained, there was greater religious freedom in colonial America than in England, and much greater freedom than in most other parts of Europe.

A role in government. In the same pamphlet in which they promised religious liberty to settlers, the founders of Carolina made another promise to induce people to move there.

> A governor and council are to be appointed among the settlers, to carry out the laws of the assembly, but the governor *is to rule but three years, and then learn to obey.* The governor has no power to lay any tax or to make or repeal any law without the consent of the settlers in their assembly. . . The settlers are to choose annually from among themselves a certain number of men, apportioned as they wish, to constitute with the governor and his council the general assembly, which shall have the sole power of making laws and laying taxes for the common good when need shall require.

The authors of this promise in 1666 were the same lord proprietors who originally planned for Carolina to be ruled by a hereditary aristocracy. It is safe to assume, therefore, that they thought it was either desirable or necessary to promise settlers a role in government.

By the time the founders of Carolina made this promise, a number of colonies already had assemblies, or legislatures. Virginia was the first. The Virginia company's charter of 1606 said that the settlers would have the same liberties "as if they had been living and born in England." In its early years, however, the company had treated the settlers as employees. They had no say at all in the running of the colony.

To attract settlers, the company made several important changes in 1618. The most important, you will recall, had to do with land. Another change gave settlers the right to elect representatives to an assembly. Along with the governor and his council, this body would make laws for the colony. The House of Burgesses, as the assembly was called, met for the first time in 1619. It was the first representative legislature in the English colonies.

There had been an assembly in the Massachusetts Bay Colony since 1634. Five years later Connecticut drew up a constitution calling for the election of a governor and a two-house legislature. Rhode Island followed suit in 1647. Even in Maryland, where Calvert had planned to rule like a lord, an elected legislature was soon set up.

Why legislatures developed. Why did legislatures develop in Britain's North American colonies? The reasons are

How the Colonies
Were First Governed

The thirteen original colonies represented three different kinds of government—proprietary, royal, and corporate. Each was similar in that it had a governor, a legislature, and some form of court system. The chief difference in the three types of colonial government lay in the method of selecting a governor. In the proprietary colonies the governor was selected by the proprietor, with the approval of the king. In the royal colonies he was appointed by the king alone. And in the corporate colonies the governor was elected directly or indirectly by the voters.

Maryland was a prime example of a proprietary colony. Control of the colony lay in the hands of the proprietor, Lord Baltimore, who had the power to govern and held title to the land both by virtue of a charter granted by the king. Lord Baltimore was to Maryland what the English king was to England. Baltimore appointed the governor and delegated to him the power to govern. Many colonies, like the Carolinas, began as proprietary colonies but then became royal colonies. By the end of the colonial period, only three colonies—Maryland, Pennsylvania, and Delaware—remained proprietary colonies.

In the royal colonies, the king appointed the governor and was able thereby to keep closer control. Several colonies, like Massachusetts Bay, started out as charter provinces, in which a charter to colonize was granted to a private company. Others, like New Jersey, were proprietary colonies for a time. But the trend after the 1680s was toward changing proprietary and charter colonies into royal colonies. By the end of the colonial period, eight of the provinces were royal colonies: New Hampshire, Massachusetts, New York, New Jersey, Virginia, North Carolina, South Carolina, and Georgia.

Corporate colonies were those with the greatest degree of self-rule. They were operated under a charter held by the colonists. Only two of the thirteen colonies—Rhode Island and Connecticut—were corporate colonies.

As Maryland's proprietor, Cecilius Calvert, the second Lord Baltimore, had far-reaching powers under a charter granted by the English king.

42

slightly different for each colony, but in general they boil down to two. First, English people were used to the idea that laws should be made by an elected legislature. One of the "rights of Englishmen" was the right to have their laws, especially tax laws, made by a body that represented them. It was natural that English settlers in North America would want the same rights. In their minds they were simply English people who happened to be living overseas.

The second reason was a very practical one. The American colonies were 3,000 miles (4,800 km) from England. Conditions in the colonies were different from those in England. Parliament, sitting in London, could not understand the problems of a wilderness settlement in Virginia or New England and make wise laws to deal with them.

Council and assembly. In some colonies, such as Carolina and Virginia, promoters freely gave settlers the right to have a legislature. In others, the right was won only after a long struggle. But by 1700, every colony had its own legislature. Most legislatures were made up of two houses. One was generally called the *council,* or *governor's council.* Its members were usually appointed by the governor, with the king's approval. The governor appointed men who would support him and the interests of the empire as a whole.

In most colonies the council was made up of the wealthiest and most important people. Often it was controlled by a few families. In Virginia, for example, almost a third of all the councillors appointed between 1680 and 1775 came from just nine families. In South Carolina, a fourth of the councillors between 1729 and 1775 came from just seven families. In New York, twenty-five of the twenty-eight appointed between 1750 and 1776 came from great landowning families.

The other house was usually called the *assembly.* Its members were elected by the colonists. The assembly had a part in making all laws. Its most important power was the power to lay taxes. No tax could be passed without its consent.

The governor was appointed either by the king or the proprietors. In only two colonies, Connecticut and Rhode Island, was he elected. But in all colonies the governor had sweeping powers. He had the right to call the legislature to meet, and he could also order it to adjourn. He could *veto,* or disapprove, laws passed by the assembly. He also could appoint many other officials in the colony, and often could make large gifts of land to favorites. The governor used both the appointments and the gifts to build up support for himself.

The right to vote. Colonists voted for their representatives to the assembly, but not all colonists had the right to vote. Voters had to be white, male, twenty-one or over, and had to own a certain amount of property. At one time or another, Catholics were not allowed to vote in five of the colonies, and Jews were not allowed to vote in four. With few exceptions, women could not vote. Indians and blacks could not vote at all.

Still, a very large number of colonists had the right to vote. Land was so cheap that most colonists could meet the property requirement. In every colony, at least 50 percent of the white adult males could vote. In Massachusetts, between

80 and 90 percent could. Governor Thomas Hutchinson, who favored limiting the right to vote, once said in disgust that in Massachusetts "everything in the shape of a man could vote."

Assembly versus governor. The assembly, or lower house, spoke for the interests of the colonists who elected its members. The governor and council, on the other hand, spoke for the interests of the king and Parliament. Often these two interests came into conflict. As a result, in many colonies there were struggles between assembly and governor.

These struggles pointed up the fact that the colonists lived under two sets of laws. One came from their own legislatures. The other was the laws and rules that Parliament made for them. Such laws governed trade, for example. During the first half of the 1600s, Parliament didn't make many laws for the colonies. Later, when it did make laws, it did very little to enforce them. So for most of the colonial period, the colonies had a great deal of freedom in running their own affairs.

When an argument between an assembly and a governor did take place, it usually concerned the right of self-government. In such a dispute, the chief weapon an assembly had was control over the spending of the colony's tax money. In many colonies, the assembly also paid the governor's salary. On a few occasions an assembly tried to reduce the governor's salary or even withhold it altogether, in order to bring him into line. These conflicts between assembly and governor became more frequent and more serious in the years just before the American Revolution.

44

CHECKUP

1. Why, as time went on, did religious toleration increase in the colonies?
2. Why did legislatures develop in the colonies? How did the two houses of most legislatures differ?
3. Who were the voters in the colonies? Who could not vote?

The Colonial Economy

Nine tenths of all Americans farmed for a living. True to the promise of America, the large majority of them owned their own land, either through purchase or headright. There was another very large class of small farm owners, however, who did not get their land in either of those ways. These persons were called *squatters*. They simply moved out to the edge of settlement, or the frontier, cleared a piece of land, and farmed it without buying it or otherwise getting a legal claim to it. Some of these frontier people were new immigrants who had headed straight for the backcountry. Some were sons and daughters of farmers from older communities where the best lands were already taken. And some were simply restless people, always moving on—people who felt crowded if there was another farmhouse in sight of their own dwelling.

Squatters lived in the backcountry of every colony. In Pennsylvania alone there were about 100,000 squatters by 1726. Having settled and improved the land, squatters felt it was rightfully theirs. Often, in time, it did become theirs. But in the meantime, squatting led to fights and lawsuits between those who lived on the land and those who legally owned it.

Geographic mobility. Benjamin Rush, a Philadelphia doctor, traveled through Pennsylvania's backcountry in the eighteenth century. Describing the squatter he wrote: "The first settler in the woods is generally a man who has outlived his credit or fortune in the [settled] parts of the state." Rush was pointing out something important about life in America. That is the ease and freedom with which people moved from place to place. It was far different in European countries, where land was scarce. There most people remained fixed in one place all their lives.

The ability to move from place to place is called *geographic mobility.* A society in which it is easy to move about, as it was in colonial America, is said to be geographically mobile. Geographic mobility is closely connected to opportunity. Do you see how? Rush's description gives you a strong clue.

Farming in the South. Because of climate and geography, farming differed from one part of the country to another. The South was a region mainly of large plantations and small farms. Plantations sometimes ranged from 1,000 to 6,000 acres (400 to 2,400 ha), and sometimes more. They specialized in raising pay crops. In Maryland, Virginia, and North Carolina, the pay crop was tobacco. Rice and indigo were the pay crops of South Carolina and Georgia. Until the 1680s, much of the work on these plantations was done by white indentured servants. After that date, it was performed more and more by black slaves.

Most plantations were located along the South's many rivers. Each had its own dock. Tobacco and other crops could be loaded directly onto the ships that would carry them to England and other lands.

Large plantations provided for almost all their own needs. George Washington's Mount Vernon is a good example. To feed his slaves, Washington raised wheat, cattle, and hogs, and set up nets in the Potomac River to catch fish. Slave blacksmiths, carpenters, and bricklayers made all the materials for the buildings. Cider and liquor were stored in barrels made on the plantation. Wheat was ground into flour in a mill on the plantation. There was also a weaving shed, where wool and flax, a plant fiber, were turned into material for clothing for the slaves.

Virginia planters oversee the loading of casks of tobacco on a ship bound for England. The rich soil and the long growing season in Virginia made tobacco farming a profitable activity.

Plantation owners like Washington dominated southern life, but there were possibly nine or ten times more small farm owners. Most southern farms were between 100 and 200 acres (40 and 80 ha); some were smaller. Many were acquired through headrights. Some were located between the large plantations, near the coastal areas. Others were further inland, along the backcountry.

Most small farmers raised enough food for their own needs and also raised a small pay crop besides. Usually that crop was tobacco. Small farmers probably raised more than half the tobacco grown in the South. They sold or exchanged it for farming tools, salt, and other needed items. Usually they farmed the land themselves, without the help of slaves or indentured servants.

Farming in the North. Except for a few large estates, the lands in New England and the middle colonies were owned and worked by small farmers. In New England, where the soil was rocky and the growing season short, farming was less profitable than it was elsewhere. Most New England farms were also smaller, running between 70 and 100 acres (28 and 40 ha). The main crop was corn, which was eaten by both humans and animals.

The labor force was the family. Husbands, wives, and children—and here and there an occasional hired hand—worked together to gain a living from the sometimes unwilling soil. On farms this small, there was little demand for indentured servants. Most farm families succeeded in raising enough for their own needs, with a little left over for sale. In the evenings family members made

their own household furnishings and farming tools.

In contrast to New England, the soil and climate of the middle colonies—New York, New Jersey, and Pennsylvania—were ideal for farming. Farms in this region were larger than in New England, generally between 150 and 200 acres (60 and 80 ha). The following account by one farmer describes farming in the middle colonies.

My farm gave me and my whole family a good living on the products of it; and left me, one year, with . . . one hundred and fifty silver dollars, for I never spent more than ten dollars a year, which went for salt, nails, and the like. Nothing to wear, eat, or drink, was purchased, as my farm provided all. With this saving, I put money to interest, bought cattle, fatted and sold them, and made great profit.

Some of the wheat and corn that farmers like this one grew for sale fed residents of cities, such as Philadelphia and New York. Because England grew enough wheat and corn for its own needs, the rest of it was shipped to the West Indies and to countries in southern Europe. Since the middle colonies were the main producers of food for export, they came to be known as the "bread colonies."

Because farms in the middle colonies were large, there was a great need for labor. Farmers in this region relied heavily on indentured servants. Many came voluntarily, happy to sell several years of their labor for passage to America. Others did not come voluntarily. Some of those were orphan children sent by the English government, which did not wish to support them. Others were children sent by parents who were

New England fishermen lay their catch out to dry. Dried fish was a major article in colonial trade.

too poor to raise them. British judges sometimes sentenced convicts to forced labor in America. All told, somewhere between 60 percent and 75 percent of white immigrants before the Revolution were indentured servants. The majority of these wound up in Pennsylvania and the other middle colonies.

In addition, farm owners hired workers for wages. How did such hired workers fare? The following account by one farm owner tells us something about their condition.

> As to labor and laborers . . . you must give them what they ask: three shillings per day in common wages and five or six shillings in harvest. They must be at your table and feed . . . on the best you have.

Do you see any connection between this farmer's complaint and the two lines of the old English poem at the beginning of this chapter?

Trade and commerce. While more than 90 percent of the people lived on farms or in farming villages, 10 percent did not. The rise of cities added another side to the opportunity of America. For one thing, the trade and commerce of the cities was next only to farming in importance in the colonial economy. For another, the cities provided a good living for skilled and unskilled workers, merchants, and seamen.

Much of the commerce was among the thirteen colonies themselves. Fish and meat from New England and wheat, flour, and iron goods from the middle colonies were shipped to the plantations of the South. Payment was made either in cash or in crops—tobacco or rice—that were then sold in other markets, either in the North or in Europe.

Colonial merchants carried on an active trade with the West Indies and southern Europe. West Indian planters exchanged sugar, molasses, and gold and silver coins for the fish, meat, and grains they needed to feed their slaves. The coins were especially welcome because the American colonies were always short of currency. Fish were also in great demand in the Catholic countries of southern Europe, where Catholics were forbidden to eat meat on Fridays and various holy days. Northern merchants also shipped grain, meat, and lumber to these countries. In payment, they received wine, and fruits, and sometimes silver and gold coins.

England was one of America's main markets. Although England did not need the products of northern farms and fisheries, northern merchants had an active trade carrying the South's rice and tobacco to England. They also carried to that country sugar and molasses they had received in the West Indies. These goods were exchanged for such manufactured goods as cloth, furniture, and finished iron products.

You may have noticed that some of the trade of the colonists was triangular, or three-cornered. That is, it involved northern ports, southern ports, and the West Indies; or northern ports, the West Indies, and England. There was another triangular trade in which a few colonial merchants were involved. That was the slave trade. A ship captain might carry rum from his home port of Bristol or Newport, Rhode Island, to the Guinea Coast of Africa. There he exchanged the rum for slaves, at the rate of about 100 gallons (380 liters) for a young male. With his human cargo, the captain set sail for the West Indies, where he sold the slaves for money and molasses. From there it was home to Rhode Island. In dozens of small distilleries the molasses was made into rum, which would be taken by other ships to Africa, and so on.

Jobs for all. The shipping and shipbuilding industries provided numerous jobs. In 1760, between 300 and 400 ships were built in New England towns. That meant a demand for shipbuilders and carpenters, ropemakers and sailmakers, captains and sailors. It also meant work for unskilled dockworkers who loaded and unloaded ships.

As city populations grew, so did the demand for skilled workers of all kinds. Many left crowded English cities for American towns, where their skills as shoemakers, bakers, and printers brought higher wages. Occasionally a town even offered skilled workers land, a house, and a guaranteed amount of work if they would settle there. Wages paid to skilled and unskilled workers in America were two to three times higher than those paid in England. Once again, the two lines of the poem on page 39 give you the reason.

Other colonists made a living from what a generous Nature gave. The sea provided a living for New England fishermen. Forests yielded lumber and such forest products as pitch, tar and turpentine, used by shipbuilders in

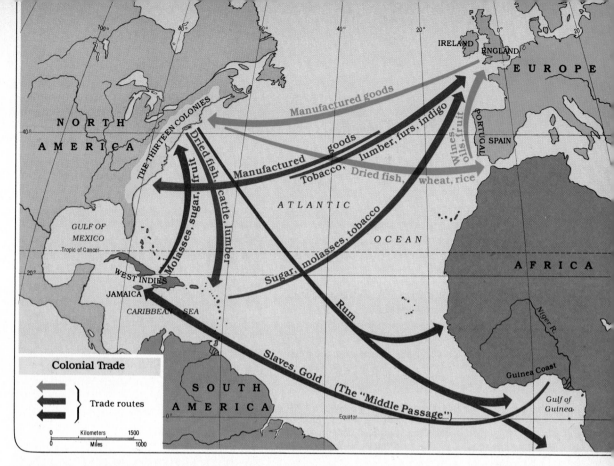

Foreign trade during America's colonial period consisted largely of the export of raw materials and the import of manufactured goods. Much of this trade was carried on with England. However, in order to make the best use of their sailing ships, owners worked out a pattern of triangular trade routes. How many examples of triangular routes can you trace out on the map above?

England and America. And in the backcountry of all the colonies, fur trapping and trading with Indians became an important business.

Finally, small manufacturing industries developed in several colonies. The making of rum from molasses was centered in a number of New England port cities, especially in Rhode Island. In several of the middle colonies, iron and iron products, such as kettles, nails, and stoves, were manufactured in dozens of small foundries.

A shortage of women. One of the important facts of life in America was the shortage of women in many of the colonies. When a shipload of 90 young women seeking mates arrived in Jamestown in 1619, it was a major event. As late as the mid-1600s, men outnumbered women in Virginia by six to one. Of the 10,000 indentured servants who left for America from one English port between about 1650 and 1680, males outnumbered females by more than three to one. Single women were generally reluctant

49

to leave England for the American wilderness. Even in New England, where typically whole families migrated from England, males were in a three to two majority.

Promoters made special efforts, therefore, to attract women to the colonies. The tasks they performed were essential to the survival of the new settlements. The proprietors of Carolina included the following paragraph in their advertising pamphlet.

If any maids or single women desire to go over to Carolina, they will think themselves in the Golden Age, when men paid dowries for their wives, for if they are only civil and under fifty years of age, some honest man or other will purchase them for their wives.

Women in colonial America not only were skilled in making clothing and in doing other kinds of work in their homes but also performed ably in other jobs vital to the colonial economy.

The writer's aim was to attract women to America. Without realizing it, he is also telling us a great deal about the position of women in England in the seventeenth century. See how much you can learn about women's status there from that paragraph.

Women's rights. Gradually the ratio of women to men improved. By the time of the Revolution, women made up nearly half the population. Partly because of the shortage of women in the colonies, their position was better than in England. Not that they had equal rights with men. Women could not vote. A wife had few legal rights over her children. The law gave husbands almost absolute power over their wives. And once women married, any property they owned passed to their husbands. For example, a wealthy Virginian named Daniel Custis died, leaving a large fortune to his widow Martha, and another large sum to their daughter "Patsy." When Martha married a young man named George Washington some years later, control of Martha's fortune passed to him. He also gained custody of the money left to Martha's daughter when the latter died shortly after Martha married George. Thus George Washington, already comfortable, was on his way to becoming one of the wealthiest men in America.

Still, women's property rights were better protected in America than in England. It became the custom that a husband could not sell or give away his wife's property without her consent. Single women and widows could own property of all kinds, could sue or be sued in colonial courts, and could run their own businesses.

Husbands had a higher status, but wives were by no means considered to be servants. One husband, who told his wife that "she was none of his wife, she was but his servant," was reported by his neighbors and fined forty shillings. Such an event was not an everyday occurrence, and by today's standards it seems a minor advance for women. At the time, however, it was an important step forward.

Women and the economy. A number of women owned and ran their own farms and business. Newspaper ads of the time show that there were women silversmiths, blacksmiths, gunsmiths, shoemakers, shipbuilders, printers, eyeglass makers and even undertakers. Many women sold goods that they sewed, ran taverns, and owned shops in which everything from hardware to foods and wines were sold. Many were widows who took over their husband's businesses or women who never married. A great many other women whose identities are lost to history worked in such trades alongside their husbands. Several large planters in the South were women, and women often helped manage their fathers' and husbands' plantations.

In colonial America almost all women married, and at an early age. Large families were the rule, for children were considered to be an advantage, helping with farm work. Thus the population

By the mid-1700s, about 1,300,000 people lived in the thirteen English colonies. To the south was Spanish Florida, and to the north lay Canada, under French control until 1763. Note that several of the colonies had more than one capital.

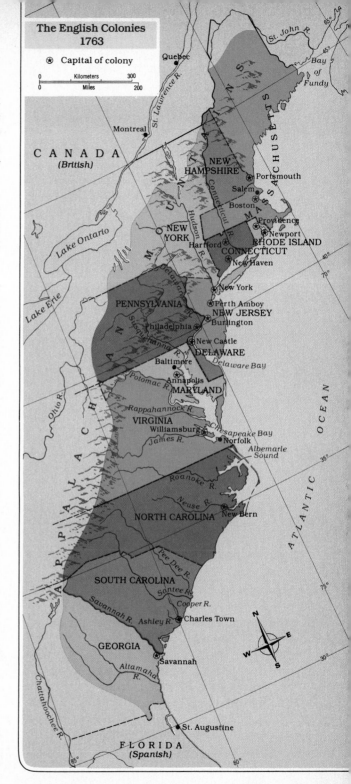

The English Colonies 1763

⊛ Capital of colony

51

doubled every generation. However, childbearing took its toll, and many women died young.

By far most women were members of farm families. The farm family was an economic unit, with defined jobs for each member. For women, these included the usual household tasks of cooking, spinning, weaving cloth, and a number of farming chores as well. Most women, however—always excepting slaves—did not work in the fields except at harvest time. These tasks were absolutely essential for the survival and well-being of the colonial family. Colonial males understood that, but few acknowledged it in the way one gentleman did in his diary of 1778.

My wife's conduct verifies that old saying that "women's work is never done." [Among the tasks she performs are] getting prepared in the kitchen, baking our bread and pies, meat, etc. . . . cutting and drying apples . . . making of cider without tools . . . seeing all our washing done, and her fine clothes and my shirts, which are all smoothed by her . . . her making of twenty large cheeses, and that from one cow, and daily using milk and cream, besides her sewing, knitting, etc.

The closer to the frontier, the more blurred was the line between male and female roles. Women there had to know how to handle a plow and a rifle as well as a spinning wheel.

By no stretch of the imagination, however, can it be said that American conditions changed traditional male-female roles or greatly changed male-dominated institutions in the colonial era. This song of the American frontier suggests a woman's view of how much, or little, change had taken place:

The heart is the fortune of all womankind,
They're always controlled, they're always confined.
Controlled by their families until they are wives,
Then slaves to their husbands the rest of their lives.

The best "poor man's country." Despite America's abundance, colonial society had its poor in both countryside and city. Among them were farmers who had been unlucky enough to have bought poor land. And while some farm workers earned as much as the one the farmer complained about on page 47, others had to scrape for a living.

The poor were more noticeable in cities and towns than on farms. When trade and business declined, many of the unskilled went without work. Others fared poorly also. The fact that colonial cities and towns raised taxes for "poor relief" and built almshouses—homes for the poor—tells us that the penniless existed.

In the late 1750s, Boston, a city of 16,000, reported that "the poor supported either wholly or in part by the town . . . will amount to the number of about 1,000." In 1775 the city of Philadelphia was providing poor relief to 700 of its 35,000 people. These numbers do not include others who received help from churches or private groups. In at least one city there was an official whose job it was to discourage the poor from settling there.

Once again, however, our standard of comparison must be the England of that day. One third of England's population lived in poverty. Its cities were filled with beggars, who roamed the streets and found shelter in cellars and back alleys.

52

The Zenger Case

The case of John Peter Zenger, a printer, is a landmark in the struggle for freedom of the press. Born in Germany, Zenger came to America as a youth and was apprenticed at the age of fourteen to a printer. After learning the printing trade, he set up his own shop. In time he became the publisher of a newspaper, *The New-York Weekly Journal.*

In 1735 Zenger was brought to trial, charged with printing newspaper articles criticizing William Cosby, the royal governor of New York. Zenger was accused of criminal libel. (Libel is the publishing of material that damages someone's reputation.) Under English law, all that had to be proved to establish guilt was that Zenger's newspaper had printed the material damaging to Governor Cosby.

In the trial, Andrew Hamilton, Zenger's lawyer, frankly admitted that Zenger had printed the material that damaged the governor's reputation. But then Hamilton introduced a new idea. He declared that the statements printed in Zenger's newspaper were true. Because they were true, said Hamilton, and because men should be free "to complain when they are hurt," this was *not* a crime. The jury agreed with Hamilton's argument and found Zenger not guilty.

The verdict did not change the law. However, it did encourage newspaper writers to criticize those in authority—when the criticism was true. The Zenger case gave a great boost to the idea of freedom of the press.

This hand press was used in the shop where Benjamin Franklin learned the printing trade.

Nowhere in white colonial America did such conditions exist.

Touring England and Scotland in 1772, Benjamin Franklin noted the great wealth of a few and the poverty of the many.

> . . . the bulk of the people [are] tenants, extremely poor, living in the most sordid wretchedness, in dirty hovels of mud and straw, and clothed only in rags.

Franklin went on to compare that scene to America.

> I thought often of the happiness of New England where every man . . . had a vote in public affairs, lives in a tidy warm house, has plenty of good food and fuel, with whole clothes from head to feet, [made perhaps by] his own family.

Joseph Trumbull of Connecticut made a similar observation while traveling in England in 1764.

> We in New England knew nothing of poverty and want, we have no idea of the thing, how much better do our poor people live than seven eighths of the people of this much-famed island.

Indeed, the standard of living for ordinary people in the American colonies was probably higher than in any other country in the world. Because of the opportunities for so many, America came to be known throughout Europe as "the best poor man's country."

Although America opened up great opportunities, they were not unlimited. And they were not equally open to all. Indeed, opportunities for many often came at the expense of others who did not share them. This helped to create inequalities within America. In the next chapter, you will read about both the limits of opportunity and the growth of inequalities.

CHECKUP

1. How did most people in colonial America make a living? How was geographical mobility connected to opportunity?
2. In what ways did farming differ in the North and in the South?
3. Describe the trade patterns that developed in colonial America.
4. How was the status of women different from that of men in colonial times?

Key Facts from Chapter 3

1. There was increasing religious freedom in colonial America, and despite some serious restrictions, religious toleration was greater than in most European countries.
2. By 1700 each of the English colonies had its own legislature, usually composed of an upper house whose members were appointed by the governor and a lower house whose members were elected by the colonists.
3. The right to vote in colonial America was held, with few exceptions, by adult white males who owned property.
4. Though women played an important role in the development of the colonies, they were subject to many restrictions as compared to men.

★ REVIEWING THE CHAPTER ★

People, Places, and Events

Review Questions

1. Why did religious toleration gradually increase in America? *P. 39*

2. Why did legislatures develop in the English colonies? *P. 41*

3. How were members of the governor's council selected? *P. 41*

4. What were the qualifications for voting in the colonies? Could many people satisfy those requirements? Explain your answer. *P. 43*

5. Why did conflict develop between the colonial assembly and the governor? What power did the assembly use as a weapon in a conflict? *P. 44*

6. How were squatters different from other landowners? *P. 44*

7. How did farming differ from one part of the country to another?
   Pp. 45–47

8. With whom did the colonial merchants trade? What goods and products were traded? *Pp. 47–48*

9. Look at the map on page 49. Molasses and sugar were one side of a triangular trade route. Starting with the exportation of those products, trace the triangular trade.

10. Describe the role women played in the colonial economy. *Pp. 51–52*

Chapter Test

*On a separate piece of paper, write **T** if the statement is true and **F** if the statement is false.*

1. All people, regardless of their faith, were guaranteed religious freedom in colonial America.

2. Most colonial governors, councils, and assemblies were elected by the colonists in the same manner in which we elect the President and members of Congress today.

3. The power to control taxation gave the colonial assembly a strong hold over the governor.

4. All male colonists over the age of 21 could vote.

5. Squatters had no legal claim to their land.

6. Southern farmers grew pay crops of rice, tobacco, and indigo.

7. The middle colonies were called the bread colonies because they learned to make corn bread from the Indians.

8. Free labor in the colonies was supplemented with indentured servants and slaves.

9. Merchants carried on an active trade with southern Europe, England, the West Indies, and Africa.

10. Women were an important part of the colonial economy, but they did not have equal rights with men.

11. The chief difference in the three types of colonial government—proprietary, royal, and corporate—lay in the method of selecting a governor.

12. The case of John Peter Zenger is considered a landmark in the struggle for freedom of religion.

55

THE LIMITS OF OPPORTUNITY

T O EUROPEANS the discovery of the New World meant opportunity. To the native peoples who had lived there for thousands of years it meant catastrophe. The coming of the Europeans brought death to millions of Indians and destroyed entire tribes.

The first recorded contact between Europeans and the native peoples of the Americas came when Columbus's men set foot in the New World in 1492. In his first report Columbus described the people he met as gentle and loving. But he also made this ominous observation:

> These people are very unskilled in arms . . . with fifty men they could all be subjected and made to do all that one wished.

Columbus, of course, was describing only one Indian tribe. There were many others, some of them not so gentle and peaceful. But belligerent and peaceful alike, the Indians fell victim to European invaders over the next 400 years.

You have already read of the Spanish conquest of the native peoples of Central and South America. Forced by the Spaniards to work in the gold and silver mines under terrible conditions, the Indians died by the thousands. The Spaniards also used Indian slaves on sugar and tobacco plantations and on ranches. What the Spaniards did in most of Central and South America, the Portuguese did in Brazil.

The tragic results of the Indian encounter with Europeans in the sixteenth and seventeenth centuries in South and Central America can be put this way: Thousands fell to European guns. Hundreds of thousands died from overwork and mistreatment. Millions—perhaps many millions—died from such European diseases as smallpox, measles, and diphtheria, to which they had never before been exposed.

Indians and Colonists

The story of the encounter between the original native peoples of North America and the English and other European settlers does not read much better. There were some 600 different groups native to North America, speaking as many as 2,000 languages and dialects. Some were farming people, some fishing people, and some hunters. Among many of them there was fierce rivalry leading to frequent warfare. In fact, one of the reasons why Europeans were eventually able to conquer the continent was that the separate Indian tribes failed to unite against white settlers.

Estimates of the number of Indians in North America in 1492 range from 1 million to 10 million. The largest number lived in the western part of present-day United States. Far fewer lived in the Southeast. Fewer still were in the Northeast, where the English first settled.

Changing feelings. The pattern of English-Indian relations was pretty much the same wherever the two peoples met. Often the Indians were friendly at first and helped the Europeans adjust to the strange, new environment, teaching them to grow corn and other crops.

57

The map above shows the names and home regions of only a few of the hundreds of native-American tribes that lived, at the time of European exploration, in what is now the United States. Population estimates vary greatly, ranging from about 850,000 to several times that number.

This first period of good feelings soon gave way to mistrust and hostility. English greed was often the cause. Not satisfied with the lands the Indians offered or sold them, white settlers took more by force. Indian resistance and bloody warfare followed.

Warfare in Virginia. In Jamestown, the English foolishly angered the Indians, thus adding to the danger and misery of the first years of settlement. Peaceful relations were restored after an Indian princess, Pocahontas, saved the life of Captain John Smith, who had been captured in 1607. Her father, who was called Powhatan from the name of his tribe, became even more friendly with the English when his daughter married a Virginia planter, John Rolfe.

The period of peace ended after Powhatan's death in 1618. The Indians had come to realize that more English settlements would push them out of their lands. In 1622 the Powhatans launched an attack to drive the English

58

from the area. The warfare was fierce. Despite the loss of a third of the settlers, the Jamestown settlement survived. The white settlers quickly struck back. "Now we have just cause to destroy them by all means possible," said one white leader. From that time on, warfare between Indians and whites in Virginia was continuous. Of the estimated 30,000 Indians who had lived in the area when the English first arrived, there were but 2,000 some 60 years later.

Warfare in New England. Indian resistance in New England flared up from time to time in the 1600s. Most Puritans thought the Indians were agents of the devil. The settlers angered the Indians not only by taking their land but by trying to force them to accept English ways and Puritan beliefs. Indians were punished if they hunted and fished on Sundays, and they were put to death if they used God's name in vain.

The Pequot War was the same kind of turning point in Indian-white relations in Massachusetts as the war in 1622 had been in Virginia. In 1637, without warning whites attacked a Pequot Indian village near the Mystic River in Connecticut. They set fire to the village, burning 600 men, women, and children alive.

Indian resentment erupted in 1675 in King Philip's War. By that time there were 90 white settlements in New England. Under the lead of King Philip, chief of the Wampanoags, a number of tribes were secretly united. The Indians then attacked more than half of the settlements, destroying twelve and killing hundreds of whites. One tenth of the grown white males in Massachusetts were either killed or captured.

The colonists responded with a vengeance. They destroyed Indian villages, beheaded chiefs (including King Philip), and sold hundreds of Indians as slaves to the West Indies. With the death of King Philip, Indian resistance in New England was crushed.

In every colony at one time or another, white settlers attempted to make Indian captives slaves. It rarely worked. For one thing, Indians did not do well in captivity, often falling victim to European diseases. For another, escape was easy, as the Indians could melt into the familiar forests and find their way back to their people.

Taking the Indians' land. How did Europeans, many of whom were religious people, justify the taking of Indian land?

This portrait of Pocahontas, a Powhatan princess, was painted in England where she went with her husband, John Rolfe, a Virginia planter. A year later, Pocahontas died of smallpox.

Solomon Stoddard, a Massachusetts minister, dealt with this question in a pamphlet he wrote in 1722.

> *Question VII.* Did we do any wrong to the Indians in buying their land at a small price?
>
> *Answer 1.* There was some part of the land that was not purchased, neither was there need that it should; it was vacant . . . and so might be possessed by virtue of God's grant to mankind. . . . The Indians made no use of it but for hunting. . . .
>
> *Answer 2.* The Indians were well contented that we should sit down by them. . . .
>
> *Answer 3.* Though we gave them but a small price for what we bought, we gave them . . . their price. And, indeed, it was worth but little; and had it continued in their hands, it would have been of little value. It is our dwelling on it, our improvements, that have made it to be of worth.

How does Stoddard justify the taking of some of the land without paying anything for it? How does he justify paying so little for the land that the English settlers did buy from the region's native Americans?

Less than human? Beneath such justifications was an attitude that many white settlers held about Indians. It was expressed by Henry Brackenridge of Pittsburgh, who went on a military expedition against the Indians in 1782.

Natives of the eastern woodlands go about their daily activities. The woman in the foreground is grinding corn in the top of a hollowed log. What else does the picture tell about these people?

[I offer] some observations with regard to the animals called Indians. . . What use do these ring-streaked, spotted and speckled cattle make of the soil? Do they till it? Revelations [a part of the Bible] said to man "thou shalt till the ground." This alone is human life. It is favorable to population, to science, to the information of a human mind in the worship of God . . . before you can make an Indian a Christian you must teach him agriculture and reduce him to a civilized life. To live by tilling is more [human], by hunting more [beast-like].

Can you see how making the Indians appear to be less than human would help Europeans justify to themselves taking over the Indians' land? Of what importance was the fact that the Indians were not Christians?

A circle of prejudice. Of course, the Indians bitterly resented the English view that they were less than human. They responded with hostility. Their hostility was proof to the whites that Indians were "savage" and should be treated as less than human. The circle of prejudice was complete. Using justifications like these, Europeans took more and more land, pushing the Indians steadily westward. From time to time, organized warfare would flare up. More usually there were simply isolated killings on both sides in the silence of the forest. Hate was answered with hate, and blood with blood.

Not all colonists believed it should be this way. Benjamin Franklin noted the source of the white prejudice against the Indians: "Savages we call them, [simply] because their manners differ from ours." Franklin also pointed out the illogic of warring on and mistreating all

Indians just because of the actions of some.

If an Indian injures me, does it follow that I may revenge that injury on all Indians? . . . if the French, who are white people, would injure the Dutch, are [the Dutch] to revenge it on the English because they are white people? The only crime [of the Indians] seems [to be] that they had a reddish-brown skin and black hair; and some people of that sort, it seems, had murdered some of our relations. If . . . any man, with a freckled face and red hair [should kill my wife], would it be right for me to revenge it by killing all the freckled red-haired men, women, and children . . . I met with?

Franklin's question answered itself, but few Americans were interested in either the question or the answer.

CHECKUP

1. How did the pattern of English-Indian relations change during the earliest years of colonization?
2. Where and why was King Philip's War fought? What was the outcome?
3. What views were put forth by those English who justified taking land from the Indians?

Blacks and Whites

For millions of black Africans, as for the Indians, the opening up of the New World meant not opportunity but disaster. Torn from their villages and packed onto ships like so many cattle, they—and their descendants—became slaves in distant lands.

Slavery in early times. Slavery had existed for centuries in the western world. The ancient Greeks and Romans

An African raiding party marches its captives to the coast, where they are to be sold into slavery. The slaves will then be transported across the Atlantic to become laborers in New World lands.

enslaved the peoples they conquered. Moslems and Christians in the Middle Ages did the same. But that type of slavery differed from the African slavery of modern times in two important ways. First, it was not based chiefly upon race. And second, the children of slaves did not always automatically become slaves themselves.

A slave trade existed in Africa from early times, too. For centuries Africans had captured other Africans and sold them into a slavery, first to the Roman Empire in Europe and later to the Arabs and Moors in the Middle East. By the 1300s, however, this trade was quite small. Even when the Portuguese began to take Africans to Spain and Portugal in the mid-1400s, the slave trade remained small.

The changing slave trade. The European discovery of the New World changed the African slave trade dramatically. As their Indian slaves in the mines and plantations died off in the 1500s, Spanish and Portuguese colonists turned to Africa for laborers.

The Portuguese continued to be the main slave traders, but before long all the great trading nations of Europe— Holland, France, Sweden, and England —entered this profitable business. England, a latecomer, entered the trade in a big way in the last half of the seventeenth century. By the 1790s English ship captains dominated the business.

There is no exact record of how many Africans were brought to the Americas. The best estimate seems to be between 9 and 10 million. Of this number, 60 percent went to the Spanish and Portuguese colonies in South and Central America, and another 35 percent worked on the plantations of the West Indies islands. About 5 percent, or 500,000, went to the area that later became the United States.

It is hard for us today even to imagine the cruelty of the slave trade. It began with the capture of Africans by other Africans, as prisoners of war. As the demand for slaves increased, African tribes along the coast, working with the slave traders, sent bands into the interior to kidnap people. The captors chained their prisoners one to another and marched them single file to the slave-trading ports. There, ship captains and slave-trading companies purchased them, giving in payment iron bars, copper pans, cotton cloth, rum, guns, gunpowder, and the like. The captives were branded with a red-hot iron carrying the mark of their buyer.

The middle passage. The slaves were then herded onto ships for the voyage across the Atlantic. The trip from Africa to the West Indies was called the *middle passage*. It was the middle part of a triangular route that a slave ship usually followed. (See the map on page 49.)

The picture on this page explains better than words how tightly slaves were packed aboard these ships. Ships like this usually had several decks. Slaves were kept below decks for fear of mutiny,

These diagrams of a slave ship show how the maximum number of Africans were loaded for the passage to the Americas. The slaves were usually chained, hands and feet, and permitted only enough exercise to provide for their survival. Even so, many of them died en route to the New World, the victims of disease.

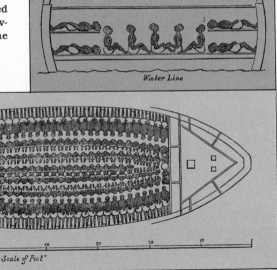

Water Line

Scale of Feet

and were allowed on deck only for feeding and exercise. One officer of a slave ship has left us this description of their treatment:

> Some commanders . . . are [forever] beating and curbing them, even without the least offense . . . which [makes] those poor wretches desperate, and besides their falling into [sickness] through melancholy often is the occasion of destroying themselves.

We will never know how many slaves died in the middle passage. Estimates are that anywhere from 15 percent to 25 percent failed to make it to America alive. If that is correct, and if 9 to 10 million did reach the New World, then somewhere between 1.5 million and 3 million Africans died aboard these slave ships. That fact alone is powerful evidence of the horrors of the slave trade.

The meaning of *black*. The tragic relationship between African blacks and English whites in British North America may have been set even before they met. For centuries the word *black* carried a negative meaning in the English and other European cultures. One writer has noted:

> Black was the color of death, . . . of the devil; it was the color of bad magic and melancholy, of poison, of mourning, forsaken love, and the lowest pit of hell. There were black arts and black humors, blackmail and blacklists, blackguard and black knights, the Black Death . . . and there were countless legends of men turning black from sin and of black races sprung from hell.

One could add to the list from other English expressions: a black day, a black mood, a black sheep in the family,

a black mark against one's name. Always, black meant "foul, wicked, sinful." *White*, on the other hand, stood for purity and good. Angels were clothed in white. Brides wore white. The dove of peace was white.

Thus when the English finally met black Africans, they already had a *prejudice* about them—that is, they had prejudged the Africans on the basis of their skin color. And the fact that the Africans were not Christian certainly reinforced the belief that they were sinful and connected with the devil.

White Europeans quickly noted other differences in appearance too, and placed a meaning on them.

> . . . the Europeans do not only differ from the . . . Africans in color . . . but also in their hair . . . in the shape of their noses, lips, and cheek bones, as also in the very outline of their faces and the mold of their skulls. They differ also in their natural manners, and in the internal qualities of their minds.

Different. Different in appearance, in religion, in customs, in language, in "the internal qualities of their minds." And different meant inferior.

It was not inevitable that the English would enslave such people. But when belief in the blacks' inferiority was combined with a severe shortage of labor, and with the example of the Spanish and Portuguese in Central and South America, slavery was not an illogical outcome.

Slavery in the English colonies. The first Africans to arrive in English North America landed in Jamestown in 1619. The Dutch ship that carried them had been bound for an island in the Caribbean Sea, but was blown off course. With workers in short supply, Jamestown settlers were glad to buy the services of these twenty black Africans, just as they bought the services of white indentured servants from England. The English called the Africans "Negroes," a term borrowed from the Portuguese and the Spanish word meaning "black."

More Africans came to Virginia and to Maryland during the next few decades, but they did not form a large part of the population. As late as 1650, only 300 of Virginia's 16,000 people were blacks.

Because of the sketchy records of that time, we know very little about these earliest Afro-Americans. It appears that at least some were treated as indentured servants and were freed after their terms of service. But it is also clear that even these blacks were treated differently than were white servants. For one thing, their terms of service were longer. For another, they were given more severe punishments. Also, black women were made to work in the fields—something that white women were not generally expected to do.

We know also that within twenty years of the first arrival of blacks in Jamestown, some were made slaves for life. A Maryland law of 1639 refers to "slaves." Records of the Virginia House of Burgesses indicate there were slaves in that colony in 1644. Virginia court records of the 1640s and 1650s also refer to slaves. But bits and pieces of evidence like these are all we have. We do not know who and how many blacks were slaves. And we know almost nothing about their lives.

It is clear, however, that by 1660 slavery was fairly widespread in Virginia and

The first blacks arrive at Jamestown in 1619. The Dutch ship carrying them to the West Indies had been blown off course by a storm.

Maryland. In that decade, both colonies established slavery by law. In 1662 a Virginia law provided that

> . . . all children born in this country shall be held [slave] or free only according to the condition of the mother.

With those words, slavery became an inherited condition for all children born to a slave mother. Maryland passed a similar law a few years later. During the next half century, slavery was made legal in all the English colonies.

Indentured servants—or slaves? At first there was no great increase in the number of slaves in the North American colonies. Most landowners preferred indentured servants from England. They

65

were of the same culture, spoke English, and were familiar with English ways of farming. Also, the initial cost of a slave was much higher. The price of an indentured servant's passage was only one fifth as much as the cost of an African slave. For the small planter without capital, that was a great difference.

In the latter part of the 1600s, the labor situation in the southern colonies changed sharply. With the formation in 1672 of the Royal African Company, a slave-trading company, British ships began to bring large numbers of slaves to the Americas. The price of slaves dropped. At just about the same time, white indentured servants began to be attracted to newer colonies—Pennsylvania, for example—where opportunities for their future seemed brighter.

The spread of slavery. Large tobacco planters now turned to black slaves for their work force. So did rice growers in South Carolina, who found it hard to get white men to do the backbreaking, unhealthy work in rice fields. The number of slaves increased rapidly. Maryland offers a good example of the change from white to black workers. In the 1670s, white indentured servants in that colony outnumbered black slaves by at least three to one. Thirty years later, black slaves outnumbered white indentured servants, 4,600 to 3,000.

By 1750, blacks made up 20 percent of the total population of England's North American colonies. By far most of the blacks were in the southern colonies, where they made up more than 40 percent of the population. Most slaves were located in the two main tobacco colonies, Virginia and Maryland.

The Number of Slaves in the Colonies 1650—1770

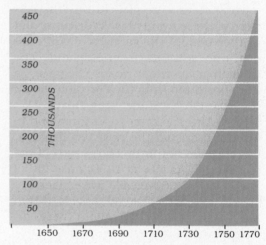

Slavery did not gain as great a hold in the colonies north of Maryland. The chief reason lay in the shorter growing season, which was not suited to plantation crops like tobacco and rice. Slaves in the North worked mainly as household servants, coach drivers, and porters. They were distributed unevenly. Slaves made up 14 percent of New York's population and about 10 percent of Pennsylvania's and New Jersey's. Rhode Island's population was also about 10 percent slave, but in the rest of New England, slaves made up only 2 percent of the population.

Slave codes. By the early 1700s almost all the American colonies had adopted special laws called slave codes. Under these laws slaves were treated differently from all others, including indentured servants. Servants had rights under their indentures—which were contracts—and they could use the courts to enforce those rights. And of course, once their service was ended they had the same rights as all other free persons.

Not so the slaves. Except in New England, slaves were not allowed to own property or to engage in any business. They could not testify in court, except in rare cases. Slaves were prohibited from gathering together in public places for fear they might plot a revolt. For the same reason, they were not allowed to have guns. In certain colonies they were forbidden to learn to read, lest they pick up dangerous ideas about freedom.

Many of the laws were aimed at keeping slaves from running away. Slaves were forbidden to leave their plantations without written permission. A South Carolina law required overseers to whip any slave on their plantations who did not have proper identification. Anyone —even a white person—who helped a slave to escape was subject to harsh punishments.

Slaves codes changed the status of blacks from human to a form of property. Slaves had almost no legal rights. Their marriages were not recognized in law, except in New England. Wives could be sold from their husbands, and children from their parents. Punishments set by law were severe, but that was only the half of it. The cruel treatment handed out by some owners was limited only by the master's imagination.

Nor could slaves look to the courts for protection. In Virginia and the Carolinas, if a master killed a slave while punishing him or her, the master was not subject to any penalties. Even for the outright murder of a slave by a master, there was usually only a light fine or other form of penalty.

The quarters for slaves were usually at a distance from, but within sight of, the plantation house. Cabins were small and poorly furnished and often lacked wooden floors.

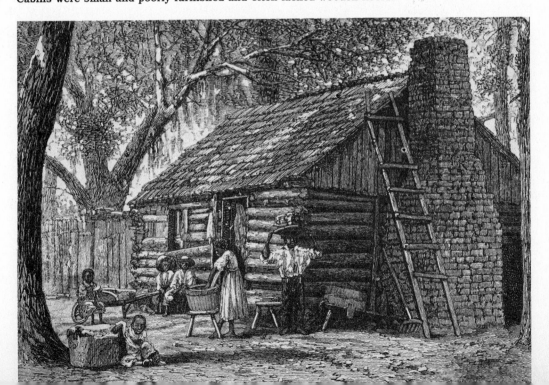

Restraints on free blacks. With the status of slave passing from mother to child, the system was absolutely closed. A slave's only chance for freedom was to run away, or to be freed by a master. Both those things did happen, and there were indeed several thousand free blacks in the colonies, north and south. But for most of them life was little different than it was for slaves. They held low-paying jobs as house servants, dock workers, and sailors. If they wandered far from home, they could expect to have to prove they were not runaway slaves. At times, failure to prove this could result in their being made slaves again. They often could not join the colonial militia, could not vote, and often could not testify in court against whites. Even though free, they were subject to the same racial prejudice as slaves, which held that *black* meant "inferior."

To Americans of African descent—even free blacks—the call of opportunity that many Europeans heard from across the ocean was but a cry of despair.

CHECKUP

1. Describe the process by which slaves were brought to America.
2. How did the status of indentured servants and slaves differ?
3. Why did slavery gain a greater hold in the South than in the North?

Opportunity Is Not Equality

The picture of colonial America as a land of opportunity was, except for Indians and blacks, fairly accurate. It is important, though, not to confuse the idea of opportunity with the idea of equality.

English writers of the seventeenth century pictured America as a land where all could find opportunity. But you would search their writings in vain for a promise that all persons in America would be equal. The reason is simple. The idea of equality did not figure much in the thinking of seventeenth century England.

English society. Society in England was made up of a number of ranks, or classes. It might help to think of them as a series of layers. In the top layer were the nobility. Great landowners, they held titles like duke, earl, and baron, which passed from father to son. In the next layer were the gentry, or landed middle class, including great merchants and professional men, like lawyers. Below them were the artisans, or skilled workers, as well as the small independent farmers called yeomen. The yeomen made up the largest class in England. In the bottom layer were the poor—farmers without land and workers without skills.

Although some persons managed to move up from one layer to another, most people lived out their lives in the layer into which they were born. Everyone, from top to bottom, was expected to be content to remain in his or her "proper station" in life. Those in the upper layers were the rulers; those in the lower were the ruled. People at the bottom were expected to "defer" to their "betters"—that is, to accept the views and the leadership of the upper classes in all matters. Members of the upper ranks did not mingle much with those of the lower. Laws even required that the people in the lower ranks dress differently.

The system of ranks by which the upper classes received the deference of the lower classes was accepted as right and necessary by all levels of English society. One might curse one's luck for having been born into a lower class, but few argued that the system should be changed. In seventeenth-century England, inequality, not equality, was the cement that held society together.

American society. Not all the layers of English society were carried over to America. Very few people in the top layer—the nobility—came. For those who had it so good, there was little reason to leave. Also, for reasons that are not known, few in the very lowest layer of English society came. These were the vagrants, the outcasts, the most wretched of the poor. The majority who came were from the middle and lower layers—yeoman farmers, skilled workers, and the farm and city laborers who came as indentured servants.

It was natural that the English who came would carry with them their ideas about rank and deference. John Winthrop, the Puritan leader of the Massachusetts Bay Colony, gave a little speech to his people in 1645 about how society should be run.

> God Almighty in his most holy and wise providence has so disposed the condition of mankind, as in all time some must be rich, some poor, some high and eminent in power and dignity; others mean and [controlled by their superiors].

Winthrop was making clear to his listeners that a system of ranks was in the natural order of things. The "gentlemen" who were among the first arrivals in Jamestown never doubted that others should defer to them. When a lowly tailor in that colony tried to enter his horse in a race in 1674, a judge fined him 100 pounds (45 kg) of tobacco. The reason the judge gave was that it was "contrary to law for a laborer to make a race, it being a sport only for gentlemen."

As in England, clothing was a sign of rank. The son of a poor carpenter gave us a good picture of Virginia society in the mid-eighteenth century when he wrote this paragraph in his memoirs:

> We were accustomed to look upon, what were called gentle folks as being of a superior order. For my part, I was quite shy of them, and kept off at a humble distance. A periwig [a white wig] in those

In colonial times, only the upper classes took part in this kind of musical activity.

days, was a distinguished badge of gentle folks—and when I saw a man riding the road, near our house, with a wig on, it would so alarm my fears, and give me such a disagreeable feeling, that I would run off, as for my life. Such ideas of the difference between the gentle and simple, were, I believe, universal among all of my rank and age.

Why did this carpenter's son run away when the man with the periwig appeared? How would you describe his attitude? Does this help you understand the ideas of rank and deference?

Deference and politics. Did the idea of deference carry over into political life in America? That is, did Americans of the colonial era accept the idea of a ruling class? One place to look for an answer is in the makeup of colonial legislatures or assemblies.

In Chapter 3 you read how and why the legislatures developed. You read also that in most colonies the majority of white adult males had the right to vote. Since most voters in each colony were farmers, you might expect that they would send farmers like themselves to the legislature.

Is that what happened? John Adams, a Massachusetts colonial leader and later President of the United States, gives us the answer for the New England colonies.

Go into every village in New England and you will find that the office of justice of the peace, and even the place of representative, which has ever depended on the freest election of the people, have generally descended from generation to generation, in three or four families at most.

What Adams saw in New England was equally true elsewhere. Candidates for office were almost always from "the better sort," or upper classes. It was understood that "the meaner sort," or common citizens, would choose between such gentlemen. In Virginia, for example, small farmers were in the great majority. But three fourths of all the men they elected to the House of Burgesses in the 1700s owned more than 10,000 acres (4,000 ha) of land each.

This does not mean that there were no farmers at all in the legislatures. There were. And as time went on, farmers from the western parts of many colonies demanded more seats for their sections. But for the most part, the idea of deference remained strong. Only rarely did a small farmer run against a gentleman. All in all, one would have to agree with the historian who wrote: "The governing class consisted of the wellborn who had wealth, prestige, and power. They monopolized the dominant offices of government."

The standard of wealth. By the early 1700s an upper class had developed in each colony. America's upper class, however, was not like England's. One big difference was that membership in the upper class in America was based mainly on wealth, not on birth. And in America, there were great opportunities for wealth. Some members of the upper class had gained their wealth through gifts of land or other special privileges from the King of England or from the proprietor or governor of a colony. The largest land gifts of all were made by the governor of New York. Several ran to

Wealthy Southern planters in colonial times often lived in elegant homes like the one shown above.

hundreds of thousands of acres. Three amounted to more than a million acres each. Needless to say, those who received them became instant members of America's wealthiest class.

But not all entered the upper class in this way. A good many families made their fortunes on their own. What they had in common was energy, ambition, some money, and an eye for the right opportunity. Family fortunes were often based on land inherited from parents and grandparents. Some families sold off part of this land as its value rose. They then used the money to buy still more unsettled lands that would later become valuable. Others used their large landholdings to raise pay crops. Many did both.

Prospering in the South. In the South, where slaves provided more and more of the labor, owning slaves was as impor-

tant to success as owning land. Those who had saved or inherited enough money to buy slaves had an advantage over those who had not. With their profits, the owners then bought more slaves in order to raise more tobacco and rice, and their advantage widened.

By the early 1700s a powerful planter aristocracy had formed in Virginia, Maryland, and South Carolina, and to a lesser extent in North Carolina and Georgia. Robert "King" Carter was one of the wealthiest of these planters. Robert's father had settled in Virginia in 1649. With money he had brought from England, he bought land. He married five times, acquiring more land with each marriage. He also bought slaves to farm the land. His son Robert built on that solid base. When "King" Carter died, in 1732, he owned 600 slaves, at least 60,000 acres (24,000 ha), and 10,000 pounds in cash.

71

A few southern planters made it to the top in a single generation. Abraham Wood worked as an indentured servant for a planter who also traded with the Indians. When he became a free man, Wood did the same, only better. He collected thousands of acres, became a planter, traded with Indians, and speculated in western land. He became one of Virginia's most prominent men.

Not many made it as Wood did. The Carter family's path to wealth was more typical, though few families rose as high.

Prospering in the North. In the North it was the merchants who were able to take advantage of opportunity and who formed a new aristocracy of wealth. The northern merchants were not jacks-of-all-trades, but they were jacks-of-many. They sent ships with colonial products to the far corners of the world and then sold the goods the ships brought back. They loaned money, sold land, made rum, and bought and sold ships. When British trade laws stood in the way of profit, they were not above smuggling.

Here, too, inheriting money from an earlier generation was an advantage. But New England history is also filled with tales of poor Yankee lads who became rich merchants. John Hull and Thomas Hancock were but two examples. John Hull came from England in the 1630s with his father, a blacksmith. John himself became a silversmith. After a number of years, he branched out. He bought his own trading ships that went to the West Indies, Spain, and England and he sold goods in Boston. When he died, Hull was one of the wealthiest men in Boston.

Thomas Hancock arrived at the same point by a different path. The son of a Congregational minister, Hancock had the advantage of coming from a family of fairly high status, though not wealth. He was apprenticed to a bookseller at fourteen, and after learning the business, Hancock set up his own store. His marriage to the daughter of one of Boston's richest bookdealers added to his advantages. Hancock used her money and business connections to buy a fleet of ships, and was soon trading in many lands.

Elias Hasket Derby of Salem, Massachusetts, was typical of the merchants who made fortunes through foreign trade. His sailing ships took American products to Russia, China, and many other lands and brought back the goods of those countries for sale in American markets.

The growth of a wealthy upper class of merchants in Boston can be seen in the table below.

Distribution of Wealth in Boston		
Percentage of Taxpayers	Percentage of Wealth Held	
	1687	1771
Bottom 30%	2	0.1
Low—mid 30%	11	9
Upper—mid 30%	40	27
Top 10%	47	63
(Top 1%	10	26)

Were the bottom 30 percent in Boston better off in 1687, or in 1771? How had the top 10 percent fared in that time? What does the table tell you about the top 1 percent of Bostonians?

Social mobility. Despite the development of social classes, America's society was very different from England's. First, the distance between the bottom layer of colonial society and the top was, except for the slaves, far less. The wealthy in America, in other words, were not nearly as rich as the rich in England. And as you read earlier, the poor were far, far better off than were the poor in England. In every colony, the great majority of white families, including those in the bottom layer, owned land. Even the few who did not had reason to hope that they or their children some day would own land. At the opposite end of the social scale, few of the wealthy in America could live like the idle rich in England. Nearly all of them—even the great planters—had to continue working to take care of their properties and their fortunes.

Second, Americans were not so fixed in their social rank. That was so because rank in America did not depend so much on birth as on wealth. And in America the opportunities to improve one's economic position, and with it one's rank, were far greater than in Europe.

Indentured servants offer the best example of this fact. Earlier you read that between 60 percent and 75 percent of the European immigrants during the colonial period were indentured servants. Their life was hard. They received no wages. They could own no property, except what their masters allowed, and they could not marry without their masters' permission. They were sometimes cruelly punished, especially for running away. A great many died before the end of their terms of service. Many of those who finished their terms became farm workers or laborers in towns and cities. It is estimated that eight out of ten never became landowners or rose into the middle class.

Now there are two ways of interpreting that fact. One is to emphasize the 80 percent of indentured servants who did not rise above the lowest layer. The other is to emphasize the 20 percent who did. Of the 20 percent, half became farm owners, and half became skilled workers who made a good living. For an age when most people in most countries remained fixed in their rank, this is an astonishing fact. Further, of the 80 percent who did not rise above the lowest class, the children and grandchildren of many did. Benjamin Franklin, whose grandparents were indentured servants,

In America, even the poorest families might own land and could hope to rise in wealth and rank.

is the best known of these, but there were thousands of others.

The movement from one layer of society to another is called *social mobility*. In colonial America there was more social mobility than anywhere on earth. For example, the same carpenter's son who fled at the sight of a periwig (see page 70) rose to become an Anglican minister and one of Virginia's most important religious leaders.

In this highly mobile society, movement could go both upward and downward. Able and ambitious people could and did rise in wealth and rank. But a poor crop, a bad investment in land, or the loss of a ship at sea could wipe out a person's wealth, and with it one's high social status.

Opportunity—does it exist today? At the start of this unit, you read that America became identified with the idea of opportunity at the beginning of its history. Did the United States remain a land of opportunity between colonial times and the present? Does it remain a land of opportunity today? You noted earlier that the very opportunities in colonial America helped to make for inequalities in wealth. These inequalities grew during the next hundred years as fortunes were made in fur trading, commerce, industry, railroads, and real estate. Wealth was distributed more unevenly in 1820 than in 1775, and still more unevenly in 1850 than in 1820. In fact, in 1850 the top 1 percent of wealth holders owned 26 percent of the wealth of the United States; the top 2 percent owned 37 percent of the wealth. Although the distribution has become less uneven since 1850, it has continued to be a matter of concern.

Unquestionably there have been greater opportunities for people at the top than for those at lower levels. Yet there is evidence that opportunity has continued to exist for the great majority of Americans. A powerful proof of this fact is that from colonial times to the present day, millions of immigrants have continued to come to America. Had they not had the opportunity to better themselves, they surely would have stopped coming. Other evidence can be found in studies of wealth in America in more recent times. These studies show that while wealth in America is still distributed very unevenly, the average person has made real gains in wealth during his or her life.

In judging the extent to which opportunity exists in America today, one must keep in mind, too, that opportunity is not measured by wealth alone. Opportunity has come to be measured today less by the chance to own land than by the chance to gain skills and education, to be free to enter a profession or other field of work, and to find a job where there is a chance to grow.

One of America's great challenges today is to open and keep open the door of opportunity, particularly to those groups to whom it has been shut. That is one of the nation's unfinished tasks. How well it is performed will determine whether America will be able to fulfill its promise to all as a land of opportunity.

CHECKUP

1. Explain how English society in the seventeeth century could be described as "a series of layers."
2. To what extent was society in the American colonies like society in England? How was it different?
3. Compare the ways of becoming wealthy in colonial times in the North and in the South.

Key Facts from Chapter 4

1. The coming of European settlers to America brought on the decline of the native peoples (Indians) whose lands were occupied by the colonists.
2. The first blacks in the colonies landed in 1619 in Jamestown, coming possibly as indentured servants. Within a short time, however, blacks were treated as slaves.
3. Colonial society was made up of a number of layers, ranging from the wealthy upper class to the lower class of farm and city workers who came as indentured servants. Below white indentured servants were black slaves and Indians.
4. It was easier in America than anywhere else in the world to rise in rank. The movement from one level to another is called social mobility.

★ REVIEWING THE CHAPTER ★

People, Places, and Events

Pocahontas   *P. 58*

Powhatan   *P. 58*

Pequot War   *P. 59*

King Philip's War   *P. 59*

Middle passage   *P. 63*

"Negroes"   *P. 65*

Indentured servants   *P. 65*

Royal African Company   *P. 66*

Slave codes   *P. 66*

Free blacks   *P. 68*

"Proper station"   *P. 68*

Social mobility   *P. 73*

Review Questions

1. What caused the conflict that developed between the Indians and the colonists? *Pp. 57–58*

2. How did the English justify seizing Indian lands? *Pp. 59–61*

3. Describe the journey of the Africans from their home in Africa to slavery in the New World. *Pp. 63–64*

4. How did the English feel about the word *black*? Why did they feel that way? *P. 64*

5. Why did many plantation owners decide to use slaves instead of indentured servants? *P. 66*

6. Compare the classes, or layers, of society in seventeenth-century England with society in America. *Pp. 68–69*

7. How did America's upper class differ from England's upper class? *Pp. 70–71*

8. Who represented colonial America's wealthy class in the South? in the North? *Pp. 71–72*

9. Why was there greater social mobility in colonial America than in England? *P. 73*

Chapter Test

In the first section below is a list of people and terms found in the chapter. In the second section is a list of descriptions. Match each person or term with the appropriate description. Write your answers on a separate sheet of paper.

1. Social mobility
2. King Philip's War
3. Slave code
4. Royal African Company
5. "Negroes"
6. Powhatan
7. Prejudice
8. Middle passage
9. Merchants
10. "Proper station"

a. Leader of the Indians of Virginia who helped the settlers

b. New England conflict between settlers and Indians

c. Members of the wealthy upper class in the northern colonies

d. Movement from one level of society to another

e. Slave-trading business

f. Trip from Africa to the West Indies

g. An idea popular in seventeenth-century England that one should stay in the layer of society to which one was born

h. Special laws to control the blacks in colonial America

i. An opinion formed without taking time or care to judge fairly

j. A term borrowed by the English from the Portuguese and the Spanish, meaning "black"

76

FOCUS ON

Great Americans

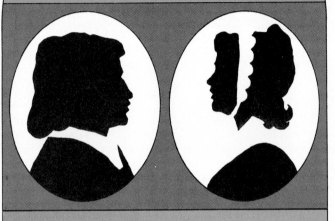

CHRISTOPHER COLUMBUS

JOHN SMITH

ROGER WILLIAMS

ELIZA LUCAS PINCKNEY

BENJAMIN FRANKLIN

★ CHRISTOPHER COLUMBUS ★

Admiral of the Ocean Sea

History is filled with unlikely and possibly undeserving heroes. Is Christopher Columbus one of them? After all, his discovery of America was a complete accident. One writer calls Columbus a successful failure—perhaps the most successful and luckiest in world history. And his biographer says, "we now honor Columbus for doing something that he never intended to do, and never knew that he had done." However, this writer adds, "we are right in so honoring him." Why? The answer lies in the life story of this remarkable sailor (see page 8).

The man we know as Columbus was born Cristoforo Colombo in Genoa, Italy, in 1451. Little is known about his childhood. His father was a weaver, as his grandfather had been, and at an early age both Christopher and his younger brother Bartholomew were taught the family trade. Christopher had little if any schooling, and he did not learn to read and write until many years later.

The Genoa of Columbus's youth was one of Europe's important seaports, and Christopher was naturally drawn to the sea. Listening to returning sailors tell their stories about faraway places set many a young Genoese boy to dreaming of adventure. This must have been especially so for Christopher, since he believed that he was destined for an important mission in his life. Most likely he pictured himself carrying the message of Christianity to other peoples, for he was a deeply religious young man.

At the age of fourteen or fifteen, Columbus began to hire on as a sailor on ships bound for other Mediterranean ports. For the next eight or nine years, he continued to work as a weaver but took jobs on ships whenever he could.

One such trip at age twenty-four was the turning point in Columbus's life. He had hired on to a merchant ship bound for northern Europe. Off Portugal, his ship was attacked and sunk. Columbus was wounded, but he was able to kick toward shore on a floating timber. Finally, exhausted, he made it to land near the town of Lagos, Portugal.

This fifteenth-century portrait of Columbus is inscribed "discoverer of a new world."

On recovering, Columbus made his way to Lisbon, the capital city of Portugal. There his brother Bartholomew worked as a chartmaker. For anyone interested in the sea and adventure, there was no better place in the world than the port of Lisbon. This town had been the home of Prince Henry, often called Henry the Navigator. (See the portrait on page 9.) Henry had brought together the best mapmakers, astronomers, and sea captains to explore, as he put it, "through all the watery roads." Henry died in 1460, when Columbus was only nine. But Portugal, as well as the rest of Europe, benefited greatly from the interest of Prince Henry and the work of his explorers. Portuguese sea captains had sailed into the unknown Atlantic and discovered the Canary Islands and the Azores. They also charted much of the west coast of Africa, and they opened up a rich trade with these regions. In 1487 Bartholomew Dias rounded the southern tip of Africa, making possible an all-water route to India, Japan, and the rest of the Far East.

In Lisbon the brothers Columbus became partners in a chartmaking business of their own. At that time, chartmaking was far from an exact science because instruments of navigation were not very precise. Information came mainly from seamen just back from their voyages. Chartmakers talked with these explorers and studied any rough sketches they might have made at sea. From those sources, the chartmakers would piece together information about coastlines, islands, the depth of water, and so on. Christopher Columbus quickly became very good at this work.

Also during these years, Columbus eagerly studied anything that would help broaden his knowledge of the sea and of sailing. Now in his late twenties, he learned to read and write. He studied mathematics. He learned astronomy so that he could sail by the stars, and he learned about shipbuilding and the rigging of sails. Most important, Columbus sailed. As a captain of merchant ships flying the Portuguese flag, he learned the seas from Iceland in the north to the equator in the south, from Greece in the east to the Azores in the west. By the time he was thirty, Columbus had become one of the most skilled captains in the Portuguese merchant fleet.

It was about this time—we do not know exactly when—that Columbus began to consider the idea of reaching the Far East by sailing *west*. This became the single great purpose of his life. He pored over maps. He read all available geography books. He sought information from navigators and from sailors who had traveled west.

Columbus's idea of reaching the east by sailing west was based on the belief that the earth was round. This belief was hardly new. It was shared by almost all educated people of the time. Why, then, had no one come up with the same idea? And why did people not support the idea once Columbus proposed it? Distance is one answer. Columbus thought the distance around the earth was much less than most other people believed it was. In fact, he thought the earth was much smaller than it really is. He also thought the landmass of Asia was larger than it is. Columbus figured the distance from Europe to Japan was about 2,400 miles (3,840 km). Such a

The Lisbon waterfront may have looked like this in 1493 when Columbus landed for repairs and supplies. He had been at sea in ships similar to these for 213 days on his first voyage of discovery.

distance would make the voyage difficult but not impossible. The estimate made by most geographers was much closer to the actual distance of 10,600 miles (16,960 km). But no one guessed that an entire continent stood in the way. Events worked out strangely. The best geographers were correct in believing the trip could not be made. So they did not try and they discovered nothing. Columbus, being incorrect, insisted on trying—and so discovered a new world!

In 1484, Columbus laid his plan before King John II of Portugal. Advised that Columbus was wrong about the distance to Japan, John turned him down. The king may also have felt that the Genoan's price was too high. It was usual for kings and queens to pay only for the costs of a voyage of exploration. Columbus, however, was anything but bashful in his demands. He wanted to be made governor of all lands he might discover and to be named "Great Admiral of the Ocean." In addition, he asked for 10 percent of all gold and silver he might find.

Columbus next went to Spain for support. After delaying him for five years, Queen Isabella turned Columbus down in 1490. The voyage, said her advisers, would be at least 10,000 miles (16,000 km) rather than 2,400 (3,840). It would take three years. There was not a ship afloat in all of Europe that could make such a trip.

Columbus was disappointed and angry. He was ready to turn to the King of France, but a friend persuaded him to try Isabella one more time. Again the queen listened to Columbus. Again her answer was No. This time the queen might have approved, but Columbus's demands were too steep. Earlier he had dropped his price and was willing to sail for expenses. Now he raised his demands, asking even more than he had of King John of Portugal.

Columbus set out for France. Even as he did, one of Isabella's advisers was urging her to change her mind. True, the adviser reasoned, this man from Genoa was asking for the moon. But what if he were to succeed? His price would then seem quite small compared with what Spain and the crown would gain. The queen reconsidered and agreed. She sent a messenger to catch up with Columbus. Thus it was that when Columbus set sail on August 3, 1492, he did so under the flag of Spain.

After a stop at the Canary Islands for fresh supplies, Columbus set a westward course for his ships—the *Niña*, the *Pinta*, and the *Santa Maria*. By September 6, the last bit of land had slipped from view. It is hard to imagine the courage it took to go onto the unknown seas. After a time, Columbus's men became restless. For Columbus, driven by belief in his destiny, each mile took him that much closer to the Indies. For the men, each mile took them that much farther from home. To keep his men calm, Columbus deceived them about the distance they had traveled. Each day, in a phony log meant for the eyes of his men, he recorded fewer miles than he entered in his own, secret log.

As it happened, Columbus overestimated his speed. Therefore the distances that he recorded in the phony log were more accurate than those recorded in the log he kept for himself!

After a month out of sight of land, the frightened men had had enough. Not all of them believed that the world was round. They threatened a mutiny and demanded that Columbus turn back. A summary of his journal gives Columbus's answer to the terrified sailors. He "cheered them as best he could, holding out good hope of the advantages they might have; and he added it was useless to complain since he had come to go to the Indies, and had to continue until he found them, with the help of Our Lord."

Some days later came an encouraging sign—branches of trees, their leaves still green, floating in the water. Then at 2:00 on the morning of October 12 came the cry from the lookout on the *Pinta*: "¡Tierra! ¡Tierra!" The white sand cliffs of an island in the Bahamas had been spotted in the moonlight. Surely, thought Columbus, this must be an island near Japan. He named the island San Salvador (Spanish for "savior") and claimed it for King Ferdinand and Queen Isabella of Spain. Then Columbus confidently sailed southward in search of Japan. During the next two months he reached the islands now known as Cuba and Hispaniola. Early in 1493, Columbus headed for home. Only two ships made the return voyage. The *Santa Maria* had been wrecked on reefs.

Columbus returned to Spain in triumph. Crowds cheered the man they believed had reached the Far East by sailing west. Queen Isabella showered honors upon him. Plans were made for a

Printed in 1507, this is the first known picture to show the discovery of the New World. On his four voyages, Columbus returned from America with Indians and many things unfamiliar to Europeans: sweet potatoes, tobacco, iguana, trunk fish, tree rats, and parrots.

second expedition. In the fall of 1493, seventeen ships under the command of the new Admiral Christopher Columbus journeyed west.

For the next two years, Columbus sailed from island to island in the Caribbean, still looking for Japan and for gold. He found neither. On his return to Spain this time, the welcome was far less royal. Clearly Columbus had found something, but people wondered if it was anything worthwhile. Queen Isabella and King Ferdinand also were impatient. Where were the gold, the spices, the silk, and the other valuable goods of the Far East?

Nevertheless, Columbus twice more persuaded the Spanish rulers to finance his voyages to the west, one in 1498 and one in 1502. Each time, he came back without the awaited treasures. He and his men had found many things never before reported by travelers to the Far East. That could have been a clue to Columbus that he had stumbled onto an entirely different place. But the same single-mindedness and persistence that had led him to try to reach the Indies by sailing west now kept him from seeing that he had not reached the Far East. Only on his third voyage, when he found the continent of South America, did he think he might have made a whole new discovery. Columbus returned from his final voyage in 1504. Ridiculed by many for his false claims and ignored by others, he died two years later a bitter, disappointed man.

Columbus was wrong in his belief that he had discovered a western route to the Far East. Why, then, does his biographer say that we are "right in honoring him"? The answer lies in the qualities of man. "No other sailor of his time," explains this writer, "had the persistence, the knowledge, and the sheer guts to sail thousands of miles into the unknown ocean until he found land."

CHECKUP

1. What experiences, skills, and studies contributed to Columbus's knowledge of sailing and the sea by the time he was thirty?
2. On what beliefs did Columbus base his idea of sailing west to reach the Far East?
3. What is meant by the statement "we honor Columbus for doing something that he never intended to do, and never knew that he had done"?

★ JOHN SMITH ★

Promoter of English Colonies in America

The Englishman lay stretched out on the ground, helpless. Around him stood his Indian captors, awaiting only an order from their sachem, or chief, to beat him to death. This was to be his punishment for wandering onto the land of Powhatan, grand sachem of the Powhatan Indians.

Suddenly from the watching crowd the eleven-year-old daughter of Chief Powhatan rushed forward. She threw herself across the prisoner. If he was to be killed, she cried, then his executioners must kill her as well. No one knows what thoughts ran through Powhatan's mind at that moment. Perhaps he believed his daughter's action was a sign from the gods. After a few chilling moments, Powhatan gave his order: set the Englishman free. (See the portraits on pages 20 and 59.)

That, at least, is how Captain John Smith told of his rescue by Pocahontas. In later years, however, some people expressed doubts about his story. Smith claimed the dramatic rescue took place in December 1607. Just a few months later, he wrote a book about his experiences in Virginia but made no mention of this adventure. Not until ten years had passed, in fact, did Smith add this story to his book. At that time, the same Pocahontas was visiting England. She was then the famous wife of John Rolfe, the Englishman who had started tobacco farming in Virginia. Everyone in England, it seemed, was curious to meet this daughter of an Indian chief. Now,

Smith was a man with a burning desire for honors and fame. He was also known to exaggerate a good story. Perhaps, said the doubters, he made up this colorful tale to share the popularity and fame of Pocahontas. Some people pointed to details in the story that didn't quite fit with other known facts. And they noted that when Smith wrote another book in 1624, he dressed up the story of this rescue with still more color and drama.

John Smith also has his defenders. They point out that doubts have been raised about other stories in Smith's

In his book about Jamestown, Smith included this illustration of his rescue from death by Pocahontas. The letters "C.S." identify Captain Smith. The Powhatan Indians lived in longhouses like this building made from trees and vines.

King Powhatan comands C.Smith to be slaine, his daughter Pokahontas beggs his life his thankfullnes and how he subiected 39 of their kings. reade y history.
printed by Iames Rowe

JOHN SMITH **83**

books. These defenders claim that evidence showing the truth of his writings has usually come to light in later years. And so the debate over whether John Smith's life was really saved by Pocahontas has continued.

John Smith was a man of many accomplishments. As much as he hoped for fame, he would have been disappointed to learn that he is remembered mainly for the Pocahontas story. He was an adventurer, a soldier, an explorer, a colonizer, and an author of eight books. He may well have done more than any other Englishman for the cause of colonization. In fact, this man with the most common of English names was one of the most uncommon men of his time.

John Smith was born in England in 1579, one of three children of a small farm family. He attended school until age sixteen, when his father arranged for him to serve as an apprentice to an important merchant in a nearby town. Many an English boy of John Smith's class would have given his eyeteeth for such an opportunity. Entry into the merchant class offered a secure future. After only a few months, however, John knew that he could never be happy in this work. More than anything else, he longed for a life of adventure.

John left both his job and England. For the next four years, he was a mercenary—that is, a soldier for hire. By age eighteen, John was doing battle in the service of the King of France against the armies of Spain. Later he fought for the Dutch against the same foe. Very quickly he gained a reputation for leadership and daring. After one battle in which outnumbered Dutch forces fought their way to victory, the Dutch commander gave full credit to the young Englishman. The mercenary troops, he reported, "were inspired by the example of Sergeant John Smith who laid about him with such rapid strokes that he left a path of Spanish dead in his wake."

More than skill and daring set John Smith apart from his fellow soldiers. He had great curiosity and an unusual thirst for learning. In his travels through Europe, he learned to speak several languages. He also learned all he could about geography and exploration. On his return to England in 1601, this twenty-one-year-old met and exchanged information with some of the leading explorers and geographers of the land. One was Henry Hudson, who later, sailing under the Dutch flag, discovered the Hudson River in present-day New York. Another was Richard Hakluyt (see page 12), the greatest geographer of the age.

Less than a year after returning home, Smith was off again. This time he hired himself out to fight against the invading Turks in central Europe. He was given the rank of captain, with command of a company of 250 men. Though John would receive many other titles in his lifetime, this was the one by which he would always call himself. As before, Smith's commander praised him for his "feats of daring" in battle.

In 1603, Smith's forces were trapped by the Turks near the Hungarian border. John was taken prisoner and made a slave. A Turkish official then sent Smith to Constantinople—as a gift! This turned out to be a lucky stroke for Smith, for his new owner, a woman named Tragabigzanda, treated him well. After some months, Tragabigzanda sent Smith to her brother, believing that he,

This stamp, issued in 1907, commemorates the founding of Jamestown and two plants important to its survival. Corn (right) was a vital food source adopted from the Indians. Tobacco (left) became a prosperous cash crop.

too, would deal with the English slave kindly. The new owner turned out to be cruel, however. One day after being severely beaten by this man, Smith rose up and killed him. He then fled for his life. After two weeks, he had made his way through the Turkish lines and into Russia, where he stayed for several months before making his way back to England. The following year Smith and a small band left for Morocco, where they rescued an Englishwoman being held as a slave by a Turkish official.

When Smith returned to London from this latest exploit in 1605, he received a hero's welcome. He was befriended by nineteen-year-old Prince Henry, who was next in line for the English throne. Over the following months, Smith met with King James I and Queen Anne, with dukes and lords, and with clergymen and scholars. At the age of twenty-six, two years before he set foot on Vir-

ginia soil, John Smith was already well known in England and had lived enough adventures for a lifetime.

Smith probably became interested in America through Hakluyt and Sir Walter Raleigh. Raleigh's earlier efforts to found a colony in America had failed, but his stories fired the imagination of the young adventurer. Smith invested in the Virginia Company of London. Always seeking new worlds to conquer, he joined the first group of colonists to leave for Virginia in December 1606.

Smith was only one of a number of leaders among this group. Aboard ship, his habit of giving orders, his insensitivity to the feelings of others, and his boasting led to trouble. At one point, the others threatened to hang him. While this threat was not carried out, for several months Smith was kept off the governing council to which he had been named by the Virginia Company.

It is not an exaggeration to credit John Smith with keeping Jamestown alive through that first year of great troubles. While jealous leaders quarreled and other men wasted time hunting for gold and silver, Smith opened a trade with the Indians. His knack for languages helped him greatly as he exchanged knives, axes, iron pots, and glass beads for food and furs. The furs were to be sold in England to provide a return for the London investors. As for the food, one settler later wrote that "the corn he [Smith] obtained kept the men of Jamestown alive that autumn and winter."

On one of Smith's trading and exploring trips, his small party was ambushed. Two of the men were killed, and Smith himself was taken prisoner. It

JOHN SMITH 85

was on this occasion, Smith later said, that he was saved by Pocahontas.

When Smith returned to Jamestown from his captivity, he found that his enemies in the colony had taken control. They immediately charged him with responsibility for the death of his two men. Smith was tried, found guilty, and sentenced to be hanged the next day. That very evening, ships bearing supplies and new settlers arrived from England. The commander of the fleet put a stop to the nonsense and ordered Smith freed. Once again, John Smith had barely escaped death.

Over the next few months, Smith emerged as the real leader of the colony. Eventually, he was made president of the governing council. Under his "no work, no eat" order, the Jamestown settlement began to deal with its problems of survival. Defenses were improved, buildings were repaired, and corn was planted. Smith established friendly relations with Powhatan, and trade with the Powhatan Indians provided food. Furs and lumber were sent back to London for sale. Smith also shipped some of the colony's troublemakers back to England. Meanwhile, Smith explored the rivers and coastlines of the region and made careful maps. At that time it was still believed that North America was only a few hundred miles wide and that there might be a river through it that would lead to the Far East.

Somehow, while doing all these things, Smith managed to find time to write a book about the Virginia colony's first year. In June 1608 he sent it to London on a returning ship. Later that year it was printed. Smith also sent back his maps of the coastline to his friend Henry Hudson. Hudson used them the following year on his own voyage of exploration in the New World.

In London, the directors of the Virginia Company did not see eye to eye with Smith. They wanted a quick return on their investments. While they demanded that the search for gold and silver be pressed, Smith was asking them to send carpenters and honest workers who could help the struggling new colony to survive. Their feelings about Smith were also poisoned by those troublemakers that Smith had sent back to England. In 1609 the investors decided to replace Smith. Even so, Smith planned to stay on in Virginia. But when his gunpowder accidentally blew up and left him badly burned, he returned to England to recover (see pages 19–23).

America was now in John Smith's blood. For the rest of his life, he was connected with the New World in one way or another. In 1614 he persuaded some merchants to finance a whaling voyage to the waters off New England. There he continued to explore, making careful maps of the coastline and charting the waters. Smith's men took no whales, but they did return with enough fish and furs to earn his backers a good profit.

The next year, a group put up money for Smith to start a colony in New England. But the ships were damaged in a storm and the people had to turn back. Losses to the investors were heavy, and they decided to pull out. Smith set out for New England once more in 1615. This time he was captured by pirates. He escaped after several months but never was able to return to America.

Smith drew this map of the New England coast from Cape Cod (then named Cape James) to Penobscot Bay (shown here as Penbrocks Bay). Can you find Plymouth and the Charles River? We have added the color to make Smith's original map easier to read (see the map on page 28).

By the 1620s, Smith realized that he would never succeed in starting a colony. He believed in the future of this new land, however, and wrote several more books about it. Through them, he encouraged English people of all classes to leave Europe and take up life in the New World (see page 29).

Smith died in 1631. He was only fifty-two, yet he had lived a life as full of adventure as anyone could hope for. And through his example and his writings, he probably did more than any other person to encourage the English settling of America.

CHECKUP

1. What did John Smith do to keep Jamestown alive through the first year of troubles?
2. What were his personal traits as a leader?
3. What did he do to encourage the English settling of America?

★ ROGER WILLIAMS ★

Religious Freedom in America

Freedom of religion—the right to worship as we please or, indeed, not to worship at all—has a long history in America. In that history one person, Roger Williams, towers above all others. By both word and example, he helped to shape the American character (see page 39).

Roger Williams was born in London, England, probably in 1603. We do not know the exact year because his birth record was burned in the great London fire of 1666. Roger grew up in a family that was comfortably off but by no means wealthy. His father was a shopkeeper who bought and sold cloth. In the custom of the day, Roger and his two brothers learned their father's trade and helped in the family business. Even as a boy, however, Roger had less interest in business than in studies, especially religious studies. For a serious-minded boy to be caught up in the religious controversies sweeping England in the early 1600s was not unusual. By the age of twelve, Roger had formed quite definite religious ideas, which were shared by Separatists of the time (see page 23).

At about thirteen or fourteen, Roger learned the newly invented skill of shorthand. This became important in Roger's life, because his skill came to the attention of Sir Edward Coke. Coke was one of the great legal scholars of the day and a leader in the effort to limit the powers of the English king. Impressed by young Williams's ability and earnestness, Coke hired him to take shorthand notes in

court. He became quite fond of the boy and later spoke of Roger as his son. When Roger was eighteen, Coke sent him to a private school. Two years later Roger went on to Cambridge University. Next he trained for the ministry, finally leaving Cambridge University in 1629.

England was not a comfortable place for Puritans or for Separatists at that time. And Williams was by now a strong Separatist. He followed with great interest the founding of the Massachusetts Bay Colony by English Puritans in 1629. Like the Puritans, he saw the New World as a place to build a society based on his own religious beliefs. On a chilly December day in 1630, Roger, his wife of one year, and eighteen other passengers boarded a supply ship in Bristol, England, bound for Boston.

Williams's reputation as a scholar and preacher had preceded his arrival in February 1631. Soon after, the citizens of Boston offered him the important position of teacher and minister to their congregation.

Had Roger Williams been an ordinary man, he would have accepted the post. But as Roger Williams would prove many times in his life, he was no ordinary man. He stunned the Boston Puritans by turning down their offer. Though they had rejected many of the beliefs and practices of the Church of England, they had not separated from it. Nothing less would do for Williams. His principles would not allow him to minister to "an unseparated people." Williams added that he also opposed the use of government to force religious beliefs upon its citizens, as the government of the colony was doing.

Shock turned quickly to anger among Bostonians. The warm welcome of only weeks before was no longer extended to Williams. Who was this ungrateful newcomer to spurn their generosity and to lecture them as well? Also, the Puritans feared that Williams's strong opposition to the Church of England might cause the king to cancel the charter of the young colony. When Separatists in the nearby settlement of Salem asked Williams to lead their church, pressure from Boston forced Salem to withdraw the invitation. Indeed, the leaders in Boston wanted Williams out of the Massachusetts Bay Colony altogether.

Williams then moved to the Plymouth colony, which was outside the boundaries of the Bay Colony. (See the map on page 28.) For the next two years, he lived among the Pilgrims, who were Separatists. He earned a living by farming and by trading with the Indians, whose language he learned. Williams came to have a deep respect for Indian culture and a love for the Indians among whom he lived. These feelings the Indians returned. Some years later, he wrote a guidebook to the Indian language entitled *A Key into the Language of America.*

Even in Plymouth, however, things did not go entirely smoothly for Roger Williams. From time to time he was invited to preach to the congregation, but he was never asked to be its minister. Governor Bradford, the colony's leader, wrote that although the Pilgrims admired Williams as a "godly man," his "strange opinions" sometimes "caused controversy between the church and him."

In 1633, Roger Williams, his wife, and their newborn child moved to Salem. The congregation there, over the objections of the leaders of the Bay Colony, had once again asked him to be its minister. For two years Williams wrote and spoke his mind freely. And for two

This is the title page of Williams's book about the language and culture of the Narragansett and other Indians near Boston. Williams had the book published on a trip to London in the 1640s.

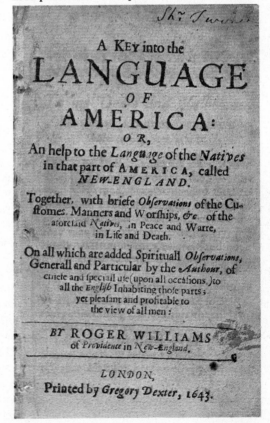

A KEY into the
LANGUAGE
OF
AMERICA:
OR,
An help to the *Language* of the *Natives* in that part of AMERICA, called NEW-ENGLAND.

Together, with briefe *Observations* of the Customes, Manners and Worships, &c. of the aforesaid *Natives*, in Peace and Warre, in Life and Death.

On all which are added Spirituall *Observations*, Generall and Particular by the *Authour*, of chiefe and speciall use (upon all occasions,) to all the *English* Inhabiting those parts; yet pleasant and profitable to the view of all men:

BY ROGER WILLIAMS of *Providence* in *New-England.*

LONDON,
Printed by *Gregory Dexter*, 1643.

years his opinions increased his troubles with the leaders of the Massachusetts Bay Colony.

Williams sharpened his attack on the churches in the colony for not separating from the Church of England. He also repeated his belief in the separation of church and state. One's duty to God was not the business of the state, he declared. It was wrong for the government to interfere in religious affairs, and it was wrong for church leaders to try to run the business of government. "No one," insisted Williams, "should be bound to worship against his own consent." Neither the Puritans nor any other religious group, he continued, had a monopoly on religious truth. For all anyone knew, God found the religions of the Indians and many other peoples just as acceptable as Christianity. All religions, said Williams, should be tolerated.

Williams also insisted that the land in the New World belonged to the Indians who had long lived there. No mere "discovery" of North America by a sailor flying an English flag could give title to the king. Of all Williams's ideas, this one struck most dangerously at the very foundation of the colony. The colony existed on a gift of land from the king. If the land had never been the king's to give, then the people of Massachusetts Bay had no right to the land they lived on. Williams argued that the colonists had rightful claim only to land that they had *bought* from the Indians.

It was bad enough that Williams held such views. But as a minister and a man of conscience, he refused to keep them to himself. To Puritan leaders he was no longer just a nuisance, he was a danger and must either be silenced or driven out. Leading Puritan ministers attacked him as an "offensive rebel" against the church and as a "man delivered up to Satan." The Massachusetts General Court, or legislature, warned him to stop spreading his "dangerous ideas." Williams refused, and in October 1635, the General Court ordered him to leave the colony. Because he was ill, and his wife was expecting their second child, the legislature gave him until spring to leave. But he was ordered to stop spreading his "new and dangerous opinions."

Williams, however, could not remain silent. He continued to preach. He even interested twenty men and women of Salem in starting a colony on Narragansett Bay, outside of Massachusetts, where they could worship freely.

This was finally too much for the leaders of the Massachusetts Bay Colony. They sent soldiers to seize Williams and place him on a ship about to sail for England. Secretly warned of the coming arrest, Williams fled into the wilderness. He was soon joined by his followers. After more than three months of walking through the New England woods in snow and bitter cold, Williams and his friends crossed the Massachusetts border at the Seekonk River. There, early in 1636, on land given by a chief of the Narragansetts, Williams founded the settlement of Providence (see page 27).

The new town quickly became a model of democracy and religious freedom. All heads of families had equal voice. Church and state were completely separate. People of all beliefs were welcome.

Over the next several years other individualists who were driven from Massachusetts for their religious beliefs made their way to the Narragansett Bay

In 1636, Williams founded Providence on the Seekonk River, where he received a friendly welcome and a gift of land from the Narragansett Indians. His arrival is depicted in this nineteenth-century woodcut.

area. Among them was Ann Hutchinson (see page 27). Out of their fondness for Roger Williams, local Indian chiefs sold land to these people very cheaply. By 1643, four settlements had been founded on the bay.

Meanwhile, in Massachusetts, Puritan leaders watched these developments with growing annoyance. Fearing the example of these communities and desiring the rich land for their own people, leaders of the Massachusetts Bay Colony made plans to persuade Parliament to extend their boundaries to take in the entire area. To head off this move, Roger Williams went to England. There, in 1644, he won from Parliament a charter that united the four towns and surrounding areas into the colony of Rhode Island. Twenty years later a new king, Charles II, officially granted a royal charter to Rhode Island.

Throughout his life in Rhode Island, Roger Williams held some public office, always without pay. He served as the colony's president for three successive terms. Rhode Island became, as Providence had been, a refuge for all who were

ROGER WILLIAMS **91**

In 1658, the first Jewish congregation in America was founded in Rhode Island. Members of the original congregation built Touro Synagogue, shown here. Still used today, it is America's first synagogue.

©John Hopf

persecuted because of their religion. While Williams was president of the colony in the 1650s, the first Jews arrived. They were followed two years later by Quakers, then among the most persecuted of all groups. In neighboring Massachusetts, Quakers were whipped and threatened with death. All peoples— Jews, Quakers, Catholics, believers and nonbelievers alike—were full citizens in the colony of Rhode Island. In some of his best-known writing, Williams held that religious liberty was a natural right of humankind.

Roger Williams had always tried to keep peace between the English settlers and his Indian friends. As the leading citizen of Rhode Island, he championed the Indians' right to the land, even when this put him at odds with his fellow colonists. In time, however, even Roger Williams could not prevent a conflict. Friendly Indian chiefs died and were replaced by men who were determined to drive out those who were taking their land. Incident followed incident, and in the mid-1670s, open war broke out. Though Williams was past seventy at the time of King Philip's War (see page 59), he led the defense of Providence against Indian attack. A large part of the settlement, including Williams's own house, was burned. Williams continued in service to the town for the remaining years of his life.

By the time of Roger Williams's death in 1683, religious liberty had begun to take root in America. There were many practical reasons why this happened (see page 39). Roger Williams, however, was the first American to argue that freedom of religion was not only practical but right. This argument and the example of his own life give Roger Williams a proud place in the history of religious liberty in America.

CHECKUP

1. In what ways did Roger Williams distinguish himself as a teenager?
2. Why did Williams turn down the Boston citizens' offer to become the teacher and minister of their congregation?
3. Why did he leave the Bay Colony? In what ways was Providence, which he founded shortly thereafter, a model of democracy and religious freedom?

★ ELIZA LUCAS PINCKNEY ★

Founder of the Indigo Industry

"I have the business of three plantations to transact," explained Eliza Lucas in 1739 in a letter to an English friend, "which requires much writing and more business . . . of all sorts than you can imagine. . . ." Managing these properties was indeed a large job. Located in South Carolina, the properties totaled nearly 4,000 acres (1,620 ha) and had 86 slaves. Each of the three plantations

was like a small village in itself, providing for nearly all of its own needs. The plantations also produced lumber, beef, pork, butter, and corn for export to islands in the West Indies.

The fact that the plantations were managed by a woman was not unusual in the colonial South. Other women took charge of family businesses when their husbands were in England on business,

Later in life, Pinckney spent much of her time visiting here at Hampton Plantation, owned by her widowed daughter. Her son Charles was widowed also, and Eliza helped rear his daughters here. The mansion still stands in McClellanville, just up the coast from Charleston, South Carolina.

in the colonial capital holding public office, or away at war. This responsibility also fell to some widows. Even when men did run the plantations, women had the large job of managing the household side of plantation life. What made this plantation manager unusual was not her sex but her youth. At the time Lucas took charge of this large operation, she was not yet seventeen.

The job of running the three plantations had been given to Eliza by her father, George Lucas. Earlier the Lucas family had lived on the British West Indies island of Antigua, in the Caribbean Sea. The family was fairly well off. George's father had been an important sugar planter in the British island colony. George himself held the rank of major in His Majesty's Army and later became a lieutenant colonel and governor of Antigua.

Eliza Lucas was born in Antigua in 1722. Much of her early life was spent there. Later the family lived for a number of years in England, where Eliza continued her schooling. She read many of the English classics and developed a love for reading and an interest in ideas, which remained with her through life. She also learned French, and she became an accomplished musician on the harpsichord.

A few years after their return to Antigua, Mrs. Lucas's health became poor. Believing she might do better in a different environment, Major Lucas moved his family to the smallest of their three South Carolina plantations late in 1738. This was a 600-acre (240-ha) tract some 6 miles (9.6 km) from Charleston. Located on Wappoo Creek, it came to be called Wappoo Plantation.

Major Lucas had expected to stay at Wappoo indefinitely. Less than a year after their arrival, however, Great Britain went to war against Spain, and Major Lucas was called back to duty in Antigua. Rather than move the family back, the major decided that his older daughter should manage his properties and take care of her mother and a younger sister. Eliza Lucas measured up to the task.

The work kept Eliza extremely busy. But, she wrote, "by rising very early I find I can go through much business. . . ." She made time to keep up with her reading and her music. She also made time for another interest, that of experimenting with crops. "I love the vegetable world extremely," she wrote. Her father encouraged this interest. At that time, South Carolina's economy was based on one crop—rice, which could be grown only in the swampy, low country. If Eliza could find a profitable way to grow other crops in South Carolina, Major Lucas advised, she would do something of great benefit to many people.

Beginning in the spring, Eliza Lucas experimented with seeds her father had sent from Antigua. These included ginger, cotton, alfalfa, and indigo. Eliza later reported to her father that the alfalfa and ginger turned out poorly, but she "had greater hopes from the indigo than any of the rest of the things I had tried."

Indigo is a weedy plant from which a highly valued blue dye is made to color cotton and wool. There was a large market for indigo in England, where it was used to dye army and navy uniforms and dress coats. The plant was common in certain parts of India. The name *indigo,* in fact, is a Spanish form of "India." Cultivation of the plant had been tried in South Carolina's low country about seventy years earlier without much success. When planters found rice to be a better cash crop, they dropped efforts to grow indigo. By 1740, Britain had to buy its indigo mainly from the French West Indies and some Spanish colonies.

Eliza's first efforts to grow indigo were by trial and error. She did not know the best time to plant or the best soil for the crop. Her first planting in March 1740 was killed by a late frost. In April, a second planting was cut down by worms. But Eliza stuck to it, and a third planting that spring led to some success. With the tiny black seeds saved from this small crop and some additional seeds sent from the West Indies, Eliza planted a half acre (.2 ha) in 1741. The crop, though small, yielded enough indigo for the experiment in making the blue dye.

Eliza's father sent Nicholas Cromwell to help make the dye, but Cromwell turned out to be an unhappy choice. He was an experienced dye maker from Montserrat, an island in the French West Indies which depended on the indigo trade with Britain. Thus Montserrat's economy might be ruined if South Carolina should start to produce indigo. Cromwell decided that since Eliza Lucas had already succeeded in growing the plant, she must not learn how to turn it into the valuable dye. Therefore, at the point in the process where lime is added

Freshly-cut indigo is steeped in water, mixed with lye, and then strained and dried to make blue dye.

to the blue juices of the soaking indigo leaves, Cromwell threw in an extra amount of lime to ruin the color.

For the next two years, Eliza continued to experiment with indigo plantings, but the crops were poor. In 1744, Eliza made large plantings of indigo on Wappoo and one of the other plantations. She hoped for a crop big enough to make dye, and this time she had success. With the help of a neighbor and another dye maker sent by her father, seventeen pounds of good quality dye was produced. Eliza sent six pounds of this dye to England, where merchants were pleased and excited to find it was of a high quality.

By the time the indigo crop of 1744 was planted, Eliza Lucas had married Charles Pinckney. Charles, some twenty years older than Eliza, was a noted lawyer and leading citizen of Charleston, South Carolina. He and his first wife had been close friends to young Eliza ever since she arrived in 1738. They exchanged letters and visits regularly, and Charles Pinckney lent Eliza books. In the fall of 1743, Mrs. Pinckney became seriously ill and died some months later. Soon after, Charles Pinckney asked Eliza to marry him.

As part of his wedding gift, George Lucas gave Charles and Eliza Pinckney, all the indigo crop growing on his plantations. Eliza let the crop go to seed; then she gave the seed away to any South Carolina planter who promised to raise and export it. In this way, indigo cultivation spread quickly. By 1747, South Carolina was able to export 134,000 pounds (60,300 kg) of the dye to England in a single year.

No longer dependent on France for indigo, the British government was pleased to be free of its old enemy. To encourage further development of this indigo trade, Parliament voted to give producers in the colonies a bonus of six pence for every pound (.45 kg) sent to England. This was in addition to the price they would normally get. Planters eagerly began cultivating indigo, especially since the prices they received for their rice crops had dropped sharply in recent years. By 1754, South Carolinians were shipping 217,000 pounds (97,650 kg) of dye to England annually. By the mid-1760s, they were shipping over a million pounds (450,000 kg) annually. (See the map on page 49.) Some indigo planters found that they were able to double their net worth every three years (see page 108).

Thus, almost entirely through the work of Eliza Lucas Pinckney, a new crop was established in South Carolina. Rice continued to be grown in the low, swampy areas, and it remained the colony's main crop. But Eliza Pinckney had shown the way to grow a profitable crop on the high ground, which was unsuited to rice (see page 45).

After her marriage, Eliza Pinckney moved from Wappoo to a new home that her husband built for her in Charleston. Even so, Eliza continued her experiments on one of her husband's seven plantations, where she turned to raising silkworms. For the most part, however, Eliza devoted herself to the then-traditional role of wife and mother during this period of her life. Between 1744 and 1750 she bore four children, one of whom died soon after birth. In 1758, however, Charles Pinckney died. A widow at thirty-six, Eliza took over the

The Charleston waterfront, seen from East Bay, looked like this just before the American Revolution. The columned mansion is the home that Charles Pinckney built for Eliza after they were married.

management of her husband's seven plantations until her sons were able to take responsibility for them.

In the years leading up to the separation of the American colonies from Great Britain, Eliza Pinckney hoped that the two sides would patch up their quarrel. When her sons became leaders in the Patriot cause, however, she joined that side. During the Revolutionary War, both sons served in the American army. The Pinckneys were thus known as leaders of the rebellion. When British troops invaded the South, they raided nearly all the Pinckney plantations. They destroyed buildings and their contents, making off with other belongings and most of the slaves. In Charleston, the Pinckney home was seized. After the war, however, the lands and homes were restored to the Pinckneys.

Eliza Lucas Pinckney was widely known at the time of her death in 1793. Her important contribution to the country was known to President Washington, who asked to take part in her funeral service. Pinckney gave to her children her own public-mindedness. She had lived to see one son become governor of South Carolina. Her other son had helped to write the Constitution of the United States while representing South Carolina at the Constitutional Convention of 1787.

You may have noticed that no portrait of Pinckney is shown. No painting or description of her is known to have existed at the time of her death. Several of her dresses, which have been preserved, provide some clues to her appearance. She was short and slim and probably had dark hair. But that is all we know. Although she left no likeness of herself, Eliza Lucas Pinckney left her mark on the economic development of South Carolina.

CHECKUP

1. What was unusual about Eliza Lucas in her role as colonial plantation manager?
2. What did she do to begin and to promote the growth of the indigo industry in South Carolina?
3. What part did the British government play in these developments? Why?

The First American

Benjamin Franklin has often been called the "First American." One reason for being called this is a proposal he made in 1754 known as the Albany Plan of Union. In an age when most colonists thought of themselves as Virginians or New Yorkers or Pennsylvanians, Franklin urged them to unite for certain common goals. To deal with problems as American problems was a new idea. A more important reason for calling Franklin the "First American" is that his life story bears out the American faith in opportunity.

Benjamin Franklin's beginnings were certainly humble enough. He was born in 1706, the tenth of fifteen children of a Boston candle and soap maker. His education was started early at home. At eight he went to school. But two years of formal schooling was all the family could afford. Ben was apprenticed to his brother James to become a printer at the age of twelve. As an apprentice, Ben would learn the trade while serving his teacher.

Franklin's lifelong attention to self-improvement began in those early years. In his autobiography, he tells how he worked toward his goal of becoming a good writer. First he would write down the main points of an essay by a writer whose style he liked. Some days later he would try to write a piece based on his outline. Then he would compare his work with the original essay, note how his work might be improved, and make corrections.

In 1721 James Franklin started a newspaper, *The New England Courant*, only the fourth in Britain's North American colonies. Ben's jobs as an apprentice were to help set the type and to sell the newspapers in the streets. Ben wanted to write also, but his brother would have none of it. So Ben wrote letters to the editor, using the name "Silence Dogood," and slipped them under the door of the shop at night. James liked the letters and printed them, much to Ben's secret pleasure. A year after beginning the newspaper, James was jailed for criticizing the government. During the month that fol-

This painting of the Peace of Paris in 1783 was never completed because the British commissioners refused to pose. The American delegates (left to right) are John Jay, John Adams, Ben Franklin, Henry Laurens, and their secretary.

lowed, sixteen-year-old Ben put out the newspaper by himself.

Ben did not get along with James, however. With three years of his apprenticeship still left to run, Ben struck out on his own. When James persuaded other Boston printers not to hire his brother, Ben left Boston.

Franklin arrived in Philadelphia in 1723 with barely a dollar in his pocket. He found work with Samuel Keimer, one of only two printers in the town at that time. After a year he went to London, where he spent the next two years learning more about printing and trying to save enough money to set himself up in business. He returned to Philadelphia in 1726 and again worked for Keimer. In 1728, at the age of twenty-two, Franklin borrowed money, took a partner, and started his own printing business. The following year he bought a small newspaper, *The Pennsylvania Gazette*, which had been doing poorly.

The newspaper quickly became a profitable business through Franklin's talent and hard work. He took care to be sure that people thought of him as hardworking, even by carrying newspapers through the streets of Philadelphia in a wheelbarrow to sell them. In 1730, Ben Franklin bought out his partner, and within a few years he had started three more newspapers—one in Rhode Island, one in South Carolina, and the third, a German-language paper, in Philadelphia. In addition, he printed many pamphlets and books and won printing contracts from the governments of Pennsylvania, Delaware, and New Jersey.

Thus Franklin was already a successful printer when he began printing the

This drawing from the *Almanack* illustrates three of Poor Richard's sayings that praise industry. It shows men and women working side by side as blacksmiths and builders.

book that brought him both fame and fortune, *Poor Richard's Almanack*. First printed in 1732, *Poor Richard's Almanack* was an immediate success. It was published every year for the next 33 years, selling about 10,000 copies each year. The *Almanack* was a collection of all sorts of odds and ends. It included a calendar, weather predictions, useful bits of general information, jokes, and "The Sayings of Poor Richard." These were proverbs and sayings drawn from other books. Franklin usually shortened and rewrote them in his own catchy style. You may know many of the sayings. "The used key is always bright." "Little strokes fell great oaks." "God helps them that help themselves." Soon the phrase "as Poor Richard says" was in common use. Franklin's name became a household word in all the colonies. Translations of *Poor Richard's Almanack* into other languages led to Franklin's popularity in Europe as well.

Many of *Poor Richard's* sayings preached the values of thrift, hard work, and self-improvement. They reflected their author's own outlook on life. Franklin was always undertaking programs to improve himself and to practice his values. There was nothing he paid more attention to than improving his character. At twenty, he drew up a guide for conduct. The original has been lost, but four points of it are known: (1) be thrifty "til I have paid what I owe"; (2) "speak truth" always; (3) work hard at "whatever business I take in hand"; and (4) "speak ill of no man whatever, not even in a matter of truth."

In the following years, Franklin worked on a useful way to reason with people. In his youth, he had been very fond of argument, but it spoiled conversation and often made enemies. Later he found a way to win support for his ideas and projects. In his autobiography, Franklin explained how he would speak.

> . . . never using . . . the words *certainly, undoubtedly* . . . but rather say . . . it appears to me, or . . . *it is so, if I am not mistaken.* This habit, I believe, has been of great advantage to me when I have had occasion to inculcate [teach] my opinions.

This art of conversation served Franklin well in private and business dealings and in his later years in diplomatic and public life.

When nearly thirty, Franklin undertook another part of his self-education. With the same success he had in teaching himself most things, he learned French, German, Italian, Spanish, and Latin.

At about this time, Franklin began a project "of arriving at moral perfection." He drew up a list of thirteen virtues including frugality, industry, sincerity, justice, moderation, tranquillity, and humility. He resolved "to give a week's strict attention to each of the virtues successively" for thirteen weeks. Then he would start at the head of the list again, allowing him to go through the whole list four times a year!

In the same spirit of improvement, Franklin threw himself into the life of Philadelphia. With members of a group he formed, he discussed important questions of the day. They organized the first lending library, which became the model for a system that spread throughout North America. Franklin helped to found the first fire company in North America in 1736 and the first fire insurance company in 1752. He helped to found the Pennsylvania Hospital and also a school that later became the University of Pennsylvania. And he led the effort to get the streets of Philadelphia paved. Serving as the postmaster of Philadelphia, he made the delivery of mail in the city efficient and profitable. Later he did the same for the whole postal system in the North American colonies.

In 1748, Franklin decided to retire from the daily cares of his printing business. He wanted time, he wrote, "to read, study, and make experiments on such points as may produce something for the common benefit of mankind." As he wrote to his mother in 1750, he would rather that people said of him, "he lived usefully, than he died rich." To keep the business healthy and going, Franklin made one of his workers a partner. The partner served as manager, while Franklin drew a share of the profits. After eighteen years, the partner would become full owner.

Franklin had always had an endless curiosity about science and nature. For years he made careful observations of such things as ocean temperatures and currents, storms, and agriculture. He devised theories about them, which he shared with scientists on both sides of the Atlantic Ocean.

By the mid-1740s he had become especially interested in electricity. Little was known about electricity at the time. He did a number of experiments and came up with several important theories, which later proved to be correct.

Franklin gained worldwide fame in 1752 when two French scientists proved his theory that lightning was electricity. Shortly after, Franklin tested his theory with his famous kite experiment. He fixed a sharp, pointed wire to the top of a kite and flew the kite during a thunderstorm. Sure enough, the wire drew the electricity from the lightning and conducted it down the wet kite string to a metal key that Franklin had hung on the bottom end.

Harvard and Yale gave honorary doctor's degrees to Franklin. And the Royal Society of London honored him with a gold medal. Although Franklin was always modest about his scientific discoveries, they ranked among the most important of the age.

Franklin's scientific interests often took a practical turn. Indeed, he seemed to be happiest when working on an invention that might better the lot of hu-

The Library Company of Philadelphia, founded by Franklin and friends, moved into this new building in 1790. A statue of Franklin can be seen in the niche above the door.

manity. He invented a metal stove that greatly cut down the loss of heat. He called it the Pennsylvania fireplace, but to most people it was known, as it is today, as the Franklin Stove. Among his other inventions were the lightning rod and bifocal glasses.

Franklin never patented or made money from his inventions. "As we enjoy great advantage from the invention of others," he explained, "we should be glad of an opportunity to serve others by any invention of ours, and this we should do freely and generously."

Even though Franklin was interested in the practical side of science, he defended scientific studies that did not appear to have any usefulness. Once while observing another scientist's experiment, he overheard another man scoff, "What good is it?" Franklin turned to the man and replied, "What good is a newborn baby?"

By the mid-1750s Franklin was being drawn very much into public affairs.

His interests, genius, and able way with people suited him well for public office. With his election to the Philadelphia Assembly in 1751, Franklin began forty years of public service. One of his first diplomatic duties was to negotiate a treaty with the Iroquois Indians. Franklin respected the Indians (see page 61), and he admired the union for self-defense that the six Iroquois tribes had formed. He drew on their ideas for his own Albany Plan of Union in 1754.

In 1757 the Pennsylvania legislature sent him to London to speak for the interests of that colony with Parliament. Later, other colonies asked Franklin to serve as their agent as well. Franklin remained in England for eighteen years. In 1766 he helped to persuade Parliament to repeal the Stamp Act (see page 116). During the next nine years he tried to get the British government to understand America's desire for self-rule. Finally tiring of Franklin's arguments on behalf of the colonies, King George III accused him of disloyalty and sent him home to America.

Franklin had been back in Philadelphia only one day when he was elected to the Second Continental Congress. After independence was declared, Congress sent Franklin to France to win support for the Revolution. By then Franklin was the best-known private citizen in the world, and he was very popular among the French. In dealing with the French government, he skillfully used his fame and popularity to the advantage of his country. Later, with John Adams and John Jay, he negotiated the Peace of Paris, which ended the war with England (see page 162). On his return to Philadelphia in 1785, his adopted city held a week-long celebration in honor of its world-famous citizen.

Franklin was a delegate to the federal Constitutional Convention of 1787. Already eighty-one, he was aware that this would probably be his last service to the American people. Like the other delegates, he was also aware that the future of the United States would be shaped by their work. When there was disagreement among the delegates, Franklin worked for compromise. Meeting for more than three months, the convention completed its work successfully. While the delegates, each in turn, signed the Constitution of the United States, Franklin made a final brief statement. From his seat, he could see a painting of the sun on the back of the chair of the presiding officer, George Washington. "I have often," said Franklin, ". . . looked at that [sun] behind the President without being able to tell whether it was rising or setting. But now at length I have the happiness to know that it is a rising, and not a setting sun." Three years later, still active with public matters, Benjamin Franklin died after a visit from Thomas Jefferson, who was en route to New York City to take his post as the country's first Secretary of State.

CHECKUP

1. What experiences and personal projects could be called the "education" of Benjamin Franklin?
2. What personal traits helped Franklin become successful in business and public affairs?
3. Explain the statement, "Franklin's life story bears out the American faith in opportunity."

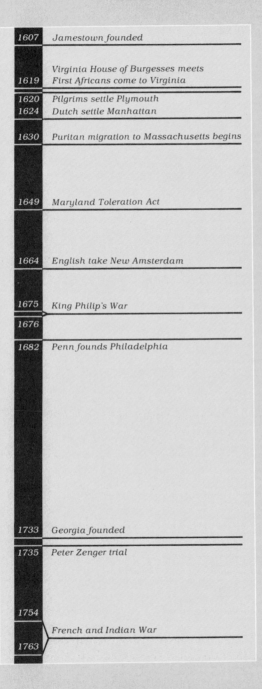

1607	Jamestown founded
1619	Virginia House of Burgesses meets First Africans come to Virginia
1620	Pilgrims settle Plymouth
1624	Dutch settle Manhattan
1630	Puritan migration to Massachusetts begins
1649	Maryland Toleration Act
1664	English take New Amsterdam
1675	King Philip's War
1676	
1682	Penn founds Philadelphia
1733	Georgia founded
1735	Peter Zenger trial
1754	
	French and Indian War
1763	

The first discoverers of America were the people Columbus called Indians. However, not until after Columbus's voyage in 1492 was there lasting contact between America and other lands. During the next century, explorers from Spain, Portugal, France, Holland, and England laid claim to vast territories in the New World.

The English were the most active colonizers. To them America meant opportunity—a place where settlers could own land, where they could worship God as they pleased, and where traders could make profits. Between 1607 and 1733, the English established permanent colonies along the Atlantic Coast, all the way from northern New England to Georgia. By 1700 every colony had its own legislature. Farming was the principal occupation, but trade and commerce were also important.

America's opportunities were not equally available to all. Voting was largely restricted to white, landowning males. Women were subject to many restrictions. Indians were forced from their lands by the colonists and were reduced in numbers by warfare and disease. Though the first Africans may have come as indentured servants, blacks were soon treated as slaves.

American society had various layers. The upper, or ruling, class was based largely on wealth. Yet there was opportunity for many in the lower classes to rise. In America there was more social mobility—movement from one layer of society to another—than anywhere else on earth.

103

Skills Development: Creating a Time Line

Thinking clearly about time sequences is important in studying history. A good way to study sequences is through the use of a time line. A time line is a kind of schematic drawing that shows when an event happened and the time relationship of that event to other events.

Each time line is drawn to a certain scale. The scale depends on what you want to show. Let's compare the scales used for time lines in this unit. Look at the time line on page 103. Measure the distance for the years 1607 to 1630. What does 1 inch (2.5 cm) represent? Now compare that scale with the one used in the time line on page 3. What is the scale for that time line? Approximately how many inches (centimeters) represent 100 years in the time line on page 103? on page 3? On which time line would there be more space to record the events of a century?

The important point to remember about scale is that it must be consistent within the particular time line. If, for example, 1 inch (2.5 cm) stands for 50 years, then that scale must be maintained throughout the time line. So before you draw a time line, you need to decide on the scale to be used in recording the events.

Drawing a Time Line

Now that you understand the importance of scale, try your hand at drawing a time line. The necessary information is provided in the right-hand column: a chronological listing of some famous explorers and their achievements. Before you begin to draw your time line, plan the scale carefully. You might wish to use different colors to show the countries for which each explorer sailed. Title your time line.

104

c.1000	Leif Ericson believed to be the first European to reach the North American coast (Iceland)
1488	Dias first European to round Cape of Good Hope (Port.)
1492	Columbus visited West Indies (Sp.)
1497	Cabot reached Canada (Eng.)
1498	Da Gama first European to reach India by sea (Port.)
1499	Vespucci sailed to West Indies and South America (Sp.)
1500	Cabral claimed Brazil for Portugal
1513	Balboa crossed Isthmus of Panama and sighted Pacific Ocean (Sp.)
1513	de León explored Florida (Sp.)
1519	Cortes conquered Mexico (Sp.)
1520	Magellan commanded first voyage around the world (Sp.)
1524	Verrazano first European to see Hudson River (Fr.)
1525	Pizarro explored Peru (Sp.)
1535	Cartier sailed up St. Lawrence River (Fr.)
1540	Coronado explored Southwest and sighted Grand Canyon (Sp.)
1541	De Soto crossed the Mississippi (Sp.)
1565	St. Augustine founded by the Spanish
1572	Drake sailed around the world (Eng.)
1576	Frobisher searched for northwest passage to India (Eng.)
1584	Raleigh visited Virginia (Eng.)
1585	English settlers left on Roanoke Island
1603	Champlain sailed up St. Lawrence River (Fr.)
1607	Settlement of Jamestown (Eng.)
1609	Hudson explored Hudson River (Hol.)

Unit  2

Americans and Revolution

THE STRUGGLE FOR INDEPENDENCE

DOWN THE ROAD TO REVOLUTION

BENJAMIN FRANKLIN spent much of the 1760s in London as the agent in Parliament for the American colonies. During one of his appearances there, the following exchange took place.

Question: What was the temper of America toward Britain before the year 1763? *Answer:* The best in the world. They submitted willingly to the government of the Crown, and paid in all their courts obedience to the acts of Parliament. . . . They had not only respect, but affection for Great Britain; for its laws, its customs, and manners, and even a fondness for its fashions, that greatly increased commerce.

The American Colonies in 1763

Franklin's statement was no doubt accurate. American colonists in 1763 were, for the most part, quite content to be British subjects. For one thing, more than half of them were of English origin. Many still had relatives in England. They were also tied to England by language and culture. English authors were their authors, and English artists their artists. Even though few of them had ever been to England, most spoke of it as "home." Among those colonists from other lands, most were speaking English by then and were becoming used to English ways.

The basic rights. When colonists boasted that they had the "rights of Englishmen," this was not a hollow term. It meant they enjoyed rights and liberties such as no other people on the earth enjoyed in that age. Among these were

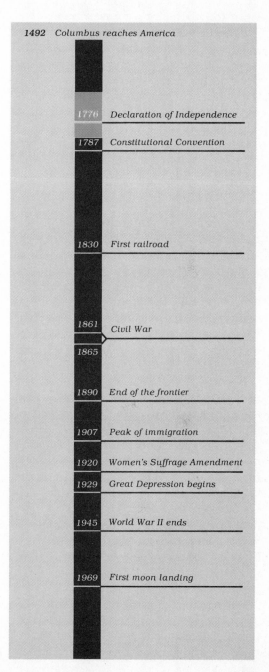

1492 Columbus reaches America

1776 Declaration of Independence

1787 Constitutional Convention

1830 First railroad

1861 Civil War
1865

1890 End of the frontier

1907 Peak of immigration

1920 Women's Suffrage Amendment

1929 Great Depression begins

1945 World War II ends

1969 First moon landing

private property, trial by jury, the right to meet together peaceably, and the right to petition their government.

Because of these "rights of Englishmen," Americans could not be taxed unless their representatives approved; in other words, "no taxation without representation." Their rights were guaranteed not only by the British constitution but also by the charter of each colony. Religious toleration in the colonies was not complete. Yet there was more of it there than anywhere else in the world.

The powers of government. The colonies also enjoyed a great deal of self-government. If a colonist were white, male, and the owner of a certain amount of property—and most white males were—he had the right to vote for his own representatives. Each colony had its own legislature and made most of its own laws. Only rarely did the British Parliament or king overrule these laws.

By the year 1763, Britain and the American colonies had worked out a compromise on dividing the powers of government. The king and Parliament were to control foreign affairs, war and peace, and overseas trade. The colonies, in most other matters, were to make their own laws. By 1763, colonial governments had won the right to levy their own taxes, appoint most of their own officials, and control their own militia. They had far more self-government than did the Spanish and French colonies in the New World.

Furthermore, most American colonists were rarely bothered by British officials. These officials were few in number and tended to be stationed in the larger seaport towns. Ninety percent of the colonists were farmers who lived in the countryside. They seldom saw a British official.

Economic advantages. American colonists also enjoyed certain trading advantages as members of the greatest empire in the western world. For one thing, the British government gave the colonists a monopoly on the sale in England of certain American products. Tobacco was one. English and Irish farmers were not allowed to raise it. And Britain placed a heavy tax on tobacco from any place except America.

Also, over a period of time, Parliament passed a number of laws to put in order the trade of the empire. They were called the Navigation Acts. They aimed to make the British empire both well-to-do and self-sufficient.Under these laws, the colonies were expected to produce raw materials for the empire and to buy manufactured goods from England. One act required that goods traded within the empire be carried only in ships made in England or America. As a result, the colonial shipbuilding industry boomed.

Britain also paid the colonists to produce certain products. Among them were indigo, used by British textile manufacturers, and tar and turpentine, needed for the British navy. That navy itself was one of the great advantages of being part of the British empire. It provided protection for American trading ships against pirates and foreign navies.

Some restrictions. It is true that the Navigation Acts restricted the colonists in some ways. They were not allowed to sell certain items, such as tobacco, rice,

Shipbuilding was a thriving industry along the Delaware River in Philadelphia. In colonial America—with its plentiful supplies of oak and pine—ships could be built more cheaply than in Britain.

indigo, and furs, to any countries outside the empire. Moreover, any goods they wished to buy from another European nation had to pass through England first. There, a special tax was placed on many of them. But all in all, the laws usually worked in the interests of the colonists as well as of the English. When they didn't, the colonists simply got around them by smuggling. That was not hard to do, because Britain had only a small number of officials in the colonies to enforce its laws.

Even British laws that discouraged or prohibited the making of certain goods in the colonies did not work much hardship—except, of course, for the few people engaged in such manufacturing. Generally, Americans were content to

buy their manufactured goods from England. England was the most advanced industrial country in the world. It could make most products more cheaply than any other nation.

A few disagreements. There were, of course, some disagreements between Britain and the American colonists. A number of them involved the colonial governments. Colonists chose their representatives to the lower house of their colonial legislatures. But most governors were appointed to office—by the king in royal colonies and by the proprietor in proprietary colonies. Because of this, the legislative and executive branches battled constantly over which had the right to do what.

109

Governors insisted that their instructions from London should be carried out to the letter. The colonists, on the other hand, wanted to be consulted. They felt that they should have a chance to modify the instructions to the governor. Americans also objected to the fact that they could not choose their own judges. Judges were appointed by the king and could be removed only by him.

A stunning turnabout. But by and large the colonists were well satisfied with life within the British empire in 1763. There was little talk of disloyalty to the king. Thinking back to that time, Benjamin Franklin later recalled, "I never heard in any conversation from any person, drunk or sober, the least expression for separation from England."

Thirteen years later the American colonies declared their independence. Why? One historian has this to say:

New soil had produced new wants, new desires, new points of view, and the colonists were demanding the right to live their own lives in their own way. As we see it today the situation was a dramatic one. On one side was the [unchanging and rigid] system of the mother country, based on precedent and tradition and designed to keep things comfortably as they were; on the other, a vital dynamic organism, containing the seed of a great nation, its forces untried, still to be proved. It is inconceivable that a connection should have continued long between [the] two. . . .

What shapes the course of events? That explanation contains an important idea about human affairs. It is the idea of *inevitability.* In this view, the course of events is not decided through acts and decisions of individuals nor by circumstances nor by chance. It is decided by great underlying forces and factors. Thus, the argument that the American colonies would have remained under English rule "if the colonists hadn't sent their troops to Lexington" or "if rabble-rousers like Sam Adams hadn't stirred up trouble" has no real importance. Things didn't happen differently, because they *couldn't* have happened differently. It was inevitable that the American colonies would seek their independence from Great Britain.

There is a problem with that view. We can never "do" history over again. We cannot bring back the exact circumstances of a time and place. Therefore, we cannot try out other approaches to see if the results would have been different. All we can ever know is what in fact *did* happen. And there is the problem. For the theory of inevitability tempts one to say that whatever did happen was bound to happen.

Was it bound to happen? Was the American Revolution as inevitable as the historian suggests above? We cannot know. What we do know is that in 1763 there was little or no talk of separating from England. Ten years later there was a great deal of talk. And in 1776 the colonies declared their independence.

Even if it were true that separation was inevitable, it was the events of those years that determined when separation would come, and why. It was those years that decided what kind of a revolution the American Revolution would be, and over what issues it would be fought. And that experience, in turn, had much to do with shaping America's attitudes about revolution for years to come.

110

1. How did most American colonists in 1763 feel about being British subjects?
2. When colonists talked of having the "rights of Englishmen," what rights were they referring to?
3. What economic benefits did Americans have from their association with Britain? What restrictions were placed on them?

A Growing Distrust

The stage for the events of 1763–1776 was set in the previous ten-year period. In 1754, for the fourth time within three quarters of a century, Britain and France went to war. The stakes were high: control of nearly all the North American continent. In 1756 the European allies of each side entered the war. For the next seven years the battle raged on four continents— North and South America, Europe, and Asia.

The French and Indian War. Nowhere was the fighting more fierce than in North America, where the war first broke out. Known in Europe as the Seven Years' War, the conflict, in America, was called the French and Indian War. It was so named because of the number of Indian tribes that fought for France (see pages 179–180).

The upper map on this page shows the areas of North America controlled by the big powers in 1700. The lower shows the area each controlled in 1763. American colonists had often expressed the

After the French and Indian War, which nation gained the most territory by the peace treaty? What other country made significant gains?

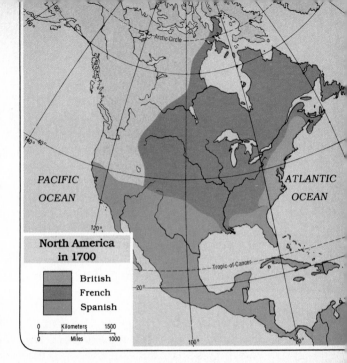

North America in 1700

- British
- French
- Spanish

0 Kilometers 1500
0 Miles 1000

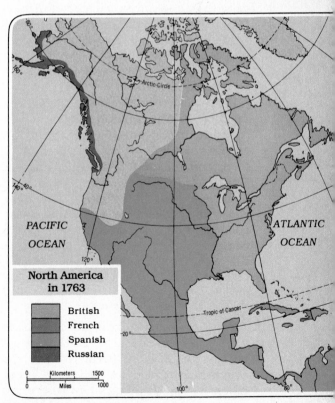

North America in 1763

- British
- French
- Spanish
- Russian

0 Kilometers 1500
0 Miles 1000

fear that they were being encircled by the French. Can you see why?

Even though Britain's American colonies had a large stake in the outcome, they contributed few soldiers and little money to the fight. It was British troops and British money that won the war. In the peace treaty of 1763, France gave up all its territory on the North American continent. Britain and Spain now shared control of the continent except for a thin strip claimed by Russia along the Pacific coast.

Paying the bills. The victory over France had been achieved at a great cost. During the war, Britain had run up a huge debt that now must be paid. Further, the cost of defending and running the British empire was five times what it had been before the war. To help pay these expenses, Britain looked to its American colonies.

It was the colonies who had benefited most by the removal of the French from America. It seemed only right that the colonies should now pay their fair share to defend the newly expanded empire. The money would come from two sources. One was new taxes. The other was better collection of the old taxes the colonists had been evading. This would come through stricter enforcement of the Navigation Acts and a general tightening up of Britain's control over its empire.

Threats to liberty? These moves came at just the wrong time for the colonies. As long as the French threat existed, the colonies depended on British military power to protect them. They were in no position to argue with their protector

about taxes. But with the French threat gone, the colonies' attitude was quite different. They quickly objected to paying more taxes.

By this time a deep distrust had begun to develop between the American colonists and the British. In Britain's eyes, the new import taxes and tighter law enforcement were only fair and right. To the colonists, however, they were anything but fair. These actions, Americans believed, aimed at robbing them of their money and their property. American colonists believed there was a close connection between their property and their liberty. In their minds, therefore, these threats to their property were threats to their liberty, too.

They also objected to the *writs of assistance*, used by the British in enforcing the Navigation Acts. A writ of assistance was a kind of search warrant, often used in looking for smuggled goods. In the past, before searching for such goods, officials had been required to obtain a search warrant in court. Before they could get a warrant, they had to offer proof that there were indeed smuggled goods in the building or on the property they intended to search. Now, they no longer needed to offer such proof. Armed with a writ of assistance, British officials could search for smuggled goods anywhere they wished and at any time. They could even enter private homes. Was not that, thought a good many Americans, another threat to their liberty?

The Stamp Act. You can sense the growing distrust in the words of John Adams, Massachusetts lawyer and political leader, after Parliament passed the

The required use of special tax stamps—like the one at left—aroused bitter opposition throughout the colonies. At right, New Hampshire citizens cheer the hanging in effigy of a tax collector.

Stamp Act of 1765. This law required the colonists to purchase special tax stamps for use on all newspapers, pamphlets, and legal documents. (We use similar tax stamps today on cigarette packages, packs of playing cards, and liquor bottles.) Special tax collectors sold the stamps. The money raised from the stamps was to be sent to England to help pay for the British troops stationed in America.

John Adams was no hothead. He was a thoughtful man, not given to exaggerated charges and fears. Yet here is how Adams interpreted the British motive behind the Stamp Act.

> There seems to be a direct and formal plan under way to enslave all America . . . to strip us in large measure of the means of knowledge . . . and to [take] from the poorer . . . people all of their little income and [confer] it on a set of stamp officers, distributors, and their deputies.

More than a tax? "Enslave." "Take from the poorer . . . people." "Strip us . . . of the means of knowledge." Those are strong words about a simple tax measure. But John Adams and other colonists were beginning to see in such actions something more than a tax.

Parliament had never before placed a direct tax on the colonies. Was this the first of more to come? English subjects were not supposed to be taxed without the consent of their representatives. That might happen to conquered peoples, but not to free English subjects. Yet here was a tax imposed on them by a Parliament in which they were not represented. Was this the start of an attempt to take away the "rights of Englishmen"? Further, those who broke the law were to be tried in a special kind of court in which there was no jury. Was not this another violation of the "rights of Englishmen"?

113

The conspiracy theory. The Americans were beginning to suspect that there was a plot, or conspiracy, to rob them of their liberty. Their suspicion is evident in the pamphlets and newspapers published in America between 1773 and 1776. In those, the British rulers are pictured as bent upon a conspiracy. Its aim was to deprive the Americans of their property and their rights as free people and to turn them into slaves.

At the center of this scheme—so the conspiracy theory went—were the king's ministers. These power-hungry men wished to destroy liberty both in Britain and in America. One way they planned to do this was to increase the number of British officials in America. Thus, the colonists, instead of governing themselves in most matters, would increasingly be governed by British officials. The salaries of these officials would be paid by taxing the colonists more. Slowly the Americans would have their property taken away, and they would be enslaved.

According to those who believed there was a conspiracy, the king's ministers would also undermine American liberties by working through American officials sympathetic to them. Promises of pensions, money, and titles of nobility would be used to bribe these colonial officials to do the bidding of the British.

Thomas Hutchinson, Lieutenant Governor and later Governor of the Massachusetts colony, was considered by many to be such an official. In truth, he was not. Yet in his private letters that American newspapers got hold of, Hutchinson had suggested the colonists' "rights of Englishmen" might have to be reduced if the British empire were to be preserved. A sellout of American liberties, claimed the accusers of Hutchinson.

Were British troops needed? The conspiracy theory also had an explanation for the presence of British troops in America. Britain kept more soldiers in America after the French and Indian War than ever before. British ministers claimed they were needed to protect the colonists against the Indians on the frontier. But the colonists wondered. The war with France was over and won. There was a need not for more troops but for fewer—unless, of course, the king's ministers had other plans for them.

After a few incidents between troops and civilians occurred, a writer in a Boston newspaper in 1768 reported:

The inhabitants of this town have been of late greatly insulted and abused by some of the officers and soldiers. Several have been assaulted [for trifling reasons] and put under guard without any lawful warrant for so doing. A physician of the town walking the streets the other evening was jostled by an officer, when a scuffle ensued. He was afterward met by the same officer in company with another, both as yet unknown, who repeated his blows and (as is supposed) gave him a stroke with a pistol and so wounded him as to endanger his life. . . . *Here, Americans, you may behold some of the first fruits springing up from that root of bitterness, a standing army. Troops are quartered upon us in a time of peace, on pretense of preserving order in a town that was as orderly before their arrival as any one large town in the whole extent of his majesty's dominions; and a little time will discover whether we are to be governed by the martial [military] or the common law of the land.*

British troops disembark from Royal Navy ships in Boston Harbor in 1768. Their role was "to keep order," but their presence in the city led to clashes that heightened already tense feelings.

Do you think the writer held to the conspiracy theory? Was he justified in fearing the presence of a standing army?

Was there really a plot? New Englanders had their own special version of the conspiracy theory. Many of the original Puritan settlers, you will recall, had come to America to escape the persecution of the Anglican church. Now a fear spread through New England that Anglican bishops might be sent to make that church the official, established church in all the American colonies.

Looking back on the events of the 1760s, we know now that there was no British conspiracy to enslave the Americans. It is, however, not things as they are but as people imagine them to be that often determine the course of events. And once people begin to see the world through the lens of a conspiracy, there is no end to what they can imagine.

As you read of the events that followed, ask yourself how the colonists might in each case have applied their conspiracy theory.

CHECKUP

1. What effect did the French and Indian War have on the control of North America?
2. Why did Britain place new taxes on the colonies? What was the reaction of the colonists?
3. What was the conspiracy theory, in which some Americans believed?

British Measures and American Reactions

The Stamp Act was met by violence and by political and economic protests. A new group, the Sons of Liberty, came into being to fight the act. They threatened and bullied tax collectors, and sometimes tarred and feathered them.

115

Massachusetts asked that the colonies send delegates to meet in New York in 1765 to consider a common course of action, and nine colonies did. It was the first time this many colonies had met to discuss their common problems. The Stamp Act Congress, as it was called, asked Parliament to repeal the act. Meanwhile, many merchants refused to buy English goods, and colonists balked at buying the tax stamps. As a result, hardly a penny was raised.

Franklin on the Stamp Act. In the face of this opposition, Parliament took up the matter again. Among the things they considered was the testimony of Benjamin Franklin, who served as the colonial agent in England:

Question: If the act is not repealed, what do you think will be the consequences?
Answer: A total loss of the respect and affection that the people of America bear to this country, and all the commerce that depends on that respect and affection.
Question: How can the commerce be affected?
Answer: You will find that, if the act is not repealed, they will take very little of your manufactures in a short time.
Question: Is it in their power to do without them?
Answer: I think they may very well do without them.
Question: Is it in their interest not to take them?
Answer: The goods they take from Britain are either necessaries, mere conveniences, or [unnecessary luxuries]. The first, as cloth etc. with a little [effort] they can make at home; the second they can do without till they are able to [make] them . . . themselves; and the last . . . they will strike off immediately. They are mere articles of fash-

Benjamin Franklin—scientist, inventor, and diplomat—was the best-known man in colonial America. Although he had only two years of school, he never stopped educating himself.

ion. . . . The people have already struck off, by general agreement, the use of all goods fashionable in mourning.

Franklin rested his argument on the American refusal to buy English goods. In doing so, he hoped to worry British merchants so that they would ask Parliament to repeal the law. Read again Franklin's explanation of how the colonists could get along without "necessaries" from England. Do you see why English cloth manufacturers might also be worried?

In 1766 Parliament bowed to American pressure and repealed the Stamp Act. Just so there would be no question as to who was boss, however, the British passed the Declaratory Act on the same day. This act stated that Parliament had full authority over the American colonies "in all cases whatsoever."

The Quartering Act. Another British measure that angered colonists had to do with the support of the 10,000 troops the British planned to keep in North America. It seemed entirely reasonable to the British that the colonies should bear some of the costs for their own defense. Supplies and shelter would be needed for the troops. The most direct way to provide them, and the least costly way to the British government, was to require the Americans to furnish them.

This Parliament did in the Quartering Act of 1765. Some time later the British passed another act, permitting these troops to be quartered in inns, alehouses, and unoccupied buildings. When the New York legislature refused to furnish funds to supply the British troops, Parliament ordered the legislature shut down until it did as told. In this case, the order was never carried out. However, it is not hard to imagine how the colonists viewed an order to their representatives to knuckle under to Parliament.

The Townshend Acts. Still, taxes had to be raised, and so in 1767 the British tried again with the Townshend Acts. This time taxes were placed on certain imported goods such as tea, paper, paint, and lead. The money raised was to be used to pay the salaries of colonial governors and other royal officials. One of the acts set up in Boston a board of customs officials to crack down on colonists who were escaping the law. The British also set up more courts. There, violators would be tried—once again without the right of trial by jury.

The Townshend Acts fitted nicely into the conspiracy theory. Until now, the governor's salary in some colonies had been paid by the colonial legislature. The colonists believed control over a governor's salary gave them a powerful weapon. They could sometimes influence the governor by threatening to hold up his salary. What would happen when the governor no longer depended on the legislature for his salary?

Furthermore, Boston had been the spearhead of the anti-Stamp Act movement. Was it coincidence that the tough new customs officials were being sent to Boston? When the Massachusetts legislature sent a letter to the other colonies opposing the Townshend Acts, the British ministry reacted strongly. The royal governor was ordered to dissolve the legislature, and soldiers were sent into Boston. Was there any longer a doubt, the colonists asked, why the British were stationing so many soldiers in North America?

"All confidence is ended. . . ." Writing to an English friend, a Boston minister named Andrew Eliot expressed the feelings of many Bostonians in 1768.

> To have a standing army! Good God! What can be worse to a people who have tasted the sweets of liberty! . . . There will never be harmony between Great Britain and her colonies that there has been. All confidence is ended, and the moment any blood is shed, all affection will cease. . . .
>
> Tamely to give up our rights and allow ourselves to be taxed at the will of people so far away, and to be under military government is to consent to be slaves.

Do you see any evidence of the conspiracy theory in the Reverend Andrew Eliot's statement?

117

Rising opposition. The Townshend Acts stirred greater opposition in the colonies than ever before. Once again American merchants agreed not to import British goods. England's trade with New York dropped by seven eighths, and with Pennsylvania and New England by one half.

To produce some of the goods they needed, American women began to manufacture clothing at home. A record of what happened has been left us by Peter Oliver, a Bostonian who sided with the British.

> [The clergy] were also set to Work, to preach up Manufactures instead of the Gospel. They preached about it and about it; until the Women and Children, both within Doors and without, set their Spinning Wheels a whirling in defiance of *Great Britain.* The female Spinners kept on spinning for 6 days of the Week . . . they generally clothed the Parson and his Family with the Produce of their Labor. This was a new Species of Enthusiasm and might be justly termed the Enthusiasm of the Spinning Wheel.

Why would New England ministers have taken the side of protestors? Does that account by an American who supported the British give us an indication of how widespread and deep the protest was?

The Boston Massacre ". . . the moment any blood is shed, all affection will cease." Two years after the Reverend Andrew Eliot wrote those words, the tension between the Americans and the British soldiers resulted in bloodshed.

As might be expected, Boston was the scene. Brawls between the redcoats and civilians had been going on there and elsewhere for some time. On the night of March 5, 1770, an angry, shouting crowd began throwing snowballs at British sentries. When the crowd would not stop, the soldiers called for help. In the noise and confusion, the soldiers, acting in fear and without orders from

In 1772, the burning of the British customs ship *Gaspee* increased tension between Britain and the colonies. While chasing a smuggler, the ship ran aground in Narragansett Bay. A group of Americans boarded the stranded *Gaspee*, removed the crew, and burned the ship to the waterline.

their commander, opened fire. Five Americans were killed. Among them was Crispus Attucks, the first black man to die in the Revolution. The colonists' leaders were quick to call the episode — for propaganda purposes — the Boston Massacre. To many Americans, the Boston Massacre was further proof of the conspiracy they believed in.

The Daughters of Liberty. Tensions between Britain and America relaxed temporarily after that incident. Britain once again retreated from its tough policy. In 1770 Parliament repealed all the Townshend duties except the one on tea. The colonists, responding measure for measure, ended their boycott of all goods except tea.

Groups of women calling themselves the Daughters of Liberty were especially active in seeing to it that the tea boycott was observed. They operated in a number of the larger colonial cities. In Boston, this public notice appeared.

The following Agreement has lately been come into by upwards of 300 Mistresses of Families in this Town; in which Number the Ladies of the highest Rank and Influence. . . .

Boston, January 31, 1770
. . . we join with the very respectable Body of Merchants and other Inhabitants of this Town . . . in their Resolutions, *totally* to abstain from the Use of TEA: And as the greatest Part of the Revenue arising [from the latest acts from England] is produced from the duty paid on Tea . . . We the Subscribers do strictly [agree] that we will totally abstain from the Use of [Tea] (Sickness excepted) not only in our respective Families; but that we will absolutely refuse it, if it should be offered to us upon any occasion whatsoever.

What do you suppose was the aim of publishing this agreement in the newspaper? Why was it important to note that the group included "Ladies of the highest Rank and Influence"? To answer that question, you might want to think back to what you read about "deference" in Unit 1.

Samuel Adams's role. With the repeal of the Townshend duties, and except for the boycott on tea, business returned to normal. From mid-1770 to 1773 things remained quiet. Many colonists thought the crisis had passed. But not Samuel Adams. A distant cousin of John Adams, Samuel Adams was a leader of the Sons of Liberty. He had played a major part in anti-British activities.

During the lull in the tensions with Britain, Adams wrote a series of newspaper articles to alert Americans to the dangers they still faced. This one appeared in the *Boston Gazette* in 1771.

I believe that no people ever yet groaned under the heavy yoke of slavery except when they deserved it. . . . The truth is that all might be free if they valued freedom and defended it as they ought. . . .

The liberties of our country, the freedom of our civil constitution, are worth defending at all risks. . . . It will bring an everlasting mark of disgrace on the present generation . . . if we should allow them to be wrested from us by violence without a struggle, or be cheated out of them by the tricks of false and designing men. At present we are in most danger of the latter. . . . Instead of sitting down satisfied with the efforts we have already made, *which is the wish of our enemies*, the necessity of the times, more than ever, calls for our utmost carefulness, deliberation, fortitude, and perseverance.

119

Adams worked hard to keep anti-British sentiment alive. To do so, he hit upon a clever scheme. In each Massachusetts town, a committee was formed to keep other towns in the colony informed whenever the British violated American liberties. These committees were called Committees of Correspondence. Later the idea was extended so that the several colonies could keep in touch with one another in the same way. These "engines of revolution," as they were called, became the machinery for organizing revolution throughout the land.

The dispute over tea. When the British blundered with the Tea Act of 1773, the Committees of Correspondence were ready to do their work. The British tax on tea, you will remember, was the only one of the Townshend duties not repealed. Britain kept that duty to show that Parliament had the right to tax the Americans. Just as stubbornly, the colonists refused to buy British tea—to show that Britain did *not* have the right of taxation. They bought their tea from the Dutch instead and smuggled it into the colonies.

This tug of wills might have gone on for years had not a new situation come up. The British East India Company was an important trading company. It controlled all trade in tea between India and the rest of the British empire. The company was being hurt by the American boycott. Finding itself with tons of unsold tea on hand, the company appealed to the British government for help. Parliament responded with an act that gave the company a monopoly on the sale of tea in America.

Since the colonists were not buying tea from the British, that act would not in itself do much good. But Parliament also lowered the price of British tea. The new price, even after the hated tea tax was added, would be cheaper than that of the Dutch tea the colonists were smuggling. By offering bargain prices, the British hoped to get Americans to buy their tea—and, at the same time, pay the tax. The Tea Act also named certain pro-British merchants in America, like the sons of Governor Thomas Hutchinson, as the only ones who could handle the sale of the tea. That shut out the Whig merchants. (An American who objected to British control and supported colonial interests was often referred to as a Whig. Many Whigs belonged to the Sons of Liberty.)

Opposing the tea tax. The colonists would have no part of the offer. They were *not* going to pay that tea tax, no matter what. When British tea ships began arriving in America, the Committees of Correspondence alerted the local Sons of Liberty to prevent the ships from unloading. In Charleston, South Carolina, the tea was unloaded but was then placed under guard so that it could not be sold. At Portsmouth, New Hampshire, and at Philadelphia, Americans forced the tea ships to turn back.

How this was done can be seen in this letter. It is addressed to Captain Ayres of the ship *Polly*, bound from London to Philadelphia.

Sir: We are informed that you have [unwisely] taken charge of a quantity of tea which has been sent out by the [East] India Company, under the auspices of the Ministry, as a trial of American virtue and [will].

Now, as your cargo, on your arrival here, will most assuredly bring you into hot water, and as you are perhaps a stranger to these parts, we have concluded to advise you of the present situation of affairs in Philadelphia, that . . . you may stop short in your dangerous errand, [protect] your ship against the rafts of combustible matter which may be set on fire and turned loose against [it]; and more than all this, that you may preserve your own person from the pitch and feathers that are prepared for you.

In the first place, we must tell you that the Pennsylvanians are, to a man, passionately fond of freedom, the birthright of Americans, and at all events are determined to enjoy it.

That they sincerely believe no power on the face of the earth has a right to tax them without their consent.

That, in their opinion, the tea in your custody is designed by the Ministry to enforce such a tax, which they will undoubtedly oppose, and in so doing, give you every possible obstruction.

The Sons of Liberty made their point. Captain Ayres decided not to land.

The Boston Tea Party. In Boston, Samuel Adams and the Sons of Liberty were determined to have a show of force over the tea tax. The result was the Boston Tea Party in December 1773. During a town meeting, citizens demanded that two tea ships that had entered the harbor be sent back to England. When Governor Hutchinson refused this demand, Bostonians disguised themselves as Mohawk Indians, boarded the vessels, and threw the trunks of tea into the harbor.

A few years earlier, an act like this might have shocked many colonists. But by 1773, attitudes had hardened. John

The Boston Tea Party is pictured on this block of four postage stamps, issued on its 200th anniversary in 1973. Outraged Patriots throw cases of the hated tea into the harbor.

Adams recorded his feelings in his diary the day after the event.

This is the most magnificent move of all. There is a dignity, a majesty . . . in this last effort of the patriots that I greatly admire. The people should never rise without doing something to be remembered, something notable and striking. This destruction of the tea is so bold, so daring, so firm, intrepid, and inflexible, and it must have such important and lasting consequences that I can't help considering it a turning point in history.

Adams then went on to justify this act. As you read his words, again look for evidence of the conspiracy theory. Note also how Adams presents the choices available. Were there any other choices possible?

The question is whether the destruction of this tea was necessary? I think it was, absolutely and indispensably. They could not send it back. The Governor, Admiral, and Comptroller would not permit it. . . . Then there was no alternative except to destroy it. To let it be landed would be giving

121

up the principle of taxation by Parliamentary authority against which the Continent has struggled for 10 years . . . and subjecting ourselves and our posterity forever . . . to desolation and oppression, to poverty and servitude.

As Adams predicted, the Boston Tea Party did become a "turning point in history." Relations between Britain and America grew worse. In America, the Whigs hoped this act of defiance would cause Britain to soften its policy. Resistance had done so in the past. In Britain, however, public opinion went against the colonists. The king himself was furious. "The die is now cast," wrote George III. "The colonies must either submit or triumph."

The Intolerable Acts. To punish the Americans, Parliament in 1774 passed a number of new acts. They were called the Intolerable Acts by the Whigs. One was the Boston Port Act, which shut down the port until Bostonians paid for the tea they had destroyed. Another was the Massachusetts Government Act. This act took away many of that colony's rights of self-government. It also made a British military man, General Thomas Gage, the new governor of the colony of Massachusetts.

Two other acts, passed at about the same time, further angered the colonists. One was a new Quartering Act, which allowed royal governors to board troops in occupied buildings. Under that act, colonists could even be required to put up soldiers in their own homes. The second was the Quebec Act of 1774. This law turned over the area north of the Ohio River to the newly formed British province of Quebec. The

law deprived several colonies of their land claims in the West.

To colonists all over America, these acts came as a shock. They were regarded as further proof that a conspiracy against the colonists' liberties did exist. Two of the acts seemed to place the colonies under military rule. And all of them punished the entire colony of Massachusetts for the acts of a small number of people.

Were not these measures, Americans asked, acts of tyranny? Did they not deprive citizens of Massachusetts of their "rights as Englishmen"?

The First Continental Congress. The colonists' answer to the Intolerable Acts was to call on delegates from all the colonies to meet in Philadelphia in September 1774. This meeting was the First Continental Congress.

Most of the delegates were men who had been resisting Britain for some time. From Massachusetts came the two Adamses, Samuel and John; from Pennsylvania, Joseph Galloway and John Dickinson. Virginia sent George Washington, Patrick Henry, and Richard Henry Lee. New York's James Duane and South Carolina's Christopher Gadsden were also there. If the Continental Congress had done nothing else, it was important for bringing together for the first time many of the men who, within their own colonies, had long been opposing Britain.

But the Congress did more. Like the Committees of Correspondence, it became another part of the machinery of revolution. Members voted for another boycott of British goods, called the Continental Association. They also called for

Virginia lawyer and orator Patrick Henry, shown here arguing a case in court, was a fiery leader of the Patriot cause. In 1775 he urged resistance to Britain in these now famous words: "I know not what course others may take; but as for me, give me liberty, or give me death!"

repeal of the hated Intolerable Acts. They spoke out strongly against taxation without representation. Finally, they asked that the colonial militias be strengthened. (The militia was the group upon which each colony depended for its defense. It was made up of the colony's able-bodied men, who served as part-time soldiers.) The militias were urged to get new members and to arm and train them. This last measure was just short of war.

Theories of empire. But few Americans were yet ready to break cleanly away from England. Indeed, what they said over and over was that they wanted only to enjoy the "rights of Englishmen." What they sought was a way to protect those rights against the attacks of the king's ministers. To do so, they proposed various theories of empire.

During the meeting of the Continental Congress, Joseph Galloway, who would side with England when the revolution began, proposed to create an American government within the colonies. There would be a president chosen by the king, and a grand council, or congress, chosen by the colonial assemblies. Each colony would still run its own affairs. The president and grand council would manage affairs among the colonies. Most important, Parliament could not make laws affecting the American colonies unless the grand council had approved of them. The plan was voted on by the Continental Congress, but it lost out by a single vote.

Shortly after the congress adjourned, John Adams put forward another theory of empire. The colonies, he said, were not really part of the British Kingdom. Therefore they were not subject to Parliament. In Adams's plan, each colony would be considered entirely independent and would make its own laws. Each would be tied to the empire, however, by allegiance to the King of England.

This later became known as the *dominion theory of empire.* During the nineteenth and twentieth centuries this theory became the basis for the British Commonwealth of Nations. Adams was proposing the exact relationship that Canada and Australia have to Great Britain today. But in the 1770s, the British were not willing to consider the idea.

By the beginning of 1775 it was plain that Britain and its American colonies could not agree on measures that would keep the empire intact. The scene was now set for the final break between the two. In the next chapter we shall see how that break came about.

CHECKUP

1. What did each of the following provide for: the Stamp Act? the Quartering Act? the Townshend Acts? the Intolerable Acts?
2. In what ways did the colonists react to these measures?
3. Describe two events in Boston that contributed to rising tensions.

Key Facts from Chapter 5

1. Before 1763, American colonists were content, for the most part, to be British subjects. The Americans enjoyed many rights and liberties as well as economic advantages.
2. After 1763, when Britain won control of Canada and the French-held territories to the Mississippi, the attitude of many Americans toward Britain gradually changed.
3. Britain believed the American colonies should pay a larger share for the expenses of the French and Indian War, and took various steps to accomplish this goal.
4. The American colonists regarded the British actions as attempts to rob them of their money, their property, and even their liberties.
5. The Boston Massacre in 1770 and the Boston Tea Party in 1773 inflamed the feelings of both the Americans and the British toward each other.
6. By the beginning of 1775 it was plain that Britain and the American colonies could not agree on measures to keep the empire intact.

★ REVIEWING THE CHAPTER ★

People, Places, and Events

Review Questions

1. Why were the American colonists generally content to be British subjects before 1763?   *P. 107*

2. Explain what is meant by the phrase "rights of Englishmen."   *Pp. 107–108*

3. As British subjects, what trade advantages did the colonists enjoy? What trade restrictions did the British impose on the colonists?   *Pp. 108–109*

4. Look at the maps on page 111 and describe how the peace treaty changed the face of North America.

5. How did British policy change toward the colonies after the French and Indian War? Why?   *P. 112*

6. Why did Americans object so strongly to the Stamp Act? Why did the British repeal the act?   *Pp. 112–113; 115–116*

7. What was the role of Samuel Adams?   *P. 119*

8. List the accomplishments of the First Continental Congress.   *Pp. 122–123*

9. Suppose you were a Patriot and your best friend were a Loyalist. (A Loyalist was one who sided with the British.) What arguments might you use to win him or her away from the Loyalist cause?

Chapter Test

*On a separate piece of paper, write **T** if the statement is true and **F** if the statement is false.*

1. Before 1763, there was little or no talk of the American colonies separating from England.

2. Under the Navigation Acts, the colonies were expected to produce manufactured goods for the empire and to buy raw materials from England.

3. After the French and Indian War, Great Britain gained the most territory by the peace treaty.

4. The colonists thought that, by taxing them without their consent, Parliament was trying to take away their political rights.

5. During the Boston Massacre, the French killed many inhabitants of that city.

6. Samuel Adams warned the colonists not to revolt against British laws.

7. Under the Intolerable Acts, British troops could be quartered in colonial homes.

8. The First Continental Congress brought together many of the people who would, in time, lead the Revolution.

9. By the time the Revolutionary War began, all American colonists were united in their opposition to British rule.

10. Life in the New World had produced new desires and new points of views that led the colonists to demand the right to live their own lives in their own way.

125

CHARLES TOWN

BOSTON

KING GEORGE III had his own theory of empire. He expressed it this way in 1774: "The New England governments are in a state of rebellion. . . . blows must decide whether they are to be subjects of this country or independent." For King George, there was no middle ground.

The Outbreak of War

Blows did indeed decide the fate of the empire. The first one came on April 19, 1775, when British soldiers and American militiamen faced each other for the first time. British General Thomas Gage learned that the Americans were secretly storing up guns and bullets in Concord, Massachusetts. On the night of April 18, he sent out soldiers from Boston to take them.

But even as the British marched through the darkness, American militiamen were arming to meet them. These Minutemen—so-called because they were to be ready at a minute's notice—had been warned by Paul Revere and others. Revere was a member of the Sons of Liberty. He and two companions had ridden along the country roads, awakening sleeping Patriots. (The Patriots were those Americans who resisted British control of the colonies.)

Shortly after dawn the British troops reached Lexington, on the road to Concord. There they found fifty Minutemen lined up across the village green. For a moment, the two groups—one large, uniformed, and well armed; the other small, in rough dress, and with fewer weapons—stood facing each other.

Two views of Lexington. Today we know that what happened next marked the beginning of the American War of Independence. Just what did take place? We have two conflicting accounts. For what we know about the exact details, we must rely upon them. One account was in a Massachusetts newspaper.

> At Lexington . . . a company of militia . . . mustered near the meeting house. The [British] troops came in sight of them just before sunrise; and running within a few rods of them, the Commanding Officer [Major Pitcairn] accosted the militia in words to this effect: "Disperse, you rebels—damn you, throw down your arms

After the Lexington encounter, a clash occurred at Concord. Why, do you think, did the poet Emerson describe the battle at North Bridge as "the shot heard round the world"?

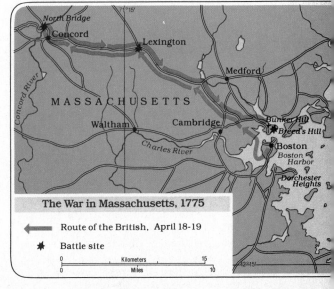

The War in Massachusetts, 1775

← Route of the British, April 18-19

✷ Battle site

and disperse"; upon which the troops huzzaed, and immediately one or two officers discharged their pistols, which were instanteously followed by the firing of four or five of the soldiers, and then there seemed to be a general discharge from the whole body. Eight of our men were killed and nine wounded. . . .

In Lexington [the British] . . . also set fire to several other houses. . . . They pillaged almost every house they passed. . . . But the savage Barbarity exercised upon the bodies of our unfortunate brethren who fell is almost incredible. Not contented with shooting down the unarmed, aged, and infirm, they disregarded the cries of the wounded, killing them without mercy, and mangling their bodies in the most shocking manner.

The second account was printed in a British newspaper in London.

Six companies of [British] light infantry . . . at Lexington found a body of the country people under arms, on a green close to the road. And upon the King's troops marching up to them, in order to inquire the reason for their being so assembled, they went off in great confusion. And several guns were fired upon the King's troops from behind a stone wall, and also from the meeting-house and other houses, by which one man was wounded, and Major Pitcairn's horse shot in two places. In consequence of this attack by the rebels, the troops returned the fire and killed several of them. . . .

On the return of the troops from Concord, they [the rebels] . . . began to fire upon them from behind stone walls and houses, and kept up in that manner a scattering fire during the whole of their march of fifteen miles, by which means several were killed and wounded. And such was the cruelty and barbarity of the rebels that they scalped and cut off the ears of some of the wounded men who fell into their hands.

Newspaper accounts must often be used by the historian to discover what actually happened in any historic event. But their usefulness is limited. Do these two stories tell why? Do you suppose it at all likely that the first would have been written by a British soldier, and the second by an American?

Enter George Washington. The Second Continental Congress met in May 1775, fresh on the heels of this clash. It adopted as its own army the ill-organized force of New England militiamen that had now penned the British troops inside Boston. One of its main decisions was to choose George Washington as commander in chief of the army.

Washington was well equipped to handle the task because of his background, training, and personal qualities. The son of a well-to-do Virginia planter, he entered military service at the age of nineteen. He fought in the French and Indian War for five years, returning as Virginia's most celebrated hero. Following the war, he settled on his estate at Mount Vernon. There he gained valuable experience running a huge plantation. As a member of the Virginia legislature he took part in anti-British protests and helped train the Virginia militia.

Washington's abilities as a leader qualified him to become commander in chief. He had a cool head in an emergency and never lost his sense of dignity and bearing. His devotion to duty enabled him to carry on even during the darkest and most discouraging times of the war. And his strong will and

Fort Ticonderoga

At the time of the American Revolution, Fort Ticonderoga, in northern New York State, was regarded as the gateway to Canada. Lying at the foot of Lake Champlain, the fort was on the north-south military route that made use of Lake Champlain, Lake George, and the Hudson River. Built by the French in 1755, Fort Ticonderoga had been the scene of fighting during the French and Indian War.

At the outbreak of the Revolutionary War, a British force was occupying the fort. Soon after the events at Lexington and Concord, Americans made plans to take Ticonderoga. Two capable officers led the expedition. One was Benedict Arnold, who headed a force of Massachusetts militia. The other was Ethan Allen, leader of a rough-and-tumble group of Vermont men known as the Green Mountain Boys.

On the evening of May 9, 1775, the expedition reached Lake Champlain, across from Fort Ticonderoga. There were only a few boats available and only about eighty men were able to cross the lake during the night. But Arnold and Allen, determined to surprise the British, attacked at sunrise without waiting for the rest of their force. Although the main gate was locked, a small one was open. The Green Mountain Boys overpowered the sentries, and took the fort without the loss of a man.

Henry Knox, the commander of the Continental Army's artillery, had the idea of using the big guns from Fort Ticonderoga to drive the British army out of Boston. In December 1775, 43 cannon and 16 mortars were placed on sledges drawn by oxen and dragged for 300 miles (470 km) across Massachusetts. Once the Americans seized Dorchester Heights, most of Boston and its harbor would have been within range of Knox's artillery. The British, faced with this possibility, decided to get out of Boston and sailed with their army to Halifax, Nova Scotia.

Ethan Allen, waving his sword aloft, demands the instant surrender of Fort Ticonderoga from its surprised British commander.

Washington's taking command of the army was hardly as impressive as the artist has pictured it. It would be many months before the troops were as well trained and disciplined as shown here.

determination held the army together when others lost hope.

Bunker Hill. Before Washington took over his new command, however, an important battle had been fought. General Gage's troops in Boston were surprised when the Americans seized Breed's Hill in Charlestown. This hill, one of the many overlooking Boston, was located just below Bunker Hill, across the river from the city.

The British were determined to drive the untrained Americans from the commanding heights. On June 17, in what has become known as the battle of Bunker Hill, British troops charged the high ground three times before taking it. The Americans were finally forced to fall back after running out of gunpowder. The cost of this victory to the British was frightful. One eighth of all the British officers killed in the Revolutionary War died that day.

The battle had an electrifying effect on both sides. The Americans gained confidence in their fighting ability after they inflicted such heavy losses upon Britain's best soldiers. In England the great shedding of blood caused the government to become more determined to defeat and punish the colonists.

A reluctance to break away. In view of the fighting that had occurred by the end of 1775, you might find it surprising that most Americans still were not talking about breaking away from the British empire. They insisted, to be sure, that the old rules of empire were over. They maintained that there would have to be a new system, one that would protect their rights.

Yet at the same time most Americans hoped to find a way to remain within the empire. And they remained loyal to their king. It was not, they assured each other, George III who was responsible for Britain's harsh policies, but his evil ministers. Many still spoke of their affection for the king, and of their acceptance of the idea of monarchy.

Thomas Paine's pamphlet. Thomas Paine, a recent immigrant from England, destroyed whatever regard Americans still had for the king and monarchy. Early in 1776 he published a pamphlet called *Common Sense.* In harsh words he laid the blame for all that had happened directly at the door of the "royal brute of Britain," George III.

Paine urged Americans to stop fooling themselves that monarchy would ever bring a just government. Monarchy, said Paine, was an absurd form of government. One honest man, he wrote, was worth "all the crowned ruffians that ever lived." It was monarchy that was reducing the world to blood and ashes. Americans should abandon it forever and create a republican form of government. This meant throwing off completely all connection with Britain. Besides, added Paine, it was ridiculous that a continent—North America— should be ruled by an island—Britain. To those who still wanted to keep ties with Britain, Paine wrote:

> Men of passive tempers look somewhat lightly over the offenses of Great Britain, and still hoping for the best, are apt to call out, "Come, come, we shall be friends again in spite of this." But examine the passions and feelings of mankind . . . and then tell me whether you can hereafter love, honor and faithfully serve the power that has carried fire and sword into your land?

Paine followed this argument with a ringing defense of freedom.

> O, ye that love mankind! Ye that dare oppose not only the tyranny but the tyrant, stand forth! Every spot on the Old World is overrun with oppression. Freedom hath been hunted round the globe. Asia and Africa have long expelled her. Europe regards her like a stranger, and England has given her warning to depart. . . .
>
> But in America we have it in our power to begin the world over again. A situation similar to the present has not happened from the days of Noah until now. The birthday of a new world is at hand, and a race of men, perhaps as numerous as all Europe contains, are to receive their portion of freedom from the outcome of a few months.

Remember that Paine was writing to encourage reluctant Americans to break with Britain and to set up a republic. Does this help you understand why he wrote that freedom will be "the outcome of a few months"?

The impact of *Common Sense*. In our day, when we are bombarded with arguments and information from a dozen different directions by television, radio, newspapers, movies, and magazines, it is hard to grasp the impact that this one little pamphlet had. In all, some 300,000 copies were sold. That would be comparable to 24 million today.

In *Common Sense*, Thomas Paine urged independence for the colonies. In the *Crisis* papers, he called upon all Americans to support wholeheartedly the Revolutionary cause.

For every copy sold, there were probably several readers. In fact, a biographer of Paine estimated that one in every two Americans read it. Thomas Jefferson, John Adams, Samuel Adams, and several other colonial leaders had recently been putting forward the same ideas that Paine expressed. But none presented them with such force and passion as Paine. People talked about *Common Sense* on street corners and in taverns and inns. Paine may well have doubled the number of Americans who favored independence.

CHECKUP

1. Where did the first clash between American and British troops take place? Why?
2. How did American and British newspaper accounts of the encounter differ?
3. What views did Thomas Paine put forth in *Common Sense?* What effect did this pamphlet have?

Independence Is Declared

By the spring of 1776, the Second Continental Congress was moving boldly toward independence. In March, it gave *privateers* permission to attack British shipping. Privateers were privately owned vessels that were authorized by the government to be used as naval ships and to capture ships of other nations. Privateering was a form of legalized piracy. That meant that Congress was now authorizing acts of war against Britain at sea as well as on land. In May, Congress sent word to the assembly of each colony that it should write a new *state* constitution and set up a state government. In other words, each of the colonies was urged to be a colony no more.

National Portrait Gallery, London

Now fitting for a

Privateer,

In the Harbour of *BEVERLY*,

The BRIGANTINE

Wafhington,

A ftrong, good veffel for that purpofe and a prime failer.

Any Seamen or Landmen that have an inclination to

Make their Fortunes in a few Months,

May have an Opportunity, by applying to

JOHN DYSON.

Beverly, September 17th, 1776.

As a result of this broadside, the *Washington* quickly signed a crew. Half the proceeds from the sale of captured ships and cargoes usually went to the privateer's owner. The other half was shared by the ship's officers and crew.

By this time the colonies as a whole had practically made their break with Britain. All that remained was to declare it before the rest of the world. A small committee was appointed by the Second Continental Congress to write a declaration of independence. The committee turned over the task to one of its members, a quiet thirty-three-year-old Virginia lawyer and planter named Thomas Jefferson.

Explaining the Revolution. The rebellion of colonies was an extraordinary act, one that had not occurred before in modern times. Therefore, one of Jefferson's main purposes was to explain and justify the act in the eyes of the world.

He did this in two ways. One was to present a theory of government and society that explained when revolution is justified. Jefferson spelled out the theory in the first part of the declaration. There he made these five points:

- All men are created equal.
- People have a right to life, liberty, and the pursuit of happiness.
- The reason government was created in the first place was to protect people in the enjoyment of those rights.
- Government has to be based on the consent of the governed.
- When a government no longer follows the wishes of its people and becomes tyrannical, the people have a right to get rid of it and to set up a new one.

These ideas were not new when Jefferson set them down. Indeed, Jefferson calls them "truths" that are "self-evident"—that is, so obvious that they need no proof. People had long talked about these ideas. Political theorists and philosophers had written books about them for nearly a hundred years. But nowhere in the world had anyone dared actually to put them into practice. No people had fought a revolution on these principles or created a new government based on them.

The second means by which Jefferson explained and justified the American Revolution was to list the many ways the colonists believed the British had wronged them. Following Tom Paine's lead, Jefferson blamed all the wrongs on King George III rather than on his ministers or on Parliament. That list of wrongs takes up most of the Declaration of Independence, as you can see on the following pages.

The Declaration of Independence

☆ ☆ ☆ ☆ ☆ ☆ ☆ ☆ ☆ ☆ ☆ ☆ ☆

When, in the course of human events, it becomes necessary for one people to dissolve the political bands which have connected them with another, and to assume, among the powers of the earth, the separate and equal station to which the laws of nature and nature's God entitle them, a decent respect to the opinions of mankind requires that they should declare the causes which impel them to the separation.

*W*e hold these truths to be self-evident; that all men are created equal, that they are endowed by their Creator with certain unalienable rights, that among these are life, liberty, and the pursuit of happiness. That to secure these rights, governments are instituted among men, deriving their just powers from the consent of the governed; that whenever any form of government becomes destructive of these ends, it is the right of the people to alter or to abolish it, and to institute new government, laying its foundation on such principles, and organizing its powers in such form, as to them shall seem most likely to effect their safety and happiness. Prudence, indeed, will dictate that governments long established should not be changed for light and transient causes; and accordingly all experience hath shown that mankind are more disposed to suffer while evils are sufferable, than to right themselves by abolishing the forms to which they are accustomed. But when a long train of abuses and usurpations, pursuing invariably the same object, evinces a design to reduce them under absolute despotism, it is their right, it is their duty, to throw off such government, and to provide new guards for their future security.

*S*uch has been the patient sufferance of these colonies; and such is now the necessity which constrains them to alter their former systems of government. The history of the present king of Great Britain is a history of repeated injuries and usurpations, all having in direct object the establishment of an absolute tyranny over these states. To prove this, let facts be submitted to a candid world.

He has refused his assent to laws the most wholesome and necessary for the public good.

He has forbidden his governors to pass laws of immediate and pressing importance, unless suspended in their operation till his assent should be obtained; and when so suspended, he has utterly neglected to attend to them.

He has refused to pass other laws for the accommodation of large districts of people, unless those people would relinquish the right of representation in the legislature, a right inestimable to them, and formidable to tyrants only.

He has called together legislative bodies at places unusual, uncomfortable, and distant from the depository of their public records, for the sole purpose of fatiguing them into compliance with his measures.

He has dissolved representative houses repeatedly, for opposing, with manly firmness, his invasions on the rights of the people.

He has refused, for a long time after such dissolutions, to cause others to be elected; whereby the legislative powers, incapable of annihilation, have returned to the people at large for their exercise; the state remaining, in the meantime, exposed to all the dangers of invasion from without and convulsions within.

He has endeavored to prevent the population of these states; for that purpose obstructing the laws for the naturalization of foreigners, refusing to pass others to encourage their migrations hither, and raising the conditions of new appropriations of lands.

He has obstructed the administration of justice, by refusing his assent to laws for establishing judiciary powers.

He has made judges dependent on his will alone for the tenure of their offices, and the amount and payment of their salaries.

He has erected a multitude of new offices, and sent hither swarms of officers to harass our people and eat out their substance.

He has kept among us, in times of peace, standing armies, without the consent of our legislatures.

He has affected to render the military independent of, and superior to, the civil power.

He has combined with others to subject us to a jurisdiction foreign to our constitution and unacknowledged by our laws, giving his assent to their acts of pretended legislation:

For quartering large bodies of armed troops among us;

For protecting them, by a mock trial, from punishment for any murders which they should commit on the inhabitants of these states;

For cutting off our trade with all parts of the world;

For imposing taxes on us without our consent;

For depriving us, in many cases, of the benefits of trial by jury;

For transporting us beyond seas, to be tried for pretended offenses;

For abolishing the free system of English laws in a neighboring province, establishing therein an arbitrary government, and enlarging its boundaries, so as to render it at once an example and fit instrument for introducing the same absolute rule into these colonies;

For taking away our charters, abolishing our most valuable laws, and altering fundamentally the forms of our governments;

For suspending our own legislatures, and declaring themselves invested with power to legislate for us in all cases whatsoever.

He has abdicated government here, by declaring us out of his protection and waging war against us.

He has plundered our seas, ravaged our coasts, burned our towns, and destroyed the lives of our people.

He is at this time transporting large armies of foreign mercenaries to complete the works of death, desolation, and tyranny already begun with circumstances of cruelty and perfidy scarcely paralleled in the most barbarous ages, and totally unworthy the head of a civilized nation.

He has constrained our fellow-citizens, taken captive on the high seas, to bear arms against their country, to become the executioners of their friends and brethren, or to fall themselves by their hands.

He has excited domestic insurrection among us, and has endeavored to bring on the inhabitants of our frontiers, the merciless Indian savages, whose known rule of warfare is an undistinguished destruction of all ages, sexes, and conditions.

In every stage of these oppressions we have petitioned for redress in the most humble terms; our repeated petitions have been answered only by repeated injury. A prince whose character is thus marked by every act which may define a tyrant is unfit to be the ruler of a free people.

Nor have we been wanting in attentions to our British brethren. We have warned them, from time to time, of attempts by their legislature to extend an unwarrantable jurisdiction over us. We have reminded them of the circumstances of our emigration and settlement here. We have appealed to their native justice and magnanimity; and we have conjured them, by the ties of our common kindred, to disavow these usurpations, which would inevitably interrupt our connections and correspondence. They, too, have been deaf to the voice of justice and consanguinity. We must, therefore, acquiesce in the necessity which denounces our separation, and hold them, as we hold the rest of mankind, enemies in war; in peace, friends.

We, therefore, the representatives of the United States of America, in General Congress assembled, appealing to the Supreme Judge of the world for the rectitude of our intentions, do, in the name and by the authority of the good people of these colonies, solemnly publish and declare that these United Colonies are, and of right ought to be, free and independent states; that they are absolved from all allegiance to the British crown, and that all political connection between them and the state of Great Britain is, and ought to be, totally dissolved; and that, as free and independent states, they have full power to levy war, conclude peace, contract alliances, establish commerce, and do all other acts and things which independent states may of right do. And, for the support of this declaration, with a firm reliance on the protection of Divine Providence, we mutually pledge to each other our lives, our fortunes, and our sacred honor.

John Hancock, President
(MASSACHUSETTS)

NEW HAMPSHIRE
Josiah Bartlett
William Whipple
Matthew Thornton

MASSACHUSETTS
John Adams
Samuel Adams
Robert Treat Paine
Elbridge Gerry

NEW YORK
William Floyd
Philip Livingston
Francis Lewis
Lewis Morris

RHODE ISLAND
Stephen Hopkins
William Ellery

NEW JERSEY
Richard Stockton
John Witherspoon
Francis Hopkinson
John Hart
Abraham Clark

PENNSYLVANIA
Robert Morris
Benjamin Rush
Benjamin Franklin
John Morton
George Clymer
James Smith
George Taylor
James Wilson
George Ross

DELAWARE
Caesar Rodney
George Read
Thomas McKean

MARYLAND
Samuel Chase
William Paca
Thomas Stone
Charles Carroll
  of Carrollton

VIRGINIA
George Wythe
Richard Henry Lee
Thomas Jefferson
Benjamin Harrison
Thomas Nelson, Jr.
Francis Lightfoot Lee
Carter Braxton

NORTH CAROLINA
William Hooper
Joseph Hewes
John Penn

SOUTH CAROLINA
Edward Rutledge
Thomas Heyward, Jr.
Thomas Lynch, Jr.
Arthur Middleton

CONNECTICUT
Roger Sherman
Samuel Huntington
William Williams
Oliver Wolcott

GEORGIA
Button Gwinnett
Lyman Hall
George Walton

A nation is born. Once Jefferson's task was completed, Congress prepared to act. On July 2, Congress voted in favor of independence. On July 4, it adopted Jefferson's Declaration of Independence.

The deed was done. At the end of the declaration, Jefferson wrote that, to the cause of American independence, "we mutually pledge to each other our lives, our fortunes, and our sacred honor." Those were not empty words to the fifty-six men who signed the document. Each well knew what would happen if the rebellion did not succeed. None summed up the need for unity better than Benjamin Franklin. "Gentlemen," he remarked, "we must all hang together, else we shall all hang separately."

CHECKUP

1. Who wrote the text of the Declaration of Independence?
2. According to the Declaration of Independence, when is revolution justified?
3. When was the Declaration of Independence adopted?

The Opposing Sides

In the chapter before this you considered whether some events and outcomes are bound to happen. Was it inevitable that American colonists would want to become independent of Great Britain? You noted then the difficulties in answering such questions for sure.

We can say for certain, however, that it was *not* inevitable that the Americans would win the war after independence had been declared. This is what General Washington wrote at the end of the war.

It will not be believed that such a force as Great Britain has employed for eight years in this country could be baffled . . . by numbers infinitely less, composed of men oftentimes half starved; always in rags, without pay and experiencing at times, every species of distress which human nature is capable of undergoing.

What were the disadvantages of the American side, according to Washington? Do Washington's remarks help you understand why many people at the start of the war thought the American rebels could not win it?

Comparing the armed forces. You need only look at the military picture at the start of the war to understand Washington's statement. In the fall of 1775, Britain's plans called for enlarging its army to 55,000 soldiers. More were added as the war went on. At the same time, Britain added 12,000 more sailors to its already large navy.

The British army also included *mercenaries*—that is, hired soldiers from other countries. The use of such soldiers was a common practice in those days. Over the course of the war, Britain hired 30,000 German troops. Most of them were from the German province of Hesse and were called Hessians. Some 50,000 Loyalists—Americans who remained loyal to King George III—took up arms for Britain. Most of the strong Indian tribes could also be counted upon to support the British. Furthermore, the British army was well trained and highly disciplined.

America's military power at the start of the war was, by comparison, pitiful. There was no army in existence. Washington had to build one from scratch. Even after an army was recruited, it was outnumbered by the

British, five to one. It was made up not of professional soldiers but of farmers, artisans, and merchants—men who were military amateurs.

On the high seas, the British navy was the finest in the world. British naval ships outnumbered American ships by a hundred to one. American naval vessels were often forced to sail shorthanded or with untrained crews.

Other British advantages. Great Britain's population was far greater than America's. There were about 9 million people living in Britain in 1775 compared with about 2.7 million Americans in the rebelling colonies. The latter included about 500,000 black slaves and a half-million Loyalists who would not or could not fight for the American cause. As a strong military power, Britain also had large amounts of war goods on hand. Britain was also far wealthier than the colonies. That meant its army could be well equipped. By comparison, the American army lacked gunpowder, food, and uniforms.

There was another reason for the difference in the equipment of the two armies. The British government had long since established its right to tax its people. During the war, then, it could raise the money it needed. But the Americans had started this rebellion largely over the issue of taxes. They were not ready to give the American Congress the same power to tax that they had denied to the British Parliament.

Without the power to tax, Congress had to ask the states to put up money and supplies. The state governments did so, but not in large enough amounts. Congress had to pay for supplies by bor-

rowing money from the public, and by seeking loans and gifts from foreign countries. It also printed paper money. That led to other problems, as you will read in the next chapter.

What all this meant for America's war effort is summed up in this letter from General Washington to Congress early in the conflict.

. . . my situation is inexpressibly distressing, to see the winter fast approaching upon a naked army, the time of their services within a few weeks of expiring, and not provision yet made for such important events. Added to this, the military chest is totally exhausted; the paymaster has not a single dollar in hand; the commissary-general [the officer in charge of food and daily supplies] assures me he has strained his credit to the utmost for the subsistence of the army. The quarter-master general [the officer in charge of quarters, clothing, and transportation] is precisely in the same situation; and the greater part of the army are in a state not far from mutiny (because they have not received what they were promised) . . . if the evil is not immediately remedied . . . the army must absolutely break up.

All through the war years, General Washington wrote letters like that to Congress.

The geographical factor. Against those British advantages, Americans had only a few. The greatest American advantage was geography. The supply line of the British army stretched 3,000 miles across the Atlantic. In many campaigns, troop movements were delayed because supplies were slow in arriving. Also, it took nearly six months to replace a British soldier who was killed or wounded in action. That was likely to

Paul Revere, Craftsman

To most Americans today, Paul Revere is known best as the rider on horseback who roused the countryside around Lexington with the cry, "The British are coming." But in his own time, he was better known as a craftsman. A genius at working with metals, Revere was a skilled silversmith, engraver, inventor, and even a maker of dental plates.

Revere fashioned many silver pieces for use in homes. The wide range of his household articles was astonishing. He made teapots, sugar bowls, salt shakers, trays, plates, and candlesticks.

In his shop in Boston, Revere used the tools of his trade to produce things of great beauty that, at the same time, expressed his political ideas. When ninety-two Patriots defied the Massachusetts governor before the Revolution, Revere made a handsome silver punch bowl honoring "the Immortal 92." After the Boston Massacre, Revere engraved a drawing showing British soldiers firing into a group of unarmed Boston citizens. He designed the first official seal used by the united American colonies as they waged their struggle for independence.

Revere's career mirrored that of the rising new nation. During the Revolutionary War, Revere used his skill to cast cannon for the Continental Army. After peace came, he turned to casting church bells. When the United States started building a navy to protect its trading vessels in the 1790s, Revere began rolling copper sheets to cover the bottom of warships. Later he began manufacturing copper boilers for the steamboats that Robert Fulton was sailing up the Hudson River. Revere also produced the sheet copper to cover the dome of the State House in Boston.

Revere typified the colonial craftworker of his day. Most Americans wanted to become farmers, and few entered the crafts and trades. The shortage of skilled artisans meant there could be little specialization. Anyone working with metal, like Revere, was called on to do many different things. Yet Revere's pride in anything he made was such that, no matter what he turned his hand to, it became a work of art.

This portrait of Paul Revere was painted in 1769 by the artist John Singleton Copley.

make a British general think twice before committing his troops to battle.

The vast expanse of the American continent gave the Americans endless space into which they could retreat. Thomas Paine likened the strategy that this space allowed to a game of checkers. "We can move out of *one* square to let you come in," he taunted a British general, "in order that we may afterwards take two or three for one; and as we can always keep a double corner for ourselves, we can always prevent a total defeat."

Fighting on familiar ground, with the feeling that they were protecting their families and homes, was also an advantage to the Americans. And most Americans were used to handling firearms.

Adding up the advantages and disadvantages of each side, the balance in 1776 seemed much in Britain's favor. Wars, however, are won not on the balance sheet but on the field of battle. That is where the great testing of American will and skill was to take place.

The militia. The American colonies had long opposed having standing armies in their midst in peacetime. Instead they relied on the local militia for their defense. The militia was made up of civilians who served as part-time soldiers.

During the Revolutionary War, the states continued to depend on the militia to fight many of the battles in their own areas. A total of about 165,000 militiamen saw service during the war.

The record of the militia members as fighters was mixed. In some situations, they proved to be useful. They could be called together quickly to meet a sudden attack nearby. Even if the British did take over an area, the militia made it hard for them to hold it. Once the British army moved on, it could control the territory only by leaving behind a large number of soldiers to guard against the local militia.

But the militia had serious weaknesses as a strong fighting force. Most militia members were short-term soldiers. They signed up for only three, six, or nine months under their state laws. And they didn't always stay that long. Once the British moved on to other states and the homes of the militia members were safe, the militia usually disbanded.

Washington himself had little faith in the militia. In the fall of 1776 he wrote to the President of Congress:

> To place any dependence upon militia is assuredly resting upon a broken staff. Men just dragged from the tender scenes of domestic life [are] unaccustomed to the din of arms, totally unacquainted with every kind of military skill, which . . . makes them timid and ready to fly from their own shadows.

The Continental Army. The backbone of the American military effort was the Continental Army. This was the national force raised by Congress. Altogether, 230,000 served in it as soldiers during the war, but there were never more than about 20,000 under arms at any one time. Continentals signed up for longer periods of service than militia members, usually from one to three years. They also served farther away from home. For these reasons, recruiting was difficult.

Among the soldiers who served in the Continental Army were 5,000 blacks. Some were free black men from the

North, but others were slaves. The latter were usually given their freedom after their military service. More probably would have served, except that Congress and several states worried about putting guns in the hands of blacks. For a time, enlistment by blacks was discouraged. Only when the British army began recruiting slaves with the promise of freedom did the American policy on recruiting blacks change.

Washington's leadership. Despite all these problems, Washington managed to shape the Continental Army into an effective fighting machine. He succeeded by the sheer force of his personality. He looked the part of a military commander. One of his acquaintances had described him earlier in life as follows:

> Measuring six feet two inches in his stockings and weighing 175 pounds . . . his frame is padded with well-developed muscles, indicating great strength. . . . His head is well-shaped, though not large, but is gracefully poised on a superb neck. . . . His movements and gestures are graceful, his walk majestic, and he is a splendid horseman.

One of the secrets of Washington's success as commander in chief was his ability to get along with Congress. He remained patient when he had good reason to be annoyed with that body. At all times he subordinated his needs as a military man to the civil authority of Congress. Members of Congress respected him for his high qualifications as a military commander.

Women and the war. Another important factor in the American military effort was the support accorded the Patriot

In celebration of the Declaration of Independence, joyful citizens raise a liberty pole, a flagstaff with a variety of decorations.

cause by American women. This support took many forms.

Some women joined their husbands in the army camps. They did not have military duties, although there are records of a few who actually served in combat. For example, Deborah Sampson Gannett dressed herself like a man, enlisted in a Massachusetts regiment, and served in the Continental Army. But women played important roles in other ways. They cooked, washed, and kept conditions in the camps as clean and as sanitary as possible. The importance of these activities can best be explained by the fact that in those years fifteen or twenty times as many soldiers · died from sickness as from battlefield wounds. Many women served also as nurses, tending the wounded in hastily built hospitals.

The heroic services of women during the Revolution are recalled by this monument at Moores Creek Bridge, North Carolina. It overlooks the grave of one of those women, Polly Slocumb. On this spot in February 1776, the Patriots defeated a Loyalist force in a battle often called "the Lexington of the South."

Women also made most of the uniforms and other clothing for soldiers. They helped make gunpowder by producing some of the ingredients within their homes.

Perhaps most important of all, women helped to keep the colonial economy going. Many a woman was left to run the family farm while her husband was off serving in the army or militia. The planting, cultivating, and harvesting that formerly had been done by husband and wife now had to be done by the woman alone. A remarkable fact of the period is that despite the loss of men to the army, farm production remained high.

In the next chapter we shall see how Americans were tested to the utmost on both the military and home fronts in waging the War of Independence.

CHECKUP

1. As the war got under way, what advantages did the British have? What advantages did the Americans have?
2. Distinguish between the militia and the Continental Army. Which was more effective as a fighting force?
3. In what ways did women make major contributions to the Patriot cause?

Key Facts from Chapter 6

1. The American War of Independence began on April 19, 1775, when British soldiers clashed with American militiamen at Lexington and Concord in Massachusetts.
2. Many Americans read and were influenced by Thomas Paine's pamphlet *Common Sense*, urging independence for the colonies.
3. The Declaration of Independence, written by Thomas Jefferson, was adopted on July 4, 1776.
4. The balance of strength between Britain and the American colonies in 1776, as measured by population, wealth, and the size of the armed forces, was much in Britain's favor.
5. The leadership of George Washington was a major factor in shaping the Continental Army into an effective fighting force.

★ REVIEWING THE CHAPTER ★

People, Places, and Events

Review Questions

1. Why did the Second Continental Congress choose George Washington as commander in chief? *P. 128*

2. Review the arguments given by Thomas Paine in favor of independence from Great Britain. What was the impact of *Common Sense*? *Pp. 131–132*

3. Describe the theory of government and society that Thomas Jefferson included in the Declaration of Independence. *P. 133*

4. How did Congress finance the war? *P. 140*

5. At the start of the war, why did many people think that the American rebels could not win? *Pp. 139–140*

6. What advantages did the Americans have in the war? *Pp. 140, 142*

7. Suppose you were an American military officer and you were to lead a campaign against the British. Your superior officer gives you a choice of either **(a)** 500 regular troops and 100 militiamen, or **(b)** 500 militiamen and 100 regular troops. Which combination would you pick and why? *P. 142*

8. Explain the roles women played in the war effort. *Pp. 143–144*

Chapter Test

In the first section below is a list of descriptions. In the second section is a list of people and terms found in the chapter. Match each description with the person or term associated with it. Write your answers on a separate piece of paper.

1. Silversmith, engraver, and inventor
2. Writer of Declaration of Independence
3. Body representing all the colonies
4. British leader in Boston
5. Legal piracy
6. Hired soldiers
7. First armed conflict
8. Author of *Common Sense*
9. National military force
10. Part-time soldiers

a. Hessians
b. Lexington and Concord
c. Militia
d. Thomas Paine
e. Paul Revere
f. George Washington
g. Second Continental Congress
h. Thomas Jefferson
i. General Thomas Gage
j. Privateers
k. Continental Army
l. Parliament
m. Benjamin Franklin

145

WASHINGTON REALIZED that the Continental Army was the symbol of the American cause. As long as it remained in the field, independence was possible. If it collapsed or was crushed, the cause of independence was lost. Washington, therefore, with great good sense fought a defensive war much of the time. He did not risk his troops in all-out battles. Not until the final campaign did he change his strategy.

The British opened the war with a different strategy. To win, they had to defeat the American army and take control of territory. That meant that the British must attack. In carrying out such a plan, their navy played a big part. With the navy, the British could easily move their troops. They could land along the coast, take key points, and march inland to pursue the American army.

In the British view, large cities on the coast were major goals. Holding them would provide ports for landing supplies. It would also, they thought, weaken the spirit of the Americans—particularly if they took control of the capital, Philadelphia.

Years of Strife

In the first two years of the war, the main military campaigns took place in the North. During those years, the British occupied America's three largest cities—Boston in 1775, New York in 1776, and Philadelphia in 1777. They gave up Boston and Philadelphia after less than a year, but they controlled New York up to the end of the war.

Early setbacks. The battle for New York in 1776 could have been the war's most important battle. The action began when a large British force under General William Howe landed on Long Island in late August. Had Howe acted decisively, he might have trapped Washington's army and ended the war then and there. However, he allowed the American troops to escape, under cover of darkness and fog, from Long Island into New York City. The British chased the American troops northward, skirmishing at Harlem Heights and fighting an inconclusive battle at White Plains. Washington's army then fled across the Hudson River to New Jersey.

The British pursued Washington's army, but never caught up for a clear-cut battle. In late autumn, the Americans withdrew farther, crossing the Delaware River into Pennsylvania. With winter coming on, Howe abandoned the campaign. He took most of his troops back to New York City for the winter, leaving some outposts in New Jersey.

Trenton and Princeton. Realizing that the enemy detachments in New Jersey were exposed, Washington struck a daring blow. On Christmas night in 1776, his small army recrossed the ice-choked Delaware River. The Americans surprised the British-paid Hessian troops at Trenton and took 900 prisoners.

Washington followed up this battle ten days later with an equally successful attack on the British troops at Princeton, New Jersey. Neither of those two victories, brilliant as they were, was a

147

major step toward winning the war. But they were the first American victories after a long string of defeats. As such, the battles at Trenton and Princeton were an important boost to the morale of the Patriots.

A three-pronged attack. In 1777 the British came up with a grand plan to end the war. They would launch a three-pronged attack centered on the Hudson River valley. One army, under General John Burgoyne, was to march south from Canada by way of Lake Champlain toward Albany. A second force under Colonel Barry St. Leger, was to hurry east from Lake Ontario through the Mohawk Valley toward the Hudson. There it would link up with Burgoyne. General Howe, stationed in New York City, would go up the Hudson River and meet the other two. In this way, the British would drive a wedge between the southern states and New England, and control the state of New York. This was the area they considered to be the heart of the rebellion.

The plan made sense, but the British bungled it. A large part of the fault was General Howe's. Instead of going up the Hudson to trap the American army that lay between him and Burgoyne, he decided first to capture Philadelphia. There would still be time, he thought, to turn north and aid Burgoyne. But there wasn't time. The Philadelphia campaign occupied Howe until late September. By then Burgoyne's army had gotten as far south as Saratoga, New York. He was more than a hundred miles from his Canadian base, out of food, and harried by the Americans. Burgoyne had to surrender his entire army of 5,700. In the meantime, St. Leger's advance had been halted at Oriskany by General Nicholas Herkimer's militiamen.

How many times did Washington's army meet the British in battle during 1776 and early 1777? In which battles were the Americans the victors?

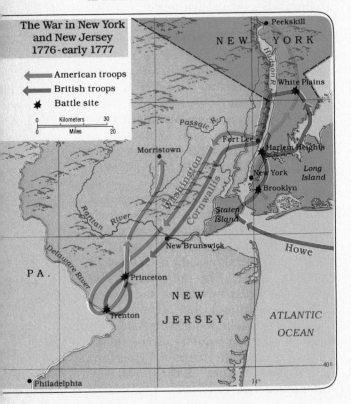

The War in New York and New Jersey 1776-early 1777

American troops
British troops
Battle site

Kilometers 0 30
Miles 0 20

NEW YORK
Peekskill
White Plains
Hudson R.
Fort Lee
Harlem Heights
New York
Long Island
Brooklyn
Staten Island
Morristown
Passaic R.
Washington
Cornwallis
Raritan River
New Brunswick
Howe
PA.
Delaware River
Princeton
Trenton
NEW JERSEY
75°
ATLANTIC OCEAN
Philadelphia
74°
40°

The turning point. The surrender of Burgoyne's army on October 17, 1777, was the turning point of the war. Britain's old enemy, France, had been watching the American rebellion with more than passing interest. From the beginning of the war, the French had been secretly providing money and

General John Stark and his men prepare to meet a largely Hessian force near Bennington, Vermont. The force, sent by General Burgoyne to seize an American supply depot, was nearly wiped out.

supplies to the colonists. More than anything else, France wished to see Britain humbled. However, the French would not openly join the war until they were convinced that the colonies had a reasonable chance to win. Saratoga convinced them. For the first time, the Americans had defeated and captured a large British army.

The next year, in 1778, the French made an alliance with the United States and entered the war. That changed the entire character of the conflict. The United States had been at a great disadvantage because of the power of the British navy. Now the French fleet could help offset America's lack of seapower.

America's European allies. From the moment that France entered the conflict, the Revolutionary War became a world war. In 1779 Spain joined the United States and France in fighting Britain. The combined fleets of France and Spain outnumbered the British by far. Thus the navy that had controlled the seas from the beginning of the war found the tables turned. Britain was forced to defend itself against invasion at home, as well as to protect its colonies in America, Africa, and Asia.

In 1780, Holland followed France in recognizing America's independence and declared war on Britain. By this time, the British were on bad terms with practically every important European country trading on the Atlantic. The Royal Navy had abused the ships of many countries when Britain ruled the waves. Now, faced with many enemies, Britain was no longer able to commit its full resources against the Americans.

149

FOREIGN HEROES OF THE REVOLUTION

Marquis de Lafayette, a French nobleman, became a major general in the Continental Army at the age of twenty. Wounded at Germantown, he later led troops at Yorktown. Washington regarded Lafayette almost as a son.

Thaddeus Kosciusko of Poland, an army engineer, built the defenses at Saratoga and West Point. A true champion of freedom, he bought slaves in order to free them. He later fought for the independence of Poland.

Johann Kalb, a native of Germany, came to America with Lafayette. He served with Washington at Brandywine, Germantown, Valley Forge, and Monmouth. He died from wounds suffered in battle at Camden, South Carolina.

Friedrich von Steuben, a Prussian army veteran, gained fame as a drill-master during the winter at Valley Forge. As a major general, he led troops at Monmouth and Yorktown. Later he became a United States citizen.

Casimir Pulaski, a Polish patriot who joined the Continental Army, headed a cavalry-infantry unit called Pulaski's Legion. Wounded while leading a cavalry charge at the siege of Savannah, he died two days later.

A change in British strategy. Under these new circumstances, the British changed their strategy. During the first two years of the war, they had launched a number of operations in the North from their base in New York City.

Their one notable success had been in taking Philadelphia. In the late summer of 1777 General Howe's army had moved by ship to the head of Chesapeake Bay and marched on Philadelphia. In a battle at Brandywine Creek, Washington's army failed to block Howe, whose troops advanced into Philadelphia. Three weeks later the Americans tried to re-take the city, but were turned back at Germantown.

Despite this success, the British saw that their strategy of capturing large cities was failing. Tom Paine had pointed out the weakness of that strategy. Paine published a number of pamphlets called *The Crisis*. In one, he included this open letter to Howe.

> By what means, may I ask, do you expect to conquer America? . . .
>
> In all the wars which you have formerly been concerned in you had only armies to contend with; in former wars, the countries followed the fate of their capitals; Canada fell with Quebec, and Minorca [a Mediterranean island seized by Britain in 1708] with Port Mahon or St. Phillips; by subduing these, the conquerors opened a way into, and became masters of the country; here it is otherwise; if you get possession of a city here, you are obliged to shut yourself up in it, and can make no use of it, than to spend your country's money in [it] . . . This is all the advantage you have drawn from New York; and you would draw less from Philadelphia, because it requires more force to keep it, and is much farther from the sea.

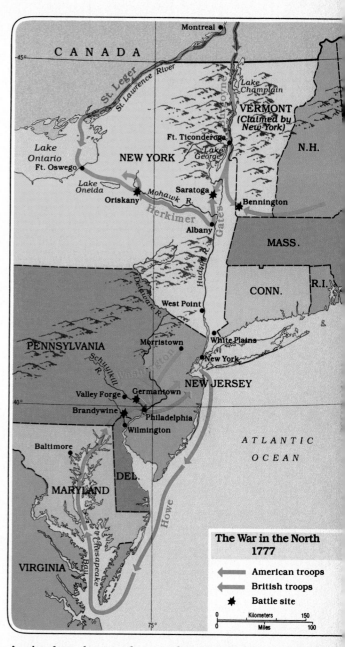

The War in the North 1777

← American troops
← British troops
✹ Battle site

| 0 | Kilometers | 150 |
| 0 | Miles | 100 |

Armies have long made use of waterways as invasion routes. What waterways did Burgoyne's army use? How would the map be different if Howe had done what he was supposed to do?

George Rogers Clark's Northwest Campaign

When war broke out, the territory west of the Appalachian Mountains was mostly unsettled. During the war, however, the region became a battleground because British frontier posts were located in the Illinois country. From forts at Kaskaskia, Cahokia, Vincennes, and Detroit, the British and their Indian allies launched bloody raids upon American settlements. The goal of the British was to win complete control of the wilderness region.

George Rogers Clark, a Virginian who had explored and settled beyond the mountains in the Kentucky region, got approval to strike back. In the summer of 1778 he led an expedition through the wilderness and captured the British forts at Kaskaskia, Cahokia, and Vincennes. Colonel Henry Hamilton, the British commander at Detroit, resolved to win back the forts. He and his Indian allies retook Vincennes in December 1778. Planning to recapture the other forts in the spring, they settled down there for the winter. They were confident that control of the Illinois country was now within their grasp.

Clark's winter camp was at Kaskaskia, 180 miles away. He was working on a plan to attack Detroit in the spring when he heard of Hamilton's capture of the fort at Vincennes. Even though it was the middle of winter, Clark decided to strike at once. Gathering a band of about 180 men, he set out on one of the most amazing marches in American military history. A mid-winter thaw had caused the Wabash River to flood, turning much of the route into a huge lake. Nevertheless, Clark led his men in the dead of winter through icy floodwaters, sometimes shoulder high. Wet to the skin, exhausted, and hungry, the men survived the march. They surprised the British in February 1779, and Hamilton was forced to surrender the fort.

Clark's victory helped win this territory for the United States. When the peace treaty was signed in 1783, Britain gave up its claims to the region.

This postage stamp, issued in 1929, shows George Rogers Clark and his band of frontiersmen receiving the surrender of the British commander, Colonel Henry Hamilton, at Vincennes. To reach the British-held fort, Clark marched his men in the dead of winter through the icy floodwaters of the Wabash Valley. This amazing feat of endurance helped win the Northwest for the United States.

The new British strategy called for moving the fighting out of the North and into the South. There were, the British felt, a large number of Loyalists in that region. They hoped that those Loyalists would rise up to support a "friendly" invasion of British troops. At the same time, the British could depend more on their sea power to supply their troops in the South and to transport them from place to place. Finally, Britain decided that the war in America would have to take second place to the struggle in other parts of the world against its long-time enemy, France.

The southern campaign. The British southern campaign got off to a good start. In 1778 the British captured Savannah, Georgia. The next year they turned back a joint force of American soldiers and the French fleet, who tried to retake the city. The British then overran most of the state of Georgia.

Much of the state of South Carolina also came under British control after Charleston fell in 1780. In Charleston the Americans met with their worst defeat of the war when an army of 5,500 had to surrender. With almost no Continental Army force left in the area, Britain's southern strategy seemed to be working.

But Britain had not counted on the military ingenuity of the Americans. They now fought back with guerrilla warfare. Bands of militiamen swarmed over British outposts in a series of hit-and-run raids. When pursued, the Americans fled into nearby swamps and forests, where they could not be followed. Led by officers like Francis Marion of South Carolina, who earned the name Swamp Fox, these roaming bands kept the British off balance with their attacks.

Greene's strategy. To take charge of the new Continental Army formed in the South, Washington appointed Nathanael Greene, a Rhode Islander. Next to Washington, Greene was the most gifted general in the army. On taking command in North Carolina, Greene outlined his strategy.

> I am determined to carry the war immediately into South Carolina. The enemy will be obliged to follow us, or give up their posts in that state. If the former takes place, it will draw the war out of this state and give it an opportunity to [recruit men for the army]. If [the British] leave their posts to fall, they must lose more there than they can gain here.

The strategy was to fight and retreat, fight and retreat, always drawing the British farther away from their base. After one of Greene's generals dealt a British force a smashing defeat in 1781 at the battle of Cowpens in South Carolina, the British commander, Lord Cornwallis, determined to run down Greene's army. Although Cornwallis gave chase, he was never able to catch the American general.

Victory at Yorktown. Since it appeared that Greene was getting many of his men and much of his supplies from Virginia, Cornwallis moved north to invade that state. He marched to Yorktown, where he took up a position on the peninsula between the York and James Rivers. There he could count on being supplied from Chesapeake Bay by the British navy and, if necessary, rescued

153

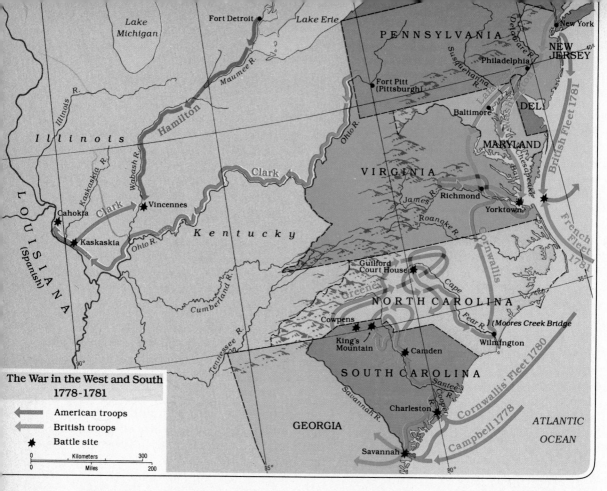

The War in the West and South
1778-1781

⬅ American troops
⬅ British troops
★ Battle site

| 0 | Kilometers | 300 |
| 0 | Miles | 200 |

The location of Yorktown was a vital factor in bringing the War for Independence to a close. What opportunity did Cornwallis see that made him decide to take a stand there with his army? What opportunity did Washington see in that situation? Which general realized his opportunity?

by it. At least this was what he planned.

Washington decided it was now time to use French seapower and the French army to trap Cornwallis. The army France had sent moved south from its base in Newport, Rhode Island. Racing his own army south from New York, Washington joined up with the French and cut off Cornwallis by land. Admiral de Grasse, the French naval commander, bottled up Chesapeake Bay. Thus there was no chance for Cornwallis to

escape by sea. A British fleet tried to rescue Cornwallis, but De Grasse fought it off. Confronted by more than 16,000 troops and 36 French warships, Cornwallis surrendered his army of 7,000.

British power in America was by no means ended by this defeat at Yorktown. The British still controlled much territory and held such major cities as New York, Charleston, and Savannah. But after years of fighting and the loss of two armies, the British were no closer to

John Paul Jones and the War at Sea

When the Revolutionary War broke out, there was no American navy. Slowly Congress began to build one. In the fall of 1775, four merchant vessels were purchased and armed. In December of that year, thirteen frigates were ordered built. The Continental Navy eventually put out to sea some fifty or sixty ships, although not all at one time.

Besides the Continental Navy, several states built their own navies. The navies in all totaled about forty ships. Together with the ships of the Continental Navy, these vessels sank or captured nearly 200 British craft. They were facing a British navy that numbered about 270 ships in 1775, and more than 460 in 1783.

The Continental Navy, although outnumbered, showed great seamanship and fighting qualities. Its most brilliant exploits were carried out by John Paul Jones. Born in Scotland with the full name of John Paul, Jones added his last name when he came to America. He probably did so to hide his true identity because he had been accused of murder in the death of a sailor. Appointed a lieutenant in 1775, Jones was soon given command of his own ship. He was later promoted to captain, and commanded a small squadron.

Jones boldly hunted enemy ships off the British coast, and even went ashore with raiding parties. In 1779 his vessel, the *Bonhomme Richard*, clashed with a bigger British warship, the *Serapis*, in the North Sea. When the *Bonhomme Richard* was almost sinking, Jones had it lashed with lines alongside the *Serapis* and continued the fight. After three hours of combat, the British commander called on Jones to surrender. Jones is said to have replied. "I have not yet begun to fight." The British ship finally surrendered, but the *Bonhomme Richard* was so badly damaged that it sank two days later.

Jones's efforts and those of the continental and state fleets were aided by another American naval force—the privateers (see page 132). More than 2,000 American craft became privateers. By the close of the war, these armed ships had sunk or captured more than 600 British vessels.

John Paul Jones raised this flag over the *Serapis*.

Chicago Historical Society

The surrender of the British at Yorktown is shown in this painting by John Trumbull. General Benjamin Lincoln prepares to receive the surrender from General O'Hara, second-in-command to Cornwallis.

breaking the rebellion. British citizens were weary of the war. With other foes to face in Europe, Britain was now ready to seek peace. A peace treaty did not come until 1783. Yet in 1781, six years after the first shots rang out on the Lexington green, the War of Independence was, for all practical purposes, won.

Some battlefield "ifs." As we noted at the start of the previous chapter, there was nothing inevitable about the outcome of the Revolutionary War. If General Howe had moved quickly against Washington in New York City in 1776, the rebellion might have been crushed before the ink had dried on the Declara-

tion of Independence. Several times during the war Howe had a chance to smash Washington's army, but he always let the Americans slip away.

Had the British succeeded in their plan to split New England from the southern states, there would have been no American victory at Saratoga—and probably no French-American alliance. Without French help, it is doubtful that the United States could have won. At the battle of Yorktown, for example, there were more French soldiers and sailors surrounding the British than there were Americans. One could build a long list of battlefield "ifs." After the war the British generals no doubt did.

1. Why were the battles at Trenton and Princeton so important to the Patriot cause?
2. What grand plan did the British formulate in 1777 to end the war? What success did it have?
3. How did British strategy change in the later years of the war? Why did this strategy fail?

Obstacles Overcome

Battles aside, there were times when the Continental Army could easily have collapsed. Always short of supplies, and with few victories to encourage them, the soldiers at times lost heart.

The plight of Washington's army was never worse than at its winter camp in Valley Forge, Pennsylvania, in 1777–1778. There, a shortage of food led to near starvation. For want of shoes, soldiers walked barefoot in the snow. Others, lacking clothing to protect them from the weather, remained penned up in miserably crowded cabins.

The money problem. There were also problems on the home front that might have lost the War of Independence. One was inflation. We have already noted that Congress printed paper money to pay for the war. This money was issued as Continental paper dollars.

At that time, the money that people trusted most was gold and silver. People did not like to accept paper money unless they felt sure they could exchange it for gold or silver. If the war was won and a new, strong government that could raise money was set up, there was a fair chance that people would be able to exchange their paper money for gold or silver. But if the rebellion failed—and for much of the war it looked that way—the paper money of Congress would be worth nothing.

Accepting paper money was, therefore, a gamble. People wouldn't take it for payment unless they were offered a lot more of it than of gold. And the more paper money Congress printed, the lower it fell in value. This table shows the amount of paper money Congress issued each year. It also shows the number of paper dollars it took each year to buy as much as a dollar in gold would buy.

Year	Paper Money Issued	Value of Paper Money to Gold
1776	$19 million	1 to 1
1777	$13 million	3 to 1
1778	$63 million	7 to 1
1779	$90 million	42 to 1

By the end of 1780, it took nearly 100 Continental paper dollars to buy as much as a dollar in gold would buy. Four months later, it took nearly 150. Since Congress was buying military supplies with Continental dollars, prices skyrocketed. Washington once commented that if one had a rat in the shape of a horse, one could probably sell it for 200 pounds. Some soldiers who were paid with these nearly worthless Continental dollars deserted; others mutinied.

State rivalries. Still another problem that might have led to an American defeat was *localism*—that is, the placing of a state's interests ahead of the national interest. You will remember that each state raised its own army, in the form of militia. Each state had its own navy and raised money for its own defense. With such division of effort, it was hard to get states to pull together in a single national effort. Each state was convinced that it was doing more than its share while others were doing less.

There were also boundary disputes between several of the states. Both New York and New Hampshire claimed what is now the state of Vermont. Virginia and Maryland argued over the former's claims to land west of the Alleghenies. Sometimes it seemed the states were busier quarreling with each other than fighting with the British.

A civil war. As soon as the Declaration of Independence was signed, the conflict between Great Britain and the Americans became—at least to the Patriots—a war between two countries. At the same time, however, another kind of war was going on at home. That was the civil war between the Loyalists and the Patriots.

Not all Americans, you will remember, favored independence. A large number remained true to the king and the British empire. Perhaps as many as 500,000, about one fifth of the white population, were Loyalists—or Tories, as they were scornfully called by the Patriots.

Loyalists came from all walks of life. A group of Loyalists arrested in New York City on suspicion of plotting to assassinate George Washington included the following: the city's mayor, a number of farmers, some tavernkeepers, two doctors, two tanners, two gunsmiths, a

Hero . . . and Traitor

Every war produces heroes and traitors. The Revolutionary War was no exception. In the careers of Nathan Hale and Benedict Arnold, one can see a clear example of this pattern.

Nathan Hale was born in Connecticut and attended Yale College. He was teaching school when war broke out, but entered military service in July 1775. Promoted to captain six months later, he went on duty near New York City. When General Washington called for a volunteer to spy on the British, Hale offered his services. Disguised as a Dutch schoolmaster, he visited enemy camps on Long Island and in New York City and drew sketches of fortifications.

This statue of Nathan Hale stands in New Haven, Connecticut, where Hale attended Yale College.

On the night of September 21, 1776, Hale was captured by British soldiers. His drawings were found hidden in his shoes, and he was sentenced to die. The next morning, as he faced death by hanging, he was allowed to speak. Tradition has it that Hale, with the rope around his neck, uttered these stirring words: "I regret that I have but one life to lose for my country."

The devotion of Nathan Hale to the American cause was not shared by Benedict Arnold, another native of Connecticut. Before the war, Arnold was involved in trade and managed a book- and drugstore. Once the war began, he quickly became an exceptional military leader. In the fall of 1775 he led a march of about 1,000 men through the Maine wilderness into Canada. In a swirling snowstorm in late December he and his men attacked the walled city of Quebec. Although the attack failed, Arnold's courage and daring were recognized, and he was promoted to brigadier general. He added to his reputation as a fiery leader in the campaign around Lake Champlain and in the battle of Saratoga. Although he was badly wounded at Saratoga, Congress recognized his worth and promoted him to major general.

But Arnold felt he had not been given the credit due him for the victory at Saratoga. Stories spread that he leaned toward the Loyalists, in part because he had married the daughter of one. Pennsylvania officials also accused him of overstepping his authority. Brooding over these matters, Arnold decided to cast his lot with the British. While in command of West Point in 1780, he worked out a plan to surrender that im-

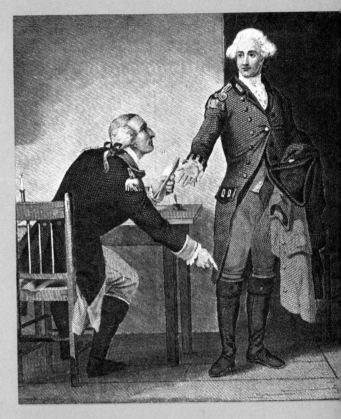

Benedict Arnold suggests to British spy John André that the defense plans for West Point be concealed in André's boot. Arnold's treachery was revealed when American soldiers stopped André, searched him, and found the papers.

portant fort to the enemy. When the plot was exposed, Arnold fled to the British.

After being made a British brigadier general, Arnold led the forces that burned Richmond, Virginia, and New London, Connecticut. Once the war was over, he went to England, where he became a merchant in the West Indies trade. He died in London in 1801, burdened by business debts and scorned by Americans as a traitor.

159

former schoolteacher, and a man described as "a damned rascal." Most Loyalists, like most Americans in general, appear to have been small farmers. A good many prosperous merchants and large landholders were also Loyalists. So were nearly all members of the Anglican clergy.

There were Loyalists in every colony, but there were more in certain areas than in others. A great many lived in the West, along the frontier. There were also large numbers in the coastal areas, especially in the middle colonies of New York, New Jersey, and Pennsylvania. The cities of New York and Philadelphia were Loyalist strongholds. The South also had a large number of Loyalists, especially in and around Charleston.

Loyalists proved to be a serious military threat to the Patriot cause. It is estimated that as many as 50,000 served with the British army. They took part in many of the war's major campaigns. There were Loyalists with Burgoyne's army at Saratoga. Loyalist soldiers fought in Savannah and aided in the capture of Charleston. They took part in the sacking of Connecticut towns, and in raids in Virginia.

Enemies within. Yet most Loyalists did not take part in the fighting. They tried to live as normally as possible during the war. Nevertheless, they were regarded by the Patriots as enemies within. The reason for this becomes apparent in this 1779 newspaper article. The article also gives you some idea of how high feelings ran.

Who were the occasion of this war? The Tories! Who persuaded the tyrants of Brit-

ain to prosecute it in a manner before unknown to civilized nations, and shocking even to barbarians? The Tories! Who prevailed on the savages of the wilderness to join the standard of the enemy? The Tories! Who have assisted the Indians in taking the scalp from the aged matron, the blooming fair one, the helpless infant, and the dying hero? The Tories!

The same article went on to describe other practices in which the Loyalists supposedly participated.

Who hold treasonous correspondence with the enemy? The Tories! Who send them daily intelligence? The Tories! Who take oaths of allegiance to the States one day, and break them the next? The Tories! Who prevent your battalions from being filled? The Tories! Who persuade those who have enlisted to desert? The Tories!

There was no wrong under heaven, apparently, for which the Loyalists were not to blame.

The treatment of Loyalists. With feelings like those, it is hardly surprising that people siding with the British were handled roughly. Their homes were sometimes looted or destroyed. Their moves were carefully watched. They were often kept from moving around freely. Those suspected of political or military acts were jailed, kept in their homes, or removed to faraway places. If one was caught returning home for a secret visit, the whole family might be sent into exile.

Those who served in the British army or gave aid to the enemy in other ways during the war were tried for treason. When convicted, they were sentenced to death. Such sentences were rarely carried out, and few Loyalists were actually executed. One reason for this was that General Washington urged that they not be. He feared that if Patriots executed Loyalists, the British would execute British-born American soldiers they had captured.

In the course of the war, the property of some wealthy Loyalists was seized. States passed laws confiscating the estates of certain offending Loyalists. Millions of acres were taken in this way. Usually the states sold the land at auction and used the funds to pay for the costs of the war. Some Loyalists were compensated by the British government for their losses, but many were not.

During the war, between 80,000 and 100,000 Loyalists left the United States so they could continue to live within the British empire. Some went "home"— that is, to England. Most, however, stayed in the Western Hemisphere, moving to Canada or to the West Indies.

It is clear the Loyalists suffered considerably. Yet, except for those who served with the British army, few lost their lives. Considering the bitterness of feelings in this civil war, that is a remarkable fact.

New governments. Once independence was declared, the former British colonies lost no time in writing state constitutions and setting up state governments. In 1776 alone, eight of them wrote new constitutions and two changed older ones. The remaining states followed within the next few years.

The experience of the recent arguments with Great Britain was stamped all over these constitutions. Colonists had gone to war to preserve the "rights of Englishmen." Now they wrote these rights securely into their constitutions. The following rights were guaranteed in most state constitutions.

- Trial by jury
- Bail
- A free trial in open court
- Writs of habeas corpus. These documents would protect citizens from being kept in prison without cause by requiring the authorities to explain to a judge why they were being held.
- Freedom of the press
- Freedom of religion
- The right to meet together peaceably and to petition the government

All constitutions, in addition, accepted the principle that government must be based on the consent of the governed. There were, however, limits to that idea. A person had to own a certain amount of property or pay a tax in order to qualify for voting. And in all but one state, the right to vote belonged only to adult white males.

The first restriction was not as great as might first appear. Most white male citizens were able to meet the property or tax requirement. In Massachusetts, for example, more than 80 percent owned enough property to give them the right to vote.

Restricting the vote to white males was far more limiting. Blacks, Indians, and women were all left out. The only exception was in New Jersey. There the constitution did not say "male," and for a time women could and did vote. In 1807, however, the constitution was changed and women could no longer vote. In spite of all those limitations, however, it remained true that nowhere in the entire world was representative

161

government as advanced as in the United States.

At the same time, a constitution was drawn up for the nation. It was called the Articles of Confederation. You will study more about the Articles in the next unit. Here we need note only that the Articles were completed in 1777, but they could not go into effect until all thirteen states *ratified*, or approved, the document. That did not occur until 1781. By that time the war was almost over. Thus, throughout most of the war the Continental Congress operated as the national government.

The Peace of Paris. In September 1783, almost two years after Yorktown, Great Britain and the United States signed the Peace of Paris. Britain acknowledged that the United States was now an independent nation. The treaty set boundaries that were very favorable to the new nation. To the north, the Great Lakes; to the south, the border of Spanish Florida, at roughly 31° north latitude;

and most important, to the west, the Mississippi River. This gave the United States the whole area between the Allegheny Mountains and the great river. Other terms had to do with American fishing rights off British-owned Newfoundland and the question of American treatment of Loyalists after the war was over.

The Peace of Paris brought forth something new in the world: the first modern nation born in revolution. That fact would forever affect the history of Americans and of the world. In the next chapter you will see several important ways in which this was so.

CHECKUP

1. How did inflation threaten to undo the struggle for independence? How did localism threaten it?
2. Who were the Loyalists? What role did they play in the war?
3. When new state constitutions were drawn up, what rights were generally guaranteed in them?

Key Facts from Chapter 7

1. During much of the War of Independence the British were on the offensive and the Americans on the defensive.
2. American victories at Trenton and Princeton were important in boosting the Patriots' morale.
3. The American victory at Saratoga was the turning point of the war. It induced France to come openly to America's aid.
4. The victory of the Americans and their French allies at Yorktown in 1781 was the last major battle of the war and assured American independence.
5. New state constitutions, written after independence was declared, guaranteed such basic rights as trial by jury, freedom of the press, and freedom of religion.

★ REVIEWING THE CHAPTER ★

People, Places, and Events

Gen. William Howe
P. 147

Trenton   P. 147

Princeton   P. 147

Gen. John Burgoyne
P. 148

Col. Barry St.
Leger   P. 148

Saratoga   P. 148

Gen. Nicholas
Herkimer   P. 148

Brandywine   P. 151

Germantown   P. 151

The Crisis   P. 151

George Rogers
Clark   P. 152

Savannah   P. 153

Charleston   P. 153

Francis Marion
P. 153

Gen. Nathanael
Greene   P. 153

Cowpens   P. 153

Lord Cornwallis
P. 153

Yorktown   P. 153

Admiral de Grasse
P. 154

John Paul Jones
P. 155

Valley Forge   P. 157

Nathan Hale   P. 158

Benedict Arnold
P. 159

Peace of Paris
P. 162

Review Questions

1. Compare Washington's war strategy with the British strategy.   P. 147

2. Define the purpose of the British three-pronged attack.   P. 148

3. What was the significance of the British defeat at Saratoga?   Pp. 148–149

4. Did the American victory at Yorktown end British power in America? Explain your answer.   P. 154

5. Describe America's money problem during the war years.   P. 157

6. How did rivalries between various states affect the war effort?   Pp. 157–158

7. How did the Patriots feel toward the Loyalists? How were the Loyalists treated?   Pp. 158; 160

8. List the individual rights included in the new state constitutions.   P. 161

Chapter Test

Complete each sentence. Write the answers on a separate piece of paper.

1. The strategic battles at _____ and _____ in New Jersey were the first American victories after a long string of defeats.

2. The surrender of Burgoyne's army at _____ convinced the French to join openly the Americans in their war for independence.

3. The British southern campaign got off to a good start with the capture of _____, Georgia.

4. _____, nicknamed the "Swamp Fox," and his band darted out of the marshes to attack the British and then disappeared before the redcoats could strike back.

5. _____, an American naval hero, commanded the *Bonhomme Richard* in a successful attack on the British warship *Serapis*.

6. Washington appointed _____ _____, one of the most gifted generals, to take charge of the new Continental Army formed in the South.

7. The surrender of Cornwallis at _____ forced the British to seek peace with America, although occasional fighting between the two sides continued for a time.

8. Those Americans who remained true to the King and the British empire were called _____.

9. America financed the war by printing paper dollars called _____.

10. Great Britain acknowledged that the United States was an independent nation with the signing of the _____ _____.

THE ENDURING REVOLUTION

Don't give up the Ship

THE AMERICAN REVOLUTION is the single most important event in the history of the United States. Without it, there would have been no United States. The American Revolution has also had a great effect on the way people in the United States have thought about themselves and about other countries. It has become the standard by which Americans judge all other revolutions.

What, then, was the meaning of the American Revolution? What kind of revolution was it? Perhaps as important, what kind of revolution *wasn't* it? Now that you have studied the course of events between 1763 and 1783, you will be able to find answers to those questions.

The Nature of the American Revolution

There are a number of ways to get at the true nature of a revolution. One is to study its leaders—to find out about their backgrounds, their social and economic positions, their occupations, and so on. Suppose we were to discover that the leaders of a revolution were all small farmers. That would suggest that farm problems were an important cause of the revolution. Suppose we found that a very large number of the leaders came from one part of the country—say, the South. That might be a clue that matters of special interest to that section had something to do with the revolution. If a great many of the leaders were from the poorer classes, what kind of clue might that give us?

Leaders of the American Revolution. What kind of people were the leaders of the American Revolution? Since we can't possibly consider all of them here, we have selected a sample. Our sample is drawn from the fifty-six signers of the Declaration of Independence—surely among the leaders of the Revolution. Here are short descriptions of twenty-eight—or one half—of the signers.

John Adams Graduate of Harvard College. Well-to-do lawyer; member of Massachusetts legislature.

Samuel Adams Graduate of Harvard College. Son of a wealthy brewer; most powerful leader in the legislature of Massachusetts.

Josiah Bartlett Doctor: colonel in the militia; member of the New Hampshire Provincial Congress.

Charles Carroll Attended colleges in France. Important landholder and political leader in Maryland; religious leader among American Catholics.

Samuel Chase Leading lawyer in the colony of Maryland; member of Maryland legislature.

George Clymer Prominent Philadelphia merchant and a leading Pennsylvania politician.

Benjamin Franklin Pennsylvania publisher; internationally known scientist.

Elbridge Gerry Graduate of Harvard College. Wealthy Massachusetts merchant and political leader.

Lyman Hall Graduate of Yale College. Doctor; minister; planter in Georgia.

John Hancock Graduate of Harvard College. Merchant; one of the richest men in Massachusetts.

165

KEY 1. Richard Stockton, N.J.; 2 Josiah Bartlett, N.H.; 3. Thomas Nelson, Jr., Va.; 4. George Clymer, Pa.; 5. Francis Lightfoot Lee, Va.; 6. John Penn, N.C.; 7. Abraham Clark, N.J.; 8. John Morton, Pa.; 9. George Ross, Pa.; 10. James Smith, Pa.; 11. Samuel Adams, Mass.; 12. Robert Treat Paine, Mass.; 13. Button Gwinnett, Ga.; 14. Robert Morris, Pa.; 15. Benjamin Harrison, Va.; 16. Carter Braxton, Va.; 17. John Hart, N.J.; 18. John Adams, Mass.; 19. Roger Sherman, Conn.; 20. James Wilson, Pa.; 21. Thomas Jefferson, Va.; 22. Charles Thompson, (Secretary); 23. John Hancock, Mass.; 24. Francis Hopkinson, N.J.; 25. William Ellery, R.I.; 26. Edward Rutledge, S.C.; 27. Benjamin Franklin, Pa.; 28. Charles Carroll, Md.; 29. Richard Henry Lee, Va.; 30. George Read, Del.; 31. George Taylor, Pa.; 32. Stephen Hopkins, R.I.

Members of the Continental Congress met in Philadelphia to approve the Declaration of Independence. The serious expressions on their faces show how gravely they viewed a break with Great Britain.

Joseph Hewes A well-to-do North Carolina shipowner and merchant; a member of the North Carolina assembly.
William Hooper Graduate of Harvard College. A wealthy lawyer in North Carolina; member of North Carolina legislature.
Stephen Hopkins Wealthy merchant; chief justice of Rhode Island; chancellor of Rhode Island College.

Thomas Jefferson   Graduate of William and Mary College. Owner of large plantation in Virginia; member of Virginia legislature.

Richard H. Lee   Educated in England. Owner of large plantation in Virginia; member of Virginia legislature.

Philip Livingston   Graduate of Yale College. Member of wealthy New York family that owned large amounts of land and had powerful ties with political leaders.

Arthur Middleton   Educated in England. Son of one of the richest families in South Carolina; member of the South Carolina legislature.

Robert Morris   Philadelphia merchant; partner in one of the largest firms in America doing business in Britain; member of Pennsylvania Assembly.

Thomas Nelson, Jr.   Educated in England. Merchant and planter; member of Virginia Council; colonel in militia.

William Paca   Graduate of College of Philadelphia (now University of Pennsylvania). Owner of a large plantation in Maryland; lawyer and politician.

Robert T. Paine   Graduate of Harvard College. A well-known Massachusetts lawyer.

Caesar Rodney   Well-to-do Delaware landowner. Member of provincial legislature; general in Delaware militia.

Benjamin Rush   Graduate of College of New Jersey (now Princeton University) and University of Edinburgh (medical degree) in Scotland. Philadelphia physician; professor of chemistry.

Edward Rutledge   Studied law in England. Owner of large plantation; member of one of the richest and most powerful families in South Carolina.

Roger Sherman   At first a shoemaker; later a lawyer, judge, and legislator in Connecticut.

William Whipple   Well-to-do merchant in New Hampshire; active in New Hampshire politics.

John Witherspoon   Graduate of University of Edinburgh. President of College of New Jersey; prominent church leader.

Oliver Wolcott   Graduate of Yale College. Lawyer and judge; colonel in Connecticut militia.

Let's say that these twenty-eight are a fair representation of those who led the American Revolution. What generalizations can you make about them? What could you say about their social position—that is, were they in the upper class or the lower? their economic position—were they well-off or not well-off? their educational backgrounds? In answering that last question, you will want to keep in mind that less than one percent of the total population of the American colonies attended college. College was usually for the upper classes only. Would you say that such people would be likely to make a revolution to change the economic system? Would they be likely to seek ways to redistribute wealth and property from those who had it to those who did not?

Power—before and after the Revolution. A second way to get at the true nature of a revolution is to see whether it brought a new group of people to power. Suppose, before a revolution, people of one religious group, or one social class, or one economic group were in power. Then, after the revolution, we found they were no longer in power. Might not that lead us to certain conclusions?

Or suppose those with certain values or beliefs—say, the value of republicanism, perhaps, or of rule by religious leaders—were in power before a revolution. Then, after it, we found people with very different values were in power. Might not that also lead us to certain conclusions? On the other hand, if the same persons, or type of persons, were in power both before and after a revolution, that would give an important clue about the meaning of the revolution.

You know, of course, that the chief aim of the American Revolution was to

Rhode Island

Office	Officeholder Before Revolution	Officeholder During and/or After Revolution
Governor	Joseph Wanton	Nicholas Cooke
Lt. Governor	Darius Sessions	William Bradford
Secretary	Henry Ward	Henry Ward
Treasurer	Joseph Clark	Joseph Clark
Attorney General	Henry Marchant	Henry Marchant
Chief Justice	Stephen Hopkins	Metcalf Bowler
Associate Justices	Job Bennett, Jr.	Shearjashub Bourne
	Metcalf Bowler	Jabez Bowen
	William Greene	William Greene
	Joseph Russell	Thomas Wells, Jr.
Assistants	John Almy	James Arnold, Jr.
	Peleg Barker	Thomas Church
	John Collins	John Collins
	John Congdon	John Jepson
	David Harris	Ambrose Page
	William Potter	William Potter
	Jonathan Randall	Jonathan Randall
	William Richmond	Peter Phillips
	John Sayles, Jr.	John Sayles, Jr.
	Thomas Wickes	Simeon Potter

end the power of the English king and Parliament over the colonies. It did that quite successfully. But within America itself, did power shift from one group to another? To answer that question, let us look at some Americans who held power before and after the Revolution.

Once again, we cannot examine here all the political leaders in each colony and state. We have selected leaders from two states, Rhode Island and Connecticut. For this example, a political leader is one who held high office in the colony or state at some time.

Connecticut

(Note that several people held more than one position.)

Office	Officeholder Before Revolution	Officeholder During and/or After Revolution
Governor	Jonathan Trumbull	Jonathan Trumbull
Lt. Governor	Matthew Griswold	Matthew Griswold
Secretary	George Wylls	George Wylls
Treasurer	John Lawrence	John Lawrence
Attorney General	None	None
Chief Justice	Matthew Griswold	Matthew Griswold
Associate Justices	Eliphalet Dyer	Eliphalet Dyer
	Samuel Huntington	Samuel Huntington
	William Pitkin	William Pitkin
	Roger Sherman	Roger Sherman
Assistants	Shubael Conant	Samuel Huntington
	Abraham Davenport	Abraham Davenport
	Eliphalet Dyer	Eliphalet Dyer
	Jabez Hamlin	Jabez Hamlin
	James A. Hillhouse	Richard Law
	Jabez Huntington	Jabez Huntington
	William Samuel Johnson	William Williams
	William Pitkin	William Pitkin
	Elisha Sheldon	Elisha Sheldon
	Roger Sherman	Roger Sherman
	Joseph Spencer	Joseph Spencer
	Oliver Wolcott	Oliver Wolcott

Jonathan Trumbull was governor of Connecticut before, during, and after the Revolution. This portrait was painted by his son John, one of the outstanding artists of the period.

Not all the states would show results quite like those for Rhode Island and Connecticut. Judging by the record in those two states, however, would you say that there was, or was not, a major change of leaders during and after the Revolution? Keep in mind that death and retirement would account for the disappearance of at least some who held office before the Revolution.

The degree of change. There is a third way to get at the real meaning of a revolution. That is to see whether really great changes did take place in government and society during and after the revolution. Suppose an entirely new kind of government came into being. That would tell us a great deal about the revolution. If property were taken from one group and given to another, that would also tell us something important. If a social class that was formerly at the bottom of the heap was raised up, and one that was formerly at the top was pulled down, that would surely tell us something about the meaning of the revolution. If such changes did *not* take place, that, too, would be important to know.

Clearly, one change brought about by the American Revolution was the end of monarchy in America. Were there other important changes in government? Look back at page 161 where we talk about the new state governments, and decide.

Seizure of property. As for seizing the property of one group, you will recall that there was some of that. Estates of many wealthy Loyalists were seized by a number of state governments. That might suggest that a sweeping change in property ownership took place.

But two things must be noted. The first is that not all Loyalists lost their lands. In fact, most did not. The second is that when states did take land from wealthy Loyalists, they did not give it to those with little or no property. Generally, the lands were sold. Often wealthy people and speculators bought them.

Condition of the slaves. The condition of the lowest class in American society, the slaves, was not much changed by the Revolution. A small number gained their freedom by serving in the Continental

Army. And a number of northern states, including Rhode Island, Pennsylvania, Massachusetts, and Connecticut, took steps to abolish, or end, slavery. But in those states there were few slaves anyway.

In the parts of the country where most slaves lived, slavery remained. The most important change affecting slavery during the Revolution took place in Delaware, Virginia, Maryland, and South Carolina. These states agreed not to bring in any more slaves from Africa.

The colonists' rights. There is still another way to learn about the real meaning of a revolution. That is to see what those who made it *said* it was about.

Think back to events between 1763 and 1775. What were the colonists' grievances against England? What did they mean when they spoke of the "rights of Englishmen"? What did they believe was happening to those rights? What part did this play in their decision to rebel?

CHECKUP

1. What generalizations can you make about the backgrounds of the leaders of the American Revolution?
2. To what extent did the Revolution bring a new group of people to power?
3. What changes were brought about by the Revolution?

The Significance of the American Revolution

From what you have learned so far, it is clear that the American Revolution, compared with many modern-day revolutions, did not bring great social or economic change. Yet Americans thought their revolution was an event of great significance. They saw it as such not only for themselves but for the rest of the world. And they were right. The American Revolution has been one of the three or four most important revolutions in the past two hundred years.

A surge of pride. For one thing, the Revolution had a great effect on the way Americans thought about themselves. Before that time, Americans had felt themselves inferior in many ways to Europeans. It was to Europe, and especially to England, that the colonists had looked for leadership on almost all things. If America lacked what Europe had, Americans had regarded this as a sign of America's weakness, not Europe's. Thus, when the English said that the absence of an aristocratic class, of an established church, and of a polished high society were marks of America's backwardness, many Americans had agreed. Some had tried to imitate England. The term Yankee, which the English used for the colonists, was one of ridicule, meaning something like "hick" or "hayseed."

All that changed with the Revolution. The Americans lost their inferiority complex. "It was," says one writer, "as if the colonists blinked and suddenly saw their society in a new light." Those characteristics that stemmed from their century and a half as colonists were no longer viewed as weaknesses. They were now seen as strengths. The American differences from the Europeans became pluses instead of minuses.

It was true that there was no American aristocracy—the better to form a new society. It was true that they had no national church—the better to develop religious freedom. The absence of that sign of national power and pride, a standing army, meant that there would be civilian and not military rule in America. As for the simple American life, it was well suited to a true republican form of government. Within such a government, liberty and equality for all citizens could be achieved.

The term Yankee now became one of pride, and Americans made "Yankee Doodle" one of their favorite patriotic songs. There was a swelling of national pride. Americans, boasted Alexander Hamilton, were a "young people" whose greatness lay ahead of them. England, he said, had already seen its best days.

A model for the world. Just as the Revolution affected the way Americans thought about themselves, it affected the way they were to think about revolutions in other countries. Americans believed their republic, dedicated to popular rule and liberty, would serve as a model for the rest of the world. Many expected that Europeans would soon overthrow kings and set up republican governments of their own. Thus, America would lead the world into a new golden age of freedom.

One historian has commented on the boldness of this view.

The audacity [boldness] of the revolutionaries of 1776 in claiming that their little colonial rebellion possessed universal significance is astounding. After

During the French Revolution, armed Parisians prepare to storm the Bastille, a prison that held many political prisoners. Most Americans approved the revolutionists' goals, if not their methods.

all, those thirteen colonies made up a tiny part of the Western world, containing perhaps two-and-a-half million people huddled along a narrow strip of the Atlantic coast, living on the fringes of Christendom. To think that anything they did would matter to the rest of the world was the height of arrogance.

Yet the fact is that other peoples *did* look upon the American Revolution as Americans did. They watched the American experiment with much interest. And they were greatly influenced by it.

Support for revolutions. For many years, Americans looked with favor upon revolutions that appeared to be modeled on their own. They voiced approval in 1789 as the French removed their king and set up a republic. The public executions that followed shocked many Americans. Still more became disillusioned when the French republic ended in the dictatorship of Napoleon. But Americans were not discouraged by what happened in France. To them, it was simply a case of a promising revolution gone wrong.

Americans likewise saw the uprisings of Spain's colonies in South and Central America in the early 1800s as carbon copies of their own revolution. And the United States experience was in fact a powerful example for the new South American republics. Venezuela, the first of the Spanish colonies to become independent, even modeled its constitution after the Constitution of the United States.

In nineteenth-century Europe, too, Americans were sure they could see the inevitable march of republicanism. In

Americans were favorably disposed toward the revolutions led by Simon Bolivar in South America. They compared those struggles against Spain with their own struggle against Britain.

1821 they greeted with wild enthusiasm the outbreak of the Greek rebellion against Turkish rule. Long before the outcome was certain, South Carolina asked Congress to recognize Greece's independence. One leading American even asked that the United States lend a fleet to aid the Greeks in their fight for liberty. In his message to Congress in 1822, President James Monroe went out of his way to praise the Greek struggle for independence. Americans greeted the revolutions that broke out in a number of European states in 1848 with the same enthusiasm.

173

The Visit of Louis Kossuth

The feelings of Americans about revolution in the mid-nineteenth century can be seen in their reaction to Louis Kossuth. In 1848 Kossuth, a Hungarian patriot, led an uprising in the Austro-Hungarian Empire. He wanted to separate Hungary from Austria and to free his homeland from the rule of the Hapsburg monarchs. The revolution failed, but a sympathetic United States government sent a naval vessel to bring Kossuth from Turkey, where he had fled, to the United States for a visit.

Arriving in New York in 1851, Kossuth received a hero's welcome. Whenever he appeared in public, huge crowds—recalling their own country's struggle for independence 75 years earlier—turned out to cheer him. Countless banquets and parades were held in Kossuth's honor. Americans eagerly copied his clothes and hair style. Stores sold Kossuth hats and Kossuth overcoats, and men grew Kossuth beards. Hungarian music and dances became all the rage. It would be many years before Hungary would become independent, yet to Americans Louis Kossuth embodied the dreams they had had since 1776 of leading the peoples of other lands away from the rule of kings and queens.

A million Americans turned out to catch a glimpse of—and to cheer—Louis Kossuth when the Hungarian revolutionist was given a parade in New York City soon after his arrival in the United States. In the scene below Kossuth waves his plumed hat to admirers gathered outside New York's City Hall.

A changing attitude. The twentieth century has witnessed more revolutions than any previous age. But in this century, the attitude of Americans toward the idea of revolution has become more mixed. Some revolutions, like the anticolonial movements in Asia in the 1940s, were applauded by Americans. To others, they have given only lukewarm support. To still others, like the Russian Revolution of 1917–1918 and the revolution that brought the Chinese Communists to power in the 1940s, Americans were opposed.

Why? The answer is complex. Some believe it is because American feelings toward revolution have changed. More likely, it is because revolutions themselves have changed. The goals that were so important to Americans in their Revolution play little part today in many revolutions around the world.

Few modern revolutions aim to bring about representative government and real elections. Few have anything to do with the "rights of Englishmen"—free speech and free press, trial by jury, protection against illegal searches and arbitrary jailing, and other civil rights. Most modern revolutions have brought about sweeping changes. They have often been aimed against those classes that controlled the government and owned property. And they have often been accompanied by bloody executions.

How are Americans likely to feel about a particular revolution in our time? Again, there are many factors that will determine that. But one of them is the way Americans view that revolution in the light of their own. The more similarities they see to the goals of the Revolution that gave birth to their republic, the more sympathetic they are likely to be.

That fact alone attests to the vitality of the American Revolution today, and to its continued hold on the American mind.

CHECKUP

1. How did the Revolution affect the way Americans thought about themselves?
2. How has the American Revolution affected the way Americans think about revolutions in other countries?

Key Facts from Chapter 8

1. The American Revolution is the single most important event in the history of the United States.
2. Most of the leaders of the American Revolution were well educated and well-to-do and were regarded as leaders in their colonies.
3. The Revolution brought about the end of monarchy in America.
4. The Revolution did not result in widespread economic and social change.
5. The Revolution gave Americans a feeling of great national pride.
6. Americans have generally judged revolutions in other countries by how similar their goals were to the goals of the American Revolution.

★ REVIEWING THE CHAPTER ★

People, Places, and Events

Review Questions

1. What are three ways to evaluate the true nature of a revolution? *Pp. 165, 167, 170*

2. As you studied the information about the signers of the Declaration of Independence, what conclusions did you reach about **(a)** their social position, **(b)** their economic position, **(c)** their educational background? Would these people usually be the ones to start a revolution? Why, or why not? *Pp. 165–167*

3. Look at the list of political leaders for Rhode Island and Connecticut on pages 168–169. Compare office holders before the Revolution with those during and/or after the Revolution. What conclusion can you reach about the group in power before and after?

4. What effect did the Revolution have on the condition of slaves? *Pp. 170–171*

5. Why did Americans give Louis Kossuth a hero's welcome? What does the reaction of the American people to Kossuth tell you about their attitude toward revolutions in the nineteenth century? *P. 174*

6. Why did Americans tend to change their attitude toward revolutions in the twentieth century? *P. 175*

Chapter Test

On a separate piece of paper, write **T** *if the statement is true and* **F** *if the statement is false.*

1. The chief aim of the American Revolution was to end the power of the English King and Parliament over the American colonies.

2. When compared to many modern revolutions, the American Revolution did not bring great social or economic changes.

3. The leaders of the American Revolution were mostly farmers without much formal education.

4. The Revolution brought a new group of political leaders into power in the American colonies.

5. As a result of the Revolution, many poor people were given land that had been taken away from the Loyalists.

6. As a result of the Revolution some northern states took steps to end slavery, but, in general, the condition of slaves in America did not change much.

7. The Revolution gave Americans a real sense of national pride that they had never had before.

8. In the eighteenth and nineteenth centuries, Americans looked with favor upon revolutions that appeared to be modeled after their own.

9. Americans were opposed to the Russian Revolution of 1917–1918, because the goals that were so important to them in the American Revolution played little part in the Russian Revolution.

10. Few modern revolutions aim to bring about representative government and real elections.

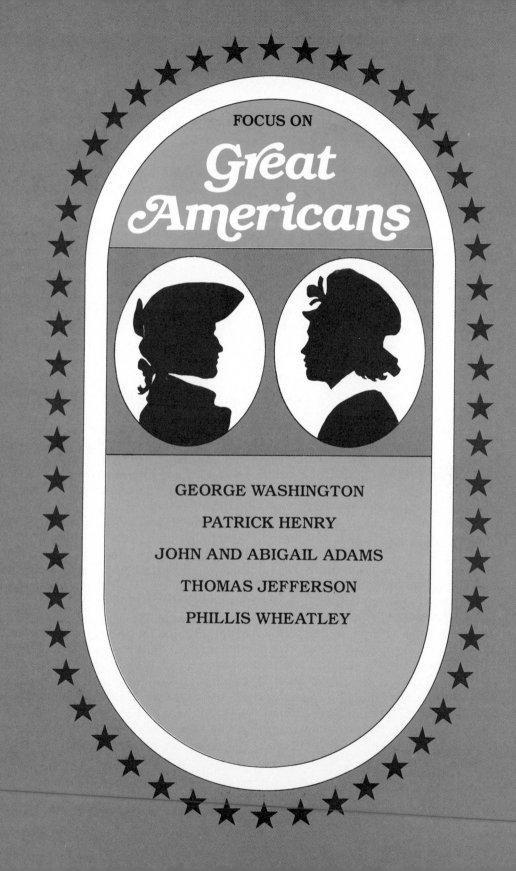

FOCUS ON

Great Americans

GEORGE WASHINGTON

PATRICK HENRY

JOHN AND ABIGAIL ADAMS

THOMAS JEFFERSON

PHILLIS WHEATLEY

★ GEORGE WASHINGTON ★

Father of His Country

With at least 7 mountains, 8 streams, 10 lakes, 33 counties, 9 colleges, and 121 towns and villages in the United States named after him, George Washington is surely one of the most honored figures in our history. He may also be among the least truly known of this group. As Americans turned the man they called the Father of His Country into a historical monument, the real Washington became ever harder to find. Tall tales like that of young George and the cherry tree—meant to illustrate his honesty and character—hide the full story of his childhood. Paintings that show an unsmiling, aloof adult—meant to show his dignity—present but half the man. Fortunately, careful biographers have done much to rescue Washington from these myths. As a result, wrote one of them, Americans will be "relieved" to learn "that Washington was sometimes violent, emotional, resentful—a human being and not a monument in frozen flesh."

George Washington was born in 1732 to Augustine Washington, a Virginia planter, and his second wife, Mary. With about 10,000 acres (4,000 ha) and fifty slaves by the time George was ten, the Washingtons were members of Virginia's upper class.

We do not know a great deal about George's youth. His education appears to have been spotty. From private tutors, and from his father, he learned to read, write, and do simple arithmetic between the ages of seven and eleven. His spelling was poor and always would be, but he was especially good at mathematics. His reading came to include the leading novels of the day as well as history, biographies, and military tactics.

The world of eleven-year-old George must have seemed to come apart when his father died suddenly in 1743. George—always insecure, sensitive to criticism, hot-tempered, and stubborn—did not get along with his mother—a narrow, self-centered, and demanding person. For most of the next half-dozen years, George decided to live with relatives, mainly with his older half brother, Lawrence, whom George idolized. On their father's death, Lawrence had inherited Mount Vernon, where George went to live. During these years, the younger Washington combined his talent for mathematics and his love for the outdoors by becoming a land surveyor. At fifteen he was being hired for small surveying jobs.

George received his first important assignment at sixteen. Lawrence had married into the wealthy Fairfax family. Lord Thomas Fairfax invited George to help survey his 5 million acres (2 million ha) of Virginia land. Soon after, with the influence of Lord Fairfax, George was made surveyor of Culpeper County. This work took him into the frontier and kindled a lifelong interest in western land. Although he never realized his dream of becoming a great landowner in the West, Washington did speculate in land throughout his career.

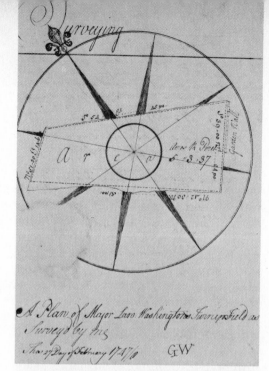

During these teenage years, George began his practice of keeping careful records of his earnings and expenses. His account books show an orderliness and attention to detail that became characteristic of Washington throughout his life. He was so accurate that his Revolutionary War account books—showing personal expenses of 24,700 English pounds over a period of eight years—were off by less than 1 pound!

In 1752 tuberculosis took the life of Lawrence Washington and removed from George the person who had been the most important influence on him since his father's death. This development indirectly shaped George's future in two ways. One was that with the death of Lawrence's daughter and wife shortly after, the estate of Mount Vernon passed to George. The second was far more important for Washington's future country. Ever since Lawrence had served as a captain in the war between England and Spain in 1740, George had been drawn toward a military career. It would offer adventure and a chance to gain recognition. At the time of his death, Lawrence was an officer in the Virginia militia. George now asked the governor to appoint him to Lawrence's place. Thus early in 1753 at the age of twenty, George Washington became a major in the Virginia militia.

If Washington had sought this post to gain recognition, his timing could not have been better. England and France were bitter rivals over the Ohio country, and each was trying to strengthen its claim and strategic position by building forts. In the winter of 1753, Governor Robert Dinwiddie of Virginia sent Washington to warn the French not to move

Surveyors provided official records for claims to American soil. Above is a plan Washington drew while practicing for this vocation. Later he surveyed lands in the Northwest Territory. He was a frontier colonel in that area, serving in the Virginia militia. Later, at age forty, he wore that uniform for this first known portrait.

in on British territory. After a five-hundred-mile trip by horseback and canoe into western Pennsylvania, Washington and his party of six reached the French commander, who politely rejected the warning. The return trip to Virginia was filled with danger. They were forced to walk much of the way when the horses gave out. En route, Washington was shot at by an Indian, was almost drowned when knocked off a raft into the ice-filled Allegheny River, and was nearly frozen to death in his soaked clothing. Once back to safety, Washington wrote an account of his trip, which brought him a measure of fame in America and England.

In 1754, Governor Dinwiddie made Washington a lieutenant colonel in the Virginia militia and sent him west with 150 men to reinforce a small fort at the junction of the Allegheny and Monongahela rivers. En route, Washington received word that the French had captured the fort, strengthened it, and renamed it Fort Duquesne. Although lacking enough men to retake the fort, Washington rashly went on. He surprised and defeated an advance party of 30 French, but was soon faced by a superior army of French and Indians from Fort Duquesne. Washington's troops fell back to a makeshift camp called Fort Necessity. But after nine hours under attack in a driving rain, Washington was forced to surrender. He and his men were allowed to return to Virginia only after he signed a paper stating he had started the fighting. Thus, although Washington fought bravely, his first military campaign ended in disaster. This small action was the start of the French and Indian War.

Faulted by British officials for unwise tactics and for signing the admission, Washington lashed out at his critics. Relations between Governor Dinwiddie and Washington cooled, and in October 1754 he resigned his commission.

The following year, however, Britain sent 2,200 regular troops under the command of General Edward Braddock to retake Fort Duquesne. Washington sought and received an invitation from Braddock to join his staff. Once again Washington was in uniform as the troops marched to the West. A few miles from Fort Duquesne, Braddock's army ran into an ambush by the French and Indians. The British were routed with heavy casualties. Although weak from illness, Washington fought bravely, recklessly exposing himself to danger. Two horses were shot from under him, and four bullets passed through his clothing. Miraculously, he was not hit. General Braddock was killed.

Following Braddock's death, Dinwiddie appointed the twenty-three-year-old Washington a colonel and commander in chief of all Virginia troops. The title was grand, but the job was anything but glamorous. When the British army retreated all the way to Philadelphia, Washington was left with the task of protecting the entire Virginia frontier against attack by the French and Indians. With just 300 men he succeeded skillfully, gaining important experience in making the most of limited resources.

As Washington matured, he continued to display some of the weaknesses of his youth. Recognition by others was still very important to him, and he remained sensitive to any criticism or slight. When British officers of

Just before Braddock's army was ambushed by French and Indian forces, Washington had been ill and confined to bed for seventeen days. Here, on horseback, he takes command after Braddock's fatal wound.

lower rank refused his orders because he was a mere colonist, Washington was especially angered. But he also grew in these years. He learned to curb his temper and to be patient. Washington was already known for his fearlessness and skill in battle. Now he gained a reputation for strength of character, integrity, and leadership.

Military duties took only part of Washington's time during these years. He was developing the plantation of Mount Vernon, and by 1757 had put 4,000 acres (1,600 ha) under cultivation. Washington put military ambitions aside entirely

in 1758 after he helped command a British force that succeeded in taking Fort Duquesne. He resigned from the militia and took up life as a full-time Virginia planter. In 1759 he married Martha Dandridge Custis, a wealthy widow with two children. Washington never had children of his own, but he bestowed a father's love on those of his wife. He could not have grieved more over the death from epilepsy of sixteen-year-old Patsy Custis had she been his own child.

The next sixteen years were surely the happiest of Washington's life. He managed his plantation with great success.

Washington enjoyed family life at Mount Vernon. He is shown here with Martha and her grandchildren, whom he adopted. During most of the Revolution, as while President, Washington was home very little.

Like most other gentlemen farmers, Washington was interested in scientific farming. He was among the earliest to rotate crops and to plant grass to renew the soil. When extra hands were needed in the field, often he would roll up his sleeves and work along with his slaves. He gave careful attention to the business side of plantation life, beginning his day at 4:00 A.M. with the account books and his correspondence.

Washington also enjoyed the social side of plantation life. During one seven-year period, the Washingtons entertained two thousand guests at Mount Vernon, many of whom stayed overnight. In addition to the fox hunting and horseback riding that were part of the life of the gentry, Washington en-joyed dancing, card playing, and the theater.

Like many other wealthy planters, Washington took part in colonial politics. On his third try, in 1759, he was elected to the Virginia assembly, and served continuously until the Revolution. From the beginning, he took the Patriot position on issues that divided England and the colonies. He opposed the Stamp Act, observing that Parliament had "no more right to put their hands into my pocket, without my consent, than I have to put my hands into yours for money." Although Washington did not approve of the destruction of property in the Boston Tea Party, he opposed the British measures to punish Boston. In 1774 Washington told members of the Virginia assembly, "I am ready to raise 1,000 men . . . at my own expense and march at their head to Boston."

Washington was elected to both the First and Second Continental Congresses. He attended the second congress in uniform, as if to make clear that he would welcome being called to command. His service in the French and Indian War was still remembered, and he was among the best-known military figures in America. At least in part, however, he owed his choice as general of the American armies to the fact that New Englanders such as John and Samuel Adams believed it was necessary to give command to a Southerner in order to unify the colonies. In accepting this appointment, Washington announced that he would accept no salary.

Few generals have been faced with a more difficult task than that which lay before Washington. To fight one of the world's strongest military powers, he would have to mold an army mainly from untrained volunteers, most of whom enlisted for only short periods. For this task, time was needed. By nature, Washington was inclined to take the offensive, but he knew that his country's only hope lay in fighting a defensive war, delaying when possible, retreating when necessary. He also knew he would need to win occasional victories to throw the British off guard, keep up morale, and win the support of foreign governments. Washington did all this brilliantly. Through shrewd strategy and tactics, and through the strength of his own character and example, Washington kept an army in the field until he had developed it into a military instrument

that could hold its own against the British. It is hard to imagine the United States winning the Revolutionary War without Washington.

At the end of the war, Washington returned to Mount Vernon, which had suffered from poor management during his absence. He would have been content to remain there for the rest of his days, but he was called to preside over the Constitutional Convention of 1787 and then to serve as the new nation's first President (see page 251). Even after his eight-year Presidency, Washington's service to his country did not end. In 1798, when war with France seemed possible during the XYZ affair (see page 262), President John Adams appointed Washington commander of the American army. This time, fortunately, the dispute was settled, and he did not have to don a uniform again.

Washington's death came suddenly, after a short illness, only seventeen days before the new century was to open. In memory of the first President of the United States, Congress voted to erect a marble monument. Today, the Washington Monument graces the skyline of Washington, D.C., both named for the man who was "first in war, first in peace, and first in the hearts of his countrymen."

CHECKUP

1. What qualities of character helped Washington to be a successful leader? How did he improve during his life?
2. What tasks faced him as the American commander? What strategies did he develop to win the Revolutionary War?
3. Describe other ways and times that Washington served his country loyally.

★ PATRICK HENRY ★

Patriot, Lawyer, Public Servant

In the making of a revolution, words are as important as weapons. You will remember how Thomas Paine's *Common Sense* and Thomas Jefferson's Declaration of Independence won support for the American Revolution. As Paine and Jefferson put their pens at the service of the struggle for independence, so Patrick Henry used the spoken word in the same cause.

Those who heard Henry were unanimous about his oratorical powers. "He is by far the most powerful speaker I ever heard," wrote fellow Virginian George Mason. "Every word he says not only engages, but commands the attention; and your passions are no longer your own when he addresses them." A Connecticut leader called him "the completest speaker I ever heard." A lawyer wrote that sitting in a courtroom, "I could write a letter [or do other tasks] with as much accuracy as I could in my office, . . . *except* when Patrick rose . . . I was obliged to lay down my pen and could not write another word until the speech was finished." Thomas Jefferson said that "his powers over a jury were . . . irresistible."

Unlike most of Virginia's revolutionary leaders, Patrick Henry did not come from one of the colony's powerful and wealthy upper-class families. His family, however, were anything but poor. Their home area was Hanover County, where the Henry name was important and respected. John Henry, his father, who was the son of a well-to-do Scottish fam-ily, had come to America in 1727. He had bought some land and acquired still more through marriage into a wealthy Virginia family. By the time Patrick, the second of eleven children, was born in 1736, John Henry owned 27,000 acres (11,○○○ ___ ___ land and a number of slav__ ___ ___ dded to these holdings.

Pa___ ___ed a school until age ten. ___ ___ t five years he was taug___ ___ y his college-educated fathe___ ___ an age at which sons of m___ ___us planters went to colleg___ ___ k had no interest in further study. ___ ent to work as a clerk in a nearby crossroads store. The following year he and his older brother opened a store of their own. Within a year, the business failed, partly because the brothers had granted credit too freely.

This was to be the first of several reverses that Patrick suffered. At eighteen, he married sixteen-year-old Sarah Shelton and received 300 acres (120 ha) and six slaves as a wedding gift from the bride's father. The land was not very productive, however, and Henry struggled to make a living for three years. Then a fire swept through their house and burned everything they owned. Patrick turned to storekeeping again, but this business, like his earlier store, soon failed. He then went to work in a tavern owned by his father-in-law, tending bar and playing the fiddle to amuse the guests. It is not likely that many who knew Patrick Henry at this time would have guessed what his future held.

At twenty-four, Patrick Henry decided to try a career in law. He did not study very hard. Later he admitted that he knew very little law when he presented himself for examination after only six weeks of study. Despite their doubts, the examiners passed him.

Henry opened a law practice in his home county. For the first time he tasted success in the world of affairs. In his first year he had nearly two hundred cases, and soon averaged nearly four hundred a year. Many of his cases came from members of his family and their friends, for the Henrys were important and well-connected in Hanover County. But clearly the main reason he prospered was that word of his ability to sway juries and judges quickly spread.

Patrick Henry first gained wide attention in Virginia in 1763, through a case known as the Parsons' Cause. The Anglican Church, the established church in Virginia, was supported by the taxpayers, whether Anglican in religion or not. The clergy were paid in tobacco. Each received about 16,000 pounds (725 kg) of tobacco per year.

A small tobacco harvest in 1758 caused the price per pound to rise from about two cents to nearly four cents. The clergy were not very popular, and many Virginians resented what amounted to a doubling of their pay. The Virginia assembly therefore passed the Two Penny Act. For the year 1758, the clergy could be paid in cash at the rate of two pennies for each pound of tobacco due them.

The clergy asked the King of England to disallow the law, and in 1759 the king did so. Then in 1763 an Anglican minister, the Reverend James Maury, sued in a Hanover County court to collect the additional pay that he was due for 1758. The judge—none other than John Henry, Patrick's father—agreed that the Two Penny Act had not been legal. That left it up to a jury to decide how much was owed to Reverend Maury.

At that point the taxpayers hired Patrick Henry to take over their case. John Henry was still the judge. (It was not unusual in local Virginia courts for a lawyer and a judge to be related. In fact, Patrick Henry was related to six of the twelve judges in Hanover County.) Henry promptly challenged the king's action in

This portrait of Patrick Henry commemorates his plea in 1775 for Virginians to form a militia to defend the Patriot cause against the British.

Shelburne Museum

Patrick Henry *(left)* denounces the Stamp Act in 1765. Jefferson sat among the Virginia Burgesses who heard Henry claim that only they had the "right and power to lay taxes . . . on the colony."

disallowing the Two Penny Act. The act had been a fair and good law for Virginians, he said. A king who disallows such laws becomes a tyrant and has no right to expect his subjects to obey him any more.

This reasoning would later be at the heart of the colonists' case in the Declaration of Independence. In 1763, however, it was daring talk. The opposing lawyer and many others in the courtroom shouted that Henry was speaking treason. The jury, however, did not think so. After only five minutes it awarded damages to Reverend Maury in the amount of —one penny!

Henry's role in this case made him very popular. In 1765 he was elected to the Virginia House of Burgesses (see page 70). Only nine days after taking his seat—on May 29, 1765, his twenty-ninth birthday—Henry presented resolutions to protest the recently enacted Stamp Act. These resolutions stated that Virginians were entitled to all the rights of Englishmen, including the right not to be taxed without representation. One said that only the assembly of the colony had any right to tax Virginians (see page 43).

Henry's resolutions touched off a heated debate and led to one of the most famous, if confused, moments in the history of the House of Burgesses. With no official record of what was said, we must rely on private accounts of what happened. Arguing for his resolutions, Henry said, "Caesar had his Brutus, Charles the First, his Cromwell, and George the Third . . . ." At this point, according to one account, the speaker of the assembly cried out, "Treason! Treason!" Looking the speaker in the eye, Henry finished his sentence, ". . . may profit by their example! If this be treason, make the most of it!"

A visiting Frenchman who heard the debate from the hallway entered a different version in his journal. When the speaker said that Henry's words were treason, he wrote that Henry begged the pardon of the speaker and the assembly. Henry also protested his undying loyalty to the king, according to the Frenchman's account.

Which version is correct? In fact, it matters little how Henry ended his speech. In winning passage of the Stamp Act Resolves by his oratory, Patrick Henry put Virginia on the long road toward independence. Most of the other colonies soon followed Virginia's lead with Stamp Act resolutions of their own.

Henry's speech made him more popular than ever. A traveler in Hanover County reported that there was "a great deal said about the Noble Patriot Mr. Henry, who lives in this county, the whole inhabitants say publicly that if the least injury was offered to him they'd stand by him to the last drop of their blood." Henry's fame quickly spread throughout the colony. From that time on, he was probably the most influential member of the assembly. He and other young members, like Thomas Jefferson and Richard Henry Lee who both later signed the Declaration of Independence, pressed for a firm stand against Parliament and the king during the following years. He supported the creation of a Virginia Committee of Correspondence in 1773 and served as a member.

In 1774 Henry was a delegate to the First Continental Congress in Philadelphia. In that body he was but one of many able men, and the records do not show that he made any special mark on it. He was among those who wanted the colonies to unite in a strong stand rather than seek a compromise with England. "The distinctions between Virginians, Pennsylvanians, New York-

ers, and New Englanders," he told the Congress, "are no more. I am not a Virginian but an American."

Not all of Henry's time and effort during these years was occupied with the public business. He continued to practice law. He also acquired a good deal of land. In colonial Virginia, you will remember, that was the chief way to wealth and social position (see pages 70–71). By the mid-1770s, Henry owned a large tobacco plantation, two other farms, 10,000 acres (4,000 ha) of land in western Kentucky, and some thirty slaves. Thus, although he was extremely popular with lower- and middle-class Virginians, Henry was in fact a prosperous planter in his own right and a rising member of Virginia society.

Even as Henry was rising in Virginia society, personal tragedy struck the Henry family. In 1772, Patrick's wife, Sarah, began to show signs of mental illness. Within two years she became insane. In those days the mentally ill were usually kept at home. Few asylums existed where patients could receive good care. Furthermore, mental illness was then thought to bring shame on an entire family. So the sick family member was often hidden away. Whether for either or both of these reasons, Sarah was kept at the Henry plantation house, where she was cared for by family servants. She died in early 1775.

Following his wife's death, Henry plunged back into the Patriot cause. A special convention of Virginia's leaders met in Richmond in the spring of 1775 to discuss the crisis. Henry took the lead in opposing British rule. By this time he believed fighting was bound to come. He proposed that a colonial militia be formed and that the colony immediately be put in a state of readiness. More cautious members feared that this would make a clash with British troops almost certain. Several of them spoke against Henry's resolutions.

Then Patrick Henry took the floor to reply. Once again there is no exact record of his words, and we must rely on the memories of different people. All agree, however, that Henry's speech was one of the greatest they had ever heard. One person, who was not even friendly to Henry, remembered that his oratory "blazed so as to warm the coldest heart. . . . Henry [spoke] as man was never known to speak before." The final sentences of Henry's speech remain today among the most famous in our history.

> Gentlemen may cry peace, peace—but there is no peace. The war is actually begun! The next gale that sweeps the north will bring to our ears the clash of resounding arms. Our brethren are already in the field! Why stand we here idle? What is it the gentlemen wish? What would they have? Is life so dear, or peace so sweet, as to be purchased at the price of chains and slavery? Forbid it, almighty God! I know not what course others may take; but as for me . . . give me liberty or give me death!

Later that spring Henry served as a Virginia delegate to the Second Continental Congress. He was also named commander-in-chief of the new Virginia militia. Henry's abilities, however, did not lie in military leadership, and some months later he resigned. In June 1776 he was elected the first governor of the new state of Virginia. The choice was fitting, for no person had done more than the popular Henry to lead the colony on the road to independence. He served for three consecutive one-year terms, the maximum allowed by the new state constitution.

Although Patrick Henry had been a leader of the Revolution, he did not seek important social changes as governor. He opposed Jefferson's bill for religious freedom. Like most Virginia slaveowners of the time, Henry questioned the morality of slavery, but he did not favor ending it. Indeed, he gained twelve additional slaves with his second marriage, in 1778, and bought others later.

Henry was succeeded as governor by Thomas Jefferson. The two men had worked together in the revolutionary cause; however, near the end of Jefferson's second term, the two clashed. Henry, who was then in the assembly again, joined in a demand for an investigation of Jefferson's conduct as governor. The investigation showed that Jefferson had behaved properly, but it left bitter feelings between Jefferson and Henry for as long as the two men lived.

Patrick Henry later served two more terms as governor. He was also chosen to serve in the federal Constitutional Convention of 1787. He declined, however, and later opposed the new constitution in the Virginia ratifying convention (see page 220). Henry's main objection was that the constitution would create a strong central government at the expense of the sovereign states (see pages 215–219). Despite his statement to the Continental Congress in 1774, Henry was always a Virginian first. He spoke of Virginia as "my country." During the month-long convention, Henry spoke nearly every day, on some days as many as five times. For one of the few

Henry gave his cry for liberty or death in Richmond's St. John's Church in 1775. He urged: "Gentlemen may cry, peace, peace; but there is no peace. The war is actually begun!. . . Why stand we here idle?"

times in his life, however, his oratory failed to carry the day, and Virginia ratified the Constitution.

Henry returned to the assembly in 1788, as popular and powerful as ever. George Washington wrote that Henry had more power in the Virginia assembly than the King of France had in his country. "He has only to say let this be law," said Washington, "and it is law." After two terms, however, Henry decided to retire from public life. He spent the remaining years of his life in the building up of a personal estate to leave to his sixteen children and numerous grandchildren. He was in great demand as a lawyer and earned large fees. He also added to his landholdings. In the 1790s, he was among the hundred wealthiest men in Virginia, with 22,000 acres (9,000 ha) of land and more than sixty slaves.

During these years President Washington asked Henry to serve as Secretary of State, Chief Justice, and ambassador to Spain. Henry declined each offer. Late in life, his rivalry with Jefferson led Henry to move into the camp of the opposing party, the Federalists. Although in failing health, he ran once again for the Virginia assembly in 1799. He was easily elected, but died before he could take office.

CHECKUP

1. What views did Patrick Henry put forth in the Parsons' Cause and in his Stamp Act Resolves?
2. When did Henry argue for military readiness to defend against the British? Why?
3. Explain how Patrick Henry's life reflects this statement: "In the making of a revolution, words are as important as weapons."

✶ JOHN AND ABIGAIL ADAMS ✶

Partners for American Independence

"John and Abigail, Abigail and John—their names are as inseparably linked as those of any human pair in history." So begins *The Book of Abigail and John,* a collection of letters between Abigail Adams and her husband, John, second President of the United States. John and Abigail Adams were indeed a remarkable couple. They were the first of four generations of Adamses who served their country and made the Adams family perhaps the most famous of American families. More than a century and a half after the death of John and Abigail, their letters remind us of what it was like to live through both the great and the ordinary events of the early years of America's history.

Abigail Smith was born in Weymouth, Massachusetts, in 1744. Her father was a well-to-do minister. On her mother's side, the family traced its history to the early settlers of the Massachusetts Bay Colony. Abigail and her sisters were not sent to school but were taught at home by their grandmother. Abigail always resented the fact that in education, as in almost everything else, sons got "every assistance and advantage" while "daughters are wholly neglected." But she made the best of things, and for the most part educated herself. Her father had a large collection of books that she was allowed to use. Abigail read all the great English writers. She also taught herself to read French.

The Smith homestead is Abigail's birthplace and home. There John courted her until they married.

Abigail was the first American woman presented at the courts of France and England after the Revolution. Led by his belief in the right to a fair trial, John served as defense lawyer to the British soldiers charged with manslaughter in the Boston Massacre. Though a Patriot, John won acquitals for all but two of the nine men.

Abigail Smith met John Adams in 1759. The Adams family had lived in neighboring Braintree for four generations, beginning in 1636. John, nine years older than Abigail, was just getting started as a lawyer. The two were married in 1764.

At just about this time the quarrel between the American colonies and Great Britain was breaking out. John at first resolved to stay out of politics, but events would not let him. He became a leader in the fight against the Stamp Act in 1765. In the following years he became closely connected with the Patriot cause. When Britain passed the Intolerable Acts to punish Boston for the Tea Party, Massachusetts sent John to the First Continental Congress. Later he served in the Second Continental Congress.

Beginning in September 1774, John and Abigail were separated for most of the next two years. Through their letters, one can see how the colonial mood changed from one of resisting the British government to one favoring independence. John's letters are from Philadelphia; Abigail's are written from the family farm in Braintree.

John to Abigail, September 8, 1774:
There is in the Congress a collection of the greatest men upon this continent. . . .

Abigail to John, September 14, 1774:
The Governer is making all kinds of warlike preparation, such as mounting cannons upon Beacon Hill. . . . The people are much alarmed. . . .

John to Abigail, September 20, 1774:
Let us eat potatoes and drink water. Let us wear canvass . . . rather than submit. . . .

John to Abigail, October 9, 1774:
Congress is [boring] beyond expression. This assembly is like no other that ever existed. Every man in it is a great man and therefore every man upon every question must show [his talents]. . . . I believe if it was moved and seconded that . . . three and two make five we should [debate] the subject for two whole days. . . .

Then, on April 19, 1775 blood was shed at Lexington and Concord (see page 127). Following this and other fighting between the Patriots and the British troops, John and Abigail exchanged the following letters.

John to Abigail, May 2, 1775:
In case of real danger . . . fly to the woods with our children.

Abigail to John, May 24, 1775:
The report was . . . that 300 [British troops] had landed [in Braintree] and were upon their march into town. The alarm flew [like] lightning, and men from all parts came flocking down till 2,000 were collected. . . .

Abigail to John, June 16, 1775:
[General Gage's army] is now eight thousand strong. . . . We live in continual expectation of alarms.

John to Abigail, June 17, 1775:
I can now inform you that the Congress [has] made choice of the . . . generous and brave George Washington Esq., to be the General of the American Army. . . . This appointment will have a great effect in cementing and securing the union of these colonies.

Abigail to John, June 18, 1775:
The day, perhaps the decisive day is come on which the fate of America depends. . . . Charlestown is laid in ashes. The battle began upon . . . Bunker Hill, a Saturday morning about 3 o'clock and has not ceased yet and 'tis now 3 o'clock Sunday afternoon. . . . How many have fallen we know not—the constant roar of the cannon is so distressing that we cannot eat, drink, or sleep. [See the painting on page 126.]

Abigail to John, June 22, 1775:
Does every member [of Congress] feel for us [in Massachusetts]? Do they realize what we suffer?

John to Abigail, July 7, 1775:
. . . every year brings us fresh evidence that we have nothing to hope for from our loving mother country [Britain] but cruelties. . . . Your description of the distresses of the worthy inhabitants of Boston, and the other seaport towns, is enough to melt a heart of stone.

Abigail to John, March 17, 1776:
Every foot of ground which [the British] obtain now they must fight for, and may [they pay for it at] a Bunker Hill price. [See page 130.]

Abigail to John, March 31, 1776:
I long to hear that you have declared an independency. . . .

John to Abigail, April 14, 1776:
As to declarations of independency, be patient.

John to Abigail, April 28, 1776:
. . . we are hastening rapidly to great events.

John to Abigail, July 3, 1776:
Yesterday the greatest question was decided which ever was debated in America. . . . A resolution was passed without one dissenting colony that these united colonies are, and of right ought to be, free and independent states.

John to Abigail, July 3, 1776:
. . . I am well aware of the toil and blood and treasure that it will cost us to maintain this declaration, and support and defend these states. Yet through all the gloom I can see the rays of ravishing light and glory.

Two of Abigail's letters during this time show her as an early supporter of equal rights for women. She wrote her husband that, in making laws for a new country, "I desire you would remember the ladies, and be more generous and favorable to them than your ancestors. Do not put such unlimited power into the hands of all husbands. Remember all men would be tyrants if they could." In another letter, five weeks later, she reminded John, "While you are proclaiming peace and good will to men, emancipating all nations, you insist upon retaining an absolute power over wives."

Although John Adams was a superior statesman and a leader in the movement for independence, he did not want a career in public life. On one occasion, in fact, he wrote to Abigail that "I am determined to avoid public life." And he made no secret of his desires after the First Continental Congress ended. "I bid farewell to great affairs," he wrote Abigail. "I had rather chop wood and make fences on my little farm."

But it was not to be. People like John Adams could not be spared by the struggling new nation, either during the war or in the decades afterward. Except for brief periods at home, John and Abigail were to be separated for another eight years. For the first two years after the Declaration of Independence, John served in the Congress in Philadelphia. Then in 1778 he was sent on a mission to France, where he joined Benjamin Franklin as an American representative to the French government. John took his ten-year-old son, John Quincy, to Europe with him. Later, he helped to negotiate the treaty of peace with Great Britain, and served as United States minister to that country.

During these years, Abigail ran the family farm and looked after all business matters. "I know not what would become of me and mine," John wrote her in 1777, "if I had not such a friend to take care of my interests in my absence." Indeed, Abigail would continue to take care of the family's farming and business affairs for the entire period of John's public service—twenty-six years.

Abigail managed so well that the Adamses were able to buy a larger house in Braintree in 1787. Abigail described the new property with pride: "There are 108 acres [44 ha] in the whole, 50 [20 ha] of which is fine woodland. The garden contains the best collection of fruit

The Adams farm in Braintree is where John was born and where Abigail managed the family business.

During the XYZ affair, President Adams avoided war while taking a strong stand against France. This 1799 poster states his position: "Millions for our defence, not a cent for tribute."

in the town." A grandson later credited her energy and good judgment with saving the family from the financial ruin experienced by so many people who gave their lives to public service in those years (see page 199).

The years of separation were difficult for Abigail. Several times during John's absence, disease swept Massachusetts. During one especially bad stretch, Abigail reported that "in six weeks, five of my near connections [were] laid in the grave." Among them were her mother, one of John's two brothers, and a niece. During this time there were "three and four funerals in a day for many days." And always, even when all were in good

health, there was loneliness without John.

In 1784, with the war over, Abigail and the remaining children went to Europe to join John and their son John Quincy. The next five years were spent in Europe, where John represented the new United States government in various offices. The Adams family returned to the United States in 1789. John was promptly elected Vice President and went to New York City to serve in that office (see page 251). In 1796 he was elected the young nation's second President (see pages 262, 264–265. His term was nearly at an end when the capital was moved to Washington, D.C. Abigail and John thus became the first First Family to live in the White House when, in November 1800, they moved in to the still unfinished building. (See the portrait on page 266.)

In 1801 John and Abigail Adams retired to their farm in Braintree, which by then was known as Quincy. There the couple lived out their years. Abigail died in 1818. John lived long enough, however, to see their son John Quincy Adams become the sixth President of the United States, in 1825.

CHECKUP

1. Give examples from the Adamses' letters that show their feelings about American independence, sacrifice, cooperation, determination, hope, and victory.
2. How did Abigail feel about the rights and treatment of women in the American colonies?
3. While Abigail managed the Adamses family business, what positions did John hold between the Declaration of Independence and his retirement?

★ THOMAS JEFFERSON ★

Author of the Declaration of Independence

In the course of his long life, Thomas Jefferson received numerous honors and held many high offices. He was governor of Virginia and a United States congressman. He served as United States Minister to France. He was the country's first Secretary of State, its second Vice President, and its third President. Yet as he approached death in his eighty-third year, it was not those achievements for which he most wished to be remembered. He wrote out his instructions for the inscription to appear on his simple gravestone:

> Here was buried Thomas Jefferson, author of the Declaration of American Independence, of the statute of Virginia for religious freedom, and father of the University of Virginia.

That Jefferson should choose these three achievements to be remembered by tells a great deal about this unusual man.

Jefferson was born in Albemarle County, Virginia, in 1743, third of the ten children of Peter and Jane Randolph Jefferson. The Randolphs were one of Virginia's most important and wealthiest families, so the Jefferson children's membership in the gentry class was assured. Although Peter Jefferson's family had neither wealth nor social position, Peter had done well as a surveyor and tobacco planter. As a result, he owned a good deal of land in western Virginia.

Thomas Jefferson was taught by private tutors, for there were no public schools and few private ones in the rural South of the 1700s. His father died in 1757, and Tom, at age fourteen the oldest surviving son, inherited 2,750 acres (1,100 ha) of land and a large number of slaves. He also had the responsibility of looking after other lands his father left.

In 1760, Tom Jefferson entered William and Mary College in Williamsburg, Virginia. The young student found the world of books and ideas so agreeable that in his second year he regularly studied fifteen hours a day. By the time he graduated, in 1762, he could read Greek and Latin well, and knew some Italian and French also. He had learned a good deal of science. And he had read the works of nearly all the great ancient thinkers and many of the modern ones. The love that Jefferson acquired for books and learning remained a lifelong passion.

On graduation, young Jefferson turned to the study of law. In those days there were no law schools. One became a lawyer by studying with a person who already was one, and then by taking an examination. Jefferson was taken on by George Wythe, one of the great lawyers of the time, who lived only a few blocks from William and Mary. Two others to study under Wythe within the next thirty years were John Marshall, later Chief Justice of the United States, and Henry Clay, who became a leader in the United States Senate. While studying law and legal history, Jefferson looked after his plantations and kept up his other reading. He also taught himself architecture.

In 1767, at the age of twenty-four, Jefferson began a successful law practice. During his first year he handled sixty-eight cases, an unusually large number for a new lawyer to get—and to accept. His reason seems to have been money, for he had just begun construction on the house he had dreamed of for years. This home on a mountaintop he named Monticello, which is Italian for "little mountain." Jefferson designed and supervised the construction of the house and everything in it, down to the furniture and curtains. Over the years he invented many gadgets for his home, which still delight the thousands who visit there each year. The main house was not yet finished when Jefferson moved to Monticello in 1771. The following year he married Martha Skelton.

Jefferson made this sketch while planning Monticello. Begun in 1768, the house was remodeled several times before it was completed in 1809.

By this time Jefferson had become deeply involved in the struggle between Great Britain and the American colonies. From the first, he sided with the colonists. He was elected to the Virginia House of Burgesses in 1769. At his suggestion the next year, that body set up a Committee of Correspondence. When the British closed Boston harbor in 1774, Jefferson asked Virginians to pray and fast for a day "to give us one heart and one mind firmly to oppose . . . every injury to American rights."

It was Jefferson's belief that Parliament had no right to make any laws at all for the colonies. The only connection between England and America was that they had the same king, whom the Americans voluntarily accepted. In 1774 these views were printed in a pamphlet called *A Summary View of the Rights of British North America*. Even though most colonials were not yet ready to go this far, Jefferson's brilliant presentation of the case brought him to the notice of people in the other colonies.

In 1775 Jefferson was a Virginia delegate to the Second Continental Congress. He was the third youngest member of the Congress, and probably the quietest one, for he rarely spoke from the floor. Because of his reputation as a writer, however, he was elected to help prepare a declaration of independence. The other members chosen for that task, including Benjamin Franklin and John Adams, then appointed Jefferson to write a draft. When he protested that the better-known John Adams should do it, Adams told him, "You write ten times better than I do."

During the next two and a half weeks Jefferson, drawing heavily on his wide

In designing Monticello, Jefferson borrowed heavily from classical European buildings that he had studied. The house is fitted with his devices, including a calendar clock that still works today.

reading of political thinkers, produced the draft which, with a few changes, became the Great Declaration (see page 133). As he later explained, his aim was not to say anything new but to write down those ideas most Americans were already agreed upon. He would "place before mankind the common sense of the subject, in terms so plain and firm as to command their assent. . . ." There is no question that he succeeded.

Soon after independence was declared, Jefferson returned to Virginia. He wished to be closer to his family and also to have a part in shaping the laws of the new state. He was elected to the legislature and served for three years.

Jefferson helped bring about important changes in Virginia's laws. He believed ownership of land should be widespread. His ideal was a republic of independent small farmers (see page 254). Two laws carried over from centuries of English practice worked against this. One allowed a landowner to declare that the lands never be divided, not even after that person's death. The other law was called *primogeniture*, which came from the Latin meaning "first-born." Under this law, if a landholder died without leaving a will, all the person's property went to the eldest son. If an owner had declared that these lands never be divided, the son could not give any of them to his brothers and sisters, even if he wished to. Such laws encouraged the building of huge estates. Jefferson believed this would hurt the new country, and his view won enough support to end both laws in Virginia.

Jefferson, who believed in a God, believed religion was a personal matter and wrote the law for religious freedom in Virginia. What a person believed was no one else's business. "It does me no injury," he wrote, "for my neighbor to say there are twenty gods, or no God. It neither picks my pocket nor breaks my leg." The law was passed six years after he left the legislature.

THOMAS JEFFERSON **197**

This victory flag celebrates the 1800 election of Jefferson to the Presidency. He brought a less formal style to the office. While other Presidents had bowed, he was the first to shake hands.

Jefferson worked for other changes in Virginia. He led a successful effort to make the criminal laws more simple, and to reduce the number of crimes that could be punished by death. But Jefferson was unable to win approval for two other important ideas. One was his plan for free education. Under this plan, all children would have received several years of schooling and the most able pupils would continue on at state expense. Another idea was to rid the young country of slavery, which Jefferson, although he was a slave owner himself, viewed as evil. His plan would have ended slavery gradually by providing that children of slaves be born free (see pages 422—423, 426).

Jefferson was elected governor of Virginia in 1779 and served two one-year terms; however, he did not find this a happy life and returned to Monticello to be with his family and his books, and to look after his farms. He had given up the law some years earlier, and now he depended on his farms for a livelihood. The same was true of many other leading figures in our early history. Thus, among Jefferson's letters today can be found hundreds to and from such men as George Washington, James Madison, and John Adams. They exchanged thoughts about great issues of the day— and about how to grow better crops!

Jefferson was especially interested in scientific farming. He was among the first in North America to rotate crops. He also practiced contour plowing to check erosion. He was continually experimenting to discover plants and trees from other parts of the world that would grow well in Virginia. He imported olive, apricot, and orange trees for his orchard, and wine grapes for his vineyard. He also later invented an improved wooden plow.

Jefferson applied the same scientific approach to other things. All his life he recorded his observations of the weather, the stars, and the world of nature around him. During these years of private life at Monticello he wrote a book about his state's geography, animal and plant life, government, and economy. The book is called *Notes on the State of Virginia*, and today it remains a good source of information about Virginia.

Thomas Jefferson would probably have been happy to remain in private life at Monticello for the rest of his days. But a sad event changed that. Tragedy had been no stranger to Thomas and Martha Jefferson in their ten years of marriage. Only three of their six children had survived. Now in 1782 Martha herself died. For months afterward Thomas Jefferson was plunged into a deep grief. Finally, he buried his grief by entering public service once more. He served one term in Congress. In 1785 he agreed to serve as United States Minister to France.

Jefferson followed Benjamin Franklin in this job. Franklin had been very popular and had taken France by storm. When a French official asked Jefferson, "*You* replace Benjamin Franklin?" Jefferson gave a modest reply. "No one can replace him, sir," he said. "I am only his successor." For the next five years Jefferson was a successful minister. He also traveled through Europe, making notes on everything he saw, and sending still more trees and seeds back to America.

When in 1790 Jefferson returned to the United States for a visit, President Washington asked him to serve as Secretary of State. Jefferson stayed in this job until the end of 1793. In 1796 he was elected Vice President and in 1800, President. You will read about this part of Jefferson's career in Chapters 10 and 11.

In 1809 Jefferson left the presidency. For seventeen more years he lived at his beloved Monticello. He continued his agricultural experiments. He kept up an active correspondence, receiving and replying to about 1,300 letters a year. He also entertained a great many visitors, at great expense.

Jefferson soon ran into financial problems. To pay his debts, he offered to sell to the government his personal library of 10,000 books on almost every subject. This was the start of the Library of Congress, the greatest library in the United States today. Still later, when Jefferson's debts mounted again, he prepared to sell some of his land. News of his troubles brought gifts from citizens all over the land, and soon most of the bills were paid.

Jefferson's final great project was the creation of a state university, which he persuaded the state legislature to found in 1819. He himself designed the campus and its buildings. Believing modern public education would help build a secure country, Jefferson sought the best scholars and teachers for the university he called "his child."

Jefferson's last letter was to several men who were organizing a celebration for the 50th anniversary of the Declaration of Independence. In this letter, Jefferson stated what he believed was the main message of the declaration for the world. It summed up the democratic faith of a lifetime: ". . . the mass of mankind [have] not been born with saddles on their backs, nor a favored few booted and spurred, ready to ride them. . . ." On the date of the celebration, July 4, 1826, Thomas Jefferson died (see page 288).

CHECKUP

1. What important changes did Jefferson bring about in Virginia laws? Describe his views on freedom of religion.
2. What did Jefferson aim to do in the Declaration of Independence and how did he come to be the one to write it?
3. List Jefferson's personal interests and projects, and explain how they contributed to the public good.

★ PHILLIS WHEATLEY ★

African-American Poet

The publication of a book of poems in the England of 1773 was hardly an unusual event. But there was something about this volume. On the opening page was a message which read in part:

> We . . . do assure the world that the poems specified in the following pages were . . . written by Phillis, a young negro girl who was, but a few years since, brought . . . from Africa, and has ever since been . . . serving as a slave in a family in this town.

The message was signed by eighteen well-known citizens of Boston in the colony of Massachusetts, including the governor, lieutenant governor, and seven ministers. It was written because the publisher feared that readers might otherwise not believe that Phillis Wheatley, a mere slave, could have written those poems!

Life in American began for Phillis as it did for hundreds of thousands of other black Americans—at the auction block. She was only seven years old when she was taken from her family and village in Africa and packed, with seventy or eighty other captives, into the hold of a slave ship. The ship's captain delivered his human cargo to Boston in 1761. There Phillis was bought by a wealthy merchant tailor named John Wheatley. The Wheatleys had several household slaves, but Mrs. Wheatley, then in her fifties, wanted a youth who could be trained as a personal servant for her later years. The family gave their young slave the name Phillis.

The task of teaching Phillis to speak English and to carry out the household duties fell to the Wheatleys' seventeen-year-old daughter, Mary. Phillis learned not only to speak but to read and write English very quickly. Within sixteen months she had read the entire Bible.

By then the Wheatleys realized that their young slave was a most unusual person. Fortunately, the Wheatleys were also unusual. Rather than keep their slave from learning, as most masters did, they encouraged Phillis. Mary instructed her in history, geography, and astronomy. Soon Phillis was reading in those subjects on her own. At age twelve she took up the study of Latin, and within a few years had translated a Latin book into English. Before long, Phillis was a slave in name only.

Phillis Wheatley began to write poetry at thirteen. She was, and always remained, a deeply religious person. Many of her poems had spiritual and moral themes. In 1770 she wrote a poem to mark the death of George Whitefield, the English minister whose sermons in America had helped spark the Great Awakening (see page 41). This poem brought attention to Phillis, who was then only sixteen. It appears to have been the first poem by a black person to have been published in North America.

The Wheatleys were proud of Phillis's accomplishments. She was already one of the better-educated young women in Boston. Visitors to the Wheatley home were eager to meet the young black poet.

A number of the Wheatleys' friends also invited Phillis to their homes. She quickly gained a reputation for good conversation and wit. Before long, this teenage girl had met with some of Boston's leading figures. She also became a member of the Old South Church in Boston, at a time when slaves were not admitted to membership.

Word of this Boston slave who wrote poetry spread to other American colonies too. Benjamin Rush, a Patriot and a prominent doctor in Philadelphia, spoke of Phillis Wheatley's "genius and accomplishments." He noted that "several of her poems have been printed and read with pleasure by the public."

In 1773, Phillis became ill. The family doctor advised that she needed "sea air." Since Nathaniel Wheatley, Mary's twin brother, was soon to go to England, it was decided that Phillis would go also.

In England, Phillis was received by a number of leading members of English society. One of them, the Countess of Huntingdon, arranged for the publication of a book of Wheatley's poems, entitled *Poems on Various Subjects, Religious and Moral.* This book, mentioned earlier, was the first ever published that was written by a black person, slave or free, from North America.

Phillis Wheatley was not yet twenty at this time. It was probably the happiest period of her life. But it did not last long. She had been in England only five weeks when word came that Mrs. Wheatley was seriously ill. Phillis quickly returned to America to be with the woman who had been more her mother than a mistress. The next year, Mrs. Wheatley died. Four years later, John Wheatley died also, and

Phillis Wheatley's portrait appears opposite the title page in her book of poems, published in 1773.

Publiſhed according to Act of Parliament, Sept. 1.1773 by Arch.ᵈ Bell.
Bookſeller Nᵒ 8 near the Saracens Head Aldgate.

POEMS

ON

VARIOUS SUBJECTS,

RELIGIOUS AND MORAL.

BY

PHILLIS WHEATLEY,

NEGRO SERVANT to Mr. JOHN WHEATLEY,
of BOSTON, in NEW ENGLAND.

LONDON:
Printed for A. BELL, Bookſeller, Aldgate; and ſold by
Meſſrs. COX and BERRY, King-Street, BOSTON.
M DCC LXXIII.

in the same year, Mary also passed away. The family life that Phillis had always known was now no more. Furthermore, as time went on, Phillis Wheatley was no longer the novelty in Boston that she once had been.

Sometime between 1774 and 1778, the Wheatley family had officially declared Phillis to be free. In 1778 she married John Peters, a free black from Boston. It was an unhappy marriage. John could not find or make steady work. He left his wife, returned, and left again. In the meantime, Phillis had three children, two of whom died.

Wheatley was writing few poems now. She had tried without success to publish a second book of poems, which she had written earlier. To support herself and her remaining child, Phillis took a job in a cheap boarding house. Never in good health, she became ill in late 1784. At the age of thirty-one, Phillis Wheatley died. Her last child died with her that same day. In 1784, Phillis was buried in Boston in an unmarked grave.

Although Phillis Wheatley was, at least in name, a slave for much of her life, she wrote little about slavery. Only one poem deals with the cruelty of the slave trade. Here she expresses the hope that parents in Africa should never again feel the pain hers must have felt when she was taken away from them.

I, young in life, by seeming cruel fate
Was snatch'd from Afric's fancy'd happy seat:
What pangs excruciating must molest,
What sorrows labour in my parent's breast?
Steel'd was that soul and by no misery mov'd
That from a father seiz'd his babe belov'd:

Such, such my case. And can I then but pray
Others may never feel tyrannic sway?

Most often, however, Phillis Wheatley's poems express her joy in having been converted to Christianity and in being in America. She also wrote about many popular events and figures. A tribute to George Washington as commander in chief of the American armies brought about a meeting with the general.

Phillis Wheatley was, of course, hardly a typical slave. Because of her unusual talent, because she was a curiosity, and because the Wheatleys were unusual owners, Phillis Wheatley could do things that other slaves could not do. From a study of her life, therefore, one can learn little if anything about what it was like to be black, whether slave or free, in a northern American colony.

Phillis Wheatley's only book of poetry and many of her other poems have been published in various forms ever since *Poems on Various Subjects, Religious and Moral* first appeared. But Wheatley is not a major poet. Why then is she remembered? The answer is that she was the first in a long line of black poets and writers who have enriched American literature. Later black authors would choose to write about the black experience in America and the views of their people.

CHECKUP

1. What was unique about the publication of Wheatley's book of poetry in 1773?
2. How was her life unusual for a black person in America during this period?
3. Why is Phillis Wheatley an important poet? Describe some subjects of her poetry.

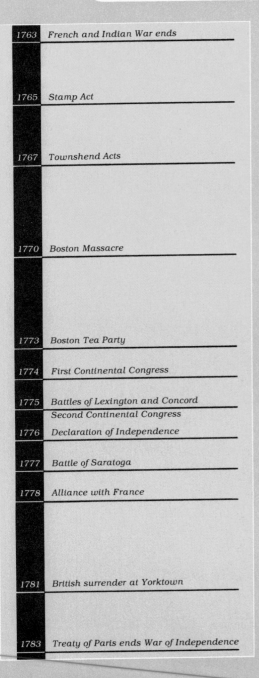

1763	French and Indian War ends
1765	Stamp Act
1767	Townshend Acts
1770	Boston Massacre
1773	Boston Tea Party
1774	First Continental Congress
1775	Battles of Lexington and Concord
1776	Second Continental Congress
1776	Declaration of Independence
1777	Battle of Saratoga
1778	Alliance with France
1781	British surrender at Yorktown
1783	Treaty of Paris ends War of Independence

The 1760s saw rising tension between Britain and its American colonies. Britain put new taxes on the colonies. Most Americans regarded those taxes and other British measures as threats to their well-being and their liberty. The Boston Massacre in 1770 and the Boston Tea Party in 1773 inflamed the feelings of both British and Americans.

War began in 1775 when British soldiers clashed with American militiamen at Lexington and Concord. Soon afterwards George Washington of Virginia was made the leader of the American troops. Independence soon became the goal of the Patriots. On July 4, 1776, the Declaration of Independence—written by Thomas Jefferson—was adopted.

At first, Americans fought a defensive war. They won few victories but avoided a crushing defeat. A victory at Trenton in December 1776 and another at Princeton a week later boosted Patriot morale. The turning point of the war was the American victory at Saratoga in 1777. After that battle, France openly supported the American cause. In the later years of the war, fighting shifted to the South. The victory of the Americans and their French allies at Yorktown assured American independence.

The Revolution is the single most important event in United States history. It brought about the end of monarchy in America, but it did not cause great social or economic change. In later years, Americans have usually judged revolutions in other countries by how similar their goals were to the goals of the American Revolution.

203

Skills Development: Reading a Map

The Treaty of Paris, signed in 1783, recognized the independence of the United States and established its new boundaries. Study the map and then answer the following questions.

1. What were the two largest cities in 1783? Which cities had a population between 10,000 and 30,000?

2. Which city is located near the intersection of 40°N 75°W?

3. In 1783, which was the westernmost state? the southernmost state?

4. In 1783, which European nations owned land bordering on the United States?

5. The Appalachian Mountains extend through how many of the thirteen original American colonies?

6. Using the scale of miles, measure the distance from Baltimore to Charleston; Newport to Richmond.

7. What geographical feature formed the westernmost boundary of the United States in 1783?

8. Name the states eventually carved out of The Old Northwest and The Old Southwest. If you need help, refer to the map on pages 550–551.

The United States in 1783

Population

- ● Cities over 30,000
- ● Cities 10,000 to 30,000
- · Cities under 10,000

Unit 3

Americans and Limited Government

THE MAKING OF A NATION

CREATING A STRONG UNION

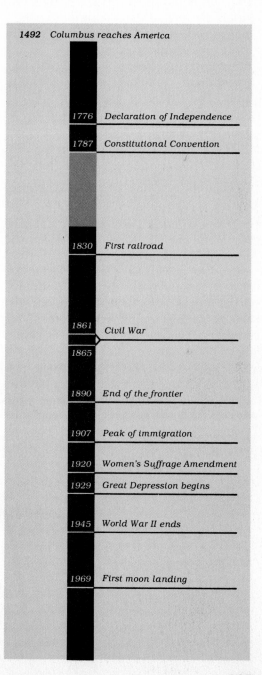

1492 Columbus reaches America

1776 Declaration of Independence

1787 Constitutional Convention

1830 First railroad

1861 Civil War

1865

1890 End of the frontier

1907 Peak of immigration

1920 Women's Suffrage Amendment

1929 Great Depression begins

1945 World War II ends

1969 First moon landing

ON APRIL 21, 1967, a group of military men overthrew the democratic government of Greece. The new government leaders quickly limited the freedom of the Greek people. One of their first steps was to abolish elections. They then moved to silence opposition. They censored newspapers, drove unfriendly editors from the country, and jailed political opponents. They even regulated personal conduct, forbade certain clothing, and dictated hair styles.

Very likely you reacted strongly to what you just read. Have you thought about why? Really, it is a matter of values or beliefs. A government had taken unlimited power over its citizens. In doing so, it had taken from them their liberty. And if you are like most Americans, that runs counter to your idea of what a government has a right to do.

No one has ever put the case against government power more strongly than Thomas Paine, the author of *Common Sense*. "Government," wrote Paine, "even in its best state, is but a necessary evil; in its worst, an intolerable one." Thomas Jefferson, author of the Declaration of Independence and third President of the United States, expressed his distrust of government only a little less strongly. "That government governs best," said Jefferson, "which governs least."

Government power—how much? In the two hundred years since Paine wrote, the world has changed in many ways. Most of us understand that government performs many important tasks in a modern society. Even those who believe that government has too much power and does too many things today would agree that there are certain things government must do.

But few Americans would want the government to have power without limit. The title of a book written by a college president in America's bicentennial year probably expresses the concerns of many: *An Overgoverned Society.* Plainly there is a lingering distrust of government power.

In few if any other countries do people debate so seriously and so often the question whether their government has too much power. Newspaper accounts often tell of some person or group that claims the government has exceeded its power. Monday, the day the Supreme Court hands down its decisions, usually brings rulings on whether some government agency or official—or even Congress itself—has the power to do certain things.

Few things stir up Americans more than the belief that government officials have abused their power. When the Watergate scandal of 1973–1974 revealed that President Richard Nixon had engaged in doubtful and probably illegal activity, public opinion turned against him. Faced with impeachment by Congress, Nixon resigned on August 9, 1974, less than two years after he had been reelected by a huge majority.

A United States senator phrased the concern of Americans this way in a speech at one of the national party conventions in 1976:

The issue this year, quite simply, is this: How much government is too much government? How many laws are too many laws? How much taxation is too much taxation? How much coercion [force] is too much coercion?

One of the landmarks of self-government by European colonists in America was the agreement by 41 adult males on the Pilgrim ship *Mayflower* to work for "just and equal" laws. The signing of the Mayflower Compact, as shown here, is as an artist imagined it many years later.

A deeply rooted belief. Our belief that limits should be placed on the power to govern carries over into almost every organization we form, from school groups to fan clubs. Nearly all of them quickly draw up rules which limit the powers of the officers.

The belief in limited government is rooted deeply in the American past. When colonists spoke of the "rights of Englishmen," they meant personal rights that no government could take away. At the bottom of the American Revolution was the question of government power. And the idea of limited government is at the very heart of the Declaration of Independence. You have already read that when Americans created their new state governments, they carefully set down which powers the governments had—and which they did not have. They did the same in writing the Articles of Confederation, the constitution of the new national government.

The Articles of Confederation

Those who wrote the Articles had to deal with another question. It was agreed that certain powers were to be denied to all governments, state as well as national. But of the powers that *would* be granted, which should be given to the national government, and which should be kept by the states?

A system in which powers are divided between a central government and local governments is called a *federal system*. The chief problem in federalism is deciding which powers should be given to each level of government. That may look easy, but it is really quite difficult. England and the North American colonies wrestled for a dozen years over the question of which powers should belong to the government in London, and which should be left to the colonial governments. When an answer could not be found, Britain lost much of its American empire.

Limiting the central government. In striking a balance in the Articles of Confederation, its writers came down on the side of local government. By no means, however, was the central government left without power. Congress could maintain an army and navy and thus could make war and peace. It could make treaties and alliances with other countries. It could regulate coinage, borrow money, establish a post office, and manage affairs with the Indians.

However, it is the powers *denied* to Congress that show the effect of America's unhappy experience with Britain's strong central government. Those who wrote the Articles, remembering how Britain had used the power to regulate trade with America, denied that power to their own central government. Recalling their quarrels over the Parliament's claim to levy taxes, they denied that right to the new Congress. Believing that the Parliament's control of the money supply had made for hard times, they gave the states the right to issue their own money. And with their grievances against George III fresh in mind, they decided the new government of the United States should have no chief executive, or president.

The Articles gave each state, no matter how large or small, one vote in Congress. For any important decision, nine states had to agree. The consent of all thirteen

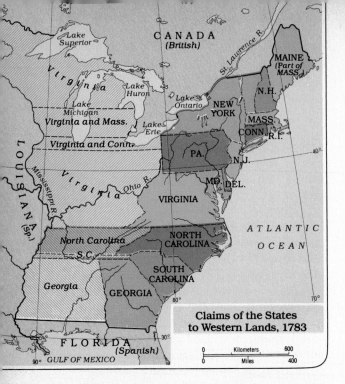

Claims of the States to Western Lands, 1783

In 1783, several of the original states still claimed land—as shown on the map above—between the Appalachian Mountains and the Mississippi River. But by 1787—as shown below—part of this region, known as the Northwest Territory, had been ceded to the federal government. By 1802, other claims were ceded.

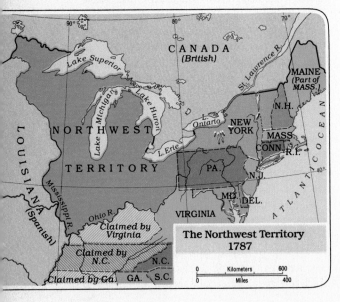

The Northwest Territory 1787

was needed to *amend,* or change, the Articles. Thus no needed power could be given to the central government if even one state objected. That gave meaning to the statement in the Articles that "each state retains its sovereignty [supreme power], freedom, and independence."

The Articles' weaknesses. Two attempts were made to amend the Articles so that Congress could raise money through a 5 percent tax on imports. Each time, however, one state refused to go along, and the amendment failed. Without the power to regulate trade among the states, Congress looked on helplessly as some states taxed goods coming from other states.

These and other limits on the power of the central government were crippling. One of the weaknesses of the Articles was that, without the power to tax, Congress could only *ask* the states to give their share of money to pay the expenses of government. Since the states could not or would not do so, the central government was always without money. To make either the citizens or the states obey its laws, it had to depend on state courts, because the Articles did not set up federal courts. The states, in fact, often paid no attention to the wishes of Congress, and Congress could do nothing about it.

Despite these weaknesses, the government under the Articles of Confederation did win the war and gain a favorable peace. That was no small feat.

The Northwest Territory. The government also dealt wisely with the problem of western lands. Before the Articles went into effect, seven states had made claims—based on their colonial charters—to land west of the Allegheny Mountains. Some of these claims overlapped, and most of them were vague. Maryland refused to ratify the Articles until those states agreed to turn over their land claims to the new national government.

Congress passed two important laws dealing with the western region known as the Northwest Territory—that is, the lands west of Pennsylvania and Virginia and north of the Ohio River. The Land Ordinance of 1785 set up the policy for the sale of this land. It was divided into townships 6 miles (9.6 km) square—that is, each township was 36 square miles (93.6 square km). Each township was further divided into "sections" of 640 acres (256 ha), or 1 square mile (2.6 square km). The land was to be sold at auction in 640-acre units for a minimum of one dollar an acre. Congress required that one section of each township be set aside to maintain public schools. The law was more favorable to land companies than to small farmers, who found it hard to scrape up $640 at one time. But it did open the way for an orderly settlement of the region. The sale of land also provided much-needed revenue for the new government.

The Northwest Ordinance. The second and more important land law was the Northwest Ordinance of 1787. This law set up the system for governing the Northwest Territory. Under the law, Congress would appoint the governor and other officials until such time as there were 5,000 adult males in the territory. At that point, the settlers could choose their own legislature and send a

Land Survey in the Northwest Territory

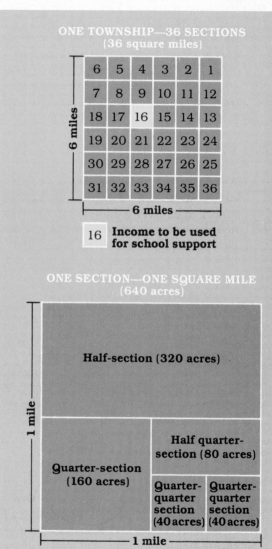

ONE TOWNSHIP—36 SECTIONS
(36 square miles)

6	5	4	3	2	1
7	8	9	10	11	12
18	17	16	15	14	13
19	20	21	22	23	24
30	29	28	27	26	25
31	32	33	34	35	36

6 miles (vertical) — 6 miles (horizontal)

16 — Income to be used for school support

ONE SECTION—ONE SQUARE MILE
(640 acres)

Half-section (320 acres)

Quarter-section (160 acres)

Half quarter-section (80 acres)

Quarter-quarter section (40 acres)

Quarter-quarter section (40 acres)

1 mile (vertical) — 1 mile (horizontal)

The rectangular system of survey devised for the Northwest Territory is used in most states west of the Appalachians. The system makes it possible to identify precisely any given piece of land. Roads sometimes follow section lines. The surveyed townships, six miles square, do not always conform with political townships.

211

non-voting delegate to Congress. When the number of people in the territory reached 60,000, the people could draw up a constitution and ask Congress to admit their region to the Union as a state, on equal terms with all other states. Not less than three nor more than five states were to be created from this territory. Equally important, the law prohibited slavery in the Northwest Territory.

A weak government? The Confederation government satisfied a great many Americans. Ever suspicious of strong, distant, central government, a majority were satisfied to leave the main powers to the state governments, which were closer to home.

Yet, a growing number of Americans were beginning to wonder if the central government was not ineffective. In 1784, many blamed the government's weakness for the beginning of a *depression*—a time when business is poor and many people cannot find jobs. That was not entirely fair, since the government had nothing to do with crop failures that occurred in several parts of the country. On the other hand, lack of any power to regulate foreign trade probably did contribute to the economic troubles. While Britain sold all it wished in American markets, American merchants were blocked from freely selling in the British empire. This was because the American minister to England, unable to speak for all the states, could not win from Britain a favorable trade treaty. One Englishman mockingly asked why the United States did not send 13 ministers to represent them in London instead of just one.

The weakness of the United States did not go unnoticed elsewhere. Most European governments did not expect the United States to last. Several cast hungry eyes on its territory. Spain, which already held Florida and the land west of the Mississippi, hoped to slice off the region between the Appalachians and the Mississippi, south of the Ohio River. And England was not about to pull out of its profitable trading and military posts in the Northwest Territory, no matter what the Treaty of Paris said.

Many Americans found this situation humiliating. An increasing number were thinking of themselves less as Virginians or Pennsylvanians and more as Americans. They wanted a government that would express this growing national feeling. They wanted a government strong enough to command the respect of its own citizens as well as that of other nations.

Shays's Rebellion. An event in western Massachusetts in the fall of 1786 added to the growing belief that the central government could not govern. Falling crop prices that year hit small farmers there very hard. Many of the farmers had borrowed money to buy their land. After paying high taxes on their land, many of them did not have enough left to make mortgage payments. When those who held the mortgages took the farmers to court, judges ordered that the farmers' land be sold to pay off their debts. Some farmers were sent to debtor's prison. The Massachusetts legislature, meanwhile, turned a deaf ear to the farmers' requests for tax relief and for the printing of paper money that would help raise the price of their crops.

Several thousand desperate farmers, led by a Revolutionary War veteran named Daniel Shays, took matters into their own hands. In several small towns they kept the courts from opening, so that judges could not order the sale of any more of their lands. The troubles kept on for several months. In December 1786, Shays and his followers tried to seize arms from a government arsenal in Springfield. The state militia, however, beat them back. That broke the back of the uprising. Some farmers surrendered, and others, including Shays, fled the state. Yet many Americans took little comfort that the rebellion had been put down. They were troubled that the central government, with no army of its own, had had to ask the state militia to put down a small band of armed farmers.

Rising fears. The concerns of two important Americans may be seen in the two letters printed below. The first is from Abigail Adams to Thomas Jefferson. On hearing news of the events in Massachusetts, Jefferson had written his friends the Adamses for more information about the uprising. Abigail Adams replied:

> Ignorant, restless desperadoes, without conscience or principles, had led a deluded multitude to follow their standard. . . . Some of them were crying out for paper currency, some for an equal distribution of property. Some were for [wiping out] all debts. . . . you will see . . . the necessity of . . . vigorous measures to [put down this rebellion]. . . . these [rebels] are for undercutting the foundations of the government and destroying the whole fabric at once. . . .

The second letter is from George Washington to John Jay, a New York political leader.

> I do not believe that we can exist long as a nation without lodging, somewhere, a power which pervades the whole union. . . .To be fearful of giving Congress . . . ample authority for national purposes appears to me . . . madness. What then is to be done? Things cannot go on in the same train forever. It is much to be feared, as you observe, that the better kind of people, being disgusted in these circumstances, will have their minds prepared for any revolution whatever. . . .

The widespread discontent that brought on Shays's Rebellion in 1786 sometimes pitted neighbor against neighbor in violent disagreement over taxes, courts, and property rights.

During the eighteenth century, Wall Street in New York City became a center of commerce. The merchants who traded there wanted a government strong enough to guarantee their property rights.

. . . I am told that even respectable characters speak of a monarchical form of government without horror. From thinking proceeds speaking, thence to acting is often but a single step. . . .

Phrases like "ignorant, restless desperadoes" and "the better kind of people" tell us a good deal about the writers' attitudes and fears. George Washington was one of the largest landowners in America and a member of Virginia's upper class. The Adamses, while not rich, were among the more important families in Massachusetts because of John Adams's work as a lawyer and political leader. As leaders in the Revolution, Washington and the Adamses shared the fear of a too-strong govern-ment. But as members of an upper class, they also wanted a government strong enough to keep order and to protect their property.

That is why such people shuddered on hearing of the uprising against courts and property rights in Massachusetts. What happened in that state could happen elsewhere. Indeed, under pressure from farmers, more than half the state legislatures had already passed laws to help debtors at the expense of their creditors. The rights of property, and the right of "the better kind of people" to govern, was being challenged. "We are fast moving toward anarchy [absence of government] and confusion," wrote an alarmed Washington.

214

1. What were the weaknesses of the Articles of Confederation?
2. How did Congress deal with the sale of land in, and the government of, the Northwest Territory?
3. In what way did Shays's Rebellion contribute to rising fears over the central government?

The Constitutional Convention

In September 1786, even as Shays's Rebellion was under way, delegates from five states met at Annapolis, Maryland, to discuss problems of commerce under the Articles of Confederation. Concluding that this problem was only one of many, the delegates recommended that Congress call a general convention to revise and strengthen the Articles. Congress agreed. On May 25, 1787, what became known as the Constitutional Convention began its meetings in Philadelphia, Pennsylvania. Four months later, the new Constitution of the United States of America had been drafted, discussed, and approved by the delegates.

The Constitutional Convention was the greatest political gathering ever held in America. Chosen by their state legislatures, the fifty-five delegates were among the ablest and most experienced men in America. Many had served their country since the Revolution. George Washington, Alexander Hamilton of New York, and Charles Cotesworth Pinckney of South Carolina had been army officers. Former members of the Continental Congress included Benjamin Franklin, James Wilson, and Robert Morris of Pennsylvania, George Wythe and George Mason of Virginia, Elbridge Gerry of Massachusetts, William Livingston of New Jersey, and Roger Sherman of Connecticut.

One striking fact about these delegates was their youth. Five delegates were in their mid-twenties, and five more were in their early or mid-thirties. Franklin was the grand old man of the convention at eighty-one, but the average age was forty-two.

Also striking was their prominence and wealth. Included among them were planters, merchants, and lawyers. Their views were naturally colored by the fact that they were well-to-do.

This remarkable group was well aware of the high stakes in what its members were doing. Alexander Hamilton noted that what they did would "decide forever the fate of republican government." That is, if they could not solve the problem of federalism and failed to create a government that would work, it was unlikely that other peoples would soon experiment with republican government.

A search for balances. The story of the Philadelphia convention is the story of a search for two new balances. One was the balance between the central government and local governments. The other was the balance between liberty and order. The problem was to create a government strong enough to govern and maintain order, yet not so strong as to threaten the liberty of its citizens. Very early, the convention decided that in order to achieve these balances it would be necessary to write an entirely new constitution rather than to amend the Articles.

Nearly all the delegates agreed that the balances had to shift in the direction of centralism and order. The government had to have the power to tax so that it would no longer need to beg the states for money. It must regulate trade among the states to prevent quarrels among them. It had to control trade with other countries so that it could negotiate trade treaties for all states. It needed to be able to raise its own army, without having to depend on the states to give men and money for defense. And it must be able to make citizens and the states obey its laws by having its own courts.

A group of Indian visitors stand before Independence Hall in Philadelphia. In this building in the summer of 1787, the nation's founders drafted the Constitution of the United States.

So clear was the need to give these powers to the central government that they were added almost without debate. Most important was the agreement that the new Constitution, and all the treaties and laws made under it, was to be the supreme law of the land. It was to be superior to state laws. This is stated in what is known as the "supremacy clause" of the Constitution (see pages 236–237).

Protecting liberty. Even as the delegates tipped the balance toward centralism and order, they built into the Constitution three ways to protect citizens from a too-powerful government. One was the idea of federalism itself. By dividing up the power of government between local and central levels, no one level was to have too much power. A second was by using the written Constitution to spell out certain things the central government could *not* do. It could not, for example, put a person in jail without a hearing. It could not take anyone's property without paying a fair price for it. It could not tax exported goods.

A third way of protecting liberty was the device of *separation of powers.* The Constitution created three independent branches of government—the *executive, legislative,* and *judicial*—and divided the powers of the central government among them. Congress, the legislative branch, was to make the laws. The President, as head of the executive branch, was to carry them out and enforce them. And the federal courts, the judicial branch, were to judge and interpret the laws.

To protect against the exercise of unlimited power by any one branch, the

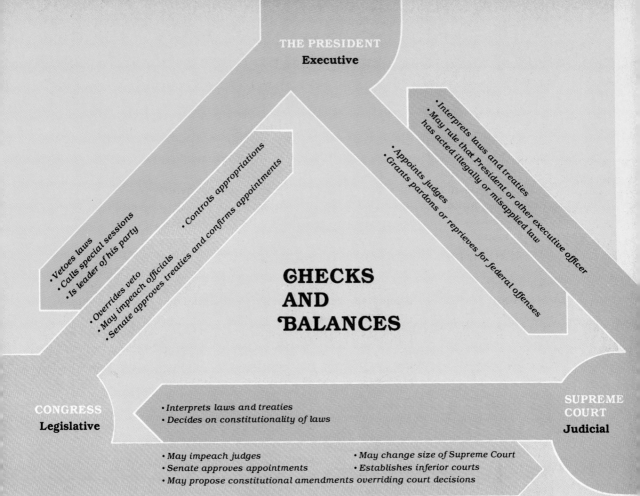

THE PRESIDENT
Executive

- Interprets laws and treaties
- May rule that President or other executive officer has acted illegally or misapplied law
- Appoints judges
- Grants pardons or reprieves for federal offenses

- Vetoes laws
- Calls special sessions
- Is leader of his party

- Overrides veto
- May impeach officials
- Senate approves treaties and confirms appointments

- Controls appropriations

CHECKS
AND
BALANCES

CONGRESS
Legislative

- Interprets laws and treaties
- Decides on constitutionality of laws

SUPREME
COURT
Judicial

- May impeach judges
- Senate approves appointments
- May propose constitutional amendments overriding court decisions

- May change size of Supreme Court
- Establishes inferior courts

Constitution provides ways by which each branch may check and balance the others. The chart above shows the separation of powers. Can you see how the President may be checked? How may the Congress be checked? What means are there for checking and balancing the courts? Do you think there may be disadvantages as well as advantages in a system of checks and balances such as this?

None of these ideas—federalism, a written constitution, and the separation of powers—was new. In combining the three as they did, however, the delegates to the convention made their unique contribution. In doing so, they invented a new government.

The Great Compromise. Not all was harmony at the convention. On several subjects there was bitter disagreement. Delegates threatened at times to walk out of the convention, and it appeared the whole effort might fail. But in the end, compromises saved the day.

One major disagreement had to do with representation in Congress. Two ideas were put forth. The Virginia, or large state, plan would base representation in Congress on population. A state with twice as many people as another,

217

would have twice as many seats. On the other hand, the New Jersey, or small state, plan said that each state would have an equal voice in Congress, just as under the Articles. Thus, Rhode Island, with its population of less than 70,000, would have as many representatives as the largest state, Virginia, with more than 10 times as many people.

This issue nearly wrecked the convention. But finally Roger Sherman of Connecticut came forward with a plan that was adopted. Under the so-called Great Compromise, there would be two houses of Congress. In the upper, or Senate, each state would have equal representa-

Roger Sherman of Connecticut was one of two men who signed all three of these great documents: the Declaration of Independence, the Articles of Confederation, and the Constitution. The other was Robert Morris of Pennsylvania.

tion. In the lower, or House of Representatives, representation would be based upon population. Such a lawmaking body made up of two houses is known as a *bicameral* legislature.

The slavery problem. Two disagreements involved slavery. One was whether to count slaves as part of the population when determining the number of members each state should have in the House of Representatives. Clearly, to do so would give additional seats to Southern states. Northern delegates argued that since slaves had no political rights, they should not be counted. It was finally proposed that for purposes of assigning seats in the House of Representatives, every five slaves would count as three persons. To count a slave as three fifths of a person plainly did not make sense. Yet to reach agreement on a new constitution, delegates accepted this three-fifths compromise.

The second disagreement on slavery was whether or not the importing of slaves into America should continue. The compromise in this case was to prohibit Congress from passing a law on that subject for twenty years. After that, Congress would be free to stop the trade if it chose.

Executive power. Another compromise had to do with the Presidency. Some delegates felt that one executive would be little different from a king—especially if the term of office was a long one. They wanted an executive branch made up of several people. Some favored leaving the choice of the executive to Congress on the grounds that the people were not qualified to make such a choice. Other delegates said that for Congress to choose the executive would destroy the idea of the separation of powers.

In the compromise it was agreed there would be one executive known as the President. The President would be chosen for a four-year term by an indirect method—an electoral college—rather than directly by the people. Finally, it was agreed that the Constitution could be amended by a vote of two-thirds of each house of Congress and three-fourths of all the states.

Its work completed, the convention sent the Constitution to the Congress. Congress forwarded the document to a specially elected convention in each state. The delegates to these conventions were asked to *ratify*, or approve, the Constitution. It would go into effect after nine states ratified it.

CHECKUP

1. What generalizations can you make about the delegates to the Constitutional Convention?
2. In what three ways did the delegates act to protect citizens from a too-powerful government?
3. What were some of the compromises made in drawing up the Constitution?

The Struggle Over Ratification

Those who favored the Constitution were called *Federalists*. They knew that ratification would not be easy, for most Americans still felt more loyal to their states than to the central government. Many Americans viewed the proposed new government as merely the old British tyranny in a new form.

A heated exchange. Debates in the state ratifying conventions often became heated. This exchange in the Massachusetts convention was typical of those that took place everywhere. Amos Singletary voiced the fears of the *Anti-Federalists*, as those who opposed the Constitution were called.

> We [fought against] Great Britain—some said for a three-penny duty on tea; but it was not that. It was because they claimed a right to tax us and bind us in all cases whatever. And does not this Constitution do the same? Does it not take away all we have—all our property? Does it not lay *all* taxes? . . .
>
> These lawyers, and men of learning, and moneyed men, that talk so finely and gloss over matters so smoothly, to make us poor illiterate people swallow down the pill, expect to get into Congress themselves. They expect to be the managers of this Constitution, and get all the power and all the money into their own hands. And then they will swallow up all us little folk . . . just as the whale swallowed up Jonah. . . .

Jonathan Smith, a Federalist, took a different point of view.

> I have lived in a part of the country where I have known the worth of good government by the [lack] of it. There was a black cloud [Shays's Rebellion] that rose in the east last winter, and spread over the west. . . . It brought on a state of anarchy. . . . People that used to live peaceably, and were before good neighbors . . . took up arms against the government. . . . They would rob you of your property, threaten to burn your houses; oblige you to be on your guard night and day. Alarms spread from town to town; families were broken up; the . . . mother would cry, O my son is among them!

Now . . . when I saw this Constitution, I found that it was a cure for these disorders. It was just such a thing as we wanted. . . . I got a copy of it and read it over and over. I had been a member of the convention to form our state constitution, and had learned something of the checks and balances of power; and I found them all here. . . .

I don't think the worse of the Constitution because lawyers, and men of learning, and moneyed men are fond of it. I don't suspect that they want to get into Congress and abuse their power. . . .

These lawyers, these moneyed men, these men of learning, are all embarked in the same cause with us, and we must all sink or swim together. And shall we throw the Constitution overboard because it does not please us [all] alike?

How does Smith's view of American society differ from Singletary's?

For and against ratification. The Anti-Federalists made three points. One was that the convention in Philadelphia had gone beyond its powers in writing an entirely new constitution. A second was that the Constitution did not have a bill of rights setting forth the basic liberties of the people—for example, freedom of speech and religion. The third was that the Constitution made the central government too strong and the state governments too weak. Among the Anti-Federalists were some of the leading Revolutionary figures—among them, Samuel Adams of Massachusetts and Patrick Henry and Richard Henry Lee of Virginia. Anti-Federalist arguments had the greatest appeal to small farmers, western frontier people, and debtors.

Federalists claimed that only a strong central government could prevent unrest at home and win respect for America abroad. Their strongest support came from merchants, businessmen, lawyers, land speculators, and southern planters. Generally speaking, the wealthier and more educated people favored ratification. The Federalists numbered in their ranks such well known men as Washington, Alexander Hamilton, James Madison, and John Jay.

The Federalists carry the day. Although the Anti-Federalists probably outnumbered the Federalists, the Constitution

This cartoon compares the ratification of the Constitution to the building of a dome held up by pillars. It was drawn at the time that eleven states had approved the document and two had not.

Father of the Constitution

James Madison was five feet four inches in height and weighed about one hundred pounds. Yet among those who founded the federal government, he was a giant. He deserves the title "Father of the Constitution" on several counts—as a debater and a recorder of events at the Constitutional Convention and as a leader in winning ratification of the Constitution.

Madison was well grounded for the vital role he played at the Constitutional Convention. Ten years earlier he had helped draft a new constitution for Virginia. Serving in both the Virginia legislature and the Continental Congress, he was regarded in each body as one of its ablest members.

Madison was thirty-six when he arrived in Philadelphia in 1787 as a Virginia delegate to the Constitutional Convention. During the debates he was a vigorous spokesman for a strong central government and for the separation of powers. The Virginia, or large state, plan was mostly his work. A number of its ideas were included in the new United States Constitution.

The debates were kept secret from the public, but Madison took notes at each session. Every evening he wrote out a full account of the day's happenings. His record, made public after his death in 1836, proved to be far more complete than the official record. Madison's account is the best we have of the Constitutional Convention.

Returning home from Philadelphia, Madison went to work to see that the new Constitution was approved by the people. He, Alexander Hamilton, and John Jay wrote *The Federalist,* a brilliant set of essays urging adoption of the Constitution. Many of the essays appeared in New York newspapers. They were then collected and published in book form. Thomas Jefferson called *The Federalist* "the best commentary on the principles of government which has ever been written."

This medallion shows James Madison as President. For his vital role in the creation and ratification of the Constitution, Madison was already assured a lasting place in American history.

was ratified. How was this possible? For one thing, many of the Anti-Federalists simply did not take the trouble to vote for delegates to the state ratifying conventions. Only one-sixth of the adult white males voted in those elections. The Anti-Federalists also failed to organize their supporters. They were widely scattered throughout the country, and never found a single issue around which they could rally.

The Federalists, on the other hand, showed a genius for organization. They held the key political positions in many states, and they made the most of them. Many Federalists were leaders in their local communities. They had a large influence in the ratification debates. In many states they were able to quiet doubts by promising to add a bill of rights to the Constitution.

Delaware ratified the Constitution in December 1787. It was the first state to do so. Within eight months, ten more states did the same, and the new Constitution became the law of the land. North Carolina ratified it in 1789, and Rhode Island followed in 1790.

We know today that the founders of our government were amazingly successful in striking a workable federal balance. They provided a flexible constitution. Today it is the oldest written constitution in the world. In 1788, however, that was all in the untold future. Setting up the new government, breathing life into the words of the Constitution was the task of the moment. It was to that job that the victorious Federalists now turned. In the chapter that follows, you will see how that urgent undertaking was carried out.

CHECKUP

1. What arguments were put forth in favor of ratification of the Constitution?
2. What arguments were put forth in opposition to ratification?
3. Why were the Federalists able to bring about ratification of the Constitution?

Key Facts from Chapter 9

1. A system in which powers are divided between a central government and local governments is called a federal government.
2. The Articles of Confederation, which was the first constitution of the United States, gave the main powers to the state governments and severely limited the powers of the central government.
3. To strengthen the central government, delegates chosen by state legislatures met in Philadelphia in 1787 and drew up a new constitution.
4. Under the Constitution, the balance of power moved in the direction of the central government.
5. Under the Constitution, the powers of the central government were divided among the executive, legislative, and judicial branches.
6. The Constitution became the law of the land in 1788, after nine states had ratified it.

★ REVIEWING THE CHAPTER ★

People, Places, and Events

Articles of Confederation   *P. 209*

Northwest Territory   *P. 210*

Land Ordinance of 1785   *P. 211*

Northwest Ordinance   *P. 211*

Shays's Rebellion   *P. 212*

Constitutional Convention   *P. 215*

Great Compromise   *P. 217*

Virginia Plan   *P. 217*

New Jersey Plan   *P. 218*

Three-fifths compromise   *P. 218*

James Madison   *P. 221*

Review Questions

1. What powers were given to the central government under the Articles of Confederation? What important powers were denied?   *P. 209*

2. How did the weaknesses of the central government under the Articles affect American relations with foreign nations?   *P. 212*

3. Why did the delegates to the Philadelphia convention write an entirely new constitution rather than amend the Articles?   *P. 215*

4. Under the Constitution, what new powers were given to the central government?   *P. 216*

5. In what three ways did the Constitution protect citizens from a too-powerful government?   *P. 216*

6. How did the issue of slavery create disagreement at the convention? What compromises were made?   *P. 218*

7. Compare the viewpoints of the Federalists and the Anti-Federalists on the subject of the ratification of the Constitution.   *P. 220*

Chapter Test

In the first section below is a list of names and terms found in the chapter. In the second section is a list of descriptions. Match each name or term with the appropriate description. Write your answers on a separate piece of paper.

1. Virginia Plan
2. Bicameral legislature
3. Articles of Confederation
4. Anti-Federalists
5. Executive, legislative, judicial
6. New Jersey Plan
7. Federal system
8. Supremacy clause
9. Bill of Rights
10. Northwest Ordinance

a. Those who opposed ratification of the Constitution

b. Representation in Congress based on equal voice for each state

c. A system for governing western lands

d. Powers divided between a central government and local governments

e. Those who favored ratification of the Constitution

f. Protects basic liberties of the people

g. Representation in Congress based on population

h. Lawmaking body made up of two houses

i. Gave power to the state governments and limited the powers of the central government

j. Constitution was to be superior to state laws

k. Three independent branches of the government

223

The Constitution of the United States

We the people of the United States, in order to form a more perfect union, establish justice, insure domestic tranquility, provide for the common defense, promote the general welfare, and secure the blessings of liberty to ourselves and our posterity, do ordain and establish this Constitution for the United States of America.

ARTICLE I

SECTION 1.

All legislative powers herein granted shall be vested in a Congress of the United States, which shall consist of a Senate and House of Representatives.

SECTION 2.

The House of Representatives shall be composed of members chosen every second year by the people of the several States, and the electors in each State shall have the qualifications requisite for electors of the most numerous branch of the State legislature.

224

No person shall be a representative who shall not have attained to the age of twenty-five years, and been seven years a citizen of the United States, and who shall not, when elected, be an inhabitant of that State in which he shall be chosen.

Representatives and direct taxes shall be apportioned among the several States which may be included within this Union, according to their respective numbers, which shall be determined by adding to the whole number of free persons, including those bound to service for a term of years, and excluding Indians not taxed, three fifths of all other persons.* The actual enumeration shall be made within three years after the first meeting of the Congress of the United States, and within every subsequent term of ten years, in such manner as they shall by law direct. The number of representatives shall not exceed one for every thirty thousand, but each State shall have at least one representative; and until such enumeration shall be made, the State of New Hampshire shall be entitled to choose three, Massachusetts eight, Rhode Island and Providence Plantations one, Connecticut five, New York six, New Jersey four, Pennsylvania eight, Delaware one, Maryland six, Virginia ten, North Carolina five, South Carolina five, and Georgia three.

When vacancies happen in the representation from any State, the executive authority thereof shall issue writs of election to fill such vacancies.

The House of Representatives shall choose their speaker and other officers, and shall have the sole power of impeachment.

SECTION 3.

The Senate of the United States shall be composed of two senators from each State, chosen by the legislature thereof,† for six years; and each senator shall have one vote.

Immediately after they shall be assembled in consequence of the first election, they shall be divided as equally as may be into three classes. The seats of the senators of the first class shall be vacated at the expiration of the second year, of the second class at the expiration of the fourth year, and of the third class at the expiration of the sixth year, so that one third may be chosen every second year; and if vacancies happen by resignation, or otherwise, during the recess of the legislature of any State, the executive thereof may make temporary appointments until the next meeting of the legislature, which shall then fill such vacancies.†

No person shall be a senator who shall not have attained to the age of thirty years, and been nine years a citizen of the United States, and who shall not, when elected, be an inhabitant of that State for which he shall be chosen.

Qualifications. Must a candidate live in the district he wants to represent? What chance of election would he probably have if he did not live there?

Apportionment. "Those bound to service" were indentured. Who were the "three fifths of all others"? Did they pay taxes? Should they have been represented? On what basis? How did Amend. 13 change this?

What is the "enumeration" called today? When was the most recent one taken?

No amendment has changed "one for every thirty thousand," but Congress limits the House to 435. Without that limit, how many members would there be? Each representative represents an average of how many people?

Vacancies. Why may a governor appoint a Senator but not a representative?

Officers; impeachment. Impeach = accuse of wrongdoing. Who may be impeached (Art. II–4)?

THE SENATE

Membership; term. Under Amend. 17, who chooses the senators? Since when?

Expiration of term; vacancies. Only one third of the Senate is replaced or re-elected at each election, but each Congress is "new." What are some benefits or drawbacks of not having a totally new Congress each time? A governor may fill a vacancy until his legislature directs a new election. See Amend. 17.

Qualifications. How do the qualifications for senator and representative differ? Why are they different?

NOTE: Items that have been changed or replaced are underlined.
* Changed by the Fourteenth Amendment
† Changed by the Seventeenth Amendment

The Vice President of the United States shall be president of the Senate, but shall have no vote, unless they be equally divided.

The Senate shall choose their other officers, and also a president pro tempore, in the absence of the Vice President, or when he shall exercise the office of President of the United States.

The Senate shall have the sole power to try all impeachments. When sitting for that purpose, they shall be on oath or affirmation. When the President of the United States is tried, the Chief Justice shall preside: and no person shall be convicted without the concurrence of two thirds of the members present.

Judgment in cases of impeachment shall not extend further than to removal from office, and disqualification to hold any office of honor, trust or profit under the United States: but the party convicted shall nevertheless be liable and subject to indictment, trial, judgment and punishment, according to law.

SECTION 4.

The times, places, and manner of holding elections for senators and representatives shall be prescribed in each State by the legislature thereof; but the Congress may at any time by law make or alter such regulations, except as to the places of choosing senators.

The Congress shall assemble at least once in every year, and such meeting shall be on the first Monday in December,* unless they shall by law appoint a different day.

Officers. As the Vice President may not be there, the president *pro tempore* acts as Senate president. Senators take daily turns presiding. Only the Vice President may break tie votes.

Impeachment. Note that the Senate acts as a court in impeachment; House appointees prosecute the case.

Punishment. What is the only punishment the Senate can give in impeachments? What might the U.S. Attorney General do after a conviction in the Senate?

ELECTIONS

Regulating elections. Remarkably, the first of many election laws was not passed until 1842. It set up election districts.

Assembly. This contrasted with the king's calling and dissolving Parliament at will.

* Changed by the Twentieth Amendment

SECTION 5.

Each house shall be the judge of the elections, returns and qualifications of its own members, and a majority of each shall constitute a quorum to do business; but a smaller number may adjourn from day to day, and may be authorized to compel the attendance of absent members, in such manner, and under such penalties as each house may provide.

Each house may determine the rules of its proceedings, punish its members for disorderly behavior, and, with the concurrence of two thirds, expel a member.

Each house shall keep a journal of its proceedings, and from time to time publish the same, excepting such parts as may in their judgment require secrecy; and the yeas and nays of the members of either house on any question shall, at the desire of one fifth of those present, be entered on the journal.

Neither house, during the session of Congress, shall, without the consent of the other, adjourn for more than three days, nor to any other place than that in which the two houses shall be sitting.

SECTION 6.

The senators and representatives shall receive a compensation for their services, to be ascertained by law, and paid out of the Treasury of the United States. They shall in all cases, except treason, felony and breach of the peace, be privileged from arrest during their attendance at the session of their respective houses, and in going to and returning from the same; and for any speech or debate in either house, they shall not be questioned in any other place.

No senator or representative shall, during the time for which he was elected, be appointed to any civil office under the authority of the United States, which shall have been created, or the emoluments thereof shall have been increased during such time; and no person holding any office under the United States shall be a member of either house during his continuance in office.

SECTION 7.

All bills for raising revenue shall originate in the House of Representatives; but the Senate may propose or concur with amendments as on other bills.

Every bill which shall have passed the House of Representatives and the Senate, shall, before it become a law, be presented to the President of the United States; if he approve he shall sign it, but if not he shall return it, with his objections to that house in which it shall have originated, who shall enter the objections at large on their journal, and proceed to reconsider it. If after such reconsideration two

RULES AND PROCEDURES

Admitting members; quorum. The election winner must be accepted by the house he is elected to. Research: Sen. Hiram Revels, an interesting case of challenge. Since the power to punish is judicial, it cannot extend outside Congress. Explain.

Journals. The daily *Congressional Record* is the published journal. But since members can and do add to, change, or omit their remarks, no "reliable, accurate journal" exists.

Adjournments. This prevents one house from holding up the work of the other, as in Parliament under Charles II.

PAY, PRIVILEGES, AND LIMITS

Pay; privileges. In 1969, Congress raised top-level salaries, including its own, by 42% to 100%. Research these in an almanac. Safeguarding members from arrest is based on English experience. How does this affect the people?

Limitations. In parliamentary republics, one person can run two or more executive departments. What must an American official do if he wishes to change jobs or get a raise?

LEGISLATION

Bills for raising money. In which house must tax bills originate? Why?

Bills into laws. Describe the ways in which the President may veto a bill. When Congress overrides a veto, how large a majority must there be in the House? in the Senate? Which part of this clause is best

thirds of that house shall agree to pass the bill, it shall be sent, together with the objections, to the other house, by which it shall likewise be reconsidered, and if approved by two thirds of that house, it shall become a law. But in all such cases the votes of both houses shall be determined by yeas and nays, and the names of the persons voting for and against the bill shall be entered on the journal of each house respectively. If any bill shall not be returned by the President within ten days (Sundays excepted) after it shall have been presented to him, the same shall be a law, in like manner as if he had signed it, unless the Congress by their adjournment prevent its return, in which case it shall not be a law.

Every order, resolution, or vote to which the concurrence of the Senate and House of Representatives may be necessary (except on a question of adjournment) shall be presented to the President of the United States; and before the same shall take effect, shall be approved by him, or being disapproved by him, shall be repassed by two thirds of the Senate and House of Representatives, according to the rules and limitations prescribed in the case of a bill.

SECTION 8.

The Congress shall have power to lay and collect taxes, duties, imposts and excises, to pay the debts and provide for the common defense and general welfare of the United States; but all duties, imposts and excises shall be uniform throughout the United States;

To borrow money on the credit of the United States;

To regulate commerce with foreign nations, and among the several States, and with the Indian tribes;

To establish a uniform rule of naturalization, and uniform laws on the subject of bankruptcies through the United States;

To coin money, regulate the value thereof, and of foreign coin, and fix the standard of weights and measures;

To provide for the punishment of counterfeiting the securities and current coin of the United States;

To establish post offices and post roads;

To promote the progress of science and useful arts by securing for limited times to authors and inventors the exclusive right to their respective writings and discoveries;

To constitute tribunals inferior to the Supreme Court;

To define and punish piracies and felonies committed on the high seas, and offenses against the law of nations;

To declare war, grant letters of marque and reprisal, and make rules concerning captures on land and water;

To raise and support armies, but no appropriation of money to that use shall be for a longer term than two years;

To provide and maintain a navy;

---

described as a "pocket veto."

Of what value is the taking and recording of a roll-call vote when Congress overrides a veto?

Veto power. This stops Congress from bypassing a possible veto under the pretense of passing a resolution. Why is a constitutional amendment the only legislation the President need not see?

POWERS OF CONGRESS

Taxes; defense; welfare. Research: "pork barrel." **Borrowing.** Jefferson called bonds "taxation without representation." Explain. **Commerce.** The tribes are likened to foreign nations. What is their situation now?

Naturalization; bankruptcy. If states say who may vote, why not who may be a citizen?

Money; standards. How is the guarantee that your money is real a kind of freedom? There are no official U.S. standards of weights and measures.

Copyrights; patents. How do these promote progress? Are they fair? Explain.

Courts; law. Highjacking = piracy. What laws do you recommend to control it?

War; armed forces. The President can send troops into foreign action without a declaration of war by Congress. How can Congress' "power of the

228

To make rules for the government and regulations of the land and naval forces;

To provide for calling forth the militia to execute the laws of the Union, suppress insurrections and repel invasions;

To provide for organizing, arming, and disciplining the militia, and for governing such part of them as may be employed in the service of the United States, reserving to the States respectively the appointment of the officers, and the authority of training the militia according to the discipline prescribed by Congress;

To exercise exclusive legislation in all cases whatsoever, over such district (not exceeding ten miles square) as may, by cession of particular States and the acceptance of Congress, become the seat of the government of the United States, and to exercise like authority over all places purchased by the consent of the legislature of the State in which the same shall be, for the erection of forts, magazines, arsenals, dockyards, and other needful buildings; and

To make all laws which shall be necessary and proper for carrying into execution the foregoing powers, and all other powers vested by this Constitution in the government of the United States, or in any department or officer thereof.

purse" curb such actions? **Navy.** Congress authorized a navy only when war with France was likely in 1798. **Militia** = National Guard, under command of governors until the President nationalizes them. **Captures.** In 1849 the Supreme Court ruled that the U.S. may not gain territory or property by right of conquest.

National capital. Maryland and Virginia both gave land for a national capital. Virginia took back its part in 1846.

Elastic clause. This is the famous battleground for contenders over how strong the central government shall be.

229

SECTION 9.

The migration or importation of such persons as any of the States now existing shall think proper to admit, shall not be prohibited by the Congress prior to the year one thousand eight hundred and eight, but a tax or duty may be imposed on such importation, not exceeding ten dollars for each person.

The privilege of the writ of habeas corpus shall not be suspended, unless when in cases of rebellion or invasion the public safety may require it.

No bill of attainder or ex post facto law shall be passed.

No capitation, or other direct,* tax shall be laid, unless in proportion to the census or enumeration herein before directed to be taken.

No tax or duty shall be laid on articles exported from any State.

No preference shall be given by any regulation of commerce or revenue to the ports of one State over those of another; nor shall vessels bound to, or from, one State be obliged to enter, clear, or pay duties in another.

No money shall be drawn from the Treasury, but in consequence of appropriations made by law; and a regular statement and account of the receipts and expenditures of all public money shall be published from time to time.

No title of nobility shall be granted by the United States: and no person holding any office of profit or trust under them, shall, without the consent of the Congress, accept of any present, emolument, office, or title of any kind whatever, from any king, prince, or foreign State.

SECTION 10.

No State shall enter into any treaty, alliance, or confederation; grant letters of marque and reprisal; coin money; emit bills of credit; make anything but gold and silver coin and tender in payment of debts, pass any bill of attainder, ex post facto law, or law impairing the obligation of contracts, or grant any title of nobility.

No State shall, without the consent of the Congress, lay any imposts or duties on imports or exports, except what may be absolutely necessary for executing its inspection laws: and the net produce of all duties and imposts laid by any State on imports or exports, shall be for the use of the Treasury of the United States; and all such laws shall be subject to the revision and control of the Congress.

No State shall, without the consent of Congress, lay any duty of tonnage, keep troops, or ships of war in time of peace, enter into any agreement or compact with another State, or with a foreign power, or engage in war, unless actually invaded, or in such imminent danger as will not admit of delay.

* Changed by the Sixteenth Amendment

FORBIDDEN POWERS

This was new! Kings were often curbed, but never a legislature. **Slavery.** In 1794 exports were banned; imports continued to 1865, despite the law of 1808.

Habeas corpus = you have the person; writ = written order. The writ's addressee must bring the prisoner promptly before the judge who issued the writ and who will decide if detention is legal. With right to counsel (Amend. 6), this clause ensures due process. Who can suspend this right? When? Why is it the most basic of civil rights? What others can be exercised without it? *Ex post facto* laws, passed after the act, make an innocent act a crime, make a lesser crime worse, increase the penalty, change rules of evidence to ensure conviction, and/or take away legal protections the accused would otherwise have had. Research: "due process of law."

POWERS FORBIDDEN STATES

With Secs. 8 and 9, this aims to help the States operate effectively without conflict among themselves or with the federal government. Study these sections to understand which powers are granted to or withheld from Congress, the States, or both. **Prohibited actions.** The outstanding part of this clause is "impairing the obligation of contracts." Research: contract. In hard times, Confederation legislatures often postponed payments of any debts. How would this affect interstate commerce? How else might State action affect interstate commerce?

ARTICLE II

SECTION 1.

The executive power shall be vested in a President of the United States of America. He shall hold his office during the term of four years, and, together with the Vice President chosen for the same term, be elected as follows:

Each State shall appoint, in such manner as the legislature thereof may direct, a number of electors, equal to the whole number of senators and representatives to which the State may be entitled in the Congress: but no senator or representative, or person holding an office of trust or profit under the United States, shall be appointed an elector.

The electors shall meet in their respective States, and vote by ballot for two persons, of whom one at least shall not be an inhabitant of the same State with themselves. And they shall make a list of all the persons voted for, and of the number of votes for each; which they shall sign and certify, and transmit sealed to the seat of the government of the United States, directed to the president of the Senate. The president of the Senate shall, in the presence of the Senate and House of Representatives, open all the certificates, and the votes shall then be counted. The person having the greatest number of votes shall be the President, if such number be a majority of the whole number of electors appointed; and if there be more than one who have such

PRESIDENT, VICE PRESIDENT

Terms. There was no executive under the old Articles of Confederation. Should the President's term be longer? Explain.
Presidential electors. Candidates for electors are chosen in various ways from State to State. All States determine electors by popular vote.

Electing executives. This entire paragraph was superseded by Amend. 12, ratified in 1804, which required electors to vote separately for President and Vice President. The amendment was seen to be necessary in 1800, when Thomas Jefferson and Aaron Burr were tied for first place, thus throwing the election into the House of Representatives. Only on the 36th ballot did Jefferson win. How-

231

majority, and have an equal number of votes, then the House of Representatives shall immediately choose by ballot one of them for President; and if no person have a majority, then from the five highest on the list the said house shall in like manner choose the President. But in choosing the President, the votes shall be taken by States, the representation from each State having one vote; a quorum for this purpose shall consist of a member or members from two thirds of the States, and a majority of all the States shall be necessary to a choice. In every case, after the choice of the President, the person having the greatest number of votes of the electors shall be the Vice President. But if there should remain two or more who have equal votes, the Senate shall choose from them by ballot the Vice President.*

The Congress may determine the time of choosing the electors, and the day on which they shall give their votes; which day shall be the same throughout the United States.

No person except a natural-born citizen, or a citizen of the United States, at the time of the adoption of this Constitution, shall be eligible to the office of President; neither shall any person be eligible to that office who shall not have attained to the age of thirty-five years, and been fourteen years a resident within the United States.

In case of the removal of the President from office, or of his death, resignation, or inability to discharge the powers and duties of the said office, the same shall devolve on the Vice President, and the Congress may by law provide for the case of removal, death, resignation, or inability, both of the President and Vice President, declaring what officer shall then act as President, and such offer shall act accordingly, until the disability be removed, or a President shall be elected.

The President shall, at stated times, receive for his services a compensation, which shall neither be increased nor diminished during the period for which he shall have been elected, and he shall not receive within that period any other emolument from the United States, or any of them.

Before he enter on the execution of his office, he shall take the following oath or affirmation:—"I do solemnly swear (or affirm) that I will faithfully execute the office of President of the United States, and will to the best of my ability, preserve, protect and defend the Constitution of the United States."

SECTION 2.

The President shall be commander in chief of the army and navy of the United States, and of the militia of the several States, when called into the actual service of the

* Changed by the Twelfth Amendment

ever, Amend. 12 does not alter the fact that the people of the U.S. do not elect the President and Vice President but are required to elect others to do it for them.

Election day. By law, the election is held on the Tuesday after the first Monday in November every fourth year from 1788. The day on which the electors (Electoral College) meet to vote is the Monday after the second Wednesday in December.

Presidential qualifications. Except for the first (why?), the President must be a native. Washington was a native, but many well-qualified men of his era were not. Research: which signers of the Constitution were not natives? **Disability.** Amend. 25, ratified in 1967, enlarges upon this clause.

Salary. The intent is to avoid his catering to Congress or to the state governments for a raise or gifts.

Oath of office. "Or affirm respects Moses' commandment and Jesus' words in Matthew: "Swear not at all [say only] Yea ...Nay...more than these come of the evil one."

PRESIDENTIAL POWERS
Military powers; reprieves, pardons. Executive departments accounted for 95% of the 3 mil-

United States; he may require the opinion, in writing, of the principal officer in each of the executive departments, upon any subject relating to the duties of their respective offices, and he shall have power to grant reprieves and pardons for offenses against the United States, except in cases of impeachment.

He shall have power, by and with the advice and consent of the Senate, to make treaties, provided two thirds of the senators present concur; and he shall nominate, and by and with the advice and consent of the Senate, shall appoint ambassadors, other public ministers and consuls, judges of the Supreme Court, and all other officers of the United States, whose appointments are not herein otherwise provided for, and which shall be established by law: but the Congress may by law vest the appointment of such inferior officers, as they think proper, in the President alone, in the courts of law, or in the heads of departments.

The President shall have power to fill up all vacancies that may happen during the recess of the Senate, by granting commissions which shall expire at the end of their next session.

SECTION 3.

He shall from time to time give to the Congress information of the state of the Union, and recommend to their consideration such measures as he shall judge necessary and expedient; he may, on extraordinary occasions, convene both houses, or either of them, and in case of disagreement between them with respect to the time of adjournment, he may adjourn them to such time as he shall think proper; he shall receive ambassadors and other public ministers; he shall take care that the laws be faithfully executed, and shall commission all the officers of the United States.

lion federal civilian employees in the early 1970's. How is the restriction on pardons part of checks and balances? How can Congress control the commander in chief?

Treaties; appointments. Who are some appointed officers not named in the Constitution? Research: some instances when the Senate refused its consent. How are checks and balances built into this clause?

Filling vacancies; interim appointments. How does this clause exemplify checks and balances?

PRESIDENT AND CONGRESS

Other duties. The President makes one or more reports to Congress soon after it meets each year. Usually he gives a State of the Union message to a meeting of both houses.

233

SECTION 4.

The President, Vice President, and all civil officers of the United States, shall be removed from office on impeachment for, and conviction of, treason, bribery, or other high crimes and misdemeanors.

ARTICLE III

SECTION 1.

The judicial power of the United States shall be vested in one Supreme Court, and in such inferior courts as the Congress may from time to time ordain and establish. The judges, both of the Supreme and inferior courts, shall hold their offices during good behavior, and shall, at stated times, receive for their services, a compensation which shall not be diminished during their continuance in office.

SECTION 2.

The judicial power shall extend to all cases, in law and equity, arising under this Constitution, the laws of the United States, and treaties made, or which shall be made, under their authority;—to all cases affecting ambassadors, other public ministers and consuls;—to all cases of admiralty and maritime jurisdiction;—to controversies to which the United States shall be a party;—to controversies between two or more States;—between a State and citizens of another State;—between citizens of different States,—between

IMPEACHMENT

Removal of officers. Which elected officers may not be impeached? Why? Which appointed officers?

JUDICIAL BRANCH

FEDERAL COURTS

Judicial power; federal judges. These judges are the only U.S. officers to hold lifetime jobs; their salaries cannot be reduced. How do these two facts help the parties in a lawsuit?

FEDERAL JURISDICTION

Federal cases. How do federal court cases differ from State court cases? In 1798, Amend. 11 stopped anyone from suing a State in federal court. Equity, a judicial method of seeing that justice is done when a law causes specific injustice or hardship, is found only where

EQUAL JUSTICE UNDER LAW

234

citizens of the same State claiming lands under grants of different States, and between a State, or the citizens thereof, and foreign States, citizens or subjects.

In all cases affecting ambassadors, other public ministers and consuls, and those in which a State shall be party, the Supreme Court shall have original jurisdiction. In all the other cases before mentioned, the Supreme Court shall have appellate jurisdiction, both as to law and fact, with such exceptions, and under such regulations as the Congress shall make.

The trial of all crimes, except in cases of impeachment, shall be by jury; and such trial shall be held in the State where the said crimes shall have been committed; but when not committed within any State, the trial shall be at such place or places as the Congress may by law have directed.

SECTION 3.

Treason against the United States shall consist only in levying war against them, or in adhering to their enemies, giving them aid and comfort. No person shall be convicted of treason unless on the testimony of two witnesses to the same overt act, or on confession in open court.

The Congress shall have power to declare the punishment of treason, but no attainder of treason shall work corruption of blood, or forfeiture except during the life of the person attainted.

ARTICLE IV

SECTION 1.

Full faith and credit shall be given in each State to the public acts, records, and judicial proceedings of every other State. And the Congress may by general laws prescribe the manner in which such acts, records, and proceedings shall be proved, and the effect thereof.

SECTION 2.

The citizens of each State shall be entitled to all privileges and immunities of citizens in the several States.

A person charged in any State with treason, felony, or other crime, who shall flee from justice, and be found in another State, shall on demand of the executive authority of the State from which he fled, be delivered up to be removed to the State having jurisdiction of the crime.

No person held to service or labor in the State, under the laws thereof, escaping into another, shall, in consequence of any law or regulation therein, be discharged from such service or labor, but shall be delivered up on claim of the party to whom such service or labor may be due.*

* Changed by the Thirteenth Amendment

Anglo-American law prevails—Americans traveling or residing in other countries, beware!

Supreme Court jurisdiction. If a defendant objects to a court verdict, he may appeal to the next higher court. The Supreme Court is the highest U.S. court of appeals.

Jury trials. Amend. 5, 6, and 7 add further detail to the right of trial by jury in the State where the crime occurred.

TREASON
Definition. A professor said he hoped the Communists would win the Vietnam war. Was he a traitor? What about war protesters? spies?

Punishment. Treason penalties include fines, prison, and death. In old times, the State took a traitor's property.

THE STATES

RELATIONS OF THE STATES
Full faith and credit. Will an Iowa marriage be legal in Utah? If Idaho acquits a man of a specific crime, can Oregon try him for it?

DUTIES OF STATE TO STATE
Citizens' privileges. A State may not discriminate unreasonably against nonresidents. **Fugitives.** Returning fugitives is extradition. Why might a governor refuse extradition?

Persons held to service. This provision refers to runaway slaves. How does this clause show that strong disagreements already existed over slavery?

SECTION 3.

New States may be admitted by the Congress into this Union; but no new State shall be formed or erected within the jurisdiction of any other State; nor any State be formed by the junction of two or more States, or parts of States, without the consent of the legislatures of the States concerned as well as of the Congress.

The Congress shall have power to dispose of and make all needful rules and regulations respecting the territory or other property belonging to the United States; and nothing in this Constitution shall be so construed as to prejudice any claims of the United States, or of any particular State.

SECTION 4.

The United States shall guarantee to every State in this Union a republican form of government, and shall protect each of them against invasion; and on application of the legislature, or of the executive (when the legislature cannot be convened) against domestic violence.

ARTICLE V

The Congress, whenever two thirds of both houses shall deem it necessary, shall propose amendments to this Constitution, or, on the application of the legislatures of two thirds of the several States, shall call a convention for proposing amendments, which, in either case, shall be valid to all intents and purposes, as part of this Constitution, when ratified by the legislatures of three fourths of the several States, or by conventions in three fourths thereof, as the one or the other mode of ratification may be proposed by the Congress; provided [that no amendment which may be made prior to the year one thousand eight hundred and eight shall in any manner affect the first and fourth clauses in the ninth section of the first article, and] that no State, without its consent, shall be deprived of its equal suffrage in the Senate.

ARTICLE VI

All debts contracted and engagements entered into, before the adoption of this Constitution, shall be as valid against the United States under this Constitution, as. under the Confederation.

This Constitution, and the laws of the United States which shall be made in pursuance thereof; and all treaties made, or which shall be made, under the authority of the United States, shall be the supreme law of the land; and the

ADMISSION OF NEW STATES

Formation; admission. Can New York City become a new State, as many wish? How? Which States were formed from others?

Territories; federal property. Congress can either govern a territory directly or authorize it to set up a legislature and a court system.

PROTECTION OF THE STATES

Guarantees. What does "republic" tell about how representatives are chosen or whom they represent? Explain the phrase *democratic republic.*

AMENDMENTS

Amending the Constitution. In another world's first, a government set up ways in which it could be changed without violence. Describe two ways in which the Constitution may be amended. (*Note:* The Supreme Court says that "two thirds of both houses" means only members present, not entire membership.) What parts could not be changed before 1808? When were these parts changed? How?

GENERAL PROVISIONS

Confederation debts. The Constitution guarantees payment of all debts contracted under the Articles of Confederation.

Supreme law. Why are treaties part of the supreme law of the land? How has the U.S. kept its treaties with the Indians? Re-

236

judges in every State shall be bound thereby, anything in the Constitution or laws of any State to the contrary notwithstanding.

The senators and representatives before mentioned, and the members of the several State legislatures, and all executive and judicial officers, both of the United States, and of the several States, shall be bound by oath or affirmation to support this Constitution; but no religious test shall ever be required as a qualification to any office or public trust under the United States.

ARTICLE VII

The ratification of the conventions of nine States shall be sufficient for the establishment of this Constitution between the States so ratifying the same.

Done in Convention by the unanimous consent of the States present the seventeenth day of September in the year of our Lord one thousand seven hundred and eighty-seven, and of the independence of the United States of America the twelfth. In witness whereof we have hereunto subscribed our names.

George Washington, President
(VIRGINIA)

MASSACHUSETTS
Nathaniel Gorham
Rufus King

NEW YORK
Alexander Hamilton

GEORGIA
William Few
Abraham Baldwin

DELAWARE
George Read
Gunning Bedford
John Dickinson
Richard Bassett
Jacob Broom

VIRGINIA
John Blair
James Madison

PENNSYLVANIA
Benjamin Franklin
Thomas Mifflin
Robert Morris
George Clymer
Thomas FitzSimons
Jared Ingersoll
James Wilson
Gouvernor Morris

NEW HAMPSHIRE
John Langdon
Nicholas Gilman

NEW JERSEY
William Livingston
David Brearley
William Paterson
Jonathan Dayton

CONNECTICUT
William Samuel
  Johnson
Roger Sherman

NORTH CAROLINA
William Blount
Richard Dobbs Spaight
Hugh Williamson

SOUTH CAROLINA
John Rutledge
Charles Cotesworth
  Pinckney
Charles Pinckney
Pierce Butler

MARYLAND
James McHenry
Daniel of
  St. Thomas Jenifer
Daniel Carroll

search: what those treaties promised the Indians.

Oath; religious test. How does State officials' support of the Constitution protect everyone? Banning religious tests was a first in world law. Was that a good idea? Why were religious tests banned?

RATIFICATION

Conventions, 1787–1790

Del.	7 Dec 87	Unanimous
Pa.	12 Dec 87	46–23
N.J.	18 Dec 87	Unanimous
Ga.	2 Jan 88	Unanimous
Conn.	9 Jan 88	128–40
Mass.	6 Feb 88	187–168 *
Md.	28 Apr 88	63–11
S.C.	27 May 88	149–73
N.H.	21 Jun 88	57–46 *
Va.	25 Jun 88	87–76 *
N.Y.	26 Jul 88	30–27 *
N.C.	21 Nov 89	187–77
R.I.	29 May 90	34–22

* Strongly urged Bill of Rights

FIRST AMENDMENT—1791

Congress shall make no law respecting an establishment of religion, or prohibiting the free exercise thereof; or abridging the freedom of speech, or of the press; or the right of the people peaceably to assemble, and to petition the government for a redress of grievances.

Religion; speech; assembly. Some other democracies tax everyone to support religion. Why doesn't the U.S.? Discuss: "There can be no freedom of speech, press [etc.] for the foes of socialism."—Soviet official A. Vishinski, *The Law of the Soviet State*. Compare that with this Supreme Court comment: "Freedom...protect[s] criticism and agitation for [change], but it does not [protect him] who counsels...the violation of the law...."

SECOND AMENDMENT—1791

A well-regulated militia, being necessary to the security of a free State, the right of the people to keep and bear arms, shall not be infringed.

Right to bear arms. Are handguns or rifles of greater value to a militia? If you were a dictator, what would you do about privately owned firearms? Why?

THIRD AMENDMENT—1791

No soldier shall, in time of peace, be quartered in any house, without the consent of the owner, nor in time of war, but in a manner to be prescribed by law.

Housing troops. Explain how quartering soldiers in private homes could be a method of controlling the nation's civilian population.

FOURTH AMENDMENT—1791

The right of the people to be secure in their persons, houses, papers, and effects, against unreasonable searches and seizures, shall not be violated, and no warrants shall issue, but upon probable cause, supported by oath or affirmation, and particularly describing the place to be searched, and the persons or things to be seized.

Unlawful search. Do you think that the use of electronic "snooping" devices, including wiretapping, by the police violates a person's right to be "secure...against unreasonable searches"? Explain your answer.

238

FIFTH AMENDMENT—1791

No person shall be held to answer for a capital or otherwise infamous crime, unless on a presentment or indictment of a grand jury, except in cases arising in the land or naval forces, or in the militia, when in actual service in time of war or public danger; nor shall any person be subject for the same offense to be twice put in jeopardy of life or limb; nor shall be compelled in any criminal case to be a witness against himself, nor be deprived of life, liberty, or property, without due process of law; nor shall private property be taken for public use without just compensation.

Rights of accused. Jeopardy begins as a jury is sworn, and ends on acquittal; if jury can't agree, if a mistrial occurs, or if conviction is reversed on appeal, **due process** (= legal fair play) begins anew. Only Anglo-American law assumes accused is not guilty until so proved and stops anyone's being forced to witness against oneself. Each step of proof must protect accused's rights.

SIXTH AMENDMENT—1791

In all criminal prosecutions, the accused shall enjoy the right to a speedy and public trial, by an impartial jury of the State and district wherein the crime shall have been committed, which district shall have been previously ascertained by law, and to be informed of the nature and cause of the accusation; to be confronted with the witnesses against him; to have compulsory process for obtaining witnesses in his favor, and to have the assistance of counsel for his defense.

Criminal procedure. There are so many cases that years may elapse between indictment and trial. Should there be a cut-off time when, if there has been no trial, the indictment is dismissed and the accused is free? Why should the accused have the aid of counsel? Explain the proverb: He who is his own lawyer has a fool for a client.

SEVENTH AMENDMENT—1791

In suits at common law, where the value in controversy shall exceed twenty dollars, the right of trial by jury shall be preserved, and no fact tried by a jury shall be otherwise reexamined in any court of the United States, than according to the rules of the common law.

Civil suits. Many parties to civil suits prefer to let a judge decide. But no judge or appeals court can set aside a civil jury's decision. Jury trials are costly—should the lower limit of $20 be changed? Why? How much?

EIGHTH AMENDMENT—1791

Excessive bail shall not be required, nor excessive fines imposed, nor cruel and unusual punishments inflicted.

NINTH AMENDMENT—1791

The enumeration in the Constitution of certain rights shall not be construed to deny or disparage others retained by the people.

TENTH AMENDMENT—1791

The powers not delegated to the United States by the Constitution, nor prohibited by it to the States are reserved to the States respectively, or to the people.

ELEVENTH AMENDMENT—1795

The judicial power of the United States shall not be construed to extend to any suit in law or equity, commenced or prosecuted against one of the United States, by citizens of another State, or by citizens or subjects of any foreign State.

TWELFTH AMENDMENT—1804

The electors shall meet in their respective States, and vote by ballot for President and Vice President, one of whom, at least, shall not be an inhabitant of the same State with themselves; they shall name in their ballots the person voted for as Vice President, and they shall make distinct lists of all persons voted for as President and of all persons voted for as Vice President, and of the number of votes for each, which lists they shall sign and certify, and transmit sealed to the seat of government of the United States, directed to the president of the Senate;—The president of the Senate shall, in the presence of the Senate and House of Representatives, open all the certificates and the votes shall then be counted;—The person having the greatest number of votes for President shall be the President, if such number be a majority of the whole number of electors appointed; and if no person have such majority, then from the persons having the highest numbers not exceeding three on the list of those voted for as President, the House of Representatives shall choose immediately, by ballot, the President. But in choosing the President, the votes shall be taken by States, the representation from each State having one vote; a

Bail, penalties. England forbade bails and fines so high as to deprive one of one's home or means of livelihood. Is death a "cruel punishment"?

People's rights retained. This amendment answers those who were against aiding a bill of rights. What must their arguments have been? Which of these do we still hear?

Reserved powers. This guarantees the pre-Constitutional sovereignty of the States. Why was this important to the early Republicans?

Suing States. This amends Art. III–2. Any nonresident must sue a State in that State's own courts, not in federal or other out-of-state courts.

Separate election of President and Vice President. Must an elector vote for the candidates who win the popular election in his district? This amends Art. II–1–c. Amend. 20 changes March 4 to January 20, and tells what to do if neither a President nor a Vice President has been chosen by inauguration day.

quorum for this purpose shall consist of a member or members from two thirds of the States, and a majority of all the States shall be necessary to a choice. And if the House of Representatives shall not choose a President whenever the right of choice shall devolve upon them, before the fourth day of March next following,* then the Vice President shall act as President, as in the case of the death or other constitutional disability of the President. The person having the greatest number of votes as Vice President shall be the Vice President, if such number be a majority of the whole number of electors appointed, and if no person have a majority, then from the two highest numbers on the list, the Senate shall choose the Vice President; a quorum for the purpose shall consist of two thirds of the whole number of senators and a majority of the whole number shall be necessary to a choice. But no person constitutionally ineligible to the office of President shall be eligible to that of Vice President of the United States.

THIRTEENTH AMENDMENT—1865

SECTION 1.
    Neither slavery nor involuntary servitude, except as a punishment for crime whereof the party shall have been duly convicted, shall exist within the United States, or any place subject to their jurisdiction.

SECTION 2.
    Congress shall have power to enforce this article by appropriate legislation.

Slavery prohibited. Some laws passed to enforce this amendment deal with peonage, under which a person in debt to another must work without pay until the debt is "worked out." Isn't this an old-fashioned idea that no longer applies to anyone? If you don't think so, explain.

* Changed by the Twentieth Amendment

241

FOURTEENTH AMENDMENT—1868

SECTION 1.

All persons born or naturalized in the United States, and subject to the jurisdiction thereof, are citizens of the United States and of the State wherein they reside. No State shall make or enforce any law which shall abridge the privileges or immunities of citizens of the United States; nor shall any State deprive any person of life, liberty, or property, without due process of law; nor deny to any person within its jurisdiction the equal protection of the laws.

Citizens and the States. This, with the Preamble and Art. VII, reinforces the idea that the foremost political relationship is between the people and the federal government, which the people authorize. Before the Civil War, all States, not just southern ones, restricted citizenship to whites. How would States' Righters feel about this amendment?

SECTION 2.

Representatives shall be apportioned among the several States according to their respective numbers, counting the whole number of persons in each State, excluding Indians not taxed. But when the right to vote at any election for the choice of electors for President and Vice President of the United States, representatives in Congress, the executive and judicial officers of a State, or the members of the legislature thereof, is denied to any of the male inhabitants of such State, being twenty-one years of age, and citizens of the United States, or in any way abridged, except for participation in rebellion, or other crime, the basis of representation therein shall be reduced in the proportion which the number of such male citizens shall bear to the whole number of male citizens twenty-one years of age in such State.

Apportionment. This amendment adds to Art. I–2–c by saying that if a State denies the vote to any group, that State's delegation in Congress shall be reduced. If such reduction never took place in a State that denied blacks the vote for a hundred years, were the senators and representatives of that State legally present in Congress? (*Note:* Courts refuse to make decisions on this "political" question. Congress has never challenged a member for being elected under discriminatory laws or situations.)

SECTION 3.

No person shall be a senator or representative in Congress, or elector of President and Vice President, or hold any office, civil or military, under the United States, or under any State, who, having previously taken an oath, as a member of Congress, or as an officer of the United States, or as a member of any State legislature, or as an executive or judicial officer of any State, to support the Constitution of the United States, shall have engaged in

Dealing with rebels. This section denies the privilege of serving in any public office to any former officeholder who took part in the rebellion of the 1860's (See Art. VII.) Congress removed the disability in 1898 so that former Confederate officers could serve in the Spanish-American War.

242

insurrection or rebellion against the same, or given aid or comfort to the enemies thereof. But Congress may by a vote of two thirds of each house, remove such disability.

SECTION 4.

The validity of the public debt of the United States, authorized by law, including debts incurred for payment of pensions and bounties for services in suppressing insurrection or rebellion, shall not be questioned. But neither the United States nor any State shall assume or pay any debt or obligation incurred in aid of insurrection or rebellion against the United States, or any claim for the loss or emancipation of any slave; but all such debts, obligations and claims shall be held illegal and void.

Civil War debt. The Confederate states sold bonds and issued paper money. Can any of those former Confederate states pay off those bonds or redeem that money today? Explain your answer. (*Note:* In this section is the only use of the word *slave* in the Constitution.)

SECTION 5.

The Congress shall have power to enforce, by appropriate legislation, the provisions of this article.

FIFTEENTH AMENDMENT—1870

SECTION 1.

The right of citizens of the United States to vote shall not be denied or abridged by the United States or by any State on account of race, color, or previous condition of servitude.

Right to vote. This third and last Reconstruction amendment was meant to guard the people against the misuse of State power. Look up "Jim Crow laws" and "Grandfather clause" to see how some States tried to evade this amendment.

SECTION 2.

The Congress shall have power to enforce this article by appropriate legislation.

SIXTEENTH AMENDMENT—1913

The Congress shall have power to lay and collect taxes on incomes, from whatever source derived, without apportionment among the several States, and without regard to any census or enumeration.

Income taxes. This amendment gets around Art. I and its requirement for equal apportionment of taxes.

SEVENTEENTH AMENDMENT—1913

The Senate of the United States shall be composed of two senators from each State, elected by the people thereof, for six years; and each senator shall have one vote. The electors in each State shall have the qualifications requisite for electors of the most numerous branch of the State legislatures.

When vacancies happen in the representation of any State in the Senate, the executive authority of such State shall issue writs of election to fill such vacancies: Provided, that the legislature of any State may empower the executive thereof to make temporary appointments until the people fill the vacancies by election as the legislature may direct.

Direct election of senators. Corruption in state legislatures and deadlocked votes often allowed seats to remain vacant for long periods. How was this harmful to the people of the State?

EIGHTEENTH AMENDMENT *—1919

SECTION 1.

After one year from the ratification of this article the manufacture, sale, or transportation of intoxicating liquors within, the importation thereof into, or the exportation thereof from the United States and all territory subject to the jurisdiction thereof for beverage purposes is hereby prohibited.

SECTION 2.

The Congress and the several States shall have concurrent power to enforce this article by appropriate legislation.

SECTION 3.

This article shall be inoperative unless it shall have been ratified as an amendment to the Constitution by the legislatures of the several States, as provided in the Constitution, within seven years from the date of the submission hereof to the States by the Congress.

Prohibition. Forbidding the sale of intoxicating liquors was first proposed in the mid-nineteenth century. The Prohibition party was organized in 1869. By 1906, 18 states had at one time or another adopted prohibition, though only a few still retained it. The amendment resulted from the efforts of temperance organizations such as the Woman's Christian Temperance Union and the Anti-Saloon League.

This was the first amendment to include a time limit for ratification. Up to this time, about 1,500 proposed amendments had been sent to the States. How many had been approved?

* Repealed by the Twenty-first Amendment

NINETEENTH AMENDMENT—1920

SECTION 1.

The right of citizens of the United States to vote shall not be denied or abridged by the United States or by any State on account of sex.

SECTION 2.

Congress shall have power, by appropriate legislation, to enforce the provisions of this article.

Women's suffrage. Suffrage = right to vote. Women's votes were not new in the U.S. Women had voted in Wyoming since 1869; Colorado, 1893; Utah and Idaho, 1896; Washington, 1910. Montana sent Jeannette Rankin to the House in 1916, four years before this amendment went into effect.

TWENTIETH AMENDMENT—1933

SECTION 1.

The terms of the President and Vice President shall end at noon on the 20th day of January, and the terms of senators and representatives at noon on the 3d day of January, of the years in which such terms would have ended if this article had not been ratified; and the terms of their successors shall then begin.

SECTION 2.

The Congress shall assemble at least once in every year, and such meeting shall begin at noon on the 3d day in January, unless they shall by law appoint a different day.

SECTION 3.

If, at the time fixed for the beginning of the term of the President, the President-elect shall have died, the Vice

Terms of President, Congress. One big change made by this amendment was that Congress was already in session when the President took office. Thus, the outgoing President would no longer have to call a special session for the Senate to confirm new Cabinet appointments. The time between election and the beginning of terms was shortened by about one fourth of a year. What developments had made this possible as well as desirable?

This amends Amend. 12 by providing for the failure of both the President-elect and the Vice President-elect to

245

President-elect shall become President. If a President shall not have been chosen before the time fixed for the beginning of his term, or if the President-elect shall have failed to qualify, then the Vice President-elect shall act as President until a President shall have qualified; and the Congress may by law provide for the case wherein neither a President-elect nor a Vice President-elect shall have qualified, declaring who shall then act as President, or the manner in which one who is to act shall be selected, and such persons shall act accordingly until a President or Vice President shall have qualified.

SECTION 4.

The Congress may by law provide for the case of the death of any of the persons from whom the House of Representatives may choose a President whenever the right of choice shall have devolved upon them, and for the case of the death of any of the persons from whom the Senate may choose a Vice President whenever the right of choice shall have devolved upon them.

SECTION 5.

Sections 1 and 2 shall take effect on the 15th day of October following the ratification of this article.

SECTION 6.

This article shall be inoperative unless it shall have been ratified as an amendment to the Constitution by the legislatures of three fourths of the several States within seven years from the date of its submission.

TWENTY-FIRST AMENDMENT—1933

SECTION 1.

The eighteenth article of amendment to the Constitution of the United States is hereby repealed.

SECTION 2.

The transportation or importation into any State, territory, or possession of the United States for delivery or use therein of intoxicating liquors, in violation of the laws thereof, is hereby prohibited.

SECTION 3.

This article shall be inoperative unless it shall have been ratified as an amendment to the Constitution by conventions in the several States, as provided in the Constitution, within seven years from the date of submission hereof to the States by the Congress.

qualify and for the possibility of deaths among candidates when the Electoral College has failed to elect a President and Vice President.

Prohibition repealed; local option guaranteed. The Prohibition Amendment, passed 13 years earlier, had been widely violated. It had resulted in bootlegging—the illegal manufacture and sale of intoxicating beverages. Organized gangs had taken over the business of supplying illegal liquor, with a great rise in crime. The amendment repealing prohibition was swiftly ratified. But states and communities still have the option to prohibit the sale of alcoholic beverages within their boundaries.

TWENTY-SECOND AMENDMENT—1951

No person shall be elected to the office of the President more than twice, and no person who has held the office of President, or acted as President, for more than two years of a term to which some other person was elected President shall be elected to the office of the President more than once.

But this Article shall not apply to any person holding the office of President when this Article was proposed by the Congress, and shall not prevent any person who may be holding the office of President, or acting as President, during the term within which this Article becomes operative from holding the office of President or acting as President during the remainder of such term.

TWENTY-THIRD AMENDMENT—1961

SECTION 1.

The District constituting the seat of government of the United States shall appoint in such manner as the Congress may direct:

A number of electors of President and Vice President equal to the whole number of senators and representatives in Congress to which the District would be entitled if it were a State, but in no event more than the least populous State; they shall be in addition to those appointed by the States, but they shall be considered, for the purposes of the election of President and Vice President, to be electors appointed by a State; and they shall meet in the District and perform such duties as provided by the twelfth article of amendment.

SECTION 2.

The Congress shall have power to enforce this article by appropriate legislation.

Two-term limit for Presidents. No President sought a third term until Franklin D. Roosevelt did so in 1940. Amend. 22 came about largely because Roosevelt broke this unwritten tradition. Roosevelt, a Democrat, was elected not only to a third term but to a fourth. When the Republicans gained control of Congress a few years later, they introduced this amendment. Note that it was worded so as not to apply to Harry S. Truman, the President at the time that it was proposed and adopted.

Presidential vote for D.C. When the Constitution was drawn up, there was no District of Columbia. The right to choose electors for President and Vice President was granted only to the states. Amend. 23 finally gave the citizens of the District of Columbia the same rights in presidential elections that the citizens of the states had always possessed.

TWENTY-FOURTH AMENDMENT—1964

SECTION 1.

The right of citizens of the United States to vote in any primary or other election for President or Vice President, for electors for President or Vice President, or for senator or representative in Congress, shall not be denied or abridged by the United States or any state by reason of failure to pay any poll tax or other tax.

SECTION 2.

The Congress shall have power to enforce this article by appropriate legislation.

Poll tax. *Poll* is an old German word for head.

TWENTY-FIFTH AMENDMENT—1967

SECTION 1.

In case of the removal of the President from office or his death or resignation, the Vice President shall become President.

SECTION 2.

Whenever there is a vacancy in the office of the Vice President, the President shall nominate a Vice President who shall take the office upon confirmation by a majority vote of both houses of Congress.

SECTION 3.

Whenever the President transmits to the president pro tempore of the Senate and the speaker of the House of Representatives his written declaration that he is unable to discharge the powers and duties of his office, and until he transmits to them a written declaration to the contrary, such powers and duties shall be discharged by the Vice President as Acting President.

SECTION 4.

Whenever the Vice President and a majority of either the principal officers of the executive departments or of such other body as Congress may by law provide, transmit to the president pro tempore of the Senate and the speaker of the House of Representatives their written declaration that the President is unable to discharge the powers and duties of his office, the Vice President shall immediately assume the powers and duties of the office as Acting President.

Thereafter, when the President transmits to the president pro tempore of the Senate and the speaker of the House of Representatives his written declaration that no

Presidential succession. When the Vice President should take over the President's duties in case of disability had never been defined. Some Presidents have had private agreements; others have not. But the numerous illnesses of Dwight Eisenhower in the 1950's and the tragic death of J. F. Kennedy in 1963 were behind the movement that resulted in this amendment.

inability exists, he shall resume the powers and duties of his office unless the Vice President and a majority of either the principal officers of the executive department or of such other body as Congress may by law provide, transmit within four days to the president pro tempore of the Senate and the speaker of the House of Representatives their written declaration that the President is unable to discharge the powers and duties of his office. Thereupon Congress shall decide the issue, assembling within 48 hours for that purpose if not in session. If the Congress, within 21 days after receipt of the latter written declaration, or, if Congress is not in session, within 21 days after Congress is required to assemble, determines by two-thirds vote of both houses that the President is unable to discharge the powers and duties of his office, the Vice President shall continue to discharge the same as Acting President; otherwise, the President shall resume the powers and duties of his office.

TWENTY-SIXTH AMENDMENT—1971

SECTION 1.

The right of citizens of the United States, who are eighteen years of age or older, to vote shall not be denied or abridged by the United States or by any State on account of age.

SECTION 2.

The Congress shall have power to enforce this article by appropriate legislation.

Eighteen made voting age. For the past 30 years the nation had been drafting young men below the age of twenty-one and sending them to war. Rarely were they allowed to vote. That, in addition to the fact that modern communications have resulted in a more knowledgeable and better educated group of under-21's, brought strong support for Amend. 26.

CHAPTER 10

THE FEDERALISTS TAKE CHARGE

THE UNITED STATES OF AMERICA during the decade of the 1780s was not really a nation. States that had joined together in a common war for independence were soon putting *tariffs* —or import taxes—on each other's goods. New York and New Hampshire fought over Vermont lands, even while Vermonters themselves wanted to become a separate state. John Adams spoke of the United States as a house with thirteen clocks that had to be set to strike at the same time.

Washington's leadership. One reason the thirteen clocks began striking at the same time under the new Constitution was the leadership of George Washington. More than any other person in America, Washington had the trust of the people. In war, his character and conduct won him their loyalty. In peace, time and again he put his country ahead of his own self-interest. One reason why the delegates in Philadelphia were willing to give large powers to the office of the President was that they counted on Washington to take the job. Once the Constitution went into effect, Washington was the choice of every elector for President. His reelection in 1792 would be equally one-sided.

Filling In the Constitution

As Congress and the new President assembled in New York, the nation's temporary capital, in the spring of 1789, everyone realized that much must be done to fill in the new Constitution. All those in the government were very much aware that every one of their actions might set a *precedent*, or pattern that would be followed in the future.

Mr. President. Members of Congress agonized, for example, over how to address the President. Vice President John Adams suggested that he be called "His Highness, the President of the United States of America and Protector of Their Liberties." Others thought "His Excellency" was just about right.

The diary of Senator William Maclay of Pennsylvania gives us a glimpse into the feelings on this issue. We have changed a few of Maclay's words in order to make the meaning clearer.

May 1. The minutes of yesterday's session were being read. When we came to the report of Washington's speech it was worded, "His most gracious speech." The secretary was going on. I interrupted him. "The words prefixed to the President's speech are the same that are usually placed before the speech of His Britannic Majesty. I consider them as improper. I therefore move that they be struck out."

If such a thing appeared in our minutes, the enemies of the Constitution would not fail to represent it as the first step to royalty.

In the end it was agreed to address Washington simply as "Mr. President." Today this matter seems more amusing than important. But it was taken very seriously in 1789.

Setting precedents. Among the precedents that were to have a lasting effect on the American government was the

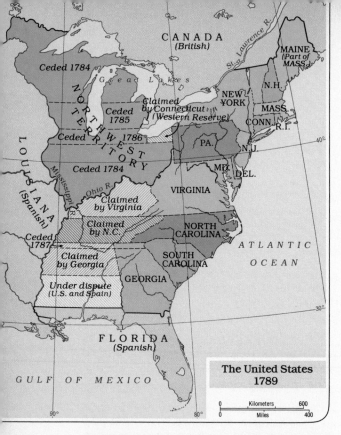

When Washington became President in 1789, the boundaries of the thirteen original states, though often poorly defined, were—except for Virginia—much as they are today. West Virginia was separated from Virginia in 1863.

creation of a *cabinet.* The Constitution says that the President may seek advice from his department heads. As early as 1791, Washington began calling his department heads together to talk with them about a whole range of matters. They came to be known as the cabinet. American Presidents ever since have turned to their cabinets for advice.

Washington established another precedent some years later when he decided not to seek a third term as President. The two-term tradition he started lasted for nearly 150 years. It lasted until Franklin D. Roosevelt served a third term and part of a fourth. In 1951 the Twenty-second Amendment was added to the Constitution, limiting all future Presidents to two terms.

The Bill of Rights. In the Congress, James Madison of Virginia was the leader in taking steps to give the Constitution life. One step was the addition of a bill of rights. During the debates on ratification, delegates in several states had agreed to ratify the Constitution only because of a promise that such a bill would be added. Madison now proposed several amendments upholding the rights of individuals against actions by the federal government.

Ten of those amendments were ratified in 1791. Together, they are known as the Bill of Rights (see pages 238–240). Among the rights protected by these amendments are freedom of speech, freedom of religion, and freedom of the press. The Bill of Rights also protects the rights of citizens to assemble peaceably, to petition the government, to bear arms, to be tried by a jury, and to have certain safeguards when accused of a crime.

The Judiciary Act of 1789. One of Congress's first acts was to use its taxing power to place a 5 percent tax on imported goods. Next, it set up federal courts under the Judiciary Act of 1789. There would be thirteen district courts—one for each state. There would be three circuit courts, and a Supreme Court with six judges. The number of district and circuit courts has been changed over the years. So has the number of judges on the Supreme Court. However, the framework of the court system has remained pretty much the same. The law set forth the kinds of cases that could be appealed from the district courts to the circuit and Supreme courts. Most important, it gave the Supreme Court of the United States the power to review the decisions of state courts. It could then declare unconstitutional those state laws that it felt violated the Constitution, acts of Congress, or United States treaties. This law, in other words, put teeth in the Constitution's "supremacy clause," which makes the document the supreme law of the land.

The Judiciary Act, however, did not deal with an important question. That was whether the Supreme Court had the power to review and declare unconstitutional acts of Congress, a co-equal branch of the government. But in 1803, in the case of *Marbury* v. *Madison* (which you will read about in the next chapter), Chief Justice John Marshall ruled that the Supreme Court did have this power.

CHECKUP

1. What were some of the precedents that were set in government while Washington was President?
2. Why was the Bill of Rights passed? What did it guarantee?
3. Describe the framework of the court system under the Judiciary Act of 1789.

Hamilton and Jefferson

The Constitution, while referring to department heads, left to Congress the job of deciding what kind of and how many departments there would be. Under Madison's leadership, Congress in 1789 set up the departments of Treasury, State, and War, and made them parts of the executive branch of government. It created the posts of Attorney General and Postmaster General as well.

To head two of the new executive departments, Washington chose two of the most able people in America. Alexander Hamilton of New York, his former military aide, became Secretary of the Treasury. Thomas Jefferson of Virginia was named Secretary of State. These two men disagreed on almost every important policy, and became bitter foes. They, and their points of view, became the rallying points for two groups that later became political parties.

A nation of factories—or farms? To begin with, Hamilton and Jefferson saw America's future differently. In a 1791 report favoring a protective tariff, Hamilton spelled out to Congress his hopes for the United States.

. . . the labor employed in agriculture is, in a great measure, periodical and occasional, depending on the seasons, and liable to various and long intermissions; while that occupied in many manufactures is constant and regular, extending through the year, employing, in some instances, night and day.

. . . machinery forms an item of great importance. . . . It is an artifical force brought in aid of the natural force of man; and . . . is an increase of hands. . . . in general, women and children are rendered more useful, and the latter more early useful, by manufacturing establishment, than they would otherwise be. . . . Workers would probably flock from Europe to the United States, to pursue their trades and professions. . . .

Contrast that view with Jefferson's version of the good society. We have changed a few of Jefferson's words in order to make his meaning clearer.

> Those who labor in the earth are the chosen people of God, if ever He had a chosen people. . . . Corruption of morals in the mass of farmers is something of which no age nor nation has furnished an example. . . . While we have land to labor, then, let us never wish to see our citizens occupied at a workbench. . . . Let our workshops remain in Europe.
>
> . . . .
>
> I think our governments will remain honest for many centuries; as long as they are chiefly agricultural. . . . When people pile upon one another in large cities, as in Europe, they shall become corrupt, as in Europe.

Which of the two wanted the United States to become a nation of cities and factories? What does he see as the advantages of manufacturing? Based on these writings, which one would you think wanted America to become a great trading nation?

How much power? The two men differed also on how much power the central government should have.

In Jefferson's view, the country was too big to be run by a single government. Public officials far away from the people would be tempted to be dishonest. He wanted the central government to be small and simple. Most governing power, he thought, should be left with the states.

Hamilton, on the other hand, favored a strong central government. He feared that strong, jealous states would keep the central government from acting effectively and would pull the union apart.

Paying the nation's debts. Hamilton's management of the new nation's financial affairs was brilliant. His first goal was to restore the government's credit, which was very low. During the Revolutionary War, Congress had borrowed heavily both from other countries and from American citizens. It raised money by selling certificates of indebtedness. These were a kind of bond, or IOU, promising to pay the money back at a later date. However, the Confederation government was never able to do so. So, the new government still owed $12 million to France, Spain, and Holland. It owed another $42 million to its own people. Many doubted the debts would, or could, be paid, at least in full.

Yet Hamilton proposed exactly that—full payment of the debts. Certificates of indebtedness were to be turned in for new interest-bearing United States bonds. Those bonds were to pay the original value of the certificates plus all unpaid interest. Money to pay off the new bonds was to be raised by new taxes. Hamilton's plan was known as the *funding program.*

The funding proposal touched off heated debate. It was not about whether the debts should be paid. Rather it was about to whom payments should be made. Many of the original lenders to the government, hard pressed for cash and discouraged about their chances of being paid back, had sold their certificates. They had done so for a small part of the original cost. James Madison, among others, felt that those who had originally lent the money to the government should get payment in full—rather than the speculators, who had bought the certificates from them at low prices. But Hamilton's plan was approved by Congress. The new bonds went to speculators and others who were holding the certificates.

Suspicions and objections. The credit of the United States government was soon restored among the nations of the world. But in the United States, the funding program left hard feelings and suspicions. The speculators, informed of the plan by Hamilton before it was made public, had hurried into the backcountry to buy certificates from unsuspecting farmers. Some of the speculators were the very Congressmen who later voted for the plan. Farmers who sold their certificates to those people at low prices rightly felt cheated.

Hamilton also proposed that the national government *assume*, or take over, responsibility for state debts left over from the war. The debts had been incurred for a national cause, he reasoned. Now they should be paid by the nation. The *assumption program*, as it was called, was also passed, but not without objection. Several states had already paid most of their debts. Virginia had paid all of its debt. Such states objected to being taxed by the federal government to pay off the debts of other states. In the end, enough votes were won to pass the bill by a compromise. Southern states, including Virginia, voted for assumption in exchange for northern votes to locate the permanent capital of the United States on the Potomac River.

A national bank. The split between Hamilton and Jefferson widened when Congress accepted Hamilton's plan to

Alexander Hamilton, the first Secretary of the Treasury, devised programs that placed the new nation on a solid financial foundation.

charter a national bank. The bank, to be called the Bank of the United States, would have a charter to operate for twenty years. This bank was to have the power to issue bank notes that would circulate as money. It would also lend funds to the government when necessary, and serve as a place to deposit the government's money. Since the bank would help the nation's businesspeople, it was an important part of Hamilton's vision of the United States as an industrial and commercial nation.

255

The creation of a national bank was part of the program drawn up by Alexander Hamilton. The main office, shown above, was located in Philadelphia.

Did Congress have the right, under the Constitution, to charter a bank? President Washington had his doubts; the Constitution did not include this power among those given to Congress. Before signing the bill, Washington asked Hamilton and Jefferson for their opinions. In their statements, both referred to the so-called *elastic clause*— the last paragraph of Article I, section 8 of the Constitution. (You will find it on page 229.) This paragraph gives Congress the power "to make all laws . . . necessary and proper for carrying into execution the . . . powers" listed in the previous paragraphs of section 8. The key words in that clause are "necessary" and "proper."

Hamilton held that the Constitution *implied* that Congress had the power to set up a national bank, even if it did not state the power in so many words. Congress was expected to carry out the duties assigned by the Constitution. It was free to choose the means to do that as long as it didn't choose a means that the Constitution prohibited. In this case, setting up a national bank was a "necessary" and "proper" means to help collect taxes, regulate trade, and provide for defense—all of which were jobs of Congress.

Jefferson's view, however, was this:

I consider the foundation of the Constitution as laid on this ground—that *all powers not delegated to the United States by the Constitution, nor prohibited by it to the states, are reserved to the states or to the people. . . .*

The incorporation of a bank, and the powers assumed by this bill, have not, in my opinion been delegated to the United States by the Constitution.

The second general phrase is "to make all laws *necessary* and proper for carrying into execution the enumerated powers." But they can all be carried into execution without a bank. A bank therefore is not *necessary*, and consequently not authorized by this phrase.

Hamilton's belief that Congress has certain "implied powers" that are not stated by the Constitution has come to be known as the *loose interpretation* of the Constitution. Jefferson's position is known as the *strict interpretation*. Which of these two views is closer to the idea of limited government? In this case, Washington sided with Hamilton and signed the bill creating the Bank of the United States.

Who should govern? Hamilton's program was related to his ideas about which people could best run the government. On this subject, he and Jefferson were once again worlds apart. Here are Hamilton's ideas on popular rule:

All communities divide themselves into the few and the many. The first are the rich and wellborn; the other, the mass of the people. The voice of the people has been said to be the voice of God. But that . . . is not true. The people are turbulent and changing; they seldom judge correctly. . . .

Hamilton believed that the new government could succeed only if it won the support and participation of the wise,

the rich, and the wellborn. His way of winning them over was to offer them positions in government, and to make participation in government pay for them. By helping the government, they would be helping themselves.

Think back to Hamilton's plan. What class of people would hold most of the bonds under the funding program? Would they have reason to help the new government succeed? When the federal government assumed the state debts, which level of government did those same people want to see strengthened —state or federal? Which groups in society were most likely to benefit if the national bank and the new government succeeded? Describing Hamilton's position, one historian has said that Hamilton "proposed to use the federal government to enrich a class, in order that this class might strengthen the federal government."

Jefferson also believed that the ablest people should hold government office. But he did not believe they could be found only among the rich and the wellborn. And he had confidence that the people would have the good judgment to choose able leaders.

I have such reliance on the good sense of the body of the people and honesty of their leaders that I am not afraid of their letting things go wrong to any length in any cause.

. . . .

Whenever the people are well-informed, they can be trusted with their own government; whenever things get so far wrong as to attract their notice, they may be relied on to set them to rights.

With Jefferson holding this view, it is not surprising that he differed with

257

Hamilton about who should run the government. Said Jefferson:

> Every government degenerates when trusted to the rulers . . . alone. The people themselves are its only safe depositories.
>
> . . . .
>
> I am not among those who fear the people. They and not the rich are our dependence for continued freedom.

Which of these two men, Hamilton or Jefferson, was more in favor of limiting government? Which do you think was more democratic-minded?

CHECKUP

1. What differing views did Hamilton and Jefferson have on the kind of country the United States should be?
2. How did Hamilton restore the credit of the federal government?
3. How did Hamilton and Jefferson justify their views on the right of Congress to charter a national bank?

The Rise of Political Parties

Differences over the program of Washington and Hamilton, the question of government power and the future of the country led to the rise of two political groups. One was called the Federalists. While they took the same name as those who had supported ratification of the Constitution, they were a different group of people. By and large they shared Hamilton's views on popular rule, industry and commerce, and government power. Those sharing Jefferson's views on these matters formed the second group. They were called the Democratic-Republicans.

Members of these two groups did not divide neatly along occupational, class, or sectional lines, any more than today's political parties do. There were Federalist farmers as well as Democratic-Republican farmers. Nevertheless, it is safe to say that most of the strength of the Federalists came from New England and the coastal parts of the Northeast, and they were supported heavily by merchants, businessmen, and lawyers. The Democratic-Republicans drew most of their support from the small farmers, plantation owners, and frontier people of the South and West.

The French Revolution. Political divisions were further sharpened by foreign affairs. No event of the time had a greater impact upon Americans than the French Revolution. In 1789 the French overthrew their king and proclaimed the principles of liberty, equality, and brotherhood. They then set up a republican form of government. News of the event was received joyously by most Americans. They believed their own Revolution had served as an example for the French.

But in 1793 the French Revolution took a violent turn. First the King of France was executed. Then in the space of a few months, 17,000 others, including some of the revolution's own leaders who had fallen out of favor, were put to death. In that same year, France declared war on Great Britain. Except for a few short truces, their struggle lasted for the next twenty-two years. The Anglo-French conflict had a great effect on America's domestic and foreign politics.

The American reactions. Federalists were disgusted by what they felt were the disorder, mob rule, and godlessness

In Paris during the French Revolution, persons suspected of being disloyal to the government are arrested and taken to jail. Americans were divided in their reactions to events in France.

of the French Revolution. Some Americans were proud of the example the United States had given to France. However, the Federalists worried about the example the French might be setting for Americans. In the eyes of the Federalists, Britain remained the ideal society. It was ruled by the upper classes and was stable. It respected tradition and property. So, when the Anglo-French war broke out, the Federalists favored Britain.

Hamilton in particular disliked the French Revolution. He believed that America's prosperity depended upon good relations with England. Most of America's trade was still with Britain. The tariff collected from British imports was the main source of income for the United States. If it were cut off, Hamilton's entire funding program would be wrecked—and with it the credit of the United States.

Thomas Jefferson and the Democratic-Republicans, on the other hand, were pro-French. Before the French Revolution, Jefferson had visited France and had seen the terrible conditions there. Although he opposed the violence, he felt the revolution was justified because it replaced a monarchy with a republican government. "The liberty of the whole earth," said Jefferson, "was depending on the outcome of the contest, and was ever such a prize won with so little innocent blood?"

The Neutrality Proclamation. Most of the American people were pro-French. Some wanted to wage war on Britain.

259

But other American citizens wanted the United States to side with Britain. Emotions were aroused further when a very enthusiastic minister from the French Republic, Edmond Genêt, arrived in America to ask for aid. Genêt was greeted by such huge crowds that he soon believed that he, rather than Washington, spoke for the American people. He even tried to recruit men and ships for the French cause without asking permission. President Washington finally had to ask the government of France to recall Genêt.

Washington, believing that America must have peace, steered a middle course. In 1793 he announced that the United States would remain neutral. The Neutrality Proclamation was unpopular, but history has shown that it was the wisest course to follow.

Britain, in the meantime, had begun to violate America's neutral rights on the seas. British captains stopped American ships and searched them. They seized those with cargoes for France. Americans on the western frontier had their own grievances against Britain. The British still held the forts they had promised to give up in the Treaty of Paris. Frontier settlers believed, with some justification, that the British were inciting the Indians against them.

Jay's Treaty. Once again, there was talk of war. And once again, Washington turned a deaf ear to it. In 1794 he sent John Jay, Chief Justice of the United States, to England to try to settle the differences between the two countries. Jay came back with a treaty some months later and almost immediately became the most unpopular man in America.

In truth, Jay's Treaty did not settle many issues. The British again agreed to leave the military posts on American territory in the Northwest. They allowed a few American ships to trade in the rich British West Indies market. But they added so many conditions to this trade that they greatly limited it. The treaty also referred several troublesome matters, such as the pre-Revolutionary War debt claims and boundary disputes, to boards of arbitration. The great accomplishment of the Jay Treaty, however, was not to be found in its words but in the fact that it prevented war.

Jay's Treaty outraged the pro-French Democratic-Republicans. They attacked it as the "death warrant of American liberty." The treaty also turned many people against Washington. One member of Congress even said the President should be impeached for signing it.

The first political party. The anger over Jay's Treaty caused the Democratic-Republicans to form a full-scale political party. They founded newspapers, formed local political clubs, and held rallies to influence voters. Those seeking local, state, and national offices agreed to help each other by running as members of the same party.

The chief builder of the new party was James Madison. With Jefferson, he had organized the opposition to Hamilton's program in 1791. Madison remained in Congress through both of Washington's terms and led the opposition to Federalist policies there. He also stayed in close touch with Jefferson after the latter retired as Secretary of State in 1793 and returned home to Monticello, Virginia.

The Whiskey Rebellion

An early test of the strength of the federal government under the new Constitution came in 1794 when the Whiskey Rebellion broke out in western Pennsylvania. Three years earlier Secretary of the Treasury Alexander Hamilton had gotten Congress to place a tax on a number of goods to help pay for his funding program. Among the taxed products was whiskey. The tax fell heavily on western farmers who distilled their grain into whiskey before shipping it to the East. They did this because of the difficulty of transportation. A pack horse could carry only 4 bushels (35 liters) of rye or corn in the form of grain, but 24 bushels (211 liters) in the form of whiskey.

To the frontier farmers, this tax on the product of their labor was unfair. In Pennsylvania, west of the Allegheny Mountains, they rose in rebellion. Mass meetings were held, and riots broke out. When the governor of Pennsylvania refused to send the state militia to restore order, President Washington, urged on by Hamilton, called upon 15,000 militia troops from neighboring states to do so. The rebellion was quickly put down. Two ring leaders, charged with treason, were pardoned by Washington.

In crushing the uprising, the federal government showed not only that it was strong enough to deal with an armed rebellion but also that it had the will to do it. The government's action in Pennsylvania was far different from the feeble way it had dealt with Shays's Rebellion.

The Whiskey Rebellion had another result that was not so pleasing to the Federalists. It made nearly all the western farmers angry with Hamilton and his Federalist supporters. Therefore, in the elections of 1796 and 1800, the western frontier people backed Jefferson and the Democratic-Republican party. After Jefferson became President in 1801, the whiskey tax was repealed.

In Maryland, Washington reviews the troops gathered to put down the Whiskey Rebellion.

It is ironic that the first American political party was led by these two men. Jefferson had once said that if forming a party was the only way to get to heaven, he would rather not get there. Madison had often written that parties were undesirable. As one of the main authors of the Constitution, he had hoped that that document would discourage the growth of political parties.

Jefferson and Madison's views about political parties were shared by most leaders of their generation. They knew that disagreements among interest groups and among sections were bound to arise. They hoped, however, that the disagreements would never lead groups to form permanent political parties. Their main goal was national unity. To them, nothing threatened unity more than political parties.

Yet by 1796 they and others had decided that only by forming a party could they hope to block policies they opposed and promote policies they favored. And only through belonging to a political party could they expect to win election to office to seek those goals.

Adams succeeds Washington. In September 1796, Washington announced his plan to retire, and gave his farewell address. Among other things, he warned against the bad influence of party spirit. He was already too late, for the Democratic-Republicans were gearing up for the 1796 campaign. They nominated Jefferson for President. The Federalists were not yet organized enough to be called a party. Federalist members of Congress, however, chose Vice President John Adams as their candidate. In a close contest, Adams re-

ceived 71 electoral votes and became President. Under the electoral system in use at that time, Jefferson, with 68 votes, became Vice President.

A dispute with France. John Adams proved to be a courageous President. His four-year term was one of the stormiest in American history. It was marked by an angry dispute between France and the United States. The French felt that the treaty of alliance they had made with the United States during the American Revolution meant that the United States must help France in its war against Britain. The French had become bitter when, in 1793, Washington had proclaimed neutrality. They were further angered when the Senate approved Jay's Treaty with their enemy, England.

Soon afterward, the French began to attack American shipping. Tension between the two countries mounted. President Adams sent three commissioners to Paris to try to settle matters peaceably. Talleyrand, the French foreign minister, refused to talk with the Americans. Instead, he appointed three agents to do so. These three, who became known as X, Y, and Z, demanded a large bribe as part of any deal. The Americans refused and broke off talks with the French.

An undeclared war. When Adams reported the XYZ affair to Congress in April 1798, Americans, angry and insulted over the bribery demand, prepared for war. Washington came out of retirement to head the army. Hamilton called for war and dreamed of leading an army against the French. American privateers received permission to attack

262

Charles Willson Peale

Patriot, portrait painter, naturalist, museum founder—these were some of the roles played by the remarkable Charles Willson Peale during the early years of the United States.

A native of Maryland, Peale was apprenticed to a saddle maker for seven years as a youth. However, he became interested in art, and showed much talent in painting portraits. In 1767 he went to London and studied under Benjamin West, one of the best known artists of the time. Upon returning to America, Peale kept busy doing portraits, and he also plunged into patriotic, political activities. He joined the militia and during the Revolution fought at Trenton, Princeton, and Germantown. While in the army, he did portraits from life of most of America's top military and naval officers. He is known particularly for his many portraits of George Washington, executed over a 23-year period. The versatile Peale also fashioned Washington's dental plates!

An ardent nationalist, Peale wanted Americans to be well educated. He promoted an interest in natural science as well as art. When he learned of the discovery of a mastodon skeleton in New York, he organized a scientific expedition to dig up the bones and put them on display. The museum that Peale opened in Philadelphia was one of the first of its kind in America. There he exhibited specimens of birds and animals, which he had stuffed and mounted, as well as many of his portraits.

To encourage American art, Peale helped to establish the Pennsylvania Academy of Fine Arts, one of the country's first public art galleries. He firmly believed that anyone could be taught to paint. Among those he instructed were members of his own family. Four of his sons, like their father, were both painters and naturalists. His niece, Sarah Miriam Peale, was very likely the first professional woman portrait painter in America.

In this self-portrait, Charles Willson Peale presents his Philadelphia museum.

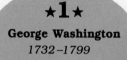

★1★

George Washington
1732–1799

Born in VIRGINIA
In Office 1789–1797
Party NONE

Elected and reelected by unanimous electoral vote. Helped erect government departments, agencies, and courts. Advised the United States to stay clear of permanent foreign alliances.

French ships because of France's seizure of American ships. For the next two years, an undeclared war was fought on the high seas. President Adams told Congress: "I will never send another minister to France without assurance that he will be received, respected and honored as the representative of a great, free, powerful, independent nation."

Still, Adams, like Washington before him, knew that war would be a disaster for the struggling young nation. So while others shouted for war, Adams quietly looked for peace. Word came to

him that Talleyrand would now properly receive an American minister. Without consulting his cabinet, Adams chose a minister to go to France. The move made him very unpopular among the other Federalists. They divided into two groups—one supporting him and the other favoring Hamilton.

Adams's second try at bringing about peace with France was successful. In the Convention of 1800, France and America agreed to end the alliance of 1778. Nothing further was said about the damage that the French had done to American shipping, but it was understood that the naval war would now end. As with Jay's Treaty, the most important achievement of this agreement was that it kept the young United States out of war. Adams himself said that this was his most important act as President.

The Alien and Sedition Acts. Affairs at home were as stormy as those abroad. Taking advantage of the war hysteria in 1798, Federalists in Congress passed a series of laws aimed at the Democratic-Republicans. Together, these laws are known as the Alien and Sedition Acts. One of them—the Naturalization Act—increased from five years to fourteen the time a foreigner had to live in the United States before becoming a citizen. Many new citizens had been siding with Jefferson and his party, and this would keep them from adding more voters to their ranks. The Alien Act gave the President the power to deport any foreigner whom he thought "dangerous to the peace and safety of the United States." The Sedition Act made it a crime for anyone to criticize the United States government, the President, or the Congress. Its aim was to silence Democratic-Republican newspaper editors.

Adams never deported any aliens, but the Sedition Act was used against newspaper editors. Twenty-five were tried. Ten were convicted and sent to jail by Federalist judges.

The Kentucky and Virginia Resolutions. The Alien and Sedition Acts raised a wave of disapproval among most people. Democratic-Republicans charged that the laws violated the guarantees of free speech and free press in the Bill of Rights. Jefferson and Madison wrote resolutions and had them passed by supporters in the Kentucky and Virginia legislatures. The Kentucky and Virginia Resolutions declared that the Alien and Sedition Acts were unconstitutional and would not be obeyed in those states. They also invited other states to pass such resolutions.

The resolutions were really intended more as political propaganda than anything else. But in claiming that a state had the right, by itself, to decide which federal laws would be obeyed within its borders, these resolutions put forth an idea—*states' rights*—that was filled with danger for the Union. You will read more about that idea in Unit 5.

The election of 1800. In the election of 1800, the Federalists were divided. John Adams failed to win a second term. Unexpectedly, however, Thomas Jefferson, the Democratic-Republicans' presidential candidate, and Aaron Burr of New York, the vice-presidential candidate, each got 73 electoral votes.

At that time, electors voted for two candidates, without distinguishing be-

★2★
John Adams
1735–1826

Born in MASSACHUSETTS
In Office 1797–1801
Party FEDERALIST

Avoided a war with France, but was harshly criticized. To curb criticism, he helped pass unpopular Alien and Sedition Acts. Failed to win second term. First president to live in the White House.

tween President and Vice President. It had been expected that at least one of the Democratic-Republican electors would vote for Jefferson and not for Burr, avoiding a tie. But none did.

Under the Constitution, when no candidate has a majority, the final choice is made in the House of Representatives. At such times, each state has one vote. It took thirty-five ballots before Jefferson received the necessary majority. To prevent such an occurrence in the future, the Twelfth Amendment was added to the Constitution in 1804.

As the first woman to live in the White House, the well-informed, witty Abigail Adams enjoyed the give-and-take of the political scene.

It provided for electors to vote separately for President and Vice President.

The election of 1800 marked the end of Federalist rule. From 1789 to 1800, the Federalists had made impressive achievements. They had organized the new government. They had maintained peace in the face of serious threats from Britain and France. They had built a strong financial foundation for the new nation. It remained to be seen whether their opponents, the Democratic-Republicans and Thomas Jefferson could provide similar leadership.

CHECKUP

1. What were the first two American political groups called? How did they differ on foreign affairs?
2. What steps did Washington and Adams take to keep the nation out of war?
3. Why did the Alien and Sedition Acts arouse so much controversy? What were the reactions in Kentucky and Virginia?

Key Facts From Chapter 10

1. George Washington was the unanimous choice of the electors as the first President of the United States.
2. The first ten amendments to the Constitution are known as the Bill of Rights.
3. The Bill of Rights, ratified in 1791, guarantees to the people—against the power of government—certain basic liberties, including freedom of speech, religion, and the press and the right of assembly.
4. The differing ideas of Secretary of State Thomas Jefferson and Secretary of the Treasury Alexander Hamilton led to the formation of two political groups: the Federalists, who shared Hamilton's views, and the Democratic-Republicans, who shared Jefferson's views.
5. The Democratic-Republicans developed into the first political party in the United States.

★ REVIEWING THE CHAPTER ★

People, Places, and Events

Review Questions

1. What two precedents were established by George Washington during his Presidency?   *Pp. 251–252*

2. List the rights of the people that are protected by the Bill of Rights.   *P. 252*

3. What were the three main points in Alexander Hamilton's financial plan?   *Pp. 254–255*

4. Contrast Hamilton's and Jefferson's views on **(a)** the future of America; **(b)** the amount of power the central government should have; and **(c)** who should run the government.   *Pp. 253–254, 257*

5. How did Hamilton and Jefferson differ in their interpretation of the power granted to the Congress under the Constitution?   *Pp. 256–257*

6. What was the XYZ affair and how was it settled?   *Pp. 262, 264*

7. What was the significance of the Kentucky and Virginia Resolutions?   *P. 265*

8. Why was the Twelfth Amendment added to the Constitution?   *P. 265*

Chapter Test

*Write **H** if the phrase refers to Alexander Hamilton and **J** if the phrase refers to Thomas Jefferson. Use a separate piece of paper for your answers.*

1. Secretary of the Treasury

2. Favored a small central government with most power left to the states

3. Supported the idea of a national bank

4. Wanted the United States to become a nation of cities and factories

5. People with his political views were called the Democratic-Republicans.

6. Believed in a strict interpretation of the Constitution

7. Proposed the funding program to pay the nation's war debts

8. People with his political views were called the Federalists.

9. Belived that "those who own the country should govern it"

10. Secretary of State

11. Opposed the creation of a national bank

12. Favored a strong central government

13. Believed the average citizen was capable of holding government office

14. Wanted the United States to remain a nation of farmers

15. Supported the French Revolution

16. Proposed the assumption program to pay the state debts left over from the Revolutionary War

17. Opposed the French Revolution

18. Believed in a loose interpretation of the Constitution

19. Became the third President of the United States

20. Wrote the Declaration of Independence

THE PERIOD OF REPUBLICAN RULE

WHEN THOMAS JEFFERSON took office in 1801, he opened a long era of Republican control of the government. (The party name *Democratic-Republican* had by this time generally been shortened to simply *Republican*.) The Federalists would never again win the Presidency. Their belief in rule by an upper class made up mostly of merchants and large landowners was out of tune with the growing democratic spirit in the country. By 1816 the Federalists would fade from the scene completely.

The Republicans, who appealed more to small farmers, skilled workers, and plantation owners, were in command for the next twenty-four years. After eight years in office, Jefferson was succeeded by his friend James Madison. Madison also served two terms and was followed by James Monroe for another two. Because all three came from Virginia, their presidencies came to be called the Virginia Dynasty.

Jefferson's Program

Jefferson called his election "the Revolution of 1800." That was an exaggeration, of course. But it did point up a number of changes that Jefferson and the Republicans brought about. Hamilton had called the national debt "a national blessing." He meant that it would bind the wealthy, to whom it was owed, to the success of the government. Jefferson and Secretary of the Treasury Albert Gallatin believed the debt to be a burden rather than a blessing. They made plans to pay

it off in sixteen years. Since they also favored lowering taxes, one of the chief ways to reduce the debt was to cut government costs. Jefferson reduced the number of government workers, cut the size of the Army and the Navy, and did away with a number of judgeships. Despite the unexpected cost of buying the Louisiana territory, Jefferson still was able to reduce the debt by nearly a third in his eight years in the White House.

Soon after Jefferson became President, the Republicans in Congress repealed the hated whiskey tax (see page 261). They allowed the Alien and Sedition Acts to expire in 1801. They changed the waiting period for immigrants to become citizens from fourteen years back to five. And they repealed the Judiciary Act of 1801, passed in the final days of the Adams administration. You will read more about the repeal of the act later in this chapter.

Despite these changes, Jefferson left most of Hamilton's program untouched. The funding program and the assumption of state debts still stood. The Bank of the United States, or the B.U.S. as it was generally called, was allowed to run to the end of its twenty-year charter in 1811. And in spite of what Jefferson had written in the Kentucky Resolution in 1798, he made no move, as President, to shift the balance of federalism from the central government to the states.

A call for simplicity. Jefferson was the first President to begin his term in the nation's new capital city, Washington, D.C. In 1800 the capital had been moved there from Philadelphia. An unfinished city with a handful of buildings scattered along the Potomac River, this setting was fitting for an administration that called for simple, democratic ways. Jefferson dropped the practice of elegant weekly presidential receptions. He put into effect at the White House, the rule of first come, first served—regardless of one's social standing. He thought nothing of receiving foreign and American officials in the faded, threadbare coat and carpet slippers he often wore.

Jefferson set the tone of his administration with these words from his inaugural address:

> We have called by different names brethren of the same principle. We are all Republicans, we are all Federalists. Let us, then, with courage and confidence pursue our own Federal and Republican principles,

our attachment to union and representative government. . . .

> Still one thing more, fellow-citizens— [we need] a wise and [thrifty] Government which shall restrain men from injuring one another . . . [and] shall leave them otherwise free to regulate their own pursuits. . . .

The election of 1800 had been a bitter political battle, but it was plain that Jefferson now wanted unity and harmony.

The Barbary pirates. Jefferson was a man of peace and a champion of the farmer. Yet one of his first acts as President was to use armed force to defend America's commerce.

For many years pirates from the Barbary States—Morocco, Algeria, Tunis, and Tripoli—had seized ships in the Mediterranean Sea off the coast of North

In 1804, during the Barbary War, Lieutenant Stephen Decatur led a daring raid into the harbor at Tripoli. He burned the captured American ship *Philadelphia,* which the pirates were refitting for use.

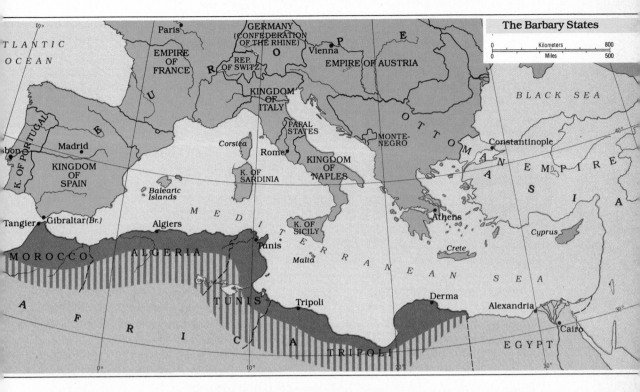

The pirates of Morocco, Algiers, Tunis, and Tripoli were a constant threat to American trading ships in the Mediterranean. After a temporary truce in 1804, pirate attacks continued off and on until 1815 when a United States fleet forced an end to pirate activity.

Africa. European nations found it easier to pay the pirates to leave the ships alone than to fight them. Under Washington and Adams, the United States had done the same.

Jefferson was opposed to paying such bribes. When Tripoli tried to raise the price for "protection" in 1801, the President put his foot down. Tripoli declared war, and Jefferson sent several naval ships to the Mediterranean Sea. The Barbary War lasted several years. The Navy failed to crush the pirates, as Jefferson had hoped. But America's show of force won new respect, and led to the end of some bribes. Tripoli made peace in 1805. Payments to the other Barbary States ended ten years later.

The Louisiana Purchase. The most important achievement of Jefferson's first administration was the purchase of the Louisiana territory. This was the vast region lying, for the most part, between the Mississippi River and the Rocky Mountains. The purchase was the result of a happy accident. Since 1763 Spain had controlled this area and also the

271

Mississippi River. The river was the western farmers' main route for getting crops to market. The crops were carried downriver on flatboats to New Orleans and were then shipped by ocean-going vessels to Atlantic ports and foreign countries.

In the Pinckney Treaty of 1795, Spain had given Americans the right to use the Mississippi. Spain also gave them the important "right of deposit" at New Orleans. This was the right to unload and store crops, without paying tariff duties, until they could be loaded onto larger ships for the ocean voyage. With about one third of its commerce going through New Orleans, the United States would have liked full control of the river and the port itself. But as long as Spain—a weak country—owned New Orleans and gave Americans permission to use the river, the United States was content with the situation.

Then, in 1802, Americans were shocked to learn that two years earlier Spain had secretly agreed to give Louisiana to France, and that the transfer would soon take place. Napoleon Bonaparte, the French dictator, wanted Louisiana to be a part of a new French empire on the North American continent. It would supply food for the sugar-rich French islands in the West Indies, especially the colony of Santo Domingo. The threat of a powerful and perhaps unfriendly nation—led by Napoleon—in control of New Orleans was cause for alarm.

Jefferson, greatly concerned, sent his friend James Monroe to Paris to join Robert Livingston, the American Minister to France. They were to try to buy New Orleans for $10 million. If they failed, Jefferson was willing to form an alliance with England to prevent the French from keeping New Orleans.

It was then that the United States had a stroke of good luck. It stemmed from a setback suffered by the French in the West Indies. On Santo Domingo, around the turn of the century, the slaves, led by Toussaint L'Ouverture, had rebelled. In 1801, Napoleon sent an army to put down the uprising; but disease and the rebelling slaves destroyed it. France lost control of the island.

Without Santo Domingo, Louisiana was of little value to Napoleon. Also, after a two-year truce, Napoleon was getting ready to make war again against England. He did not expect to be able to hold Louisiana against British attack. He therefore decided to get what he could for it. The startled American ministers, who were ready to offer $10 million for New Orleans, were told they could buy all of Louisiana for a little more money. Monroe and Livingston quickly agreed on a treaty. For $15 million, or less than three cents an acre, they doubled America's size. It was the biggest bargain in American history.

A constitutional problem. This windfall left President Jefferson with a problem. His vision of America was one of a nation of small farmers. By adding this territory, he believed that such a nation would be assured. However, Jefferson was also the champion of "strict interpretation" of the Constitution. In 1791 he had written to President Washington:

> I consider the foundation of the Constitution as laid on this ground—that all powers not delegated to the United States by

272

the Constitution, nor prohibited by it to the states, are reserved to the states, or to the people.

Yet nowhere did the Constitution say that the government had the right to acquire foreign territory.

For a while Jefferson considered a constitutional amendment that would allow the United States to buy Louisiana. He soon realized that by the time such an amendment could be ratified, Napoleon might have changed his mind. He therefore urged the Senate to approve the treaty and to worry about the constitutional problem later. The Senate did approve, and in December 1803 the United States took possession of the Louisiana Territory. It was not the last time in American history that the belief in limited government came into conflict with an opportunity or a national need. And it was not the last time that limited government came out the loser.

Among the first to explore the Louisiana territory were Meriwether Lewis and William Clark (see page 276) and Zebulon Pike. Pike explored the upper Mississippi region and, later, the Rocky Mountains. He sighted but did not climb the mountain now called Pikes Peak.

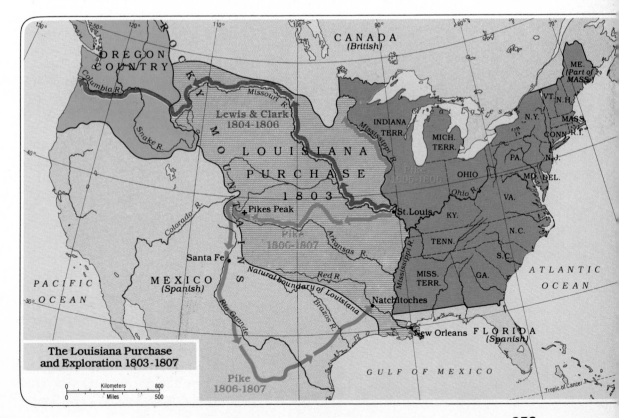

The Louisiana Purchase and Exploration 1803-1807

A minority view. Certain New England Federalists were dismayed by the purchase of Louisiana. The American West was filling up rapidly, and several new states—Kentucky, Tennessee, and Ohio—had already entered the Union. The Louisiana Purchase meant that still more western states would soon be created. The New England states, already in the minority, would then be so greatly outnumbered that they would have little influence in making national policy.

Led by Timothy Pickering of Massachusetts, these Federalists planned to lead the New England states out of the Union to form a "Northern Confederacy." When Hamilton and other leading Federalists rejected the idea, the planners turned to the ambitious Vice President, Aaron Burr. Burr wanted to run for governor of New York. The New England group approached Burr, hoping he would take his state into the proposed confederacy if he won. But Burr lost the election, with Hamilton leading the campaign against him. Nothing ever came of the confederacy scheme. But some months later, Burr had his revenge when he fatally wounded Hamilton in a duel.

Unseating the "midnight judges." With a Republican majority in Congress and a Republican in the White House, the Federalists' last stronghold was in the federal courts. That was because federal judges hold office for life. Most of the judges were Federalists who had been appointed by Presidents Washington and Adams. And as Jefferson noted, "Few die, and none resign."

In the final weeks of the Adams administration, Congress had created still more judgeships, by the Judiciary Act of 1801, and Adams filled them with Federalists. Because he was still signing their commissions, or appointment papers, the night before he left office, they came to be called the "midnight judges."

Jefferson and the Republicans were furious. The new Congress repealed the Judiciary Act of 1801, leaving all of Adams's judges without salaries or jobs. The Federalists claimed this action was unconstitutional. They said that the judges had been appointed for life, and Congress could not change the situation by eliminating their positions.

When Jefferson learned that the commissions had not yet been delivered to several of Adams's appointees, he or-

In 1792 Kentucky became the first state in the lands west of the Appalachians. Soon afterwards the building shown below was built to serve as the state house at Frankfort, Kentucky's capital.

dered Secretary of State James Madison to hold them back. One of those appointees, William Marbury, claimed that the commission was rightfully his. He asked the Supreme Court to order Madison to deliver it. The legal name for such an order is *writ of mandamus*, and the federal Judiciary Act of 1789 had given the Supreme Court the power to issue such a writ.

Marshall in *Marbury* v. *Madison*. In the case of *Marbury* v. *Madison* (1803), Chief Justice John Marshall ruled that Marbury ought to have his commission. He also said, however, that the Supreme Court could not order Madison to give it to him. The reason, said Marshall, was that the section of the Judiciary Act of 1789 giving that power to the Court was unconstitutional. Since the Constitution itself had not given this power to the Court, the Congress could not do so simply by passing a law.

Marshall's opinion was shrewd. In denying the Supreme Court a small power, Marshall had seized for it a much bigger one: the power to review acts of Congress and to declare them unconstitutional. From that time on, the Supreme Court has claimed this power. It is the power that raised the stature of the judiciary branch to the level of the other two branches of government—the executive and the legislative.

Striking at Federalist judges. Jefferson was angered by Marshall's claim of judicial power. More determined than ever to strike at Federalist judges, the President urged supporters in Congress to *impeach* a number of judges. Impeachment is the first step in removal from

John Marshall served as Chief Justice of the United States for 34 years. During that time, several decisions by the Supreme Court upheld the powers of the federal government.

office. The first target was John Pickering, a federal judge in New Hampshire. Pickering was both alcoholic and insane, but neither condition was constitutional ground for impeachment. Nonetheless, the House of Representatives impeached Pickering, the Senate convicted him, and he was removed from office.

The Jeffersonians' next target was Samuel Chase, a justice on the Supreme Court. Chase had offended the Republicans by his unfair treatment of several of them when they were tried under the Sedition Act. He had also attacked the Jefferson administration from the

The Lewis and Clark Expedition

President Thomas Jefferson began planning for exploration of the Louisiana territory even before the United States bought it. He was interested in promoting trade with the Indians in the lands west of the Mississippi. With the purchase of the territory from France in May 1803, the plans for exploration were quickly completed.

To lead the expedition, Jefferson selected Meriwether Lewis, his private secretary. Lewis chose William Clark, the younger brother of George Rogers Clark, to share the leadership with him. Both Lewis and Clark were Virginians and army officers and were used to dealing with the Indians.

The forty-five members of the expedition set out by riverboats from St. Louis in May 1804. After making their way slowly up the Missouri River, they stopped for the winter in the Mandan Indian country in what is now North Dakota. The next spring, they followed the Missouri River to its source. Then they traveled by foot, with pack horses, through the Rocky Mountains. They were helped through this wild, uncharted country by a remarkable Indian woman named Sacagawea. She and her husband, a French-Canadian trapper, served as guides and interpreters with the expedition. A member of the Shoshoni tribe, Sacagawea smoothed the way between her people and the explorers. During the trip the expedition met many different tribes of Indians, all of whom were friendly.

Lewis and Clark followed the Snake and Columbia Rivers until, in November 1805, they sighted the Pacific Ocean. Lewis wrote in his journal: "An Indian called me . . . and gave me . . . a piece of fresh salmon roasted . . . this was the first salmon I had seen and perfectly convinced me that we were on the waters of the Pacific Ocean."

The following spring the party started back. It reached St. Louis in September 1806. In the round trip the expedition had traveled 8,000 miles (12,800 km). It brought back much information regarding the geography, Indians, plant and animal life, and natural resources of the region. The trip also led to the growth of the fur trade. In later years the exploration became a basis for the United States' claim to the Oregon country.

The Lewis and Clark expedition meet a Chinook Indian party in 1805. Sacagawea, standing by Lewis, addresses the Indians in sign language.

bench, and had complained that allowing everyone to vote would cause the republic to "sink into a mobocracy." The House of Representatives impeached Chase, but the Senate did not convict him. With the failure to remove Chase, the Republicans gave up on their efforts to remove Federalist judges.

Despite the failure to root the Federalists out of the judiciary, Jefferson could look back on his first term with satisfaction. Most Americans felt the same way. In 1804 they reelected him by a wide margin over his Federalist opponent. Jefferson carried every state but Connecticut and Delaware.

CHECKUP

1. What changes in government did Jefferson bring about?
2. What did the United States achieve in the Barbary War?
3. What constitutional problem was involved in (a) the Louisiana Purchase? (b) the case of *Marbury* v. *Madison*?

Neutrality, Embargo, and War

"Peace is our passion," Jefferson once wrote. But the world was not at peace when he began his second term. France and Britain had renewed their struggle in 1803, after a two-year truce. Within a few years, Napoleon's army was the master of Europe. Britain, with its great navy, was supreme on the seas. The war then settled into a long struggle, much like a fight between a tiger and a shark, each the master in its own element.

At first the European war brought great prosperity to the United States. As the major neutral nation, it doubled its sale of goods to France and England between 1803 and 1805. Shipbuilding boomed, and America's merchant fleet grew enormously.

Soon, however, the situation changed. Since the two foes could not strike directly at each other, they tried to weaken each other by upsetting their enemy's trade. Each seized neutral ships trading with their foe. The United States was caught in the middle. Between 1803 and 1807, Britain seized 1,000 American ships, and France seized 500 more.

The impressment of seamen. Even worse than the taking of ships was the British practice of *impressment*—the seizure of sailors for service on British ships. Horrible conditions in the Royal Navy had led thousands of sailors to desert to America. Many of them went to sea again on American ships, carrying fake naturalization papers. To get their sailors back, British captains stopped American ships and took off those seamen they believed were British. Often they were not too careful about whom they took. They simply wanted manpower for their own ships. As one British naval officer explained, "It is my duty to keep my ship manned, and I will do so wherever I find men that speak the same language with me." In the ten years after the British renewed war with France in 1803, they took between 5,000 and 10,000 sailors off American ships. Probably three fourths were American citizens.

In June 1807 an incident with the British enraged Americans. The British frigate *Leopard* stopped the American naval ship *Chesapeake* within sight of the Virginia coast and demanded to search its crew for deserters. When the American captain refused, the *Leopard*

A British boarding party seizes a sailor on an American ship. Such boarding parties claimed the men they took were deserters from the Royal Navy, but the seized men were often Americans.

gress—in 1807—approved the Embargo Act. This law forbade all exports, whether in American or foreign ships. Also, no American ship was permitted to leave for a foreign port, even without cargo.

Jefferson reasoned that if there were no American ships on the high seas, Britain and France could not seize them and the British could not impress American sailors. More important, by denying American goods to the warring countries, Jefferson hoped to force them to change their policies. Boycotts had worked against Britain in the years before the Revolution. Jefferson hoped that such economic pressure would work again.

However, the Embargo Act hurt the United States far more than it hurt France or Britain. Ships lay idle, goods rotted on docks, and crops remained unsold. Exports fell to one fifth of what they had been. Sailors and others whose jobs depended on trade were thrown out of work. Merchants lost trade that, even with the seizure of some of their ships, had been profitable. Western farmers also felt the embargo's effect as the loss of European markets caused prices of their crops to drop.

Resistance to the embargo. No measure in America since the days of British rule was resisted as much as the Embargo Act. Federalists declared that the Constitution gave Congress the power to regulate trade, not to stop it. In their eyes, the embargo was unconstitutional. When ship owners and captains tried to get around the law, Jefferson used harsh measures to enforce it. He sent the militia to prevent the smuggling of goods across the Canadian border. The

fired, killing three seamen and wounding eighteen. The British then boarded the crippled ship and removed four sailors, only one of whom was British.

The Embargo Act. To Americans, this insult to their flag was the last straw. Many demanded war. Jefferson knew that would be unwise. With almost no Navy to fight back, he decided on economic pressure. On his urging, Con-

government hired officials to police the ports. Under the Force Act of 1809, federal officers could seize, without a court order, any goods they suspected were going to be shipped in violation of the embargo. Jefferson, the champion of limited government, was now using strong powers to back up his embargo policy.

Jefferson finally gave up. In the last days of his administration, Congress repealed the Embargo Act. It was replaced by the Non-Intercourse Act. This law prohibited trade with Britain and France, but it allowed trade with all other countries. Trade with either or both of the warring nations could begin again only after the violation of American rights ended.

Madison and American rights. The embargo helped revive the Federalist opposition to the Republicans in the election of 1808, but the Republicans still won handily. James Madison, the new President, was no more successful in ending the violation of our rights than Jefferson had been. When it was clear after a year that the Non-Intercourse Act was not working, Madison and the Congress tried another measure. This was Macon's Bill No. 2, passed in 1810. Under it, the United States allowed trade again with both Britain and France, even though they were still violating our rights. The law added, however, that if either country agreed to end the violations, the United States would stop trading with the other.

In 1802, only one wing of the Capitol had been completed. Both the Senate and the House of Representatives met in this modest building, and the Supreme Court convened in the basement.

For a while it seemed that this law might work. A few months after its passage, Napoleon announced that France would honor America's neutral rights. But Napoleon meant only to trick Madison. France went right on seizing American ships. Meanwhile, taking the French at their word, Madison told the British that under the terms of Macon's Bill No. 2, the United States would end its trade with Britain in early 1811. The British pointed out that the French actually had not stopped seizing American ships. This was true, but America paid no attention. Tensions between the two countries grew worse as the British continued to seize our ships and impress seamen. In the United States, the clamor for war became louder.

Western grievances. Although Britain's actions hit the ports in the East most directly, the demand for war was stronger in the West. Westerners had several grievances. They blamed British interference with American trade for falling farm prices. And they believed that the British were encouraging Indians in the Northwest to attack American settlers there.

Actually it was the settlers' greed for Indian land in the West that caused the Indians to resist. Between 1800 and 1810, through force or through trickery, Indians had been driven off 100 million acres (40 million ha) in the Ohio Valley alone. In an attempt to halt the white settlers' advance into their lands, a Shawnee chief named Tecumseh or-

Mounted troops under General William Henry Harrison attack Britain's Indian allies at the battle of the Thames in Canada. One of the casualties was the Shawnee chief, Tecumseh.

ganized Indian tribes from the Canadian border to the Gulf Coast. This Indian confederacy was effective for a time. But resistance crumbled after army troops under General William Henry Harrison fought Indians to a standstill at the battle of Tippecanoe in the Indiana Territory in 1811. That battle was only the beginning of a long, bloody period of warfare (see page 306).

Land hunger. Another reason why westerners wanted war against Britain was their hunger for even more land. Although over a million square miles (400,000 square ha) in the West had no permanent settlements, Americans along the frontier were casting hungry eyes on Canada. The belief that the British were stirring up the Indians from their base in Canada only added to the desire to take over the land. Settlers in the Southeast also saw war as a possible opportunity to seize Florida from Spain, Britain's weak ally. The United States had already seized a part of the Spanish territory in 1810.

A final factor in the West's demand for war was the desire to defend national honor. The issues of ship seizures and impressment did not affect the West as directly as they affected the East. However, westerners felt that America's honor should be defended against such British insults. In Congress these western views were expressed by a group called the War Hawks. They were led by the young Speaker of the House of Representatives, Henry Clay of Kentucky.

War is declared. Madison, like Jefferson, had hoped to avoid war. The growing demand for war was, however, too much for him to resist. On June 1, 1812, the President asked Congress to declare war on Great Britain. Seventeen days later, Congress did so. Most of the votes for war came from the South and the West. The majority of Congress members from the Northeast voted against war. Although that region had been hurt most by impressment and the seizure of American ships, its people feared that war would ruin their commerce completely.

The War of 1812 has been called a "needless war." Two days before Congress declared war, Britain had changed its policy of seizing American ships. But it took six weeks for that news to reach America. By that time, the two countries were already fighting.

Almost a disaster. The War of 1812 was almost a disaster for the young nation. Despite the demand for war, the country was ill-prepared. The army was tiny, and there were few volunteers. Leadership was poor. On the seas, Britain's navy greatly outnumbered America's. The country itself was badly divided, with New England bitterly opposing the war and withholding both money and men.

The American plans for war called for a three-way invasion of Canada. One force was to march from Detroit, a second along the Niagara River, and a third from the foot of Lake Champlain. All three invasions failed, and Americans soon were trying to keep the Canadians off American soil. Later, however, the United States won some victories in the West. American forces also defeated the Indians at the battle of the Thames in Canada in 1813 and at Horseshoe Bend in the Mississippi Territory in 1814.

Matters went badly on the sea. At first, American privateers were active, capturing 1,300 British trading ships. But the privateers were soon swept from the seas by Britain's fleet. The same happened to the small American Navy. The American frigate *Constitution,* called "Old Ironsides," won some stirring sea battles. But soon it and other naval ships were blockaded in American ports by Britain's powerful navy.

America's military fortunes reached a low point in 1814. A British force entered Chesapeake Bay, marched to Washington, and burned most of the government buildings, including the White House. James and Dolley Madison had to flee for their lives, with Mrs. Madison carrying her parrot, a picture of Washington, and some official papers.

A few bright spots. Only on the Great Lakes did American forces prosper. Control of the lakes was important because they lay along the invasion routes between the United States and Canada. In the battle of Lake Erie in 1813, Captain Oliver Perry secured command of the lakes. The next year, Captain Thomas Macdonough, with his victory at the battle of Plattsburg on Lake Champlain, prevented an invasion from Canada.

Perry's and Macdonough's victories were important in bringing the war to an end. In 1814 the British defeated Napoleon and were free to use their huge army and navy against the United States. But when the Duke of Wellington, the leading British general, advised that little could be achieved without control of the Great Lakes and the invasion routes from Canada, a war-weary Britain decided on peace.

Despite earlier military disasters, America ended the war on a note of triumph. In January 1815, General Andrew Jackson's troops won a brilliant victory at New Orleans. But the battle

When the British bombarded Fort McHenry in Baltimore Harbor in 1814, Francis Scott Key, an American who watched the attack, feared the fort would fall. When he saw the American flag waving the next morning, he excitedly composed the words of "The Star Spangled Banner."

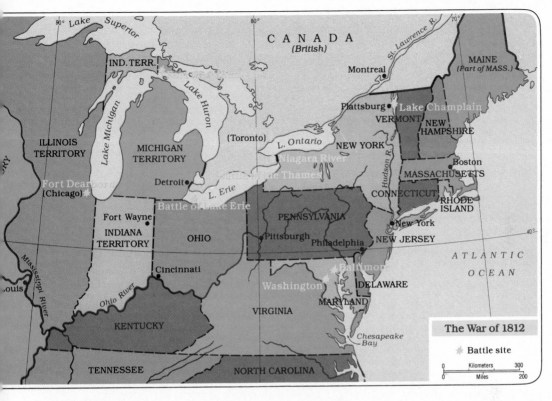

The War of 1812

★ Battle site

Though freedom of the seas was the big issue in the War of 1812, the major battles took place near the boundary between the United States and Canada. However, the only major land victory of the American forces occurred at New Orleans, far to the south of the area shown on the map.

was fought two weeks after the peace had been signed in Europe. The slow sailing ships that carried messages across the Atlantic played as important a role at the close of the war as they had played in the beginning.

The Treaty of Ghent. The peace treaty failed to settle a single question over which America and Britain had fought. By the Treaty of Ghent (1814), boundaries were to remain where they had been before the war, and all conquered

territories were returned. There was no mention at all of America's neutral trade, impressment, or blockades. But America emerged from the war with a greater sense of independence. First, Americans had won the last battle of the war. The victory at New Orleans helped them forget earlier defeats. Second, Britain showed a greater respect to the United States during the treaty negotiations and afterward. For this reason, the conflict has sometimes been called "America's second war of independence."

283

The Hartford Convention. Earlier you read of the Northeast's opposition to the war. The people in New England called it "Mr. Madison's War." In December 1814, New England Federalists met in Hartford, Connecticut, to protest the war and to propose a convention to revise the Constitution. Some of the organizers wanted New England to *secede* from—that is, to pull out of—the Union. They were in the minority, however.

The Hartford Convention proposed a number of amendments to make it more difficult for the national government to exercise certain powers. The delegates proposed requiring in each house of Congress a two-thirds majority to declare war, to admit new states, or to limit trade under such laws as the Embargo Act and the Non-Intercourse Act. They called also for limiting the President to one term, and for prohibiting successive Presidents from the same state. The latter was a slap at the Virginia Dynasty. Taken together, these proposals aimed to change the federal balance by shifting power from the national government to the states.

The delegates also adopted a statement declaring that when an act of the federal government violated the Constitution, each state was to have the right to ignore or disobey the act. The state was to be the judge of when that violation occurred. This resolution by the Federalists was little different from the Virginia and Kentucky Resolutions supported by the Jeffersonian Republicans sixteen years before.

Nothing came of the Hartford Convention except ill for the Federalists. Since they had met in secret session while the war was going on, their actions raised many suspicions. Republicans claimed the convention was really a plot to break away from the Union. Actually, the Federalists had done nothing disloyal— no more than Republicans had done during the Adams years. But the Federalists were never able to recover from the charge. When news arrived that peace had been agreed upon, they were still protesting the war and predicting a British victory. Thus they were further discredited.

The idea of limited government. The position of the Federalists in Hartford on the powers the national government should have was far different from what it had been two decades earlier. At that time, the Federalists controlled both the Presidency and the Congress. They then favored a "loose interpretation" of the Constitution and more power for the central government. At the same time, the Republicans, led by Jefferson and Madison, opposed that view.

After the Jeffersonians won the Presidency and the Congress, those positions appear to have been reversed. Then it was the Jeffersonians who stretched the Constitution to purchase the Louisiana Territory and to pass and enforce the Embargo Act. And it was the Federalists who argued for a stricter interpretation of the Constitution. The Hartford Convention climaxed their opposition.

All of this raises an important question: Just how deeply did Americans of that time believe in limited government? At first glance, it may appear that what a group believed depended on whether or not it was in power. Certainly that was true in part. It is also true, however, that a major aim of the "outs"—those who

Webster's American Language

The burst of nationalism that America experienced after the War of 1812 expressed itself in many different forms. One way was through changes in language suggested by Noah Webster, a native of Connecticut. Soon after the Revolutionary War, Webster, a graduate of Yale College, had written, "America must be as independent in *literature* as she is in *politics* . . ." He wanted to form a national "American" language that would be distinct from English. He was convinced the first step toward achieving America's literary independence would be to establish a uniform language throughout the United States. To do so, he published an American dictionary. It simplified the British spelling of many words,—for example, *honour* became *honor*. The first version of his dictionary was published in 1806, but the full work, *An American Dictionary of the English Language*, was not finished until 1825. It was published three years later.

In addition, Webster was concerned about the spoken language. If the dialects spoken in various parts of the country were allowed to become more and more different from one another, sectionalism would win out over nationalism. Realizing the binding power of a common language, Webster in his dictionary suggested a single way for pronouncing words.

Webster first became interested in words and language during the Revolutionary War when he taught school to earn money to pay for his law studies. While teaching in Goshen, New York, he noticed that most of the textbooks he used were written by English authors. An ardent patriot, he decided to remedy the situation. In 1783 he published a spelling book that standardized the spelling of many words. At the time of his death in 1843, *The American Spelling Book* had sold 15 million copies. Today the famous "blue-backed speller" is the only American book to have sold 100 million copies.

Noah Webster's dictionary carried the definitions of 70,000 words. Revised many times, it is still published and still bears Webster's name.

are out of office—is to become "ins." The fact that the "outs" believed they could win support by raising the cry of a too-strong government is an indication of the appeal that the idea of limited government had for most Americans.

CHECKUP

1. Why did Jefferson urge Congress to pass the Embargo Act?
2. Why did the Embargo Act encounter so much resistance?
3. What was accomplished by the War of 1812?

The Era of Good Feeling

The years immediately following the war saw a great burst of national pride and feeling. Americans felt they had won the war, and the way seemed open to a secure and prosperous future. Americans busied themselves with building their nation and advancing their fortunes. The absence of party fights led people then, and some historians since, to label the times "the Era of Good Feeling."

The decline of the Federalists left the Republicans in complete control of the national government. James Monroe was elected President in 1816 by 183 electoral votes to just 34 for the Federalist Rufus King. Four years later there was not even an organized opposition to Monroe's reelection, and only one elector voted against him. Jefferson's comment of 1801 that "we are all Republicans, we are all Federalists," had been only a figure of speech. By 1817 it was very nearly a political fact.

Approving a national bank. The good feelings of the times were reflected in Congress. The two parties agreed on issues that had divided them for twenty-five years. One such issue was a national bank. In 1791, Jeffersonians had fought bitterly against creating the Bank of the United States. When the bank's twenty-year charter came up for renewal in 1811, however, many leading Republicans had changed their minds. A bill to renew the charter barely failed.

The difficulties of the government in financing the war led many to see how useful it might be to have a national bank that could lend money to the government in times of crisis. In 1816, the Republican Congress—with hardly a murmer—gave a twenty-year charter to the Second Bank of the United States.

Protecting American manufacturers. The Republican view on tariffs had also changed. In 1791, Hamilton had argued for a high tariff on imported goods in order to encourage the growth of manufacturing in the United States. The tariff would raise the price of foreign (mostly English) manufactured goods. This, reasoned Hamilton, would protect America's "infant industries" against foreign competition until they could grow stronger and more efficient.

Jeffersonians, who did not want an industrial America, blocked Hamilton's plan. Ironically, the Jeffersonian policies later gave American manufacturers more protection than could have been given by any Hamiltonian tariff. Embargo, nonintercourse, and finally war almost shut out English goods from 1808 to 1815. With such protection, American manufacturing grew.

With the war over, there was fear that British manufacturers might "dump" their goods in America—that is, sell

★3★
Thomas Jefferson
1743–1826

Born in VIRGINIA
In Office 1801–1809
Party DEM.-REPUBLICAN

Agreed to Louisiana Purchase, thereby doubling size of United States. Sent Lewis and Clark to explore the Northwest. To keep out of European war, supported embargo on foreign trade.

★4★
James Madison
1751–1836

Born in VIRGINIA
In Office 1809–1817
Party DEM.-REPUBLICAN

Supported tariff to protect industry and urged national system of roads and canals. During War of 1812, had to flee from Washington when British burned the White House.

★5★
James Monroe
1758–1831

Born in VIRGINIA
In Office 1817–1825
Party DEM.-REPUBLICAN

Obtained Florida from Spain. Warned European powers against colonizing in the Americas. Monroe's two terms were called by some "the Era of Good Feeling."

---

below cost in order to drive American manufacturers out of business and recapture the American market for themselves. Republicans in Congress therefore voted a 20 percent duty on a number of imported goods. This was the first protective tariff in American history. Hamilton would have smiled.

Building roads and canals. A third subject on which Congress acted was "internal improvements"—the building of roads, canals, and the like. Such improvements would allow goods to move to and from markets, and would help tie together an expanding nation.

In 1811 work had begun on building the National Road from Cumberland, Maryland, across the Alleghenies to Wheeling, West Virginia. In 1816 Congress voted more money to extend the road to Vandalia, Illinois. Congress also passed a bill to set up a permanent fund to build internal improvements. President Madison, however, believed that this pushed the Constitution too far in the direction of government power. He vetoed the bill.

Acquiring Florida. The feelings of nationalism after the War of 1812 can be seen in the way that Florida was acquired from Spain. In 1810 and 1813, the United States had seized two small parts of West Florida, where Americans had settled. However, the rest of West Florida and all of East Florida remained in Spanish hands. This presented problems for the United States. Slaves from the southern states sometimes escaped into Spanish Florida. And Indians living there raided United States territory and then fled back to safety.

In 1818 President Monroe sent General Andrew Jackson into Florida to put a stop to these raids. Jackson defeated the Indians and also captured two Spanish forts. Spain, faced with revolts in its South American colonies, could do little to defend Florida.

Jackson's invasion strengthened the hand of John Quincy Adams, the Secretary of State. He had told the Spanish they should either control the Indians in Florida or else sell the territory to the United States. Fearing that the rest of Florida might be seized, the Spanish decided to sell. In 1819, the United States purchased Florida for $5 million. In the Transcontinental Treaty, Spain agreed also to give up its claims to territory in the Pacific Northwest.

Curbing government power. On July 4, 1826, John Adams and Thomas Jefferson died within hours of each other. They were among the last giants of the Revolutionary era to pass from the scene. Their generation gave the United States independence and guided the young nation through difficult years.

It was the generation of Adams and Jefferson that also burned into the American mind the idea of limited government. No short document ever put the case for that idea better than the Declaration of Independence. No group ever translated that idea into a workable government better than the federal Constitutional Convention.

The Revolutionary generation was not unanimous, as you have seen, on exactly what powers government should have. There were even times when circumstances led some American leaders to approve of the exercise of government powers beyond those they approved in theory. The Alien and Sedition Acts that John Adams signed almost surely violated the Bill of Rights. Jefferson's purchase of Louisiana stretched the

The United States's southeastern boundary was established by the addition of East Florida.

The Acquisition of Florida

Constitution to its limits. His embargo, and his strong enforcement of it, caused many to feel the hand of government.

Yet while there was disagreement about where to draw the line on government power, there was no disagreement at all that a line should be drawn. A useful way to gauge where Americans drew that line is to compare the United States government with others of the time. Nowhere else in the world did the power of government touch its citizens more lightly than in the United States.

That remained the case throughout the nineteenth century—except for the Civil War and the Reconstruction period—and well into the twentieth. Indeed, if Adams or Jefferson were to have returned to the United States of the 1880s, they would have found much that was familiar and comfortable in the practices of government at that time.

"How much government?" In time, industrialism, the rise of cities, and war—in short, modern society—would create the need for more positive roles for government. In our day, some of the ideas held by Jefferson and the Revolutionary generation on limited government seem almost quaint. Yet Americans are still fearful about unlimited government power. Even as government has taken on a larger role, a wary public continues to raise questions about it. Courts continue to protect the rights of individuals against abuses of governmental power. A watchful press continues to speak out when government overreaches itself.

"How much government is too much government?" asked the United States senator who was quoted at the start of this unit. It is a question that Americans have wrestled with from the very beginning. Every time it is asked, Americans approve once more the legacy of the nation's early years.

CHECKUP

1. How did the attitude of the Republicans change on (a) a national bank? (b) tariffs?
2. What action did Congress take during the Republican era regarding internal improvements?
3. How have Americans felt over the years about giving power to their government?

Key Facts From Chapter 11

1. The purchase of the Louisiana Territory from France in 1803 for $15 million doubled the size of the United States.
2. The United States went to war with Great Britain in 1812. A major reason was British interference with American shipping.
3. The War of 1812 ended without a clearcut victory for either side. It failed to settle a single issue over which the United States and Great Britain had fought.
4. A growth of national pride and an absence of party strife following the War of 1812 caused the period to be called by some "the Era of Good Feeling."

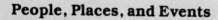

★ REVIEWING THE CHAPTER ★

People, Places, and Events

Barbary states *P. 270*

Napoleon Bonaparte *P. 272*

Robert Livingston *P. 272*

Samuel Chase *P. 275*

Embargo Act *P. 278*

Tecumseh *P. 280*

War Hawks *P. 281*

Oliver Perry *P. 282*

Andrew Jackson *P. 282*

Treaty of Ghent *P. 283*

Noah Webster *P. 285*

Second Bank of the United States *P. 286*

Review Questions

1. How was Jefferson justified in referring to his election as "the Revolution of 1800"? *P. 269*

2. Why was the Louisiana Purchase called the biggest bargain in American history? *P. 272*

3. What was the real significance of the *Marbury* v. *Madison* case? *P. 275*

4. List the grievances that caused the United States to go to war with Great Britain. *Pp. 277, 280–281*

5. Why was the War of 1812 almost a disaster for the United States? *Pp. 281–282*

6. What were the results of the War of 1812? *P. 283*

7. How did the Hartford Convention contribute to the decline of the Federalist Party? *P. 284*

8. Explain what is meant by "the Era of Good Feeling." When did it occur? *P. 286*

9. How did the United States acquire Florida? *P. 288*

Chapter Test

Select the correct answer for each statement. Write your answers on a separate piece of paper.

1. The most important achievement of Jefferson's first administration was the purchase of the (Barbary states, Louisiana Territory, Florida).

2. The case of *Marbury* v. *Madison* was concerned with the issue of ("midnight judges," impeachment, impressment)

3. Jefferson tried to keep the United States out of the European war by urging Congress to pass the (Alien and Sedition Acts, Judiciary Act of 1801, Embargo Act).

4. The Federalists lost all popular support as a result of the (Barbary pirates, Hartford Convention, "Era of Good Feeling").

5. The War of 1812 was fought between the United States and (Great Britain, France, Spain).

6. A naval hero of the War of 1812 was (Oliver Perry, Andrew Jackson, William Henry Harrison).

7. The War of 1812 was ended by the (Treaty of Paris, Pinckney Treaty, Treaty of Ghent).

8. The growth of national pride encouraged Congress to give a twenty-year charter to the (War Hawks, Second Bank of the United States, Virginia Dynasty).

9. In 1819, the United States paid $5 million to Spain for the territory of (Oregon, Florida, Louisiana).

10. The main theme of this unit has been Americans' concern about (limited government, opportunity, revolution).

FOCUS ON

Great Americans

MERCY OTIS WARREN

JOHN MARSHALL

TECUMSEH

JOHN QUINCY ADAMS

★ MERCY OTIS WARREN ★

Author for the American Nation

In a history of American feminism, Mercy Otis Warren appears as an early figure along with Anne Hutchinson and Abigail Adams. She was notable, a biographer wrote, "for her aggressive concern with public affairs and her insistence upon the right of women to have other than domestic interests." With her good friend Abigail Adams, she shared a respect for the female intellect and an impatience with the advantages given to men in education and public life. Mercy Otis Warren made important contributions to her country's struggle for independence and to its literature as well. These achievements were all the more remarkable because they were accomplished even as she performed the traditional roles of wife, mother, and keeper of the home—roles expected of her by society.

Mercy Otis was born in 1728 into a family whose roots had been planted deep in Massachusetts soil more than one hundred years before. A great-great-grandmother had come to America as a servant girl on the *Mayflower*, and a great-great-grandfather had been an early settler in the Massachusetts Bay Colony. Mercy was the third of thirteen children. The Otis family was comfortable, if not rich. Mercy's father made a good living as a farmer, merchant, and lawyer and was well respected in his town of Barnstable.

Mercy was raised as most girls were in her day. She learned household skills, which she would need later as a wife and mother. Although she learned to read and write at home, she received no formal schooling. However, Mercy tagged along with her older brothers to their tutor, and she was allowed to sit in on their private lessons. James, Jr.—the oldest of the Otis children—had a brilliant mind, and Mercy idolized him. Together they read and discussed the writings of the great political thinkers. They were especially drawn to those who wrote of liberty, limited government, and the natural rights of humankind. Those ideas were to form the foundation of the American Revolution. They were ideas that James and Mercy would support throughout their lives.

In 1754, Mercy Otis married James Warren, a merchant, farmer, and leading citizen of nearby Plymouth. They made their home in Plymouth and raised five sons there. In addition to having children, raising them, and running the household, Mercy Otis Warren managed to make time for reading. She also tried her hand at writing poetry about nature, friendship, and religion —subjects that were considered appropriate for women.

In time, Mercy's interests turned from poetry to politics. As the situation with Britain worsened in the 1760s and 1770s, leaders of the resistance in Massachusetts met regularly at her home in Plymouth. They included such men as James Otis, John Adams from nearby Braintree, Sam Adams from Boston, and of course, James Warren. (It is believed that the idea of Committees of Correspondence came from one of these meetings. See page 120.) We do not know if Mercy Warren took an active part in these meetings. Politics was regarded as the business of men. If a woman had political opinions, she might share them with her husband, as Abigail did with John. It was thought improper, however, to express those opinions publicly. Yet, at those private meetings, Mercy was among friends. It seems likely that she would have spoken her mind. Her own belief in the need to resist British authority later became clear in her writing.

It was at this time that Mercy Warren put her pen to work in the Patriot cause. Her friend John Adams admired her talent and encouraged her. She chose to write satire—using sharp wit to poke fun at the Tories in Massachusetts and hold them up to ridicule. For her first efforts, Warren chose poetry, a form familiar to her. In one poem she attacked certain well-to-do colonial women who were buying fine cloth and other goods from England in spite of the boycott (see pages 116–119). Next she moved to writing short plays in verse form. Mercy had never seen a stage performance, and her plays were meant to be read rather than acted.

In 1772, parts of her first play, *The Adulateur*, appeared in two issues of a Boston newspaper. Later it was printed and sold in pamphlet form. Her second play, *The Defeat*, appeared in the newspapers the following year. The plays were set in a fictitious land called Upper Servia. Every reader, however, knew that Upper Servia was really Massachusetts, just as they knew that the

plays' characters were the real-life villains and heroes of the American struggle. The leading villain was the hated Governor Thomas Hutchinson, the great-great-grandson of Anne Hutchinson. Mercy Warren named him "Rapatio," a name that stuck and later was used by many Bostonians to show

Mercy Otis Warren spoke out during a time when it was thought improper for women to concern themselves with public matters.

Museum of Fine Arts, Boston

displeasure with him. Warren also satirized timid citizens who believed in the Patriot cause but were afraid to stand up and be counted. The heroes, of course, were the Patriots. They were led by brother James Otis and included John Adams and Samuel Adams.

Mercy Warren's plays were published anonymously. Not only was it thought improper for women to write on political subjects but it would have been dangerous to sign one's name to writing that savagely ridiculed the governor and other powerful officials. Everyone in Mercy Warren's circle of friends, however, knew who the author was.

Sometime later, when Warren was criticized for being too outspoken for a colonial woman, she gave this reply: "Be it known unto Britain even American daughters are politicians and patriots, and will aid the good work with their female efforts."

The plays had popular appeal. Reassured by John Adams that her work was important, Mercy Warren continued to write for the Patriot cause. On April 3, 1775, just two weeks before the British marched on Concord and Lexington, her third and best play, *The Group*, appeared. As in her earlier plays, her target was the Tory leaders of Boston. *The Group* was very popular, and it was only with difficulty that Warren managed to keep her identity secret. After the Revolutionary War began, Mercy Warren wrote two plays on historical subjects. Two other unsigned plays may also have been hers.

In 1775, Mercy Warren began a project that she would not complete for thirty years. Ever since reading Sir Walter Raleigh's *History of the World* as a girl,

THE

ADULATEUR.

A

Tragedy,

As it is now acted in

UPPER SERVIA.

Then let us rife my friends, and ftrive to fill
This little interval, this paufe of life,
(While yet our liberty and fates are doubtful)
With refolution, friendfhip, Roman bravery,
And all the virtues we can crowd into it ;
That Heav'n may fay it ought to be prolong'd.
CATO's Tragedy

B O S T O N
Printed and fold at the New Printing-Office,
Near Concert-Hall.
MDCCLXXIII.

The Adulateur, the first of Warren's three Patriot plays, accurately mirrored the feelings of many Massachusetts colonists.

she had had a strong interest in history. With John Adams's encouragement, she began to write a history of the American struggle against the British king and Parliament. Even as she undertook this large task, Mercy Otis Warren was busy with her duties as wife, mother, and housekeeper. Her success lay in her dedication to the Patriot cause and her ability to organize time. In a letter to a niece, she wrote that if she carefully managed her day and wasted no time there would still be time for "the book and the pen."

After the Revolution, Mercy and James Warren became allied with the more democratic faction in Massachusetts. With Thomas Jefferson and others, they shared a belief in limited government and in the ability of the common people to govern themselves. Their beliefs put them at odds with many old friends, such as Abigail and John Adams and Sam Adams. Thus many of these people did not support James Warren when he ran for governor in 1785, and he was defeated. He lost again the next year in the race for lieutenant governor. Friendships were strained further by Shays's Rebellion (see page 212). The Adamses believed the government must crush the rebellion. Although James and Mercy Warren did not support the farmers' efforts to close down the courts in Massachusetts, they expressed sympathy for the plight that led these farmers to take such desperate acts.

Soon after, the Constitutional Convention opened in Philadelphia (see pages 215–219). No one stated the problem facing the delegates better than Mrs. Warren did in a letter to an English friend. "On the one hand," she wrote, "we stand in need of a strong federal government founded on principles that will support the prosperity and union of the colonies. On the other hand we have struggled for liberty . . . too much to limit . . . the rights of [the people]." The problem was to strike the right balance.

Mercy Otis Warren opposed the federal Constitution of 1787. She felt that the delegates had failed to protect the rights for which the Revolution had been fought. At the age of sixty, she presented her case against ratifying the Constitution in a nineteen-page essay titled *Observations on the New Constitution and on the Federal and State Conventions.* It was printed anonymously in Massachusetts and New York. Warren's main objection was that the Constitution lacked a bill of rights. She also believed that the President should not be given such great power, that there should be a limit on how long members of Congress could serve, and that there should be safeguards against a permanent standing army. In Massachusetts, a divided convention ratified the Constitution only after supporters promised to add a bill of rights. When that was done in 1791, Mercy Warren accepted the new Constitution.

Meanwhile, Warren continued with her writing. In 1790, she published a book of poems with her own name on the cover. In 1800 with eyesight failing, she turned to her history of the American Revolution, which she had worked on over the years. Now, at seventy-two, she determined to complete this work.

Five years later the book appeared— *The History of the Rise, Progress, and Termination of the American Revolution* by Mercy Otis Warren. The title was misleading, because by this time Warren's history had grown to three volumes and covered the 1780s and 1790s as well. In addition to being a history, it clearly stated her strong beliefs on natural rights, liberty, and democracy. Warren also expressed strong opinions about the people who did not share her views.

One such person was John Adams. On reading the book, the former President, then living in retirement in Quincy, exploded in anger. He was a proud man, and he believed that Mercy

This is a painting of the Warren house in Plymouth. How did the events that took place here help shape the history of the United States?

Warren had ignored his contribution to the Revolutionary cause. Worse, he was offended by the accusation that, as Vice President and President, he had "forgotten the principles of the American Revolution" and favored "monarchy." Adams told many people he regretted ever encouraging Mercy Warren to write the book. After a bitter exchange of letters, Adams cut off all dealings with his former friend. Their relationship was not patched up for seven years.

Mercy Otis Warren died at her Plymouth home in 1814. She had lived and died in a world in which a woman's interests could be satisfied only if they did not interfere with her traditional duties, and she accepted that world. Yet, unlike any other American woman of her day, she made important contributions in both the world of politics and the world of literature. This woman who never saw a play wrote at least five and possibly seven of them. In an age when women had no place in politics, her aid to the Patriot cause won the applause of men like John Adams and Samuel Adams.

When one thinks of the limits placed upon women in that age, one can only wonder: What might Mercy Otis Warren and thousands of other talented women have achieved had there been acceptance of a fuller role for them?

CHECKUP

1. Name the different forms of writing used by Mercy Otis Warren. From her writing on political topics, give examples of two of these forms.
2. What were Mercy Otis Warren's contributions to the Patriot cause? Explain how her life reflects both traditional and unusual roles for women during this period in American history.
3. List Warren's reasons for opposing the Constitution of 1787. What change led her later to accept the Constitution?

★ JOHN MARSHALL ★

Chief Justice of the United States

In a now-famous remark, a former Chief Justice of the United States noted that, while the Constitution is the law of the land, "the Constitution is what the Supreme Court says it is." Through this power to interpret the Constitution, the Supreme Court has played a major role in the development of the American government and nation. No judge did more to establish this power or used it with greater influence on the course of American history than John Marshall, Chief Justice of the United States from 1801 to 1835.

John Marshall was born in 1755 in a frontier log cabin in western Virginia. Germantown, now called Midland, was the nearest settlement. John, the eldest of fifteen children, was a cousin of Thomas Jefferson because their mothers were both Randolphs. However the Marshalls, though comfortable, did not have the wealth of the Jeffersons. John's father, Thomas Marshall, managed a large part of the land in western Virginia that was owned by Lord Thomas Fairfax. Thomas Marshall and George Washington had known each other since their youth, and Marshall had assisted Washington in surveying Lord Fairfax's land. Although the Marshalls moved twice as the family prospered, they remained in the region of the Blue Ridge Mountains. Thus John Marshall spent his entire youth within 30 miles (48 km) of his place of birth.

There were no schools in that region, but John's mother and father had had some education and taught John to read and write. His father also introduced John to literature, poetry, and history. One of Thomas Marshall's favorite writers was the Englishman Alexander Pope. Years later John recalled how he had been made to copy and memorize several of Pope's long poems as part of his education. At fourteen, John was sent to a school in Westmoreland County, about 100 miles (160 km) away. One of his classmates there was a future president of the United States, James Monroe. On his return home the next year, he continued to study English literature with his father. A local clergyman was hired to teach John the Latin classics, which educated people were expected to know. Among his friends on the Virginia frontier, John Marshall was the only one who acquired any formal education.

Marshall's parents wanted John to become a lawyer. His father bought him a copy of Blackstone's *Commentaries*, the great work on the English law. John studied this volume in his free time. Thus the future justice's introduction to the law came through self-study.

During the years of growing tension between Great Britain and the colonies, Thomas Marshall served in the Virginia House of Burgesses. When fighting broke out at Lexington and Concord, he and his eldest son organized the neighbors into a volunteer militia company, with Thomas as major and John as lieutenant. Called the Culpeper Minutemen, they took part in much of the

Even though John Marshall had little formal training for the law, his experience and brilliant mind made him an outstanding Chief Justice of the United States.

early fighting in Virginia at Great Bridge and Norfolk.

After the Declaration of Independence, John joined Washington's Continental Army as the lieutenant of a Virginia regiment. He later rose to captain. He was at Valley Forge during the cruel winter of 1777–1778 (see page 157). He also fought at Brandywine and Germantown in Pennsylvania, Monmouth in New Jersey, and Stony Point in New York. Marshall later said that it was

those experiences of fighting in so many parts of the country to create a nation that gave him his strong feeling of nationalism. During the war, he also came to know and admire George Washington. After Washington's death, Marshall wrote a five-volume biography of him. Marshall also got to know Washington's brilliant young aide, Alexander Hamilton.

When his three-year term of service was over in 1779, Captain Marshall returned to Virginia to await a new command. However, except for a brief return to duty late in 1780, his service in the war was over. Meanwhile, Marshall attended the law lectures of George Wythe for two months at the College of William and Mary in Williamsburg. This was the only formal training in law that the future Chief Justice of the United States ever received.

Even as he attended Wythe's lectures, John Marshall had his mind on other things too. On page after page of his notebooks appears the name Mary Ambler. John was twenty-four at the time; Mary was but fourteen. Three years later the two were married. In their long life together they had ten children, four of whom died. The Marshalls were a devoted couple, and when Mary became an invalid later in life, John gave her his never-failing attention.

After studying in Williamsburg, John returned to Fauquier County, Virginia, the Marshall family's home county. He was licensed to practice law there in 1780. Two years later, Marshall was elected to the Virginia legislature to represent the county as his father once had. By then, the state capital had been moved from Williamsburg to Richmond, which was Mary Ambler's home town. In 1783, John and Mary were married and set up their home in Richmond, where John also began a law practice.

Marshall had strong ideas about many issues before the country during his early years in office. As a strong nationalist, he was disappointed in the weakness of the central government under the Articles of Confederation. He also was deeply troubled by Shays's Rebellion in 1786 and its threat to property rights (see pages 212–213). He became a strong supporter of the movement for a new federal constitution and was one of the members of the Virginia convention who opposed Patrick Henry and voted to ratify the Constitution.

Following the adoption of the Constitution, Marshall concentrated on his growing law practice. He declined to run for Congress, and later turned down President Washington's offers to appoint him attorney general in 1795 and minister to France the next year. He also declined President Adams's offer to appoint him to the Supreme Court. However, with the threat of war between France and the United States in 1797, John Marshall agreed to serve as one of Adams's three commissioners on a special peace mission to France. This was the mission that led to the XYZ affair (see page 262).

In 1798 Mr. Washington invited Marshall to Mount Vernon. The invitation was actually a call to duty. Washington urged Marshall to reenter public life and run for Congress. The former President was Marshall's hero, and Marshall could hardly turn down this man who had already given half a lifetime to the service of his country. Marshall ran for Congress and was elected. Although a Federalist, he followed an independent course in Congress. He angered many in his party by voting to repeal the Alien and Sedition Acts (see pages 264–265).

In 1800, President Adams appointed Marshall Secretary of State after the Virginian had turned down the job of Secretary of War. Later that year, Oliver Ellsworth resigned as Chief Justice of the United States. Adams first offered the job to John Jay, who turned it down. Jay had been the country's first Chief Justice and thought so little of the job that he left it in 1795 to become governor of New York. The Court, Jay told Adams, would never gain enough "energy, weight, and dignity" to be really important. John Marshall suggested another person for the position, but the President decided against him. Finally, Adams turned to his Secretary of State and asked, "Who shall I nominate now?" After a few moments the President continued, "I believe I must nominate you."

Marshall officially became Chief Justice in February 1801. He stayed on without pay as Secretary of State until the end of the Adams Presidency on March 4. Thus it was Marshall who, as Secretary of State, signed the commissions of the "midnight judges" (see page 274) but failed to have William Marbury's papers delivered. The delivery was not made because the State Department's only clerk was on loan to the President for a few days! This led to the great case of *Marbury* v. *Madison*.

When John Marshall joined the Supreme Court, its unimportance in government was symbolized by its meeting place—a room in a small building far from the White House and Congress.

Only eight or nine cases a year came before the Court, which met two months out of the year.

Under John Marshall, the Supreme Court became a powerful force in American government. He immediately changed the way the Court announced its decisions. Formerly each justice had written an individual opinion for each decision the Court made. Marshall got the justices to agree to have the Court give a single opinion for the majority in each case. Thus instead of speaking with six voices, which were often in disagreement on their reasoning, the Court spoke with one voice. As a result, the Court's decisions carried more weight. These majority opinions gave the Court's final word on the meaning of the Constitution.

The Supreme Court has been meeting in this marble building since 1935. It is one of the most imposing buildings in Washington, D.C.

For thirty-four years, Marshall was clearly the leader of the Court in fact as well as in name. In the first four years, he wrote all but two of the decisions himself. Of the 1215 cases handled by the Court during his time, Marshall wrote the majority opinion in 519 of them. Partly through forceful personality and brilliant mind, the Chief Justice was usually able to get the members to agree unanimously with his view. In all those thirty-four years and 1215 cases, Marshall was in the minority only twice. This also added to the influence of the Supreme Court.

Under Marshall the Supreme Court made many decisions that dealt with the powers of the federal government. The Court established for itself the right of *judicial review*—that is, the authority to decide whether or not a law is constitutional. In *Marbury* v. *Madison* (1803), it declared a part of an act of Congress to be unconstitutional. A number of times it declared laws passed by the states to be unconstitutional. The Court also reviewed decisions of state courts when they involved constitutional issues, and it often reversed the lower-court decisions.

Like Alexander Hamilton, John Marshall favored a loose interpretation of the Constitution (see pages 256–257). He believed that the Constitution gave broad powers to the federal government. When national power came into conflict with state authority, the Court took the side of the national power, as in *McCulloch* v. *Maryland* (see page 352). In *Gibbons* v. *Ogden* (1824), he ruled that only the federal government could regulate interstate commerce. Marshall also interpreted the Constitution so as to

Mr. Ogden received sole steam navigation rights on the Hudson River from Robert Fulton, whose steamboat *Clermont* is pictured here. Mr. Gibbons objected. This led to the famous case of *Gibbons* v. *Ogden*.

protect property rights against interference by the states in *Fletcher* v. *Peck* (1810) and in the Dartmouth College Case (1819). Thus, during Marshall's long career as Chief Justice of the United States, the Supreme Court became a strong and respected branch of government, and the foundations were laid for the powers of the modern national government.

John Marshall died in the city of Philadelphia in 1835. On his funeral day, the bell atop Independence Hall, which had often rung to mark important events, sounded the nation's respect for the late Chief Justice. According to legend, the bell tolled so long that

day that it cracked, never to ring again. Today the bell is preserved in Independence National Historical Park in Philadelphia. It is known to countless millions of Americans and foreign visitors as the Liberty Bell.

CHECKUP

1. What was Marshall's education, including his training to practice law?
2. Explain the changes Marshall made in the way the Supreme Court worked. How did this help the Court become a powerful force in government?
3. Under Marshall, what positions did the Court take on issues dealing with the powers of government?

★ TECUMSEH ★

Leader of an Indian Confederacy

As one looks back upon the struggle between the American Indians and the white settlers for control of the land, only one outcome appears to have been possible. The victory of the settlers, with their technology and greater numbers, seems to have been inevitable. And so, in all probability, it was. Yet to those who took part in the struggle, especially in the early years, the outcome was not always so certain. In fact, for a brief time early in the nineteenth century, there were some on both sides who believed that the Indians might succeed in slowing, if not stopping, the advance of the white settlers (see pages 328–332). The reason was the rise of the Indian leader Tecumseh, one of the most remarkable persons in American history.

Tecumseh was born in 1768 in Old Piqua, a Shawnee village on the Miami River near the present city of Springfield, Ohio. The Shawnees originally lived in southeastern United States. They migrated to the Ohio River valley in the 1750s and soon were the most numerous tribe in the area.

Tecumseh grew up with a hatred of whites. It is not hard to understand why. The treaty that ended the French and Indian War in 1763 had reserved the Ohio Valley for the Indians. White settlers soon pushed into it anyway. Tecumseh's father and other Shawnee warriors had fought to stop this advance, but they had met defeat. In 1774 the Shawnees were forced to sign a treaty giving up their hunting grounds south of the Ohio River, in what is now Kentucky. Later that year, when Tecumseh was six, a band of white hunters killed his father in cold blood for refusing to serve as their guide. Three years later, Cornstalk, a Shawnee chief who was Tecumseh's boyhood idol, was murdered after being wrongly accused of killing a white settler. In 1780, when Tecumseh was twelve, troops led by George Rogers Clark raided Shawnee settlements north of the Ohio River and destroyed the village of Old Piqua. Two years later, Clark's soldiers did the same to the neighboring Shawnee town of Old Chillicothe. These experiences reinforced for Tecumseh the urging of his mother at his father's graveside: "Tecumseh, you shall avenge the death of your father and appease the spirit of his slaughtered brethren."

Tecumseh came of age as a Shawnee warrior as the Revolutionary War was drawing to a close. By that time, some white settlers had begun to cross the Allegheny Mountains into the Indian lands of the Ohio Valley. Tecumseh took part in a desperate guerrilla warfare to throw back those settlers. Indian warriors attacked whites in frontier settlements and forest cabins. They ambushed flatboats on the Ohio River. In turn, the Indians were attacked and massacred by settlers and army troops. The warfare between Indians and whites was cruel beyond description.

Tecumseh also took part in two successful campaigns against United States

302 *GREAT AMERICANS*

Army forces in 1790 and 1791. In 1790, General Josiah Harmar and about 1,400 men went into Indian country north of the Ohio River to put the United States government in control there. The main tribes in Ohio combined to drive Harmar back. The next year, at the headwaters of the Maumee and Wabash rivers, they dealt the forces of General Arthur St. Clair one of the worst defeats in American military history. More than half of St. Clair's 1,700 soldiers were killed or wounded, and the rest fled.

But in 1794, General "Mad" Anthony Wayne, with 3,600 men, defeated the Indians at Fallen Timbers, near present-day Toledo, Ohio. This broke the power of the Indians in the Old Northwest. At a peace council in Greenville, Ohio, the following spring, twelve Indian chiefs gave up their claims to the lower half of Ohio and to scattered plots of land around government forts in Upper Ohio. In exchange, they received goods worth about $20,000 plus the promise of small yearly payments to the tribe. These annual payments, which were called *annuities*, were a usual way of tempting poor Indians to sign over their rights to land. By the Treaty of Greenville, an area of about 25,000 square miles (65,000 square km) of land changed hands. That is an area larger than the state of West Virginia.

Tecumseh, who had fought at Fallen Timbers, refused to attend the peace conference at Greenville, He believed the land belonged to all Indians and that the chiefs had no right to sign it away. Yet he knew he could do nothing about it. As white settlers poured into Ohio, he, too, moved to the Indian side of the treaty line, into what is now Indiana.

The Treaty of Greenville brought a period of peace in the Northwest Territory. But Tecumseh knew it would not last. White settlers continued to arrive. In 1801, President Jefferson appointed William Henry Harrison, who later became the ninth President of the United

This portrait, based on an eyewitness description and sketch, shows Tecumseh wearing a British uniform and medal as well as traditional Shawnee headdress and ornaments.

States, as governor of the Indiana Territory. The very next year Harrison began pressuring individual chiefs to sign over pieces of land in exchange for small annuities. Desperately poor, weakened by sickness and by the white people's whiskey, the Indians seemed powerless to resist. Bit by bit, land was handed over to the white settlers.

During these years, however, events were occurring that held out hope for a change in the Indians' fortune. More and more, the younger Indians were looking to Tecumseh as their leader. He was already known for his deeds as a warrior. According to one who knew him well, he was "perfectly fearless of danger. He always inspired his companions with confidence." To this was added a reputation as an orator of great power. Although he knew English, he refused to speak publicly in anything but his own tongue. Those who understood Shawnee said that as a frontier orator he was the equal of Henry Clay. He also used his commanding appearance to good effect. "When Tecumseh rose to speak," reported one white eyewitness, " . . . he appeared one of the most dignified men I ever beheld. While this orator of nature was speaking, the vast crowd preserved the most profound silence."

At the councils of white and Indian leaders, Tecumseh was a militant defender of Indian rights. He denounced outrages suffered by the Indians and recounted the trail of broken treaties since Jamestown. The Indians would observe the Treaty of Greenville, he said, even though it was not a just treaty. But they would be pushed back no farther. "These lands are ours. No one has a right to remove us," said Tecumseh,

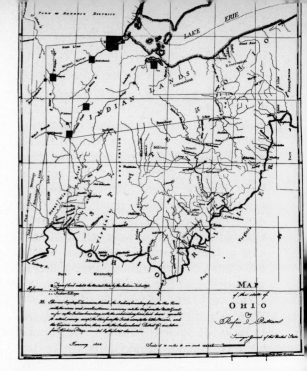

Ohio became a state in 1803. This map, drawn in 1804, shows the territory in the northwestern part of the state that was still Indian land at that time.

"because we are the first owners. The Great Spirit above has appointed this place for us, on which to light our fires, and here we will remain."

Meanwhile, Tecumseh's younger brother, Tenskwatawa, had become a religious leader among the Indians of the Northwest Territory. He took to preaching to the Indians with such great energy and effect that he became known as the Prophet. Indians had lost their lands and had fallen low, he told them, because they had forsaken Indian ways for the ways of the whites. Only when the Indians gave up their wicked ways, especially drinking, would their lands be restored to them. He told them to stop fighting among themselves and live in harmony with the "Master of

Life." The Prophet's preaching, along with his mystical visions, led to a kind of religious awakening among the Indians. Tenskwatawa's following increased greatly after 1806, when he foretold the eclipse of the sun. Two years later, hundreds of Indians went with Tenskwatawa and Tecumseh to live at Prophet's Town, a village on the Tippecanoe River in Indiana Territory.

The religious revival began tightening the bonds of friendship among the Indian tribes. But Tecumseh knew that a plan of action would be needed to save the land. As long as the United States government could deal with Indian tribes one at a time, it could defeat them in battle or take advantage of them in treaties. If all the tribes united in one great confederation, they could stand firm against threats to their lands. Tecumseh's plan included becoming allied with Great Britain, which also opposed United States control of the Northwest Territory. With British aid and support, Tecumseh felt he could build a strong and armed defense against the white settlers.

By 1807, this plan for an Indian confederation had become the driving purpose in Tecumseh's life. Traveling by horse, by canoe, and on foot, he visited every tribe east of the Mississippi River from the Great Lakes to the Gulf of Mexico during the next four years to win the tribes to his plan. Among the Ottawa, Potawatomi, Winnebago, Kickapoo, Wyandot, Delaware, Sauk, Fox, Miami, Chippewa, and Menomini, he met with success. These, along with his own Shawnee tribe, were the tribes that occupied the Northwest Territory— present-day Ohio, Indiana, Illinois,

Michigan, and Wisconsin. The Southern tribes and the Iroquois of New York, however, did not go along. Meanwhile, the United States government moved to get the Indians to give up another large area of land. While Tecumseh was away in 1809, Governor Harrison called for a great council of chiefs to meet at Fort Wayne. There, with the aid of whiskey and the promise of more annuities, he got the desperately poor Indians to part with another 4,700 square miles (12,200 square km) on the Wabash and White rivers. The total cost to the United States in gifts and annuities was $10,550. That came to less than half a cent an acre!

When he returned, Tecumseh was enraged to learn what had happened at Fort Wayne. In an angry meeting with Harrison, Tecumseh demanded that the treaty be torn up. The land, he said, "belongs to all, for the use of every one. No groups among us have a right to sell, even to one another. . . ." At another point he exclaimed, "Sell a country! Why not sell the air, the clouds, and the great sea, as well as the earth? Did not the Great Spirit make them all for the use of his children?" But Harrison would not budge.

Once again, Tecumseh headed south to win support for his confederacy. Tirelessly, he pushed for union among the powerful Indian tribes so that they would not fall, one by one, before the white advance as in the past. "The annihilation of our race is at hand, unless we unite in one common cause against the common foe," he warned. But while the younger warriors spoke in support, the more cautious chiefs held back. Some were already receiving annuities.

Sir Isaac Brock, victorious British leader at the battle of Detroit, was encouraged by Tecumseh to attack the fort. Tecumseh was admired as a military man and a leader of his people.

Others believed they could not win a war against the United States government.

Harrison watched the activities of Tecumseh and the Prophet with concern. He feared that if the Indians united they might wipe out the white settlements in Indiana. He also believed the British were responsible for arming and encouraging the Indians. In the fall of 1811, Harrison marched on Prophet's Town with an army of 900. Tecumseh, who was again in the South, had left the Prophet with orders to avoid a battle. All the Indians must be united first to fight together. But some of the Prophet's followers wanted to do battle, and Harrison's forces then destroyed Prophet's Town in the battle of Tippecanoe.

Tecumseh first learned of what had happened when he returned and found his home in ruins. He was furious with his brother for allowing the Indians to attack, but the damage had been done. The defeat at Prophet's Town took much of the steam out of the movement for union.

As tensions grew between Great Britain and the United States during these years, Great Britain tried to keep the friendship of the Indians. In 1812 fighting broke out between the two countries. Tecumseh urged the Indians of North America "to form ourselves into one great combination and cast our lot with the British in this war." A number of tribes in the Northwest fought with the British under Tecumseh's leadership. They played an important part in stopping General William Hull's invasion of Canada and in the later capture of Detroit.

In 1813, Tecumseh was killed in the war at the battle of the Thames River in southern Canada (see the picture on page 280). The dream of an Indian confederacy died with Tecumseh. Perhaps such a union could never have been achieved. And it may well be that even such a union could not have changed the course of the struggle. But for a few brief years, at least, Tecumseh provided the Indian tribes in the United States a hope, an example, and a vision.

CHECKUP

1. Describe how Tecumseh's life was an example of strength and support for the Indian way of life in the early nineteenth century.
2. What was Tecumseh's plan for an Indian confederacy?
3. What events led to Tecumseh's death in 1813?

⋆ JOHN QUINCY ADAMS ⋆

Raised to Be President

If ever a person was brought up to be President, it was John Quincy Adams. Born in 1767, this eldest son of John and Abigail Adams grew up in the birth-time of the American nation. In later years he recalled walking as a child with his mother to the top of a hill near their Braintree, Massachusetts, farm and watching British cannons fire on Bunker Hill. The Adams household was filled with talk of the rights of Americans. In such a family, it would have been hard not to become steeped in the spirit of the American Revolution and duty to one's country.

From the first, John Quincy's parents steered him in the direction of public service. "Together," writes his biographer, "they worked to mold his character." Abigail Adams often reminded her son that he must someday be the "guardian of his country's laws and liberties." To prepare him, continues this writer, "they prescribed his education to a degree that would stagger a modern psychologist." John did not attend school. The town of Braintree had closed its only grammar school to save money for the war, and the teacher had joined the army. John was taught at home, and by age ten, he was reading English literature and knew some French, Latin, and Greek.

When John Adams was sent to France by Congress in early 1778, he took his ten-year-old son with him. Except for a brief return to Boston the following year, John Quincy spent the next seven years in Europe. In Paris he attended a boarding school. He excelled in languages, and within a few years he could read French, German, Latin, Greek, and a little Spanish. He later picked up Dutch when his father became minister to the Netherlands.

In 1781, young John's language skills brought him his first assignment to serve his country. The American representative in Russia needed an interpreter to translate and copy official letters.

Of all the men who had been President, John Quincy Adams was the first to be photographed. The picture was taken long after he had left office, when he was an old man.

The Treaty of Ghent, ending the War of 1812, was signed on Christmas Eve, 1814. John Quincy Adams represented the United States. Great Britain's chief representative was Lord Gambier.

On the recommendation of his father, fourteen-year-old John Quincy was offered the job.

After a year in Russia, John returned to Paris and served as his father's private secretary. In this position, he often found himself in the company of some of the leaders of France and America. He wrote in his diary that of all the people he met, he most enjoyed his evenings with his father's good friend Thomas Jefferson.

In 1785, John Quincy Adams returned to the United States to attend Harvard College. After graduation he studied law, and in 1790 he began a practice in Boston. However, the young Adams never enjoyed the law as his father had. He continued to read his-

tory, literature, and science, and to await an opportunity for a role in public life. When President George Washington offered him the job of minister to the Netherlands, John Quincy gladly accepted the post. Nearly three years in the Netherlands were followed by three more as minister to Prussia. His work in Holland impressed Washington, who called John Quincy Adams America's most valuable public servant abroad.

In 1801, John Quincy Adams returned to America and became involved in politics. He was elected to the Massachusetts Senate and, in 1803, to the United States Senate. Though Adams was elected as a Federalist and shared many of the views of others in that party (see pages 219–222), he was never a strict party person. He was the only New England Federalist in Congress to support the plan of Thomas Jefferson to buy Louisiana. Unlike the Federalists who feared that westward expansion would weaken New England's influence in the country, Adams put nation ahead of section (see page 274). Adams had no time for those in his party who urged New England to secede and form a new confederacy with New York State.

Adams also supported President Jefferson's policies to end England's interference with America's neutral rights. He even voted for the Embargo Act, which New Englanders bitterly opposed. To one senator who had voted with him, Adams said, "This measure will cost you and me our seats, but private interest must not be put in opposition to public good."

He was right. Angry Massachusetts Federalists refused to nominate Adams for a second term in the Senate. In his retirement in Quincy, Massachusetts, the elder John Adams was saddened. His hopes for his son's advancement in public service had been dashed. There was nothing to do now, he advised John Quincy Adams, but to return "to your office as a lawyer. Devote yourself to your profession and the education of your children." John Quincy agreed, for he also believed his public career was ended.

To his surprise, it was not. Only days after James Madison took office as President, he appointed Adams to serve as minister to Russia. Adams served in that post from 1809 to 1814. He was in Russia when the War of 1812 broke out. When the opportunity to make peace with Britain arose in 1814, Madison called on Adams to head America's peace commission. Adams was the country's most experienced diplomat at the time.

At the beginning of negotiations with Britain, there was friction among the five American commissioners, especially between Adams and Henry Clay. With his seriousness of purpose, his devotion to duty, and the self-discipline that had been drilled into him by his parents, Adams had a somewhat chilly and distant personality. No less aware of his duty than Adams, Clay was a warm and outgoing son of the frontier. He enjoyed smoking, horse racing, and gambling. Adams began each day at 5:00 A.M. by reading the Bible. That, he complained, was just about the time that Clay's card party was breaking up down the hall. Nonetheless, the commissioners grew to respect one another. Together they won a better peace treaty than many had thought possible (see page 283). At the end of the negotiations, President Madison appointed John Quincy Adams minister to England.

In 1816, James Monroe was elected President. He promptly called Adams home to serve as Secretary of State. It was a fitting appointment. Adams was probably the most qualified man in the country for the job. In Massachusetts, John and Abigail Adams learned the news with joy. Both Madison and Monroe had moved from Secretary of State to President, and people widely viewed the office as a natural stepping-stone. Abigail proudly wrote her son that people were now mentioning him as one "worthy to preside over the counsels of a great nation."

Adams gave his most valuable service to the country during eight years as

Secretary of State. He succeeded in acquiring East Florida from Spain. He also dealt with a number of problems left unsettled in the Treaty of Ghent, including an agreement with England about the border between Canada and the United States as far west as the Rockies.

Another notable achievement in which Secretary of State Adams shared was the Monroe Doctrine. Nearly all of Spain's colonies in Central and South America had rebelled and set up their own governments by 1820. However, these governments were still weak, and the United States was concerned that some European nations might try to take control of them. Adams proposed that the United States tell the world that it opposed interference in the Western Hemisphere. President Monroe gave this message to Congress in 1823:

> . . . the American continents, by the free and independent condition which they have assumed and maintain, are henceforth not to be considered as subjects for future colonization by any European powers. . . .
>
> . . . The political system of the allied powers [in Europe] is essentially different . . . from that of America. . . . We owe it, therefore, . . . to declare that we should consider any attempt on their part to extend their system [of government] to any portion of this hemisphere as dangerous to our peace and safety.

In short, John Quincy Adams and President James Monroe told Europe, "Hands off the New World."

In 1825, John Quincy Adams became the sixth President of the United States. Abigail had died in 1818, but John lived to see the fulfillment of his and Abigail's dreams and ambitions for their son.

Unhappily, John Quincy Adams's Presidency could not be called a success (see pages 339–341), and he was defeated for reelection.

Embittered by this rejection, Adams retired to Quincy, once again believing his public career was over. The citizens of his district wished otherwise. In 1831 they asked Adams to represent them in the House of Representatives. He was elected for eight additional terms.

John Quincy Adams was the only President ever to serve in the House after his Presidency. As one might expect, he voted on measures without regard to party, always putting nation ahead of section, and principle above party. His chief concern in these years was to restrict the spread of slavery in the West (see Chapter 13). Adams even opposed the annexation of Texas—which as President he had tried to buy from Mexico—because it would mean the expansion of slavery.

On February 21, 1848, while at his seat in the House of Representatives, Adams suffered a stroke. He died two days later without regaining consciousness. If this man, driven always by his sense of duty, could have chosen his own end, most certainly he would not have wished it otherwise.

CHECKUP

1. Explain how Adams's childhood reflects the phrase "Raised to be President."
2. What did John Quincy Adams do to serve his country before and after he was President of the United States?
3. List positions that he took on public issues while in Congress, and explain how those positions show that Adams put nation before section.

1787	Constitutional Convention
	Northwest Ordinance
1789	New government goes into effect
1791	Bill of Rights adopted
1795	Jay's Treaty
1800	Washington becomes capital
1803	Louisiana Purchase
1805	Lewis and Clark reach the Pacific
1807	Embargo Act
1812	
	War of 1812
1814	
1815	Battle of New Orleans
1819	Acquisition of Florida completed

Under the Articles of Confederation, which went into effect in 1781, the United States government was weak and ineffective. In 1787 a group of state delegates met in Philadelphia to revise the Articles. Instead, those at the meeting, now known as the Constitutional Convention, wrote a new constitution. It became the law of the land in 1788. The Bill of Rights was added in 1791.

George Washington, as the first President, oversaw organization of the federal government. Secretary of State Thomas Jefferson and Secretary of the Treasury Alexander Hamilton differed on many issues. Out of their differences there developed, in time, the first political parties. Washington and his successor, John Adams, kept the United States neutral during troubles in Europe. Adams had a stormy term of office, and failed to win reelection.

Thomas Jefferson's election in 1800 ushered in twenty-four years of Republican rule. In 1803 the purchase of the Louisiana Territory from France doubled the size of the United States. Freedom of the seas became a crucial issue when war between Britain and France threatened American shipping. Measures taken by Jefferson and his successor, James Madison, to meet the situation were unpopular. The issue of freedom of the seas brought on the War of 1812 with Britain. Though neither side could claim victory, the United States emerged with an upsurge of national pride. James Monroe's administrations (1817—1825) were called by some "the Era of Good Feeling."

311

Skills Development: Analyzing Source Material

The following primary source material presents excerpts from President Jefferson's letter of instructions to Meriwether Lewis. Lewis, along with William Clark, led an expedition that explored the vast Louisiana Purchase. Read the source material and then answer the questions.

The object of your mission is to explore the Missouri River, and such principal stream of it, as, by its course and communication with the water of the Pacific Ocean may offer the most direct and practicable water communication across this continent, for the purposes of commerce.

Your observations are to be taken with great pains and accuracy, to be entered distinctly and intelligibly for others as well as yourself to comprehend all the elements necessary. . . . Several copies of these [observations] . . . should be made at leisure times and put into the care of the most trustworthy of your attendants. . . . A further guard [against accidental loss] would be that one of these copies be written on the paper of the birch, as less liable to injury from damp than common paper.

The commerce which may be carried on with the [Indians] renders a knowledge of these people important. You will therefore endeavor to make yourself acquainted . . . with the names of the nations and their numbers; . . . their language, traditions, monuments; their ordinary occupations in agriculture, fishing, hunting, war, arts, and the implements for these; their food, clothing, and domestic accommodations; the diseases prevalent among them . . . and articles of commerce they may need or furnish and to what extent.

Other objects worthy of notice will be: the soil and face of the country, . . . the animals of the country generally, and especially those not known in the U.S.; . . . the mineral production; . . . volcanic appearances; climate. . . .

. . . treat [the Indians] in the most friendly and conciliatory manner which their own conduct will admit; . . . make them acquainted with . . . our wish to be neighborly, friendly, and useful to them. . . .

As it is impossible for us to foresee in what manner you will be received by those people, whether with hospitality or hostility, so is it impossible to prescribe the exact degree of perseverance with which you are to pursue your journey. . . . To your own discretion, therefore, must be left the degree of danger you may risk, and the point at which you should decline, only saying we wish you to err on the side of safety, and to bring back your party safe, even if it be with less information.

1. Based on the evidence in the source material, tell how you think Jefferson felt about the following things.

   a. Relations with the Indians
   b. Knowledge of the new land's physical geography
   c. The value of keeping records
   d. The expedition's success compared with the explorers' safety
   e. Opening up trade routes and expanding American commerce

2. Write a paragraph describing the kind of person Jefferson must have been, as revealed by these instructions.

Unit

4

Americans: A People on the Move

EXPANSION, DEMOCRACY, AND INDUSTRIALISM

CHAPTER
12
WESTWARD THE FRONTIER

STRETCHING FROM THE CAROLINAS on the East Coast to southern California on the West Coast is an arc of warm land called the Sunbelt. This area occupies about a third of the United States. It is the fastest-growing part of the country today. In the 1960s the population of the states in the Sunbelt grew one and a half times as fast as that of the other states.

Increases during the 1970s were even greater. By 1975 the population had gone up by the following percentages: Arizona, 25.3; Texas, 9.3; Florida, 23; South Carolina, 8.8; New Mexico, 12.7. During this same time, northern states such as Pennsylvania, Illinois, Indiana, New Jersey, Ohio, and Iowa were barely holding their own, and New York was losing ground.

This shifting of population is part of a much larger pattern. Today one of every three Americans lives in a state other than the one in which he or she was born. Of the remaining two out of three, a good many have moved from one place to another within the same state. Every year one in five Americans changes residence. One writer has suggested, perhaps not entirely in jest, that the national symbol is not the eagle but the moving van.

Our very language is the language of a people on the move. One widely used book on American slang uses thirteen columns of the index just to list all the slang expressions with the word *go* in them.

One writer has summed up this American characteristic in this way:

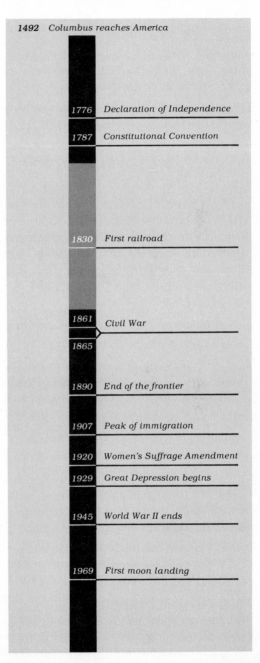

1492   *Columbus reaches America*

1776   *Declaration of Independence*

1787   *Constitutional Convention*

1830   *First railroad*

1861   *Civil War*

1865

1890   *End of the frontier*

1907   *Peak of immigration*

1920   *Women's Suffrage Amendment*

1929   *Great Depression begins*

1945   *World War II ends*

1969   *First moon landing*

. . . Americans have moved and have kept moving from farm to farm, from state to state, from town to town, back and forth, from job to job, around and around. There is a fever in our blood. We have itching feet. Here today and gone tomorrow. Let's go. 'Scuse our dust. Fill 'er up. Freewheeling. Howdy, stranger.

In short, Americans are the most mobile people on the face of the earth.

A restless people. The restlessness of Americans is nothing new. Travelers to our country have made note of it for 150 years. A South American visitor in the 1840s commented that "if God were suddenly to call the world to judgment He would surprise two thirds of the American population on the road like ants." A visitor from France had observed ten years earlier:

> [The American man is] not only a worker, he is a migratory worker. He has no root in the soil; he is a stranger to the worship of one's birthplace and family home; he is always in the mood to move on, always ready to start in the first steamer that comes along from the place where he had just now landed. He is devoured with a passion for movement; he cannot stay in one place; he must go and come. . . .

The most famous of all traveler accounts is *Democracy in America*, written in 1835 by a young Frenchman, Alexis de Tocqueville. In it, he said:

> In the United States a man builds a house in which to spend his old age, and he sells it before the roof is on; he plants a garden and [rents] it just as the trees are coming into bearing; he brings a field into tillage and leaves other men to gather the crops; he embraces a profession and gives it up; he settles in a place, which he soon afterwards leaves to carry his changeable longings elsewhere.

How can one account for the restlessness of Americans? One explanation may lie in the fact that America was populated by people from other lands. They had broken away from the village or piece of land to which their ancestors were tied for hundreds of years. Thus they were rootless. With no ties to any one place, they were always on the move.

Perhaps the restlessness comes from being part of a culture that stresses opportunity and rising in the world. Newspapers, political leaders, Fourth of July orators—all speak glowingly of America's opportunities. In such a society, the reasoning goes, one must be ready to seize the opportunity that arises, whether that be moving to lands in the West or to the growing cities. Perhaps that is what Tocqueville had in mind when he wrote:

> The American has no time to tie himself to anything. He grows accustomed only to change, and ends by regarding it as the natural state of man. He feels the need of it, more, he loves it; for the instability, instead of meaning disaster to him, seems to give birth only to miracles all about him.

Across the Mountains

Whatever may be the cause of the restlessness of Americans, much of their history is tied directly to this quality. More than anything else, it is the restlessness of the people that gave America its present-day boundaries. It affected our relations with other nations. It contributed to the tragic history of the native peoples of North America. It leveled forests, raised up cities, and settled a continent in an incredibly short time.

Daniel Boone

One of the first pioneers to venture into the wilderness across the Appalachian Mountains was Daniel Boone. As a youth on the North Carolina frontier, he first heard of a land called Kentucky. In 1769 he and his brother set out along an Indian trail. It led them through the mountains by way of a natural pass called Cumberland Gap. The country they came to was all that Boone had dreamed of. The soil was rich. Buffalo grazed on the bluegrass. Deer and panther roamed the forests. Great flocks of passenger pigeons darkened the skies.

Six years later, Boone guided the first permanent settlers to Kentucky. They founded a settlement called Boonesborough. The paths over which the group had traveled became the Wilderness Road, by which many later settlers made their way west.

Boone spent an adventurous life along the frontier, ranging as far west as the Yellowstone River. He became the most famous pioneer of his day. No one has caught the spirit of this legendary frontiersman and his times better than the poet Stephen Vincent Benét, who wrote:

When Daniel Boone goes by, at night,
The phantom deer arise
And all lost, wild America
Is burning in their eyes.

Daniel Boone was a fine shot with his favorite Kentucky rifle that he called *Tick-Licker*.

317

The Applachian barrier. After the colonists had gained a foothold on the continent, they began to push the line of settlement steadily westward. By the time of the American Revolution, the frontier reached the Appalachian Mountains, about 300 miles inland from the Atlantic seaboard. A few pioneers had crossed the mountains in Pennsylvania and Virginia. Altogether, perhaps a few thousand made it to the western side of the mountains in the 1760s and 1770s. But for most, the Appalachians were a major barrier.

For a time, the westward movement slowed. Clearly, though, Americans regarded the mountains as a place to pause, not to stop. They had made that clear after the French and Indian War when King George III issued the Proclamation of 1763, forbidding settlement west of the Alleghenies. The colonists' anger over this act had added to the growing split with Great Britain.

An avalanche of people. Over the next twenty years Americans fought a war for independence and set up a government. During the first decade of independence, the government was engaged in clearing away the influence of the British and Spanish from its western lands, and in making treaties with Indian tribes. Those things accomplished, an avalanche of people began to roll down the western side of the mountains. From Virginia and North Carolina, they crossed through passes into Kentucky and Tennessee. To the north, settlers trekked from Massachusetts and Connecticut across New York to Ohio. From there, they soon pushed on to the Mississippi River, the nation's western boundary. To the south, planters moved westward into Alabama and Mississippi.

The table below reveals the speed of western settlement between 1790 and 1819. Of the new states listed there, only Vermont lay east of the Appalachians.

New States Formed from the Original Territory of the United States, 1791–1819

State	Population in 1790	1800	1810	1820
Vermont (1791)*	85,000	154,000	218,000	236,000
Kentucky (1792)	74,000	221,000	407,000	564,000
Tennessee (1796)	36,000	106,000	262,000	423,000
Ohio (1803)	—	45,000	231,000	581,000
Indiana (1816)	—	6,000	25,000	147,000
Mississippi (1817)	—	8,000	31,000	75,000
Illinois (1818)	—	—	12,000	55,000
Alabama (1819)	—	1,000	9,000	128,000

*The year in which each state entered the union is in parentheses. Under the terms of the Northwest Ordinance of 1787, sixty thousand people were required before a territory could become a state. (In the case of Illinois, the population requirement was not enforced.)

In his inaugural message in 1801, President Thomas Jefferson had written that the United States had "room enough for our descendants to the thousandth and thousandth generation." So rapidly was the frontier being pushed back, however, that many people doubted there was room enough for the second and third generations. With good prices being paid for wheat, corn, and cotton, there was money to be made. Northern farmers and southern planters bought up western land as fast as the government put it up for sale. By 1819, states had been created in all the original territory of the United States, except for the area in the northwest that later became Michigan, Wisconsin, and Minnesota.

By the time Ohio became a state, however, Jefferson had completed the deal for the Louisiana Purchase. Sixteen years later, Florida was acquired from Spain. With these two additions, the territory of the United States was increased by more than 150 percent. Soon new states were being carved out of the newly acquired lands: Louisiana in 1812, Missouri in 1821.

The pattern of settlement. Western settlement followed a pattern. Typically, hunters and trappers were the first whites to enter an area and mark out trails. After the supply of furs ran out they departed, leaving no permanent settlement behind. Following them came the men and women pioneers. Often they were squatters. They moved to the edge of the frontier, threw up shelters, cleared patches of land, planted crops, and grazed their hogs in the nearby forest. To add to their food supply, the pioneers hunted animals. After a number of years, they moved on for a variety of reasons. Perhaps others were moving too close for their liking. Perhaps they could get a good price for the land they had improved. Or perhaps they had heard of still better lands beyond.

These men and women of the frontier might make half a dozen such moves in their lifetime. Thomas Lincoln was fairly typical. Born in western Virginia, he grew up in the central part of Kentucky. He had no schooling, but he knew something about farming and carpentering. In 1806 Thomas Lincoln married Nancy Hanks, an illiterate daughter of a farming family. He and Nancy settled on a farm in the western part of Kentucky. In 1809 their son Abraham was born. In 1816 the Lincolns moved to the southern part of Indiana. After "squatting" for a year, they bought land and built a log cabin without windows and with a roof made of mud and dry grass. Nancy Lincoln died, and Thomas remarried. In 1830 the Lincolns moved again, this time to Illinois. By then, Abraham was old enough to strike out on his own.

The permanent settlers. After the frontier people came the permanent settlers. These were the people who had enough money to buy the land and the tools they would need for farming. They finished the clearing, dug out the tree stumps, built fences, put up frame houses. As their harvests increased, they often bought extra land to sell at a profit at a later date. There was a bit of the speculator in most American farmers. Normally, these farm families expected to stay; but they were always prepared to

The Brooklyn Museum

The pioneers' first task was to clear the land for planting crops. They often killed the trees by cutting grooves around the trunks.

move if the fertility of their soil gave out or if they got a very good price for their land.

Whether one was a rootless pioneer or a permanent settler, it was a hard life. Why, wondered an Englishman, would anyone want to put up with all the hardships of the frontier?

The rugged road, the dirty hovels, the fire in the woods to sleep by, the pathless ways through the wilderness, the dangerous crossing of the rivers. . . .

And for what?

To boil their pot in gipsy-fashion, to have a mere board to eat on, to drink whiskey or pure water, to sit and sleep under a shed far inferior to English cowpens, to have a mill at twenty miles' distance, . . . and a doctor nowhere.

There were a number of answers to the Englishman's question, not all of them the same for each person who went to the frontier. Some of the answers you will find in the following items.

By a Connecticut farmer in the eighteenth century:

Our lands being thus worn out, I suppose to be one reason why so many are inclined to Remove to new Places that they may raise Wheat: As also that they may have more Room, thinking that we live too thick.

By a New England traveler to the West, eighteenth century:

Those who are first inclined to emigrate are usually such as have met with difficulties at home. These are commonly joined by persons who, having large families and small farms, are induced, for the sake of settling their children comfortably, to seek for new and cheaper lands. To both are always added the discontented, the enterprising, the ambitious, and the [greedy]. . . . Others, still, are [attracted] by the prospect of gain, presented in every new country to the [wise], from the purchase and sale of new lands: while not a small number are influenced by the brilliant stories, which everywhere are told concerning most [lands] during the early progress of their settlement.

One historian has written that the lure of the West made for a kind of "gold-rush mentality." Do these two accounts help you to see why?

320

1. What were the major obstacles to western settlement in the early years of the United States?
2. Who were usually the first people to move to the frontier? What groups then followed?
3. Why did so many Americans leave settled areas and move to the frontier?

Speeding Western Settlement

During the first 150 years after Jamestown was settled, the frontier had been pushed westward at a rate of 2 miles (3.2 km) a year. After 1790, it moved westward at a rate of 17 miles (27.2 km) a year. Three things contributed to this amazing increase: an important invention, developments in transportation, and changes in government land policy. Underlying all was the continuing land hunger of a people on the move.

The cotton gin. One development that speeded western settlement was the invention of the cotton gin in 1793 (see page 322). It made cotton raising highly profitable, and the production of cotton rose rapidly to meet the demand from English factories. From less than 4,000 bales in 1790, production climbed to 260,000 bales in 1816. Because cotton farming used up the fertility in the soil in just a few years, planters in South Carolina and Georgia were soon moving onto the rich coastal plains of Alabama, Mississippi, and Louisiana. Some large plantations were carved out of this land, but a good many smaller farms were located there, too. By 1820, half of America's cotton was grown in these newly opened lands.

Roads to the West. A second development that speeded western settlement was improved transportation. Beginning in the 1790s, a number of roads

Most early roads were dirt trails wide enough for a wagon. They were often muddy and developed deep ruts. The best of the major highways was the National Road. For most of its route, it was paved with stone and covered with gravel.

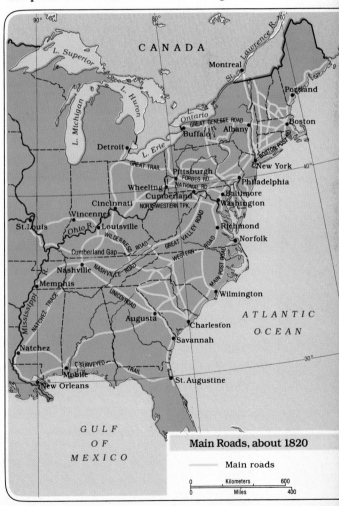

Main Roads, about 1820

Main roads

Kilometers 600
Miles 400

Inventions that changed the face of America

The Cotton Gin

Before the 1790s, not much cotton had been grown in America because processing it was difficult. Before cotton can be made into thread, the tiny seeds must be removed from the fluffy, white fibers. With "long-staple," or "Sea Island," cotton, the black, slippery seeds can be separated from the fiber by running the cotton between rollers much like those of an old-fashioned clothes wringer. However, this kind of cotton grew well only in small areas along the South Carolina and Georgia coasts. "Short-staple" cotton would grow well almost anywhere in the South, but its fuzzy seeds were so sticky that they had to be picked out by hand. Even a good worker could clean only a few pounds of cotton a day.

In 1793 Eli Whitney, a young Northerner, born in Massachusetts and educated at Yale College, went south to be a tutor on a plantation. While in Georgia, he became aware of the difficulty of removing seeds from short-staple cotton. Whitney had a mechanical bent, and within two weeks he had designed a hand-operated machine to do the job. The wire teeth of Whitney's engine—or as it came to be called, "gin"—tugged the cotton fibers through narrow slots. The seeds, however, were too large to pass through. A revolving brush then removed the fibers from the teeth. With Whitney's cotton gin, one person could clean as much as fifty pounds of cotton in a day.

The invention had electrifying effects. Cotton now became a profitable crop, and the South's faltering economy came to life. Planters, seeking fresh soil for cotton cultivation, moved westward. Mill towns grew up in the North to spin and weave the cotton. And the increased need for labor fastened the slavery system on the South. You will learn more in Unit 5 about the consequences of this last effect of Eli Whitney's invention of the cotton gin.

The cotton gin was a simple machine that any blacksmith could duplicate. Though Whitney held a patent on the machine, it was widely copied. He received little of the wealth that his invention brought for others.

were built to connect east and west. Usually they were built by private interests who charged a toll. State and local governments often helped pay the costs of road building. The federal government itself built one important highway—the National Road. Its first section was from Cumberland, Maryland, to Wheeling, on the Ohio River.

Paved with stone and gravel, these roads were a great improvement over the trails that early settlers had followed through the wilderness. Even so, they were crude affairs. In rainy seasons, they turned to mud. Some farmers in northern climates held their crops until winter, when they could ship them by sleigh over the snow-covered roads. It was also very expensive to ship goods over these roads. In fact, it was cheaper to send goods 3,000 miles (4,800 km) across the ocean than 30 miles (48 km) overland!

The steamboat. After 1800, improvements in transportation occurred that are important enough to justify the term *Transportation Revolution.* One was the invention of the steamboat. Rivers had long offered obvious avenues for transporting goods. However, because of the river current, traffic only went one way. In 1807, for example, 1,800 boats and rafts went downstream on the Mississippi River; only 11 went up. That same year, Robert Fulton, a Pennsylvania-born engineer, built the first practical steamboat. That invention turned rivers into two-way highways of commerce. Within twenty years, steamboats were plying the waters of nearly every large river in the country and giving western farm goods outlets to world markets.

Metropolitan Museum of Art, Gift of Mrs. John Sylvester, 1936.

This toll road ran between Baltimore and Reisterstown in Maryland. Coaches, wagons carrying freight, horses with riders, and even travelers on foot streamed through the busy tollgate.

Canal building. Another development in transportation that aided western growth was the digging of several thousand miles of canals. This created water highways where there were no rivers. The greatest canal was the Erie, running across New York State and connecting Buffalo to Albany. Building the Erie Canal was an enormous task. Every foot of its 364 miles (582.4 km) had to be dug by hand. With its opening in 1825, goods were transported to Buffalo from villages all along the shores of Lake Erie. From Buffalo, the goods went by canalboat to Albany and then down the Hudson River to New York City. In this manner, goods could travel by an all-water route from the Old Northwest to the nation's largest seaport and trading center.

Before the Erie Canal, the cost of shipping a bushel (35.2 l) of wheat overland from Buffalo to New York City was three times the value of the wheat itself. The canal reduced the cost to a few pennies, thus cutting the cost of shipping by 90 percent. In this way, canals encouraged settlement in the regions

323

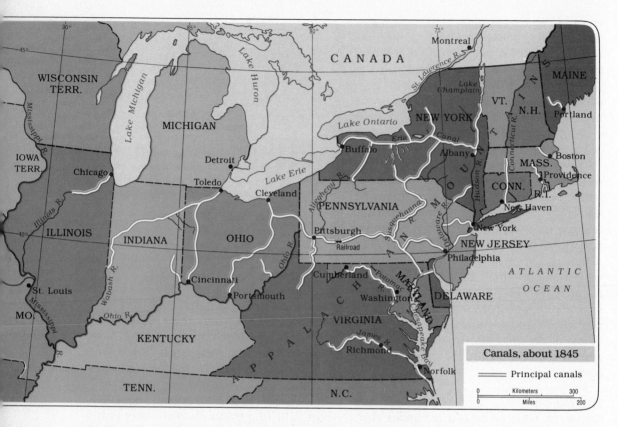

The success of the Erie Canal in New York State induced many other states to undertake canal building. Few of those canals proved to be profitable, but they contributed greatly to the development of the nation. Note that many canals followed the routes of rivers.

around the Great Lakes, for farmers now knew they could ship their products to market cheaply.

The railroad. The transportation development that was the most important of all in opening up the West was the railroad. The first American railroad line was built in Baltimore in 1830 and was all of 13 miles (20.8 km) long. By 1840, 2,200 miles (3,520 km) of track had been laid. The railroad was now begin-

ning to be a serious rival to the canal and the steamboat. During the next ten years, more than 6,000 miles (9,600 km) of track were added. By 1860, the United States had more than 31,000 miles (49,600 km) of track.

At first, railroad lines went from cities to the nearby countryside, much like spokes in a wheel, with each wheel separate from the other. Later, lines began to connect the hubs of these wheels—that is, the cities. By 1860, all the major cities of the North were tied to each other by rail.

Building railroads was expensive. Private investors from both the United States and England put up a good deal of the money. States and cities, believing that railroads would add to their prosperity, also bought stock in railroad corporations or loaned them money. Of the billion dollars spent in railroad building by 1860, perhaps one fourth came from public funds. In 1850 the federal government also began to support railroad building with grants of land to the companies.

Railroads opened up areas that were far from rivers and canals by providing cheap transportation for farm goods. One three-county area of rich farmland in Illinois, for example, had a population of only 8,500 in 1840. Farmers there raised 750,000 bushels (26,400 kl) of wheat and corn. Shortly after, a railroad line was built nearby. By 1860, there were 38,000 people living in these three counties. Farmers now raised more than 6,200,000 bushels (218,240 kl) of wheat and corn. Many eastern farmers found they were no longer able to compete with western farmers, who could now ship their crops cheaply. Therefore, those eastern farmers often pulled up stakes and moved west themselves.

Together, the steamboat, canal, and railroad lowered transportation costs dramatically. Before 1820, it had cost about twenty cents to ship a ton (.9 t) of goods one mile (1.6 km). By 1860, the cost had dropped to a penny, and the goods arrived five to ten times sooner. At the same time, passengers could be carried west for about one cent a mile and could go as far in six days as they used to go in three weeks.

The first steam locomotive to operate on a commercial rail line was the *Tom Thumb* of the Baltimore and Ohio Railroad. In 1830 the *Tom Thumb*, designed by the New York inventor Peter Cooper, raced a horse. The horse won the race when the steam locomotive broke down.

By 1860, America's railroads connected practically all the major cities east of the Mississippi River, and were pushing westward.

Government land policy. Another important development that speeded western settlement was government land policy. Following the Revolutionary War, the federal government controlled vast lands in the West. In Chapter 9 you

learned how Congress, in 1785, set up a system for surveying and selling the land of the Northwest Territory to private individuals. The land was marked off into squares measuring a mile (1.6 km) on each side. Each square contained 640 acres (256 ha) and was called a section. Under the 1785 law, one had to buy an entire section at $1 an acre (.4 ha). That was more land than most settlers needed, and $640 was more money than they could afford. Most of the land was bought by *speculators.* These were people who bought the land not for their own use but in the hope it would rise in value so that they could sell at a profit.

Individuals and private land companies also owned huge tracts of land that they had acquired during colonial times or had bought from the states shortly afterward at bargain prices. Massachusetts, for instance, sold six million acres (2.4 million ha) to one buyer at about three cents an acre. A group called the Ohio Company arranged to buy 750,000 acres (300,000 ha). Not all such investors did well. Some bought unwisely and lost money. One of the investors, Robert Morris of Pennsylvania, spent several years in a debtor's jail after he went broke on land schemes. But many landowners made out quite well. They usually sold the land to settlers in quarter sections— 160 acres (64 ha)—at a good price, and provided credit terms.

Most of the land by far, however, remained in the control of the federal government. Over the years, westerners pressured the federal government to sell land in smaller lots and at lower prices. How successful they were can be seen in the table at the top of page 327.

Requirements for Purchase of Land from the United States Government

Year of Law	Minimum Number of Acres to Be Bought	Minimum Price per Acre	Terms
1785	640	$1.00	Cash only
1796	640	$2.00	One half in cash, balance in one year
1800	320	$2.00	One fourth in cash, one fourth per year
1804	160	$2.00	One fourth in cash, one fourth per year
1820	80	$1.25	Cash only
1832	40	$1.25	Cash only

How much money did a settler need to buy land from the government in 1804? in 1820? in 1832? You can see how these changes in the law might have aided western settlement. Of course, settlers needed money for other things, too—tools, fencing, and so on. But by the early 1800s, farmland was within the reach of thousands, not only to raise crops on but to buy and sell for profit. The federal government set up land offices in various places where settlers could buy their land. During boom years, when land was in great demand, buyers lined up to purchase their land, giving us the phrase that we use today to describe a very good business—"a land-office business." In a two-year period during the land boom of the 1830s, the United States government sold 40 million acres (16 million ha) of land to settlers.

The growth of towns and cities. As settlers occupied the farmlands of the West, towns developed to provide goods and services to farmers. Some towns— like St. Louis, Cincinnati, and Pittsburgh—started as trading or military posts along rivers and at key road crossings. In some areas, towns were started even before the arrival of many farmers. Speculators bought land at places they thought would make good town sites and then advertised heavily, assuring buyers that the sites were certain to become great cities. Some places did. Most did not. Those people who guessed right became wealthy. The others moved on again to try their luck at other places.

The Erie Canal contributed greatly to the growth of towns and cities along its path. Buffalo, on Lake Erie, boomed. It was at the western end of the canal. Only a small village in 1780, Buffalo grew to a town of 12,000 by 1832. Rochester, New York, also owed much of its early growth to its location near the canal. By increasing traffic on the Great Lakes, the canal was responsible for the growth of a number of cities on the lakes. Cleveland, Ohio, hardly a village before the canal

At Lockport, New York, on the Erie Canal, a boat carrying passengers approaches the locks to be "lifted" upward. The steep incline there required locks at five levels.

opened, was a thriving city by 1840. Detroit and Milwaukee had a similar growth.

CHECKUP

1. How did the invention of the cotton gin affect western settlement?
2. What is meant by the term *Transportation Revolution*? In what ways did this development aid western growth?
3. How did the federal government's land policies affect western settlement?

Pushing the Indians Westward

Americans were fond of talking about the "empty" continent that lay to the west. Thomas Jefferson wrote cheerfully in 1801 about settling "the extensive country still remaining vacant within our limits." Of course, as Jefferson and every frontier family knew, the continent was not empty at all. Indians inhabited much of it. Western settlement could advance only as the native Americans were moved out of the way.

Jefferson had written earlier that "it may be taken for a certainty that not a foot of land will ever be taken from the Indians without their own consent." That was an odd statement even then, since so much had already been taken without the consent of the Indians. In any case, American behavior made a mockery of Jefferson's statement. Time after time, white settlers pushed into Indian land and then cried "treachery" when the Indians resisted. Thousands on both sides paid with their lives in warfare that has few rivals for cruelty.

To satisfy the settlers' hunger for more land, the United States government pushed the Indians farther and farther to the West. The history of western advance can be told as a romantic story of a people on the move, clearing land, enduring hardships, and conquering a continent. It can also be told as an endless succession of broken treaties with Indians. Both stories are true.

Treaties—made and broken. After the American Revolution, the United States government had made a number of treaties with Indian tribes living within the boundaries it had won at the Peace of Paris. In each case, white settlers were forbidden to cross the treaty lines. They soon did, however, and fighting broke out. For a while the Indians held their own, and in 1790 and 1791 they defeated United States forces in a series of battles in the Ohio Territory. But in 1794 they were defeated at the battle of Fallen Timbers by General "Mad Anthony" Wayne. A year later, twelve tribes in the Northwest Territory signed the Treaty of Greenville with the United States by which they gave up most of the region.

This treaty set a boundary between the Indian lands and the lands open for settlement. It was only then that settlers poured into the Ohio Territory in large numbers (see pages 302–306).

The years from 1800 to the 1830s were a disaster for the Indians. In the first decade, a dozen tribes were defeated in battles with the United States Army. In 1803, tribes in Indiana Territory were forced to sign a treaty giving up some of the lands granted to them only eight years earlier in the Treaty of Greenville.

For a brief time it appeared that the Indians might successfully draw a line. But the battle of Tippecanoe in 1811, followed by the death of Tecumseh in 1813 (see page 306), ended that hope. At about the same time, General Andrew Jackson was crushing the Creek Indians in Alabama Territory and forcing them from their lands. Jackson and General William H. Harrison, the hero of Tippecanoe, would later become Presidents of the United States. They owed much of their popularity to their reputations as Indian fighters.

Indian Territory. In 1825 Congress adopted a new Indian policy. It set aside land west of the Mississippi River, in present-day Oklahoma, to which all Indian tribes east of the river were to move. This was to be the "permanent Indian frontier." The lands would be "secured and guaranteed to them," with no white settlers allowed.

Indian nations to the East were pressured to give up their homelands in exchange for land in the Indian Territory. If they chose not to move, it was made clear that they would have to abide by

329

the laws and the ways of the settlers. Desiring to keep their own culture, the Indians had little choice. In the eight years that Jackson was President, Indian tribes signed 94 treaties, all of which added up to a transfer of millions of acres from Indian nations to the United States government. Having signed, they set out for Indian Territory. Indians called it the Trail of Tears. About 25 percent of the Cherokees and the Creeks who set out on the sad journey died along the way.

To the north, the Sauk and Fox tribes suffered the same fate as the southern Indians. They were removed from their lands in the upper Mississippi Valley. By 1840, all Indian tribes except the Seminoles in Florida had been pushed to areas beyond the Mississippi. In a series of fierce battles between 1835 and 1842, the Seminoles, too, were crushed, and their land was opened to white settlers.

A few whites spoke out against this treatment of the native Americans. One of them was James Barbour, Secretary of War under President John Quincy Adams. He wrote bitterly that "our promises have been broken . . . the happiness of the Indian is a cheap sacrifice to the acquisition of new lands."

The Seminoles attack an Army fort in Florida about 1835. Most of them were later forced to move to the West. In 1970 the Seminoles were awarded $12 million for the lands taken from them.

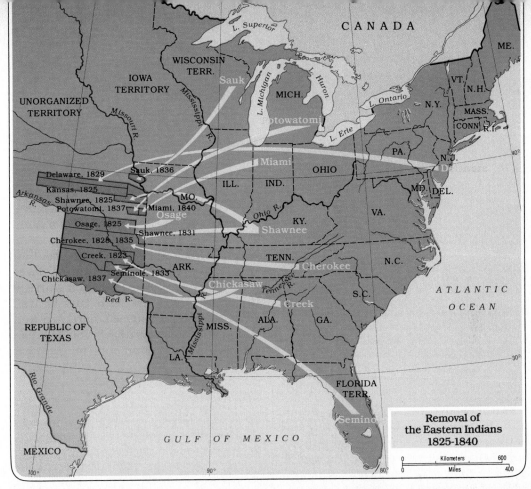

By 1840, most of the Indians east of the Mississippi had been forced to give up their lands and go to present-day Oklahoma. The Cherokees called their route to the West the Trail of Tears. The Seminoles resisted strongly, and a few hundred were allowed to stay in Florida.

But to most Americans, Indians were simply "wretched savages" who stood in the way of "civilization, of science, and of true religion."

The racism that infected white America's dealings with the Indians was never expressed more clearly than by President Jackson in 1833.

They have neither the intelligence, the industry, the moral habits, nor the desire of improvement which are essential to any favorable change in their existence. Established in the midst of another and a superior race . . . they must necessarily yield.

And yield the Indians did. Within seven years of the removal of the Sauk and Fox tribes, there were 75,000 settlers in the Iowa and Wisconsin territories. Ten years later there were a half million. Iowa became a state in 1846; Wisconsin, in 1848. Minnesota, a part of the Wisconsin Territory, gained statehood in 1858.

331

Osceola led the Seminoles in their resistance to moving west. When invited to discuss peace under a flag of truce, he was treacherously siezed and thrown into prison, where he died.

next ten years and became a state in 1836. Florida, where the Seminoles had been crushed in 1842, became a state three years later.

The first American West was created, as you have seen, by the optimism, drive, and greed of a people on the move. In time, these people demanded a hand in shaping the policies of the federal government. The election of the first Westerner as President, Andrew Jackson, was a sign of that section's arrival in national politics. With that arrival, the old balance between northern and southern states was upset. You will read about these developments in the next chapter.

Farther south, planters quickly moved into the rich cotton lands after the departure of the Indians. Mississippi's population, 136,000 in 1830, increased by more than 200,000 in ten years. Arkansas, a territory of 30,000 in 1830, more than tripled its population in the

CHECKUP

1. In what respects were the 30 years or so after 1800 "a disaster for the Indians"?
2. What effect did the Indian policy adopted by Congress in 1825 have on native American tribes?
3. How did most Americans attempt to justify their treatment of the Indians?

Key Facts from Chapter 12

1. During colonial times, the Appalachian Mountains were the greatest obstacle to westward settlement by Americans.
2. After the American Revolution, hunters and trappers moved across the mountains, followed by restless pioneers, and finally by permanent settlers.
3. Among the developments that helped bring about movement into the West were the inventions of the cotton gin, the steamboat, and the railroad, and the building of canals.
4. The policy of the United States government in making western lands available at low cost led many Americans to move to the frontier.
5. As settlers moved into the West, the Indians were ruthlessly forced off their homelands and made to settle in other areas.

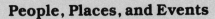

★ REVIEWING THE CHAPTER ★

People, Places, and Events

Review Questions

1. What explanations does the text offer for why Americans in general are such a restless people? *P. 316*

2. Describe the typical pattern of settlement of western lands. *P. 319*

3. Tell in what specific way each development encouraged western settlement of the United States: **(a)** invention of the cotton gin, **(b)** invention of the steamboat, **(c)** canal building, **(d)** railroad building. *Pp. 321–325*

4. How did the Erie Canal contribute to New York City's development as an important trade center? *Pp. 323–324*

5. How was railroad construction financed in the nineteenth century? *P. 325*

6. Why was the federal government's land policy of 1785 unsatisfactory for the ordinary settler? *P. 326*

7. What was the attitude of white Americans toward the Indians in the nineteenth century? How did this attitude affect government policy toward the Indians? *Pp. 329–331*

Chapter Test

*On a separate piece of paper, write **T** if the statement is true and **F** if the statement is false.*

1. Many white people justified the removal of Indians from their lands on the grounds that they were ignorant savages unable to improve the land.

2. Andrew Jackson and William Henry Harrison first gained national attention as Indian fighters.

3. The Seminoles of Florida were the last tribe to resist the federal government's efforts to move them west of the Mississippi to Indian Territory.

4. The National Road, built by the federal government to connect Washington, D.C., with Philadelphia, made it less expensive to ship goods between the two cities.

5. Eli Whitney's cotton gin was largely responsible for improving the prosperity of the South.

6. Fallen Timbers was an important lumbering company that helped western settlers clear their land for homesteading and farming.

7. The Appalachian Mountains kept people from moving westward until the middle of the nineteenth century.

8. The Erie Canal, built by engineer Robert Fulton and his crew, connected Buffalo and Albany.

9. Between 1785 and the 1830s, the federal government eased the requirements for land purchase to enable more settlers to own land.

10. The Sunbelt occupies about a third of the United States and is the fastest-growing part of the country today.

THE AGE OF JACKSON

FROM THE TIME of the Revolution, the West was a factor in national politics. The two major acts of Congress under the Articles of Confederation had to do with western lands. Getting the British out of the West and pushing back the Indians through war and treaty were important aims of the government under President Washington. It was the votes of the two western states of Kentucky and Tennessee that made Thomas Jefferson President. Later still, it was Westerners who led the cry for war against Great Britain in 1812. Even so, with few states and few seats in Congress, Westerners had little direct voice in politics at the national level.

The Growth of Sectionalism

The minor role of the West in national politics was sharply changed between 1810 and 1820 by the flood of restless Americans that rolled onto the lands between the Appalachians and the Mississippi River. During those years the population of the West went from one million to two million. Five new western states entered the Union. By 1820, there were three sections of the country with enough votes in Congress and enough electoral votes to have a voice in national politics. The North, the South, and the West each had developed differently. Each had its own special needs and desires. Each, therefore, now tried to use its say in national politics to advance its own interests and attain the goals that it felt were important.

Issues between North and South. The chief interest of the North was the growth of its industries. The North wanted Congress to place high import taxes, or tariffs, on goods brought in from other countries. These high tariffs would bring in money for the government. Their main purpose, however, would be to make the price of foreign goods so high that those goods could not compete with the products of northern industries.

The South, on the other hand, was bitterly opposed to high tariffs. As a planting rather than a manufacturing section, it bought its manufactured goods elsewhere, often from England. High tariffs pushed the prices of imported goods up to, or above, the prices of northern-made goods. Thus, whether southerners bought in the North or from England, they paid more because of the tariffs.

The South had another reason for opposing high tariffs. The South exported two thirds of its cotton to England. If Americans bought fewer goods from England because of high tariffs, England would be able to buy less cotton from the South.

A goal of even greater importance to the South was to protect slavery. The South wanted the federal government to do nothing that would interfere with slavery or with its spread into new territories. Northerners had no wish to interfere with slavery in the southern states. But they did oppose its spread into the territories, for they did not want more slave states to be created.

335

The West's interests. Slavery and the tariffs, burning issues in the two older sections, held little interest for Westerners. They were far more concerned with issues that bore on the development of their own section. In Chapter 12, you read of two of these. Westerners wanted internal improvements—roads and canals that would get their goods to eastern markets directly, quickly, and cheaply. Even more, they wanted the federal government to sell western lands cheaply, or even to give them away.

The North was generally in favor of internal improvements, for roads and canals would lead to more trade between the West and such states as New York and Pennsylvania. The South was more divided on this issue. Although some Southerners were in favor of internal improvements, others complained. They declared that the money paid by the federal government to build these improvements came from the tariff duties they, the Southerners, were paying. Still the issue of internal improvements was not as important to either of the older sections as it was to the West.

On land policy, neither North nor South agreed with the West. To both older sections, western land was part of the national treasure, to be sold at good prices. The North was especially opposed to a cheap land policy. Northerners felt it would encourage people to move west. That, they feared, would reduce the Northeast's population and thus its representation in Congress. Northern manufacturers felt, too, that such migration would make labor for their factories more scarce and costly.

Two other subjects of great importance to the West were banking and Indian policy. You have already read about the West's demand for Indian removal. Later in this chapter you will read about the West's position on banking and credit.

These were the issues at the bottom of the three-cornered rivalry that had been created by a people on the move. No one section was strong enough to control the federal government, but any two could outvote the third.

The explosive slavery issue. The strongest rivalry was between the North and the South. They became involved at this time in the first of the sectional issues to explode into national politics. This was the issue of the spread of slavery into the western territories.

In 1819 the territory of Missouri asked to enter the Union as a state under a constitution that allowed slavery. Congressman James Tallmadge of New York proposed an amendment to admit Missouri only if slavery were gradually abolished there. The House of Representatives approved Tallmadge's amendment, but the Senate blocked it. The debate—and the deadlock—went on for more than a year.

Tallmadge's amendment brought into focus differences between North and South on the issue of slavery. Missouri was part of the Louisiana Purchase, where slavery had existed under the French. Since the purchase, in 1803, Congress had made no law about slavery in the Louisiana Territory. Most people, however, thought of the Ohio River as the unofficial boundary between South and North—between slave states and free states. Missouri lay north of the latitude of the Ohio River. If Missouri came in as a slave state, argued Northerners, then other areas north of that latitude might become slave states, too. If so, the South would have greater power in Congress. Northerners complained that the South already had more seats in the House of Representatives than it was fairly entitled to. This was a result of the three-fifths clause in the Constitution (see page 218).

Southerners, on the other hand, were concerned that the population of the northern states was growing much more rapidly than that of the southern states. In the House of Representatives, members from the North outnumbered those from the South, 105 to 81, and that margin seemed sure to grow. With two senators from each state, the Senate was evenly divided, with eleven free states and eleven slave states. Slaveholders felt it was crucial that Northerners not get an advantage in the Senate, for then the North would control both bodies of Congress. It would then be able to pass laws harmful to the interests of the South.

The Missouri Compromise. Henry Clay of Kentucky, the Speaker of the House, finally arranged a compromise. Clay put the nation's interests, as he understood them, ahead of sectional interests. Maine, which had long been a part of Massachusetts, was also ready for statehood, so it was agreed to admit the two

In 1820 the Missouri Compromise seemed to solve the issue of the spread of slavery. But the solution was only temporary, and the issue would arise again after the Mexican War.

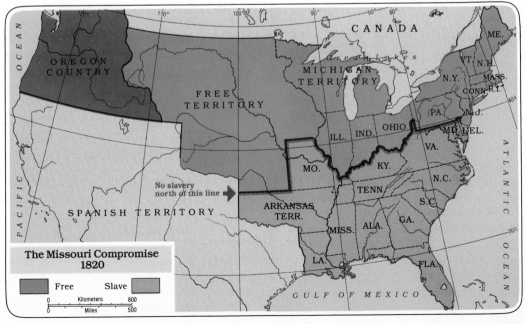

The Missouri Compromise
1820

Free   Slave

together, Missouri as a slave state and Maine as a free state. Thus the balance in the Senate would be kept. It was agreed, too, that slavery would not be allowed in the rest of the Louisiana Purchase north of latitude 36°30′, which served as Missouri's southern boundary.

The 1824 presidential candidates. The rivalry among the sections could be seen most clearly in the presidential contest of 1824. The Federalists were by then no longer a national party. Only the Republican party remained. Four Republicans, however, ran for the Presidency, each representing the outlook of a section. Northerners supported John Quincy Adams, Monroe's Secretary of State and son of the second President. William Crawford of Georgia, Secretary of the Treasury under both Madison and Monroe, spoke for the South. From the rising West came two men, Congressman Henry Clay of Kentucky and Senator Andrew Jackson of Tennessee.

Jackson was popular in the West not for his views—few knew what they were—but for what he was. Born in a cabin in the South Carolina backcountry in 1767, Jackson was a self-made man. By the age of twenty, he was practicing law, and soon afterward he was making money buying and selling land in western Tennessee. Jackson had led an army against the Creek Indians in 1814. He was also the hero of the battle of New Orleans (see page 282). Jackson believed in plain people. He judged people by their achievements, not by their family background. Westerners saw in him a man who shared their beliefs in individualism, equality, and democracy. Jackson's qualities brought him support in other sections of the country as well.

Clay's "American System." Of the four candidates, only Henry Clay had put together a program to appeal to more than one section. Clay called it the American System. It was based on a vision of a growing, self-sufficient America, with each section's interests tied to the well-being of the others. In his plan, a protective tariff would help manufacturing develop in the Northeast and make northern workers prosperous. Western farmers and southern planters would not need to depend on foreign markets, for the Northeast would become a dependable home market for western foodstuffs and southern cotton. Money raised by the tariff would pay for roads and canals that would bring farm goods to the East and manufactured goods to the West cheaply and quickly. A national bank would see that a sound currency and credit system helped the economy of all sections grow. There was less in this program for the South than for the East and West. Still it was the closest thing there was to a national program.

The election of 1824. The outcome of the election followed sectional lines. Adams took the New England states and New York. Crawford, who had suffered a stroke during the campaign, won Georgia and Virginia. Jackson won much of the West and a good part of the South. Clay, who was probably the second choice in most states, was the first choice of only three. The electoral vote stood 99 for Jackson, 84 for Adams, 41 for Crawford, and 37 for Clay.

338

Since no one had a majority, under the Constitution the House of Representatives had to choose from the top three candidates, with each state having one vote. Jackson's backers said that since he had won the most popular votes, the House should choose him. Clay, however, persuaded his supporters to vote for Adams, who shared many of Clay's ideas about the American System. Adams was thus elected. When Adams appointed Clay his Secretary of State—an office that had been the stepping stone to the Presidency for every President since 1808—Jackson's followers charged that the two had made a "corrupt bargain." There is no evidence that this was true, but the charge dogged Adams throughout his four years in office.

Adams as Chief Executive. As President, John Quincy Adams showed little interest in gaining advantage for his own section of the country. He tried to be a truly national President. Adams favored internal improvements that would tie the country more closely together. In his belief that the federal government should give encouragement and financial aid to agriculture, science, and education, he was a century ahead of his time.

Except for internal improvements, which Congress supported, Adams made little headway. This was partly due to his own shortcomings as a political leader. Perhaps no President could have succeeded in bridging the sectional differences of the time. But Adams was especially unsuited to the task. A cold and uncompromising man, he lacked the political skills needed to build sup-

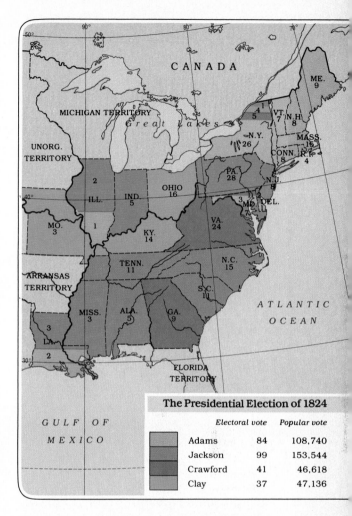

The Presidential Election of 1824		
	Electoral vote	Popular vote
Adams	84	108,740
Jackson	99	153,544
Crawford	41	46,618
Clay	37	47,136

The totals in the key above show why Jackson's supporters were outraged over the outcome of the 1824 election. Jackson received almost 45,000 more popular votes and 15 more electoral votes than did John Quincy Adams.

port for his nationalist views. Moreover, Jackson supporters in Congress had one main goal, and that was to elect their man in 1828. They spent the full four years of Adams's term blocking his

339

Born in MASSACHUSETTS
In Office 1825—1829
Party NAT. REPUBLICAN

Elected by the House of
Representatives after no
candidate won a majority of
electoral votes. His programs
met opposition, and he was
defeated in his bid for
reelection.

★ ★ ★ ★ ★ ★ ★ ★

plans and trying to embarrass him. By
the midpoint of Adams's term, Congress
had divided into two groups. Supporters
of Adams came to be known as National
Republicans, while those backing Jackson
took for themselves the old Jeffersonian name of Democratic-Republicans, or more simply, Democrats.

The tariff of 1828. The one important
act of Congress in the Adams administration was the tariff bill passed in 1828.
This act placed higher rates than ever
before on imported manufactured goods.

To win western support, it also protected western goods like raw wool
and hemp (from which rope was made)
from foreign competition. Southern opponents called the law the "Tariff of
Abominations."

The most bitter foes of the protective
tariff came from southern coastal states.
These states were having economic
problems and were losing population.
The main reason for their troubles was
that their cotton lands were wearing
out. As a result, their cotton could not
compete with cotton raised on the more
fertile lands to the west—Alabama, Mississippi, Louisiana, and Missouri. Failing to understand this, however, the
leaders of the Southeast fixed the blame
for their problems on the tariff. They
even argued that the tariff laws were an
unconstitutional use of federal power.

Calhoun and states' rights. The Southerner who made the strongest argument
against the tariff was John C. Calhoun
of South Carolina. In a long statement
written in 1828, Calhoun stated that a
state had the right to *nullify*, or declare
invalid, any federal law it believed to be
unconstitutional. This was based on the
claim that the Constitution was simply
a *compact*, or an agreement, among
sovereign states. In entering the Union,
so the claim held, the states had not
given up their rights. Most especially,
they had kept the most important right
of all—the right to secede.

This extreme statement of the *states'
rights* position was not new in American
history. The Virginia and Kentucky resolutions of 1798 had set forth similar
views. Some New England Federalists
during the War of 1812 had also talked

of nullification and secession. Never before, however, had the idea been so fully developed and so carefully argued.

Calhoun's statement, which was called the South Carolina Exposition and Protest, was adopted by the South Carolina legislature in 1828. That body, however, did not try to act upon its theory. Also, Calhoun's authorship was kept secret. The reason was that Calhoun, who was then Adams's Vice President, was running for that office again in 1828, this time on the Democratic ticket with Andrew Jackson. Southerners hoped that he would be able to persuade General Jackson to adopt their point of view on the tariff. Jackson, at the age of sixty-two, was the oldest candidate ever to run for the Presidency. Moreover, he was in poor health: he carried lead in his body from a frontier duel. Many thought he would be a one-term President, at most, and that Calhoun would succeed him.

The election of 1828. The election of 1828 pitted Jackson, the Democrat, against Adams, who was seeking a second term as a National Republican. The campaign was a mudslinging affair that did little credit to either party or candidate. Each side made charges about the honesty, decency, and morality of the other. Jackson supporters painted their man as the champion of ordinary people and Adams as an aristocrat.

In the end, the popular Jackson won a big victory. He carried every part of the country except New England, New Jersey, and Delaware. Westerners had voted for him as a son of their own section. Southern planters felt he would understand their problems, since he, too, was a planter and slaveholder. Small business people looked to him as a self-made man who would encourage opportunity. City workers hoped for his support for certain laws that would improve their lot. Everywhere, Americans saw in Jackson a hero and a man of the people.

CHECKUP

1. What were the major sectional issues that confronted the nation by 1820?
2. Whose supporters made charges of a "corrupt bargain" following the election of 1824? Why?
3. What were the differing views put forth by North and South on the tariff of 1828?

This drawing, mocking John C. Calhoun for his strong stand on states' rights, pictures the South Carolina statesman as the biblical Joshua commanding the sun to stand still.

Jacksonian Democracy

"I never saw anything like it before," said Massachusetts Senator Daniel Webster about the crowds that gathered in Washington for Jackson's inauguration on March 4, 1829. "They really seem to think the country is rescued from some dreadful danger." After the swearing-in at the Capitol, the cheering thousands followed the new President to the White House for a celebration. Jackson's supporters paraded across the carpeted floors in muddy boots, knocked over punch bowls, and stood on chairs to get a look at the President. A Washington woman who was present wrote this description of the scene.

> The President, after having been *literally* nearly pressed to death & almost suffocated & torn to pieces by the people in their eagerness to shake hands with Old Hickory. . . . escaped to his lodgings. . . . Cut glass and china to the amount of several thousand dollars had been broken in the struggle to get the refreshments. . . . Ladies fainted, men were seen with bloody noses & such a scene of confusion took place as is impossible to describe,—those who got in could not get out by the door again, but had to scramble out of windows.

"It was a proud day for the people," wrote a supporter of the new President. "General Jackson is *their own* President." But a conservative Supreme Court Justice saw it differently. The rule of "King Mob," he said, had now begun.

Rise of the common man. Jackson's Presidency has often been connected with the phrase "the rise of the common man." What that phrase meant is that in Jackson's time ordinary people came to have a greater say in government than ever before. The colonies and the new states, you will recall, limited voting to taxpayers and owners of property. As late as 1803, only Connecticut, Maryland, Vermont, and the new western state of Ohio allowed all adult white males to vote. In the years following the war of 1812, however, the growing democratic spirit led to broad changes. Between 1816 and 1821, six new western states entered the Union with no property qualifications on voting or holding office. At about the same time, older states dropped these requirements from their constitutions. By the late 1820s, all but a few states allowed all adult white males to vote. Most also dropped religious tests for holding office.

These changes appear far more limited today than they did at that time. The right to vote did not apply to women, who were half the population. It seldom included free blacks. In fact, in those very years, four states *took away* the vote from free blacks. By 1838, blacks could vote only in New England states. Yet in spite of these limits, in no country in the world was democracy more widespread at the time than in the United States. Visitors to America were struck more by this feature than any other. You may remember that the French author Alexis de Tocqueville called his book *Democracy in America.*

A broadening of democracy. Along with broader voting rights came a change in popular attitude that was just as important. In earlier times, you will recall, ordinary people were expected to vote for their "betters"—people of wealth and social position. Even the democratic

This George Caleb Bingham painting, showing the announcement of election results, catches the spirit of the time when "the common man" came to play a more active role in politics.

Thomas Jefferson expected that ordinary people would be wise enough to choose those with special ability and training as their leaders. By Jackson's time, however, Americans no longer deferred to their betters nor looked to people with special training. Why should they not choose leaders from among their own—people who were like them, who shared their experience, their values, their prejudices?

When people voted for Jackson, they were voting for such a man. He was the first President who did not have a background of social importance or family wealth. Jackson sprang from the plain people. They felt close enough to call him by a nickname—Old Hickory. It would never have occurred to anyone to do that to Washington, Adams, or any other earlier President.

Such changes in popular thinking broadened the meaning of democracy. Candidates for office now had to appeal to the desires, the pride, and the prejudices of ordinary people. After this time, it would be impossible to imagine someone like Alexander Hamilton—who had said, "Your people, sir, is a great beast"—long remaining in politics.

Changes in nominating and electing. The way in which Presidents were nominated and elected also became

343

more democratic. Since Jefferson's time, every candidate for President had been chosen in a *caucus*, or meeting of the party's congressmen. This method allowed a few insiders to keep control. The caucus system broke down in the 1820s and was soon replaced by the nominating convention. First used in 1831 by a minor party, the Anti-Masons, the nominating convention was adopted by both major parties the following year. The convention allowed much broader participation in the choice of candidates than had the caucus.

The manner of choosing presidential electors—those people who actually cast the ballots in the electoral college—also changed. By 1828, South Carolina was the only state in which electors were still chosen by the legislature. In all other states, they were elected by the people. These electors were publicly pledged to vote for one or another of the presidential candidates. This was very nearly the same as having the people vote for the President directly.

All these changes had happened, or were well underway, before the election of 1828. Thus it should be clear that it was not Jackson's election that brought about the rise of the common man. It was, rather, the rise of the common man that made possible Jackson's election to the Presidency.

There was an irony in this, for in many ways Jackson himself was anything but a common man. Despite his humble beginnings, he owned a large cotton plantation and slaves, and had long been a member of Tennessee's upper class. Many who knew Jackson commented on how he carried himself like an aristocrat.

The spoils system. Yet it is certainly true that Jackson glorified the common man and thought of himself as the champion of ordinary people. "Never for a moment believe," he said once, "that the great body of the citizens . . . can deliberately intend to do wrong." His faith in the ability of ordinary folks can be seen in his policy on federal officeholding. Shortly after taking office, Jackson replaced about 900 of the 10,000 federal jobholders, many of whom had opposed his election. He replaced them with his own supporters. Turning out officeholders and putting one's own supporters in was an old practice, and every previous President had done it. During his two terms, Jackson replaced 10 percent of the federal civil employees, about the same percentage that Thomas Jefferson had replaced. Jackson's political friends frankly justified the practice on the simple ground that "to the victor belong the spoils." From that phrase has come the term *spoils system.*

But Jackson explained the practice in democratic terms. No officeholder, he said, had a right to keep a government job as though it was private property. In fact, the public would gain from removing those who had stayed in office so long that they forgot they were supposed to serve the people. Most important, no class of people had a monopoly on the skills needed to work for the government. "The duties of all public officers are . . . so plain and simple," said Jackson, "that ordinary people of intelligence could perform them." Jackson further argued that it was desirable to "rotate" the offices among many people, so that more could have this "valuable training in citizenship." It is not a criticism of Jackson to note that many politicians then and later would use "rotation in office" not for "citizenship" but as a way of letting as many supporters as possible get on the federal payroll.

Jackson and the Presidency. Jackson brought to the Presidency a different view of that office than earlier Presidents had held. Congressmen might vote the interests of their districts, and senators of their states. But according to Jackson's view, only the President, elected by all the people, could look after the interests of all. To do that, the office of President must be one of strength and power. The President must make his own judgment of the meaning of the Constitution or of the wisdom of a bill. He must not simply accept the views of the other branches of government.

As a result, Jackson vetoed twelve bills—more than all the Presidents before him put together. He also tangled with the Supreme Court more than once. Because of these views, Jackson's foes called him King Andrew I.

Continued sectionalism. The election of Andrew Jackson, with support from nearly every part of the country, did not mean the end of the sectional struggle. Indeed, during Jackson's Presidency the struggle for sectional advantage heightened.

To their demands for lower land prices, Westerners had recently added two new proposals intended to speed settlement of their section. One proposal called *preemption*, was to allow frontier squatters first right to buy the land they were living on when the government put

This bitter Whig cartoon pictures Andrew Jackson on a pig growing fat on political spoils.

it up for sale. The second was to reduce the price of unsold land each year, with the government giving away any that was left over after four or five years. This plan was called *graduation*. Neither became law during Jackson's Presidency, but Congress did provide for preemption after 1841.

Northeastern interests, on the other hand, continued to oppose the rapid settlement of the West. In December 1829, Senator Samuel Foot of Connecticut proposed that the sale of western lands be stopped for the time being. Westerners in the Senate were enraged. Led by Senator Thomas Hart Benton of Missouri, they charged that the Foot Resolution was part of a manufacturer's plot to keep labor in the Northeast and prevent the growth of the West.

345

Hayne versus Webster. Seeing a chance to split the North and West, the South entered the debate. The North's policies, argued Senator Robert Y. Hayne of South Carolina, were a threat to both the South and the West. Should not the two sections therefore make common cause? Let the West join in opposing high tariffs, and in exchange, the South would support a cheap land policy.

Hayne then went on to invite the West to support the idea of nullification—that is, that within its own borders a state could nullify a federal law. This brought Senator Daniel Webster of Massachusetts into the debate. Soon the Foot Resolution and the question of land policy were forgotten as the debate turned to the meaning of the Constitution and the nature of the Union. For nearly a week Hayne and Webster argued their views before a packed gallery in the Senate. Hayne, repeating Calhoun's arguments, insisted that the Union was made up of sovereign states. Each, he said, was free to nullify an act of Congress or even to pull out of the Union. Webster insisted the opposite—that the Union had been formed by the people, not by the states; that it was perpetual; and that nullification and secession were not possible.

Although the debate did not solve anything, it drew the issue squarely. Either the states were finally sovereign or the nation was. It remained to be seen if the West would accept the South's hand and Calhoun's view of the Constitution.

Jackson's stand. Many people now looked to President Jackson, the West's champion, for an answer. The South-

In Jackson's day, western roads were crude. In the picture below, note the stumps still standing in the road and, at right, the logs serving as a roadway over a marsh or stream.

erners hoped that the President would side with them. In his inaugural address, Jackson had expressed himself in favor of a federal government of limited power. Warning against stretching the Constitution, he had spoken of the "legitimate sphere of State sovereignty."

But on the matter of preserving the Union and the supremacy of the federal government, Jackson was like a rock. At the Democratic party's Jefferson Day dinner in April 1830, Jackson gave his answer. Staring directly at Calhoun, the President proposed his toast: "Our Federal Union—it must be preserved!" Calhoun accepted the challenge. "The Union," he replied, "—next to our liberty, the most dear. May we all remember that it can only be preserved by respecting the rights of the states and distributing equally the benefits and burdens of the Union."

Relations between Jackson and Calhoun had been cool for some time. Their differences on this issue, plus several personal differences that arose later, left them enemies.

The Maysville Road veto. Westerners had reason to be satisfied with their President. He shared their outlook on most things. He agreed with their views on land policy. No one could ask for a stronger supporter of Indian removal. On the issue of internal improvements, however, the President disappointed the West. Jackson did favor roads and canals, but he thought that building them was mainly the job of the states rather than of the federal government.

In May 1830, Jackson's views became clear when he vetoed a bill to help pay for a 60-mile (96-km) road in Kentucky, between Maysville and Lexington. The road was expected to be a link in a future interstate highway. For the present, however, it lay entirely within one state. Thus, Jackson said, this road was "local," rather than "national," in character. For the federal government to pay for projects of this kind, he felt, would lead to waste, corruption, and a too-powerful central government. Jackson may also have had another reason for this veto. It allowed him to strike a blow at his main rival, Senator Henry Clay, whose home state was Kentucky.

Although Jackson lost some support in the West because of this veto, most Westerners remained loyal to him. Later, he approved bills for building roads in the territories and for extending the National Road. By the end of his two terms, he had approved more such spending than any President before him.

The nullification crisis. The opposition of Southerners to tariffs remained strong, and Calhoun and his fellow South Carolinians continued to nurse their grudge against Jackson. Actually, Jackson privately agreed that the tariff was too high. In late 1831 he urged Congress to reconsider it. Congress did pass a new tariff law in 1832, but it did little to lower rates.

South Carolina was now certain that the South could not hope for a low-tariff bill from Congress. Therefore, the state moved to put into practice the theories of the South Carolina Exposition. A specially elected convention met in November 1832 and passed the Ordinance of Nullification. It declared that the federal tariff laws of 1828 and 1832 were of no effect in South Carolina. It also forbade the collection of tariffs in that state after February 1, 1833. If the federal government were to try to force South Carolina to obey the tariff laws, warned the convention, that would be grounds for withdrawing from the Union. Meanwhile, John Calhoun resigned the Vice Presidency, and South Carolina sent him back to Washington as its Senator.

There was never a question about what President Jackson's response would be. If the United States government were to allow this challenge to its authority to stand, the union of states would, he believed, be ended. Jackson warned South Carolina that nullification was not possible under the Constitution. Federal law, he said, would be enforced. Resistance to it was treason. The President sent a warship with reinforcements to the forts in Charleston Harbor, and said he stood ready to lead an army, if necessary. Privately, he threatened to hang Calhoun.

Seeking a compromise. In Congress, meanwhile, Henry Clay led an effort to find a compromise. In March 1833, Congress passed a bill to lower the tariff, over a ten-year period, to its 1816 levels. On the same day, the Force Bill was passed. This act allowed the President to use troops if necessary to enforce the law in South Carolina.

Although South Carolina had invited other southern states to follow its lead, none did. Standing alone against the United States government, South Carolina accepted the compromise. The convention met again and repealed its ordinance nullifying the tariff. But in a final act of defiance, it passed another ordinance nullifying the Force Bill.

Both sides claimed victory. Unionists declared that they had faced down the challenge. Southerners pointed out that they had won their objective, a lower tariff. Often it is desirable to have an outcome in which each side can feel it has won something. In this case, however, such an outcome may have done more harm than good. It left the key question of states' rights versus federal power unanswered. That question would rise again and again over the next quarter century. The answer would not finally come until the blood of hundreds of thousands had been shed.

CHECKUP

1. In what ways was Jackson's administration different from earlier ones?
2. Why did Jackson veto a bill to help pay for the Maysville Road?
3. How was the nullification crisis of 1831—1832 settled?

Jackson and the Bank

One of the biggest struggles of the Jackson period concerned the Second Bank of the United States. To understand Jackson's war against the Bank, you will need to know something about money and banking in those days. The main money was gold and silver, also called *specie* and "hard money." Banks added to this money supply by printing paper money called bank notes. On the face of each note was stated the amount and the promise of the issuing bank to redeem, or convert, the note into dollars of gold or silver on demand. As long as people were confident that a bank could and would redeem its notes in hard money, few would bother to convert

Andrew Jackson spent his last years at the Hermitage, his home near Nashville, Tennessee.

them. The notes were just as good as hard money. A bank could safely issue several times as much in bank notes as it had gold and silver in reserve. It was unlikely that all of its noteholders would redeem their notes at one time.

The more notes a bank printed, the more money it had to lend. The more it lent, the more it could earn through interest charges. You can see the temptation, then, for a bank to print a lot of notes. On the other hand, if a bank issued too many notes, it ran the risk of not having enough gold or silver to redeem them when presented. If that happened, the bank would have to go out of business. A well-run bank, therefore, would not issue more than three or four times as much in notes as it had specie in its vault.

Easy-credit practices. Not all banks, however, were well run. In fact, not all people wanted them to be well run. Those who wanted easier credit were in favor of banks printing a great number of bank notes. The more paper money there was, the easier it would be to borrow.

That was the case in the West after the War of 1812. You will recall that high prices for cotton and farm products led to a great demand for land. Settlers bought more than they needed, planning to sell at a profit later. Speculators also bought up large pieces of choice land. Westerners, short on cash, financed these purchases by borrowing. This was easy to do, for state banks in the West—privately owned banks that operated under state charters—followed reckless practices. They printed and lent far more bank notes, and required far less security for the loans, than was wise. Since people could borrow easily to buy land, demand for land rose. And as demand rose, prices soared.

Second Bank of the United States. What did the Second Bank of the United States have to do with this? The Bank was chartered by Congress in 1816 for a twenty year period. It was like other banks in a number of ways. It took deposits, issued notes, and made loans.

But it was different in important ways. The Bank of the United States was the only bank chartered by the federal government, which also owned one fifth of the stock. With a capital of $35 million and deposits several times that much, the Bank of the United States was far larger than any other bank in the nation. It was the only bank that had branches—twenty-nine in all—in every part of the country. It held the deposits of the United States government, which could amount to several million dollars at any one time.

Most important, it had great power over other banks. This was because in the normal course of its large business the Bank of the United States received great numbers of the notes of other banks. At any time, the Bank would present notes for thousands of dollars to an issuing state bank and demand gold or silver in exchange. State banks all over the country therefore had to think twice before printing great amounts of paper money.

In the first few years of its life, the Bank did not use its power to redeem notes in gold or silver. In fact, between 1816 and 1818 its western branches overissued and overlent bank notes just as the state banks were doing. Thus the Bank helped to fuel the speculation and rising land prices in the West.

The Panic of 1819. Finally realizing that this was not sound banking, the Bank of the United States put the brakes on credit in 1818. It reduced its bank notes and cut down its loans. It also presented to the state banks large numbers of their notes for payment in gold and silver. This put the Bank in healthy condition again, but it forced out of business a number of state banks that didn't have enough hard money to redeem their notes. It also led the remaining state banks to cut down their note issues by half in less than two years. Fewer notes meant fewer loans; fewer loans meant fewer buyers of land; and less demand for land meant falling prices. Those who had counted on paying off bank loans by selling lands at high prices were caught in the squeeze. Thousands lost their lands and farms.

As word got out that the banks were in trouble, people hurried to convert bank notes into hard money. That only made more banks go under all the sooner. The Panic of 1819 was on. A depression followed that lasted in the West for two years.

The speculation probably would have led to a crash sooner or later, even had there been no Bank of the United States. But the Bank's action had clearly helped to bring it on. Westerners—farmers and bankers alike—were bitter about the Bank ever after. They agreed with the person who noted, "The Bank was saved and the people were ruined."

Differing views on the Bank. In 1823, Nicholas Biddle, a wealthy Philadelphian, became president of the Bank of the United States. Under his able leadership, the Bank became prosperous while performing important services to the American economy. It held one third of all the bank deposits in the United States, and it made one fifth of all the loans. These loans helped hundreds of small businesses to grow. The Bank's notes, as sound as gold or silver coin, added to the money supply. By helping to keep prices stable and the economy strong, the Bank won many supporters.

The Bank, however, also had many foes. State banks in all parts of the country were unhappy about having to compete for business against the branches of the Bank of the United States. Those who wanted to see more paper money and easier credit were against the Bank. Such "soft-money," or "cheap-money," people included not only farmers in the West and South but also rising business people in eastern cities. And hard-money supporters opposed the Bank because it allowed paper money to circulate at all. Many of those people were eastern workers.

There was also growing opposition on the grounds of privilege and power. The Bank of the United States was the only bank with a federal charter, and it had a monopoly on the government's deposits. This privilege brought great profits for its stockholders. Most of them were wealthy Northeasterners, and a good

Jackson attacks the Bank, shown as a many-headed serpent. The heads are those of Bank officials.

★7★
Andrew Jackson
1767—1845

Born in SOUTH CAROLINA
In Office 1829—1837
Party DEMOCRATIC

A symbol of the common man. Resisted South Carolina's nullification of federal tariffs. Killed the Bank of the United States. Used the spoils system in filling government jobs.

number were English investors. Further, although the directors of the Bank had great power over the whole American economy, they were not accountable to the public.

A rechartering proposal. President Jackson understood little about banking. A bad experience with paper money at the age of thirty had left him a hard-money man. "I do not dislike your Bank any more than all banks," he told Biddle. That, of course, was not much consolation for the Bank's president.

Early in his term, Jackson stated that he thought the Bank was not constitutional. In the Supreme Court case of *McCulloch* v. *Maryland* in 1819, Chief Justice John Marshall had ruled that it was. But Jackson believed the President had an equal right with the Court and Congress to decide on such questions for himself. Biddle worried about the Bank's future, tried to win support by granting loans to lawmakers and journalists on very favorable terms.

Biddle then made a fatal mistake. Henry Clay was planning to run as a National Republican against Jackson in 1832 and was looking for a winning issue. He believed the Bank would be one. Clay urged Biddle to ask Congress to recharter the Bank in 1832, four years before the old charter would expire. Clay knew that Congress would do so. Then, if Jackson signed the bill, the President would lose support in the West and South. If he vetoed it, he would lose support in the Northeast. Biddle agreed to ask for the recharter.

In July 1832 Congress passed the recharter bill. Jackson understood the strategy well. "The Bank, Mr. Van Buren, is trying to kill me," he said to his political ally and Secretary of State, "but I will kill it." Jackson vetoed the bill. Although his veto message was addressed to Congress, it was really aimed over Congress's head at the American people. The Bank, said Jackson, was unconstitutional because it was not really "necessary and proper." It was un-American, declared the President, because it had a large number of foreign stockholders. It was undemocratic because it put great "power in the hands of a few men irresponsible to the people."

Perhaps most important, Jackson argued, it was wrong for the government to give monopoly privileges to a few of its citizens—namely, the stockholders of the Bank.

> . . . when the laws [are used] . . . to make the rich richer, and the potent more powerful, the humble members of the society—the farmers, mechanics, and laborers—who have neither the time nor the means of securing like favors to themselves, have a right to complain of the injustice of their government.

Henry Clay had his issue. He could not have made a bigger mistake. Clay was able to rally Bank supporters to his side. But Jackson, by his veto message, once more appeared to be the champion of the common people and the foe of privilege. And in this new day of broader voting rights, there were many more common people than friends of the Bank. In the 1832 election, Jackson and his running mate, Martin Van Buren, overwhelmed Clay, 219 electoral votes to 49.

The "pet banks." The election of 1832 doomed the Bank of the United States to end when its charter ran out in 1836. Jackson, however, decided not to wait. On his orders, government deposits were withdrawn from the Bank and placed in certain state banks, which the opposition called "pet banks." Stripped of its business with the government, the Bank of the United States was little more than an empty shell by the time its charter ran out in 1836.

All together, 89 state banks received government deposits. They were supposed to have been chosen for political reasons, and a good number of the banks were less than sound. With the government's gold in their vaults, they could issue many more bank notes. Even those state banks that did not hold government deposits could do this, for the Bank of the United States was now without power to stop them. In the West, new "wildcat banks" sprang up—unreliable banks, issuing large numbers of notes with almost no specie to back them. Borrowing was easy. Between 1829 and 1836 the amount lent by state banks rose from $137 million to $475 million. These loans touched off wild speculation, especially in land. Government land sales doubled and then doubled again within a single year. Many buyers paid the United States Treasury with the cheap and nearly worthless paper money of the wildcat banks. And where was this money deposited? In the pet banks, which promptly lent it out again, adding to the speculation.

The Specie Circular. Hard-money men were aghast. They had cheered the death of the Bank because it issued paper money. Now they beheld the results of their victory—a country awash in cheap paper money. To stop this situation, President Jackson issued an order in July 1836 known as the Specie Circular. From that time on, said the order, the Treasury would accept only gold or silver as payment for public land.

The Specie Circular caused the sale of public lands to fall off sharply, for few people had gold or silver. Further, it led to a rush to convert bank notes into gold or silver. The weakest banks could not do this and quickly went under. At the very same time, Congress passed a law known as the Distribution Act. Receipts from land sales had paid off the national debt and left the United States government with a surplus, and this act provided that it be distributed to the states. This meant that the pet banks, among which the surplus was deposited, had to pay out a lot of money to the states at the very time they were feeling the effect of the Specie Circular.

The Panic of 1837. Soon panic spread, just as it had in 1819. The Panic of 1837 quickly turned into a depression. Struggling to survive, banks refused to renew old loans or to make new ones. Businesses failed. Thousands were thrown out of work. Unemployed workers in Philadelphia and New York rioted. Construction on roads and canals stopped, throwing thousands more out of work. Farm prices fell. Cotton, which had brought fifteen cents a pound in 1836, slid to six cents a pound by 1842.

In large part, the panic and depression were results of Jackson's policies. Killing the Bank of the United States removed an important check on the "cheap-money" tendencies of state banks. The speculation that followed would probably have led to a crash sooner or later, but it was Jackson's Specie Circular that made it sooner.

Van Buren as President. Fortunately for Jackson's popularity, he had left office by the time the panic and depression hit. The new President was Martin Van Buren, Vice President during Jackson's second term. Van Buren was called by some The Little Magician for his skills as a politician. A long-time political leader in New York State, he had been one of the first to understand the changes that

the rise of the common man would bring to politics. He was one of Jackson's early supporters for the Presidency, and with Old Hickory's backing had easily won the Democratic party nomination in 1836.

The Democrats were opposed by the Whig party, a collection of groups and individuals that had little in common except opposition to Jackson. The Whigs took their name from the British party that had opposed George III, claiming that they, too, stood for liberty— against the authority of King Andrew I.

Knowing there was little chance of defeating Van Buren in a head-to-head race, the Whigs ran sectional favorites in different parts of the country. The hope was that together the candidates would win enough votes to keep Van Buren from getting a majority and thus throw the election into the House of Representatives. The plan failed. Only General William Henry Harrison, the Whig candidate in the West, ran well.

Van Buren was in office less than three months when the panic broke. In those days it was believed that a depression, like a common cold, had to run its course. It was felt there was nothing the government could do, or should do, to deal with it. Thus, during the next four years, Van Buren watched helplessly as the depression racked the country and wrecked his Presidency.

The election of 1840. The scent of victory was in the air as the Whigs gathered to choose their candidates for the 1840 election. To oppose Van Buren, they named General William Henry Harrison. The Indian fighter and hero of the battle of Tippecanoe had shown strength in

★8★
Martin Van Buren
1782—1862

Born in NEW YORK
In Office 1837—1841
Party DEMOCRATIC

First President who made a career of politics. Depression struck the nation soon after he took office, and it lasted throughout his term. He failed in his attempt to win reelection.

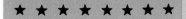

★9★
William Henry Harrison
1773—1841

Born in VIRGINIA
In Office 1841
Party WHIG

Won fame fighting Indians at Tippecanoe and British in War of 1812. Served Ohio in Congress. At sixty-eight, the oldest man to be elected President. Served one month.

★10★
John Tyler
1790—1862

Born in VIRGINIA
In Office 1841—1845
Party WHIG

First Vice President to become President on death of Chief Executive. A former Democrat, he clashed with Whigs after becoming President. Signed bill annexing Texas.

the West in 1836. To carry the South, the Whigs chose for the Vice Presidency John Tyler, a states' rights Virginian. The party wrote no platform, for the varied elements in the party could not have agreed on one.

The campaign showed that the Whigs had learned well the strategy of politics in the new democratic age. Although Harrison was a country gentleman, living in a sixteen-room mansion in Ohio, the Whigs presented him as a simple man of the frontier, born in a log cabin. Meanwhile, Van Buren was pictured as a man with aristocratic tastes and no feeling for the common people who were suffering in the depression. It was a rerun of 1828, but with the sides reversed. The Whigs, with their slogan "Tippecanoe and Tyler too," claimed to be standing for the ordinary people against "Van, Van, the used up man."

Harrison won by a large majority of electoral votes, although the popular vote was somewhat closer. Shortly after taking office, however, Harrison died, and Tyler completed the term. Tyler's administration was marked by many quarrels with the leaders of his own party. Four years later they refused to renominate him.

The Jacksonian era witnessed a great broadening of democracy. Also, it was a time of broadening opportunities for many Americans. Seeking fulfillment of a national destiny as well as opportunity for themselves, Americans were a people on the move. They pushed steadily toward the nation's western boundary—first the Mississippi River and then, after the Louisiana Purchase, the Rocky Mountains.

Opportunity lay not only in the open spaces of the West, however. It was to be found also in the towns and cities of the East and Middle West. Thousands upon thousands moved to cities, starting the rapid growth that would eventually make the United States an urban nation. Many people were lured by the opportunities created by the growth of commerce and manufacturing. Still small at the start of this era, manufacturing was firmly established by its end. In the next chapter you will learn about America's industrial beginnings. You will also learn how the westward movement and the War of 1812 spurred industrial growth.

CHECKUP

1. What were the strengths and the weaknesses of the Second Bank of the United States?
2. Why and how did Jackson "kill" the Bank? What was the effect of his action against the Bank in the 1832 election?
3. What part did Jackson's policies play in bringing on the Panic of 1837? How was Van Buren affected?

Key Facts from Chapter 13

1. As the nation's borders expanded during the early 1800s, three sections—the North, the South, and the West—developed differently with different interests.

2. Sectionalism—the attempt of each section to advance its own interests on the national scene—became a strong but divisive force in American politics and government.

3. Sectional issues included the tariff, slavery, government land policy, internal improvements, and banking policy.

4. The extension of the right to vote to almost all white adult males made possible the election of Andrew Jackson as President.

5. Jackson championed the cause of the "common man." During the Jacksonian era, ordinary people gained greater influence and participation in government.

6. Jackson's fight against the Bank of the United States was popular, but killing the Bank indirectly helped to bring on the Panic of 1837.

7. One issue that came to the fore during Jackson's administration was that of states' rights, especially the right of a state to nullify a federal law within its own borders.

★ REVIEWING THE CHAPTER ★

People, Places, and Events

Review Questions

1. Why did Missouri's request for admission as a slave state cause so much controversy? *Pp. 336–337*
2. What were John Quincy Adams's particular strengths and weaknesses as President? *Pp. 339–340*
3. Why is Jacksonian democracy described as "the rise of the common man"? *P. 342*
4. How did the procedures for nominating and electing a President change during the 1820s and 1830s? *Pp. 343–344*
5. What were Jackson's views about the role of the President? *P. 345*
6. Contrast the two points of view about the nature of the federal union as expressed by Hayne and Webster in their debate. *P. 346*
7. Why were so many Americans opposed to the Second Bank of the United States? *Pp. 351–352*
8. Why did Clay push for a rechartering of the Bank in 1832, when its charter did not expire until 1836? *P. 352*
9. Why was the Whig party formed, and when was it successful? *Pp. 354–355*

Chapter Test

For each sentence, write the letter of the correct ending. For some sentences, there may be more than one correct ending. Use a separate piece of paper.

1. The Specie Circular caused **(a)** the sale of public lands to fall off sharply, **(b)** a rush to convert bank notes into hard money, **(c)** the "Tariff of Abominations."
2. Robert Hayne and Daniel Webster argued their views on **(a)** slavery, **(b)** nullification, **(c)** specie.
3. President Jackson vetoed the **(a)** Distribution Act, **(b)** Maysville Road Bill, **(c)** Ordinance of Nullification.
4. The North and the West generally agreed on the following issues: **(a)** high tariffs, **(b)** internal improvements, **(c)** rapid western settlement.
5. The South objected to **(a)** high tariffs, **(b)** cheap land, **(c)** the spread of slavery.
6. The Missouri Compromise was arranged by **(a)** Andrew Jackson, **(b)** Daniel Webster, **(c)** Henry Clay.
7. John C. Calhoun's South Carolina Exposition and Protest upheld **(a)** the spoils system, **(b)** sectionalism, **(c)** states' rights.
8. Westerners opposed the strict money policies of **(a)** the Bank of the United States, **(b)** "pet banks," **(c)** "wildcat banks."
9. Jackson's Presidency has often been connected with **(a)** the rise of the common people, **(b)** the slavery issue in Missouri, **(c)** the spoils system.
10. Andrew Jackson was succeeded in office by **(a)** John Quincy Adams, **(b)** Martin Van Buren, **(c)** William Henry Harrison.

AMERICA'S INDUSTRIAL BEGINNINGS

I N ONE SENSE, there had been manufacturing in America as long as there had been British colonies. Almost from the beginning, some Americans had made their living from iron forges and blacksmith shops, from flour mills and sawmills.

The overwhelming majority of Americans, however, took their living from the soil and the sea throughout the seventeenth and eighteenth centuries. Thus when Thomas Jefferson wrote of his vision of the ideal America as a nation of small farmers, he was describing the America that actually existed. It was Alexander Hamilton who set forth a vision of a changed America—an America with factories. In his "Report on Manufactures," he proposed measures to make that vision a reality.

The First Factories

Today we can see that Jefferson's vision of America as a nation of small farmers was doomed from the beginning. As population in the West increased, the need for manufactured goods would increase also. The South, investing its capital in cotton lands, also required manufactured goods. Sooner or later American capital would be attracted into manufacturing to supply these increasing needs. Even as Jefferson was praising agriculture and deploring the appearance of factories, events were moving America toward industrialism. Indeed, the first factory in America had appeared in 1790, during George Washington's first term as President.

Slater's cotton mill. In 1788, Samuel Slater was a textile worker in a cotton mill in England, where the Industrial Revolution had begun. At that time, the British were trying to keep their ideas secret about machines and manufacturing so that they would have no competition. Parliament passed laws prohibiting textile workers and textile machinery from leaving the country.

However, Slater was lured to America by the promise of a rich reward for anyone who knew Britain's industrial secrets. Disguised as a farm boy, the twenty-one-year-old Slater slipped out of England. Soon after arriving in America in 1789, he built a spinning machine completely from memory. He helped set up America's first cotton mill in Pawtucket, Rhode Island.

In 1791, Alexander Hamilton and others tried to advance manufacturing dramatically by helping to organize the Society for Establishing Useful Manufactures. The society founded the city of Paterson, New Jersey, as a center for manufacturing in America. With crude machinery, the society began producing such items as yarn, cloth, and hats. The goods were of poor quality, however, and the machinery was undependable.

Effects of the War of 1812. The real beginning of America's industrial revolution came with the War of 1812. Before that time, the United States had been forced to rely upon Britain for most manufactured goods. American manufacturers lacked capital, for Americans with money were more likely to invest it

359

in land speculation or trade. There was a shortage of labor, for most people preferred to become farmers rather than to work in factories. Also, manufacturers found it hard to get their goods to market.

The War of 1812 changed many of these conditions. The embargo, the Non-Intercourse Act, and the war itself shut off the supply of British goods from 1808 to 1815. With the scarcity of imported products, Americans were encouraged to go into manufacturing. In 1800 there were but 7 mills making cotton thread in the United States. But in the single year 1809—when the embargo was followed by the ban on trade with Britain and France—89 new mills were built. By the end of the war, there were 213 such mills. Other manufacturers were soon making cloth, nails, guns, and other products. This was the start of America's industrial revolution. From these small beginnings, the United States was to rise to the top of all industrial countries in less than a century.

Advantages of the Northeast. Most American manufacturing was located at first in the Northeast—the New England states and New York, New Jersey, and Pennsylvania. The region had abundant waterpower. Since most early machinery was driven by the power of falling water, the river valleys became centers of industry. Mills making cotton and woolen cloth were built on such New England rivers as the Connecticut, the Merrimack, and the Housatonic.

When the War of 1812 cut off trade and commerce, many well-to-do merchants in the Northeast turned to manufacturing, and supplied the capital

that had been lacking earlier. In the words of one historian, they made the shift from "the wharf to waterfall," as they built their mills to run with waterpower. Most of the important banks and other financial institutions were also located in this part of the country.

The Northeast had numerous other advantages for starting manufacturing. In the 1820s, almost half of all Americans lived in that part of the country, and many began to look to the factories for work. The Northeast also had larger cities, bigger ports, and more roads and canals than other parts of the country. And in the states of New York, New Jersey, and Pennsylvania there were big deposits of coal and iron.

The Waltham factory. In 1814 a group of wealthy men known as the Boston Associates built a textile factory in Waltham, Massachusetts. It was the first factory to bring under one roof all the steps in manufacturing cloth, from spinning the raw cotton to dyeing the finished cloth. Most of the factory's machines were driven by waterpower. The Boston Manufacturing Company, as it was called, was a success from the start. In the late 1820s the Boston Associates built more factories at a Massachusetts site named Lowell after one of the Associates.

After the successes in Waltham and Lowell, textile-mill towns sprang up in New Hampshire and Rhode Island as well as in Massachusetts. When New Englanders moved westward into the Mohawk and Hudson river valleys of New York State, they took the system of textile manufacturing with them. By 1830, the United States had 800 cotton mills.

CHECKUP
1. How did Hamilton's vision of America differ from Jefferson's?
2. Why did the War of 1812 help to bring on America's industrial revolution?
3. In what part of the country was most American manufacturing located at first? Why?

The Expansion of Industry

At first, factories were pretty much confined to the Northeast. The South lacked capital, which was tied up in land and slaves. The lightly settled West lacked both capital and labor.

A westward move. In time, however, people moved westward. The states carved out of the Northwest Territory provided a larger market. They also provided a greater labor supply and a growing number of cities from which goods were distributed. Some of these cities began processing the farm goods grown in the region. This gave rise to such new industries as flour milling, lumber manufacturing, meat-packing, and the making of leather goods.

As population increased in the West, there developed a belt of manufacturing rivaling that of the Northeast. Stretching from Pittsburgh to St. Louis, the industrial buildup was especially strong along Lake Erie and in the Ohio River Valley. Besides meat, flour, and lumber products, the factories of the region manufactured farm machinery, whiskey, bagging, and other things. In most cases, these industries could manufacture products and sell them in the West more cheaply than they could be imported from the East.

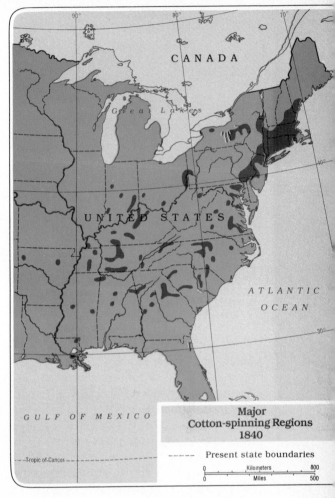

Major
Cotton-spinning Regions
1840

----- Present state boundaries

By 1840, cotton spinning was a major industry in the United States. Most spinning mills were in the river valleys of the Northeast.

The effect of inventions. A number of inventions spurred the rapid expansion of America's industry. As early as 1804, Oliver Evans, a mechanic and shopkeeper from Delaware, had revolutionized flour milling. His inventions included a conveyor-belt system, an elevator,

361

Industry developed rapidly in Pittsburgh where the Allegheny and Monongahela rivers join.

and a new grinding process. These operations were all automatic, and by combining them, Evans devised the first *automated* factory.

Between 1825 and 1850, there was a rash of new inventions and processes. In 1844, Charles Goodyear succeeded in making rubber that could withstand heat and cold. This made it possible to produce such articles as raincoats and rubber boots. In 1846, Elias Howe received a patent for his sewing machine, thereby providing the basis for a ready-made clothing industry. Hundreds of smaller inventions, including friction matches, lead pencils, the Colt pistol, and screw-making machines, served as the start for new industries.

In Europe, wage earners often feared such new inventions. They thought technological advances might cause

them to lose their jobs. British visitors to the United States were therefore surprised to find that American workers "hail with satisfaction all mechanical improvements." The reason, of course, was that American working people saw inventions as the agents of progress and material well-being.

Machinery on the farms. Inventions also led to greater production on farms. In 1819, Jethro Wood, a farmer in central New York, patented a cast-iron plow that was an important advance over the centuries-old wooden plow. In 1847, John Deere built the first all-steel plow. At his factory in Moline, Illinois, he was soon making thousands of plows each year to meet the demand.

Another major development in agriculture was the invention of the reaper. This machine did the work in reaping grain that had hitherto been performed by men with scythes. In the 1830s, Obed Hussey of Ohio and Cyrus McCormick of Virginia patented reaping machines that were much alike. But by the 1850s, McCormick's reaper dominated. He established a manufacturing plant in Chicago, and by 1860, about 100,000 of his machines had been sold. Another 250,000 came into use within the next five years. "The reaping machine," according to one report of that period, "is a saving of more than one third the labor when it cuts and rakes."

The American system. America's great progress in technology and industry was soon noticed throughout the world. In 1851, the British held a large industrial fair at the Crystal Palace in London. Among the American products shown there were the McCormick reaper, the Colt revolver, and some Goodyear rubber products. The British were amazed. A London newspaper wrote: "Their reaping machine has carried conviction to the heart of British farmers. Their revolvers threaten to revolutionize military tactics."

So impressed were the British that they sent a committee to the United States to investigate the reasons for America's economic progress. One main reason they discovered was that Americans applied the ideas of *mechanization* and *division of labor* to all processes of manufacturing. Wherever possible, Americans used machines rather than human hands to perform a task. Americans also tended to break down the process of production into separate steps. A machine performed a single operation on the raw material, which would then be moved on to the next step.

Americans also employed labor-saving devices in moving materials through the factory process. As the British committee observed:

". . . everything that could be done to reduce labor in the movement of materials from one point to another was adopted. This includes mechanical arrangements for lifting materials from one floor to another, carriages for conveying materials on the same floor, and the like."

America's system of manufacturing also included the idea of *interchangeable parts.* Eli Whitney (the same person who devised the first cotton gin) had used this idea in his Connecticut firearms factory as early as 1798. Before that time, a gun was manufactured by a gunsmith, who made each part separately. If any part of the gun was broken, a new part had to be made to fit that particular gun. To meet a contract deadline for supplying guns to the government, Whitney hit upon the idea of manufacturing identical parts. Each part would fit any gun of the type being made. This meant that the broken gun could be repaired very quickly simply by slipping in a new part. Moreover, with large numbers of identical parts on hand, unskilled workers could assemble the guns.

This approach to manufacturing, sometimes called the "American system," was soon applied to hundreds of machines. It paved the way for mass production in the factory system. The procedure proved to be one of the most important developments in America's industrial history.

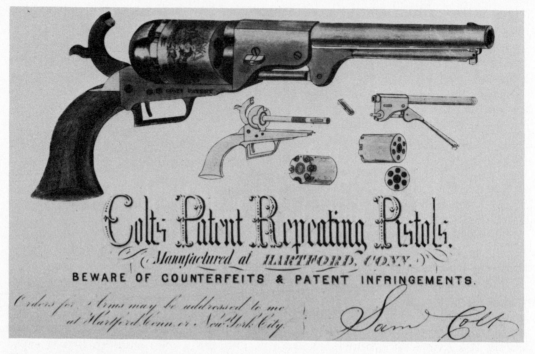

The revolver that Samuel Colt of Connecticut invented was assembled by a series of workers, each of whom did a single task. Thus the assembly line was added to the "American system."

Rise of corporations. Another development in the mid-1800s was the rise of the corporation as a form of business organization. Up to about 1850, the two most common types of business organization were the single ownership and the partnership. But now, for several reasons, the corporation became increasingly popular. First of all, a business could raise large amounts of money by selling stock, or certificates of ownership, in the corporation. Secondly, a corporation received a charter; this gave it lasting life, so that its business was not interrupted by the death of the owner or the death or withdrawal of a partner. Finally, a person who invested in a corporation had only a limited liability—that is, if the corporation failed, the stockholder would lose only the amount of money that he or she had invested. In a partnership, each of the partners was personally accountable for all the debts.

Because of all these advantages, the corporation came into wide use as a form of business organization. During the 1850s, the number of corporations in manufacturing doubled.

American railroads. One industry that boomed in the mid-nineteenth century was the railroad industry. During the 1850s, railroad companies pushed their lines from the Atlantic Coast deep into the interior. In 1851 the Erie was the world's longest railroad, with 537 miles (859 km) of track. It linked the Hudson River north of New York City and Lake Erie. The following year, the Baltimore and Ohio connected Baltimore and Wheeling, West Virginia. In 1853, the New York Central was formed out of eight small lines, tying together Albany and Buffalo. And in 1858, the Pennsylvania Railroad ran its line across the Appalachian Mountains from Philadelphia to Pittsburgh.

By 1860, most of the nation's 31,000 miles (49,600 km) of track linked the Northeast to the Old Northwest. (This development had political as well as economic meaning, in that the two sections were tied together before the Civil War.) The rail network connected New York, Philadelphia, and Baltimore to such cities as Chicago and Cincinnati. About half of the lines were west of the Appalachian Mountains. Because of its strategic location. Chicago became the great railroad center of the Midwest.

Railroads had a great economic effect on the country. They made it possible to ship raw materials to factories over long distances. Manufacturers could also reach out to larger and more distant markets to sell their goods. Passengers could travel quickly and easily. In 1855 one could go by rail from the East Coast to Chicago or St. Louis in forty-eight hours. Thirty years before, such a trip would have required two or three weeks.

The railroads themselves were now big business. In many states they were the most important corporations with the largest amounts of capital. More than $1.2 billion was invested in railroad lines between 1830 and 1860, much of it coming from Europe. Public funds also went to the railroad industry. Local and state governments gave loans, or grants or purchased railroad stock. In 1850, Congress passed a bill providing for the first of many federal land grants. To help finance a railroad through Illinois, the federal government gave that

A train of the Michigan Central line is about to leave a sidetrack in the railroad yards in Chicago. The location of that Middle Western city made it a foremost railroad center.

state 3 square miles (7.8 square km) of federal land in alternate sections on both sides of the proposed line. This set an important precedent for future federal aid. By 1860, about 28 million acres (11.2 million ha) of federal lands had been given to the states to help them build railroads.

The iron and steel industries. The manufacture of locomotives, rails and other railway equipment, and machinery for America's factories required great amounts of iron. Iron had been produced in small quantities for many years, but the industry did not expand significantly until after the War of 1812. Then the introduction of machinery permitted manufacturing operations to be carried out on a larger scale. Also, new coal and iron deposits were discovered in western Pennsylvania and in the Ohio River valley.

After the 1820s, the iron industry boomed. High tariffs kept out foreign iron imports. As the textile industry grew, so did the demand for textile machinery. Iron stoves came into common use, and by 1850, more than 300,000 were being made each year. The growth of the railroad industry was an important factor in the the growth of the iron industry. In 1860, railroads purchased about $15 million worth of iron in the form of locomotives, rails, and other equipment. This was nearly half the nation's iron output.

As the iron industry grew in size, it became more concentrated in location. Pennsylvania produced almost half of America's iron by 1860, with Ohio ranking second. Pittsburgh gained a permanent place as a leader in the iron

and steel industries. But the output of steel was still small compared with that of iron. In 1860, steel output was only 12,000 tons (10,800 t).

Foreign trade. In the depression that followed the Panic of 1837, America's foreign trade fell to a thirty-year low. Beginning in 1843, however, foreign trade surged. Almost every year from then until 1860 saw a large gain over the year before, both in imports and exports. Much of the increase in exports was in western wheat. The United States still imported far more in manufactured goods than it sold abroad. However, a small but growing part of its export trade came from American industry.

Almost three-fourths of that foreign trade was carried in American sailing ships, which were the best in the world. America's sleek packets made the Atlantic crossing from Liverpool, England, to New York in an average of 33 days, nearly half the time of the shorter, stubbier British vessels. Sleekest of all the sailing vessels were the clipper ships. Long and trim, and topped by broad sails and the tallest masts that could be fashioned, the clippers' graceful hulls sliced through the waters in record time. Clippers cut the sailing time from New York to San Francisco via Cape Horn from 159 days to less than 90.

The growth of cities. Foreign trade had a direct effect on immigration and the growth of America's cities. The great increase in the number of ships made it possible for the millions who wished to migrate to America to find passage. A large percentage of those immigrants moved directly into America's cities,

American clipper ships, like the one shown above, were the fastest sailing ships of their time. The vessels were called clipper ships because they "clipped off" the miles.

helping their population to soar. Boston, a city of 93,000 in 1840, reached 178,000 in 1860. New York City grew from almost 400,000 to over a million in the same period. Philadelphia's population went from 94,000 to more than half a million. Inland cities, such as Cincinnati and St. Louis, also grew rapidly. Many of the new immigrants became workers in America's factories.

Industry at the takeoff point. American industry by 1860 was, despite its growth in the previous decade, still only in the early stages of development. Though some mills made steel and other "heavy industry" articles, most American manufacturing continued to be directed toward the simple processing of farm products. Factories were usually small, averaging about ten workers each. Moreover, America was still a large importer of foreign manufactured goods because it could not satisfy its own needs.

The 1860 census showed more than 140,000 manufacturing places and 1.5 million workers in industry. Nearly 60 percent of America's labor force was still involved in agriculture, but the picture was changing rapidly. The United States was on the verge of a great industrial breakthrough, which would change the country from a farming to a manufacturing nation.

CHECKUP

1. What were some of the inventions that led to the expansion of industry and the increase in farm production during the nation's first century?
2. What were some of the factory processes that brought worldwide attention to the American system of manufacturing?
3. How did the growth of foreign trade affect the growth of cities?

The Dark Side of Industrialism

Not all Americans agreed that tons of steel or yards of cloth were the proper measure of progress, either for the nation or for individuals. Surely, they believed, there were measures of greatness other than material goods—for example, things of the mind and of the spirit.

Thoreau's criticism. One of these critics was Henry David Thoreau, a native of Massachusetts. Thoreau believed that the scramble for wealth was changing American society and destroying both human and natural resources. The new emphasis on "getting ahead" was, according to Thoreau, a false value. He wrote:

> There is no more fatal blunderer than he who consumes the great part of his life getting a living. . . . It is not enough to tell me that you worked hard to get your gold. So does the Devil work hard.

And at another time, Thoreau wrote:

> Most men are so occupied with the . . . cares and . . . hard labors of life that its finer fruits cannot be plucked by them.

All these bad effects were, to Thoreau, the evil products of industrialism. To him, the railroad, symbol of progress to so many Americans, was the symbol of a change that was making people the slaves of machines. "We do not ride on the railroad," he wrote. "It rides upon us."

In 1846, Thoreau built a hut in the woods at Walden Pond, near Concord, Massachusetts. There he lived alone for more than two years, free from machines, government, and the products of modern civilization. Thoreau later explained his purpose:

> I went to the woods because I wished to live deliberately, to front only the essential facts of life, and see if I could not learn what it had to teach, and not, when I came to die, discover that I had not lived.

Some years afterward he published *Walden*, a classic book about his ideas and experiences during that period.

Emerson and Melville. Another who expressed concern about the changing American values was Thoreau's friend, Ralph Waldo Emerson. Also a native of Massachusetts, and a writer and philosopher, Emerson was the most famous public lecturer of his day. Emerson did not dislike industrialism as did his friend Thoreau. But Emerson was much troubled by the growing emphasis in America upon material things. To him, the measure of progress lay in such things as the growth of democracy, of individualism, and of self-reliance. These were the true values that Americans should hold high.

Thoreau declared that Americans, intent on success, were basing their lives on false values.

368

The Lyceum Movement

Education has long been part of the American Dream, but it has not always taken place in the classroom. In the late 1820s the desire for more knowledge and culture led to the rise of groups known as lyceums. The lyceum movement was an effort to spread popular learning among adults who were interested in improving their minds.

The movement actually began in Great Britain and then spread to America. In the United States its father was Josiah Holbrook of Connecticut, a traveling lecturer and part-time schoolmaster. He founded the first American lyceum in 1826 in Millbury, Massachusetts. Within six years, there were more than three thousand lyceums in America.

In the lyceums, people could hear talks or debates on such public issues as capital punishment, school curriculum reform, and popular science. Ralph Waldo Emerson, Oliver Wendell Holmes, and other outstanding thinkers and writers gave lectures. Musical artists performed, and scientists gave demonstrations of their experiments. Holbrook often supplied lyceum groups with pamphlets on various subjects and with mathematical and scientific materials that he had made himself.

The lyceum movement thus became a powerful force for social and political reform. Lyceum groups conducted discussions, established libraries, and lobbied for better schools. In some instances, the lyceums were responsible for setting up educational institutions. The Lowell Institute of Boston and Cooper Union in New York both began as lyceums. The lyceum movement faded after the Civil War. In its day, however, it satisfied the thirst for knowledge and culture that many Americans deeply felt.

The famous writer and philosopher Ralph Waldo Emerson lectures at a Massachusetts lyceum.

Herman Melville, one of America's greatest writers, was another who rejected the idea that material plenty necessarily meant progress for a society. In one of his essays, Melville described the lives and working conditions of young girls in a paper mill. His essay was a protest against the way humans were becoming secondary to machines.

As famous writers and lecturers, Thoreau, Emerson, and Melville could make their criticisms heard. But there were thousands of other people whose doubts that industrialism was bringing progress to America were never heard. These were the working poor who labored in America's factories and mines.

Factory workers. In 1800, nearly nine of every ten Americans were members of farm families. Although the remaining one in every ten included some skilled and unskilled workers in the cities, there was no large, ready pool of labor from which the rising new industries could draw. Workers in the early factories were therefore drawn from the poorer farm families nearby. Sometimes whole families were hired. More often it was just the women and children.

In Samuel Slater's first American factory, most of the workers were children. By 1820, about half of all the factory workers were children of nine or ten. Working from sunup to sundown six days a week, they received less than a dollar for their week's work. Yet at a time when children often worked full days on farms, few people thought it was bad for children to work in factories. The work was not considered hard, and the children's earnings, however small, added to their families' income.

The Lowell girls. The Boston Associates followed a different path in their factories, especially in the Lowell mills. Several of the Associates had visited England and had been horrified by the miserable working and living conditions of factory workers there. They hoped to avoid the development of such a permanent, depressed, wage-earning class in America. Therefore, they hired mostly young, unmarried women from New England farm families. During their employment, usually a year or two, the girls lived in company boarding houses. These lodgings were so well kept and supervised that parents were willing to allow their daughters to work and live in Lowell. Rules were strict: no drinking or card playing, everyone in bed by ten o'clock, and church attendance on Sundays. To improve their minds, the girls were encouraged to read books, to write letters, and to listen to lectures. Employees even published a magazine of their own poetry and other writings. Of their weekly wages of $2.50 to $3.00, about half went for room and board. The rest they saved, sent to their families, or spent.

For a time, Lowell was a showplace for foreign visitors. One visitor in 1842 was the famous English writer Charles Dickens. A short time before, Dickens had written a novel dealing with the desperate condition of the English working class. But after touring the mills in Lowell during his American tour, he wrote that he saw "no face that bore an unhappy and unhealthy look."

Yet other reports and events suggest that all was not what it seemed in the New England mills. A visitor to another cotton mill of the Boston Associates, in

Two "Lowell girls" operate looms in one of the textile mills that the Boston Associates built along the Merrimack River. The mills gave employment to hundreds of young women in New England.

Manchester, New Hampshire, wrote: "The atmosphere . . . is charged with cotton thread and dust, which, we are told, are very injurious to the lungs." And another visitor, writing about the Lowell girls shortly before Dickens did, reported that "the great mass wear out their health, spirit, and morals without becoming one whit better off than when they started."

In 1834, about one thousand Lowell girls walked off their jobs to protest a 15 percent wage cut. A few years later, several thousand were forced to leave the company boardinghouses after they formed an association to fight against worsening conditions in the mills. On another occasion, the Lowell girls tried without success to get the Massachusetts legislature to limit their workday to ten hours.

A changing industrial scene. Meanwhile, hundreds of other factories were rising elsewhere in America. They appeared not only in rural communities like Lowell and Manchester but, more and more, in such large cities as Boston, New York, and Philadelphia. In these places, bright, clean factories and comfortable boardinghouses were seldom, if ever, found. Instead, dark, dirty mills and slum housing were the rule. Moreover, during the 1840s and 1850s, the work force changed. Instead of farm girls who came to the factories for a year or two, there developed a wage-earning class made up mostly of immigrants. Soon the company boardinghouses of Lowell disappeared. It had now become clear that the experiment of the Boston Associates was not the pattern that American industry would follow.

A supervisor instructs a child laborer in her duties at a textile mill. During the 1800s, children made up a significant part of the labor force in factories of this kind.

At the same time, the rise of factories dealt a blow to the artisan class. This group consisted of independent skilled workers who until then had made most of America's clothing, boots, furniture, and other goods in their homes and small shops. By the middle of the nineteenth century, artisans were finding it impossible to compete with goods made by machines run by low-paid workers. A few artisans were able to get enough capital to hire other workers and even to start factories of their own. Most, however, had to give up their independent businesses. They were pushed down into the wage-earning class, although at a higher level than that of the unskilled worker.

Women and children in the mills. In most factories of the 1800s, hours were long—in fact, a 70-hour workweek was normal! Wages were low, and working conditions were grim. Women made up probably 20 percent of the factory work force. They were most numerous in four industries: boots and shoes, ready-made clothing, cotton textiles, and woolens.

Children made up another large percentage of the workers. Beginning in the 1830s, child labor in the factories began to be a matter of deep concern. This was partly because factory conditions for child labor were growing worse. Seth Luther, a labor reformer, described what a visitor to a cotton mill in 1832 might expect to see.

He might see, in some instances, the child taken from his bed at four in the morning, and plunged into cold water to drive away his slumbers . . . After all this, he might see that child robbed, yes, robbed of a part of his time allowed for meals by moving the hands of the clocks backwards or forwards, as would best accomplish this purpose. . . .

The other part of the concern over child labor had to do with the growing awareness that education of the young was important. And as one person noted, "If thirteen hours actual labor is required each day, it is impossible to attend to education. . . ."

The birth of unions. Workers responded to the conditions of industrialism in the 1820s by forming "workingmen's organizations." These were the first American labor unions. Most of them were made up of skilled workers who were no longer independent but were employed by others. These workers organized to protest lower wages and also their loss in status. At first, the workers in a given trade—weaving or printing, for example—organized locally. They also took part in local politics. In 1828 a political party called the Workingmen's party was formed in Philadelphia. There were local labor parties in at least fifteen states.

Soon these local organizations were banding together to form national unions of printers, carpenters, and other skilled workers. And in 1834 these groups came together to form the National Trades Union. However, size was deceiving. This national union was, in fact, weak. A depression that began in 1837 (see page 282) dealt this national movement a blow from which it did not recover.

In 1842 the labor movement made an important gain. Before that time, the courts had held that workers' organizations were "conspiracies"—that is, criminal plots—and therefore unlawful. But in *Commonwealth* v. *Hunt,* a Massachusetts court ruled that it was legal for workers to form unions. This gain, however, was limited. First of all, it applied only in Massachusetts. Secondly, when unions tried to use the weapons of the strike and the boycott, the courts ruled against them.

The growth of unions during this period lagged. Hostile newspapers, unfavorable public opinion and court decisions, and the use of strikebreakers by employers—as well as court decisions—held down union growth. So also did the fact that many workers did not yet see themselves as a group with a common interest that could be advanced through common action. Therefore, by the middle of the nineteenth century, the number of workers who joined unions was small. Most who did join were skilled workers. The organization of unskilled factory workers would not come until many years later.

Two new groups. By the mid-1800s, no one could dispute that America, measured in material terms, had made great progress in half a century. Millions of Americans counted their blessings that they were living at such a time.

Accompanying these growing national riches was the appearance of two new groups: industrialists and factory workers. A disturbing aspect of this development was the uneven way in which the earnings of industry were divided. Parke Godwin, a newspaper writer, provided this picture of the growing gap between wealth and poverty in America in the 1840s.

> Walk through the streets of any of our crowded cities; see how within a stone's throw of each other stand the most marked and frightful contrasts. Here, look at this marble palace reared in a pure atmosphere and in the neighborhood of pleasing prospects. . . . Look you, again, to that not far distant alley, where some ten destitute and diseased families are nestled under the same rickety and tumbling roof; no fire is there to warm them; no clothes to cover their bodies. . . . the rain and keen hail fall on their almost defenceless heads. . . . Look you, at this, we say, and think that unless something better than what we now see is done, it will grow worse!

At the time Godwin was writing this, the wealth of America was spread more unevenly than ever before. By 1850, the top 1 percent of wealth holders owned 26 percent of the wealth in the United States. And the top 2 percent of wealth holders owned 37 percent of the nation's wealth.

In every country, industrialism has come at a high human price. As you have seen, America was no exception. At the same time, it is important to note that the human cost was lower in America than elsewhere. Workers in America, though by no means well-off, were far better-off than workers in other industrial countries. Proof of that fact lies not only in the statistics on wages but in the statistics on immigration of European workers to the United States.

While industrialism was changing the face of much of the eastern part of the nation, another drama was unfolding in the Far West. There, Americans were pursuing a vision of a nation that extended from ocean to ocean. In Chapter 15 you will read how that vision became reality.

CHECKUP

1. How did Thoreau, Emerson, and Melville feel about the growth of industrialism?
2. In what ways did the lives of the workers differ in the first mills in Lowell and in later factories?
3. Why were the first American labor unions formed? Why had they grown little by the mid-1800s?

Key Facts from Chapter 14

1. The first American factories, powered by falling water, were located alongside the rivers of the Northeast.
2. By cutting off trade with other countries, the War of 1812 stimulated America's industrial development.
3. The "American system" of manufacturing stressed the use of machinery, the division of labor, and the interchangeability of parts. It paved the way for mass production.
4. The factory system brought material plenty to many Americans, but to many others it brought grim working and living conditions.
5. Workers reacted to the ills of industrialism by forming labor unions.

People, Places, and Events

Samuel Slater *P. 359*

Boston Manufacturing Company *P. 360*

Charles Goodyear *P. 362*

Elias Howe *P. 362*

John Deere *P. 362*

Cyrus McCormick *P. 363*

Pittsburgh *P. 366*

Lowell girls *P. 370*

Review Questions

1. Why was Samuel Slater important in the development of American industry? *P. 359*

2. How did the War of 1812 stimulate America's industrial development? *Pp. 359–360*

3. Name five important inventors and their inventions of the first half of the nineteenth century. *Pp. 361–363*

4. Exactly what is meant by the "American system"? *P. 363*

5. What form of business organization became popular in the mid–1800s? Why? *P. 364*

6. Explain the role of the iron and steel industries in the economic development of the nation. *P. 366*

7. What specific criticisms of industrialism did the following people make: **(a)** Henry David Thoreau **(b)** Ralph Waldo Emerson **(c)** Herman Melville? *Pp. 368, 370*

8. What were working conditions like in the early factories? How did workers try to protect themselves against such conditions? *Pp. 372–373*

9. What two new social groups emerged in America as a result of the industrial growth of the 1800s? *P. 373*

Chapter Test

Copy the statements below and complete them by filling in the blanks. Use the vocabulary that has been introduced in this chapter.

1. In the 1820s, workers banded together to form "workingmen's organizations" and these became the first American _____.

2. The event that brought about the real beginning of America's industrial revolution was the _____.

3. _____, an English textile worker, who brought to America his knowledge of the latest machines, helped set up America's first _____ in Rhode Island.

4. Most American manufacturing was located in the _____ because this region had abundant _____.

5. The invention of the sewing machine by _____ provided the basis for a ready–made clothing industry.

6. One reason why the _____ came into wide use as a form of business organization was the fact that it had unlimited life.

7. By 1860, the state of _____ produced almost half of America's iron.

8. The growth of industrialism changed the United States from a _____ to a _____ nation.

9. Two important inventions that led to greater agricultural production were John Deere's first _____ and Cyrus McCormick's _____.

10. The three major characteristics of the "American system" were _____ _____, and _____.

FROM SEA TO SHINING SEA

MANY AMERICANS BELIEVED that their nation had a special mission to lead the rest of the world toward free institutions and a republican form of government. The nation's founders believed this mission would be fulfilled by example. A half century later their confident descendants declared that America should fulfill its mission not only by example but by "extending the area of freedom." With almost religious fervor, they proclaimed that more land should be brought under the American flag. To match such a grand vision, no boundary short of the Pacific Ocean itself seemed suitable.

The idea of the nation extending to the Pacific was not entirely new to Americans in the 1830s. When the United States was making the Transcontinental Treaty with Spain in 1819 (see page 288), Secretary of State John Quincy Adams told a cabinet meeting that it was a "law of nature" that all of North America should come under the American flag. Soon what Adams was saying privately was being said openly. There was nothing bashful about the way Americans stated their claims. Here, for example, is a speaker at a political convention in 1844.

Make way, I say, for the young American Buffalo—he has not yet got land enough; he wants more land as his cool shelter in summer—he wants more land for his beautiful pasture grounds. I tell you, we will give him Oregon for his summer shade, and the region of Texas as his winter pasture. Like all of his race, he wants salt, too. Well, he shall have the use

of two oceans—the mighty Pacific and the turbulent Atlantic shall be his. . . . He shall not stop until he slakes his thirst in the frozen ocean.

A member of Congress was just as open in a speech to the House of Representatives. Many of that body, he predicted, would live to hear the phrase from the Speaker's chair, "the gentleman from Texas." He wanted them also to hear "the gentleman from Oregon." He would even go further and have "the gentleman from Nova Scotia, the gentleman from Canada, the gentleman from Cuba, the gentleman from Mexico, aye, even the gentleman from Patagonia."

Manifest destiny. A Democratic journalist named John O'Sullivan summed up the urges of this restless people in 1845 when he wrote that it was America's "manifest [that is, self-evident] destiny to overspread the continent allotted by Providence for the free development of our yearly multiplying millions." The phrase *manifest destiny* was soon on the lips of editors, politicians, clergy, and ordinary Americans. It was a phrase with which many could agree, partly because it was so wonderfully vague. To some it meant expansion to the Pacific. To others it meant spreading over all of North America. To still others it meant controlling the Western Hemisphere.

Meanwhile, some people, both in government and out, were thinking of the more practical benefits that expansion would bring. Northern farmers were interested in the rich lands on the West Coast. Southern slaveholders saw Texas

377

as a place where cotton culture and slavery could expand. The three great Pacific ports—at Puget Sound in the Oregon country and at San Francisco and San Diego in California—were seen by eastern merchants and government leaders as doorways to trade with the Far East. Most of all, the United States was aware that Great Britain was interested in acquiring the entire western area of North America. A strong European power was the last thing that Americans wanted along their country's western border.

George Caleb Bingham caught the spirit of manifest destiny in this painting of a determined band of pioneers, led by Daniel Boone, moving through Cumberland Gap on their way west.

Adding Texas and Oregon

What opened the way for the United States to "fulfill its destiny" was the crumbling of Spanish power in the Americas. Between 1808 and 1824, every Spanish colony in South, Central, and North America except Cuba rebelled and won its independence. The new Republic of Mexico inherited all of New Spain, which included the present-day American Southwest.

Settlers in Texas. One of the Mexican republic's early goals was to encourage settlement in Texas, the northern part of the state of Coahuila-Texas. A developed Texas could serve to buffer the rest of Mexico from Indian raids and from an aggressive United States. It would, moreover, strengthen Mexico's economy. The Mexican government therefore offered free land to groups of Americans who would settle there. In 1820, Moses Austin received the first land grant, but he died soon afterward. His son Stephen took over the grant and led the first groups of American emigrants into Texas. Learning that the land was good for cotton, others from nearby states in the South poured into Texas with their slaves. By 1830, there were 20,000 white Americans and 2,000 slaves in Texas. There were only a few thousand Mexicans.

The Mexican government soon realized it had made a mistake. The Americans were difficult to control and unwilling to live by Mexican law. That law forbade slavery, but American slaveholders found a way around it. The law required immigrants to be, or become, Catholic, but most of the Americans who came were Protestant, and

San Antonio developed as a typical Mexican town, with a busy square lined by adobe buildings. This painting was made soon after Texas became a part of the United States.

they remained so. The Americans hardly bothered to learn more than a few words of Spanish. It was soon clear that they thought of themselves as Americans living in a place that, for the time being, belonged to Mexico.

In 1830 Mexico halted immigration from the United States and sent soldiers to Texas to tighten the rule. A few years later Mexico's president, General Antonio López de Santa Anna, dissolved the Mexican Congress, ended local government throughout Mexico—including Texas—and took on the powers of a dictator. Meanwhile, the Mexican government had been unable to enforce its law prohibiting Americans from entering Texas. By 1835, Americans there outnumbered Mexicans, 30,000 to 3,500. The Americans were in a rebellious mood over the loss of self-government. In that year there were a number of clashes between Mexican soldiers and the Texans. In 1836, Texas declared itself an independent republic.

The Alamo. Even as Texas proclaimed its independence an event was occurring that would give the Texans their battle cry. Determined to crush the rebellion, Santa Anna had led an army of some 4,000 soldiers against a Texas force of 187 men in San Antonio. The Texans took up a position in a deserted mission known as the Alamo. Fierce fighting raged for ten days, and the Mexicans lost 1,544 men. But on March 6, the Mexicans overwhelmed the Texans. The six defenders who survived the Mexican attack were executed at Santa Anna's orders. Among those who died at the Alamo were Jim Bowie, inventor of the hunting knife that is named for him, and Davy Crockett, a former congressman from Tennessee. Thereafter, "Remember the Alamo!" became the slogan of Texas forces.

The Lone Star Republic. A short time later, Mexican troops wiped out another Texas force at Goliad, southeast of San Antonio. But in April 1836, General Sam Houston, leading an army of fewer than 800, struck at a Mexican force almost twice that size at the San Jacinto River. Houston's troops killed or captured the entire Mexican force. The Mexican army was soon driven out of Texas completely. Houston was made president of the Republic of Texas. Within a month the Lone Star Republic (named after its flag with a single star) asked the United States to annex it, or take it over.

The United States had long wanted Texas. Presidents Monroe, Adams, and Jackson had all offered to buy it from Mexico. American citizens had sent guns and supplies to the rebels. A good many Americans thought of annexation as simply bringing Americans in Texas back under the United States flag and Constitution.

By the 1830s, however, many in the Northeast were opposed to annexing Texas because they did not want to add more slave states to the Union. (You will read more about this opposition in Unit 5.) For nine years after Texas became independent, its annexation was blocked in Congress by these objections.

The annexation of Texas. Meanwhile, the young republic needed protection against a possible attempt at restoring Mexican control. Therefore, Texas developed close ties with England. England was interested in Texas as a source of raw cotton for its factories and as a market for its manufactured goods. It also saw an independent Texas as a barrier to American expansion farther west. When the United States Senate turned down a treaty of annexation in 1844, the Texans seriously thought about making an alliance with England.

Expansion became an issue in the American presidential election of 1844, however. The Democratic party and its candidate, James K. Polk of Tennessee, came out for the annexation of Texas. Henry Clay, running for the Presidency for the third time, was the Whig party candidate. Clay straddled the annexation question—that is, he did not come out clearly for or against it. When Polk won, it was generally felt that the American people had chosen him because of his stand on Texas. The retiring President, John Tyler, had long favored bringing Texas into the Union. Now, in the final days of his administration, Tyler persuaded Congress to pass a joint resolution annexing Texas. On December 29, 1845, Texas entered the Union as the twenty-eighth state.

The Oregon country. Farther to the north and west, the United States was gaining another large area. In the early nineteenth century, a number of coun-

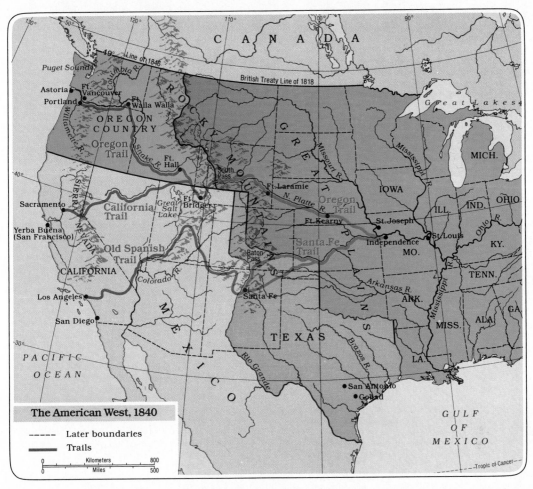

The American West, 1840

- - - - - Later boundaries
———— Trails

| Kilometers |
| 0 800 |
| Miles |
| 0 500 |

During the 1840s and 1850s, thousands of pioneers bound for Oregon and California made the grueling trip over the westward trails. As the wagon trains advanced, the trails were littered with articles cast aside to lighten the burden of the laboring horses and oxen. Alongside the rutted trails were markers over the shallow graves of those who had died along the way.

tries, including the United States and Great Britain, claimed the land called the Oregon country. It lay between the Rocky Mountains on the east and the Pacific Ocean on the west. From a southern boundary of 42° north latitude, it extended to 54°40′ north latitude, the southern boundary of Alaska. (At that time Alaska belonged to Russia.) The United States based its claim to the Oregon country mainly on the explorations of Lewis and Clark (see page 276). In 1810 an American merchant, John Jacob Astor, set up fur-

The Mountain Men

In opening the way for settlement of the Far West, the "mountain men" played a key role. They were trappers and traders who, in the early 1800s, moved into the Rocky Mountain region in search of furs. As they pushed deep into this strange and hostile land, danger was ever present. Sometimes they fought the Indians, but on other occasions they lived with them and even adopted the Indian way of life. Many of the mountain men dressed in moccasins and buckskins, took shelter in winter in lodges of buffalo skins, and married Indian women.

The big event each year for the mountain men was the spring *rendezvous*. This was a meeting of trappers, Indians, and traders in a mountain valley in Wyoming or Utah. There the mountain men and the Indians exchanged their furs for the traders' guns, ammunition, knives, traps, and such luxuries as flour and coffee. For a week or so, a holiday air prevailed. Then the gathering broke up. The traders' pack trains, laden with furs, headed eastward for St. Louis and other cities. The Indians returned to their villages. And the mountain men made their way back into the wilderness for another lonely year.

During their search for furs, the mountain men traced the great western rivers to their sources. They named many of the peaks of the Rockies, and they found passes through the towering ranges. Kit Carson charted trails to Utah, Oregon, and California. Jim Bridger became the first white man to look upon Great Salt Lake. Jim Beckwourth, a free black from Missouri, discovered the pass in California that today bears his name.

By 1840, the beaver hat had gone out of style, and the fur trade declined. The mountain men became scouts and guides. Over the trails they had used so often as trappers, they now led wagon trains of settlers into California and the Oregon country.

In 1837, trappers and traders meet for the spring rendezvous at Green River, Wyoming.

Pioneers going west prepare to encamp for the night beside a small stream.

trading posts along the Columbia River. Astor's Pacific Fur Company founded the settlement of Astoria. During the War of 1812, however, rival Canadian companies got their government to push Astor out with a show of force. After this, there was little American interest in the Oregon country for a quarter of a century.

Few people lived in the area. For that reason, the United States and Britain were willing to sign a treaty in 1818 to jointly occupy the Oregon country for ten years. In 1827 they renewed the treaty for an indefinite period, subject to cancellation on one year's notice.

In the 1830s a number of American missionaries and settlers went to Oregon. The first of them was Jason Lee, a Methodist missionary who arrived in 1833. Marcus and Narcissa Whitman were among the Presbyterians who arrived in 1836 to do work among the Indians. Four years later Father Pierre Jean De Smet arrived to represent the Catholics.

Many of the missionaries settled in the Willamette Valley and near the point where the Snake River enters the Columbia. They were soon sending word back east about the beauty of the Oregon country. Their descriptions of the

383

The territory originally claimed by the United States extended almost to the southern boundary of Alaska, then a Russian possession. However, the goal of most Oregon-bound pioneers was the fertile valley of the Willamette River.

mild climate and rich farmland aroused interest. Within a few years, Easterners had a case of "Oregon fever." In 1843 more than 1,000 people set out from Independence, Missouri, on the 2,000-mile (3,200-km) journey across plains, rivers, and mountains to the farmer's new paradise. Most of them traveled in groups for safety against Indian attacks as well as to help each other through the hardships of the five-month-long trip. By 1835, there were 5,000 Americans living in Oregon, with more on the way.

They formed a provisional government and asked the United States to take them over.

Fifty-four Forty or Fight. Expansionists soon laid claim to the entire Oregon territory. Politicians and journalists raised the cry "Fifty-four Forty or Fight," though no American lived north of the 49° line and there were solutions other than fighting. The annexation of Oregon, as well as Texas, became an issue in the election of 1844. When Polk won, he spoke out in favor of taking the entire Oregon country. Privately, however, he let it be known to the British minister that the United States would be satisfied to divide the territory at 49° north latitude. That line was the boundary between Canada and the United States from Lake of the Woods westward to the Oregon country.

The British minister rejected the offer without even consulting his government. Polk then renewed his demand for all the land up to 54°40′. The United States gave England the necessary one-year notice to end their agreement of joint occupancy. For a time it looked as if there might be war. But neither side wanted to fight, and in 1846 cooler heads worked out an agreement to divide the Oregon country at the 49° north latitude line.

CHECKUP

1. What meaning in America's history does the term *manifest destiny* have?
2. How did the United States acquire Texas?
3. What is the significance of the slogan "Remember the Alamo"? "Fifty-four Forty or Fight"?

The Mormons

Most of the pioneers who moved westward across the dry region that was then called the Great American Desert were bound for Oregon or California. But one group of people stopped and settled on the arid lands. They were members of the Church of Jesus Christ of Latter-Day Saints, more commonly known as the Mormons.

The Mormon church had been founded by Joseph Smith in western New York State in 1830. Smith's teachings met with hostility among many people, and he and his followers moved westward. In time, they settled in Nauvoo, Illinois. But disputes broke out there between the Mormons and their neighbors, and Smith was killed by a mob.

The new leader of the Mormons was Brigham Young. He determined to take his people into the western wilderness, far from other folks. In 1847 he led an advance party westward. The site that Young chose for the new Mormon community was a spot near Great Salt Lake in what was then Mexican territory. During the following months, thousands of Mormons made the long journey across the Great Plains to settle in the region they called Deseret.

A people with less discipline and dedication would not have survived. But the Mormons stressed cooperation. They worked hard to irrigate the dry lands and raise wheat and corn. By 1850, there were more than 10,000 settlers. As a result of the Mexican Cession, the region was now within the United States. It became the Territory of Utah, with Brigham Young as its governor.

On their trek to Utah, Mormon pioneers, pulling handcarts loaded with their goods, prepare to stop for the night. Earlier arrivals are starting fires for cooking the evening meal.

The War with Mexico

One reason the United States was anxious to settle the Oregon dispute peacefully was that the country was rapidly moving toward war with Mexico. Angered by the annexation of Texas, Mexico broke off relations with the United States in 1845. Furthermore, the two countries disagreed over the location of Texas's southern border. Mexico claimed it was the Nueces River. The United States held that it was the Rio Grande, the mouth of which was more than 100 miles (160 km) farther south, on the Gulf of Mexico.

Had that been the only issue there would have been no reason for war. Few Americans or Mexicans lived in the disputed area, and there was plenty of time to work out a solution. At this moment, however, President Polk was determined to acquire another piece of territory owned by Mexico. That territory was California, lying on the Pacific Coast south of the Oregon country.

Americans in California. American interest in California had built slowly since the first contacts of New England whalers and merchants in the early nineteenth century. At that time California belonged to Spain. Spain had established a string of missions in order to teach the Indians agriculture and convert them to Christianity. Spanish ranchers traded hides and tallow for the goods brought by the American merchants. This trade continued after control of California passed to Mexico in 1822. The region was sparsely settled, with only a few thousand whites—mostly Mexicans—in addition to a larger Indian population.

A few Americans settled in California in the 1830s and urged others to join them. Many were encouraged to come by the appearance in 1844 of John C. Frémont's report of his explorations in California. Frémont, an army officer, was one of a number who were exploring the Far West in those years. He had led earlier exploring parties through much of the Rocky Mountain country, Oregon, and California. Frémont's report on California made special note of the great possibilities for farming and commerce, and led many to move there over the years. By 1845 there were about 700 Americans in California. There were ten times as many Mexicans and even more Indians, but it was clear that a "California fever" was building, among Americans. Further, there were already conflicts between the Americans and the Indian and Mexican inhabitants over land and cultural differences. Many of the 700 Americans were itching to "play the Texas game." That is, they wanted to become a majority and then rebel, declare their independence, and ask the United States to take them over.

War is declared. At this point, President Polk sent a representative, John Slidell, to Mexico. He was told to work out differences over the Mexican border and other matters. He was authorized to offer to buy California and New Mexico for up to $30 million.

When the Mexican government refused even to talk to Slidell, Polk decided on war. American troops under the command of General Zachary Taylor were already camped south of the Nueces. Polk ordered them to the Rio Grande, knowing that this would pro-

United States troops under General John Wool leave San Antonio, Texas, in 1846 on their way to Mexico. The drawing was made by one of the soldiers, sixteen-year-old Sam Chamberlain.

voke a clash. The President had already prepared his message asking Congress to declare war. When the report of a battle arrived, Polk added the news to his message, claiming that "American blood has been shed on American soil." Thereupon, Congress declared war.

Waging the war. Mexico's armies were soon overpowered by the better trained, better armed, and more numerous American troops. General Taylor carried the war into northern Mexico, crushing Mexican resistance at the battle of Buena Vista in February 1847. General Winfield Scott marched his troops into the heart of Mexico and conquered the capital, Mexico City, in September 1847.

Meanwhile, the New Mexico territory had also fallen into American hands. An American army led by Colonel Stephen Kearny had moved from the East into California. There it joined a naval squadron that had taken San Francisco

387

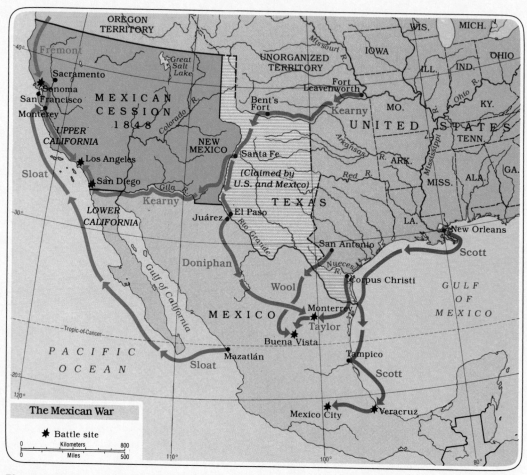

The Mexican War and the settlement that followed had unforeseen consequences for the United States. As you will see in Unit 5, the addition to the United States of the lands of the Mexican Cession revived old quarrels about slavery and thereby helped bring on the Civil War.

and Monterey. Even as the combined force was defeating the handful of Mexican troops, American settlers in California rebelled. Supported by soldier-explorer John Frémont, who was on another exploring trip to the region, they raised their bear flag (so called because it featured a picture of a grizzly

bear) and declared California to be an independent republic.

The peace treaty. In February 1848, the United States and Mexico signed the Treaty of Guadalupe Hidalgo, which ended the war. The treaty included the following terms: (1) Mexico accepted the

Rio Grande as its boundary with Texas. (2) Mexico *ceded*, or gave up, New Mexico and Upper California to the United States. (3) The United States paid Mexico $15 million for the new territory. (4) The United States paid American citizens some $3 million that the Mexican government owed them.

With the transfer of these vast territories from Mexico came a hundred thousand Mexicans who were living there. The treaty further provided that these people were free to move to Mexico, but that those who chose to stay for one year would automatically be citizens of the United States. Most of the people stayed.

One further strip of territory south of the New Mexico territory was bought from Mexico in 1853. This was the Gadsden Purchase, so called because James Gadsden, the United States minister to Mexico, arranged it. The land was wanted for a southern rail route to the Pacific. The purchase gave the United States its present southwestern boundary.

In 1848 even the most extreme believers in manifest destiny could look back upon the previous three years with satisfaction. In that brief time, the United States had increased its territory by 1,200,000 square miles (3,120,000 square km), an incredible 66 percent. That, Americans agreed, was land enough even for a restless, land-hungry people.

At the beginning of this unit, we noted that much of America's history is tied to the restlessness of its people. You have read how that restlessness gave the country most of its present land before

★11★

James K. Polk
1795—1849

Born in NORTH CAROLINA
In Office 1845—1849
Party DEMOCRATIC

Followed an expansionist policy. Directed war with Mexico, by which U.S. got California and Southwest. Settled Oregon boundary dispute. First President not to seek reelection.

the middle of the nineteenth century. Restless Americans—miners, cattle raisers, and farmers—swept over plains, deserts, and mountains to fill in half the continent in little more than one generation.

This migration, incredible as it is, tells only a part of the story of this people on the move. Another part is to be found in the growth of American cities. For no movement of this endlessly mobile people has been more continuous or greater in size than the flow of people

389

from farm and village to town and city. The movement to cities is very evident if we compare some statistics. In 1790, the year of the nation's first census, only one in thirty Americans lived in a city of 8,000 or more. Today it is very different. Nearly four out of five Americans are city dwellers.

Even this fact, however, does not give a complete picture of the moving Americans. It does not reveal the movement from one city to another. For example, the population of Boston, Massachusetts, grew from 383,000 to 448,000 between 1880 and 1890. That shows a gain of 65,000. But it does not show that nearly *fifteen times* that many— one and a quarter million—are estimated to have moved in and out of this one city during those same ten years! Studies of other cities of the time show much the same thing.

The effects of mobility. What have been the effects of this restlessness on the American people and their society? They have been many. As you have seen, there has been a clear connection between mobility and opportunity. The readiness to move about has made it possible for a

With the Gadsden Purchase of 1853, the United States great era of expansion on the continent of North America came to an end. The American people had spanned a continent. More than a century later, the state of Alaska and the offshore state of Hawaii would be added.

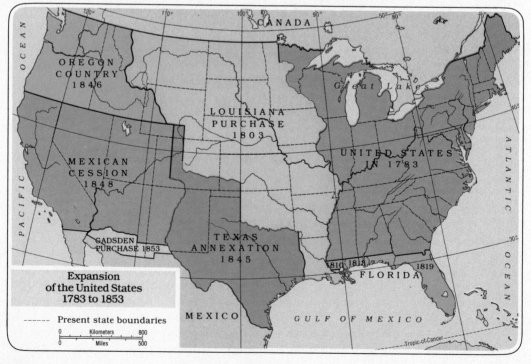

good many people to improve their positions and to rise in the world. It has also provided a safety valve for those who have not risen. Their luck, they say, will perhaps be better in the next town or in another part of the country.

Certainly all this mobility has had a great effect on the American family. We take for granted that young people will not be tied to the same place as their families. They will go wherever a job opportunity or their wish for adventure may take them. As a result, *family, home,* and *community* hardly mean the same in America as they do in a society where people are anchored to a place for generations.

Very probably this has something to do with the fact that Americans are a nation of joiners. The Elks and the Masons, churches and social clubs, may be substitutes for family, neighborhood, and village.

No doubt other possible effects of the rootlessness of Americans will occur to you. Knowing that friendships may be temporary, do Americans treat them differently? Americans are well known for their openness, their readiness to strike up new friendships, their first-name introductions to strangers. Are these traits connected to a need of an ever-moving people to form new relationships? Do Americans have less interest in local government, perhaps, or in preserving the quality of a town or neighborhood because tomorrow they may be someplace else? Does the practice of using things and then moving on affect their attitudes about conservation? These are some of the many questions that students of American society raise about the effects of mobility. Whatever may be the exact answer to any of them, it is clear that modern America has been shaped in important ways by the fact that its people, through all of their history, have been a people on the move.

CHECKUP

1. Why did the Mexican War take place?
2. How did the Mexican War alter the boundaries of the United States?
3. What territory was added to the United States by the Gadsden Purchase?
4. How has the restlessness of the American people affected American society?

Key Facts from Chapter 15

1. The term *manifest destiny* became popular during the 1840s as an expression of the expansionist goals of the United States.
2. Texas became independent of Mexico in 1836 and joined the United States in 1845.
3. A dispute between the United States and Great Britain over the Oregon country was settled in 1846 by dividing the region at 49° north latitude.
4. As a result of the war with Mexico, 1846–1848, the United States gained most of the lands that today make up the American Southwest.

People, Places, and Events

Manifest destiny P. 377

Santa Anna P. 379

The Alamo P. 379

Sam Houston P. 380

James K. Polk Pp. 380, 389

John Jacob Astor P. 381

Marcus and Narcissa Whitman P. 383

Mormons P. 385

John C. Frémont P. 386

John Slidell P. 386

Gadsden Purchase P. 389

Review Questions

1. What practical benefits could national expansion bring? Pp. 377–378
2. Why did the Mexican government encourage American settlement in Texas and then try to drive the settlers out? P. 378
3. Why was public opinion divided about the annexation of Texas by the 1830s? P. 380
4. What finally persuaded the United States to annex Texas? P. 380
5. On what evidence did the United States base its claim to the Oregon territory? Pp. 381, 383
6. What was James K. Polk's position on the issue of expansion in the election of 1844? P. 384
7. Give the following information about the Mexican War: **(a)** dates, **(b)** three causes, **(c)** American military leaders, **(d)** name of treaty, **(e)** specific terms of the treaty. Pp. 386–389
8. What have been some effects of mobility on the American people and their society? Pp. 390–391

392

Chapter Test

Match the name in the first section with the correct description in the second section. Write your answers on a separate piece of paper.

1. Winfield Scott
2. James K. Polk
3. Zachary Taylor
4. John C. Frémont
5. Sam Houston
6. John Slidell
7. Brigham Young
8. Marcus Whitman
9. Santa Anna
10. Jim Beckwourth
11. Rio Grande
12. Moses Austin
13. James Gadsden
14. John J. Astor
15. Jim Bridger
16. Nueces River

a. Mexican leader at the Alamo
b. "Mountain man" in California
c. American missionary in Oregon
d. Southern boundary of Texas, according to the United States
e. American diplomat sent to purchase California from Mexico
f. President of the Lone Star Republic
g. Expansionist President
h. Received a land grant from the Mexican government to settle in Texas
i. "Mountain man" and first white person to look upon Great Salt Lake
j. Southern boundary of Texas according to Mexico
k. American general who captured Mexico City
l. Soldier–explorer in the Far West
m. American general who first clashed with the Mexicans at the Rio Grande
n. Set up fur-trading posts in Oregon
o. Arranged a land purchase that gave the United States its present southwestern boundary
p. Mormon leader

FOCUS ON

Great Americans

CLAY, WEBSTER, AND CALHOUN

EMMA HART WILLARD

JAMES FENIMORE COOPER

SAM HOUSTON

CHAMPIONS OF REFORM

Three Giants of the Senate

The United States Senate has been the political home for some of the greatest figures in the history of our nation. Between 1830 and 1850, three senators stood out above all others. They were Henry Clay, Daniel Webster, and John C. Calhoun. Each aspired to the Presidency but did not achieve it. Each, however, left an important mark on the nation's history.

Henry Clay was born in Hanover County, Virginia, in 1777. When Henry was four, the death of his father left his mother to care for the nine Clay children. Henry helped work the family farm and got what formal schooling he could. When he was fifteen, his mother married again and the family moved to Richmond. There Henry's stepfather helped him get a job as a clerk with the state's highest court. George Wythe, one of the great lawyers of the time, noted Henry's good work and offered him a job

as his secretary. Henry worked and studied law for several years and, at the age of twenty, became a lawyer himself. He opened an office in Lexington, Kentucky. Soon after, he married Lucretia Hart, member of a well-known Lexington family.

In 1803, Clay was elected to the Kentucky legislature, his first political office. Eight years later he was elected to the United States House of Representatives. Remarkably, the members elected Clay, a first-termer, to be Speaker of the House. He served as Speaker for six terms. He left the House for a time in 1814 to help negotiate the treaty with England that ended the War of 1812.

Clay was one of the most popular orators in the House. On one occasion, when Clay was to make a speech, the United States Senate adjourned so that the members could hear him. The speech, which lasted three days, turned

Three giants of the United States Senate were Henry Clay of Kentucky *(left)*, Daniel Webster of Massachusetts *(center)*, and John C. Calhoun of South Carolina *(right)*.

This silk banner is from the 1844 presidential campaign. Henry Clay, the Whig candidate, was defeated by James K. Polk. It was Clay's third and last try for the Presidency.

out to be an important one in Clay's career. It dealt with General Andrew Jackson's invasion of Florida and his actions there. Clay spoke against the general. Jackson never forgave Clay, and was his enemy for life.

In American politics at that time, Congressmen were expected to put the feelings and interests of their home areas even above the national interests. This type of political thinking is called sectionalism. On issues and in behavior, Henry Clay expressed perfectly the mood and outlook of the West. He was easygoing, open, and friendly. He enjoyed gambling and was adventurous. Newspapers called him "The Western Star" and "Gallant Harry of the West." Clay's western temperament never changed. His development of the American System (see page 338), however, showed his growth from a sectional politician to a national statesman.

Clay, whose political career spanned almost fifty years, is best remembered as the Great Pacificator, or peacemaker. Three times he arranged sectional compromises to preserve the Union: the Missouri Compromise (see pages 337–338), the compromise tariff of 1833 (see page 348), and the Compromise of 1850 (see pages 446–448).

After running a poor fourth for the Presidency in 1824, Clay served as Secretary of State under President Adams. He entered the Senate in 1831. The next year he again ran for the Presidency and was soundly defeated by Jackson. Clay then became the chief organizer and leading figure of an opposition party, the Whigs. In 1844 the Whigs nominated Clay for his third try for the Presidency. This time he was narrowly defeated by Polk. He continued to serve in the Senate until his death in 1852.

Daniel Webster, the second of the three giants of the Senate, was born in New Hampshire in 1782. Daniel attended Dartmouth College and some years later became a successful lawyer in Portsmouth, New Hampshire. He soon turned to politics, becoming a Federalist. In 1812, a few months after the start of war with England, he was elected to Congress. Webster opposed the war. He refused to vote the money to pay for it. He even suggested that the states might nullify certain acts of Congress that were meant to support the war. But Webster never spoke of disunion, nor did he have anything to do with those New Englanders who did in 1814 (see page 284).

After the war, Webster continued to resist the spirit of nationalism that swept much of the country. He regarded himself mainly as a representative of New England shipping interests. He voted against the tariff of 1816, which both Clay and John C. Calhoun favored. A high tariff, he reasoned, would reduce the amount of goods to be imported.

Senator Daniel Webster replies to the states' rights argument of Robert Hayne during the famous Webster-Hayne debate. Senator John C. Calhoun can be seen at the far left.

This would cut into the business of the shippers who carried these goods. He also did not favor the Bank of the United States or internal improvements, two other parts of the American System. Webster would later change many of these views.

In 1816, Daniel Webster gave up his New Hampshire seat in Congress and moved to Boston, Massachusetts. There he developed a highly successful law practice. He argued and won a number of major cases before the Supreme Court. The most famous was *McCulloch v. Maryland* in 1819 (see page 352). By the 1820s, Webster was considered by most to be the best lawyer in the land.

Webster returned to Congress in 1823 as a representative from Massachusetts. Four years later he became a senator. By this time, great changes were under way in New England. Merchants had begun to invest in manufacturing. The making of cotton textiles and woolens had become important in Massachusetts. Webster now became a strong supporter of a high tariff that would protect Mas-

sachusetts manufacturers from foreign competition.

By this time also, Webster had established his great reputation as an orator. This was the golden age of oratory in the United States Senate. Many of its members were capable of holding an audience spellbound for hours. Of them all, however, Daniel Webster was commonly regarded as the greatest.

Webster was at his very best in the Webster-Hayne debate of 1830 (see page 346). His speech was widely reported and read. It brought added fame to Webster, who was already known as a leading opponent of Jackson and the Democratic party in the Senate. Along with Clay, Webster was a leader in the new Whig party. His new fame led him to think of the White House.

In 1836 the Whigs nominated four separate candidates. Each one was popular in a different part of the country. The Whigs hoped in this way to keep the Democrat Martin Van Buren from winning a majority of the electoral votes. This would throw the election into the

House, as happened in 1824 (see pages 338–339). But the plan failed. Webster only received the electoral votes of Massachusetts. Webster hoped for the nomination again in 1840 and in 1848, but the party did not turn to him.

In 1841, Webster left the Senate to become Secretary of State under President Harrison, and he stayed on under President Tyler. With great skill, Webster negotiated the Webster-Ashburton Treaty with Great Britain in 1842. This treaty settled a boundary dispute between Maine and Canada. In 1844, Webster returned to the Senate.

Webster's greatest failing was a taste for expensive living. It led him to rely on rich friends for loans and gifts. In 1844, Boston businessmen put up $100,000 so that Webster could stay in the Senate rather than return to his law practice to make money. As a Senator, he voted for measures favored by these friends. He might have voted for those measures anyway, but he could never erase doubts about his motives for doing so.

Known for his devotion to the Union, Webster made his last great effort to save it by supporting the Compromise of 1850 (see page 448). He did this even though he knew that the antislavery people of Massachusetts who had supported him would turn against him. After President Taylor's death, Webster served briefly as Secretary of State under President Fillmore in 1851. Illness forced him to retire the next year.

John C. Calhoun was born in 1782 on his father's plantation in South Carolina. When John was fourteen, his father died. For the next five years, John helped his mother manage their farmlands. Then he resumed his schooling, entering Yale College in 1802. After graduation he stayed on in Connecticut to study law. He returned to South Carolina to open a law office in 1807.

Calhoun was elected to the state legislature in 1808, and two years later won a seat in the United States House of Representatives. In 1811, Calhoun married a wealthy distant cousin, Floride Calhoun. The marriage allowed him to give up his law practice. From then until his death thirty-nine years later, Calhoun was a planter-statesman, the ideal of the Southern gentry.

The picture of Calhoun left by those who knew him is of a serious, deep, humorless man who had few pleasures in life beyond his work. "I never heard him utter a jest," wrote one friend. "He never read for pleasure or played cards." Wrote another, "There is no *relaxation* for him." In contrast to the warm and outgoing Clay, Calhoun did not care for company. He preferred to spend long hours alone thinking.

John Calhoun is usually thought of as the great champion of the South's interests and the defender of slavery. In his later years he surely was. But for his first fifteen years in national politics, he was mainly known for his strong nationalist views. Like Clay, he was a leading War Hawk in Congress. He introduced the resolution for declaring war against Britain in 1812. After the war, he favored the building of roads and canals by the federal government to "bind the republic together." He supported a national bank. He was also for a protective tariff to encourage manufacturing. These measures would not benefit the South directly, but Calhoun favored them because they would lead to a stronger and more unified country. As Secretary of War under President Monroe from 1817 to 1825, he again showed his strong nationalism.

Calhoun hoped to become President in 1824, but lacking enough support, he withdrew from the race. He ran for and won the Vice Presidency instead, serving with John Quincy Adams. In 1828 he ran for Vice President with Andrew Jackson, expecting to succeed him in four years. But soon after Jackson became President, they had a falling out that destroyed Calhoun's hopes.

There were several reasons for the break. One was the Peggy Eaton affair. John Eaton, Jackson's Secretary of War, had married Peggy O'Neale Timberlake, a beautiful daughter of a Washington tavernkeeper. Washington tongues wagged about the fact that the two had married only four months after Peggy's first husband died. Floride Calhoun, calling Peggy a "hussy," refused to receive her in the Calhoun home. She led other Cabinet wives and Washington society to snub her. President Jackson was outraged. Remembering the slanders against his own wife, Rachel, before she died, he defended Peggy Eaton. When John Calhoun sided with his wife, he earned Jackson's anger. Another cause of the break was that Jackson learned that in 1818 Secretary of War Calhoun had criticized Jackson's invasion of Spanish Florida to the Cabinet and favored punishing him.

Even had these incidents not occurred, Jackson and Calhoun would have parted company. Jackson was a strong nationalist, and by this time Calhoun had become a sectionalist. He was known to be the author of the South

Carolina Exposition and Protest (see page 341). By 1830, Calhoun was denouncing as unconstitutional some of the very measures he had earlier supported, including a tariff. In 1831, Calhoun resigned the Vice Presidency. South Carolina promptly selected him for the United States Senate (see page 348).

Throughout the 1830s and 1840s, except for brief periods, Calhoun served in the Senate. There he used his powerful mind to protect the South and slavery against the northern majority. Calhoun was uncompromising. He would preserve the Union if possible, but it must be on the South's terms. Too weak to deliver his speech opposing the Compromise of 1850, he was carried into the Senate chamber to hear it read by another senator. A short time later he died, uttering the words, "The South! The poor South!"

Within two years, Clay and Webster were also dead. The passing of these three marked the end of an era. The business of the nation would go on, and new leaders would arise. But the days when three such giants strode the halls of the United States Senate would not soon be seen again.

CHECKUP

1. How did the political views called nationalism and sectionalism differ? From each of these three biographies, give an example that shows either a nationalist or a sectionalist view.
2. What changes in their political views did each of these three men have during their Senate careers?
3. What was the attitude of each senator toward the Compromise of 1850?

✦ EMMA HART WILLARD ✦

Pioneer in the Education of Women

Abigail Adams's complaint that "daughters are wholly neglected" in education remained as true in the early nineteenth century as it had been in her own time. Girls, it was believed, needed only such education as would fit them for their future roles as wives, mothers, and homemakers. Further, it was said that women were creatures of emotion rather than reason. Their ability to understand such subjects as mathematics, the sciences, and philosophy was limited. In addition, long study of those "masculine subjects" would rob women of their charm and gentleness—and, some claimed, even their health. Because of such views about them, few women went to school above the elementary level. None were admitted to college. By the 1820s there were a few able and determined women who were working to improve educational opportunities for members of their sex. Emma Hart Willard was one of the pioneers in this movement.

Emma was born to a Connecticut farm family in 1787. She was the next to the youngest of the seventeen children of Samuel and Lydia Hart. Emma grew up learning the division of labor that was usual to such families. The men worked the fields, and the women tended the home.

Yet in some ways the Hart household was quite unusual. Samuel Hart did not share the belief that women should not have opinions about serious subjects. He encouraged sons and daughters alike to discuss ideas and political events. Lydia Hart believed that girls as well as boys should know good literature. She read the English classics to her children in the evenings. Thus Emma Hart early developed a love of reading, a thirst for knowledge, and an ability to think for herself. At thirteen, in fact, Emma taught herself geometry, one of those subjects the female mind was not supposed to understand.

Emma Hart Willard helped improve educational opportunities for women. The Troy Female Seminary, which she founded, offered courses previously considered too "difficult" for women.

Encouraged by her parents, Emma enrolled in the local academy, or high school, in 1802. Two years later, at the age of seventeen, she was teaching the young children in her hometown of Berlin, Connecticut. By the time Emma Hart was twenty-one, she was the head of a female academy, one of the first of its kind, in Middlebury, Vermont.

The next year, 1809, Emma Hart married Dr. John Willard, who was one of the chief supporters of the girls' academy. Willard was a fifty-year-old widower with four children. Emma gave up teaching for her new roles of wife, stepmother, and homemaker. The following year she had a child of her own.

If a nephew of her husband had not come to live with the Willards while he attended Middlebury College, Emma might have remained contented with her new role. But talking with the boy about his classes, discussing the ideas he was learning, and reading his books made Emma aware of the educational opportunities denied to women. Neither Middlebury nor any other college admitted women at that time.

Emma Willard was determined to do something to improve the education of women. In 1814, when her husband suffered a financial setback, she opened a boarding school for girls in the Willard home. She did all the teaching. She also taught herself college-level subjects, which she in turn taught her students.

Encouraged by her students' mastery of the "masculine subjects," Mrs. Willard soon developed her ambitious ". . . Plan for Improving Female Education." The plan called for starting a women's school to be supported with state funds, as were many men's colleges. Her plan,

later published, received the approval of such people as President Monroe, Thomas Jefferson, and John Adams.

Believing that her best chance for support lay in New York State, Mrs. Willard moved her academy from Middlebury to Waterford, New York. From there she hoped to win the attention and favor of the state government. She succeeded in winning the support of Governor DeWitt Clinton. But her lobbying efforts failed with the legislature, which refused to vote the funds. Bitterly, Mrs. Willard complained to a friend about men who "think that everything must be precisely as it has been, and that because their wives are ignorant . . . it is better that all women should be so."

Shortly, however, leading citizens of Troy, New York, urged Emma Willard to move there. The city council passed a special tax to raise funds to buy a building. "It seems now as if Providence has opened the way for the permanent establishment of the school on the plan I wish to execute," Willard wrote her mother. Housed in an old three-story building, the Troy Female Seminary opened in 1821. It had an enrollment of ninety students from seven states. Within a few years, the school added a second building, and enrollment rose to three hundred. Emma Willard was the school's director, and she continued to teach some classes. Her husband handled the school's business affairs until his death in 1825, after which Emma Willard took on that task also.

The subjects taught at the new school reflected the determination of its thirty-four-year-old founder to provide for women the kind of education that was

The Troy Female Seminary, founded by Emma Willard, was opened in Troy, New York, in 1821. The influence of the school spread as many of its students became teachers throughout the country.

available to men. Each year new courses were added—history, philosophy, trigonometry, languages, painting, chemistry, zoology. Some of the courses were more advanced than those taught at many men's colleges.

The school also reflected the traditional views of Emma Willard. Life was strictly regulated from morning to night. Students were reminded that "it is every woman's duty to look as well as she can." Table manners were carefully watched. The girls were taught "how to enter and leave a room properly, and how to rise and be seated gracefully." Most girls would marry, and Willard believed they should learn to perform the "duties of women." Students were therefore required to make their beds and clean their rooms. They were also offered training in cooking and making pastry. They received religious instruction and were required to attend a church of their choice. Every Saturday afternoon, Willard delivered a lecture on a subject such as religion, behavior, or the duties of women.

In addition to her aim to provide better education for women, Emma Willard set out to improve the quality of instruction in America's schools. Thus from its beginning the Troy Female Seminary emphasized the training of teachers. Its students were in great demand. Long before teachers colleges existed, the Seminary had provided hundreds of teachers for schools throughout the United States.

Even as Mrs. Willard was establishing her school at Troy, educational opportunities for women were broadening elsewhere. In South Carolina and Kentucky, in Massachusetts, New Hampshire, and Connecticut, female academies and seminaries were being established. None of the other schools, however, offered as complete a course of study as the Troy Female Seminary. And none of the founders achieved the fame and influence of Emma Willard.

Because the legislature did not provide funds, costs had to be borne by the families of those who attended the seminary. Tuition, room, and board for one year was $200, a sum few families could afford. Thus, while Emma Willard opened the door to educational opportunity for women, it was mainly the daughters of the well-to-do who passed through it. Hoping to extend opportunities to young women of ordinary means, Mrs. Willard continued to urge the legislatures of New York and other states to adopt her ". . . Plan for Improving Female Education." She pointed out that the states would benefit from well-trained teachers. She did not succeed, however, in winning legislative support.

In 1838, after twenty-four years of building and directing her schools for women, Emma Willard turned over direction of the Troy Female Seminary to her son and daughter-in-law and retired. In the years that followed, Willard gave all of her time to improving public schools. She traveled a good deal and gave many speeches throughout the South and West. She helped the educational reformer Henry Barnard in his efforts to improve the public schools of Connecticut. Willard lived to see women admitted to many colleges formerly closed to them and to see the establishment of a number of fine women's colleges. She died in 1870. The name of the Troy Female Seminary was then changed to the Emma Willard School in honor of its founder.

What is Emma Willard's place in the history of women's struggle for equal rights? Certainly she was not a feminist. She herself wrote that in the family the husband and father was the "natural sovereign," or ruler. She entitled one of her essays "Will Scientific Education Make Woman Less Dependent on Man?" and answered her question with a clear "No." She never questioned that men and women had different "spheres" in life. Although she recognized that laws discriminated against women, she did not join the women's movement of her day. To those women who said "Now!" she answered in these lines from one of her poems:

Let not the day be urg'd: wait God's full time. . . .
Let woman wait, till men shall seek her aid.

Yet Emma Willard is an important figure in the history of women in America. At a time when the idea was not widely accepted, she insisted that women were the mental equals of men and should have the same opportunities to develop their minds. Indeed, the success of the Troy Female Seminary proved her point and helped change public opinion on education for women. Through the schools she founded and through her personal actions, Emma Willard paved the way for greater gains for the women who would follow.

CHECKUP

1. What unusual aspects of Emma Willard's upbringing prepared her for the role of educational innovator?
2. What subjects were taught at the Troy Female Seminary? What traditional female roles were emphasized? What subjects did she introduce?
3. Why can it be said that "Emma Willard is an important figure in the history of women in America"?

And the Rise of an American Literature

"In the four quarters of the globe, who reads an American book? or goes to an American play? or looks at an American picture or statue?" Those sneering questions in a British magazine summed up Europe's view of the arts in the new nation early in the nineteenth century. Americans were a dynamic and energetic people, yes; but they had no great literature or art. They had won political independence, yes; but they were still culturally dependent on Europe and, Europeans felt, were likely to remain so.

Yet by the 1830s, that dependence was coming to an end. A number of writers, drawing on the American environment and experience, were creating a truly American literature. One of those writers was James Fenimore Cooper. Cooper was the first American to be recognized in the United States and abroad as an important writer of fiction. Cooper did not write his first novel until he was past thirty. During the remaining thirty-one years of his life, however, he wrote an average of one novel a year.

James Fenimore Cooper was the eleventh of twelve children of Judge William Cooper and Elizabeth Fenimore Cooper. Born in Burlington, New Jersey, in 1789, he grew up in Cooperstown, a village on the shore of Otsego Lake in central New York State. Cooperstown was named for James's father, who had created it from a large piece of land he acquired shortly after the Revolution. As the founder of Cooperstown, its largest landowner, and a man of wealth, William Cooper was the town's leading citizen.

The Cooper family lived in a mansion called Otsego Hall. From his parents, James Fenimore Cooper acquired the

James Fenimore Cooper's stories about the American frontier made him the first American writer to gain fame and success in both the United States and Europe.

aristocratic tastes and attitudes of a country gentleman. Also an active and adventurous boy with a love of nature, James became familiar with life in the woodlands. Cooperstown lay in the midst of a forest near the edge of the frontier. From the hunters, woodsmen, and trappers with whom he spent time, James acquired the democratic ideals of the frontier. Those two influences—aristocratic and democratic—would affect Cooper throughout his life.

After a short period of schooling in Cooperstown, James was sent to live and study with a private tutor in Albany, New York. In 1802, at the age of thirteen, he entered Yale College. He was not yet mature enough for college life, however, and was sent away after two years of making mischief and learning as little as possible.

In 1806, James and his father decided that he should go to sea to prepare for a career in the navy. James put to sea on a merchant ship bound for England and Spain. On this voyage two American-born mates of James were seized by the British and impressed into the British navy. The episode fired James's already strong patriotic feelings. After working a year on the merchant ship, James became a midshipman in the United States Navy. He spent most of the next three years on duty on Lake Ontario and Lake Champlain. Preparations were being made for possible naval warfare against Great Britain.

In 1811, James Fenimore Cooper married Susan De Lancey, daughter of a prominent New York family, and soon after left the navy. With an inheritance from his father, who had died two years earlier, Cooper was able to live the life of

a country gentleman. Because Susan Cooper did not care for the isolated existence of Cooperstown, the Coopers settled in Westchester County, near New York City.

According to a family story, it was a challenge from his wife that led James Fenimore Cooper to try writing fiction. Reading aloud to her from a new and not very good English novel, Cooper commented that he could write a better one himself. "Why don't you?" asked Susan. The result a few months later was Cooper's first book, *Precaution* (1820). The book turned out to be every bit as bad as the novel that Cooper had criticized. The new author had made the mistake of setting his story in English places he had never seen and in English society, of which he knew nothing firsthand.

Cooper did not repeat the error. For his next story he chose an American theme. *The Spy* (1821) was a novel about the American Revolution, was set in familiar Westchester County, and dealt with a patriotic theme. The story's chief character is Harvey Birch, who serves his country by pretending to be in the service of Great Britain. Only General Washington knows his true character. The dedicated patriot Birch endures danger, loneliness, and the distrust of the people around him as he moves through suspense-filled adventures.

The Spy was an immediate success, not only in the United States but in Europe, where it was translated into several languages. With this book, Cooper achieved an important aim. He had won the respect of English critics, who usually looked down their noses at American writers. He did it with a book on a patriotic theme, laid in an American setting, and featuring American characters and ways.

Two years later, drawing on his experiences at sea, Cooper wrote his first great sea story, *The Pilot*. This, too, was well received in Europe. On hearing of its favorable reception there, the American poet William Cullen Bryant wrote a friend, "I hope it is the breaking of a bright day for American literature."

It was. Cooper's greatest novels were yet to come. For those he turned to the scenes of his boyhood—the shadowy forests, the occasional clearings, and the clear blue waters of the American wilderness. *The Pioneers* (1823), *The Last of the Mohicans* (1826), and *The Prairie* (1827) dealt with purely American themes. The dangers and adventure of frontier life, the conflict between the pioneers and the Indians, the press of "civilization" upon unspoiled nature were part of those books. For a central character, Cooper created one of the immortal heroic figures in fiction. This is Natty Bumppo, a self-reliant wilderness scout known also as Leatherstocking. Fifteen years later Cooper added two more books to this group, *The Pathfinder* (1840) and *The Deerslayer* (1841). Together the five books are known as the *Leatherstocking Tales*. They trace the life and adventures of the rugged, open, and honest hero from youth to old age as he retreats along with the frontier in the face of advancing settlement. In those and his other adventure stories, Cooper followed the formula of brave action, hot pursuit, and narrow escape.

Cooper's books were a huge success in America and Europe. Europeans, al-

This illustration is from an early edition of James Fenimore Cooper's *The Pathfinder*. The frontier experience is an important element in most of Cooper's novels.

ready fascinated by the American West, gobbled up the works of this master storyteller. Cooper wrote in 1831 that his object in writing novels on American themes was his country's "mental independence." He succeeded in creating a literature that was uniquely independent of European influence. With Cooper's novels, American literature came into its own.

James Fenimore Cooper was but one of a number of writers who made the years from 1820 to 1860 a golden age of literature in the United States. Another writer, Washington Irving, had written *A History of New York by Diedrich Knickerbocker* (1809). This was not really a history but a humorous and good-natured account of the Dutch traditions of New York City, told through the stories of an imaginary historian, Diedrich Knickerbocker. In his *Sketch Book* (1820), Irving created two of his most famous characters—Rip Van Winkle in "The Legend of Sleepy Hollow" and Ichabod Crane in "The Tale of the Headless Horseman."

Edgar Allan Poe, who wrote mainly in the 1830s and 1840s, developed the short story and the mystery tale. Poe was the inventor of the modern detective story. His poem *The Raven* and his chilling short story *The Pit and the Pendulum* are classics that are still read.

Among all the great American novelists are two other writers of the time, Nathaniel Hawthorne and Herman Melville. Both advanced the art of the novel beyond the romantic adventures of the great storyteller, Cooper. They dealt with universal themes. Hawthorne dwelt on the themes of evil and sin in *The House of the Seven Gables* (1851) and *The Scarlet Letter* (1850), one of the greatest of American novels. Melville's best-known book is *Moby Dick* (1851). It is the story of Ahab, captain of a whaling ship, who spends his life in pursuit of the great white whale that has bitten off his leg. Captain Ahab finally catches up with the whale but is killed by it. The whale, Moby Dick, represents evil, and Melville's message is that humans cannot hope to destroy evil in the world, though they must heroically try.

After Irving, Cooper, Poe, Hawthorne, and Melville, no English magazine would again ask who would bother to read a book written by an American. The writers of the nineteenth century created a literature that was read not only by Americans but by people throughout the world.

The Headless Horseman pursues Ichabod Crane in Washington Irving's "The Tale of the Headless Horseman." Best known as a writer, Irving was also a lawyer, businessman, and diplomat.

CHECKUP

1. How did Cooper's early life prepare him for his later career as an American novelist?
2. What were some of the themes on which Cooper based his novels? What made those themes "American"?
3. Name some of the writers from what has been called America's golden age of literature. What major contribution did each make to American literature?

★ SAM HOUSTON ★

Statesman and Hero of the Frontier

During the two hundred years of American history, only one person has been governor of two different states, has represented both in Congress, and has served twice as president of another country! That person was Sam Houston. The country was the Republic of Texas. Houston helped to create it, and he more than any other person was responsible for making it part of the United States. Some said of Houston, who stood six feet three inches (190 cm) and weighed 240 pounds (109 kg), that his ambitions and his boasts matched his size. It can also be said that his achievements matched his size.

Born in 1793, Sam Houston lived on the family plantation in western Virginia until his early teens. In 1806 the plantation was sold to pay debts. Then Sam's father, an army officer, died suddenly. The family—now mother and nine children—had little choice but to move to the Tennessee land that had already been purchased.

During the next two years, young Sam and his two older brothers labored to turn their 400 acres (162 ha) of Tennessee woods and fields into a farm. They succeeded, but it was soon clear that Sam had no taste for farming. His brothers arranged a job for him as a clerk in a general store in nearby Maryville. Neither was that to Sam's liking. Sam Houston was restless for adventure and dreamed of doing great deeds.

For the present, however, what Sam most enjoyed was to hunt and live in the forest with the Indians. At sixteen, he left home to live with the friendly Cherokees, just across the Tennessee River from the Houston farm. The Cherokee chief Oo-loo-te-ka ("He Who Puts the Drums Away") adopted Sam as a son and named him Co-lon-neh ("The Raven"). For the next three years, with just an occasional visit home, Sam lived with the Indians. He learned their language and came to respect and understand them as few other frontier people did.

In 1812 Sam returned to Maryville. To pay off several old debts, he opened a school. The school was in a little log cabin, and Sam was its one and only teacher. His own schooling added up to only a year and a half, but he could read, write, and spell, and he did read books on his own. This was a typical background for teachers on the frontier. School ran from just after spring planting to just before harvesting. The charge was $8 per student—payable one third in cash, one third in corn, and one third in cotton. Houston did well enough to take care of his living expenses and pay off his debts.

The War of 1812 began soon after Sam Houston opened his school. The following year, Houston enlisted in the army. He was placed under the command of Captain Andrew Jackson, a man who would have a great influence on Houston's life. Houston stayed in the army after the war was over and rose to the rank of lieutenant.

SAM HOUSTON **407**

In 1817, Sam Houston was appointed as Indian agent to his Cherokee friends. An Indian agent supervised the payment of money and supplies to a tribe with which the United States had a treaty. In

Sam Houston represented the states of Tennessee and Texas in Congress, served those states as governor, and also served as president of the Republic of Texas.

San Jacinto Museum of History Association

general, an agent represented the government in its dealings with the tribe.

At the time of Houston's appointment, trouble was brewing over the treaties that several Cherokee chiefs had made with the United States. The chiefs had given up ancient Cherokee lands in eastern Tennessee in exchange for money and land west of the Mississippi River. Many braves were angry and talked of fighting rather than moving. Houston was sympathetic, but he knew that in such a fight the Cherokees could only lose. He convinced the Cherokees that they must leave. At the same time, he tried to help them get the supplies that the government had promised for the journey. To show his sympathy for their cause, he wore Indian dress when he went with the Cherokee leaders to see Secretary of War John C. Calhoun.

Houston decided he did not want to continue his army career and, in 1818, returned to Tennessee. He studied law and opened an office in Lebanon. Andrew Jackson's home, The Hermitage, was in nearby Nashville, and Houston became a favorite guest of the general and his wife, Rachel. With Jackson's support, Houston was appointed a major general in the state militia. He was also elected district attorney for the Nashville district just a year after opening his law office. In 1823 the popular Houston was elected to the first of two terms in Congress, and in 1827 he became governor of Tennessee. A year later his friend and old commander, Jackson, became President. There was talk that Houston might someday follow his path. The future could hardly have looked brighter as Governor Houston began his reelection campaign in 1829.

Suddenly, Sam Houston's fortunes changed dramatically. He had married Eliza Allen early in 1829. But only weeks after, Eliza left him and returned to her parents. To his dying day, Sam Houston never revealed the reason why his marriage broke up. Houston felt humiliated. He withdrew from the race, resigned the governorship, and quit Tennessee for the West. In what later became Arkansas, Houston rejoined the Cherokees and Chief Oo-loo-te-ka. Houston threw himself into Indian life and was made a citizen of the Cherokee Nation. Less than a year after leaving Tennessee, Houston was in Washington, D.C., wearing buckskin and blanket. He went as part of a Cherokee delegation to complain about certain Indian agents who had been cheating them. While in the capital, Houston enjoyed the chance to meet again with Jackson. Still, these were not happy years for Sam Houston. He was restless. In 1832 he bade goodby to the Cherokees and headed for Texas.

Why Texas? To this day no one can say for certain. Some believe that he was sent by President Jackson to stir a revolution against Mexico and lead Texas into the United States. Jackson had once tried to buy Texas from Mexico. Houston was known to favor a United States that spread from sea to sea. And people remembered that once he had boasted he would conquer Texas. Most evidence suggests, however, that Houston was drawn to Texas by the opportunities for people of energy and ambition. In 1833 he opened a law office in the town of Nacogdoches, near the Louisiana border, and did well. He also speculated in land. Less than a year after arriving in Texas, he wrote a cousin that he had a part interest in "about 140,000 acres [56,700 ha] of choice land"; and "beside this I own and have paid for 10,000 [4,050 ha] which is, I think, the most valuable land in Texas."

Yet if Houston did not go to Texas to stir trouble, he certainly knew that trouble was already brewing. Americans in Texas were upset by the central Mexican government's tightening rule. At a special convention at San Felipe in 1833, the Americans proposed a new constitution that would make Texas a separate, self-governing state of Mexico. Sam Houston was chairman of the committee that drew up the constitution. It was hoped that the government in Mexico City would approve this proposal. But the new president and dictator of Mexico, General Antonio López de Santa Anna, wanted more control over his country, not less. In each Mexican state, he abolished the legislature and appointed his own governor to rule. He also prepared an army of 3,000 to bring the American colonists in Texas into line.

The Americans in Texas resisted Santa Anna's plans and set up a separate government. After several small clashes, the Mexican general ordered his army to kill every Texan who had taken up arms against him. The new Texas government made Houston commander in chief with power to raise and organize an army. Other Texans were also eager to lead an army, and the government gave command of the army, or parts of it, to four different men—at the same time! Disgusted, Houston withdrew. Only after several crushing defeats and the massacres at the Alamo (see

The Alamo, a deserted mission, was the site of a bloody battle between outnumbered Texans and Mexican soldiers. "Remember the Alamo!" became the slogan of Texans set on independence from Mexico.

page 379) and Goliad did the government finally turn back to Houston for leadership.

Many Texans, including some of his own men, wanted Houston to make a stand quickly. But the commander realized his small army was not ready for a fight. Houston kept falling back, all the while recruiting and training volunteers. He was also waiting—hoping the

Mexicans would make a mistake. He talked about his plans with no one. "If I err," he wrote, "the blame is mine." At last the overconfident Santa Anna made a crucial error. He split his forces, leaving just one part of his armies to catch Houston.

At the San Jacinto River, near Galveston Bay, the two armies were in sight of each other. In those days, fighting usually started at daybreak and broke off at nightfall. Attacks were not started late in the day because there would not be enough time for a decisive battle before darkness. Thus the afternoon of April 21, 1836, found the Mexican troops resting for the expected battle the next day. Suddenly, Houston's army of 783 attacked. They caught the more than 1300 Mexican troops by surprise. In less than twenty minutes the battle was over. Half the Mexican army had been killed, and the rest had been captured, including General Santa Anna himself. Texas casualties were two dead and thirty wounded, of whom seven later died. One of the wounded was General Sam Houston, who took a bullet in an ankle.

Houston's men wanted to hang the captured Mexican leader in revenge for the Alamo and Goliad. Instead, Santa Anna was forced to agree to end the war, withdraw Mexican troops from Texas, and work toward getting his government to recognize the independence of Texas. It mattered little whether the Mexican government would be bound by Santa Anna's agreement. The war was over.

Houston was the man of the hour in Texas. He was elected president of the Republic of Texas. However, the problems he faced were huge. The state was deeply in debt. Its volunteer citizens' army had disbanded, but the threat of war from both the Indians and Mexico remained.

As president from 1836 to 1838 and again from 1841 to 1844, Houston kept government spending to a minimum. He even cut his own salary in half to help Texas get on a sound economic base. For its own reasons, Mexico chose not to renew the war with Texas. And Houston negotiated skillfully to prevent war with the Indians. Meanwhile, though working to have Texas annexed by the United States, he was also considering alliances with France and Britain.

After annexation, in 1845, Houston became a United States senator. During the next fourteen years, he spoke both for fair treatment of the Indians and for the cause of the Union. He was the only Southern senator to vote for the entire Compromise of 1850 (see pages 446–448) and against the Kansas-Nebraska Act (see page 451). Hoping to stop the growing move toward secession, Houston decided to run for governor of Texas as a Unionist. He lost in 1857 but was elected in 1859. Nonetheless, he failed to head off secession. Statewide, Texans voted by a 3-to-1 majority to leave the Union.

Houston refused to take the oath of allegiance to the Confederate government. "I love Texas too well," he said, "to bring strife and bloodshed upon her." He was therefore removed from office. Two years later, in 1863, Sam Houston died. By this time, Texans had found that his prophecy of bloodshed was all too true.

CHECKUP

1. What were the influences of Chief Oo-loo-te-ka, Andrew Jackson, and Santa Anna on the life or career of Sam Houston?
2. Describe the military strategy that made it possible for Houston's forces to win the battle of San Jacinto.
3. Analyze Houston's political performance as president of the Texas Republic and as a United States senator.

★ CHAMPIONS OF REFORM ★

Social Change in America

During the 1830s and 1840s, a small army of reformers examined America inside and out. They wanted to improve society and to better the lot of the less fortunate. Through peace societies, they hoped to end wars. Through temperance groups, they tried to limit the use of liquor, which they believed to be the main cause of poverty, crime, and broken homes. They sought improvement in prison conditions and education of the blind and the deaf. They also sought to abolish slavery (see pages 437–441). During this era of reform three of the major movements dealt with public education, care for the mentally ill, and women's rights.

As late as the 1820s, public education in America existed only in New England. Even there, education was poorly supported. Buildings were run-down, teachers were untrained, and the school term was often as short as two months a year. Most parents who could afford it either sent their children to private schools or hired private tutors. Many children received no schooling at all.

Beginning in the 1830s, educational reformers led by Horace Mann in Massachusetts and Henry Barnard in Connecticut and Rhode Island worked to provide free, tax-supported primary schools. Horace Mann was born in Franklin, Massachusetts, in 1796, and Henry Barnard was born fifteen years later in Hartford, Connecticut. Each experienced at first hand the poor public schools of his state. Henry Barnard's

district school was so long on discipline and so short on good teaching that, at thirteen, Barnard planned to run away from home rather than return to school for another day. His father was able to pay for a private school, however, and Henry continued his education. Horace Mann attended a school that held classes only two months a year.

Later, when Barnard and Mann were elected to their state legislatures, they each worked to make good education available to all children, regardless of wealth or social position. The Connecticut and Massachusetts legislatures passed laws to improve the public schools in their states. Barnard and Mann became the guiding forces of the boards of education, which carried out the laws. They spoke at public meetings and roused the public to support their plans. They made full reports to the legislatures on the state of education. Connecticut and Massachusetts built new schools and made the school year longer. They created schools for the training of teachers and improved the teachers' pay. Barnard also achieved similar results in Rhode Island.

Mann and Barnard were supported by business people, who favored free public schools. Employers needed workers who could read, write, and "figure." Support also came from associations of working people, who saw schooling as the key to advancement for themselves and their children. Mann himself often used the argument that free public education would close the growing gap between rich and poor. He said it "never did happen, and never can happen, . . . that an intelligent and practical body of men should be permanently poor." Perhaps the most important argument was that voters should be educated.

Opposition was often strong and bitter. Some people claimed that giving an education to the children of the poor would cause them to grow up lazy. Other people, raising the fear of a powerful government, objected that public schools would interfere in the relationship between parent and child. Many people saw no reason why they should pay taxes that would be used to educate other people's children.

By the 1850s, however, the majority of the states were committed to tax-supported education in elementary schools. Most states also passed attendance laws, lengthened the school year, added new subjects, and improved teaching methods. Influenced by Mann and Barnard, several states also set up schools to train teachers. Other reformers, such as Emma Willard (see page 399) and Catharine Beecher, led successful efforts in many states to improve education for women.

Reformers did not have total success, however, in the area of education. It was 1918 before every state had a public elementary school system. Many of the attendance laws were quite loose. As late as 1860, only one white child in every six actually went to school; hardly any black children received schooling. Further, these reforms touched only elementary schools. In 1860 there were barely three hundred public high schools in the country. Nearly one hundred of those were in Mann's state of Massachusetts. At the same time, there were some six thousand private academies, or high schools. The great majority of young people did not go to high school, and of those who did go, nearly all had to pay for their education.

Other reformers during the years before the Civil War worked to improve care for the insane. Dorothea Dix (1802–1887) was their leader. She was born in Maine but lived in Massachusetts most of her life. She began to teach school at fourteen. In her thirties, Dix was forced by ill health to retire from full-time teaching. At that time, she had been the head of a young ladies' seminary in Boston for nearly fifteen years. Then a friend asked her to teach a Sunday-school class for women inmates in the East Cambridge jail near Boston. Her visit to the jail on that March morning in 1841 changed her life. Dix was

Students today benefit from the reforms in education that were pioneered by such people as Horace Mann, Henry Barnard, Emma Hart Willard, and Catharine Beecher.

horrified by the conditions. Among the people held in the filthy, unheated jail were a number of insane. In an age when insanity was thought to be incurable, most communities wanted only to keep those unfortunate people where they could do no harm. Generally, that meant in jails and poorhouses, where they were either neglected or mistreated.

Dorothea Dix made the humane treatment of the insane her life's cause. During the next three years, this woman of frail health traveled 10,000 miles (16,000 km), visiting every one of the eight hundred penitentiaries, county jails, and poorhouses in Massachusetts. One entry in her notebooks tells of people held "in *cages, closets, cellars, stalls, pens! Chained naked, beaten with rods,* and *lashed* into *obedience!*"

From Massachusetts, Dix carried her work to other states, going as far west as

The "tranquilizing chair," designed by Dr. Benjamin Rush, was used in the 1800s to restrain patients suffering from mental illness.

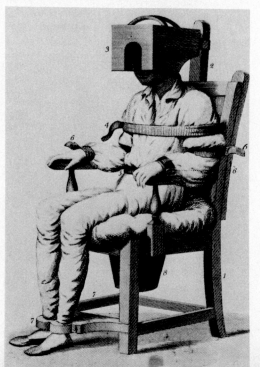

Illinois and as far south as Alabama. Her method was the same in each state. She studied the conditions thoroughly and then presented her findings to the public and the legislature in such detail that the situation could not be ignored or denied. In the years from 1843 to 1880, the number of mental hospitals in the United States increased from 13 to 123. Most of the credit belongs to this reformer. Dix died in 1887 in Trenton, New Jersey, in a state hospital that she had helped found.

Next to abolition, the reform movement that had the greatest significance for the future was women's rights. In the decades before the Civil War, the position of women was little improved from colonial times, when there were great inequities. Husbands still controlled the property of their wives. In a divorce, the husband usually kept the children. Women still could not sue in court or serve on juries. Schooling was not thought to be important for girls. Their proper path in life was felt to be marriage and homemaking. Colleges were closed to them, as were professions such as law, medicine, and the ministry. A woman might become a teacher, but her pay would be lower than a man's. Only among Quakers were women allowed to speak before mixed groups in public.

Here and there, a few determined women broke through these barriers. In 1821, Emma Hart Willard founded the first higher-level school for women in America. Angelina and Sarah Grimké (see pages 438, 440, 441), abolitionists from South Carolina, spoke in public to mixed audiences. Lucy Stone was graduated in 1847 from Oberlin College in Ohio, the first school to award college degrees to women. She became the first woman to lecture on women's rights. Elizabeth Blackwell won her struggle to enter medical school. She received a degree in 1849 and then practiced medicine. Those women were exceptions.

Many other women, however, were very active in all the great reform movements of the day. Indeed it was through work in the abolitionist movement that some women began to see parallels between their own condition and that of slaves. Abby Kelley, a Massachusetts abolitionist, said:

> We have good cause to be grateful to the slave for the benefits we have received to *ourselves*, in working for *him*. In striving to strike his irons off, we found most surely, that *we* were manacled *ourselves*: not by *one* chain only, but by many.

The point was driven home in 1840 at a world antislavery meeting in London. A number of women abolitionists were told they could watch from the balcony but could not take part in the meeting. This convention brought together two women who would lead the fight in America for women's rights. They were Lucretia Mott (1793–1880) and Elizabeth Cady Stanton (1815–1902).

Lucretia Coffin was born into a Quaker family on Nantucket Island in Massachusetts and later moved to Philadelphia. She recalled later in life that women's rights "was the most important question of my life from a very early day." In 1811 she married James Mott, who supported her in her feminist work as well as in many other reform causes all their married life. A strong abolitionist, she attempted in the 1820s to organize a boycott of products made

Lucretia Mott *(top)* and Elizabeth Cady Stanton *(bottom)* were both active abolitionists and feminists. They organized the Women's Rights Convention in Seneca Falls, New York, in 1848.

by slave labor. Later she formed the Philadelphia Female Anti-Slavery Society and helped organize the Anti-Slavery Convention of American Women. More than once she braved an antiabolitionist mob to advance her work.

The unequal treatment of women became clear to Elizabeth Cady at an early age also. And like Mott, she rebelled against it. Believing women to be the mental equals of men, she insisted that they should be legal equals as well. When she married Henry Stanton in 1840, she insisted that the word *obey* be omitted from the marriage ceremony. Later she insisted on being called Elizabeth Cady Stanton rather than Mrs. Henry B. Stanton. She believed that a woman should not have to give up her identity when she married.

Smarting from the discriminatory treatment they received at the world antislavery convention in 1840, Mott and Stanton promised each other to hold a women's rights convention when they returned to the United States. Their aim was to improve the legal status of women and to free them from the bonds of tradition. Eight years later, in July 1848, they carried out their resolve when the Women's Rights Convention was held at Seneca Falls, New York, where Stanton lived. The convention adopted a Declaration of Sentiments written by Stanton. Modeled on the Declaration of Independence, her declaration began by proclaiming that "all men *and women* are created equal." It went on to list eighteen legal wrongs suffered by women. Women demanded control of their own property and earnings after marriage, the right to enter schools and the professions, and equal rights with men before the law. In a bold move for the time, Elizabeth Cady Stanton proposed a resolution favoring woman suffrage. Even Lucretia Mott thought this was daring. Although the resolution was adopted, it was the only one that received less than a unanimous vote.

In the following decades, some of the convention's demands were won. Sev-

eral states passed laws giving married women control over their own property. During the 1850s, however, most women agreed to put the cause of abolition ahead of their own cause. Thus little progress was made in women's rights for many years. At the time of her death in 1880 Lucretia Mott was still involved in efforts on behalf of the freed slaves and of women. Elizabeth Cady Stanton remained a major figure—along with Susan B. Anthony, Lucy Stone, and others—in the women's rights movement for another twenty years.

Reform movements in education, in care for the insane, and in women's rights would have come sooner or later in the United States. The special contributions of Horace Mann, Henry Barnard, Dorothea Dix, Lucretia Mott, and Elizabeth Cady Stanton were in starting the movements when they did. The ability and dedication of these champions of reform overcame great opposition and brought about important improvements in pre–Civil War America. They also laid the groundwork for even greater advances in later years.

CHECKUP

1. Name as many problems as you can that reformers tried to remedy. List individual reformers next to the problems that they tried to solve. What do you think were the best goals stated in all the plans for reform? Why?
2. What improvements in education were achieved through the work of Horace Mann and Henry Barnard? What states benefited from their efforts?
3. What problems did the women's movement hope to solve? Explain what progress was achieved for women's rights by the early movement.

★ REVIEWING THE UNIT ★

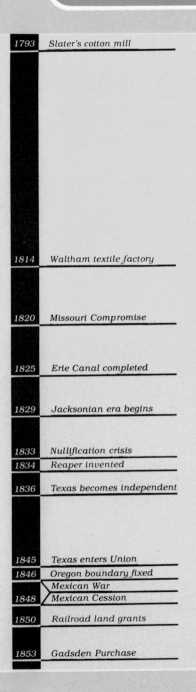

1793	Slater's cotton mill
1814	Waltham textile factory
1820	Missouri Compromise
1825	Erie Canal completed
1829	Jacksonian era begins
1833	Nullification crisis
1834	Reaper invented
1836	Texas becomes independent
1845	Texas enters Union
1846	Oregon boundary fixed
	Mexican War
1848	Mexican Cession
1850	Railroad land grants
1853	Gadsden Purchase

In the early 1800s, Americans started moving westward in large numbers. First to cross the Appalachians were hunters and trappers. Then came the pioneers and permanent settlers. The development of roads, canals, and railways hastened the westward movement. The federal government sold western lands at low prices. Tragic victims of westward expansion were the Indians, who were forced off their home lands.

Sectional rivalries arose as the North, the South, and the West developed differently. With northern backing, John Quincy Adams was elected President in 1824. Andrew Jackson, with western support, won the 1828 election. Jackson's two terms saw ordinary people gain influence in government.

As the nation grew, so did industry. The War of 1812 marked the real beginning of America's industrial revolution. No longer able to rely on Britain for manufactured goods, Americans developed their own industries. Between 1825 and 1850, new inventions and processes spurred the growth of industry.

During the 1840s, a confident America continued its expansion. It gained the Oregon country up to 49° north latitude. Texas became independent from Mexico, and in 1845 it was annexed by the United States. Following the war with Mexico (1846–1848), California and most of what is today the American Southwest were added by the Treaty of Guadalupe Hidalgo. By 1848, Americans, ever on the move, had expanded the nation's boundaries from the Atlantic to the Pacific.

417

Skills Development: Interpreting Graphs

One theme of this unit is the historical movement of the American people. As you study the graphs and answer the questions, think about how the information relates to the mobility theme.

1. What are the four regions named on the map?

2. Each bar on the graphs represents the increase in the region's population for a particular five-year period. The change is expressed in millions. For example, in the Northeast for the period 1950–55, the population increased by 2.7 million or 2,700,000.

a. What is the increase in population for the West in the period 1960–65?
b. For the North Central in 1965–70?
c. For the South in 1955–60?

3. In which five-year period did each region experience the largest increase in population? the smallest increase?

4. In 1970–75, which region had the greatest population growth? Which region had the smallest growth?

5. In which region do you live? Describe the population trend in your region during the twenty-five year period.

Population Increase for 5-Year Periods by Region: 1950–1975
(Increase expressed in millions.)

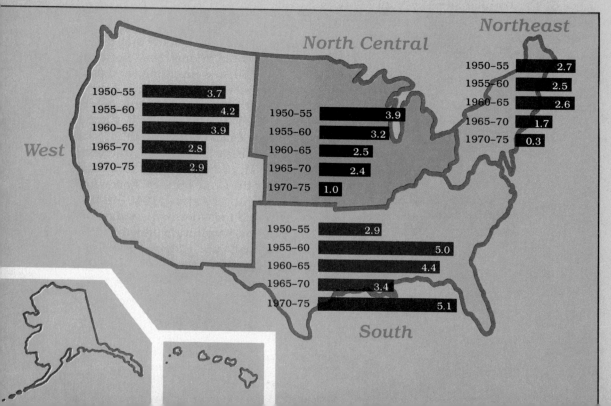

Northeast
1950–55	2.7
1955–60	2.5
1960–65	2.6
1965–70	1.7
1970–75	0.3

North Central
1950–55	3.9
1955–60	3.2
1960–65	2.5
1965–70	2.4
1970–75	1.0

West
1950–55	3.7
1955–60	4.2
1960–65	3.9
1965–70	2.8
1970–75	2.9

South
1950–55	2.9
1955–60	5.0
1960–65	4.4
1965–70	3.4
1970–75	5.1

Unit

5

Americans: Freedom and Equality

A NATION DIVIDED

CHAPTER 16

THE WORLD THE SLAVEHOLDERS MADE

"M Y LIFE had its significance and its only deep significance because it was part of a Problem," wrote a famous American in his autobiography. "But that problem was, as I continue to think, the central problem of the greatest of the world's democracies and so the Problem of the future world." The writer of those lines was a noted American scholar and public figure. He had received a Ph. D. degree from Harvard and had taught at several American colleges. He was the author of dozens of books and articles. He was also one of the founders of the best-known civil rights organization in the United States, the National Association for the Advancement of Colored People (NAACP).

The writer was William Edward Burghardt Du Bois, a black American. The "central problem" of which he wrote was the problem of race. In a larger sense, it was the question of whether a multiracial society could make good on its claims of freedom and equality for all. For Du Bois as for many others, the extent to which it fulfilled those claims was the true measure of democracy. For that reason, the history of black people in America becomes a test case of American democracy.

Du Bois wrote his autobiography in 1940. In the years since then, and especially in the most recent twenty years or so, America has taken important steps in dealing with its "central problem." The evidence is not simply in laws passed or in court decisions handed down. It can be found, among other

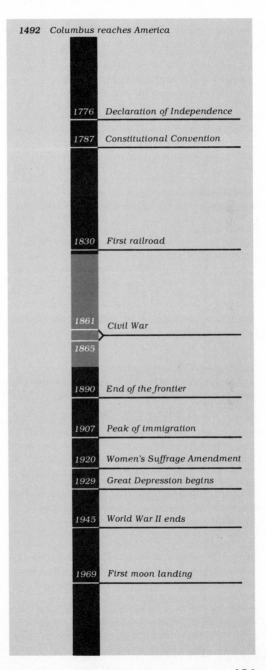

1492 *Columbus reaches America*

1776 *Declaration of Independence*

1787 *Constitutional Convention*

1830 *First railroad*

1861 *Civil War*

1865

1890 *End of the frontier*

1907 *Peak of immigration*

1920 *Women's Suffrage Amendment*

1929 *Great Depression begins*

1945 *World War II ends*

1969 *First moon landing*

places, in the statistics on college graduates, entry into the professions, distribution of income, and the holding of positions in government. It can be seen in offices, on college campuses, and in the use of public facilities.

Many of these changes came as a result of the demands and organized efforts of blacks themselves. The movement for greater rights in the 1960s and 1970s, often called the *Black Revolution,* was an important force for improving the social, political, and economic conditions of black Americans. Hispanic Americans, American Indians, and other minorities have also pressed their claims for a share in the American Dream.

It is also true that these changes, so long in coming, have by no means achieved the goal of equality. That fact, too, can be found in statistics—those on unemployment and poverty, for example. And it can be seen in a drive through cities and rural regions.

At the root of the "Problem," as Du Bois suggested, are the long-held ideas of white Americans about race—ideas that are only now changing. You explored those ideas, their sources, and some of their tragic consequences in Unit 1. In this unit you will examine those ideas further. You will learn about the experience of black people in America during the first hundred years of the nation's history. You will learn how and why slavery came to be an important issue for an ever larger number of Americans. Unable any longer to square slavery with the value of freedom, they finally ended slavery.

Most Americans of the time were content to leave the matter at that. But for a minority even then, the freeing of slaves raised a host of new questions about the meaning of freedom. Does freedom mean merely the absence of slavery? Does it—must it—mean something more? Is equality—equal rights, equal opportunity—a necessary part of freedom? Or is it possible to have freedom with something less than equality? To the free blacks during the era of slavery, these were familiar questions. You will explore them in this unit.

Slave and Free

The American Revolution had an important effect upon the black Americans. For one thing, as you read in Unit 2, several thousand slaves gained their freedom in exchange for serving in the army. Even more important, the ideas of the Revolution caused many Americans to look at slavery in a different light. How could white Americans justify black slavery while complaining that Britain was trying to "enslave" them? As Abigail Adams wrote in 1774 to her husband, John, "It always appeared [wrong] to me to fight . . . for what we are daily robbing and plundering from [the slaves. They] have as good a right to freedom as we have."

There was surely a contradiction between slavery and the Declaration of Independence, which says that "all men are created equal." Thomas Jefferson, the author of the Declaration, understood that. In an early draft of the Declaration, he had condemned King George for violating "the sacred rights of life and liberty" of Africans by enslaving them. However, Southerners in the Continental Congress—especially those from

South Carolina and Georgia, where the slave population was large—objected to this paragraph, and it was removed.

A spreading idea. Though the Continental Congress struck out Jefferson's words, it could not strike out the idea. In 1775 the first antislavery society in America was formed in Philadelphia, with Benjamin Franklin as its president. A year later the Society of Friends (Quakers) ruled that all of its members must free their slaves. Nearly all states, including those in the South, passed laws against the slave trade. During and right after the war, five northern states took steps to end slavery. To be sure, none had a large slave population. Furthermore, most did away with slavery gradually rather than at once, generally giving a slave freedom at the age of twenty-one. Still, those states were taking important steps toward freedom.

The effect of Revolutionary ideas about freedom was felt in the South, too. While Jefferson was governor of Virginia in the 1780s, he proposed that slavery be ended in that state, but the legislature did not accept the idea. Virginia and several other states did, however, pass laws making it easier for owners to set their slaves free. *Manumission* is the legal word for "setting slaves free." Many owners did this, most often in their wills. One North Carolina slave owner who freed his slaves at his death gave these reasons in his will:

Reason the first: . . . every human being . . . his or her color what it may [be], is entitled to freedom. . . . Reason the second: My conscience . . . condemns me for keeping them in slavery. Reason the third: the golden rule directs us to do unto every

One slave who became free at the time of the American Revolution was Phillis Wheatley of Boston. Brought from Africa as a child, she learned English quickly and showed a flair for writing verse. Her poetic talents were encouraged by her master's wife. Miss Wheatley's first book of poems, published in 1773, attracted much attention in both America and England.

human creature, as we would wish to be done unto. . . . Reason the fourth and last: I wish to die with a clear conscience that I may not be ashamed to appear before my master in a future world.

Free blacks. As a result of the spreading ideas about freedom, the number of free black people rose. By 1790, when the first federal census was taken, there were about 59,000 free blacks in the United States—about 8 percent of the black population. Most free blacks were in the southern states. By 1810, that number had tripled.

At the same time, it is important to understand that almost none of the

423

people who talked of the wrongs of slavery also favored equality for black Americans. Many states limited the number of free blacks or kept them from entering. Some even required that a freed slave must leave the state. Free blacks could not testify in court. Although they could vote in a number of states, they did not hold office. A few states limited the free blacks' chances to work in certain occupations. Even when laws did not limit job opportunities for them, prejudice did.

Making their way. To help themselves make their way in a society that discriminated against them, free blacks in northern cities formed their own organizations. They set up churches and schools and formed business and study groups and social clubs. Several of these organizations offered very practical help to their members—supplying insurance, making loans, and performing other services.

Through these groups, free blacks also tried to promote the cause of freedom for the slaves and equal rights for themselves. Because their numbers were small and their position was weak, the only way they had a chance of success was by persuading others to their views. One way of doing so was to set a high standard of personal conduct—

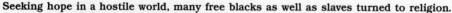

Seeking hope in a hostile world, many free blacks as well as slaves turned to religion.

hard work, a religious life, thrift, and so on. Such conduct would show that blacks were responsible citizens and deserved full rights. Another way of promoting their cause was to petition Congress and the state legislatures to end slavery and discrimination. At every opportunity, they reminded white Americans of the gap between the words of the Declaration of Independence and the condition of black people in America. One of the leaders in this effort was Benjamin Banneker, a mathematician who helped to plan the city of Washington.

Was slavery dying? At the Constitutional Convention, in 1787, a proposal by George Mason of Virginia to outlaw slavery had been defeated. In the debate, one northern delegate, also opposed to slavery, argued that Mason's plan was not necessary. "As population increases," he reasoned, "poor labor will be so plentiful as to [make] slaves useless. Slavery in time will not be a speck in our country." In the 1780s and 1790s, a good many Americans in both North and South agreed that slavery was on the way to its death.

There is some evidence to support this view. The number of slaves imported fell from an average of 6,500 a year in the 1760s to an average of fewer than 2,000 a year in the 1770s. In many parts of the South the profits of slavery shrank as overproduction of tobacco caused prices to drop and as the fertility of tobacco lands decreased. Many planters in Maryland and Virginia found themselves deep in debt. Further, as you have read, slavery was ending in the North, and the number of manumissions in the South was increasing.

Another view. On the other hand, there is strong evidence that slavery was *not* dying out. By the 1780s, southern states were having second thoughts about ending the importation of slaves. In that decade, the number of slaves brought into the United States climbed to an average of 5,000 a year. In the Constitutional Convention, southern states won a number of compromises that protected slavery. Among them were the three-fifths clause (see page 218) and the guarantee that runaway slaves would be returned.

Several of the reasons to believe that slavery would continue had little or nothing to do with profits. One of these was that slaveholders were unwilling to accept the changes in their way of living that would come with freeing slaves. Thus, even men like Thomas Jefferson and George Washington, who spoke out against slavery as a curse, did not give up their slaves until they died.

A second reason lay in the fact that most whites believed blacks to be inferior. They did not believe that a society in which blacks and whites lived side by side in equality could work. In other words, it was not just slavery that was the problem. It was that slavery and race had been tied together. Had the slaves been white, owners might well have worked out a way to free them and to live alongside them in the same society. They had done so with indentured servants. But few whites could bring themselves to do this with black people. African slavery, then, was not just a labor system. It was also a social system, with *African* having the meaning of "lower being" even when the African was not a slave.

Effects of the cotton gin. As you read in Unit 4, Eli Whitney's invention of the cotton gin had far-reaching effects. The production of cotton rose rapidly. As planters opened up new cotton lands, slaves became more valuable. In the ten years after 1795, the price of slaves doubled, and the number of slaves imported rose sharply. Between 1790 and 1800 traders brought 80,000 slaves into the United States. By the time Congress ended the slave trade, in 1808, another 100,000 had entered. And even after it became illegal to import slaves, several thousand were smuggled in each year.

Touissaint L'Ouverture, a slave for almost fifty years, led the successful slave uprising in the 1790s against the French in Saint Domingue.

While the cotton culture was fastening slavery on the South, an event in the West Indies strengthened the South's belief that slavery was the only way to control black people. Slaves in the French colony of Saint Domingue rebelled against their masters. They took over the colony, fought off French and British armies, and eventually set up in Haiti the first black republic in the Western Hemisphere. All this took place between 1791 and 1804.

The idea that slaves could rise up and take over a society was terrifying to American slaveholders. They feared that ideas of freedom might infect their own slaves. Then in 1801 an uprising almost took place. A Virginia slave named Gabriel and his armed followers planned to seize a number of key points and hold them. Other slaves, Gabriel believed, would soon join them in a general uprising. At the last moment, the plot was discovered, and Gabriel and several dozen other slaves were executed.

As news of Gabriel's rebellion spread through the South, controls on slaves and even on free blacks were tightened. Blacks away from their home plantations had to produce either papers proving they were free or passes from their masters. Most southern states also now made it more difficult for a master to free slaves.

Still, there were people in the South who believed that slavery was wrong. They were also concerned about the effect that slavery had on white Americans. Thomas Jefferson, who knew firsthand what it meant to live in a slave society, explained this concern.

There is an unhappy influence on our people produced by slavery among us.

Every exchange between master and slave always includes the worst passions on the master's part, and degrading submission on the slaves' part. Our children see this, and learn to imitate it. The parent storms, the child watches . . . and puts on the same airs to smaller slaves, and thus learns tyranny. . . . When half the people trample the rights of the other half that way . . . it makes . . . tyrants of the masters and dangerous enemies of the slaves. . . . Also the masters will get used to having other people do their work, and no country can progress if half its people will not work.

Colonization in Africa. Although men and women of conscience were troubled by slavery, few were ready to liberate blacks and live alongside them in the same society. The best answer to the problem of slavery that white Americans could come up with was to plant a colony for blacks in Africa. In 1816 the American Colonization Society was formed with the support of such leading figures as Henry Clay, James Monroe, and John Marshall. The society planned to buy land in West Africa with contributions from Congress and from individuals. It hoped to transport to that colony 50,000 freed slaves a year.

The plan did not work out. To carry out its program, the society needed $1 million a year, but in its best year it raised less than $50,000. During the society's forty-year history, it settled only 8,000 Afro-Americans in Liberia, the nation it founded in West Africa.

The idea of "returning home" never had much appeal to American blacks. For one thing, by the time the American Colonization Society was founded, most blacks in America, both slave and free,

had been born in the United States. To them, the United States, not Africa, was home. For another, some black leaders saw colonization as a means of strengthening, not ending, slavery. James Forten, a wealthy black sailmaker in Philadelphia, explained in 1818:

> Those slaves who feel they should be free and who thus may become dangerous to the quiet of their masters, will be sent to the colony; and the tame and submissive will be retained. . . . The bondage of a large portion of our brothers will thus become perpetual.

In 1830, Peter Williams, a New York minister, explained why free blacks opposed colonization.

> We are natives of this country; we ask only that we be treated as well as foreigners. Not a few of our fathers suffered and bled to purchase its independence; we ask only to be treated as well as those who fought against it.
>
> [The Colonization Society] professes to have no other object . . . than the colonizing of the free people of colour on the coast of Africa, with their *own consent*; but if our homes are made so uncomfortable that we cannot continue in them, or if . . . we are driven from them, and no other door is open to receive us but Africa, our removal there will be anything but voluntary.

Although free blacks had no wish to take part in a colonization scheme, some did favor leaving America for other lands. Between 1820 and 1825, several thousand free blacks moved to Haiti. However, Haitians thought of the new arrivals as foreigners. Moreover, the emigrants themselves found that they were more American in their ideas and customs than they had realized. After a few years, many returned to America.

427

1. What effect did the American Revolution have on black Americans? How did free blacks promote the cause of freedom?
2. Why did some people in the 1780s and 1790s feel that slavery would die out? What were some of the reasons that it did not?
3. Why was African colonization unsuccessful as a solution to the slavery problem?

Life Under Slavery

The world that the slaveholder made was filled with problems for white Americans. For black Americans, it was filled with danger and uncertainty. From the time that Africans were snatched from their homeland and packed into the cramped spaces below the decks of ships, there was never a moment's security for them.

The work routine. In the nineteenth century, about three fourths of all slaves worked the fields of the South. If they were on a small farm with fewer than five slaves, their owner often worked alongside them. Those on larger plantations worked under the eyes of an *overseer*—a manager. The overseer was often assisted by a black slave known as a *driver*. Slaves rose at daybreak, were in the fields at dawn, and usually stayed there until sunset. A break for breakfast, and two more for lunch and dinner offered a bit of relief and a chance to talk with other slaves. Such a workday was always at least ten hours long. Sometimes it was as long as sixteen hours.

As you read in Unit 1, a large plantation was much like a self-sufficient small town. Thus there was a need for many kinds of workers besides field hands.

Slaves worked as shoemakers, carpenters, cooks, barbers, nurses, housekeepers, and at many other jobs requiring special skills. Sometimes they worked closely with their masters or overseers and often received special favors, such as gifts of cast-off clothing or home furnishings. Often the skilled slaves learned English better than the field hands, and a master might teach them to read and "figure." Attractive men and women slaves worked in the main house as cooks, maids, and butlers, or as caretakers for children of ill adults. At times, masters trusted talented slaves to treat the sick or to barter and trade for the household. These house slaves were at the top of the slave social order.

The slaves that were most often freed were the household servants and the slaves with special skills. Their master knew them as people. Moreover, they were the ones in the best position to make their way in a free society. By 1830 there were about 150,000 free blacks. They were centered in the cities of Baltimore, New Orleans, Charleston, and Washington.

Survival of African culture. For a long time it was thought that the slaves' African culture simply disappeared after they landed in America. However, as we have learned more about African society, we have come to realize that a considerable amount of African culture did survive. For example, in many African societies where farming was done in groups, one person sang to set a rhythm for the others to work by. This practice was carried over into the tobacco, rice, and cotton fields of the American South.

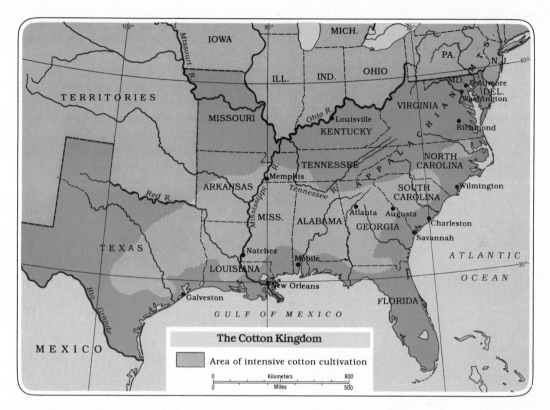

The slave population of the South was concentrated in the belt of intensive cotton cultivation.

On large plantations, slaves lived in small buildings not far from the main house. Floors were often of packed earth, and windows lacked glass. In the evenings, when the laborers came back to their quarters from the fields, there was singing and the telling of stories that had been passed on to the slaves by their parents and grandparents. The designs of the drums and stringed instruments that were used to make music were also African in origin.

Certain African religious beliefs and customs were brought to America too. When slaves were converted to Christianity, they often kept parts of their earlier religion.

African languages, too, survived for a time. Most slaves came from tribes along the western coast of Africa. Though tribal languages were different, they had some likenesses, as French and Spanish have, for example. Africans from different tribes, thrown together on large plantations, worked out new languages that combined their own languages and English. A number of African words made their way into the English language. These include *goober* (for peanut) and *yam* (for sweet potato).

429

Operation of the cotton gin on a Southern plantation was a job usually performed by slaves. At an early age, the slave children were assigned such tasks as carrying water to the older workers.

In time, English replaced the African languages. But in the low country of coastal South Carolina and Georgia, where the concentration of blacks was among the heaviest, a language called *Gullah* is still spoken. It was heavily influenced by African languages. Burial customs also show the African influence. One Afro-American cemetery in Georgia still has old grave markers that resemble West African carvings.

Role of the "Auntie." An important link in passing on parts of African culture from one generation to another was an older woman called the *Auntie*. She was often no longer able to do heavy field labor and so took care of the babies and small children of slave mothers who worked in the fields. The Auntie may have been a relative of the children she cared for. She entertained them with folktales that were frequently African in origin.

The Auntie also often served in the role that had been played in Africa by a man called the *griot*. It was the griot's job to memorize the history of births, family trees, wars, famines, and other local history. In Africa, this person was respected and protected and had no other work to do. As the griot grew old, he passed on his knowledge of local events to a successor.

The treatment of slaves. House servants were better treated than field hands. They played an important part in the family life of their owners and were in constant contact with them. Yet most owners treated field hands with some care too. The slave was a big investment. A master would indeed be very unwise not to take care of a field hand, who, by the 1850s, cost $1,700 to replace. Thus, recent studies of slave diets on large plantations show that the average slave probably got enough protein, vitamins, and calories to stay healthy. Though food was monotonous, the evidence is that slaves were not underfed.

Many masters encouraged slave marriages even though the marriages were not recognized by law. Masters did so partly because marriage conformed with their own ideas of a proper, moral life and partly because slaves with families made more stable workers. The threat to sell a member of the family also helped to discipline slaves.

Masters—kind and cruel. The most important factor in determining the treatment of the slave was the attitude of the master. Frederick Douglass, a Maryland slave who later escaped to the North, described one owner in this way:

> Instead of the cold, damp floor of my old master's kitchen, I was now on carpets. . . . I had a good straw bed, well-furnished with covers; instead of coarse meal in the morning, I had good bread and mush occasionally; instead of my old tow-linen shirt, I had good, clean clothes. I was really well off. . . . I was human, and she, dear lady, knew and felt me to be so.

But this lady was only one of several owners that Douglass had. Mr. Covey was very different.

> If at any one time of my life more than another, I was made to drink the bitterest dregs of slavery, that time was during the first six months of my stay with Mr. Covey. We were worked in all weathers. It was never too hot or too cold; it could never rain, blow, hail, or snow too hard for us to work in the field. Work, work, work was scarcely more the order of the day than of the night. The longest days were too short for him and the shortest nights too long for him. I was somewhat unmanageable when I first went there, but a few months of this discipline tamed me. Mr. Covey succeeded in breaking me.

Douglass's descriptions of these two owners are a reminder of the central truth of slavery: the power of one human, the master, over another, the

slave, was total. The slave depended on the owner for food, clothing, and care. The master decided where, when, and at what task the slave should work. The master decided whether the slave might take a mate and whether and when they would be separated from each other and from their children. The slave's very life was in the hands of the master.

Physical punishment. Since there was no control of a master's use of force, it is not surprising that angry and brutal masters often did real harm to the helpless slaves. Whipping was routinely used, even by owners who thought of themselves as kind. Slaves who had not done enough work to please their owners were given a few lashes to make them pick up their pace. Slaves who broke rules or were disrespectful to their owners might be whipped in front of other slaves to set an example. The threat of physical beatings was one of the chief means of keeping slaves under control. As one Virginia planter said, "A great deal of whipping is not necessary; some *is*."

The breakup of families. One of the cruelest parts of the slave system was the breakup of families through the sale of slaves. This was done far more often for business reasons than for punishment. However, the reason hardly made a difference to the slave family that was separated. Between 1800 and 1860, about 100,000 slaves from the declining tobacco regions in Virginia and Maryland were sold "down the river" to cotton planters in the Deep South. Probably between 15 and 30 percent of the slave couples were separated by the sale of

Prospective buyers prepare to make bids at a slave auction in 1852. Such sales were held regularly in the cities of the slaveholding states. The auctions often separated the members of slave families.

one of the mates. More often it was the strong, young slaves who were sold, because they brought the best price.

Slave families knew that separation could occur at any time. Nevertheless, many slaves were able to make family life work. On many plantations, there were several generations of a slave family. Marriage into other slave families on the plantation made for a network of aunts, uncles, cousins, and other relations. Often, husband and wife were owned by separate masters on neighboring plantations. Then the husband was able to see his wife and children only one or two evenings a week, when he was allowed visiting rights by his owner. But slaves managed to keep their families intact whenever possible. Most slave marriages were broken only by death or by forced separation.

The response of the slaves. Some slaves accepted their lot. Others resisted. Between 2,000 and 3,000 slaves ran away each year. But escape was difficult. Masters sometimes hunted slaves with trained dogs. Nor could a runaway always count on other slaves to help, for they did not want to get into trouble themselves. Also, masters tempted their slaves with rewards for turning in runaways.

Even when runaways thought they had made good their escape, they could never feel sure they were safe. Professional slave catchers might retake them months or even years later. A captured runaway might then be branded or have a foot cut off to prevent another escape. The punishment was often performed in the presence of other slaves. The message was clear.

Resistance by rebellion. Before slavery was ended, there were more than 200 rebellions or plans for rebellion. Most of these were quite small, but some were major, such as the Stono rebellion in South Carolina and Gabriel's rebellion in Virginia. The largest was Nat Turner's rebellion in 1831 (see page 441).

Rebellion had even less hope for success than running away, for the whites had the guns. And even if a rebellion succeeded, where could the slaves go? The slaveholders were even more determined to track down rebels than to catch ordinary runaways. Rebellion, then, was an act of desperation. So were individual acts taken in rage, such as killing an overseer or clubbing a master. For the slave who committed such an act, execution was swift and certain.

Other kinds of resistance. There were forms of resistance, though, that were widespread though undramatic. Slaves would work very slowly. They would break tools or set fire to the toolshed or barn. They would either pretend to be ill or deliberately let themselves become ill. Some even went so far as to cut off a hand or foot so that they could not do field work. Masters were never sure whether the slaves had planned those things or whether they occurred by sheer accident. One Louisiana doctor actually thought this behavior was the result of a special slave disease. He gave it a Latin name, *dyaesthesia aethiopica,* and described it.

Individuals affected with this complaint . . . do much mischief . . . owing to the stupidness of mind and insensibility of the nerves induced by the disease. Thus, they break, waste, and destroy everything they handle; abuse horses and cattle; tear, burn, or rend their own clothing. . . . When driven to labor the slave performs the task assigned him in a headlong, careless manner, treading down with his feet or cutting with the hoe the plants he is put to cultivate; breaking the tools he works with; and spoiling everything he touches that can be injured by careless handling.

Hence the overseers call it "rascality," supposing that the mischief is intentionally done.

Many a slave would have laughed to know of the good doctor's findings.

Quite rare was the kind of resistance shown by Frederick Douglass against Mr. Covey. You read earlier that Covey had broken Douglass. But the time came when Douglass could strike back.

Whence came the daring . . . to grapple with a man, who 48 hours before could . . . have made me tremble . . . I do not know. . . . The fighting madness had

Frederick Douglass, born into slavery in Maryland, fled to Massachusetts at the age of twenty-two. He later became an abolitionist leader.

come upon me, and I found my strong fingers firmly attached to his throat. . . . My resistance was entirely unexpected and Covey was taken all aback by it. . . . "Are you going to resist, you scoundrel," said he. To which I returned a polite "Yes, sir."

Douglass went on to describe a long fight between himself and this hated master, and the results of that fight.

He had not, in all the scuffle, drawn a single drop of blood from me. I had . . . been victorious, because my aim had not been to injure him, but to prevent his injuring me. . . . He never again laid the weight of his finger on me. . . .

I was no longer a servile coward. . . . This spirit had made me a free man in *fact* though I still remained a slave in *form*. When a slave cannot be flogged, he is more than half free. . . . From this time until my escape from slavery [more than four years later] I was never . . . whipped. . . . the easy manner in which I got off was always a surprise to me. . . . the probability is that Covey was ashamed to have it known that he had been mastered by a boy of sixteen.

The great majority of slaves, however, accepted their life. Because their masters' power over them was complete, they learned to walk, to talk, and to behave in ways that would please those masters, whatever the secret thoughts in their own hearts. And they turned to religion to find comfort in the hope of a better life in a world hereafter.

This was the world of the slave. Increasingly it became enmeshed with nearly every issue in American national politics—expansion, states' rights, and others. Finally, as we shall see in the next chapter, slavery overshadowed all other issues and eventually brought about America's most tragic conflict.

CHECKUP

1. How did the work of slaves vary on large plantations?
2. How were slaves kept under control by their masters?
3. In what ways did the slaves resist their lot?

Key Facts from Chapter 16

1. The Declaration of Independence, which says that "all men are created equal," caused many white Americans to question how slavery could be justified.

2. During the years immediately following the American Revolution, many whites came to favor freedom for slaves, and by 1810 there were close to 200,000 free blacks.

3. Among those whites who favored freedom for slaves, very few also favored equality for black Americans.

4. The invention of the cotton gin resulted in the increased planting of cotton and the need for more field labor, thus helping to fasten the slavery system on the South.

5. Many slaves accepted their lot, but many others resisted—by running away, by rebelling openly, or by doing their jobs poorly.

★ REVIEWING THE CHAPTER ★

People, Places, and Events

Review Questions

1. Why was African slavery more than just a labor system? *P. 425*
2. What effects did the cotton gin have on cotton production and the issue of slavery? *P. 426*
3. Why did Jefferson believe that slavery had a bad effect on the master as well as on the slave? *P. 427*
4. Compare the lot of the field hand with that of the house slave on a plantation. *P. 428*
5. Name four ways in which the African culture survived among the slaves in America. *Pp. 428–430*
6. What was the special role played by the Auntie in the slave society? *P. 430*
7. Besides physical punishment, what other hold did slave owners have over their slaves? *P. 431*
8. What methods could the slave use to "fight back" against the slave owner? *Pp. 432–433*

9. Why did a slave rebellion offer little hope of success? *P. 433*

Chapter Test

On a separate piece of paper, write **T** *if the statement is true and* **F** *if the statement is false.*

1. Freedom from slavery gave blacks equal rights and equal opportunity with whites.
2. Leaders of the Revolution, such as Washington and Jefferson, favored abolition of slavery and freed their own slaves to set a good example.
3. The plan to return blacks to Africa was enthusiastically supported by blacks, but colonization failed because of the lack of money.
4. The African culture survived among the slaves, and in time even became part of the white culture.
5. The Black Revolution refers to the slave uprising that took place in Louisiana during the 1830s.
6. There were no free blacks in the South before the Civil War.
7. A large plantation was much like a self-sufficient small town.
8. In general, field slaves were better treated than house slaves because field hands cost a great deal of money to replace should something happen to them.
9. A slave revolt in the French colony of Saint Domingue resulted in the eventual establishment of the first black republic in the Western Hemisphere.
10. The attitude of the master was probably the most important factor in determining the treatment of slaves.

THE ISSUE OF SLAVERY played no major part in national politics for the first thirty years after George Washington became President. Opinion was sharply divided between North and South, but most leaders were anxious to avoid an issue that might split the Union. Further, slavery was considered a local matter. Under the Constitution, each state decided for itself whether slavery would exist within its borders.

In 1819, however, slavery burst into national politics over the question of its spread into the territories. After a year of heated debate, Congress passed the Missouri Compromise. It set 36°30′ north latitude as the dividing line between slave and free territories (see page 338). Politicians breathed a sigh of relief. They believed they had now removed the dangerous issue of slavery from national politics.

The aging John Adams knew better. "I take it for granted," he wrote Thomas Jefferson, "that the present is a mere preamble—a title page to a great tragic volume." Whole chapters of that "volume" would soon follow. One of them was the nullification crisis of 1832–33 (see page 347). Although the apparent issue was the tariff, the question of slavery lay just beneath the surface. Southerners knew well that a federal government that could force a tariff on them could someday also interfere with slavery. "We are divided into slave-holding and nonslave-holding states," observed one South Carolinian at the time, "and this . . . must separate us at last."

The Antislavery Crusade

Most early opponents of slavery favored one of three approaches to the problem. They urged owners to treat their slaves more like human beings than like property. They tried to persuade owners to free slaves, at least in their wills. Or they supported colonization. By the 1820s, a small number of whites were working for *universal emancipation*—that is, the freeing of all slaves. But most of the whites proposed that this be done gradually, that slave owners be paid for their losses, and that the freed slaves be colonized. Such a person was Benjamin Lundy, a Quaker who published an antislavery newspaper.

Around 1830, however, there occurred an important change in the goals of the antislavery movement. Its leaders felt that they were making little progress and now began to demand that slavery be ended immediately.

The abolitionists. This demand that slavery be abolished right away gave antislavery reformers of the 1830s the name of *abolitionists*. Using the printing press, lecture platform, and pulpit, they spread their message on the cruelty of slavery. Many were deeply religious people for whom slavery was one of the worst of sins. Outstanding among these abolitionists was William Lloyd Garrison of Massachusetts. A former writer for Lundy's newspaper, Garrison began his own paper, *The Liberator,* in 1831. In the first issue, Garrison made clear that he no longer believed in a *gradual* freeing of slaves.

437

I will be as harsh as truth, and as uncompromising as justice. On this subject, I do not wish to think, or speak, or write with moderation. No! No! Tell a man whose house is on fire to give a moderate alarm; . . . tell the mother to gradually extricate her babe from the fire into which it has fallen—but urge me not to use moderation in a cause like the present. I will not equivocate, I will not excuse—I will not retreat a single inch—AND I WILL BE HEARD.

Garrison helped organize the American Anti-Slavery Society in 1833. He published his newspaper until the end of the Civil War.

Another abolitionist leader, a New England minister named Theodore Dwight Weld, organized abolitionist groups in New York State and the Ohio Valley. Teams of his followers held public meetings in the spirit of religious revivals. With their message that slavery was cruel and sinful, and abolition was Christian, they organized nearly 2,000 antislavery societies by 1850. Most of the members, including many of the leaders, were women.

Two sisters from a South Carolina slaveholding family, Angelina and Sarah Grimké, wrote articles and made speeches. They were ridiculed and persecuted, not only for their ideas but for their boldness. The idea of women speaking before public groups was disapproved by most at the time.

The Underground Railroad. Some abolitionists did not wait for slaves to be freed voluntarily. They became involved in the *Underground Railroad,* a network of people who helped slaves escape from the South. In time, more than 3,000 people were involved in the railroad. Slaves would run away at a time arranged in advance and then be passed from house to house along the route to some safe place—often Canada.

Stories of spectacular escapes grew up around the railroad. A Maryland slave, Harriet Tubman, escaped and then risked her life by returning to the South nineteen times in order to guide other slaves to freedom.

At the height of its operation, the railroad probably helped about 500 slaves a year to escape. Actually, owners voluntarily freed more than that number each year. But the Underground Railroad was more threatening because it freed slaves without the owners' permission.

Northern opposition. Abolitionists were hardly the darlings of the North. Operators of mills that needed cheap cotton from the South were not anxious for slavery to end. Neither were those white workers who feared that free blacks would work for low pay and drive down wages. Even many whites who disliked slavery were irritated by the "troublemaking" of the abolitionists.

As a result, abolitionist leaders were often attacked and sometimes beaten. Garrison, arriving in Boston to speak to a women's antislavery group, was dragged through the streets by an angry mob. Weld was mobbed on numerous occasions. In New York and Philadelphia, abolitionist meetings were broken up. Philadelphia city officials stood by and watched a mob burn a building where abolitionists gathered. And in Alton, Illinois, in 1837, an angry mob of whites burned the printing press of Elijah Lovejoy, an abolitionist printer, and shot him to death.

A number of slave women flee with their children on what they hope will be the road to freedom. Runaway slaves usually hid in the woods or elsewhere by day and moved northward at night.

A political approach. Most abolitionists worked outside of politics. They expected to end slavery by *moral suasion* — that is, by convincing people to end it because it was morally wrong. "If we express frankly and freely our position," said one, "[slaveholders] will give up their slaves." By the end of the 1830s, however, some abolitionists were looking to achieve their ends through politics. They formed the Liberty party and chose James Birney, a former Kentucky slave owner, as their candidate for President in 1840. Their platform did not call for immediate abolition of slavery. Instead it focused on stopping the spread of slavery into the territories.

Birney polled only 7,000 votes in 1840. Running again in 1844, however, he received 62,000 votes. In New York State he drew enough votes away from Henry Clay, the Whig candidate, to cost Clay the state and thereby swing the election to James K. Polk of Tennessee, the Democratic candidate. Still, 62,000 was barely 2 percent of those who voted. More Americans than that felt slavery was wrong—antislavery societies had many more members—but most of them did not yet feel strongly enough about the issue to leave the Whig and Democratic parties.

No thought of equality. There was no more thought of equality for blacks in the North than there was in the South. Northern states that entered the Union after 1820 prohibited slavery, but many also discouraged free blacks from living within their borders. In the 1830s, several states took away the blacks' right to vote. By 1840, only 7 percent of the North's free blacks were allowed to vote. Only in Massachusetts could a black serve on a jury. By law or by custom, there was segregation in housing, public transportation, schools, theaters, and churches. It was plain that whites in the north as well as in the South felt that blacks should be kept "in their place."

Only some of the abolitionists favored equality for blacks. Garrison frequently had dinner with black friends and campaigned for integrated schools in Boston. Angelina Grimké went to social gatherings with her good friend, Sarah Mappes Douglas, a free black woman from Philadelphia. But many white abolitionists disapproved of such mixing with black people. Some antislavery groups would not let black people join. The American Anti-Slavery Society would not have a black minister speak to its meeting in 1836 because "the time has not come to mix with people of color in public." Most abolitionists were concerned with ending the moral wrong of slavery, not with fighting for equality for the Negro.

Black abolitionists. Free black Americans were deeply involved in the struggle to end slavery. In fact, a free black named David Walker published an abolitionist pamphlet in Boston in 1829, two years before Garrison's first issue of *The Liberator*. In his "Appeal . . . to the colored citizens of the world," Walker warned that if slaves were not freed immediately they might take their freedom by force. Indeed, until the mid-1830s, black people were the main source of support for the antislavery movement. Of the first 450 subscribers to Garrison's *Liberator*, 400 were black; of the 2,300 subscribers in 1834, 1,700 were black. Black abolitionists carried their message to other blacks and to whites through newspapers, books, and lectures. Autobiographies by former slaves, such as Frederick Douglass, were found to be especially effective.

Douglass's newspaper was named for the star by which escaping slaves made their way to freedom.

Black abolitionists were aware that for many of their white colleagues the fight was *against* slavery, not *for* equality for the black American. In his newspaper *North Star,* Douglass commented, "Until abolitionists [erase] prejudice from their own hearts, they can never receive the unwavering confidence of the people of color." Especially resented was the advice of some white abolitionists about how to behave. "Better have a little of the plantation speech," one white abolitionist told Frederick Douglass. "It is best that you seem not too learned." And Henry Highland Garnet, another abolitionist who had been a slave, sent this reply to a white abolitionist who disagreed with Garnet's views:

I have dared to think and act contrary to you. . . . If . . . I must think and act as you do because you are an abolitionist, . . . then I say your abolitionism is abject slavery.

CHECKUP

1. How did the abolitionists try to attain the goal they were working for?
2. What groups in the North opposed abolitionism? Why?
3. On what matters did white and black abolitionists disagree?

The South's Reaction

Hammered by attacks from the abolitionists, the South increasingly thought of itself as a nation apart. This feeling of isolation, of being a nation threatened, was heightened by the Turner rebellion in 1831. That event reminded the South of the grim dangers of slaveholding. Nat Turner, a Virginia slave, led a group of slaves in a three-day uprising against slave owners and their families in Southampton County. Before the rebelling slaves were caught, they had killed sixty people.

Silencing the critics. The South's response to these attacks from outside and inside was to tighten once more the controls on black people. It also tried to shut off criticism. Many Southern postmasters refused to deliver *The Liberator* and other antislavery writings. Several Southern states put a price on the head of Garrison and other abolitionists in the North. In Congress, Southerners in 1836 pushed through a *gag rule,* which prevented abolitionist petitions from being read or acted upon. The rule remained in effect for eight years, until former President John Quincy Adams, now a congressman from Massachusetts, led a successful fight to repeal it.

Southern critics were silenced too. The number of antislavery societies in the South shrank from 130 in 1827 to just 3 in 1832. Such citizens as James Birney and the Grimké sisters were pressured to leave the South. Others who held similar views fell silent. The South closed ranks in defense of its way of life. The generation of Jefferson, Washington, and Monroe had regarded slavery as a curse that must one day die out. John Calhoun, however, spoke for the new generation of Southerners.

This agitation [against slavery] has produced one happy effect at least; it has compelled us in the South to look into the nature and character of this great institution and to correct many false impressions that even we had [about] it. Many in the South once believed that it was moral and

441

Sarah Grimké, born in South Carolina, was one of two sisters who championed the causes of abolitionism and women's rights. She was an effective speaker on the lecture platform.

out, had a class of people who did the hardest and most unpleasant work. The people in this class in the South, the slaves, were cared for in sickness and in health, in old age as in youth. They had perfect security. But in the wage system of the "free" North, workers had no security at all. They received nothing in illness or in old age, and they could be thrown out of work during a depression.

In the South, wrote George Fitzhugh, a leading defender of slavery, all was harmony.

> A society of universal liberty and equality is absurd and impracticable. A state of slavery . . . is the only situation in which the war of competition ceases and peace and goodwill will arise. At the slaveholding South all is peace, quiet, plenty and contentment. We have no mobs, no trade unions, no strikes for higher wages.

The Southern way of life. As their differing ideas on slavery suggest, the South and the North had been growing apart for many years. By the middle of the nineteenth century, they stood as almost two different societies. In the North, although most people were still farmers, manufacturing and commerce were growing rapidly. Increasing numbers of people lived in cities. Immigrants, many of them from Ireland and Germany, added variety to the North's population.

The South, by contrast, was still almost wholly agricultural and rural. Less than 10 percent of its people lived in towns or cities of more than 2,500 people. There was a sameness to the white population. Few immigrants were willing to go to the South and compete for jobs with slaves. Thus the 1850 cen-

political evil; . . . we see it now in its true light, and regard it as the most safe and stable basis for free institutions in the world.

The proslavery view. Southern minds and pens concentrated on creating a proslavery argument. They turned to the Bible, to the United States Constitution, to the ancient philosophers, and to the classical civilization of republican Greece (which had slavery) to find justification for their way of life.

Southerners contrasted also the treatment of their slaves with that of Northern workers. Every society, they pointed

sus showed that fewer than three Southerners in a hundred had been born outside the United States. Most white Southerners were descended from the English and Scotch-Irish who had settled in the South in the seventeenth and eighteenth centuries.

The pace of life in the South was slower than it was in the bustling, commercial North. Visitors often commented on this fact and on the warmth of the welcome they received in the homes of Southerners, rich and poor alike. *Southern hospitality* became a byword. At the same time, visitors noted the many ways in which the South seemed to lag behind the North. There were fewer newspapers and fewer schools, and illiteracy was high. Southern farms and villages often lacked the well-kept look of those in the more prosperous North.

Southern class structure. One's standing in the South was based mainly on ownership of land and slaves. The great planters, therefore, stood at the top of Southern society. They set the tone of Southern social life and held the main political offices—or chose those who did. A small, close-knit group, they were tied to each other by the bonds of blood and marriage.

The picture we often have of the wealthy plantation owner, living a life of ease in a mansion, was true for only a very few. Most owners worked hard. Usually they supervised the day-to-day operations of the plantations and kept the business records as well. While the homes of most were comfortable, they were hardly lavish. Profits were by no means certain, for the price that cotton

would bring varied from year to year. In good times a planter might make large profits. At other times he might barely break even, or possibly lose money. Planters in the older parts of the South, where the soil was worn out, were often in debt.

This planter class was quite small. Only 8,000 slave owners owned as many as fifty slaves. Fewer than 40,000, or about 12 percent of all slave owners, owned as many as twenty slaves. This was probably the minimum number of slaves needed to run a good-sized plantation successfully.

Just below these great planters was the upper-middle class. This class included planters with between five and twenty slaves, as well as the successful merchants, bankers, doctors, and lawyers, who lived in towns.

The great majority of whites belonged to the middle class, made up mainly of independent small farmers. Most of these owned no slaves at all. The few who did usually owned but one or two and worked in the fields with them. At the bottom of the social scale were the poverty-stricken whites, who scratched out a bare living from the poor soil in the pinelands or the hill country.

More than three fourths of all the white families in the South owned no slaves at all. Why, then, were Southern whites so unified in their defense of slavery? The reasons varied. Many middle-class farmers favored slavery because they hoped to rise someday into the planter class and become slave owners themselves. Poor whites were assured that, however low they might be on the social scale, as long as there was slavery there would be others below

Out of the towns and cities, social life in the South centered about the great plantations.

them. And whites of all classes were convinced that blacks were inferior people and not fit for freedom. Slavery fixed the relationship of blacks and whites. Southern whites were not able to imagine a society in which that relationship did not exist. Thus they were committed to the belief that slavery was necessary and desirable. Ending it, they believed, would threaten their very way of life.

CHECKUP

1. In what ways did the South respond to attacks on slavery?
2. How did the Southern way of life differ from the way of life in the North?
3. Why, with few exceptions, were Southern whites of all classes supporters of the slavery system?

The Argument over the Spread of Slavery

The war with Mexico resulted, as you read in Unit 4, in the addition of millions of acres of land to the United States. At any other time, such an outcome would have been the cause of unmixed joy. But the slavery issue poisoned the well.

The Missouri Compromise had supposedly settled the question of where slavery could and could not extend. It had run a line through the United States. Below that line, slavery could exist; above it, slavery was outlawed. But the newly won Mexican lands were not covered by the Missouri Compromise. Whether slavery could be brought into that region became the subject of bitter argument.

The Wilmot Proviso. The argument started even before the war was ended, when Congressman David Wilmot of Pennsylvania offered an amendment to a money bill. His amendment provided that slavery would be prohibited in all lands acquired from Mexico. The view that slavery should not be allowed in any more territories was known as the *free-soil* position. The House of Representatives, with its Northern majority, passed the Wilmot Proviso twice. The Senate blocked it both times.

Southern leaders were enraged by the Wilmot Proviso. Calhoun saw it as the opening of a Northern campaign to destroy slavery in the South. He countered with his own resolutions in the Senate. Territories of the United States belonged to all the states, he said, and all states had equal rights in them. This meant that Congress could not prohibit citizens from taking their slaves or other property into the territories. Calhoun's resolutions did not pass, but no senator could fail to understand their meaning. In Calhoun's view, even the Missouri Compromise, which prohibited slavery above 36°30' north latitude in the territory of the Louisiana Purchase, had been unconstitutional.

Search for a middle ground. Many looked for a middle ground between Wilmot and Calhoun. One proposal was simply to extend the 36°30' line to the Pacific Coast. Another, known as *popular sovereignty*, was to let the people of each territory decide for themselves whether or not they wanted slavery. This view, supported mainly in the Midwest, was held by such Senate leaders as Lewis Cass of Michigan and Stephen A.

Douglas of Illinois. It appealed to many because it appeared to be a democratic way to handle the problem. It also would take the dangerous question of slavery in the territories out of Congress, where it might divide the Union.

But supporters of popular sovereignty never made clear just *when* the people of a territory should vote on slavery. Should it be *before* slaveholders brought slaves in? Or *after* they did? The outcome of the vote would surely be different in the one case than in the other. More important, popular sovereignty ignored the fact that to more and more Northerners, slavery was a moral issue. If one person's owning another was morally wrong, a majority vote to allow it could not make it right.

The election of 1848. Both parties in the 1848 election avoided the issue of slavery expansion. The Democrats nominated Lewis Cass, an old party politician, and they wrote a platform that was silent on slavery. The Whigs, who had won with a general as their candidate in 1840, chose another war hero, General Zachary Taylor, and wrote no platform at all. Taylor, in fact, had never revealed his views on any of the important issues of the day.

In the North, a number of strongly antislavery Democrats left the party because of its stand—or rather its lack of a stand. They were called *Barnburners*, because it was said they were willing to burn down the barn (that is, destroy the party) to get rid of the rats (the proslavery Democrats). The Whigs likewise were split. One group, the *Conscience Whigs*, put the moral issue of slavery ahead of harmony with the South and the cotton trade. The other group, the *Cotton Whigs*, took a proslavery view. The Conscience Whigs left their party, and together with the Barnburners and members of the old Liberty party, they formed the Free-Soil party. Former President Martin Van Buren became their candidate. Taylor won the election. Yet the new Free-Soil party had taken more than 10 percent of the vote and had won nine seats in Congress.

The uproar about California. While Congress and the country argued about slavery in the territories, gold was discovered in 1848 in California. Within a year the population of California—still not an organized territory—reached 100,000. The area needed a government. President Taylor thought he saw a way to solve at a single stroke both California's problem and the question that was dividing the country. People could debate whether Congress had the power to block slavery in the territories. No one, however, could deny that a *state* could decide for itself whether it would have slavery. California had more than enough people to become a state. Why not, then, let California skip the territorial stage? Why not let it enter the Union directly as a state, with or without slavery, however it wished? That is what Taylor recommended.

Californians gladly took Taylor's advice. In December 1849, they asked to enter the Union with a constitution that prohibited slavery. (New Mexico prepared to do the same thing a short time later.) As Congress met that same month, Taylor declared that California's problem had been solved, and he urged Congress to admit it as a free state.

Far from solving the problem, the inexperienced Taylor set off an uproar that almost destroyed the Union. The South was furious. Taylor, a slaveholder himself, was seen as a traitor. With the more populous North already in control of the House of Representatives, the South's main stronghold in government was the Senate. There the slave and free states were evenly balanced in 1850. A free California would tip the balance to the North. Every Southerner who could read a map knew that the balance would be tipped sooner or later, for none of the remaining territories in the United States were fit for plantation slavery. One day soon, the House, the Senate, and the Presidency would all be in the hands of the North, where antislavery feeling was growing. The slave states would then be at the North's mercy. Many Southerners believed that before that day came, a bargain should be struck to protect slavery. Most felt that this was the time for such bargaining. If the North would not agree, then perhaps the South should leave the Union.

Clay's plan. Such talk alarmed Senator Henry Clay of Kentucky. Thirty years earlier, Clay had arranged the Missouri Compromise. Seventeen years earlier, he had worked out the compromise that ended the nullification crisis. Now, at seventy-two years of age, he set his talents one last time to the task of finding a middle way that both North and South could accept.

Clay hoped to settle differences not only on the territory question but on other important matters dividing the two. In January 1850, he presented his plan. It called for the following.

(1) California would be admitted to the Union as a free state.

(2) The rest of the Mexican Cession would be organized into two parts— the Utah and New Mexico territories —which would have no restrictions on slavery. Presumably, the people in each territory would eventually decide whether or not to permit slavery.

(3) Certain lands in dispute on the border between Texas and New Mexico would be given to New Mexico, but Texas would be awarded $10 million by the federal government.

(4) The trade in slaves would be forbidden in Washington, D.C., but slavery itself could continue there.

(5) A new fugitive slave law would make the recapture of runaways easier and provide for severe punishment of anyone who helped slaves escape.

(6) Congress would not interfere with the slave trade among the states.

Hour after hour, Clay urged each side to back down. To Northerners who demanded the Wilmot Proviso, Clay pointed out that the deserts, plains, and mountains of the Southwest were not suited to plantation farming. Why insist on a statement forbidding something that would not happen anyway? "You have got what is worth more than a thousand Wilmot Provisos," Clay told them. "You have nature on your side." He warned the South that secession would lead to a bloody civil war.

Calhoun's and Webster's views. John C. Calhoun, the South's greatest spokesman, had no interest in compromise. Now dying of tuberculosis, he was

In 1850 an aging Henry Clay of Kentucky urges the Senate to accept his compromise plan.

carried on a stretcher on March 4, 1850 to the Senate floor. There a younger Southern senator read his speech. The Union could be saved, said Calhoun, only by "a full and final settlement" between North and South. The North must give the South equal rights in the new territories. It must return fugitive slaves. It must "cease the agitation of the slave question." If Northern senators could not agree to these conditions, said Calhoun,

say so; and let the States we both represent agree to separate and part in peace. If you are unwilling we should part in peace, tell us so; and we shall know what to do, when you reduce the question to submission or resistance.

447

Three days later Daniel Webster, the third of the Senate's aging giants, entered the debate. Like Clay, Webster was a Unionist above all. "I wish to speak today not as a Massachusetts man, nor as a Northern man," Webster told the Senate, "but as an American." Believing that only through this compromise could the Union be saved, Webster tried to make it acceptable to the North. He himself had supported the Wilmot Proviso, he said, but saving the Union was more important than insisting on an empty statement of principle. An opponent of slavery, he urged the North to accept the fugitive slave law.

Others had their say. Senator William H. Seward of New York argued against the fugitive slave law. Though the Constitution requires the return of runaways, there is a "higher law" than the Constitution, said Seward.

The Compromise of 1850. The debate in Congress lasted several months. Outside of Congress the debate went on as well. Southern extremists meeting in Nashville, Tennessee, in June 1850 talked openly of secession. Abolitionists in Webster's native New England condemned him for his support of the fugitive slave law. But moderates in both North and South generally supported a compromise. With President Taylor opposed, however, the chances of compromise were uncertain.

Taylor's sudden death in July opened the door to a solution. His successor, Millard Fillmore of New York, favored Clay's plan. In the autumn, with Douglas of Illinois taking up the work for an exhausted Clay, the Compromise of 1850 became law.

Reaction to the Compromise. Within each section, many opposed the Compromise. In the South, the "fire-eaters" predicted the North would not live up to its bargain. They favored immediate secession, before the North could become even stronger and better able to defeat the South. In the North, abolitionists and other opponents of the Compromise vowed they would not obey the fugitive slave law.

For the most part, however, there was a feeling of relief. Many political leaders regarded the slavery question as finally settled. Some said they would never bring up the matter again.

That seemed to be the meaning of the 1852 elections. For their candidate, the Democrats set aside such well-known leaders as Cass, Douglas, and James Buchanan in favor of a little-known former senator, Franklin Pierce of New Hampshire. Their platform stressed that the party accepted the Compromise. The Whigs also accepted the Compromise, but with little enthusiasm. Once again, they turned to a military hero, General Winfield Scott. This time it did them no good. Pierce won an overwhelming victory in the electoral college, 254 to 42, though the popular vote was much closer. The Free-Soil candidate received only half as many votes as in 1848.

CHECKUP

1. What were the opposing views of Wilmot and Calhoun on the issue of slavery in the lands acquired from Mexico?
2. Why did President Taylor's plan for admitting California to the Union set off an uproar?
3. How did the Compromise of 1850 deal with the slavery issue?

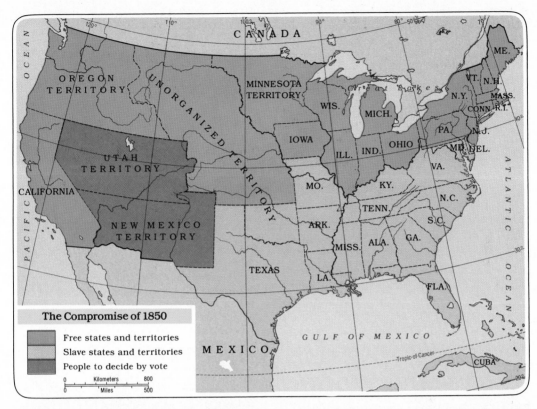

The Compromise of 1850

- Free states and territories
- Slave states and territories
- People to decide by vote

Kilometers 0 — 800
Miles 0 — 500

After the Compromise of 1850, the United States consisted of sixteen free states and fifteen slave states. The long-kept balance was slowly tipping toward the North. Events in the Western territories would eventually undermine the Compromise that Henry Clay had worked out.

The Rising Storm

Despite a general acceptance of the Compromise of 1850, careful observers could see warning signals. By 1852, there were signs that the Whig party was splitting. In the North, Conscience Whigs refused to accept the Compromise, and in the South some Cotton Whigs moved over to the Democratic party. The death of both Henry Clay and Daniel Webster in 1852 took from the scene two powerful Unionists who had held the Whig party together. It was plain that the Whigs would not survive as a political party if the slavery question were opened again.

Though the Compromise of 1850 had included a strong fugitive slave law, Northerners tried, often successfully, to block the return of fugitive slaves. In 1852, Harriet Beecher Stowe's antislavery book, *Uncle Tom's Cabin*, created a sensation (see page 450). Far from being put out, the fire that threatened the Union still smoldered, ready to burst into flame at the next incident.

449

★ AMERICA · EXPRESSES · ITSELF ★

Uncle Tom's Cabin

No book published in America ever had a greater political effect than the novel *Uncle Tom's Cabin*. The author was Harriet Beecher Stowe. At the time she wrote the book, Mrs. Stowe was living in Brunswick, Maine, where her husband was a professor at Bowdoin College. Mrs. Stowe's aim was to show how terrible slavery was. The main character of her novel is Uncle Tom, a slave, one of whose masters is the brutal Simon Legree. Among the other characters are a young slave couple who flee to Canada.

Uncle Tom's Cabin appeared in 1852 at a time when there was great controversy over the fugitive slave law. Presses ran night and day to meet the demand for the book. Within 18 months, some 1,200,000 copies had been published. The story created great sympathy for the slaves. Senator William Seward of New York, an abolitionist, urged Southerners to read the book and learn the error of their ways. Southerners, on the other hand, charged that Harriet Beecher Stowe was a fanatic without firsthand knowledge of the conditions of slavery.

In a second book, *Key to Uncle Tom's Cabin*, Mrs. Stowe attempted to show that her novel was based on fact. Before moving to Maine, she had lived for some years in Cincinnati, Ohio, on the route of the Underground Railroad by which slaves fled northward. She had also visited a Kentucky plantation.

450

Because of its effect on public opinion, *Uncle Tom's Cabin* has been called the greatest of American propaganda novels. Senator Charles Sumner of Massachusetts declared that without this book Lincoln would not have been elected President. When Lincoln himself met Mrs. Stowe during the Civil War, he is said to have greeted her with these words: "So you're the little woman who made the book that made this great war."

Millions who never read the book *Uncle Tom's Cabin* saw the widely performed stage production. As the playbill shows, this company had given more than a thousand performances.

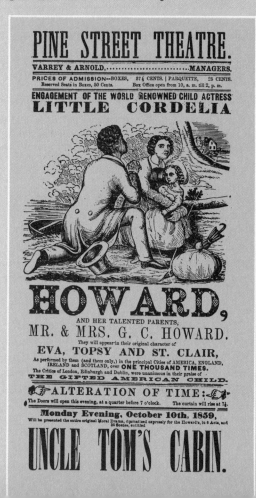

PINE STREET THEATRE.

VARREY & ARNOLD,........................MANAGERS.

PRICES OF ADMISSION--BOXES, 37½ CENTS. | PARQUETTE, 25 CENTS.
Reserved Seats in Boxes, 50 Cents.   Box Office open from 10, a. m. till 2, p. m.

ENGAGEMENT OF THE WORLD RENOWNED CHILD ACTRESS

LITTLE CORDELIA

HOWARD,

AND HER TALENTED PARENTS,

MR. & MRS. G. C. HOWARD.

They will appear in their original character of

EVA, TOPSY AND ST. CLAIR,

As performed by them (and them only,) in the principal Cities of AMERICA, ENGLAND, IRELAND and SCOTLAND, over ONE THOUSAND TIMES.

The Critics of London, Edinburgh and Dublin, were unanimous in their praise of

THE GIFTED AMERICAN CHILD.

☞ ALTERATION OF TIME: ☜

The Doors will open this evening, at a quarter before 7 o'clock.   The curtain will rise at 7½.

Monday Evening, October 10th, 1859,

Will be presented the entire original Moral Drama, dramatized expressly for the Howard's, in 6 Acts, and 30 Scenes, entitled

UNCLE TOM'S CABIN.

The Kansas-Nebraska Act. Such an incident came in January 1854. At that time, Congress was considering several routes for a railroad to California. Senator Douglas of Illinois was anxious that the line run from Chicago in his home state to the Pacific. The route, however, would take the railroad through an unorganized territory inhabited by Indians and lacking a government. Douglas therefore introduced a bill to *organize* the Nebraska Territory—that is, open it to settlement and start it on its course to statehood.

Nebraska lay north of 36°30′ north latitude in the Louisiana Purchase, however, and slavery was prohibited there. To win Southern votes for his bill, Douglas prepared to divide the land into two territories, Nebraska and Kansas. The bill specifically repealed the Missouri Compromise and provided for popular sovereignty instead. It was expected that the Northern territory of Nebraska would become a free state. With popular sovereignty, the South would have a chance to make Kansas a slave state. Supported by

Compare this map of the United States, after the Kansas-Nebraska Act, with the map on page 335, showing the nation four years earlier. Note the changes in the Western territories.

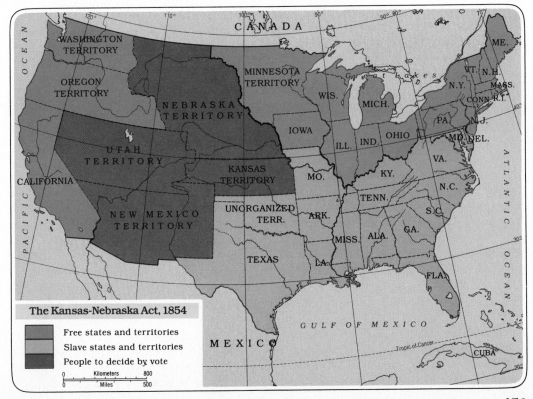

The Kansas-Nebraska Act, 1854

Free states and territories
Slave states and territories
People to decide by vote

★12★
Zachary Taylor
1784–1850

Born in VIRGINIA
In Office 1849–1850
Party WHIG

An army officer, and a national hero after war with Mexico. Though once a slave owner, he sought the admission of California as a free state. Died after sixteen months in office.

★ ★ ★ ★ ★ ★ ★ ★

★13★
Millard Fillmore
1800–1874

Born in NEW YORK
In Office 1850–1853
Party WHIG

Signed Compromise of 1850, which helped delay Civil War. But his enforcement of Fugitive Slave Law lost him Northern support, and Whigs did not make him their candidate in 1852.

★ ★ ★ ★ ★ ★ ★ ★

★14★
Franklin Pierce
1804–1869

Born in NEW HAMPSHIRE
In Office 1853–1857
Party DEMOCRATIC

Served at time of great bitterness over slavery. Supported Kansas-Nebraska Act, angering Northerners. Approved Gadsden Purchase from Mexico. Protected rights of immigrants.

★ ★ ★ ★ ★ ★ ★ ★

President Pierce and the Democratic party, Douglas pushed the Kansas-Nebraska Act through Congress.

In the North and West, the Kansas-Nebraska Act led to a storm of protest. To many people the repeal of the thirty-four-year-old Missouri Compromise to limit slavery was a betrayal. Protest meetings were held all over the North and West. Senator Douglas declared that he could have ridden across the country by the light of his burning effigies.

Antislavery Democrats and Whigs left their parties to form new local and statewide anti-Nebraska parties. Their main demand was an end to the spread of slavery into the territories. Soon these parties came together to form a new national party—the Republican party. The Whigs, meanwhile, collapsed. Many Southern Whigs now completed their shift into the Democratic party. Whigs in the North joined either the Republicans or another new party—the American, or Know-Nothing, party. The Know-Nothing party played down the slavery question and stressed its opposition to Catholics and immigrants.

452

"Bleeding Kansas." Since the question of slavery in Kansas was to be decided by the settlers themselves, both sides encouraged people to settle there. On the day set for the election of a territorial legislature, thousands of proslavery Missourians crossed into Kansas and voted illegally. They elected a proslavery territorial legislature and governor. This new body passed a slave code and set harsh punishments, including death, for anyone who interfered with slavery. Antislavery settlers, claiming fraud, held their own elections. They chose a free-state legislature and governor, and drew up an antislavery constitution. Thus, one year after the Kansas-Nebraska Act, the territory of Kansas had two legislatures and two governors.

In May 1856, the situation became violent. A proslavery band attacked the antislavery town of Lawrence, burning homes and newspaper offices. In revenge, a fiery, fanatical abolitionist named John Brown and six followers murdered five proslavery settlers at Pottawatomie Creek. This action touched off open warfare that claimed 200 lives and gave the territory the name of "Bleeding Kansas." Such was the first bitter fruit of popular sovereignty.

The violence in Kansas was soon matched in the halls of Congress. In a speech on "The Crime Against Kansas," Senator Charles Sumner of Massachusetts spoke out harshly against Senator Andrew Butler of South Carolina. Two days later, Butler's nephew, Representative Preston Brooks, walked over to Sumner at his Senate desk and beat him into unconsciousness with a cane. Sumner, seriously injured, did not return to the

In Kansas a band of antislavery settlers exchange fire with proslavery people. The upsurge of violence in this border state aroused feelings throughout the North and the South.

Senate for three years. Many Southerners thought that the abolitionist Sumner had gotten only what he deserved, and a number of them sent Brooks canes to use against other Northerners. Meanwhile, in Northern eyes, Sumner's empty Senate seat became a symbol of the brutality of the slaveholding South.

The election of 1856. Against this background of violence, the election of 1856 took place. The new Republican party had been very successful in state elections in 1854 and 1855. Now its national convention nominated John Frémont, the soldier and Western explorer, for President. The party's chief position was to keep slavery from spreading into the territories. To enlarge its appeal in the North and West, however, it added planks favoring high tariffs for growing Northern industries, free homesteads, and a railroad to the Pacific.

The leading contender for the Democratic nomination was Stephen A. Douglas of Illinois. The Kansas-Nebraska Act, however, had made him too controversial. The Democratic party therefore turned to James Buchanan of Pennsylvania, a sixty-six-year-old party politician. As minister to England, he had had the good fortune to be out of the country during the Kansas-Nebraska uproar. Buchanan was generally favorable to the South. In nominating a *dough-face*—that is, a Northerner with Southern principles—the Democrats hoped to appeal to both sections. The American party nominated Millard Fillmore.

Buchanan won with 174 electoral votes to 114 for Frémont. Fillmore carried only Maryland. Frémont won most of the free states and only narrowly lost Pennsylvania and Illinois. Had he taken those two states, he would have won the Presidency. Thus the Republican party, a sectional party, had come very close to victory in its first national election.

The Dred Scott case. Two days after Buchanan took office in March 1857, the Supreme Court handed down an important decision on slavery. In the 1830s, Dred Scott, a Missouri slave, had been taken by his owner to Illinois, a free state, and later to the Wisconsin Territory, where slavery was prohibited under the Missouri Compromise. Some years later, he returned with his owner to Missouri. Claiming that his stay on free soil had made him a free man, Scott sued for freedom in the courts. In the 1850s the case reached the Supreme Court.

In *Dred Scott* v. *Sandford,* a majority of the justices, including Chief Justice Roger Taney, held that blacks—even free blacks—were not citizens under the Constitution. Therefore it was ruled that Scott could not sue in a federal court. Further, the Court stated that whatever Scott might have been while he was in Illinois and in Wisconsin Territory, he was a slave once he returned to Missouri.

This ruling was enough to decide the case, and the Court could have stopped there. But Chief Justice Taney, believing that a clear decision by the Court might settle the slavery issue once and for all, pushed further. The Fifth Amendment to the Constitution states that no person's property may be taken away "without due process of law." Slaves were property. It followed, then, according to Taney, that Congress had no power to deny a citizen the right to take property—slaves, cattle, furniture, or whatever—into a territory. That is exactly what the Missouri Compromise had done. That act of Congress, said the Court, had therefore been unconstitutional all along.

Far from quieting the slavery controversy, the Dred Scott decision created another uproar. Southerners rejoiced. The North was stunned and angry. Republicans were especially upset, for if there was no way in which Congress could keep slavery out of the territories, the party's very reason for being had been swept away. Republicans said that the Dred Scott decision was a bad ruling, and it would not last long. They pointed out that seven out of the nine judges on the Supreme Court were Democrats and that five of the seven were from the South. A Republican President would appoint different judges, they said, and the decision would be overturned.

The Lecompton constitution. Meanwhile, the proslavery forces in Kansas met in Lecompton. They drew up a proposed state constitution and sent it to the voters. Knowing that the majority of Kansans were antislavery, they rigged the vote. No matter how the people voted, they would be approving a constitution making Kansas a slave state. Antislavery Kansans refused to take part in the voting. As a result, the Lecompton constitution was adopted. Despite this trickery, President Buchanan recommended that Congress accept Kansas into the Union as a slave state. This was too much for Senator Douglas.

★15★

James Buchanan
1791–1868

Born in PENNSYLVANIA
In Office 1857–1861
Party DEMOCRATIC

Caught up in storm over slavery. Tried to keep peace. Regarded Dred Scott decision as binding. Said states had no right to secede, but would not take action to keep them in the Union.

★ ★ ★ ★ ★ ★ ★ ★

Such action, he said, would make a joke of popular sovereignty and its idea of majority rule. Douglas split with Buchanan and the Southern Democrats, and Congress became deadlocked.

Antislavery Kansans now took matters into their own hands. They put the Lecompton constitution to a fair vote in another election, and it was voted down by a large margin. In yet another vote, ordered by Congress, the Lecompton constitution was rejected by a 6 to 1 margin. Kansas finally entered the Union as a free state in 1861.

455

"Cotton is King." Economic as well as political problems troubled the country. Overexpansion in railroads, land speculation, falling prices for grain, and problems in banking touched off a business panic and depression in 1857. It lasted for several years, and the North was hard hit. Because world demand for cotton remained high, however, the South was not as badly affected. Indeed, cotton accounted for nearly two thirds of the value of all United States exports.

The 1857 panic had important political results in both the North and the South. Northern manufacturers, more interested than ever in protective tariffs, moved to support the Republican party. Southern leaders became convinced that the real economic strength of the country rested in the cotton kingdom, with its system of slave labor. Thus they became more confident that the North would have to give in to their demands. As Senator Hammond of South Carolina said to his Northern colleagues in 1858, "You do not dare to make war on cotton. No power on earth dares to make war on it. Cotton is King." A Southerner named Hinton Rowan Helper wrote *The Impending Crisis of the South* in 1857. Because of this book, arguing that slavery actually made the South economically weaker, Helper was hounded out of the South.

Abraham Lincoln of Illinois. In the elections of 1858, Republicans made large gains in the North and West, and they won many seats in the House of Representatives. The most closely watched contest of that year was in Illinois, where Democrat Stephen Douglas was seeking reelection to the Senate. To op-

pose him, Republicans chose a young lawyer named Abraham Lincoln. He had served one term in the United States House of Representatives as a Whig during Polk's Presidency. With many other antislavery Whigs, Lincoln had shifted to the Republican party after the Kansas-Nebraska Act.

Lincoln was not an abolitionist. Nor, as he said during the campaign, had he "ever been in favor of bringing about in any way the social and political equality of the white and black races." But he did oppose slavery. "In the right to eat the bread . . . which his own hand earns," Lincoln would say, "he [the black man] is my equal, and the equal of Judge Douglas, and the equal of every living man." And while he did not believe that the federal government could interfere with slavery in the Southern states, he opposed its spread into a single foot of free territory. If slavery was thus limited, Lincoln believed, it would eventually die out.

The Freeport debate. The Lincoln-Douglas campaign featured a series of seven debates in Illinois towns. The most important one took place at Freeport. The Supreme Court had said in the Dred Scott case that Congress could not prohibit slavery in a territory. It followed that a territorial legislature, which was created by an act of Congress, could not do what Congress was prohibited from doing. Was there, then, asked Lincoln, any way in which an antislavery majority in a territory could keep slavery out? The question was a shrewd one. If Douglas said there was no way, he would be rejecting popular sovereignty, the idea on which he had built his career. If he said that slavery could still be kept out, he would be arguing against the Dred Scott decision. This would anger the South, whose support he hoped for in the next presidential election.

Douglas's reply was equally shrewd. Yes, he said, there was a way for a majority to keep out slavery, despite the Dred Scott decision. The territorial legislature could simply refuse to pass a slave code—those laws that protected slavery—for without it, slavery could not exist a single day.

Douglas's reply became known as the *Freeport Doctrine*. It satisfied enough Illinois voters for the Democrats to carry both houses of the state legislature narrowly, and it reelected Douglas to the United States Senate. But the Freeport Doctrine raised a storm among Southern Democrats, as Lincoln knew it would. No longer satisfied that slavery was *allowed* in the territories by the Dred Scott decision, they now demanded that Congress pass laws to *protect* it there. This would mean the end of popular sovereignty, and Northern and Western Democrats in Congress refused to go along. Meanwhile, despite the loss, Lincoln emerged from the election with a growing reputation.

Harpers Ferry. In the fall of 1859, John Brown—the same John Brown who had touched off the warfare in Kansas—led

Inside the arsenal at Harpers Ferry, John Brown and his men defend themselves against the militia and a company of marines. Only four out of nineteen were alive and unwounded upon Brown's surrender.

a small band of followers in an attack on a United States arsenal at Harpers Ferry in Virginia. With the guns stored there, Brown planned to arm Virginia slaves for an uprising. There was never any chance that this wild idea would succeed. Brown was quickly captured, tried for treason against the state of Virginia, found guilty, and hanged.

Most Northern citizens, political leaders, and newspapers condemned Brown's raid. Abolitionists, however, raised Brown to sainthood. He was an "angel of light," they said, whose execution would "make the gallows glorious like the cross." At their meetings, the abolitionists were soon singing:

John Brown's body lies a-mouldering in the grave,
His soul goes marching on.

It was the words of the abolitionists rather than those of Northern leaders and journals that frightened Southerners chose to hear. They were enraged to learn that some leading abolitionists had known of Brown's plan and had given him money to carry it out. That Northerners would help to bring about what Southerners most dreaded—a slave uprising—was to them further proof of the North's bad faith.

As the year 1860 opened, most of the ties that had held the Union together snapped. Every new episode, every new statement was taken by each side as proof of the aggressive designs of the other. By year's end, a sectional party would capture the Presidency, and secession of Southern states would begin. Soon after, the nation would be plunged into civil war. You will read of these events and their outcome in the next chapter.

CHECKUP

1. What were the results in Kansas of the passage of the Kansas-Nebraska Act?
2. How did the makeup of American political parties change during the 1850s?
3. In what ways did the Dred Scott case intensify the slavery controversy?
4. What were Abraham Lincoln's views on slavery?

Key Facts from Chapter 17

1. The antislavery movement was led by Northern abolitionists, both black and white. The abolitionists demanded that slaves be given their freedom.

2. As antislavery feeling became stronger, so did the defense of slavery by Southerners.

3. By the mid-1800s, the North and South were moving in different directions. The North was moving toward an industrial, urban society, while the South remained largely rural and agricultural.

4. Following the Mexican War, the overriding issue in national politics became the spread of slavery into the Western territories.

5. During the 1850s, the Republican party was formed. Its major goal was to keep slavery out of the territories.

★ REVIEWING THE CHAPTER ★

People, Places, and Events

Review Questions

1. What three suggestions did early opponents of slavery offer to settle the problem? *P. 437*
2. How were blacks treated in the North? *Pp. 439–440*
3. In what ways did blacks contribute to the abolition movement? *Pp. 440–441*
4. How did the South justify the practice of slavery? *P. 442*
5. Did most Southerners own slaves? Explain. *P. 443*
6. In what way did popular sovereignty propose to settle the argument over the spread of slavery? *P. 445*
7. What were the views of John Calhoun and Daniel Webster in regard to the compromise offered by Henry Clay in 1850? *Pp. 447–448*
8. Describe the impact of *Uncle Tom's Cabin*. *P. 450*
9. How did the Panic of 1857 influence the political attitudes of Northerners and Southerners? *P. 456*

Chapter Test

The statements below indicate events that occurred during the period 1820 to 1859. On a separate piece of paper, number 1 to 10. Beginning with number 1 for the earliest event, rearrange the events so that they are in the correct chronological order.

A. The Compromise of 1850 provided for the admission of California to the Union as a free state.

B. Open warfare between proslavery and antislavery forces claimed a number of lives in "Bleeding Kansas."

C. John Brown's raid at Harpers Ferry disturbed southern slave owners, who lived in constant fear of a massive slave revolt.

D. The Kansas-Nebraska Act specifically repealed the Missouri Compromise and provided for popular sovereignty as the method to settle slavery issue in the two newly created territories.

E. The Lincoln-Douglas debate at Freeport, Illinois argued the issues at stake in the Dred Scott decision.

F. The Missouri Compromise was the first great clash between North and South over the question of slavery.

G. Elijah Lovejoy, an abolitionist printer, was shot to death by an angry mob.

H. California sought to enter the Union as a free state.

I. As part of the decision in the Dred Scott case, the Supreme Court said that Congress could not bar slavery in any territories of the national government.

J. *Uncle Tom's Cabin* appeared at a time when there was great controversy over the Fugitive Slave Law.

459

SECESSION AND CIVIL WAR

THE ELECTION OF 1860 took place against a background of rising sectional tension. Favored to win the Democratic party's nomination was Senator Stephen Douglas of Illinois. At the convention in South Carolina in April 1860, Southern delegates pressed their demand for a law to protect slavery in the territories. When Northern delegates refused to put this demand in the platform, Southerners walked out. The convention then adjourned without choosing a candidate. Six weeks later in Baltimore the Democrats tried again, but with the same result. This time the Northern delegates remained and nominated Douglas. Southern Democrats then met separately and chose John J. Breckinridge of Kentucky as their candidate. The Democratic party had now split into two sectional parties.

This split opened the door to a Republican victory. The new Republican party needed only to hold the support of those who had voted for it in 1856 and 1858. The strategy therefore called for choosing a candidate who would not frighten voters away. Mainly for that reason, party leaders at the Republican convention passed over the best known Republican, Senator William H. Seward of New York. Seward had once spoken of an "irreconcilable conflict" between North and South, and he was considered by some to be extreme. The Republicans named instead the more moderate Abraham Lincoln. The Republican platform, while promising not to interfere with slavery in the Southern states, opposed its spread into the territories.

A fourth party, the Constitutional Union party, also entered the field. Most of its leaders were former Whigs from the states of Maryland, Virginia, Kentucky, and Missouri. Those states lay between the North and the South. The leaders of the party desperately hoped to avoid war, knowing that if it came, their states would be the battleground. The Constitutional Union party nominated John Bell of Tennessee for President, and declared simply in favor of the Constitution and the Union.

Lincoln's election. Although Lincoln received less than 40 percent of the popular vote, he easily won the election. He received 180 electoral votes to 72 for Breckinridge and 39 for Bell. Douglas, who with 29 percent was second to Lincoln in popular votes, won only 12 electoral votes. The Democrats, however, kept control of Congress.

The presidential vote showed how deeply the country was split. Lincoln was not even on the ballot in ten Southern states. In the North, Breckinridge got a mere handful of votes. At the same time, the combined vote for these two clearly sectional candidates was far greater than that for the moderates, Bell and Douglas.

The South Leaves the Union

During the campaign, many Southern leaders warned that if Lincoln was elected the South would secede. They were true to their word. On December 20, 1860, South Carolina seceded from the Union. That state was followed in the next six weeks by Mississippi, Florida, Alabama, Georgia, Louisiana, and Texas.

The Confederacy. On February 1, 1861, representatives of the seven seceding states of the Deep South met in Montgomery, Alabama, and formed the Confederate States of America. Four more Southern states—Virginia, North Carolina, Tennessee, and Arkansas—did not secede. However, they warned they would do so if force was used against the seven states that had withdrawn from the Union.

The Constitution of the Confederacy was much like that of the United States. The main differences were that the states in the Confederacy were sovereign, and slavery could never be abolished. Jefferson Davis of Mississippi, a former senator and cabinet member, became President. Alexander Stephens of Georgia, a former congressman, was made Vice President. Shortly after taking office, Stephens explained the reason why the Southern states formed the Confederate government.

> Our confederacy is founded upon the great truth that the Negro is not equal to the white man, that slavery is his natural and normal condition. This, our new government, is the first in the history of the world based upon this great physical and moral truth.

Meanwhile, the seceding states seized federal forts, post offices, and customs houses within their borders. Only Fort Sumter, in the harbor of Charleston, South Carolina, and Fort Pickens, off the Florida coast, remained under federal control. All these events took place while James Buchanan was still President. He did nothing to stop them. His position was that while secession was not possible under the Constitution, the federal government had no power under that document to stop it! Meanwhile, several compromise efforts in Congress failed.

Why the haste to secede? Why did the South hasten to secede at this time? Congress, after all, was still in the hands of the Democrats. On the Supreme Court, there was still a majority friendly to the Southern view. Even President-elect Lincoln had promised not to interfere with slavery in the Southern states. Despite the alarms of the fire-eaters, it is clear that there was no immediate threat to slavery in the South. Further, once it became a separate country, the South would have no claim at all to a share of the territories in the West. And getting back slaves who had run away to the North, now merely difficult, would then be impossible.

There are at least two reasons why the South seceded at this time. One is that its leaders were looking not to the present but to the future. Sooner or later, the rapidly growing, antislavery North would control all the branches of government. Better to leave now, said Southern leaders, than wait for that time when the North would be still stronger. A second reason is that after years of arguing with the North over tariffs, slavery, and states' rights, feelings had been built to a point where nothing but action would do. A South Carolina woman named Mary Chesnut later recalled her own feelings at that time.

462

My father was a South Carolina nullifier, Governor of the state at the time of the nullification row and then United States Senator; so I was of necessity a rebel born. . . . Come what would, I wanted them to fight and stop talking. South Carolinians had heated themselves into a fever that only bloodletting could ever cure. It was the inevitable remedy, so I was a seceder.

Would war follow? Not all Southerners shared Mary Chesnut's belief that secession would lead to war. Indeed, it was the belief that they could leave the Union without causing war that made many Southerners bold enough to take the step. In the North, many people agreed with the newspaper editor who wrote, "Let the erring sisters depart in peace." Many abolitionists were also pacifists. Further, Southerners believed that Northern manufacturers who needed cotton and Northern merchants who sold in Southern markets would never let the North go to war and ruin their businesses.

If war should come, the Southerners counted on King Cotton to give them victory. English and French textile manufacturers depended on Southern cotton. War would cut off their supply. Before England and France would allow their economies to be ruined, Southerners were sure that those nations would come into the war on the side of the South. Further, Southern slaveholders counted on the sympathetic support of the British upper class.

Lincoln's inauguration. On March 4, 1861, amid the nation's greatest crisis, Abraham Lincoln became the sixteenth President of the United States. In his inaugural address Lincoln tried to reas-

In February 1861, Jefferson Davis was sworn in as President of the Confederacy at Montgomery, Alabama. After Virginia seceded, the capital was moved from Montgomery to Richmond.

sure the South. The President declared he would agree to a constitutional amendment that the government would never interfere with slavery in the South. At the same time, he said that secession was not possible under the Constitution. His oath of office required that he hold and protect government property, and he would do so. Whether this would lead to war was, the President said, a decision that lay in the hands of the South.

The firing on Fort Sumter. Lincoln's determination was quickly put to the test. Major Robert Anderson, the army commander at Fort Sumter, reported that more arms, men, and supplies would be needed to hold the fort. Lincoln feared that sending men would cause Southern forces to open fire. Yet he was unwilling to allow the garrison to be starved into surrender. He therefore decided to send food only, and he notified authorities in South Carolina of this fact. But Confederate leaders were determined that the fort should fall. Their guns opened fire at 4:30 A.M. on April 12, before the supplies arrived. After thirty-four hours, Anderson and his men surrendered.

With the firing on Fort Sumter, Northern opinion, until now divided, rallied behind Lincoln. Two days later, the President called on the state militias for 75,000 volunteers to put down the rebellion. Virginia, North Carolina, Arkansas, and Tennessee promptly carried out their earlier threat to leave the Union. (The western part of Virginia, where Union sentiment was strong, broke away with the aid of Union troops. In 1863, it became the state of West Virginia.) Four other slave states— Maryland, Delaware, Kentucky, and Missouri—remained in the Union. Those states came to be called the *border states*. Keeping them in the Union became a chief objective of the Lincoln administration.

Within two weeks, Lincoln called for more troops and ordered a naval blockade of Southern ports. The Civil War had begun.

Confederate artillery pieces under the command of General P. G. T. Beauregard pound Fort Sumter in the harbor of Charleston, South Carolina. The barrage marked the beginning of the Civil War.

1. In what ways did the election of 1860 reflect the split over the slavery issue?
2. Why did the South hasten to secede following Lincoln's election?
3. Under what circumstances were the first shots of the Civil War fired?

Mounting the War Effort

How the war would be pursued by the two sides depended to a large degree on the resources available to each. A comparison at the start of the war shows that the Union and the Confederacy each had certain advantages.

Northern advantages. The twenty-three states remaining in the Union had a population of 22 million. In the eleven Confederate states there were only 9 million people, of whom 3.5 million were slaves. The North thus had a much larger population from which to draw soldiers.

With seven times as much manufacturing as the South, the North was able after 1862 to make all the war goods it needed, from guns to medical supplies. The South, on the other hand, had to buy many of its supplies from Europe. This was made difficult because of another of the North's advantages—its navy. Soon after the war started, the North set up a naval blockade that kept ships from entering or leaving Southern ports. Although far from airtight, the blockade became a powerful weapon.

Other Northern advantages included greater wealth to pay for a war and a better railway system. With twice as many miles of railroad lines as the South had, the North could move troops and supplies quickly. Moreover, as the war went on, Southern railroads fell into ever worse condition.

Southern advantages. A major advantage of the Confederacy was that, unlike the Union, it did not have to conquer any territory to attain its goal. To maintain independence, the Confederacy needed only to hold what it had. Thus its armies could fight a defensive war. That meant several things. One, the Confederacy's supply lines were short, while the enemy's were long. Also, the Southern soldiers fought on land they knew well. And finally, they felt that they were fighting to defend not only their way of life but their very homes, giving them a strong sense of purpose. Further, the South's strong military tradition gave it better military leadership at the start of the war. At the outbreak of the war, many officers in the United States Army were from the South. Most of those officers chose to resign and cast their lot with the Confederacy.

Raising an army: the North. Soon after the war began, it became clear to Northern leaders that they needed more than the three-month volunteers from the state militias. Lincoln therefore called for 42,000 volunteers for three-year terms in the regular army. Two months later, Congress increased the size of the army to 500,000. When enlistments slowed, Congress passed the nation's first draft law, in March 1863. There was a good deal of opposition to this law. *Peace Democrats*—Northern Democrats who opposed the war—were against it. So were many who believed that a draft violated their civil rights.

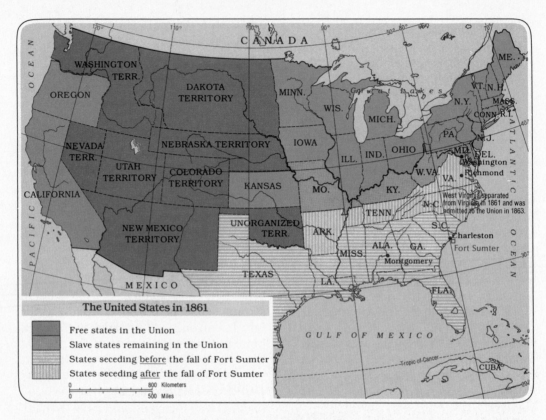

The United States in 1861

- Free states in the Union
- Slave states remaining in the Union
- States seceding <u>before</u> the fall of Fort Sumter
- States seceding <u>after</u> the fall of Fort Sumter

West Virginia separated from Virginia in 1861 and was admitted to the Union in 1863.

The Union consisted of twenty-three states following the admission of West Virginia in 1863. There were eleven states in the Confederacy. Most Western regions had territorial status.

Most opposition, though, centered on the fact that a draftee could keep from serving by paying the government $300 or by hiring a substitute to go in his place. This led some to complain that the war was "a rich man's war but a poor man's fight." In several cities there were draft riots. The worst was in New York City, where four days of rioting in July 1863 left several hundred dead. Union soldiers had to be sent to the city to restore order.

Black Americans were another source of troops for the army. At first, though, they were not allowed to enlist. When some blacks in Cincinnati tried to volunteer, they were told that "this"—a war that was about slavery—"is a white man's war!" After 1862, however, blacks were allowed to enlist. By the end of the war some 200,000, many of them former slaves, had served as members of the Union army.

Raising an army: the South. In the South, too, volunteers flocked to the colors at first. With a smaller population, however, the South had to turn to the

466

draft nearly a year before the North did. Because the law allowed persons owning twenty or more slaves to be free from military service, it was bitterly opposed by many nonslaveholders. As casualties and desertions began to mount, the Confederacy raised the draft age to fifty. By early 1865, the Confederacy became so desperate that it passed a law to draft 300,000 slaves—into the very army that was fighting to preserve slavery! But the war ended before any slaves were drafted.

Paying for the war. The cost of fighting ran into billions of dollars for both sides. Both sides used three means to pay for the war: they taxed; they borrowed; and they printed paper money. The North, with far more of its wealth in money, was the more successful. Among its taxes was an income tax, the first in the country's history. It remained law until 1872. The federal government also raised a large amount of money by selling bonds to the public. In the National Banking Acts of 1863 and 1864, the government created a system of national banks, and it required these banks to buy United States government bonds. When these methods did not provide enough funds, Congress approved the issue of paper money. By the end of the war, $450 million in *greenbacks*, so

For both North and South, raising an army was an urgent task. This poster was used to recruit Union soldiers in Vermont. The photograph shows newly outfitted Confederate recruits.

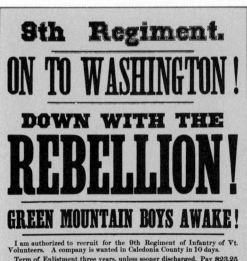

called because of their color, had been issued. Greenbacks could not be redeemed for gold or silver. Therefore, their value at any time depended on how much faith people had in the government that issued them. When the war was going poorly for the North, greenbacks were worth as little as 30 cents. As Northern fortunes improved, so did the value of the greenbacks.

The South had a much harder time raising money. Most of its wealth was tied up in land and slaves, and the North's blockade kept the South from raising much money by selling cotton. Since few farmers had much money, the Confederacy passed a *tax in kind.* This required farmers to pay one tenth of their produce to the government. The Confederate government as well as individual Southern states sold bonds. The Confederacy turned to printing money earlier than the North did, and it printed more of it. By 1864, it had issued more than $1 billion in paper money. As the South's paper dollar fell in value, prices there skyrocketed. Flour came to cost $300 a barrel, and butter, $25 a pound. By the end of the war, the value of the Confederate dollar had dropped to less than a penny.

The home front. For the families of the millions who went off to war, normal life was disrupted. Women and children had to take on the work that had been done by the menfolk. Some Southern women had always run farms and plantations. Now, many more did. To their usual tasks they also added that of helping to manufacture war goods. A Georgia woman later recalled how every household "became a miniature factory" for

making clothing after the North's blockade cut off supply lines from England and France.

A remarkable fact is that despite the absence of many men from Northern farms for long periods of time, farm production in that section actually increased during the war. That was partly due to the greater use of machinery. Much of the increased production, however, was the result of women picking up the farm work formerly done by men. A traveler to the Midwest in 1863 reported that "women were in the fields everywhere, driving the reapers, binding and shocking, and loading grain." One woman explained:

> Harvesting isn't any harder than cooking, washing, and ironing over a red-hot stove in July and August—only we have to do both now. My three brothers went into the army, all my cousins, most of the young men about here, and the men we used to hire. So there's no help to be got but women, and the crops must be got in all the same, you know.

Lincoln's leadership. One of the North's greatest strengths turned out to be the leadership of Abraham Lincoln. When he first entered the Presidency, many people thought of Lincoln as a smalltown politician who was not big enough for the job. Several of his cabinet appointees, including Secretary of State William Seward, tried to dominate the President. Seward quickly learned, however, that Lincoln intended to run the government himself and had the ability to do it. From then on, Seward was the President's loyal supporter.

Throughout the war, Lincoln faced strong political opposition in and out of

Employees leave work at the Treasury Department building in Washington, D.C., during the Civil War. At that time, many women filled government jobs that had previously been held by men.

Congress. On the one side were those Northern Democrats who opposed the war. The *Copperheads,* as the Peace Democrats were called, wanted to invite the South back into the Union on the South's terms—a guarantee of states' rights. Some opponents of the war went so far as to form secret societies and plan acts of treason. On the other side were the Radical Republicans. They made up a growing wing of the party that wanted slavery abolished and the South punished. In Congress, the Radical Republicans created and controlled the Joint Committee on the Conduct of the War. Through this committee, they kept up a steady stream of criticism of Lincoln. With great patience and skill, the President steered between those two groups, moving always toward the main objective of saving the Union.

Stretching the Constitution. In his efforts to save the Union, Lincoln stretched the constitutional powers of the President to their very limits—and even beyond. Although the Constitution gives the power to raise an army only to Congress, Lincoln took it upon himself in May 1861 to call for three-year volunteers. Congress legalized that action when it returned to Washington two months later. Lincoln also acted without congressional authority in declaring the blockade.

To prevent interference with the war effort, especially in the border states, Lincoln suspended the writ of *habeas corpus* (see page 161). As a result, more than 13,000 civilians were arrested and held without trial in military jails— some for days, some for months, and a few for years. Those who were brought

469

to trial were tried in military courts. After the war, the Supreme Court ruled in *ex parte Milligan* (1866) that military trials of civilians were illegal where regular courts were still operating.

Lincoln justified his actions by saying that in order to preserve the Constitution, he had at times to disregard parts of it. Others might use the same justification for causes that were less good or when the danger to the nation and the Constitution was less clear.

Jefferson Davis's role. Jefferson Davis, the President of the Confederacy was less successful than Lincoln in directing the war effort. One reason was that Davis lacked Lincoln's skill in dealing with the trying problems of wartime leadership. Often Davis allowed himself to become bogged down with details. Further, his attempts to provide a unified leadership for the war effort were blocked by some states that insisted on states' rights. The doctrine of states' rights was, of course, one of the founding ideas of the Confederacy. At various times, some Southern states refused to take orders from the Confederate government. Once, South Carolina even threatened to secede from the Confederacy!

Wartime diplomacy. Both sides engaged in active diplomacy with European nations. The aim of the Confederacy was to bring England and France into the war on its side, or at least to get help from them. The North's aim was simply to keep those countries neutral.

The South, you will recall, had pinned most of its hopes on the need of Britain and France for cotton. However, when the war began, both countries had large supplies of cotton on hand. By the time they were used up, Britain and France had developed new sources of cotton in Egypt and India. Also, Britain's upper classes were sympathetic to the South, as the South had expected. But that sympathy was offset by the strong antislavery and pro-Northern feelings of the English working people.

Several crises arose between England and the United States. The first occurred when the commander of a United States warship stopped the British ship *Trent* and removed two Confederate diplomats who were traveling to Europe to seek aid for their cause. The British angrily protested this violation of freedom of the seas. This was the same right over which the United States had gone to war against England in 1812. The incident, which could have led to war, ended when President Lincoln ordered the release of the two Confederates.

Another dispute arose when English shipbuilders built two warships for the Confederacy and allowed them to put to sea in violation of international law. These warships, the *Alabama* and the *Florida,* destroyed a large number of Union merchant ships. Charles Francis Adams, the United States minister to England, had to threaten war to keep the British from delivering other warships built for the Confederacy.

CHECKUP

1. What advantages did each side have at the beginning of the Civil War?
2. How did the two sides secure troops and raise money for carrying on the war?
3. With what other problems did the two wartime leaders, Abraham Lincoln and Jefferson Davis, have to contend?

The Agony of War

At the very beginning of the war, the North adopted a military plan with three parts. The first part was to blockade Southern ports. This would keep the South from sending its cotton to European nations and receiving supplies from them. The second part of the plan was to capture Richmond, Virginia. The capital of the Confederacy had been moved there from Montgomery, Alabama, after Virginia seceded. The third part of the plan was to control the Mississippi River. This would split the region lying west of the river—Texas, Arkansas, and most of Louisiana—from the rest of the Confederacy. It would deny the rebels a part of their manpower and supplies. Those Confederate states east of the Mississippi could then be squeezed between the blockade and armies moving in from west and north.

"Forward to Richmond!" Although the war began on April 12, 1861, with the firing on Fort Sumter, the first battle did not come until three months later. With the cry "Forward to Richmond!" a Union force marched out of Washington toward the Confederate capital. Civilians in a holiday mood trailed behind in their carriages, expecting to see the rebels turn and flee.

The two armies, neither of which was yet well trained, met on July 21 about 30 miles (48 km) from Washington, near a small creek called Bull Run. At first, Northern troops drove the Southern soldiers back. But one Confederate group led by General "Stonewall" Jackson held

In this pencil sketch, an unknown onlooker caught the feeling of panic that swept through the Union troops fleeing back toward Washington from Bull Run after the first big battle of the war.

its ground. With the arrival of reinforcements, Southern troops went on the attack. Northern troops retreated, and then broke in panic and ran. Soon the road to Washington was jammed with fleeing soldiers. The Southerners, however, were too inexperienced and disorganized to follow up their victory. After the battle of Bull Run, both sides settled in for a long war.

For the rest of 1861 the Eastern theater of war—the region between the Atlantic Ocean and the Appalachian Mountains—was quiet. It was plain that the Union soldiers needed training. To mold the volunteers into an effective army, Lincoln put General George B. McClellan in command.

The Western theater, 1862. In the region between the Appalachians and the Mississippi River, Union forces were more successful. Their aim there was to keep the border states of Missouri and Kentucky in the Union, while cutting the Confederacy off from the states west of the Mississippi. Early in 1862, General Ulysses S. Grant, then a little-known Union officer, moved a force into western Kentucky and Tennessee. In sharp fighting, Grant took Fort Henry on the Tennessee River and Fort Donelson on the Cumberland. Those losses forced Southern armies to withdraw into northern Mississippi. A Confederate counterattack just over the Tennessee border, near Shiloh, caught Grant by surprise and led to a bloody two-day battle. Grant's army was saved by reinforcements, however, and the Confederates had to withdraw.

Shortly afterward, a Union fleet under Captain David G. Farragut sailed up the Mississippi from the Gulf of Mexico, took New Orleans, and moved farther up river. By mid-1862, the Union controlled all the Mississippi except for the stretch between Vicksburg, Mississippi, and Port Hudson, Louisiana.

The Eastern theater, 1862. By the spring of 1862, the Confederacy was reeling. Northern victories in the West and a tightening blockade along the coast were squeezing the South. In Virginia, McClellan was preparing to move his well-trained army against Richmond. What followed, however, was a stunning reversal that revived the lagging fortunes of the Confederacy.

McClellan decided against attacking Richmond from the north. Instead, he had the navy move his troops to the York Peninsula, between the York and James rivers. From there he began a slow advance toward the Confederate capital. McClellan's caution gave Robert E. Lee, the brilliant Confederate general, time to make several bold moves. Lee sent Stonewall Jackson on raids into the Shenandoah Valley, making it appear that Washington would be attacked. The threat that Jackson posed tied up a large number of Union troops. Meanwhile, Jackson's troops, moving quickly, rejoined Lee's main forces, which now attacked McClellan's army. In the Seven Days' Battles—from June 25 to July 1, 1862—losses on both sides were severe, but Lee succeeded in halting the Union advance. A bolder commander than McClellan might have pressed on and taken Richmond. McClellan, however, withdrew. What is known as the Peninsula Campaign was thus a failure. Lincoln then removed McClellan from his

The Monitor and the Merrimac

One of the most significant naval battles in history was the engagement between the Union ship *Monitor* and the Confederate ship *Merrimac* at Hampton Roads, Virginia, in 1862. Until that time, almost all warships were made of wood. Such a vessel was the *Merrimac*, a United States naval ship at its berth in Norfolk, Virginia, when that state seceded in 1861. After the *Merrimac* was sunk by order of its commander, the Confederates raised it and covered its sides with iron plates, four inches thick. Armed with ten guns, the *Merrimac* (renamed the *Virginia* but usually called by its original name) steamed out of Norfolk harbor on March 8, 1862, to attack ships of the Union blockade. By nightfall, this strange-looking vessel with slanted sides had destroyed two Union ships and had caused another, the *Minnesota,* to run aground in shallow water.

On that very day, another ironclad was reaching Hampton Roads. This was the Union's *Monitor,* built in New York under the direction of John Ericcson, a Swedish-American inventor. The new *Monitor,* with its deck almost at water level and with a revolving gun turret, was variously described as "a cheesebox on a raft" and "a tin can on a shingle."

When the *Merrimac* moved out the next morning to attack the stranded *Minnesota,* the *Monitor* was waiting. For four hours the two ironclads blasted each other at close range. Shells clanged against the iron plates of each ship, but with little effect. Both ships finally withdrew. This first battle between ironclads made plain that the era of the wooden warship was over. To be effective, naval ships would henceforth have to be made of steel.

At point-blank range, the *Monitor* and the *Merrimac* pound each other. Nearby is the grounded *Minnesota.*

National Gallery of Art, Gift of Edgar William and Bernice Chrysler Garbisch

post. McClellan's troops were placed under the command of John Pope, a more aggressive general. But when Pope attempted another invasion of Virginia from the north, Lee defeated him badly, at the second battle of Bull Run.

Antietam. The South was hoping for a victory that would both convince England to aid the Confederacy and encourage the border states to leave the Union. In pursuit of those goals, Lee moved into Maryland. Lee's battle plans, however, fell into the hands of McClellan, now in command of the Army of the Potomac. In September 1862, McClellan and Lee met at Antietam, Maryland, and after a bloody battle the Confederates withdrew. Had McClellan pursued the re-

Nurse Clara Barton writes a letter for a Union soldier in a field hospital. This great American devoted her life to helping others. In 1881 she founded the American Red Cross.

Museum of Fine Arts, Boston

treating Lee, he might have dealt Southern armies a crippling blow. Once again, however, McClellan's caution cost the chance for a major victory. And once again Lincoln removed McClellan from command.

The Emancipation Proclamation. Although Antietam ended in little more than a draw, it was nonetheless an important battle. From the beginning of the war, both Congress and President Lincoln had stated that their object was to preserve the Union, not to end slavery. One reason for their stand was that four slaveholding states—Maryland, Delaware, Kentucky, and Missouri—had remained in the Union. To declare that the government was fighting the war to free the slaves would have led those border states to secede. Their loss would have dealt a serious blow to the Union cause. Furthermore, Northern opinion had been more ready to support a war for the Union than for emancipation. Lincoln himself favored gradual emancipation, with payments made to owners, followed by colonization of the freed slaves.

When Horace Greeley, a New York newspaper owner and an abolitionist, demanded early in 1862 that Lincoln declare in favor of emancipation immediately, the President replied in a public letter.

> My paramount object in this struggle is to save the Union, and is *not* either to save or destroy slavery. If I could save the Union without freeing *any* slave I would do it; and if I could save it by freeing *all* the slaves, I would it; and if I could do it by freeing some and leaving others alone, I would also do that.

This, said Lincoln, was his view of his "official duty." However, he continued to hold the "*personal* wish that all men everywhere could be free."

But by mid-1862, opinion throughout the North was undergoing a change. More people were now in favor of making the end of slavery a war aim. By summer, Lincoln believed the time had come to announce that slaves would be freed. However, Union armies had suffered a string of defeats, and Secretary of State Seward advised Lincoln to hold off such a statement until a Union victory. Otherwise, the announcement might appear to be a desperate act.

Antietam was not the big victory Lincoln had hoped for, but it was enough. On September 22, 1862, the President announced that all slaves in areas still in rebellion against the United States as of January 1, 1863, "shall be then, thenceforward, and forever free." On the latter date, he issued the official *Emancipation Proclamation.*

The Emancipation Proclamation did not free a single slave immediately. There was no way of enforcing it within the areas still in rebellion. And it did not apply to the border states. Nor did it apply to parts of the Confederacy already under control of Union armies. This led critics of Lincoln to say that he would only free slaves where he could not, but would not free them where he could.

Nonetheless, the Emancipation Proclamation was of great importance. It committed the United States to ending slavery. By convincing the English masses that the war was being fought for human freedom, it also ended any chance that England might enter the war on the side of the South.

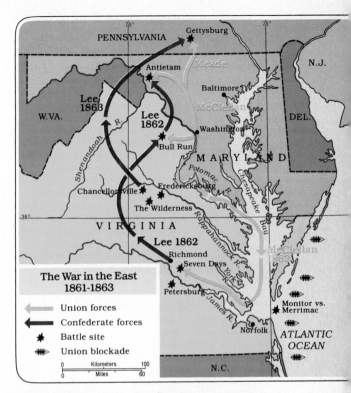

In the Eastern theater between 1861 and 1863, neither side had reason to be optimistic. The Union forces failed to take Richmond, and the Confederates failed in their invasion of the North.

Gettysburg. Lee was well aware that time was on the side of the North. He decided therefore to try for a victory on Northern soil. Such a bold action would deal a blow to the North's morale and might lead it to quit the war. Thus, after brilliant victories in Virginia—at Fredericksburg in December 1862 and at Chancellorsville in May 1863—Lee pushed on into Pennsylvania. On July 1, 1863, his army met Union forces under General George Meade near the little town of Gettysburg.

475

For three days the battle lines flowed back and forth in the fields and over the ridges of southern Pennsylvania. The climax came on July 3, when 15,000 Confederates under General George

It was in the West, where Ulysses S. Grant first made his mark, that the tide turned in favor of the Union. The most important Union victories were at Vicksburg and Chattanooga.

Pickett charged up a slope toward Union positions. The attackers failed—barely —to take the ridge and had to fall back. The next day, Lee withdrew his army. He had lost so many men that he never again would have the strength to invade the North.

Vicksburg and Chattanooga. Even while Northern armies were turning back Lee in the East, other Union forces were winning a major victory in the West. On July 4, 1863, after a siege that lasted for several months, Vicksburg on the Mississippi surrendered to General Grant. This put the entire river under Union control. Texas, Arkansas, and most of Louisiana were cut off from the rest of the Confederacy.

From the summer of 1863 on, Southern forces were mainly on the defensive. In the Western theater, Grant advanced on Chattanooga, Tennessee. This city was a key railway junction, and it stood in a gap in the Appalachian Mountains, commanding the route into Georgia. With victories at Lookout Mountain and Missionary Ridge, near Chattanooga, Grant drove the Confederate forces back. This opened the way for the Union invasion of Georgia, into the very heart of the Confederacy. After the Chattanooga operation, Grant was called to Washington and given top command of all Union armies.

Another move on Richmond. Grant now turned to the task at which so many other Union generals had failed—the capture of Richmond. Lee opposed him doggedly. In battles at the wooded region called the Wilderness, at Spotsylvania, and at Cold Harbor, the Union forces

The War in the West
1862-1863

→ Union forces
← Confederate forces
★ Battle site
⊕ Union blockade

Kilometers 0 — 250
Miles 0 — 150

ILLINOIS
INDIANA
Grant 1862
Ohio R.
Louisville
KENTUCKY
MO.
Paducah
Ft. Henry
Ft. Donelson
Cumberland R.
Pea Ridge
Nashville
TENNESSEE
Arkansas R.
Memphis
Shiloh
Chattanooga
35°
Little Rock
Corinth
Tennessee R.
ARKANSAS
A. S. Johnston
GA.
Mississippi R.
Grant 1863
ALABAMA
Red R.
Vicksburg
Jackson
Montgomery
Alabama R.
LOUISIANA
Farragut
Port Hudson
Mobile
FLORIDA
New Orleans
GULF OF MEXICO
30°
90°

Lee and Grant

The two men who rose to command of the opposing armies in the Civil War were men of vastly different backgrounds. Robert E. Lee was a member of one of Virginia's leading families. At West Point he made an outstanding record, and he fought brilliantly in the Mexican War. In the years that followed, his military reputation grew, and he was President Lincoln's choice to command the Union armies. Lee, torn between love of the Union and love of his native state, decided to stand by Virginia and fight with the Confederate forces.

By contrast, there was little in the career of Ulysses S. Grant before the Civil War to mark him as a coming leader. While at West Point, this son of an Ohio tanner did not distinguish himself. In the war with Mexico, he fought well but won no special recognition. Later, assigned to posts far from his family, Grant became lonely and took to drink. In 1854 he resigned from the army rather than face a court-martial. The start of the Civil War found him a clerk in a leather store in Galena, Illinois. Because the Union needed experienced officers, he was offered a troop command in Cairo, Illinois. After that, his great talents emerged.

In warfare, as in their early lives, Lee and Grant were a study in contrasts. Outnumbered in men and equipment, Lee used daring, surprise moves to keep the other side off balance. By comparison, Grant seemed a plodder. But unlike other Union generals, he understood that the key to victory was to put relentless pressure on the South. Thus the difference between these two great generals was as much the result of military circumstance as of personality.

Ulysses S. Grant *(left)* and Robert E. Lee *(right)* differed greatly in background and personality.

lost more than 50,000 men. But unlike the Union generals who had preceded him, Grant did not fall back. Though forced to alter his course, he kept within striking distance of Richmond.

Sherman's march. Meanwhile, farther south, the Union army that had taken Chattanooga was making rapid gains. That army, now led by General William T. Sherman, took Atlanta in September 1864 and then set off across Georgia for the coast. Abandoning its supply lines that extended back into Tennessee,

Sherman's army lived off the countryside. As the Union forces advanced, they burned cotton gins, factories, and warehouses and destroyed railroads and bridges. After reaching Savannah, the army turned northward and advanced into South Carolina. Sherman's success lifted Union hopes for victory and contributed to Lincoln's reelection in 1864.

The spring of 1865 saw Sherman's army pushing northward toward Virginia. Its goal was to link up with Grant's forces. At this point, Lee's army, short of men and supplies, had to leave

The events of 1864–1865 in the East brought the Civil War to an end. With arrows and symbols, the map shows the three major factors in the Union victory: Grant's relentless drive on Richmond, Sherman's march across Georgia and then northward, and the Union blockade.

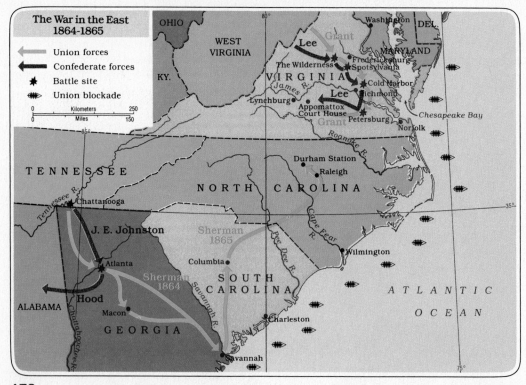

Matthew Brady, shown at lower right, is probably the best known American photographer of all time. Traveling with the Union army, he and his assistants took hundreds of photographs of soldiers, battlefields, and army camps. At upper right is the wagon that carried Brady's equipment. The other pictures are examples of Brady's work. At upper left is a black guard detail at a fort near Washington, D.C., and at lower left is a Union battery manned by troops from Connecticut.

Richmond. It was now plain that the South's position was hopeless. On April 9, Lee and Grant met in a private home at Appomattox Courthouse, Virginia. There Lee surrendered his army. As he left to join his defeated troops, the Union soldiers began a wild cheer. But Grant quickly silenced them. "The war is over," he said. "The rebels are our countrymen again."

The Civil War was the most tragic, destructive, and disruptive war in our history. About 2.5 million men served in the armies and navies at one time or another. More than 618,000 Americans were killed in battle or died of wounds. This compares with about 5,800 battle casualties among Americans in each of two previous conflicts—the War of 1812 and the Mexican War. The Civil War toll would have been even higher had it not been for the tireless work of doctors and nurses in the hospitals behind the lines and in the field.

Though the human costs had been staggering, the war had settled two main issues. The Union was preserved, and slavery was to be ended. But important questions remained. How would the seceding states be restored to the Union, and on what terms? What rights were the freed slaves to have? How would the races live together, and on what terms? Would freedom mean equality? These questions would be answered in the years immediately following. You will read about those answers in Chapter 19.

CHECKUP

1. What success did the North have in carrying out its three-part military plan?
2. Explain the importance of each of the following battles: Bull Run; Antietam; Gettysburg; Vicksburg.
3. To what extent did the Emancipation Proclamation change the status of slaves? In what other ways was this document important?

Key Facts from Chapter 18

1. The immediate cause of the Civil War was the South's determination to have its own government, the Confederate States of America, and the North's determination to keep the Union intact.
2. The Civil War started in 1861 with the firing on Fort Sumter in the harbor of Charleston, South Carolina. It ended in 1865 with the surrender of Confederate General Robert E. Lee to Union General Ulysses S. Grant at Appomattox Courthouse, Virginia.
3. The Emancipation Proclamation of January 1, 1863, put forth by President Abraham Lincoln, had no immediate effect in freeing the slaves but was important in that it committed the United States to ending slavery.
4. The Civil War was America's most tragic and disruptive war. There were more American casualties than in any other war in which Americans had fought.

People, Places, and Events

Abraham Lincoln   *P. 461*

Jefferson Davis   *P. 462*

Fort Sumter   *P. 464*

Richmond   *P. 471*

Bull Run   *P. 472*

Ulysses S. Grant   *P. 472*

Robert E. Lee   *P. 472*

Antietam   *P. 474*

Emancipation Proclamation   *P. 474*

Gettysburg   *P. 475*

Vicksburg   *P. 476*

William T. Sherman   *P. 478*

Appomattox   *P. 480*

Review Questions

1. Discuss the Presidential election of 1860 in terms of **(a)** the candidates, **(b)** the parties, **(c)** their platforms, and **(d)** the outcome of the voting.   *P. 461*

2. Which states immediately joined the Confederacy? Which states joined later?   *Pp. 461–462, 464*

3. How did the Confederate Constitution differ from the Constitution of the United States?   *P. 462*

4. Why were many Southerners convinced that there would be no war over secession?   *P. 463*

5. What effect did the course of the war have on the value of money in the North and South?   *Pp. 467–468*

6. Why was the South unsuccessful in gaining the support of Britain and France?   *P. 470*

7. List the North's strategy for winning the war and the reason for each part.   *P. 471*

8. Which issues were settled by the war? Which were not?   *P. 480*

Chapter Test

Match the names in the first section with the correct description from the second section. Write the letter of the description after the number of the name, using a separate piece of paper. Note: There may be more than one correct description for a name.

1. Robert E. Lee
2. George Meade
3. David Farragut
4. Antietam
5. Jefferson Davis
6. Abraham Lincoln
7. Bull Run
8. Ulysses S. Grant
9. William T. Sherman
10. George B. McClellan

a. Union victory that made it possible for the President to issue the Emancipation Proclamation

b. Top commander of the Confederate Army

c. Union general who captured Atlanta

d. Sixteenth President of the United States

e. Union general who failed to capture Richmond in the Peninsula Campaign

f. First battle of the war

g. Top commander of the Union forces

h. President of the Confederacy

i. Union naval leader who captured New Orleans

j. Defeated the Southern army at Gettysburg

k. Union general who took Vicksburg

l. Surrendered his army at Appomattox

m. Won the election of 1860 with less than 40 percent of the popular vote

n. Site of two important battles

ORGANIZED LIFE in the South had collapsed in the wake of the war. Travelers to that region were horrified by what they saw: blackened, burned ruins of towns and cities, uncultivated fields; torn-up railroad lines; and demolished cotton gins and factories. Describing Charleston, South Carolina, a Northern newspaperman reported:

> [It is] a city of ruins, a desolation, of vacant houses, of widowed women, of rotting wharves, of deserted warehouses, of weed-wild gardens, of miles of grass-grown streets. . . .

Capital, needed to bring the economy back to life, was not to be had. Emancipation wiped out the region's $2.5 billion investment in slaves, nearly two thirds of the South's wealth. The failure of Southern banks meant the loss of another billion dollars. Confederate currency was now worthless. With the credit system broken down, farmers were not able to buy the seed and tools they needed for planting.

Worst of all was the loss of the white South's young people. Nearly a quarter of a million men were killed, and many more were disabled for life. Of the white men in Mississippi old enough to fight, fully a third were either killed or maimed. One fifth of all the taxes taken in by that state in 1866 went to pay for artificial limbs.

The feeling of freedom. If the war devastated the Southern white society, it created both new opportunities and problems for the three million freed slaves. For many, the need to experience the feeling of freedom, to test it and be sure it was real, was overwhelming. "No, Miss," explained a former slave when asked to stay on at a South Carolina plantation, "I must go. If I stay here, I'll never know I am free." Large numbers of former slaves took to the road. For many, freedom meant the opportunity to rejoin wives, husbands, and children. To do this, most had to go no farther than to a neighboring plantation. But many hundreds set out on longer and more uncertain journeys to look for loved ones from whom they had been separated by sale.

Even so, many slaves stayed put. Of those who moved, most did not go far. The fact was that whether they moved or not, everyday life for most was not too different from what it had been before the war. They had been led by some Northerners to believe that freed slaves would receive "forty acres and a mule" to get started in their new life. That never happened. Without land of their own, therefore, the freed slaves worked for others, often their former masters, for wages or a share of the crop. And they shared in the general poverty and economic breakdown of the postwar South.

Restoring the Union

Even as the war was raging, government leaders were giving thought to how the Union should be restored. President Lincoln favored bringing the rebelling states back into the Union at the earliest

★16★

Abraham Lincoln
1809–1865

Born in KENTUCKY
In Office 1861–1865
Party REPUBLICAN

Elected on antislavery
platform. Was determined
to preserve the Union.
His leadership brought the
nation through its great
crisis—the Civil War. Killed
by an assassin.

Lincoln's plan. The great strength of Lincoln's plan was that it would restore the Union quickly. But it had a great weakness. Although it ended slavery, it left the Southern states entirely free to decide how the freed slaves would be treated and what rights, if any, black people would have. Few could doubt that the South, left to its own wishes, would manage to control the former slaves.

The Lincoln plan was quickly put into effect in states controlled by the Union army. By the end of 1864, four states had met Lincoln's requirements and set up new governments. Lincoln's plan, however, had meanwhile brought a storm of protest from most Republicans in Congress. They insisted that Congress—not the President—should decide the terms for the return of the Southern states. Lincoln's plan for a quick and easy return, most of the Republican members of Congress felt, did not make the price of the rebellion high enough.

One group in the Republican party in Congress was known as the Radical Republican wing. These Republicans were radical in the sense that they wished to bring about a sweeping change in Southern society. Their goal was nothing less than to make good on the Declaration of Independence—to raise the freed slaves to equality with the whites. That meant that blacks should have the right to vote, enjoy full civil rights, and be free of discrimination.

Two of the main Radical Republicans were Representative Thaddeus Stevens of Pennsylvania and Senator Charles Sumner of Massachusetts. You will recall that Sumner was the abolitionist senator who was beaten at his Senate

possible time. He proposed to do this by using the President's pardoning power. Under his plan, announced in December 1863, the President would pardon all—except a handful of top Confederate leaders and army officers—who took an oath of loyalty to the United States and agreed to an end to slavery. When 10 percent of the people who had voted in a state in 1860 had taken the oath, the state could draw up a new constitution, elect officials, and reenter the Union. Actually, Lincoln's view was that the states had never legally left the Union.

desk in 1856. Stevens had had a lifelong commitment to equality for blacks. He favored dividing public lands and large plantations in Southern states into forty-acre plots for the freed slaves. Only then, he believed, would they have a chance to be economically independent.

The Wade-Davis Bill. Radicals were able to get only a part of what they wanted into the Wade-Davis Bill. Passed in July 1864, it was Congress's plan for Reconstruction. For a state to be readmitted to the Union, said this bill, a majority of the white males in the state (not Lincoln's 10 percent of the voters) must take the oath of loyalty. The leaders could then meet to write a new state constitution. But no Confederate official, and no one who had willingly taken up arms against the United States could vote or hold office in the new government. Each new government must, of course, end slavery. It must also *repudiate* the state's war debts—that is, declare that they would not be paid.

Lincoln was able to keep the Wade-Davis bill from becoming law by means of a *pocket veto*. In a strong statement, however, Radical Republicans warned the President that making policy for Reconstruction was the business of Congress, not the President. Congress put teeth in what it said by refusing to seat representatives sent from the states that had followed Lincoln's plan. Congress could do this because the Constitution gives it the right to pass on its members' credentials. The stage was now set for a clash.

The election of 1864. So bitter were the Radical Republicans toward Lincoln that they tried to defeat him in the presidential election of 1864. Two years earlier, Lincoln had persuaded Republicans to join with those Democrats who supported the war in the National Union party. He himself was chosen in 1864 to head the National Union ticket. Andrew Johnson of Tennessee, a Southern Democrat who had remained loyal to the

The leaders of the Radical Republicans included (left to right) Representative Thaddeus Stevens of Pennsylvania, Senator Charles Sumner of Massachusetts, and Senator Benjamin Wade of Ohio.

Lincoln's funeral carriage, drawn by sixteen horses, proceeds through New York City.

Union, was the party's candidate for Vice President. He was chosen in order to attract the votes of Democrats. The Radical Republicans had already selected John C. Frémont, the Western explorer, as their presidential candidate. The Democrats nominated General George McClellan.

When the campaign began, Lincoln's chances were not bright. However, arguments over war aims weakened the Democrats, and the Radical Republican candidate, Frémont, decided to withdraw from the race. Union victories on Southern battlefields shortly before election day gave Lincoln's campaign a boost, and he won quite easily.

Johnson succeeds Lincoln. Less than a week after the end of the war, Lincoln was dead. He and his wife had gone to a play at Ford's Theater in Washington. During the performance, John Wilkes Booth, an actor and a Southern sym-

pathizer, stole into the box occupied by the Lincolns and shot the President in the head. The President was taken to a house across the street and died there the next morning. Booth fled from the theater and was tracked to a barn in Virginia. There he died of gunshot wounds, possibly inflicted by himself.

A few hours after Lincoln's death, Vice President Andrew Johnson took the oath of office as the seventeenth President of the United States. Johnson had started life even poorer than Lincoln had. He rose to be a congressman from Tennessee and a two-term governor of that state, where he championed the interest of the small farmers against large planters. Radicals expected him to be one of them. "Johnson, we have faith in you," said Senator Wade of Ohio. "By the gods, there'll be no trouble now."

The Radicals had guessed wrong. They had mistaken Johnson's hatred of the planter class of the South for

486

support of Radical goals. Although Johnson strongly supported the Union, he held Southern views on slavery.

Johnson's Reconstruction plan. In May 1865, Johnson announced a plan for Reconstruction very much like Lincoln's. To reenter the Union, Southern states needed only to wipe out their secession ordinances, state that they would not pay their war debts, and ratify the Thirteenth Amendment. This amendment provided for an end to slavery in the United States.

Radicals protested Johnson's plan, but they could do nothing to stop it because Congress was not in session. Johnson hoped that by the time it assembled again in December 1865, he could present Congress with an accomplished fact and the Radicals would have to accept it. By December, the Thirteenth Amendment had indeed been ratified. And all the states of the Confederacy except Texas had fulfilled most of the requirements of the Johnson plan.

Congress versus Johnson. The Republicans in Congress—Radicals and moderates alike—would have none of it. They resented Johnson's attempt to take Reconstruction out of their hands. They objected that the punishment for rebellion and war was so light. They demanded that the South repent. Proof that the Southerners had not had a change of heart was the fact that they had elected to Congress more than seventy leaders of the rebellion.

Further, Republicans deeply believed that the safety of the Union depended on their party's control of Congress. The return of Southern Democrats would threaten that control. Ironically, since an ex-slave would now be counted as a full person rather than three fifths of a person (see page 218), the South would now have fifteen *more* seats in the House than it had in 1860.

The black codes. Republicans were also angered by the *black codes* that Southern states were passing. These laws were meant to control the economic and social lives of the former slaves. The codes gave freedmen certain rights, such as to make contracts and to own property. Some of the codes also protected the freed slaves from dishonest merchants and employers. But one of the main aims of the codes was to guarantee that despite the end of slavery, there would still be a work force of blacks for Southern farms and plantations. Louisiana's code, for example, required blacks to sign contracts with employers during the first ten days of January. They then could not leave their jobs until the following January. South Carolina blacks were limited to farm jobs and housework. In a number of states a black who was considered to be a vagrant could be fined and then be required to work off the fine with months of labor. To many Northerners the black codes seemed proof that the South was still not willing to give the slaves freedom.

For all those reasons, Congress refused to accept Reconstruction as completed. It would not permit the members elected from the Southern states to take their seats. Instead, it set up the Joint Committee on Reconstruction, made up of members of both houses of Congress, to come up with a new program for Reconstruction. The state governments that were set up under Johnson's plan stayed in office and continued to govern their states. However, they had no voice in national affairs. That situation would continue for the next fifteen months.

The Freedmen's Bureau. In the spring of 1866, Republicans in Congress passed two bills dealing with Reconstruction. The first was a bill to keep the Freedmen's Bureau alive. The Freedmen's Bureau had been set up in 1865 for one year, largely to help the freed slaves get started anew. This government agency saved thousands of freed slaves and white war refugees from starvation by providing food, clothing, and medical care. It also helped the freed slaves find jobs. It protected them against those white employers who might try to take advantage of them with unfair work contracts. Equally important, it started schools in which thousands of former slaves—parents as well as children— eagerly learned to read and write. The new bill added to the power of the Bureau by allowing it to fine or imprison, without a jury trial, persons whom it found guilty of depriving blacks of their civil rights.

President Johnson vetoed this bill as unconstitutional. Congress was not able to pass it over the President's veto. In July of 1866, however, Congress passed the bill again, and this time it easily overrode Johnson's veto. Since Congress was made of the same people both times, you can see that the Republican moderates were moving away from Johnson and toward the Radicals.

In setting up the Freedmen's Bureau, the United States government became involved for the first time in aiding large numbers of people at a time of catastrophe. The Bureau, for the most part, did good work. However, it also became caught up in politics. Some of its agents became more involved with promoting the interests of the Republican party in the South than with the proper work of the Bureau. Congress ended the Bureau in 1872.

The Civil Rights Act. The second bill passed by the Republicans that spring was the Civil Rights Act of 1866. This law stated that all persons born in the United States were citizens, regardless of race. All citizens were entitled to the same legal rights.

In passing this bill, Congress had in mind both the Dred Scott decision, which had said that blacks were not citizens, and the black codes of Southern states. This guarantee of equal rights for both races, the first in American history, could be enforced by federal troops.

The Fourteenth Amendment. Many congressmen feared that the Civil Rights Act might be held unconstitutional or would be repealed by a later Congress. To be sure that the act would always be in force, Congress put its provisions into a constitutional amendment, the Fourteenth. The Radicals had hoped to guarantee the vote to black people by this amendment. This would advance not only their goal of equality for blacks but also their aim to win Republican votes in the South and keep their party in power. They could not gain enough backing to guarantee black suffrage directly by their amendment. They did, however, put in a section that

Under the Freedmen's Bureau, schools for former slaves were set up throughout the South. The drawing above is of a primary school for freed slaves in the Mississippi city of Vicksburg.

was aimed to achieve that goal indirectly. This section provided that a Southern state that denied its adult male citizens the vote would lose seats in Congress in the same proportion.

The amendment also forbade former Confederates to hold federal or state office. They could be made eligible only by a two-thirds vote of Congress. Another section provided that the Confederate war debt would not be paid, and that no one could be paid for the loss of slaves.

Approval of the Fourteenth Amendment was, in effect, the price set by Congress for the former Confederate states' reentry into the Union. Tennessee ratified it and was promptly readmitted. Encouraged by President Johnson, however, the other ten states that had seceded turned it down.

The elections of 1866. That threw the question of Reconstruction policy into the congressional elections of 1866. In

this contest, Democratic candidates were at a disadvantage. The Republican party presented itself as the party that saved the Union. It presented the opposition as the party of treason, which had brought four years of war. Stirring the emotions of war—a tactic known as *waving the bloody shirt*—Republicans urged veterans to "vote the way you shot." They pointed to recent race riots in New Orleans and Memphis as examples of how the South, if allowed to go its own way, would treat the freed slaves.

Johnson's support for Democratic candidates only made things worse for them. In an eighteen-day speaking tour of the North, he often lost his temper, took part in noisy arguments with people who jeered him, and behaved like anything but a President. In the election, Republicans gained enough seats to give them a two-thirds majority in Congress. It could now pass any bill it wished over Johnson's veto.

Born in NORTH CAROLINA
In Office 1865–1869
Party DEMOCRATIC

Favored generous treatment
for defeated South. Was
opposed by Radical
Republicans, who wanted to
punish South. Bitter feelings
led to impeachment, but he
was not convicted.

Triumph of the Radicals. Under the
leadership of Stevens and Sumner, Radical Republicans now prepared a sweeping program of Reconstruction. The Reconstruction Act of March 2, 1867,
made the Lincoln and Johnson state
governments illegal (except for Tennessee, which was back in the Union), and
placed the South under army rule. The
region was divided into five districts,
each under an army general, with troops
to enforce federal law and keep order.

To come back into the Union, each
state had to call a convention to draw up

a new constitution. Blacks as well as
whites (but not former Confederate officeholders) could vote for and serve
as delegates. The new state constitutions must include negro suffrage and
be approved by the voters. In addition,
the state must ratify the Fourteenth
Amendment. With this program, Radicals believed they were close to their goal
of equality for the ex-slaves. Once Congress approved a state's constitution,
the state could return, its congressmen
would be seated, and federal troops
would be withdrawn from within its
borders.

By 1868, seven of the Southern states
had met the terms of the Reconstruction
Act and had been readmitted to the
Union. In that year also, the Fourteenth
Amendment was ratified and added to
the Constitution. Three years later, the
last state was reconstructed.

The impeachment of Johnson. Now
firmly in control, Radicals in Congress
were determined to have no interference
from other branches of government.
To protect against the chance that the
Supreme Court might declare its program unconstitutional, they limited the
Court's power to hear certain kinds of
cases. To make sure that President
Johnson could not get around their
program with orders to the army generals in the South, Radicals passed the
Command of the Army Act. It said that
the President must put forth military
orders only through the General of the
Army, Ulysses S. Grant, who was working closely with the Radicals. Since the
Constitution makes the President the
Commander in Chief, this law was almost certainly unconstitutional. In the

Tenure of Office Act, Congress further limited the President by requiring the Senate's approval before he removed any official who had been appointed with the Senate's consent. Johnson believed this act was unconstitutional and decided to test it. He removed one of his cabinet officers, Secretary of War Edwin Stanton, who had been working hand in hand with the Radical Republicans.

For nearly a year, Radicals had been looking for an excuse to force Johnson out of office. His removal of Stanton now gave them that excuse. The Constitution says that a President may be removed from office for "treason, bribery, or other high crimes and misdemeanors." The House of Representatives put together a number of charges against Johnson. The charges centered on his alleged violation of the Tenure of Office Act. By making the charges, the House *impeached* the President—that is, formally accused him of "high crimes and misdemeanors." He then had to stand trial before the Senate.

Johnson went on trial in March 1868. The vote for conviction in the Senate was 35 to 19, just one short of the necessary two thirds. By that narrow margin, the Radicals failed to remove Johnson from office. Had they succeeded, the new President under the law at that time would have been Benjamin Wade, a Radical Republican who was president *pro tem* of the Senate.

The election of 1868. Even though the Radicals had failed to remove Johnson from office, they were still in control of Reconstruction policy. Now, in 1868, they hoped to win the Presidency as well. For their candidate, Republicans chose General Ulysses S. Grant, the war hero. Grant had cooperated with the Radical Republicans, and they felt that they could control him. The Democrats nominated Horatio Seymour, a former war governor of New York who was honest, wealthy, and colorless.

Grant won by a large margin in the electoral votes, but even with his party waving the bloody shirt, his popular majority was small—only 300,000. Without the votes of some 500,000 freedmen, giving Grant seven reconstructed states, Grant would not have had the majority of the popular vote.

The importance of the freedmen's votes was clear to the Republicans. To be sure that black men would not be kept from voting in the future the Republicans put forth the Fifteenth Amendment. No citizen could be kept from

Republican Senator James Grimes of Iowa breaks with his party by voting for acquittal in the impeachment trial of Andrew Johnson.

voting "on account of race, color, or previous condition of servitude [slavery]." Congress required the three states still not back in the Union—Virginia, Texas, and Mississippi—to ratify this amendment as a condition of their return. In 1870 the Fifteenth Amendment was added to the Constitution.

CHECKUP

1. How did Lincoln's and Johnson's plans for restoring the Union differ from Congress's plan?
2. What steps did the Southern states take to control the economic and social lives of the former slaves?
3. How did the Radical Republicans try to assure that President Johnson could not interfere with their program? What success did they have?

The Reconstructed South

Reconstruction brought about a sweeping change in the South. For the first time, black people had a political voice. Grateful to the party that brought them freedom, almost all of them voted Republican. Most whites voted Democratic, but with 150,000 whites barred from voting, black voters in the South outnumbered white voters, 700,000 to 625,000. Thus the Republican party, which in 1860 had not carried a single Southern state, was in control of all of them ten years later.

Black Reconstruction? Because blacks voted and held office, the decade from 1868 on came to be called *Black Reconstruction,* a phrase that seemed to say that blacks ruled the Southern states. That, however, was anything but the case. It was true that in every Southern

state, blacks held many such local offices as sheriff and justice of the peace. State offices such as treasurer and superintendent of education were also sometimes held by blacks. Black men even served as lieutenant-governor in the states of Mississippi, Louisiana, and South Carolina.

Overall, however, the number of blacks who held office was quite modest, considering the number of black voters. During the whole Reconstruction period, blacks held a majority in a legislature in only one state—ironically, South Carolina, the leader of the secession—and that majority was in only one house and for only a few years. Of the more than one hundred Southerners elected to Congress during the Reconstruction period, only sixteen were black. There were never more than eight black congressmen at one time. Only two, Hiram Revels and Blanche K. Bruce, both of Mississippi, were sent to the United States Senate.

Carpetbaggers and scalawags. Whites held most positions of leadership in the Republican Reconstruction governments. A number of these were Northerners only recently arrived in the South. They were called *carpetbaggers* by Southerners because they were said to have carried their few belongings in suitcases made of carpeting. These men were a mixed lot. Some had come to the South looking for business opportunities. Others, such as teachers and clergy, had come to do educational, humanitarian, and religious work among the former slaves. Still other carpetbaggers were simply adventurers who meant to take advantage of the

492

Robert Elliott of South Carolina, one of seven blacks in Congress in 1874, delivers a speech.

upset conditions in the Southern states to advance their own interests by hook or by crook.

Most of the white leaders in the new state governments, however, were native Southerners. They, too, were a varied group. At one extreme were some who had opposed secession from the beginning. At the other were certain lower-class whites who had always envied the planters and now saw the chance to gain power over them. The great majority who joined the Republicans were, however, men of some standing—business people and some planters, for example. They believed that the best way to bring back prosperity was to cooperate with the ruling group. Southern Democrats regarded the Southern white Republicans as traitors and called them *scalawags,* a term applied to runty, worthless farm animals.

Among the blacks who served in Southern legislatures were a goodly number of uneducated ex-slaves. Some of them were easily used by others, and their inexperience gave Southern and Northern white critics of Reconstruction a field day. "Seven years ago these men [the black legislators] were raising corn and cotton under the whip of the overseer," sneered one white writer. "Today they are raising points of order and questions of privilege."

493

Such criticism took no notice of the fact that about half the blacks who held office during Reconstruction were not ex-slaves but free blacks. They included ministers and others who had already achieved some education. Two such men were George T. Ruby and Blanche K. Bruce. Ruby was an educated Northerner who had emigrated to Haiti. Returning to the United States when the Civil War began, he organized schools in Louisiana during the war. Later he served as a Freedmen's Bureau agent in Texas before being elected to the Texas state senate. Bruce, who had started life as a slave in Virginia, studied briefly at Oberlin College, Ohio, and taught school in Missouri before entering politics.

Black strategy. The criticism that black lawmakers simply did the bidding of white party leaders also missed the mark. Some of these men worked hard to advance the interest of all blacks. Knowing they could not hope to bring about all the changes black people needed, they concentrated on three areas. One was education. A second was preserving the right of blacks to vote—"our only means of protection," as one black man from Arkansas put it. A third area was the protection of black people against violence.

Because they were in the minority, black politicians knew they would need the support of at least some Southern whites to achieve their goals. The strategy they usually followed, therefore, was to ally themselves with the South's business people and members of the upper classes. The black politicians provided votes in the legislatures for laws that those groups wanted. They also urged

Hiram Revels of Mississippi takes the oath of office as a United States senator during the Reconstruction period. He later served for many years as president of Alcorn University.

black voters to support those whites at election time. In return it was hoped that those whites would support black leaders in their three major areas of concern. In the end this alliance did not do much for blacks. It was not because the idea was a poor one, but because the blacks' bargaining position was so weak. Still, the strategy did make possible some small gains for a while. And once the protection of the federal government was withdrawn, it was all the Southern blacks had to lean on.

The Southern white response. Most of the white South resisted Black Reconstruction. What Northern Radicals saw as the beginning of biracial democratic government, most Southern whites saw as government by force and ignorance. Many whites were outraged at the sight of men who had been slaves but a few years earlier now voting and making laws. They resented being taxed to send black children to school, even though nearly all the schools were segregated. Basically, most white Southerners simply could not accept the idea of a society in which white and black were equal.

In 1866 the Ku Klux Klan was formed in Pulaski, Tennessee, and it spread quickly through the South. Its aim was to make the South once more a white person's country. Its weapons were the whip, the gun, the lynch rope, and fear. Wearing white robes and hoods, night-riding Klansmen struck terror among both blacks and those Southern whites who had befriended blacks. In addition to reminding blacks of their "proper place," the Klan aimed to keep them from voting. Other groups devoted to white supremacy also sprang up.

In 1870 Congress began to take action against these secret groups. The Force Act of 1870 and the Ku Klux Klan Act of 1871 gave the President the power to send troops to Southern counties that had fallen under Klan control. President Grant did so, and by the next year the Klan had very nearly disappeared.

Southern white control. By 1872, Radical Republicanism had passed its peak. The iron will by which the Radical wing had gained control of the Republican party was weakening. Thaddeus Stevens was dead, and Charles Sumner was an old man with little power left in the Senate. Much of the Northerners' interest in Reconstruction had been based on their desire to punish the South. As that desire faded, so did their interest.

The signs of change were clear. In 1872, Congress allowed the Freedmen's Bureau to expire. That same year, it passed a general Amnesty Act, granting a final pardon to all but a few hundred Confederates. The only new law to protect the rights of blacks was the Civil Rights Act of 1875. It said that all persons were to have the "full and equal enjoyment" of eating places, hotels, streetcars, and other public facilities.

Meanwhile, the Republican governments in the South were coming under heavy attack. Democrats charged them with being corrupt and inefficient. State debts and state taxes, it was pointed out, had shot upward under Republican rule. Most important, Southern white Democrats were determined to regain control of their states. To keep blacks from voting, they formed such groups as rifle clubs, the Red Shirts, and the White Leagues. Unlike the Klan, there was nothing secret about those groups. Through threats of violence and through economic pressure—such as firing or not hiring blacks who voted, and not allowing them to buy goods on credit—they kept down the black vote. By 1872, Democrats had already regained control of several Southern states. By 1876, only South Carolina, Louisiana, and Florida remained in Republican hands. That was only because federal troops remained in those three states. The following year the troops were removed, and white Democratic rule was restored.

The Compromise of 1877. The withdrawal of the last federal troops from the South came as the result of the election of 1876. For the Presidency, the Democratic party chose Governor Samuel J. Tilden of New York. Tilden, who had made his reputation by exposing political corruption in New York City, made a strong candidate. Worried by the corruption issue, Republicans passed over the popular Senator James G. Blaine of Maine, who had been involved in a shady railroad deal. They chose instead Rutherford B. Hayes, governor of Ohio.

When the returns came in, Tilden appeared to be the winner. He had 250,000 more popular votes than Hayes, and he was one electoral vote short of a majority, with twenty votes in dispute. Nineteen of those votes were from Louisiana, South Carolina, and Florida, and the twentieth was from Oregon. Each of the four states sent two sets of returns to Washington—one making Hayes the winner, and the other Tilden. In January 1877, Congress set up a special body of five senators, five representatives, and five Supreme Court justices to decide which returns should be counted. Eight of the fifteen members of the Electoral Commission were Republicans. By a straight party vote of eight to seven, the Commission declared Hayes the winner. The decision, however, still had to be accepted in Congress, and outraged Democrats there threatened to block it. Working behind the scenes, Republican and business leaders won the support of Southern Democratic leaders for the Commission report. As their price, Southerners got a pledge of at least one cabinet seat for a Southerner in the Hayes administration, promises of support for internal improvements and federal aid for a railroad, and the withdrawal of remaining troops from the South. Thus in 1877, Reconstruction came to a close.

Reconstruction—success or failure? Radical Reconstruction lasted from about 1867 to about 1877. Ever since that time, it has been a subject of controversy. It has been described by one historian as "a clash between good and evil." And which of the two it was depended on one's viewpoint and biases.

However, most historians today agree that Reconstruction was a complex series of events, neither wholly good nor wholly bad but a mixture of both.

Those who have called Reconstruction bad point out that there was much corruption in the Southern state governments. It is true that public funds sometimes ended up in the pockets of corrupt politicians. Such corruption can never be excused, yet it must be judged in the framework of the times. The years following the Civil War saw a breakdown of moral standards all over the country. During this period, corruption was actually greater in certain Northern states and cities than it was in the South. As you will see in Unit 8, corruption even tainted the federal government during the 1870s.

A second charge often made is that the Reconstruction state governments spent money recklessly, causing the public debt—and taxes—to shoot upward. While there was some extravagance, it was a very minor cause of the spiralling costs of government and taxes. All Southern state governments were confronted with costs many times what they had borne before the war. Repairing the war damages was a very expensive undertaking. Moreover, the states were now called upon to supply services on a much larger scale than ever before. Those new responsibilities accounted to a very large degree for the mounting public debt and the higher taxes.

The Reconstruction period saw a number of positive achievements by the Southern state governments. The governments were reorganized along modern lines, and certain reforms were car-

ried out. Many railway lines, factories, and other buildings destroyed during the war were rebuilt. One of the most impressive achievements was that of setting up schools in a region where public education had been almost nonexistent. In South Carolina, for example, the number of children in public schools climbed from 20,000 just before the Civil War to more than 120,000 in 1873.

It is clear that the Radical Republicans did not reach their goal of equality for black Americans. There were several

497

reasons for this failure. Full equality would have required economic independence. In a farming society like the South's, that meant owning land. Radicals did propose that the government divide up large Southern farms into forty-acre pieces for the freed slaves, but there was never a chance that such a bill would pass. Ideas about the rights of private property and about limited government were simply too strong.

More important was that most Americans—Northerners as well as Southerners—never really accepted the Radical goal in the first place. In six of seven Northern states that voted on amendments to allow blacks to vote, the amendments were defeated. A Republican congressman who voted for all the Radical Reconstruction program probably spoke for the great majority when he admitted: "I never believed in Negro equality. I believe God made us, for his own wise purposes, a superior race."

Yet Reconstruction clearly started black Americans on the long tortuous road to equality. The Fourteenth and Fifteenth amendments gave blacks legal tools to use in chipping away at the discrimination that had so long blocked their progress. As blacks developed their own leaders and movements in the twentieth century, these tools made a crucial difference.

CHECKUP

1. What part did blacks take in ruling Southern states during the Reconstruction period?
2. How did Southern whites respond to Black Reconstruction?
3. What were some of the positive accomplishments of Reconstruction?

The Aftermath of Reconstruction

In the years following Reconstruction, a number of Southerners began to talk of a New South. The South they envisioned was a prosperous region of cities, factories, and trade, supported by a diversified agriculture. Northern capital would be attracted by the hope of good returns. "The ambition of the South," said one of the boosters of the New South, "is to out-Yankee the Yankees." Many of the leaders in the new white governments of the South were business-minded men who hoped to make this New South a reality. In fact you will recall that in the Compromise of 1877 they won promises of capital for railroads and other improvements.

Some progress toward this goal was made in the 1880s and 1890s. New cities, such as Birmingham, Alabama, appeared, and older cities, such as Atlanta, Georgia, grew much larger. By 1900, mills in the South were making half of America's textiles and nearly all of its cigarettes. But the South of many factories and booming cities was still a hundred years away. Throughout the late nineteenth century, the South remained the most rural and agricultural region of the country.

The sharecrop and crop-lien systems. Nor did Southern agriculture become diversified. The lack of capital created special problems for Southern farming. Many small white farmers and nearly all freed slaves lacked the money to buy their own land or even to rent land on a cash basis. Many landowners, on the other hand, lacked the money to hire people to work their land. Out of these

As sharecroppers after the Civil War, many blacks found themselves cultivating the same fields that they had worked on as slaves. The people in this group are planting sweet potatoes.

situations there developed the *share-crop* and *crop-lien* systems. A landowner turned over a certain amount of land to a tenant. He also supplied the tenant with tools, seeds, and other supplies that had been purchased on credit from the local storekeeper. For all of this the tenant, or *sharecropper,* paid the landlord a share—usually a third to a half—of the crop he produced. To buy on credit, the landowner had to give the storekeeper a *lien* on his share of the crop. This was a pledge that whatever cash the landowner received from the sale of the crops would first go to pay off the storekeeper. To be sure of receiving payment, the storekeeper usually insisted that crops be raised that could be readily sold for cash. Such cash crops were almost always cotton and tobacco.

Because the sharecropper bought food, clothing, and other supplies on credit, he, too, gave a lien on his share of the crop. With prices and interest charges high—ranging from 40 to 100 percent—the harvest often did not bring in enough to pay off the debt completely. The sharecropper then had to pledge to work the same piece of land the next year or until the debt was paid.

The crop-lien system filled a real need in a society where credit was scarce. But it had three bad effects. It kept the South tied to a one-crop agriculture. It kept tenants from saving enough to buy their own land (70 percent of Southern farmers in 1900 were still tenants). And it caused many sharecroppers, usually blacks, to be bound to the land almost as if they were still slaves. The South's rural regions remained vast areas of poverty.

The blacks' loss of rights. The return of harmony between North and South came at the expense of black Americans. Southern whites were assured by President Hayes that the federal government would no longer "intrude" in their affairs. Soon they were exploring ways to get around the Fourteenth and Fifteeth amendments. Blacks were barred from restaurants, hotels, theaters, streetcars, and other public facilities, or they were made to sit in separate sections. Although these practices seemed clearly to

499

violate the Civil Rights Act of 1875, blacks found no protection in the courts. In the civil rights cases of 1883, the Supreme Court ruled that the law was unconstitutional, not the practices. The Fourteenth Amendment, said the Court, prohibited *states* from denying "full and equal enjoyment" of *public* accommodations, but it did not limit the acts of *private individuals.*

Soon the state governments, too, experimented with ways to get around the Fourteenth Amendment. They passed laws requiring segregation by race, arguing that this was not discrimination as long as equal facilities were provided to blacks. In *Plessy* v. *Ferguson* (1896), the Court agreed. It upheld a Louisiana law that required blacks and whites to ride in separate railroad cars. Three

years later the Court applied the same "separate but equal" doctrine to state laws that set up segregated public schools. Such laws came to be known as *Jim Crow* laws (after a black song-and-dance man); the separate and almost always unequal facilities were called Jim Crow cars, Jim Crow lunchrooms, and so on. By the turn of the century, Jim Crow had extended to, among other things, theaters, ticket windows, waiting rooms, boardinghouses, hospitals, jails, toilets, and drinking fountains. Soon afterward, witnesses in courts were sworn in on Jim Crow Bibles.

In addition to these "legal" methods, the weapons of fear were used to "keep blacks in their place." The most brutal and ugly of these was lynching—killing carried out by a mob. In the 1880s an average of 150 lynchings a year took place in the United States. Most, but not all, were in the South. In the 1890s, the yearly average was 70.

Keeping blacks from voting. The attack upon the Fifteenth Amendment, which assured blacks of the right to vote, did not come until the 1890s. Until then, many blacks in the South continued to vote. They generally supported the ruling white conservatives in return for small favors and a certain amount of protection from the worst kinds of oppression. In the 1890s, however, the reforming Populist party tried to win blacks as well as poor whites to its support. The prospect of different groups of whites bidding for black support alarmed many Southern whites. Most of the white South united during the next ten years to remove this threat to white supremacy by taking away the black

Black citizens vote in an election soon after the Civil War. In later years, the right of black men to vote was drastically curtailed through such devices as the poll tax and literacy tests.

man's right to vote. Several devices were used. The most popular were the *poll tax* and the *literacy test.* The poll tax was an annual tax that had to be paid before one could vote. The literacy test required the voter to demonstrate he could read and understand a passage—which could be made as easy or as hard as the examining official wished.

These devices would also prevent many poor whites from voting. In a number of states, however, exceptions were made that allowed whites to vote anyway. The favorite device was the *grandfather clause* (in the voting law.) Typical of this was the Louisiana law that allowed anyone to vote, even if he did not pay the poll tax or pass the reading test, as long as his father or grandfather had been a voter before March 1867. That was the date when black people were first allowed to vote in that state.

The *white primary* was still another device for keeping the vote of blacks from meaning anything. All Southern states were controlled by the Democratic party, a reaction against the Republican rule of Reconstruction days. The only election that meant anything, therefore, was the Democratic primary—the election in which the Democrats selected their candidates. By allowing only whites to vote in primaries, the blacks were effectively shut out from taking part in the democratic process.

The blacks' reaction. Here and there blacks resisted the taking away of their rights. During the first few years after 1900, blacks in twenty-five cities *boycotted* Jim Crow streetcars—that, is, they refused to use them. But these boycotts

failed. Thus, most blacks—economically powerless, turned away by the courts, forgotten or ignored by the North, and faced with the opposition of Southern whites—believed that their best hope lay in an alliance with Southern white conservatives. To be sure, these conservatives upheld white supremacy, but they were often willing to give jobs to blacks and to give money to black schools. In return, they required that the blacks "stay in their place."

Many black Americans made their peace with this system. Some, like ex-slave Booker T. Washington, even saw this arrangement as an opportunity. In 1881 he began a school for blacks in Tuskegee, Alabama. His school stressed the teaching of job skills—carpentry, blacksmithing, sewing, and other forms of manual work. Washington's school was handsomely supported by whites, both Northern and Southern. They supported his effort because Washington was able to convince them that well-trained black workers would be responsible citizens.

The Atlanta Compromise. Washington's appeal for support in training blacks met with favor, especially in the South, for another reason. Washington made plain that blacks should not ask for social or political equality but should concentrate on advancing economically. In a famous speech at Atlanta, Georgia, in 1895, Washington held out a picture of white-black relations. Holding up his hand, he explained:

> In all things that are purely social black people and white can be as separate as the fingers, yet one as the hand in all things essential to mutual progress.

501

Washington has been criticized for being willing to bargain away the rights of citizenship that had been so hard won by black Americans. Of late, however, historians have suggested that perhaps Washington was a smart politician who understood how to take the first step toward equality as preparation for the second. Often overlooked is the fact that Washington made clear that once blacks, as productive citizens, "proved themselves worthy," other steps toward equality must follow.

The approach of Du Bois. Booker T. Washington was widely looked upon as the top spokesman for black Americans in the years around the beginning of the twentieth century. But not all blacks accepted him as their leader. One who was highly critical of Washington's program of accommodation was William E. B. Du Bois. Blacks would never be able to gain self-respect, said Du Bois, while they willingly accepted the status of inferiors. They must seek full equality, not tomorrow but today. Du Bois and other militants met in Niagara, Canada, in 1905 to form the Niagara Movement. Du Bois issued a ringing declaration.

> We claim for ourselves every single right that belongs to a freeborn American, political, civil, and social; and until we get these rights we will never cease to protest and assail the ears of America.

Four years later, Du Bois and several other champions of equality—white as well as black—formed the National Association for the Advancement of Colored People (NAACP). The NAACP lobbied with legislatures and brought suit in courts to end discrimination. Its first major victory came in 1915, when the

Two leading spokesmen for black Americans in the early 1900s were Booker T. Washington *(top)* and William E. B. Du Bois. However, they had different approaches to white-black relations.

Supreme Court made the grandfather clause unconstitutional.

Until 1910 or so, most blacks favored Booker T. Washington's approach of accommodation. From then on, however, the Du Bois approach has dominated. Through appeals to conscience, through lobbying, politics, and court suits, black Americans and their white allies have worked to bring America face to face with the need to bring practice into line with idealism.

Equality can be defined differently by different people. Writing in 1903 Du Bois offered a vision of equality for the Afro-American that is startingly modern.

One ever feels his two-ness—an American, a Negro. The history of the American Negro is the history of . . . a longing . . . to merge this double self into a better and truer self. . . . The Afro-American would not Africanize America, for America has too much to teach the world and Africa. He would not bleach his Negro soul in a flood of white Americanism, for he knows that Negro blood has a message for the world. He simply wishes to make it possible for a man to be both a Negro and an American, without being cursed and spit upon by his fellows, without having the doors of Opportunity closed roughly in his face.

What William E. B. Du Bois wrote about the hopes of American blacks can be just as well applied to every other group living in the United States. It is the challenge by which, above all others, the success of this country will have to be measured.

CHECKUP

1. What were the effects on the South of the sharecrop and crop-lien system?.
2. By what means were the rights given to blacks under the Fourteenth and Fifteenth amendments taken away from them?
3. What different approaches did Booker T. Washington and William E. B. Du Bois take to bettering the position of blacks in the late 1800s and early 1900s?

Key Facts from Chapter 19

1. The immediate task of the federal government at the end of the Civil War was to bring the rebelling Southern states back into the Union.

2. Presidents Lincoln and Johnson favored a plan that would restore the Union quickly and easily without punishing the South or causing sweeping changes in Southern society.

3. The Radical Republicans favored a plan for restoring the Union that would punish the South and raise the freed slaves to a position of equality in Southern society.

4. The Radical Republicans succeeded in putting their plan into operation, but they failed in their attempt to remove President Johnson from office. They also failed to raise the freed slaves to a position of equality with whites.

5. The Thirteenth, Fourteenth, and Fifteenth amendments prohibited slavery, made blacks citizens, and guaranteed that their rights, including the right to vote, were not to be denied by the states.

6. Despite these amendments, various methods were devised during and after Reconstruction to keep blacks from voting and to deny them social equality.

★ REVIEWING THE CHAPTER ★

People, Places, and Events

Review Questions

1. What was the great strength of President Lincoln's plan to restore the Union? the great weakness? *Pp. 483–484*

2. What action did Congress take in an effort to prevent any interference with their plans for Southern Reconstruction? *Pp. 490–491*

3. Distinguish between the following Constitutional amendments: Thirteenth, Fourteenth, and Fifteenth. *Pp. 487, 488, 491*

4. Who operated Reconstruction governments in the Southern states and how effective was their leadership? *Pp. 492–494*

5. What was the problem with the election returns in 1876? How was the matter settled? *P. 496*

6. What was meant by the term *Jim Crow laws*? *P. 500*

7. What was the purpose of the poll tax and the literacy test? *P. 501*

Chapter Test

Complete each sentence using the vocabulary from this chapter. Write your answers on a separate piece of paper.

1. The House of Representatives impeached Andrew Johnson by charging that he violated the _____ ____.

2. The _____ was Congress' plan for Reconstruction, but Lincoln was able to kill the legislation by using a _____.

3. The _____declared Rutherford B. Hayes the winner of the disputed election of 1876.

4. Reconstruction came to an end when Democrats and Republicans accepted the _____.

5. The government agency established to give welfare to blacks and poor whites after the war was called the _____ _____.

6. In *Plessy* v. *Ferguson,* the _____ _____ ruled in favor of the doctrine of _____ but equal" facilities for blacks.

7. Northerners who moved to the South for political reasons during Reconstruction were called _____.

8. The _____ Amendment provided that no citizen could be kept from voting "on account of _____, color, or previous condition of servitude."

9. Segregation laws were referred to as _____ laws.

10. _____ advocated that blacks concentrate on advancing economically instead of asking for political or social equality.

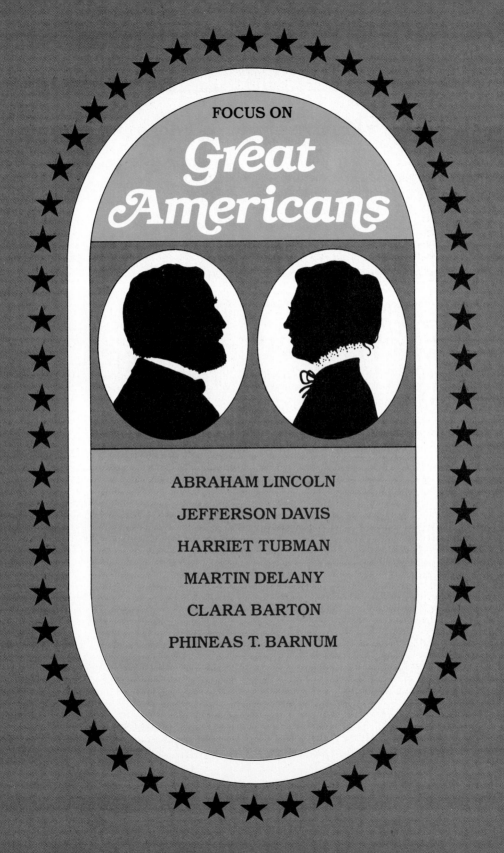

FOCUS ON

Great Americans

ABRAHAM LINCOLN

JEFFERSON DAVIS

HARRIET TUBMAN

MARTIN DELANY

CLARA BARTON

PHINEAS T. BARNUM

Frontiersman to President

Abraham Lincoln has been the subject of more writing than any other American. There are already more than 5,000 titles dealing with him, and the number is still growing. Certainly one reason for the fascination with Lincoln is that he presided over the nation in the time of its greatest danger. Another is based on his human qualities of compassion and forgiveness. But perhaps as important as any other reason is that Lincoln seems to be the perfect expression of a major American ideal. For many Americans, Abraham Lincoln is the abiding example of how someone from the humblest beginnings can rise to the highest office in the land.

Indeed, the man who was to become the sixteenth President of the United States came into the world with few advantages. Abraham, the second child of Thomas and Nancy Hanks Lincoln, was born in 1809 in a one-room log cabin about 3 miles (4.8 km) south of Hodgenville in Hardin (now Larue) County, Kentucky. His mother, a kind and deeply religious woman, was illiterate; his father could barely write his own name. Abraham Lincoln was raised in poverty.

Lincoln's father, Thomas, has often been unfairly described as lazy and shiftless. Actually, he was a hardworking man who pieced together a living by doing carpentry and odd jobs and by farming. Unfortunately, he was a poor judge of farmland. After several years of poor crops on the farm near Hodgenville,

The first known photograph of Abraham Lincoln (*above*) was taken in 1834. The last known photograph (*below*) was taken in 1865, a few days before Lincoln was assassinated.

Thomas Lincoln sold it and bought land at Knob Creek, about 8 miles (12.9 km) away. Abraham was two at the time. Of the 230 acres (93.2 ha) Lincoln bought, however, only 30 acres (12.2 ha) could be farmed. And even on that part, spring floods more than once washed out a new crop. After five hard years there, the Lincoln family moved to the Indiana Territory. This time they were squatters (see page 44) for a year before Thomas bought the land.

Like other boys on the frontier, Abe Lincoln did farm chores from an early age. Only when he and his older sister could be spared from work at home was there time for school. The schools they attended in both Kentucky and Indiana were called "blab" schools; because there were no books, the children learned by repeating what the teacher said. Abraham attended school for only short periods. His schooling probably did not total one year.

When Abraham was nine, his mother died. The following year his father married Sarah Bush Johnston, a widow with three children. She was a loving stepmother to Abraham, and he adored her. It was she who taught and encouraged him to read. Abraham Lincoln developed a strong desire to learn. He read and reread the few books the family had. He also traveled many miles to borrow books from neighbors. He did all the writing for the Lincoln family, and did much of the writing for their neighbors as well.

There was little time for reading, however, in the hard frontier life. Always tall and strong for his age, Abraham did more than his share of clearing trees and plowing the land. His father also hired him out to work for neighbors.

During those years, Abraham Lincoln's life seemed to take no special direction. At seventeen he worked as a ferryhand on a nearby river. Two years later he and two others hired themselves out to build a flatboat and float cargo down the Mississippi River to New Orleans. On his return he helped the family move to a new farm in Illinois. Abraham helped with the usual frontier

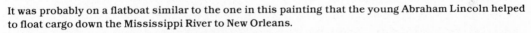

It was probably on a flatboat similar to the one in this painting that the young Abraham Lincoln helped to float cargo down the Mississippi River to New Orleans.

tasks of building a cabin, clearing the land, splitting rails to fence it, and setting a crop. Later that spring he and a cousin hired out to split 5,000 rails into fencing. He later described himself at this stage of his life as "a piece of floating driftwood."

In 1830, after a hard winter, the Lincolns moved again. This time Abraham did not accompany them. Once again he hired out to float cargo down to New Orleans. On his return in 1831, he struck out on his own. He took a job as a store clerk in New Salem, Illinois, a village of some twenty-five families about 20 miles (32.2 km) from Springfield.

Lincoln won quick acceptance in his new home through his courage and his physical strength, qualities much admired in frontier America. Challenged to a wrestling match by youths of the town, the rugged, six-foot-four-inch (193 cm) newcomer bested the leader of the group, Jack Armstrong. The young men became fast friends thereafter. Anxious to improve himself, Lincoln joined the town's debating club. He also began to read more widely and to study grammar and mathematics on his own.

When the store he worked in closed, Abe Lincoln and a partner bought a general store of their own. The store lost money, however, and closed within a year. The death of his partner then left Lincoln with all the debts. In frontier America it was not unusual for a debtor to simply move away without paying. Lincoln, however, stayed on and paid off his debts in full over the next decade. It was his conduct in that matter and other dealings that earned him the name "Honest Abe." In 1833 he was appointed the village postmaster. The

pay was hardly enough to live on, so Lincoln added to his income by hiring out as a farm worker, a mill hand, and a rail splitter, as well as by doing some surveying.

In 1832, Lincoln ran for the Illinois legislature. Because Henry Clay was his political hero, Lincoln ran as a Whig. He lost, but in 1834 he ran again and won. He was reelected three more times. In his eight years in the legislature he gained valuable experience in the political arts of persuasion and compromise. He became one of his party's leaders in the legislature.

Meanwhile, encouraged by a lawyer and fellow legislator from Springfield named John Todd Stuart, Lincoln began to study law. For two years he studied books lent to him by Stuart, and in 1836 he passed the law exams. The next year Lincoln moved to Springfield and became Stuart's partner. He was still so poor that he had to borrow a horse to make the move. Two saddlebags held all his belongings.

In 1841, Lincoln formed a partnership with Stephen T. Logan. This was an important step in Lincoln's growth. From Logan, Lincoln learned the importance of attending to detail, being precise and methodical, and carefully preparing each case. Before long, theirs was one of the leading law firms in Illinois.

After several years Lincoln opened his own law office, taking a new lawyer named William H. Herndon as his partner. Herndon later wrote one of the first biographies of Lincoln. One would never have guessed from the appearance of their office how successful the new partnership would be. The office windows were never washed. Papers were

During the 1858 senatorial campaign in Illinois, Abraham Lincoln and Stephen A. Douglas had seven debates. Douglas won the election, but the debates made Lincoln a national figure.

piled high on desk tops and tables and were scattered everywhere. Lincoln and Herndon often had trouble locating an important paper or letter. On one large envelope Lincoln wrote, "When you can't find it anywhere else, look into this." Lincoln also made a practice of stuffing letters and scribbled notes into his stovepipe hat. Once when he bought a new one, he absentmindedly threw out the old one, notes and all.

There was nothing untidy about Lincoln's mind, however. He had a remarkable ability to think a problem through to the heart and then state it briefly and simply enough for all to understand. This talent served him well in persuading juries with logic and fairmindedness. It would also be one of his greatest strengths as a political leader later on. His famed Gettysburg Address, simple yet moving, is perhaps the best example of this quality.

One of Lincoln's most famous cases was the murder trial of "Duff" Armstrong, son of the young man Lincoln had wrestled and befriended in New Salem. The witness who identified "Duff" as the murderer claimed he had seen him by the light of a full moon. Lincoln produced an almanac that showed it would have been impossible to identify the murderer by moonlight because there was only a quarter moon the night of the murder. Armstrong was acquitted.

In 1842, Abraham Lincoln married Mary Todd of Lexington, Kentucky. The two were almost opposite in background and temperament. Mary was from a well-to-do, prominent family; Abraham was from the humblest of backgrounds. Mary liked fine clothes and jewelry; Abraham was a man of simple tastes. He was easygoing; she had a stormy temper. She had frequent outbursts over small things. These were often accompanied by violent headaches, now recognized as warnings of the mental illness that overtook her near the end of her life. Yet for the most part, Abraham and Mary Lincoln were happy with each other. Lincoln's patience, understanding, and forgiveness in dealing with his wife's tantrums helped to make the marriage work. During their marriage the Lincolns shared the tragedy of the deaths of two of their four sons.

In 1846, Lincoln was elected to Congress. With other Whigs, he opposed the war against Mexico. President Polk had justified the war by claiming that "American blood has been shed on American soil." Knowing the clash had really taken place on Mexican territory, Lincoln presented several resolutions challenging the President to show the exact spot where blood had been shed. These became known as the "spot resolutions." Lincoln voted in favor of the Wilmot Proviso (see page 445). He also authored a plan for gradually abolishing slavery in Washington, D.C., but the plan failed to win enough support to be introduced in Congress. Unpopular in his home district because of his opposition to the war, Lincoln decided against seeking a second term. Thus at age thirty-nine, Lincoln believed his political career was over, and he returned to the practice of law full-time.

Although out of office, Lincoln retained his interest in politics. As the slavery issue came to the fore, his simple and eloquent statements spoke for growing numbers of citizens. Lincoln felt that slavery was a "monstrous injustice." He said, "As I would not be a *slave*, so I would not be a *master*. This expresses my idea of democracy. Whatever differs from this, to the extent of the difference, is no democracy." Lincoln once remarked privately, "Whenever I hear anyone arguing for slavery I feel a strong impulse to see it tried on him personally."

By the spring of 1856, Lincoln had switched from the Whig party to the new Republican party. Two years later he was chosen to run for the Senate. The Democratic candidate was Stephen A. Douglas. In accepting his party's nomination, Lincoln drew upon a statement from the Bible.

"A house divided against itself cannot stand." I believe this government cannot endure permanently half slave and half free. I do not expect the Union to be dissolved—I do not expect the house to fall—but I do expect it will cease to be divided. It will become all one thing, or all the other.

The campaign that followed is one of the most famous in American history. Although Lincoln was not elected, the debate made him a national figure and a strong candidate for the Presidency. Two years later, in 1860, he was nominated for and elected to that office.

You have already read about Lincoln as President during the Civil War (see pages 468–470). No President ever carried a greater burden nor carried it with greater human sympathy for the victims on both sides. This, perhaps even more than his qualities of leadership, raised him to the level of greatness. It was a greatness that many did not recognize until after he was killed. Secretary of War Stanton best expressed the loss to the nation and best foretold the place that Lincoln would have in history. Announcing the death of the President, Stanton said simply, "Now he belongs to the ages."

CHECKUP

1. Describe Lincoln's early life and education. How did he earn a living before he became a lawyer?
2. What experience did Lincoln have in government before he became President?
3. What were Lincoln's views on slavery? What effect did he think the slavery issue would have on the United States?

President of the Confederacy

Jefferson Davis was born in a four-room log cabin in Kentucky on June 3, 1808. Eight months later and less than 100 miles (160 km) away, Abraham Lincoln would be born in another Kentucky log cabin. Davis and Lincoln were destined to lead the opposing sides in America's Civil War. While that conflict raised the one man to greatness, it shattered the reputation of the other. It was the unhappy fate of Jefferson Davis to be thrust into a position he did not want, and for which he was not suited.

Jefferson Davis was the youngest of the ten children of Jane and Samuel Davis. The Davises grew tobacco and

Before becoming President of the Confederacy, Jefferson Davis had been a United States senator, a military officer, and Secretary of War under President Franklin Pierce.

raised horses in the bluegrass country, but after fifteen years, they still had not prospered. A few years after Jefferson's birth, therefore, they moved to uncleared but rich cotton land in the Mississippi Territory. Aided by a boom in cotton and guidance from Joseph, the business-minded eldest son, the Davis family became wealthy in a few years.

From boyhood, Jefferson was usually described as high-spirited, imaginative, and independent. That meant, among other things, that he didn't accept discipline readily and at times was mischievous. He did poorly in local schools before going on to Transylvania College in Kentucky. After little more than a year there, he entered West Point in 1824 at the age of sixteen. He was no doubt influenced in his choice of school by a family tradition of military service. His father had fought in the Revolution, and three brothers had served in the War of 1812. Again, Jefferson was anything but a model student. Three classmates who did better than Davis later served under him when he was commander in chief of the Confederacy. They were Generals Robert E. Lee, Albert Sidney Johnston, and Joseph E. Johnston.

After graduation in 1828, Lieutenant Jefferson Davis served at remote posts in Wisconsin and Illinois, where the main duty was to protect settlers from Indian attacks. In 1833 the young lieutenant met and fell in love with Sarah Knox Taylor, the eighteen-year-old daughter of his commanding officer,

Colonel Zachary Taylor. The two asked the colonel, who later became twelfth President of the United States, for permission to marry, but he refused. It is not clear whether Taylor changed his mind, but Jefferson Davis and Sarah Knox Taylor were married in June 1835.

In that same month Lieutenant Davis resigned from the army and headed back to Mississippi with his bride. He had received a large piece of the family land along the Mississippi River, about twenty miles (32.2 km) below Vicksburg. Jefferson Davis now looked ahead to a new life with his wife. Just three months later, however, his dreams were shattered. Sarah was dead, a victim of malaria. Jefferson had also been stricken by the disease but had recovered. For the next decade, Jefferson Davis threw himself into the task of becoming a successful planter. Often working along with his slaves, he cleared and planted his land, which he named Brierfield.

The Davis name was already associated in the state with wealth and social position, and Jefferson Davis's success added to both. Like his brother Joseph, he also took on the manners, tastes, and values of the Southern aristocracy. During those years, probably under his brother's influence, he read widely in history, politics, and military tactics as well as in literature and poetry. The brothers spent many evenings together at each other's plantations talking about books and ideas. In later years, Jefferson Davis became known as one of the best-educated men in Congress.

As a slaveholder, Davis was a mild master. In fact, neighboring planters complained that he spoiled his slaves and set a bad example. It was true that Davis treated his slaves with kindness and care. He rarely punished them, allowed them to learn to read and write, and looked after their medical care with far more concern than most masters. Nevertheless, unlike many Southern slaveholders who regarded slavery as a curse and at best a necessary evil, Jefferson Davis thought that slavery was good for both master and slave. He did not believe, as Calhoun did, that slavery should be the permanent lot of black people in the United States. But he did believe it would take several generations for slaves, through education and discipline, to be made fit for freedom. Until that distant day, he felt, slavery must be protected.

In the early 1840s, Davis became active in politics, and he was elected as a Democrat to the United States House of Representatives in 1845. That same year he married Varina Howell. The couple had six children, only two of whom outlived their parents.

With the outbreak of war with Mexico in 1846, Davis resigned from Congress to accept charge of the Mississippi Rifles, a volunteer regiment. Once again his superior officer was Zachary Taylor, his former father-in-law. We do not know what passed between these men in the years since 1835, but they seem to have become reconciled. In any case, at the battle of Buena Vista both men won military glory and national fame (see page 387). Davis, now a colonel, devised a maneuver that broke up a Mexican cavalry charge and turned possible defeat into victory for Taylor's outnumbered men. Davis was shot in the foot in this action and was on crutches for two years after.

Jefferson Davis resigned from Congress during the Mexican War to assume command of a volunteer regiment. In the battle of Buena Vista (*above*) he gained national fame and military glory.

In 1847 the governor of Mississippi named Davis to fill an unexpired term in the United States Senate. There, Davis was a strong defender of the South's interests. He opposed the Wilmot Proviso, demanded that slavery be permitted to spread into the territories, and voted against the Compromise of 1850 (see pages 446–448). Unlike the fire-eaters who favored immediate secession, Davis was willing to preserve the Union. But like Calhoun, he believed that this could continue only on the South's terms. If that could not be, then the Southern states should secede.

After being narrowly defeated in 1851 in his bid for the governorship of Mississippi, Davis returned briefly to private life. He was soon back in Washington, however, as President Franklin Pierce's Secretary of War. Ever a promoter of the South's interest, Davis favored passage of a bill by Congress to finance the building of a transcontinental railroad along a southern route. To make the route more attractive to Congress, he persuaded President Pierce to buy from Mexico a strip of land south of the New Mexico territory through which such a railroad could be built. Thus the Gadsden Purchase was made for $10 million in 1853 but to no avail, because Congress voted in favor of a central route for the railroad. Davis was also an expansionist and especially sought territory into which slavery could spread.

The sectional conflict was growing quickly when Davis was reelected to the Senate in 1857. Davis had said that if an abolitionist were elected President, Mississippi should leave the Union. Nevertheless, when Lincoln—whom Southerners regarded as an abolitionist—was elected, Davis counseled the fire-eaters to delay action until there remained no prospect of a peaceful settlement. They did not heed his advice, however, and in January 1860, Mississippi joined South Carolina, which had already seceded (see pages 461–464).

Confederacy President Jefferson Davis is shown with his Cabinet and General Robert E. Lee (*in uniform*). Davis would have preferred Lee's position as commander of the Confederate Army to the Presidency.

Three weeks later, delegates from the seven seceding states met in Montgomery, Alabama. They adopted a constitution, proclaimed the Confederate States of America, and unanimously chose Jefferson Davis to be President. It was not the job that he wanted. He had preferred to be chosen to head the Confederate Army. His wife recorded that when Davis told her of the telegram bearing the news of his selection, he spoke "as a man might speak of a sentence of death." Nonetheless, he accepted the Presidency as a duty. Davis was later elected without opposition to a six-year term by the people of the new country.

Jefferson Davis was ill prepared by his experience to be the leader of the new government. As Secretary of War, he had supervised only seven clerks and overseen an army of ten to fifteen thousand. Now as President of the Confederacy, he had to create a whole new government numbering more than 70,000 civilian employees. He allowed himself to get bogged down in details. Further, his

military experience made him feel that he was the equal of any military man. Too often he overruled generals like Joseph E. Johnston and Robert E. Lee, who were better strategists. His interference with the war department led five different secretaries of war to quit.

Some of his personal qualities were also not well suited to the Presidency. No one doubted his courage, sincerity, and integrity, but he lacked tact and flexibility. His life as an aristocrat had not prepared him for the give-and-take needed in dealing with independent congressmen and governors. He was unable to ignore criticism and always felt a need to answer back. Rather than trying to win over those who disagreed, he quarreled with them and turned them away or made enemies.

Yet it is too simple to lay the problems of the Confederacy at Davis's door. The blind devotion to states' rights by many Southerners did far more damage to the South's cause. So, also, did the self-centered actions of certain other officials who undercut the President. Vice President Alexander Stephens, who hated both the President and life in the capital city, simply left Richmond for one stretch of a year and a half. It may well be that leading the Confederacy to victory was an impossible task. At the end of the war, some Southern leaders blamed the defeat on Davis, but General Robert E. Lee did not join them. When asked if Jefferson Davis had been a good President, Lee replied, "I know of no man who could have done better."

It is certain that no one could have more steadfastly refused to concede defeat. Even after Lee surrendered, Davis was urging a group of officers to keep up the struggle. "Three thousand brave men," he pleaded, "are enough for a nucleus around which the whole people will rally." It was no use. The South was defeated.

For several months following the war, Jefferson Davis was a hunted man. Some people thought he had helped to plot Lincoln's assassination, and President Johnson offered a reward of $100,000 in gold for the capture of Davis. Federal troops caught up with him in southern Georgia in May 1865. Then it was that Jefferson Davis knew the bitter taste of defeat. With newspapers and the Northern public crying, "Hang Jeff Davis!" he was imprisoned in Fort Monroe, Virginia. His cell had a single window, and he was kept under guard around the clock. For a time, Davis was placed in leg irons. Eventually moved to better quarters, he was held for two years awaiting trial on a charge of treason until he was released on bail in 1867. Davis had been stripped of his citizenship, but a trial was never held.

Even as a freed man, Jefferson Davis lived with the bitter aftermath of defeat for most of his remaining twenty-two years. His fortune was gone. His health was poor. Brierfield was again overgrown with weeds and brush, but Davis was no longer the strong young man of twenty-seven who had first cleared it. He went to Canada and then to England, seeking a job and hoping to recover his health. On his return to America, he took a position as president of an insurance company in Tennessee. But the company failed in the depression of the 1870s. Finally, in the late 1870s, he returned to Mississippi to write his memoirs. Sales of *The Rise and Fall of the Confederate Government,* though never strong, supported him for a while. He later earned some money by delivering lectures. In time, the quiet dignity with which he had accepted his fate restored his popularity in the South. In his final years, Jefferson Davis had the satisfaction of being hailed once again as a hero at home. He died in 1889 at the age of eighty-one. Eighty-nine years later, in honor of the one hundredth anniversary of the end of Reconstruction, Congress voted to restore the rights of citizenship to this former leader of the Confederacy.

CHECKUP

1. What were Davis's views on slavery?
2. What was Davis's political career before the Southern states seceded from the Union? What positions did Davis take on issues before the Senate between 1847 and 1851? On secession?
3. What problems did Davis have as President of the Confederacy? Why was the Presidency an unfortunate position for him? What had he preferred to do? Why?

✷ HARRIET TUBMAN ✷

"The Slaves Call Her Moses"

To a white abolitionist from Massachusetts, she was "the greatest heroine of the age." Frederick Douglass, the black abolitionist leader, wrote of her that "excepting John Brown . . . I know of no one who has willingly encountered more perils and hardships to serve our enslaved people. . . ." The object of this high praise was a former slave who could neither read nor write. But Harriet Tubman had two qualities that raised her above the ordinary. She had a burning passion for freedom. And she had the courage to risk her own life time and again to help others achieve freedom.

In 1849, Harriet Tubman fled slavery and escaped to a free state. For years after, she repeatedly risked her own freedom by returning to the South to help other slaves escape.

Harriet was born about 1820. She was one of ten or eleven children of Harriet Greene and Benjamin Ross, a slave couple owned by one Edward Brodas of Dorchester County, Maryland. Brodas often hired out his slaves to others. Thus at the age of five or six, Harriet was being sent out to do housework and take care of babies in neighboring homes and plantations. Later she worked also as a cook and a field hand. She was not a very cooperative slave, for there were many complaints about her work. She was treated cruelly at times. At age thirteen or fourteen, while trying to shield a fellow slave from an angry overseer, Harriet was struck in the head with a two-pound weight. The blow fractured her skull and caused her to have sudden sleeping spells three or four times a day for the rest of her life.

Sometime in the 1830s Brodas died, and ownership of his slaves passed to a young heir. In 1849 that person died, too, and rumors quickly spread among the slaves that they were to be sold to a cotton or rice grower in the South. This meant that families might be split up. There was also a strong chance of winding up with a cruel master and of working in severe and unhealthy conditions. Apparently around this time, two of Harriet's sisters were, in fact, sold. Harriet was determined that this would not happen to her. Five years earlier she had married a free black named John Tubman. Often she had told him of her hope for freedom. Now the time had come.

She confided to her husband her plan to escape and urged him to come. But John Tubman refused. It was a heartbreaking moment for Harriet. She loved her husband, but she loved freedom more. She decided to go alone.

Some time earlier, a white woman who lived nearby and for whom Harriet had done chores had told Harriet that should the day ever come when Harriet wanted to escape, she would help. Now Harriet went to the woman's home in the dead of night. She was given a piece of paper with the names of two people and directions for getting to the house of the first. There she was to show the paper to the people who lived there. This Harriet did. When the woman at the first house looked at the paper, she gave Harriet a broom and told her to sweep the yard. This was done to disguise Harriet as a servant there. That night the husband put Harriet Tubman in his wagon, covered her over, and drove to the edge of the next town. There she got out and followed the man's directions to the second house. In this manner, Harriet made her way north—hiding by day and traveling by night. Finally she reached the Pennsylvania line—a free state at last! "When I found I had crossed that line," she said later, "I looked at my hands to see if I was the same person. There was such a glory over everything; the sun came like gold through the trees, and over the fields, and I felt like I was in Heaven."

The route that Harriet Tubman had been traveling to freedom was known as the Underground Railroad (see page 438). Over the years "conductors" had guided many thousands of slaves from "station" to "station," helping the slaves reach the free North. As she learned more about the work of the people who made up the Underground Railroad, Harriet determined to be a part of them. She especially wanted to rescue her family and friends.

Harriet's first journey of rescue was in December 1850. One of her sisters was a slave in Cambridge, Maryland, a town on the Eastern Shore of Chesapeake Bay. Shortly before Christmas, Harriet quietly entered the town along with her sister's husband, a free black. They arrived by boat. The two of them quickly hid Harriet's sister and two children in the boat and made the long, hard stretch across the bay to Baltimore. After hiding there for a few days, they continued their journey north by way of the Underground Railroad. Several months later, Harriet returned to rescue a brother and two others.

One of her great disappointments came soon after. She had once again risked her freedom by returning to the South, this time in the hope of persuading her husband to go back with her. When she found him, she discovered that he had remarried and had no wish to leave.

Just about the time Harriet Tubman was beginning her work, a new law was passed that made the operation of the Underground Railroad more difficult and dangerous in the North as well as in the South. This was the fugitive slave law. It was part of the Compromise of 1850. Sheriffs in Northern states could now *require* that citizens help them capture runaway slaves. Blacks accused of being runaways were tried without a jury before a special commissioner. Under the law, a commissioner got a five-dollar fee for ruling that the accused was not a fugitive slave; the fee was ten dollars for ruling that the slave *was* a fugitive! Many Northerners refused to obey the new law. Still it was thought safest to conduct runaways out of the country and into Canada.

In 1851, Tubman took her first group along this added line on the Underground Railroad. The party of eleven, which included a brother, went overland along the Hudson River to Albany, then westward along the route of the Erie Canal to Niagara Falls, and across the Niagara River to St. Catherines in Canada. Along this route she encountered some of the famous antislavery people of the time: in Peterboro, New York, Gerrit Smith, who provided money for the abolitionist cause; in Auburn, New York, William Henry Seward, a United States senator; in Rochester, Frederick Douglass and Susan B. Anthony, the women's-rights leader.

Harriet Tubman herself lived in St. Catherines from 1851 to 1857. Each year, however, she made at least one trip back to the South to conduct more slaves along the railroad to freedom. It is believed that she risked her own freedom on nineteen trips and helped between sixty and three hundred souls out of slavery.

In rescuing her family, Tubman would first have someone write a letter for her to a free black living in the area she was going to. Postal officials often opened mail to free blacks, so her message had to be masked. For example, when preparing to rescue three brothers in 1854, she wrote: "Read my letter to the old folks, and give my love to them, and tell my brothers to be always *watching unto prayer,* and when the *good old ship of Zion comes along, to be ready to step aboard.*" The brothers understood.

Harriet Tubman used all the tricks of an experienced and shrewd conductor. She would start on a Saturday night, because runaways were not as likely to be missed on Sunday. Even if the runaways were missed, posters to spread the

Harriet Tubman is shown with a group of people she guided out of slavery. It is believed that Tubman helped between sixty and three hundred slaves gain their freedom.

alarm couldn't be made until Monday. She traveled by night, following the North Star. On cloudy nights, she would feel the bark of trees for the soft algae that usually grew on the north side. Then she would know which way to go. She knew by heart the hiding places in the swamps and the forests, and she knew the barns and cellars that were the stations. Infants were mildly drugged so that their cries did not give the fugitives away. She even developed tricks of her own. Once, believing her group was being followed, she boarded a train heading *south*. She knew her pursuers would not suspect her of moving in that direction.

In 1858, Harriet Tubman moved to Auburn, New York, home of Senator Seward. By this time she was well-known in abolitionist circles. She often spoke at abolitionist meetings and told stories of her escapes. Harriet Tubman was simple and uneducated, but her message was powerful. A Northern abolitionist wrote of her in 1859: "The slaves call her Moses. She has a reward of twelve thousand dollars offered for her in Maryland and will probably be burned alive whenever she is caught, which she probably will be, first or last, as she is going again."

Harriet Tubman was never caught. Her last trip on the Underground Railroad was in December 1860, shortly before the Civil War began. On this trip she helped seven more slaves from Maryland to freedom.

Soon after the Civil War began, Mrs. Tubman went south with the Union armies. She helped nurse and feed the slaves who streamed into the army camp for protection. She did the same for black troops. In addition, she worked for the Union armies as a scout and a spy. She also organized a number of guerrilla raids inside the Confederate lines.

At war's end, Harriet Tubman returned to her home in Auburn, New York. She lived there for almost fifty years, most of them in poverty. The army had paid her next to nothing for her work during the war. What little money she had, or was able to get, she gave to the founding of freedmen's schools in the South. In 1869, two years after learning of John Tubman's death, she married a man named Nelson Davis. Near the end of her life, Congress finally provided her with a small pension in recognition of her war work.

For the rest of her life, Harriet Tubman was active in causes for her people as well as in the movement for women's rights. Once, when called upon to speak about her work before the war, she told her audience, "I was the conductor of the Underground Railroad for eight years, and . . . I never ran my train off the track, and I never lost a passenger." It was a splendid summary of Harriet Tubman's work. When she died in 1913, those were the words that the citizens of Auburn chose for the tablet they erected in her memory.

CHECKUP

1. How did the Compromise of 1850 affect the work of Harriet Tubman and the Underground Railroad? What tricks did Tubman use in guiding escaping slaves safely to the North?
2. What did Tubman do during the Civil War?
3. How was Tubman rewarded for the work she did between 1850 and 1865?

HARRIET TUBMAN **519**

★ MARTIN DELANY ★

Leader for Black Rights

The front page of a newspaper published in 1843 carried the motto, "Who would be free themselves must strike the blow." This expresses the lifelong belief of Martin Robinson Delany, the paper's founder, publisher, and chief writer. Although Delany did not publish his weekly paper, the *Mystery*, for very long, he devoted his entire life to the cause of black people. Even while slavery existed, Delany was speaking the language of self-determination. A free black himself, he believed that blacks in America must take the lead in winning their freedom and not depend on others.

Martin Robinson Delany was born in 1812 in Charles Town, Virginia (now in West Virginia). Although his father was a slave, his mother was free. This, under Virginia law, made Martin and her other children free. Martin's mother supported the family by sewing and taking in laundry. The Delany children did not go to school. A state law of 1819 prohibited black children from attending school and even from receiving any instruction at all. Nonetheless, Martin's mother taught her five sons and daughters to read and write from some beginner's books she had obtained in trade from a friendly white peddler. When a local court found her guilty of breaking the law, she gathered her family together and fled to Chambersburg, Pennsylvania, to avoid punishment. The next year Martin's father managed to buy his freedom. He then joined the rest of the family.

Little is known of Martin Delany's life in Chambersburg. He seems to have kept up with his studies either at home or in a segregated school. When he was nineteen he went to Pittsburgh to study with Reverend Louis Woodson. Black parents of the city had hired Woodson to teach their children, who were not allowed to attend the public schools. Martin studied with Woodson for nearly five years, learning mathematics and some Latin as well as English grammar and history. In 1833 he became an apprentice to a Pittsburgh doctor. At that time there were no black doctors in the United States. The first was to be Dr. James McCune Smith, who began a practice in New York in 1837 after training in Scotland. Delany served three years as an apprentice and then opened a practice limited to "cupping" and "bleeding." Those two procedures sound strange to us today. At that time, however, they were thought to be beneficial for all kinds of sickness.

In 1843, Delany married Catherine Richards. She came from one of the black families that had settled in Pittsburgh when it was still a village. Eleven children would be born to them. Five boys and a girl would live to adulthood. The children were given names that showed pride in their black heritage. The oldest son was named Toussaint L'Ouverture, after the liberator of Haiti; the daughter was called Ethiopia. The family was supported by Delany's medical work.

During all that time, Martin Delany was developing his interest in the cause of black people. After publishing the *Mystery* for four years, he joined the famed ex-slave and abolitionist Frederick Douglass as coeditor of Douglass's newspaper, the *North Star* (see page 441). It soon became clear, however, that Douglass and Delany disagreed on the place of white abolitionists in the movement. Douglass believed their work was necessary, not only to end slavery but also to win the struggle for equality that must follow. He felt that whites should hold many positions of leadership in the movement. In Delany's view, blacks should lead the movement and set its goals. "[The] elevation [of blacks] must be the result of self-efforts, and the work of [their] own hands. No other human power can accomplish it," he wrote. If black people wished to rise to equality in political and economic matters, they would have to speak for themselves, provide their own leadership, and not depend upon others. Only then would they truly be able to say what their own future would be. Delany realized that this would require education. Therefore he stated that young blacks had a duty to their people to educate themselves, even though they were given little opportunity to do so.

In his public speeches as well as in his newspaper articles, Delany spoke strongly in favor of self-determination for black people. To whites he said that "whatever ideas of liberty I may have, have been received from reading the lives of your revolutionary fathers." Unfortunately, his harsh criticism and scolding manner angered many of his readers and listeners. Quakers in Cincinnati and Columbiana, Ohio, refused to let him lecture in their meeting-houses, although they welcomed other black abolitionists. This led Delany to turn against the Quakers. "I cannot [believe]," he said, "that there is much Christianity where there is no humanity." But many black people also were not ready for his message of black self-determination. Delany left the *North Star* in 1849, and he and Douglass went their separate ways.

Martin Delany was the highest-ranking black field officer in the Civil War. A leader in the fight for black rights, Delany believed that blacks should lead the movement and set its goals.

In 1848, at the age of thirty-six, Delany decided to return to the study of medicine. He apprenticed with a second Pittsburgh doctor who, like his first teacher, was a member of the Pennsylvania Anti-Slavery Society. Two years later, with the backing of eighteen white doctors from the Pittsburgh area, he was admitted to Harvard Medical School. Two other black men were also admitted. Both were sponsored by a colonization society and planned to practice in Liberia. However, all three men were forced to leave the school after one term. A majority of the students claimed that the continued presence of the three would lower the reputation of the school.

In 1850, the same year that Delany was forced to leave medical school, Congress passed a new fugitive slave law. Over the next ten years more than fifty thousand free blacks and escaping slaves emigrated to Canada because they feared kidnapping and reenslavement. Ever since 1839, when he was twenty-seven years old, Martin Delany had pondered whether to stay in the United States and fight for equality or to emigrate. Now, in the 1850s, his treatment at Harvard and the fugitive slave law led him to feel that black people could not receive justice and equality in the United States. To the white abolitionist William Lloyd Garrison he wrote, "I have no hopes in this country—no confidence in the American people—with a *few* excellent exceptions. . . ."

Delany now joined those blacks, small in number, who looked to emigration from the United States and establishment of independent black nations as the only answer. Within a few years he was the leading emigrationist.

Throughout history, oppressed people had left their homes, he observed; it was time now for black Americans to do so. For Delany, emigration was a positive act. It was a step along the way to self-determination. Black people could create their own nations and thus control their own futures. "Our race is to be redeemed," wrote Delany. "But we must go from among our oppressors; it never can be done by staying among them."

During the 1850s, emigrationists held several conventions at which they discussed possible sites for a new home. Most emigrationists opposed Africa because of its association with the hated American Colonization Society. That society's purpose in creating Liberia had been to remove free black people from the United States (see page 427). However, Central America, South America, and the Caribbean Islands were favored. Each place had countries with large black populations. A nation of black Americans and West Indian blacks, for example, could raise enough cotton, sugar, and rice to compete with and destroy the economy of the South. This would also destroy slavery. Delany favored emigration to Central America in his book entitled *The Condition, Elevation, Emigration and Destiny of the Colored People of the United States, Politically Considered*, published in 1852.

Emigrationists, however, remained a small minority of black Americans. Most black abolitionists agreed with Frederick Douglass that emigration was "uncalled for [and] unwise." For better or worse, the destiny of black Americans was in the United States. Their duty was

To Martin Delany, the emigration of black people to Africa was a step toward self-determination.

to stay and help in the struggle to free their three and a half million brothers and sisters in slavery and to fight for equality and justice afterward.

But Martin Delany persisted in his support of emigration. In 1856 he moved his family from Pittsburgh to Chatham, Ontario, Canada, where he made a living practicing medicine. In those days one did not need to graduate from a medical school to practice medicine. Indeed, with his earlier apprenticeships and one term at Harvard, Delany was probably better trained than many who called themselves doctors.

By 1858, Delany had shifted the focus of his interest in emigration to Africa.

He and an assistant went on an exploring expedition up the Niger River in Africa in 1859. Delany used the information he collected on the geography of the area as the basis for a lecture before The Royal Geographical Society in London in June of 1860. He concluded that the area, called Yorubaland, would be a good place for black Americans to emigrate. When he returned to the United States late in 1860, however, he found almost no popular support. Nearly all black Americans were turning their attention to ending slavery. Delany, too, put aside emigration. In 1864 he moved his family from Canada to Wilberforce, Ohio. He wanted his children to attend

Wilberforce University, the first college in the United States run by and for black Americans.

Delany called for the formation of a separate all-black army to free the slaves. That was not to happen (see page 466). A number of states, such as Massachusetts and Rhode Island, did form black regiments, and Delany became a recruiter for several of them.

In February 1865, Delany met with President Lincoln to urge that a separate black army, led by blacks, occupy the South. Delany was given an army commission as a major. He was the first black man to receive an officer's commission and was the highest-ranking black field officer in the Civil War. His main job was recruiting black volunteers. The President and Secretary of War Stanton were interested in Delany's plan. The war ended, however, before the plan could be developed.

With the end of the war in April 1865, Major Delany was assigned to the Freedmen's Bureau (see page 488) in South Carolina. In this position Delany urged the freed slaves to stand up for their rights and to insist on a fair share of the wealth their labor produced. He helped former slaves to make contracts that protected their new rights. He favored a plan for the federal government to redistribute conquered lands and allow freed slaves to buy 40 acres (16 ha). Laws to put this plan into action were never passed by Congress.

After leaving the army in 1868, Martin Delany remained in Charleston, South Carolina. There he argued in favor of blacks having a fair share of the offices in the state government. His reasoning again lay in his goal of self-determination for his people. He said, " . . . no people have become a great people who had not their own leaders." He himself held a number of minor posts but was defeated when he tried for higher office.

In his late years, Delany again became interested in emigration to Africa. He was active in encouraging blacks from South Carolina to emigrate to Liberia. For Delany, however, the dream of returning to Africa was never to come true. After failing in an effort to be named the United States minister to Liberia, he returned to Ohio. He died there in 1885.

Martin Delany's great aim had been for black people to be able to determine their own future. He believed that would be possible only if they had a nation of their own. Not many people agreed. For one thing, says one writer, his message was "too bold—too extreme for his own people to accept at the time." For another, his own personality probably lost him support for his ideas. He was harshly critical of those who did not accept all of his ideas. It would be nearly one hundred years before large numbers of black Americans and other American minorities would join the movement for self-determination.

CHECKUP

1. What influences in Martin Delany's early life led him to believe so strongly in self-determination and education?
2. What events changed Delany from a leader in the abolitionist movement to a leader of the emigrationists?
3. What do you think was Martin Delany's most important contribution? Explain the reasons for your choice.

✦ CLARA BARTON ✦

Angel of the Battlefield

Like all wars, the Civil War produced many heroes—persons whose acts of courage and self-sacrifice raised them above others. Not all the heroes wore uniforms or carried guns. Few performed greater acts of heroism than Clara Barton, a woman barely five feet (152 cm) tall. Singlehandedly she provided medical help and comfort to thousands of wounded and dying soldiers, often at the risk of her own life. To the soldiers, she was known as the Angel of the Battlefield.

Even as a child Clara Barton seemed headed for a life of service. The youngest of five children of Stephen and Sarah Barton of North Oxford, Massachusetts, she was born Clarissa Harlowe Barton on Christmas Day, 1821. Her father, a farmer active in community affairs, was an army veteran. While other fathers told their children fairy tales and nursery rhymes, Stephen Barton filled his daughter with stories of military battles and patriotic deeds. "I early learned," Clara wrote later, "that next to Heaven, our highest duty was to love and serve our country and honor and support its laws." From her mother, a practical and warmhearted woman, Clara learned the skills of cooking, preserving food, and sewing. These skills she later put to important use during the war. From both parents she gained strong humanitarian feelings and a "passion for service." Within her family circle she had occasion to satisfy both. Beginning at age eleven, Clara spent all her time for two years as the nurse and companion of a sick older brother.

As a young girl Clara Barton was painfully shy, sensitive, and lonely. But she became determined to overcome her shyness. An excellent student herself, Clara began to teach in local schools at eighteen. This was one of the few occupations open to a young woman who wished to help others. As her confidence grew, she started her own school. She

Clara Barton, shown here in a Matthew Brady photograph, had a long and varied career. She was a teacher, Patent Office clerk, battlefield nurse, and president of the American Red Cross.

ran this school for ten years, directing the education of the children of workers employed in her brothers' sawmills.

In 1850, after eleven years of serving others, Clara Barton returned to school herself for a year. She soon became depressed. She wrote in her diary: "I contribute to the happiness of not a single object and often to the unhappiness of many and always my own, for I am never happy." By this time, and perhaps earlier, Clara Barton had come to realize that her mental health depended upon satisfying her "passion for service." Throughout her life she would experience periods of depression and even breakdowns. Always they were associated with the feeling that she was not being of use to others.

The following year she taught school in Hightstown, New Jersey. At that time, New Jersey parents had to pay to send their children to school. In 1852, Clara Barton persuaded the school board of nearby Bordentown to let her open a free school, the first in the state. Within two years, the school had grown to serve six hundred pupils. Soon, however, the school board decided that so large a school needed a principal. Since the board believed that that was a "man's job," Clara was passed over. Not long after, she resigned.

Clara Barton did not know it at the time, but her teaching career was over. In 1854 she got a job as a clerk in the United States Patent Office in Washington, D.C. She was the first woman to hold a regular appointment in the federal civil service. Here, too, she met sex discrimination. Neither President Franklin Pierce nor Secretary of the Interior Robert McLelland approved of women and men working in the same office. Supported by the Patent Commissioner, however, Clara kept her job for more than two years. A change of administration cost her the job in 1857, but she regained her position in 1860 with the backing of the two senators from Massachusetts.

Less than a year later, the Civil War broke out. For Clara Barton, now almost forty, the war presented an unparalleled opportunity for service. "The patriot blood of my father was warm in my veins," she recalled. She threw her enormous energies into the cause. She provided food and comfort to homesick soldiers from Massachusetts and elsewhere who poured into the capital in the early months of the war. She raised the supplies herself. She wrote letters home for those who couldn't write. As news of her work spread, churches and citizens' groups sent bandages and other supplies. Soon her apartment was overflowing with boxes, and she had to rent a warehouse to store the supplies.

As soldiers massed in Washington for the First Battle of Bull Run (see page 471), Clara Barton wrote her father: "I shall remain here while anyone remains, and do whatever comes to my hand. I may be compelled to *face* danger, but *never fear it,* and while our soldiers can stand and *fight,* I can stand and feed and nurse them." But Barton was not long satisfied to stay in Washington and tend the wounded who returned from battle. She sent a request to army officials that she "be allowed to go and administer comfort to our brave men" at the front. As she wrote later in the war, "My business is stanching [stopping the flow of] blood and feeding fainting men;

my post the open field between the bullet and the hospital." The officials turned down her request at first, but she kept after them until finally they consented.

She first went up to the Union front lines in August 1862, two days after the battle of Cedar Mountain, near Culpeper, Virginia. The field hospital was almost out of dressings for wounds when Barton arrived with her mule-drawn wagon filled with supplies. Of her arrival, Surgeon James Dunn wrote, "I thought that night if heaven ever sent out a holy angel, she must be the one, her assistance was so timely." Barton helped Dunn to bandage the wounded, and then fed them.

Soon Clara Barton was often on the scene of battles with her wagonloads of bandages, coffee, jellies, brandy, crackers, and cans of soup and beef. She was present at the Second Battle of Bull Run, Chantilly, Antietam (see page 474), and Fredericksburg. After the Second Battle of Bull Run, she hardly slept or ate for three days while she and several helpers cared for thousands who waited to be moved to hospitals in the rear. At Antietam she followed the cannon right down to the battle, the only woman allowed at the front. She was barely missed by a bullet that passed through her sleeve and killed a wounded soldier to whom she was giving a drink. Her wagon provided the only medical supplies available for an important period of time. For a surgeon trying to care for a thousand wounded men in near darkness, she produced four boxes of candles. At Fredericksburg, Barton again narrowly missed death when a piece of exploding shell ripped through the skirts of her coat and dress.

Covered wagons carry wounded to the crude field hospital at the battle of Fredericksburg. Clara Barton risked her life under heavy fire to answer a doctor's bloodstained note for help.

On the battlefields Clara Barton often worked for days with enormous energy and almost no sleep. She cared for the wounded in the field, in tents, houses, churches, or wherever shelter could be found. She comforted the dying and the wounded. She wrote letters home for them. And she provided for their nourishment. An army surgeon at Antietam recalled her "with sleeves rolled up to the elbows . . . [making soup] in a huge iron kettle." She became, as she later recalled, "a notable housekeeper, if that might be said of one who . . . lived in the fields and woods and tents, and wagons, with all out of doors for a cooking range, mother earth for a hearth, and the winds of Heaven for a chimney."

On her return to Washington, Barton was called to serve at Lincoln Hospital. As she entered one ward, seventy men—each of whom had received her care—rose to salute her.

During the war there were organizations that were doing the same kind of work as Clara Barton. The Women's Central Association of Relief provided bandages and emergency supplies to the army. The United States Sanitary Commission provided doctors and nurses for army hospitals and gave aid on the battlefield. Dorothea Dix organized an army corps of nurses.

Clara Barton never became a part of those organizations, preferring to work alone. As the Sanitary Commission and Dix's army nurses became more organized and experienced, they were better able to do the work that Clara Barton had been doing. Thus Barton found that her services were needed less urgently. She spent much of 1863 inactive while she accompanied Union troops that held Charleston, South Carolina, under siege. "I fear I may be spending time to little purpose," she wrote in her diary. "No one really needs me here." By 1864 she was back in Washington with nothing to do. Barton became so depressed that she even thought of suicide: "I cannot raise my spirits," she wrote in her diary. "The old temptation to go from all the world. I think I will come to that someday. . . . I want to leave all."

Late in the spring of 1864, however, General Grant began the bloody Wilderness campaign (see page 476). Clara Barton resumed the familiar work of nursing and feeding the wounded, which restored purpose to her life. Then in June, General Benjamin Butler appointed her to head the Department of Nurses for his army in Virginia.

During the war, Barton received many inquiries about missing soldiers from worried families who knew of her work in the field. Indeed, more than half the Union dead were still not identified by war's end. In the final months of the war, Barton won President Lincoln's support to set up an office to locate men missing in action. Between 1865 and 1868, she was able to identify more than 20,000 of the Union dead.

When the war ended, Clara Barton was acclaimed as one of the nation's heroes. She found herself in great demand as a public speaker. Though she confessed privately that speech making terrified her, she gave some three hundred lectures between 1866 and 1868.

Again, however, the old feelings of uselessness overtook her. In 1869 she suffered a breakdown, and her doctor ordered her to Europe for a complete rest. Clara Barton must surely have believed that she had reached the end of her useful existence.

In fact, still greater work lay ahead. While in Switzerland, Clara Barton learned about the International Committee of the Red Cross. It was a volunteer group that had been founded in 1863 to give aid to the sick and wounded of armies in time of war. Eleven countries had given their support to the Red Cross by signing the Treaty of Geneva (the Geneva Convention) in 1864. America was not one of them. But the idea excited Clara Barton, and she determined someday to set up the Red Cross in her own country. In the meantime, she returned to the battlefield service as part of the International Red Cross and helped the wounded in the Franco-Prussian War of 1870–1871.

Barton returned to the United States in 1873. Weakened by several more breakdowns during the next four years, she lived in semiretirement. By 1877, however, she was well enough again to begin her one-woman drive to have the United States join the International Red Cross. With her usual determination, she badgered government officials to win their support. She spoke to President Hayes and President Garfield about the Red Cross. To win public support, she wrote a pamphlet about it, adding a

An exhausted marathon runner is given assistance by the American Red Cross. Clara Barton helped found the American Red Cross in 1881 and served as its president until 1904.

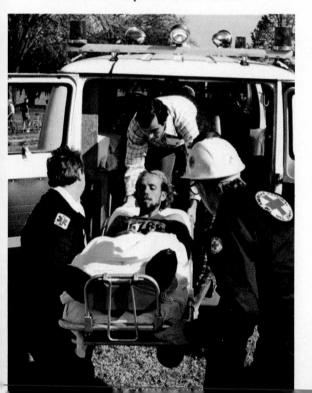

new emphasis on how the Red Cross could provide relief in times of flood, fire, epidemic, and other disasters. In 1881, she and a number of friends organized the American Association of the Red Cross. The next year, President Chester Arthur signed the Geneva Treaty, and the United States Senate ratified it. The United States became a part of the International Red Cross.

It was fitting that the first president of the American Red Cross should be Clara Barton. She remained the president until 1904, when she was eighty-two years old. During all those years, this remarkable woman led the Red Cross as it provided relief to victims of flood, hurricane, disease, and war. Even after her retirement, she remained active and alert until her death in 1912.

A lifelong feminist, Clara Barton was a friend of leaders of the women's movement, women such as Susan B. Anthony and Lucy Stone. She was a strong supporter of woman suffrage, and in her own careers in teaching and in the patent office, she had tried to open the way for women into jobs that had been closed to them. She was also a strong supporter of equal pay for equal work. However, it is for her humanitarian and patriotic work that Clara Barton is best remembered.

CHECKUP

1. Name three events from the life of Clara Barton that illustrate her "passion for service."
2. What events from the life of Barton show her interest in women's rights?
3. Trace the involvement of Barton with the International Red Cross and with the formation of the American Red Cross.

★ PHINEAS T. BARNUM ★

Showman for America

Phineas Taylor Barnum was born in Bethel, Connecticut, on the fifth of July, 1810. He missed the Fourth by only a few hours. That, Barnum always thought, was a pity. What would have been more fitting than for the greatest showman of the age to enter the world to the accompaniment of parades and fireworks?

Phineas was the oldest of five children of Irena Taylor and Philo Barnum. The boy was named for his mother's father, Phineas Taylor, a man Barnum remembered admiringly as one who "would go further, wait longer, [and] work harder" than anyone else to play a practical joke. His father, Philo, at one time or another worked at being a tailor, storeowner, tavernkeeper, and farmer but achieved little success at any of those jobs.

If there was anything that Phineas Barnum disliked more than the discipline of the local school, it was manual work on the farm. At twelve he managed to avoid both by becoming a clerk in a country store. At eighteen, with financial help from his grandfather, Phineas opened his own grocery store in Bethel. From that store, he also ran his own lottery, which was legal at that time. The next year he married a local tailor, Charity Hallett, with whom he eventually had three daughters.

The grocery business helped to shape Barnum's view of the world. His customers were hard bargainers. Rather than paying in cash, they often paid Barnum in goods they had made—hats,

cloth, and the like. "The customers cheated us in their fabrics," he recalled in his autobiography, "[and] we cheated the customers with our goods. Each party expected to be cheated, if it was possible." As it turned out, his customers got the better deal, leaving him with many unpaid bills. Then, too, Connecticut outlawed the lottery. P. T. Barnum sold the store and opened another in New York City in 1834.

The following year marked P. T. Barnum's entry into the business of entertainment. In Philadelphia a promoter was exhibiting to the paying public a slave woman who he claimed was 161 years old. She was billed to have been the nurse of George Washington. She was no such thing; but the woman, Joice Heth, was well coached and could answer all kinds of questions about "dear little George." The promoter even had a phony bill of sale from Washington's father dated 1727. On learning that the promoter was willing to sell his property, Barnum sold his store and bought Joice Heth.

Barnum arranged to exhibit Joice Heth in New York. First he flooded the city with handbills and posters, which advertised "the most astonishing and interesting curiosity in the world." He also played upon the patriotic appeal of George Washington's name. The advertisements created great interest, and the exhibition opened to a large crowd. Barnum kept the crowds coming by getting newspaper editors, who should have

known better, to write seriously about the exhibit. A profitable tour of New England followed. To keep Joice Heth's name before the public, Barnum created controversy. Using a false name, he wrote letters to the newspapers charging that Joice Heth was really made of rubber and springs and run by a ventriloquist. Then the papers published his own strong denial.

Thus early in his career Barnum was getting the public's attention by using ideas and tricks that in time he developed into a fine art. First he would announce a great discovery and make up wild stories about it. Then while keeping up the flow of news and information, Barnum would encourage controversy and doubt to hold the public's attention.

All too soon for Barnum, Joice Heth died. An autopsy showed her to have been only about eighty. Newspapers blamed Barnum for "humbugging," or tricking, the public. Barnum denied knowing the truth about Joice Heth, and he never admitted any wrong. In later years, however, he did say that the Joice Heth episode was the "least deserving of all my efforts in the show line. . . ."

There followed a short time with a traveling circus. Next he took a two-year tour of the South with his Grand Scientific and Musical Theater—which included a juggler, magician, clown, and song-and-dance man. Tired of moving around, Barnum returned to New York in 1838. Another business turned sour when Barnum's partner fled the country, leaving a pile of debts. Still another business proved more successful. But Barnum saw little of the profits because

he was again swindled—this time by his salesmen.

P. T. Barnum's great opportunity came in 1841 when Scudder's American Museum in New York City went up for sale. In nineteenth-century America, museums were places of amusement rather than institutions of science, art, and learning. Relics and curiosities were shown to the paying public, and a variety of entertainment was presented in "lecture rooms." Barnum borrowed the money to buy Scudder's. He renamed it Barnum's American Museum and began a search for performers and oddities that would lure people into his building. As he later recalled, he found "industrious fleas, jugglers, . . . gypsies, fat boys, giants, dwarfs, rope-dancers." Some of his displays were genuine fossils and animals—things that might be seen in a museum of natural history today. But Barnum could not resist a hoax. He exhibited a wooden leg that he claimed had been left on a battlefield by Santa Anna. Barnum also showed a horse with hair like sheep's wool and "the greatest Curiosity in the world"—the Feejee Mermaid, half fish and half monkey. All these he advertised with great exaggeration, false claims, and misleading illustrations.

Barnum's deceptions enraged the newspaper editors he regularly fooled but apparently not the public, who seemed to accept them as part of the entertainment. In fact, Barnum once said, "The bigger the humbug, the better people will like it." Indeed, figuring out the deception seemed to be half the fun, a fact that Barnum later turned to profit. He lectured frequently on the art of humbug. An employee said, "First he humbugs them, and then they pay to hear him tell how he did it."

Barnum's greatest spectacle was Charles S. Stratton of Bridgeport, Connecticut. When Stratton came to Barnum's attention, he was a five-year-old who stood only two feet one inch (63.5 cm) tall and weighed fifteen pounds (6.8 kg). Barnum nicknamed him General Tom Thumb, outfitted him with the uniforms of kings and generals, and taught him routines and jokes. Under the guidance of the great showman, Tom Thumb became an immediate sensation. He had a talent for impersonation, song and dance, and was intelligent and witty as well. Huge crowds came to see him at Barnum's Museum. Ten thousand showed up at the dock to see him off on a tour of Europe. In Europe, Barnum shrewdly arranged for a visit with the king or queen of each country, knowing that the publicity would bring out the crowds. At six, Tom Thumb was world famous. During his lifetime of fifty years, he and his family became rich.

Even as the American nation became divided over slavery and moved toward war, Barnum was able to delight the public more than ever. In 1850 he gave Americans the most exciting cultural event of the age. From Sweden he brought Jenny Lind, the world's most famous singer. For six months before her arrival, he ran a publicity campaign the like of which had never been seen. Lind gave a hundred concerts during her nationwide tour. Hundreds of thousands of Americans heard a great musical artist for the first time. The tour made Jenny Lind and P.T. Barnum rich.

Strangely enough, P. T. Barnum seemed unable to hold on to his prosper-ity. In the early 1850s he bought land in East Bridgeport, Connecticut. He planned to build an ideal community of homes and industries. As part of this plan, he invested in a clock manufacturing company. Within a few years, his associates walked away from the company, leaving him with debts of half a million dollars. For the third time, the man who had built a career on the gullibility of others had himself been "taken" in a business deal. This time he was financially ruined.

To recoup his fortune, Barnum took Tom Thumb on another tour of Europe. He also earned money by lecturing on the art of money making, though he said privately that he was better able to speak about money losing. Nevertheless, by 1860 he had paid off all of his debts. His return to active management of Barnum's American Museum was heralded

Jumbo, the largest elephant in captivity, was one of Barnum's most popular attractions.

by a great parade of animals and brass bands through the streets of New York—all arranged by P. T. Barnum.

Barnum's American Museum was by now a greater attraction than ever. Even England's Prince of Wales visited it on a tour of the United States. In 1865 the museum and most of the exhibits were destroyed by fire. Barnum opened a new museum in four months. When that museum burned in 1868, Barnum left the museum stage of his career.

"Like a good trouper," writes one of Barnum's biographers, "Barnum saved his best act for last"—the circus. In 1870, while America was recovering from war, a circus operator persuaded Barnum to join in organizing a great circus. Barnum agreed to lend his name and touch of magic, and soon P. T. Barnum's Museum, Menagerie, and Circus was playing to huge crowds in many American cities. This was followed a few years later by P. T. Barnum's Great Travelling World's Fair. Barnum billed this show the way he was to bill all of his later circuses, as "The Greatest Show on Earth." Barnum was now depending less on humbug and more on spectacle. There were other circuses in America, but Barnum's shows outdid them all with dazzling color, music, thrills, animals, and performers. Each year's show was more spectacular than the last.

In 1880, Barnum entered into a partnership with a competitor named James Bailey, forming Barnum and Bailey. Then in his seventies, Barnum left most of the management of the circus to others. He did, however, keep a hand in the publicity. Who but Barnum would have advertised that after seeing his circus, "There Is Nothing Left to See"? He also continued to acquire new attractions, the most famous of them being Jumbo, the largest elephant in captivity. In 1890 he made a final trip to Europe when his circus went on tour there. His health failed rapidly after that, and he died in 1891.

So fascinating was Barnum the showman that the serious side of the man was often overlooked. He was deeply religious and always insisted that his entertainments be moral and appropriate for families. At thirty-seven he became interested in the temperance movement. For the rest of his life he lectured on temperance reform wherever he could, including at his museum and his circus. He served two terms in the Connecticut legislature in the 1860s and strongly supported black suffrage in that state. He did much for the civic improvement of his adopted city of Bridgeport, and he served as its mayor for one year.

It is for his contribution to the amusement of Americans that Phineas Taylor Barnum is rightly remembered. Barnum was, without a doubt, the greatest showman of the age. He also gave to America a form of entertainment that is still very much alive.

CHECKUP

1. List the different kinds of entertainment P. T. Barnum offered the American public during his lifetime. What were his other interests and activities?
2. Explain the different ways used by Barnum to attract people to his shows, museums, and circuses. Give examples of as many ways as possible.
3. How does Barnum's life reflect his drive to succeed in show business?

1831	Nat Turner slave uprising
1846	Wilmot Proviso
1850	Compromise of 1850
1852	Uncle Tom's Cabin
1854	Kansas-Nebraska Act
1857	Dred Scott decision
1858	Lincoln-Douglas debates
1859	John Brown at Harpers Ferry
1860	Lincoln elected President
1861	Confederate States of America formed
1863	Civil War
1865	Emancipation Proclamation
1865	Lincoln assassinated
	Thirteenth Amendment
1868	Johnson impeachment trial
	Fourteenth Amendment
1870	Fifteenth Amendment
1877	Reconstruction ends

The invention of the cotton gin brought about the expansion of cotton-growing lands and increased the demand for field laborers, thus fastening slavery on the South. Yet many people—both black and white—opposed slavery and sought to abolish it. The spread of slavery into the Western territories became a major issue in national politics. Compromises in 1820 and 1850 kept a shaky balance in Congress between free and slave states. Events during the 1850s brought the issue to a head. They included the publication of *Uncle Tom's Cabin*, the formation of the antislavery Republican party, the Kansas-Nebraska Act, the Dred Scott case, and John Brown's raid on Harpers Ferry.

Soon after Abraham Lincoln, a Republican, was elected President in 1860, the Confederate States of America was formed in the South. The Civil War started in 1861 as the North sought to restore the Union. After four years of destructive conflict, the war ended in 1865 with the North victorious. The slaves became free, gaining the rights and privileges of all other American citizens.

Following Lincoln's assassination, the Radical Republicans in Congress directed the Reconstruction of the South. They tried to remove President Andrew Johnson from office but failed. Reconstruction lasted from about 1867 to 1877. It restored the Southern states to the Union but failed to assure the freed slaves of a position of equality in American society. From the 1870s onward, many of the freed slaves' rights as citizens were taken from them.

535

Skills Development: Reading a Map

Blacks and many white people who opposed slavery established a system of secret escape routes known as the Underground Railroad. People on the Underground Railroad used railroad language in the hope that they would not be found out. A "station" might be a house, a store, or a barn, where friendly people gave runaway slaves food and a place to rest. "Passengers" were the slaves themselves. They traveled mostly at night, going from station to station in secret, and led by a "conductor"—an abolitionist who knew the way. Canada was often the final destination for many escaping slaves.

As you study the map and answer the questions, try to imagine what it might have been like to be part of the Underground Railroad.

1. What does each dot on the map represent?

2. In what direction were runaway slaves traveling on the Underground Railroad?

3. As shown on this map, what is the most southern station? the most northern station?

4. Which station was located on the southwestern shore of Lake Michigan?

5. What bodies of water were routes on the Underground Railroad?

6. Trace the route an escaping slave would follow from: (a) Norfolk, Virginia to Montreal, Canada; (b) Davenport, Iowa to Chatham, Canada.

7. Using the scale of miles/kilometers, measure the distance from: (a) Chester, Illinois to Chicago, Illinois; (b) Fitchburg, Massachusetts to Montreal.

8. If the runaway slave could travel an average of 19 kilometers a day, approximately how many days would it take him or her to go from Philadelphia to Oswego, New York?

9. Why would a runaway slave be likely to head for the Ohio River?

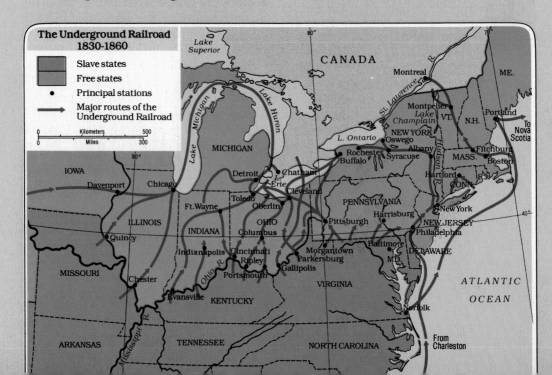

The Underground Railroad 1830–1860
- Slave states
- Free states
- Principal stations
- Major routes of the Underground Railroad

The Great Divide

THE CIVIL WAR and the Reconstruction period mark a great divide in the history of the United States. In the 270 years since the founding of the tiny settlement at Jamestown, a new people had arisen and the foundation for their nation's greatness had been laid. During that time also, distinctive American values had evolved—values such as the beliefs in opportunity, progress, liberty, and limited government.

Now, with its greatest crisis behind it, the nation would undergo important changes. The settlement of the West, hardly slowed by the Civil War, would proceed at a breathtaking pace. Dazzled by prospects of wealth in the vast area gained from France in 1803 and from Mexico in 1848, Americans would devour the West before 1900. In the name of progress, they would exploit its resources without much thought for the future. As they did, they would ruthlessly smash the Indian civilization that stood in their way.

The United States would also rapidly change from a farming nation to an industrial one. By the 1820s the Industrial Revolution in America had begun with the development of small factories in New England (see pages 359–360). It gradually spread through the Northeast and West over the next thirty years. At the start of the Civil War, the United States was still mainly a farming country, but industrial development was poised at a takeoff point. And take off it did. The last part of the nineteenth century in the United States would witness the most rapid industrial expansion in world history. Equating material abundance with progress, Americans would stun the world with the huge production of goods from their factories and mines. By the end of the nineteenth century, the United States would rank as the industrial leader of the world. It would maintain that position into the 1980s.

While America was becoming an industrial giant, it was also changing from a rural nation to an urban one. At the time of the Constitutional Convention in 1787, about 90 percent of the

American population lived in rural areas. There were then hardly five cities worthy of the name in the entire country. During the first half of the nineteenth century, however, canals, steamboats, and railroads, along with heavy immigration, helped to create many new cities and to enlarge older ones. By the time of the Civil War, America had its first city of one million—New York—and 16 percent of America's people lived in urban areas. Over the next forty years, older cities would expand rapidly and new ones would mushroom everywhere but in the South. A milestone would be passed in 1920. In that year the census would report that more people were living in cities than in rural areas. Today we are a nation of city dwellers, with some 80 percent of all Americans living in urban areas.

Still another development would be the increased involvement of the United States in world affairs. In its first hundred years America was barely concerned with events beyond its own borders. But by the arrival of the twentieth century, the country would acquire possessions far from its shores. In the new century the United States would emerge as one of the superpowers of the world.

Although much about the United States would change, much also would remain the same. America began as a nation of people of many origins and backgrounds, and so it would remain. Immigrants by the millions would continue to come to its shores from every part of the world. Americans would also remain a people on the move. Great shifts of population—to the South and Southwest as well as to the West, and from farm to city—would continue. And Americans would continue to believe in the values they had fixed early in their history. If it was true, as some critics noted, that America did not present opportunity equally to all, it was also true that the United States would offer more opportunity for equality to a far larger part of its population than any other nation.

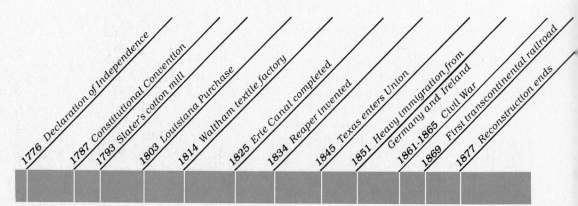

Unfinished business. On November 19, 1863, President Abraham Lincoln journeyed to Gettysburg, Pennsylvania, to dedicate a national cemetery on the site of the battle of Gettysburg. At the very beginning of his brief address, Lincoln stated what was at stake in the Civil War.

> Four score and seven years ago our fathers brought forth on this continent, a new nation, conceived in Liberty, and dedicated to the proposition that all men are created equal.
>
> Now we are engaged in a great civil war, testing whether that nation, or any nation so conceived and so dedicated, can long endure.

Could American democracy survive? Or was crusty John Adams a prophet when he wrote, many years before, "there never was a democracy yet that did not commit suicide"?

The end of the Civil War gave an affirmative answer to Lincoln's question. The nation did endure. The Union was preserved. "Government of the people, by the people, for the people" did "not perish from the earth."

Lincoln's Gettysburg Address had posed the great question of the nation's first century of life. In the next century and beyond, the changes that the United States would experience would raise a host of new questions and challenges. How would Americans adjust as their country changed from a farming to an industrial nation, from a rural society to an urban one? Could American liberties be preserved while the nation sought safety in a dangerous world? Would individualism be able to survive in a mass society? And perhaps most important, would America make good its promise of liberty and equality for all of its people? Those were some of the key questions that Americans of future generations would have to address.

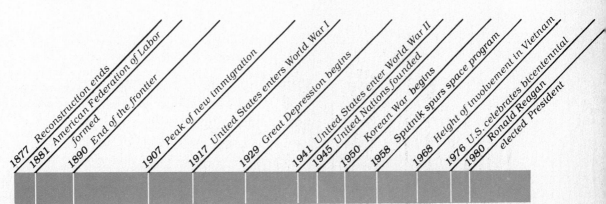

Directions

The North Pole is a very special place. It is the most northern place on the earth. North is the direction toward the North Pole.

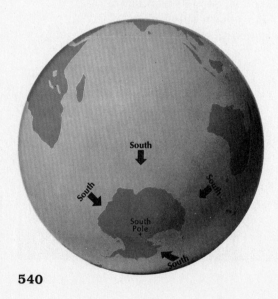

The South Pole is another very special place. It is the most southern place on the earth. South is the direction toward the South Pole. North and south are opposite each other.

North and south are directions. Two other directions are east and west. The sun seems to rise in the east and to set in the west. When you face north, east is to your right and west is to your left. East and west are opposite each other.

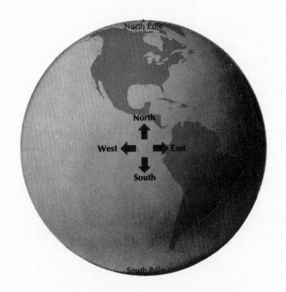

Directions help us to find places on maps and globes. Sometimes directions are shown by a small drawing on the map. This drawing is called a compass rose. Find the compass rose on this map.

In which direction would you travel to go from the state of Illinois to the state of Wisconsin? From Illinois to Indiana?

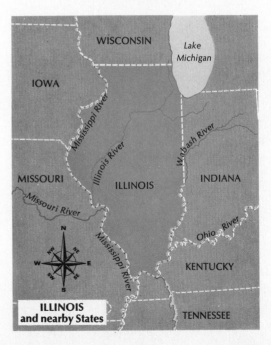

ILLINOIS
and nearby States

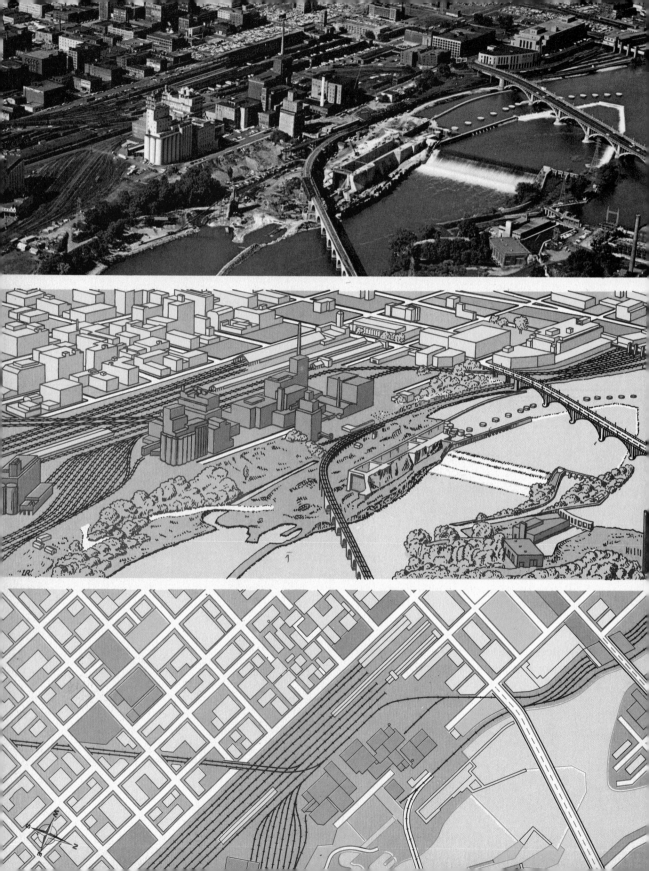

Symbols

At the top of the page is a photograph. It shows a part of Minneapolis, Minnesota. This photograph was taken from an airplane.

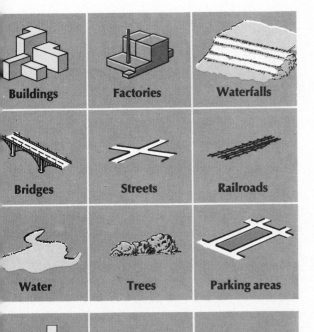

Buildings	**Factories**	**Waterfalls**
Bridges	**Streets**	**Railroads**
Water	**Trees**	**Parking areas**
Buildings	**Factories**	**Waterfalls**
Bridges	**Streets**	**Railroads**
Water	**Trees**	**Parking areas**

Under the photograph is a drawing of the same part of Minneapolis. This is a special kind of drawing. It uses symbols. The symbols stand for real things and places in Minneapolis. The key shows what real things and places the symbols stand for. What symbol is used for bridges?

The map at the bottom of the page shows the same part of Minneapolis that the photograph and the drawing show. This map, like the special drawing, has a key. The symbols in the map key are different from those in the drawing. But they, too, stand for real things and places. What symbol is used for bridges?

543

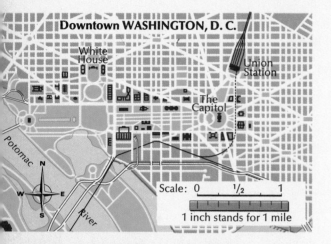

Downtown WASHINGTON, D. C.

Scale: 0   1/2   1
1 inch stands for 1 mile

Scale

The places and distances shown on maps must be smaller than their real size on the earth. So a certain number of inches on a map are used to show a certain number of miles on the earth. This way of showing size or distance on a map is called scale.

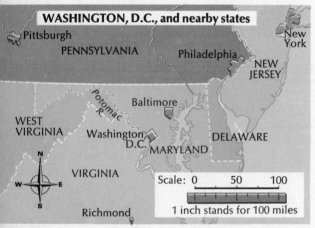

WASHINGTON, D.C., and nearby states

Scale: 0   50   100
1 inch stands for 100 miles

Each of these three maps has a different scale. The map at the top of the page has a scale of one inch to one mile. This means that a distance of one mile on the earth is shown on this map by a distance of one inch.

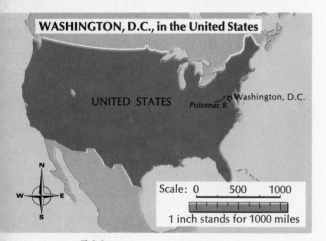

WASHINGTON, D.C., in the United States

Scale: 0   500   1000
1 inch stands for 1000 miles

What are the scales on the other two maps? Which is the best map to use if you are in Washington, D.C.?

544

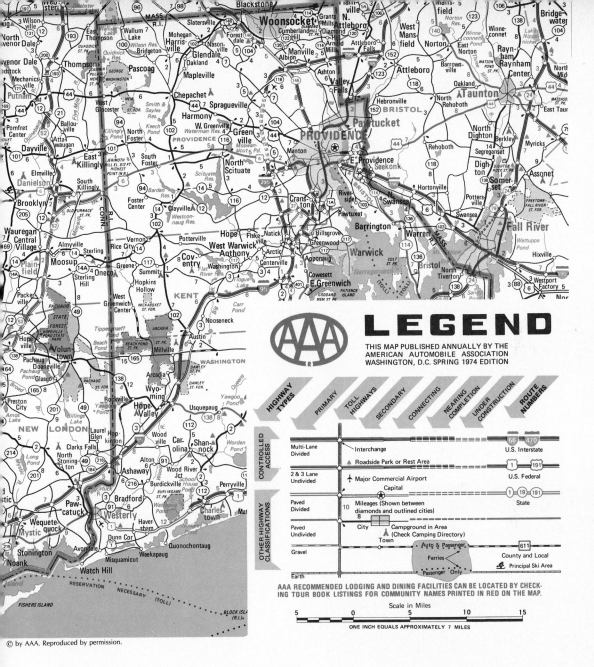

Road Map

What is the scale of miles on the road map shown above? Look at the key to this map. What symbol is used to show a state capital? What symbol is used to show a U.S. Interstate Highway?

What is the number of the route you would take if you were traveling from Fall River, Massachusetts, to Providence, Rhode Island? Why do people use road maps?

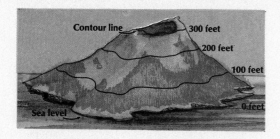

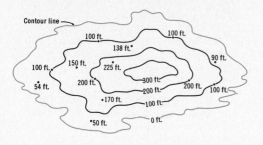

Contours

To measure your height, you would measure the distance from the bottom of your feet to the top of your head. The bottom of your feet would be your *base*. The earth's hills and mountains are also measured from base to top. The base for all the earth's hills and mountains is sea level. Find sea level (0 feet) on the drawing of the mountain. Distance above sea level is called elevation. The lines on the drawing are contour lines.

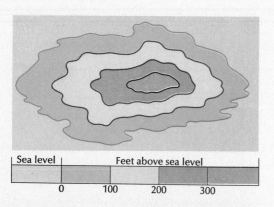

Contour lines are a good way to show elevation. All points along one contour line are the same distance above sea level. Find the 200-foot contour line on the drawing. Now find it on the contour map of the mountain. What is the highest contour line shown on the drawing? What is the highest contour line shown on the map?

Sometimes color is added between contour lines. What does the yellow color stand for? What is the elevation of the green part? Find the orange part. Can you find the same part on the drawing at the top of the page?

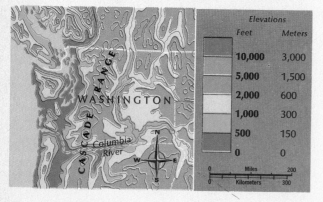

Elevation can be shown in this same way on maps of any part of the world. This is a map of part of the United States. What is the elevation of the land around the Columbia River? What is the elevation of the highest places in Washington?

Latitude and Longitude

The lines drawn on this map are called lines of latitude. The beginning line for measuring latitude is the equator. The equator is halfway between the two poles. Latitude lines extend east and west. They measure distance in degrees north and south of the equator.

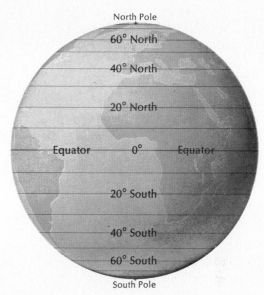

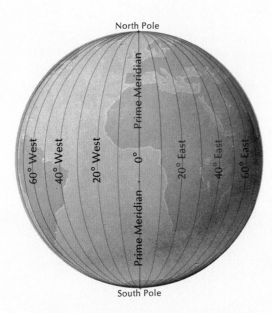

The lines drawn on this map are called lines of longitude, or meridians. The beginning line for measuring longitude is the prime meridian. Longitude lines extend north and south. They measure distance in degrees east and west of the prime meridian.

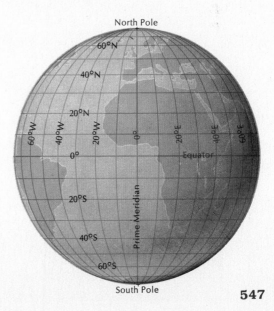

Latitude and longitude lines cross one another on maps and globes. If you know the longitude and latitude of a place, you can find it on a map or globe. Find the place where 20° south latitude and 20° west longitude cross. Find the place where 40° north latitude and 30° east longitude cross.

547

Atlas

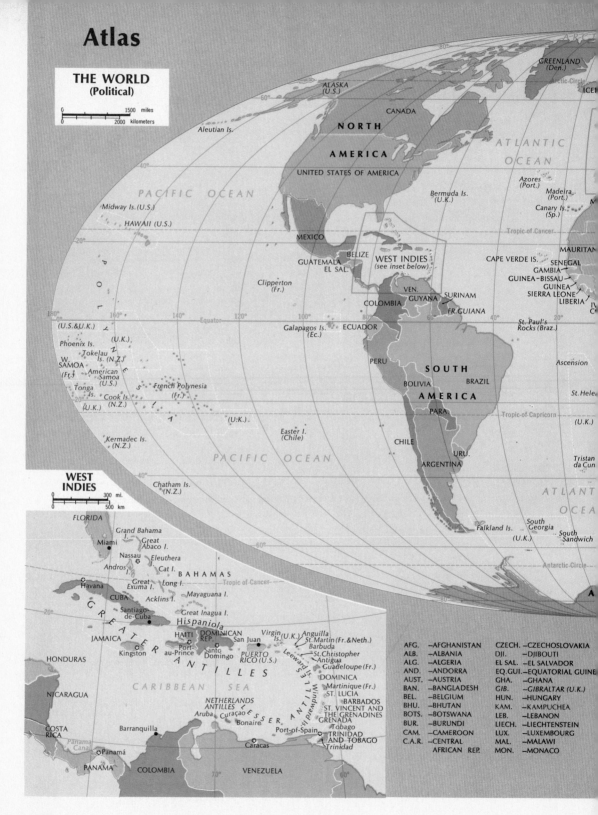

THE WORLD
(Political)

0 — 1500 miles
0 — 2000 kilometers

NORTH AMERICA

ALASKA (U.S.)

CANADA

GREENLAND (Den.)

Arctic Circle

ICEL

UNITED STATES OF AMERICA

ATLANTIC OCEAN

PACIFIC OCEAN

Aleutian Is.

Midway Is.(U.S.)

HAWAII (U.S.)

Azores (Port.)

Madeira (Port.)

Canary Is. (Sp.)

Tropic of Cancer

MEXICO

BELIZE

WEST INDIES (see inset below)

CAPE VERDE IS.

MAURITAN

SENEGAL

GAMBIA

GUINEA–BISSAU

GUINEA

SIERRA LEONE

LIBERIA

GUATEMALA
EL SAL.

Clipperton (Fr.)

VEN.

COLOMBIA

GUYANA

SURINAM

FR. GUIANA

St. Paul's Rocks (Braz.)

Galapagos Is. (Ec.)

ECUADOR

Equator

180° 160° 140° 120° 100° 80° 20°

(U.S.&U.K.)

(U.K.)

Phoenix Is.

Tokelau Is. (N.Z.)

W. SAMOA (Fr.)

American Samoa (U.S.)

Tonga Is.

Cook Is. (N.Z.)

(U.K.)

French Polynesia (Fr.)

(U.K.)

Kermadec Is. (N.Z.)

Easter I. (Chile)

PERU

BOLIVIA

BRAZIL

SOUTH AMERICA

PARA.

Ascension

St.Hele

PACIFIC OCEAN

Tropic of Capricorn

(U.K.)

Tristan da Cun

Chatham Is. (N.Z.)

40°

60°

80°

CHILE

URU.

ARGENTINA

ATLANT OCEA

A

Falkland Is. (U.K.)

South Georgia

South Sandwich

Antarctic Circle

WEST INDIES

0 — 300 mi.
0 — 500 km

FLORIDA

Miami

Grand Bahama I.

Great Abaco I.

Nassau

Eleuthera I.

Andros I.

Cat I.

BAHAMAS

Havana

CUBA

Santiago-de-Cuba

Great Exuma I.

Long I.

Acklins I.

Mayaguana I.

Tropic of Cancer

JAMAICA

Kingston

HAITI

Port-au-Prince

Great Inagua I.

Hispaniola

DOMINICAN REP.

Santo Domingo

San Juan

PUERTO RICO (U.S.)

Virgin Is.

(U.K.)

Anguilla

St.Martin (Fr.&Neth.)

Barbuda

Antigua

St.Christopher

Guadeloupe (Fr.)

DOMINICA

Martinique (Fr.)

ST. LUCIA

BARBADOS

ST. VINCENT AND THE GRENADINES

GRENADA

Leeward Is.

Windward Is.

GREATER ANTILLES

LESSER ANTILLES

HONDURAS

NICARAGUA

COSTA RICA

Panama Canal

Panamá

PANAMA

CARIBBEAN SEA

NETHERLANDS ANTILLES

Aruba Curaçao Bonaire

Barranquilla

COLOMBIA

Caracas

VENEZUELA

Port-of-Spain

Tobago

TRINIDAD AND TOBAGO

Trinidad

20°

60°

70°

60°

AFG.	—AFGHANISTAN	CZECH.	—CZECHOSLOVAKIA
ALB.	—ALBANIA	DJI.	—DJIBOUTI
ALG.	—ALGERIA	EL SAL.	—EL SALVADOR
AND.	—ANDORRA	EQ.GUI.	—EQUATORIAL GUINE
AUST.	—AUSTRIA	GHA.	—GHANA
BAN.	—BANGLADESH	GIB.	—GIBRALTAR (U.K.)
BEL.	—BELGIUM	HUN.	—HUNGARY
BHU.	—BHUTAN	KAM.	—KAMPUCHEA
BOTS.	—BOTSWANA	LEB.	—LEBANON
BUR.	—BURUNDI	LIECH.	—LIECHTENSTEIN
CAM.	—CAMEROON	LUX.	—LUXEMBOURG
C.A.R.	—CENTRAL AFRICAN REP.	MAL.	—MALAWI
		MON.	—MONACO

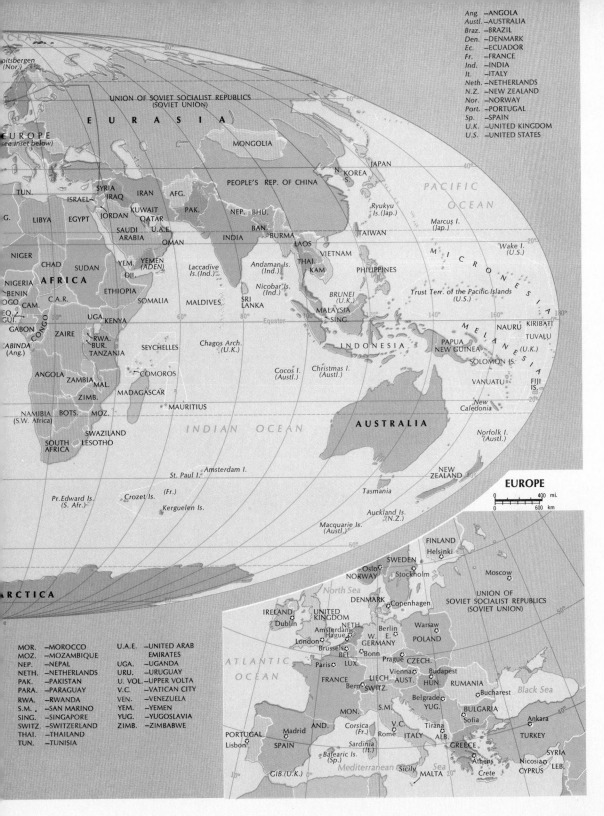

Ang. —ANGOLA
Austl. —AUSTRALIA
Braz. —BRAZIL
Den. —DENMARK
Ec. —ECUADOR
Fr. —FRANCE
Ind. —INDIA
It. —ITALY
Neth. —NETHERLANDS
N.Z. —NEW ZEALAND
Nor. —NORWAY
Port. —PORTUGAL
Sp. —SPAIN
U.K. —UNITED KINGDOM
U.S. —UNITED STATES

MOR. —MOROCCO
MOZ. —MOZAMBIQUE
NEP. —NEPAL
NETH. —NETHERLANDS
PAK. —PAKISTAN
PARA. —PARAGUAY
RWA. —RWANDA
S.M. —SAN MARINO
SING. —SINGAPORE
SWITZ. —SWITZERLAND
THAI. —THAILAND
TUN. —TUNISIA

U.A.E. —UNITED ARAB
EMIRATES
UGA. —UGANDA
URU. —URUGUAY
U. VOL. —UPPER VOLTA
V.C. —VATICAN CITY
VEN. —VENEZUELA
YEM. —YEMEN
YUG. —YUGOSLAVIA
ZIMB. —ZIMBABWE

EUROPE
0   400 mi.
0   600 km

Vancouver
C. Flattery
Olympia · Seattle WASHINGTON
Mt. Rainier 14,410 ft.
Spokane
Portland
Columbia R.
Salem
Eugene
OREGON
C. Blanco
Boise
IDAHO
Idaho Falls
Snake R.
C. Mendocino
Reno
Carson City
Humboldt R.
Great Salt Lake
Ogden
Salt Lake City
Sacramento
Berkeley
Oakland
San Francisco
San Jose
NEVADA
UTAH
Fresno
Mt. Whitney 14,495 ft.
Pt. Conception
Bakersfield
Mojave Desert
Glendale
Pasadena
Los Angeles
San Bernardino
Riverside
Long Beach
Santa Ana
San Diego

ROCKY
Great Falls
Missouri R.
Helena
MONTANA
Billings
Yellowstone R.
Grand Teton 13,766 ft.
WYOMING
Green R.
NORTH DAKOTA
Bismarck
Fargo
BLACK HILLS
Pierre
SOUTH DAKOTA
Sioux Falls
Sioux City
Cheyenne
N. Platte R.
NEBRASKA
Omaha
Longs Pk. 14,256 ft.
Denver
COLORADO
Pikes Pk. 14,110 ft.
S. Platte R.
Platte R.
Lincoln
Pueblo
Blanca Pk. 14,310 ft.
Arkansas R.
KANSAS
Topeka
Wichita
ARIZONA
NEW MEXICO
Santa Fe
Albuquerque
Amarillo
OKLAHOMA
Oklahoma City
Tulsa
Phoenix
Tucson
Rio Grande
Lubbock
Llano Estacado
Fort Worth
Dallas
Red R.
TEXAS
Waco
Brazos R.
El Paso
Austin
San Antonio
Houston
Rio Grande
Laredo
Corpus Christi

PACIFIC OCEAN

GREAT PLAINS

CANADA
MEXICO
Coastal
West longitud

ASIA
SOVIET UNION
Arctic Circle
Barrow
BROOKS RANGE
Bering Strait
Nome
St. Lawrence I.
St. Matthew I.
ALASKA
Yukon R.
Fairbanks
CANADA
Monday International Date Line Sunday
Nunivak I.
ALASKA RANGE
Mt. McKinley (Mt. Denali) 20,320 ft.
BERING SEA
Kenai Pen.
Juneau
ALEUTIAN ISLANDS
Near Is.
Rat Is.
Andreanof Is.
Fox Is.
Unimak I.
Kodiak I.
Gulf of Alaska
Alexander Arch.

0   300 mi.
0   500 km

UNITED STATES
OF AMERICA
(Physical-Political)

CONN.	—CONNECTICUT
D.C.	—DISTRICT OF COLUMBIA
MASS.	—MASSACHUSETTS
MD.	—MARYLAND
N.H.	—NEW HAMPSHIRE
R.I.	—RHODE ISLAND
VT.	—VERMONT
W.VA.	—WEST VIRGINIA

C.	—Cape
Mt.	—Mountain
Pen.	—Peninsula
Pk.	—Peak

— International boundaries
--- State boundaries
✪ National capitals
★ State capitals
● Other cities

Elevations

Feet		Meters
10,000		3,000
5,000		1,500
2,000		600
1,000		300
0		0

Miles 300
Kilometers 500

HAWAII

Same scale
as main map

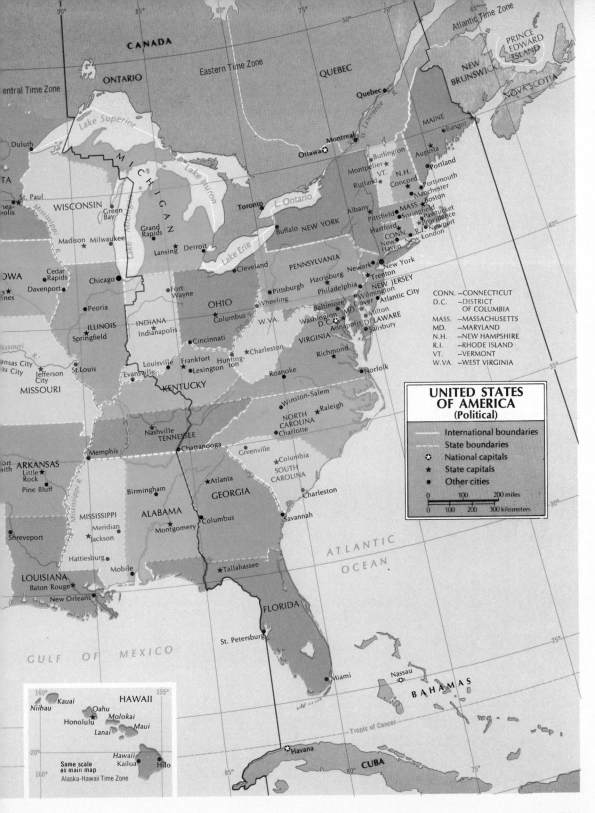

UNITED STATES
OF AMERICA
(Political)

International boundaries
State boundaries
National capitals
State capitals
Other cities

0   100   200 miles
0   100   200   300 kilometers

CONN. —CONNECTICUT
D.C. —DISTRICT
         OF COLUMBIA
MASS. —MASSACHUSETTS
MD.   —MARYLAND
N.H. —NEW HAMPSHIRE
R.I.   —RHODE ISLAND
VT.   —VERMONT
W.VA. —WEST VIRGINIA

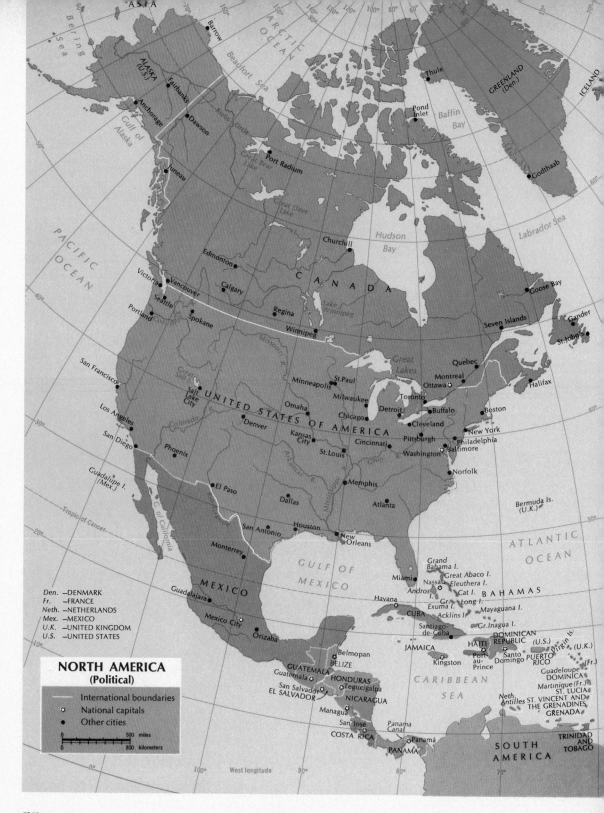

NORTH AMERICA
(Political)

——— International boundaries
✪ National capitals
• Other cities

0 ——— 500 miles
0 ——— 800 kilometers

Den. —DENMARK
Fr. —FRANCE
Neth. —NETHERLANDS
Mex. —MEXICO
U.K. —UNITED KINGDOM
U.S. —UNITED STATES

554

Barranquilla
Cartagena
Maracaibo
Valencia
Barquisimeto
Caracas
Cúcuta
San Cristóbal
Port-of-Spain
TRINIDAD AND TOBAGO
Orinoco R.

VENEZUELA

Medellín
Bucaramanga
Bogotá

COLOMBIA

Cali

Quito

ECUADOR

Guayaquil

alpelo I.
(Col.)

GUYANA

Georgetown

Paramaribo

SURINAME

Cayenne

FRENCH
GUIANA
(Fr.)

Col. —COLOMBIA
Fr. —FRANCE
U.K. —UNITED KINGDOM

Equator

Manaus

Amazon R.

Belém

São Luis

Fortaleza

Iquitos

Trujillo

PERU

Recife

Maceió

Callao
Lima

Cuzco

BRAZIL

Arequipa

Lake
Titicaca

La Paz

BOLIVIA

Sucre

Brasília
(Federal
District)

Salvador

PACIFIC

OCEAN

Chuquicamata

Belo
Horizonte

Antofagasta

PARAGUAY

Rio de Janeiro

São Paulo

Niterói

Santos

Tropic of Capricorn

San Félix I.
(Chile)

San Ambrosio I.
(Chile)

Tucumán

Asunción

Curitiba

Paraná R.

CHILE

Córdoba

Santa
Fe
Paraná

Pôrto Alegre

Valparaíso
Santiago

Rosario

URUGUAY

Juan Fernández Is.
(Chile)

Buenos Aires
La Plata

Montevideo

Río de la Plata

ATLANTIC

OCEAN

Concepción

ARGENTINA

Mar del Plata

Bahía Blanca

SOUTH AMERICA
(Political)

International boundaries
National capitals
Other cities

Falkland Is.
(U.K.)

Punta Arenas

Strait of
Magellan

West longitude

500 miles
800 kilometers

555

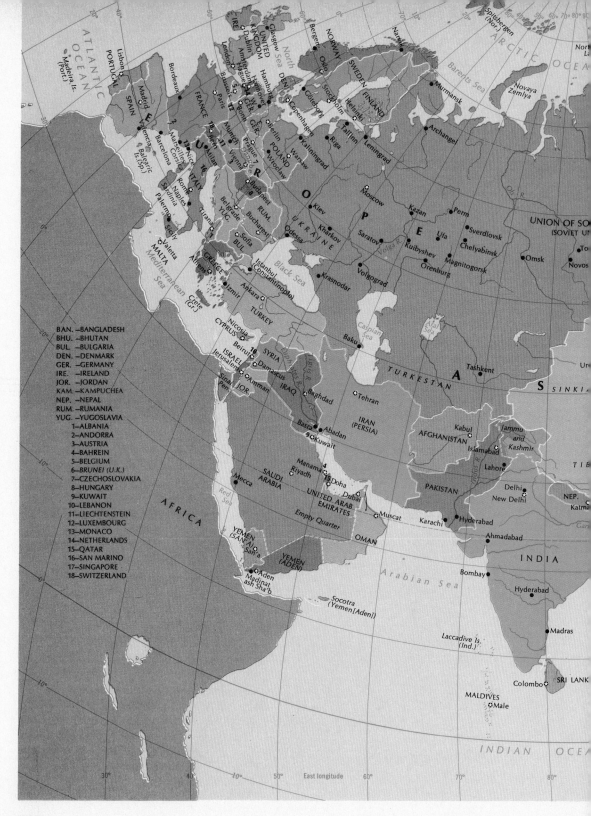

BAN. —BANGLADESH
BHU. —BHUTAN
BUL. —BULGARIA
DEN. —DENMARK
GER. —GERMANY
IRE. —IRELAND
JOR. —JORDAN
KAM. —KAMPUCHEA
NEP. —NEPAL
RUM. —RUMANIA
YUG. —YUGOSLAVIA
1—ALBANIA
2—ANDORRA
3—AUSTRIA
4—BAHREIN
5—BELGIUM
6—BRUNEI (U.K.)
7—CZECHOSLOVAKIA
8—HUNGARY
9—KUWAIT
10—LEBANON
11—LIECHTENSTEIN
12—LUXEMBOURG
13—MONACO
14—NETHERLANDS
15—QATAR
16—SAN MARINO
17—SINGAPORE
18—SWITZERLAND

Gr. —GREECE
Ind. —INDIA
Indo. —INDONESIA
Jap. —JAPANESE
Nor. —NORWAY
Pen. —Peninsula
Port. —PORTUGAL
TERR. —TERRITORY
Trust. —Trusteeship
U.K. —UNITED KINGDOM
U.S. —UNITED STATES
U.S.S.R.—SOVIET UNION

EURASIA (Political)

——— International boundaries
- - - - Indefinite or temporary
boundaries
✪ National capitals
● Other cities

0   800 mi.
0   1200 km

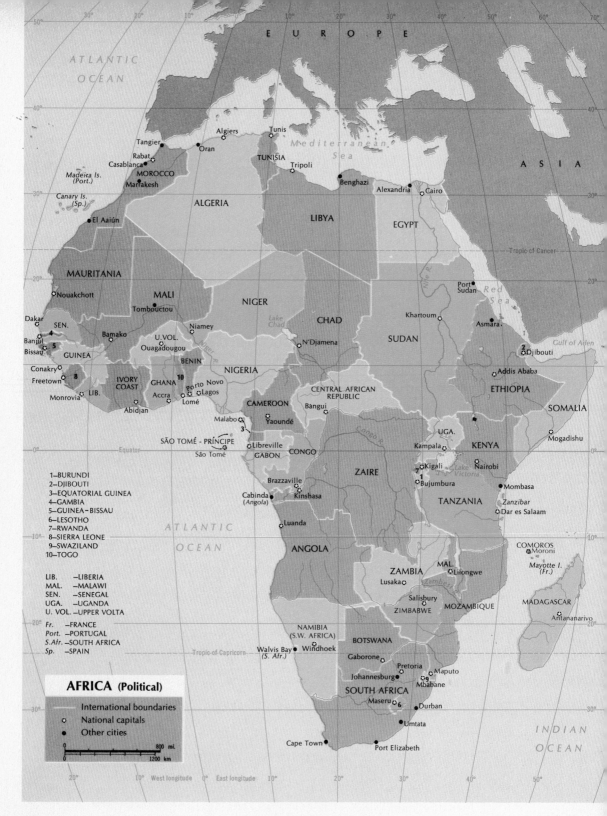

AFRICA (Political)

— International boundaries
☼ National capitals
● Other cities

| 1—BURUNDI |
| 2—DJIBOUTI |
| 3—EQUATORIAL GUINEA |
| 4—GAMBIA |
| 5—GUINEA-BISSAU |
| 6—LESOTHO |
| 7—RWANDA |
| 8—SIERRA LEONE |
| 9—SWAZILAND |
| 10—TOGO |

LIB.	—LIBERIA
MAL.	—MALAWI
SEN.	—SENEGAL
UGA.	—UGANDA
U. VOL.	—UPPER VOLTA

Fr.	—FRANCE
Port.	—PORTUGAL
S.Afr.	—SOUTH AFRICA
Sp.	—SPAIN

0   800 mi.
0   1200 km

PRESIDENTS AND VICE PRESIDENTS OF THE UNITED STATES

President	Birth-Death	State*	Term	Party	Vice President
George Washington	1732–1799	Va.	1789–1797	None	John Adams
John Adams	1735–1826	Mass.	1797–1801	Federalist	Thomas Jefferson
Thomas Jefferson	1743–1826	Va.	1801–1805	Democratic-	Aaron Burr
			1805–1809	Republican	George Clinton
James Madison	1751–1836	Va.	1809–1813	Democratic-	George Clinton
			1813–1817	Republican	Elbridge Gerry
James Monroe	1758–1831	Va.	1817–1825	Democratic-	Daniel D. Tompkins
				Republican	
John Quincy Adams	1767–1848	Mass.	1825–1829	National	John C. Calhoun
				Republican	
Andrew Jackson	1767–1845	Tenn.	1829–1833	Democratic	John C. Calhoun
			1833–1837		Martin Van Buren
Martin Van Buren	1782–1862	N.Y.	1837–1841	Democratic	Richard M. Johnson
William H. Harrison	1773–1841	Ohio	1841	Whig	John Tyler
John Tyler	1790–1862	Va.	1841–1845	Whig	. . . .
James K. Polk	1795–1849	Tenn.	1845–1849	Democratic	George M. Dallas
Zachary Taylor	1784–1850	La.	1849–1850	Whig	Millard Fillmore
Millard Fillmore	1800–1874	N.Y.	1850–1853	Whig	. . . .
Franklin Pierce	1804–1869	N.H.	1853–1857	Democratic	William R. King
James Buchanan	1791–1868	Pa.	1857–1861	Democratic	John C. Breckinridge
Abraham Lincoln	1809–1865	Ill.	1861–1865	Republican	Hannibal Hamlin
			1865		Andrew Johnson
Andrew Johnson	1808–1875	Tenn.	1865–1869	Democratic	. . . .
Ulysses S. Grant	1822–1885	Ill.	1869–1873	Republican	Schuyler Colfax
			1873–1877		Henry Wilson
Rutherford B. Hayes	1822–1893	Ohio	1877–1881	Republican	William A. Wheeler
James A. Garfield	1831–1881	Ohio	1881	Republican	Chester A. Arthur
Chester A. Arthur	1830–1886	N.Y.	1881–1885	Republican	. . . .
Grover Cleveland	1837–1908	N.Y.	1885–1889	Democratic	Thomas A. Hendricks
Benjamin Harrison	1833–1901	Ind.	1889–1893	Republican	Levi P. Morton
Grover Cleveland	1837–1908	N.Y.	1893–1897	Democratic	Adlai E. Stevenson
William McKinley	1843–1901	Ohio	1897–1901	Republican	Garret A. Hobart
			1901		Theodore Roosevelt
Theodore Roosevelt	1858–1919	N.Y.	1901–1905	Republican	
			1905–1909		Charles W. Fairbanks
William H. Taft	1857–1930	Ohio	1909–1913	Republican	James S. Sherman
Woodrow Wilson	1856–1924	N.J.	1913–1921	Democratic	Thomas R. Marshall
Warren G. Harding	1865–1923	Ohio	1921–1923	Republican	Calvin Coolidge
Calvin Coolidge	1872–1933	Mass.	1923–1925	Republican	. . . .
			1925–1929		Charles G. Dawes
Herbert C. Hoover	1874–1964	Calif.	1929–1933	Republican	Charles Curtis
Franklin D. Roosevelt	1882–1945	N.Y.	1933–1941	Democratic	John N. Garner
			1941–1945		Henry A. Wallace
			1945		Harry S. Truman
Harry S. Truman	1884–1972	Mo.	1945–1949	Democratic	. . . .
			1949–1953		Alben W. Barkley
Dwight D. Eisenhower	1890–1969	N.Y.	1953–1961	Republican	Richard M. Nixon
John F. Kennedy	1917–1963	Mass.	1961–1963	Democratic	Lyndon B. Johnson
Lyndon B. Johnson	1908–1973	Texas	1963–1965	Democratic	. . . .
			1965–1969		Hubert H. Humphrey
Richard M. Nixon	1913–	N.Y.	1969–1973	Republican	Spiro T. Agnew
			1973–1974		Agnew/Ford
Gerald R. Ford	1913–	Mich.	1974–1977	Republican	Nelson R. Rockefeller
James Earl Carter	1924–	Ga.	1977–1981	Democratic	Walter Mondale
Ronald Reagan	1911–	Calif.	1981–	Republican	George Bush

*State of residence at election

FACTS ABOUT THE STATES

State	Year and Order of Admission*	Area (sq. mi.) and Rank	Population (1980) and Rank	Represen-tatives	Capital City
Alabama	1819 (22)	51,609 (29)	3,890,061 (22)	7	Montgomery
Alaska	1959 (49)	586,400 (1)	400,481 (50)	1	Juneau
Arizona	1912 (48)	113,909 (6)	2,717,866 (29)	5	Phoenix
Arkansas	1836 (25)	53,104 (27)	2,285,513 (33)	4	Little Rock
California	1850 (31)	158,693 (3)	23,668,562 (1)	45	Sacramento
Colorado	1876 (38)	104,247 (8)	2,888,834 (28)	6	Denver
Connecticut	1788 (5)	5,009 (48)	3,107,576 (25)	6	Hartford
Delaware	1787 (1)	2,057 (49)	595,225 (47)	1	Dover
Florida	1845 (27)	58,560 (22)	9,739,992 (7)	19	Tallahassee
Georgia	1788 (4)	58,876 (21)	5,464,265 (13)	10	Atlanta
Hawaii	1959 (50)	6,424 (47)	965,000 (39)	2	Honolulu
Idaho	1890 (43)	83,557 (13)	943,935 (41)	2	Boise
Illinois	1818 (21)	56,400 (24)	11,418,461 (5)	22	Springfield
Indiana	1816 (19)	36,291 (38)	5,490,179 (12)	10	Indianapolis
Iowa	1846 (29)	56,290 (25)	2,913,387 (27)	6	Des Moines
Kansas	1861 (34)	82,264 (14)	2,363,208 (32)	5	Topeka
Kentucky	1792 (15)	40,395 (37)	3,661,433 (23)	7	Frankfort
Louisiana	1812 (18)	48,523 (31)	4,203,972 (19)	8	Baton Rouge
Maine	1820 (23)	33,215 (39)	1,124,660 (38)	2	Augusta
Maryland	1788 (7)	10,577 (42)	4,216,446 (18)	8	Annapolis
Massachusetts	1788 (6)	8,257 (45)	5,737,037 (11)	11	Boston
Michigan	1837 (26)	58,216 (23)	9,258,344 (8)	18	Lansing
Minnesota	1858 (32)	84,068 (12)	4,077,148 (21)	8	St. Paul
Mississippi	1817 (20)	47,716 (32)	2,520,638 (31)	5	Jackson
Missouri	1821 (24)	69,686 (19)	4,917,444 (15)	9	Jefferson City
Montana	1889 (41)	147,138 (4)	786,690 (44)	2	Helena
Nebraska	1867 (37)	77,227 (15)	1,570,006 (35)	3	Lincoln
Nevada	1864 (36)	110,540 (7)	799,184 (43)	2	Carson City
New Hampshire	1788 (9)	9,304 (44)	920,610 (42)	2	Concord
New Jersey	1787 (3)	7,836 (46)	7,364,158 (9)	14	Trenton
New Mexico	1912 (47)	121,666 (5)	1,299,968 (37)	3	Santa Fe
New York	1788 (11)	49,576 (30)	17,557,288 (2)	34	Albany
North Carolina	1789 (12)	52,719 (28)	5,874,429 (10)	11	Raleigh
North Dakota	1889 (39)	70,665 (17)	652,695 (46)	1	Bismarck
Ohio	1803 (17)	41,222 (35)	10,797,419 (6)	21	Columbus
Oklahoma	1907 (46)	69,919 (18)	3,025,266 (26)	6	Oklahoma City
Oregon	1859 (33)	96,981 (10)	2,632,663 (30)	5	Salem
Pennsylvania	1787 (2)	45,333 (33)	11,866,728 (4)	23	Harrisburg
Rhode Island	1790 (13)	1,214 (50)	947,154 (40)	2	Providence
South Carolina	1788 (8)	31,055 (40)	3,119,208 (24)	6	Columbia
South Dakota	1889 (40)	77,047 (16)	690,178 (45)	1	Pierre
Tennessee	1796 (16)	42,244 (34)	4,590,750 (17)	9	Nashville
Texas	1845 (28)	267,339 (2)	14,228,383 (3)	27	Austin
Utah	1896 (45)	84,916 (11)	1,461,037 (36)	3	Salt Lake City
Vermont	1791 (14)	9,609 (43)	511,456 (48)	1	Montpelier
Virginia	1788 (10)	40,815 (36)	5,346,279 (14)	10	Richmond
Washington	1889 (42)	68,192 (20)	4,130,163 (20)	8	Olympia
West Virginia	1863 (35)	24,181 (41)	1,949,644 (34)	4	Charleston
Wisconsin	1848 (30)	56,154 (26)	4,705,335 (16)	9	Madison
Wyoming	1890 (44)	97,914 (9)	470,816 (49)	1	Cheyenne

*For first 13 states, year of ratification of Constitution

Index

562

Declaratory Act, 116
Deference in colonial society, 69–70
Delany, Martin R., 520–524
Delaware, 34
Democracy, broadening of, 342–344
Democratic party, as party of Jackson, 340. *See also* names of candidates.
Democratic-Republican party, 260, 262
Democratic-Republicans: called Democrats under Jackson, 340; called Republicans under Jefferson, 269; and French Revolution, 259; support Jefferson, 258
Democrats: as name for Democratic-Republicans, 340; in Southern states, 495. *See also* names of candidates.
Depression after 1837, 354
De Soto, Hernando, 9
Dias, Bartholomew, 79
Dickinson, John, 122, 215
Dinwiddie, Robert, 179, 180
Diseases, European, 57
Dix, Dorothea, 413–414, 528
Dominion theory of empire, 124
Douglas, Sarah Mappes, 440
Douglas, Stephen A.: and Compromise of 1850, 448; and election of 1860, 461; and Kansas-Nebraska Act, 451–452; and popular sovereignty, 445; in Senate campaign, 456–457, 510
Douglass, Frederick, 431, 433–434, 440, 441, 516, 518, 521
Draft law during Civil War, 465–466, 467
Dred Scott case, 454–455
Duane, James, 122
Du Bois, William E.B., 421, 422, 502–503

Eaton, Peggy, 398
Education: public, 402, 412–413; for women, 399–402, 413
"Elastic clause," 256
Election: of 1800, 265; of 1824, 338–339; of 1828, 341; of 1840, 354–355, 439; of 1844, 380, 439; of 1848, 445–446; of 1856, 454; of 1860, 461; of 1876, 496. *See also* names of candidates.
Electors, presidential, 219, 265–266, 344
Elizabeth I, Queen of England, 12, 13
Emancipation Proclamation, 474–475
Embargo Act, 278–279

Emerson, Ralph Waldo, 368, 369
Empire, theories of, 123–124
Enclosure movement, 14
England, 7, 12. *See also* Great Britain.
Equality: lacking in English colonies, 68; meaning of, 421–422
Era of Good Feeling, 286
Ericson, Leif, 8
Erie Canal, 323, 327
Evans, Oliver, 361–362
Executive branch, 216–217, 218–219
Explorers, motives of, 7, 26

Factories, workers in, 370–372. *See also* Manufacturing.
Fallen Timbers, battle of, 303, 329
Farming: machinery and, 362–363; in middle colonies, 46–47; in New England colonies, 46; in South in late 1800s, 498–499; in southern colonies, 45–46
Farragut, David G., 472
Federalism, 209, 215–216
Federalist, The, 221
Federalists: achievements of, 266; and Constitution, 219–220, 222; decline of, 269, 286; and French Revolution, 258–259; support Hamilton, 258
Ferdinand, King of Spain, 81, 82
"Fifty-four Forty or Fight," 384
Fillmore, Millard, 448, 452, 454
Finns, 9, 32
Florida: acquired from Spain, 288, 319; becomes state, 332; Seminole Indians in, 330; settlement of, 9; and War Hawks, 281
Foot, Samuel, 345
Force Act, 279
Force Bill, 348
Fort Duquesne, 180, 181
Fort Sumter, 462, 464
Fort Ticonderoga, 129
France: and American Civil War, 470; colonies of, 9; in dispute with U.S. in 1790s, 262, 264; explorers from, 7; in French and Indian War, 111–112, 180; and Louisiana Territory, 272; Revolution of 1789 in, 173, 258; in Revolutionary War, 148–149, 154, 156; seizes American ships, 277, 280
Franklin, Benjamin: biography of, 98–102; on colonists before 1763, 107; at Constitutional Convention, 102, 215; grandson of indentured ser-

vants, 73; on independence, 139; among leaders of American Revolution, 165; on poverty, 54; and slavery, 423; on Stamp Act, 116; on treatment of Indians, 61
Freedmen's Bureau, 488, 524
Freedom, meaning of, 421–422
Freeport Doctrine, 457
Free-Soil Party, 446, 448
Frémont, John C., 386, 388, 454, 486
French and Indian War, 111–112, 180
French Revolution, 173, 258
Frontier. *See* Westward movement.
Fugitive Slave Law, 447, 517–518
Fulton, Robert, 323
Funding program, 254–255
Fur trade, 382, 383

Gabriel's rebellion, 426
Gadsden, Christopher, 122
Gadsden Purchase, 389, 513
Gage, Thomas, 122, 127
Gallatin, Albert, 269
Galloway, Joseph, 122, 123
Garnet, Henry Highland, 441
Garrison, William Lloyd, 437–438, 440, 441
Genêt, Edmond, 260
Geneva Treaty, 528, 529
George III, King of Great Britain, 122, 127, 131, 133, 318
Georgia, settlement of, 34–35
Germans in English colonies, 35, 36
Germantown, battle of, 151
Gerry, Elbridge, 165, 215
Gettysburg, battle of, 475–476
Ghent, Treaty of, 283
Gibbons v. *Ogden*, 300
Gold in California, 446
Goliad, battle of, 380
Goodyear, Charles, 362
Government: belief in limited power of, 207–209, 284, 286, 288–289; in English colonies, 41–44, 108, 109–110; federal system of, 209, 215–216; ideas of, in Declaration of Independence, 133; of states, 161
Governors in English colonies, 42, 43, 44
Grandfather clause, 501, 502
Grant, Ulysses S.: in Civil War, 472, 476–478, 480; as President, 491, 495, 496
Grasse, François de, 154
Great Awakening, 41, 200
Great Britain: and American Civil War, 470; and Confederation government, 212; in

French and Indian War, 111–112, 180; and impressment, 277–278; and Jay's Treaty, 260; and Oregon country, 381, 383, 384; in Revolutionary War, 127–130, 139–140, 147–149, 151–156; seizes American ships, 277–280; in War of 1812, 281–283, 306
Great Compromise, 217–218
Great Lakes: and Erie Canal, 323–324; growth of cities on, 327–328
Greece, 173, 207
Greeley, Horace, 474
Greenbacks, 467–468
Greene, Nathanael, 153
Greenville, Treaty of, 303, 329
Grimké, Angelina, 414, 438, 440, 441
Grimké, Sarah, 414, 438, 441
Guadalupe Hidalgo, Treaty of, 388–389

Habeas corpus, writs of, 161
Haiti, 426, 427
Hakluyt, Richard, 12, 14, 84
Hale, Nathan, 158–159
Hall, Lyman, 165
Hamilton, Alexander: and Constitution, 220, 221; at Constitutional Convention, 215; death of, 274; financial programs of, 254–257; and French Revolution, 259; and manufacturing, 286, 359; policies of, 253–258; and tariffs, 286; and Whiskey Rebellion, 261
Hamilton, Andrew, 53
Hamilton, Henry, 152
Hancock, John, 165
Hancock, Thomas, 72
Harpers Ferry raid, 458
Harrison, William Henry: at battle of Tippecanoe, 281, 306, 329; and elections of 1836 and 1840, 354–355; as governor of Indiana Territory, 303–304, 305; as President, 355
Hart, Emma. See Willard, Emma Hart.
Hartford Convention, 284
Hawthorne, Nathaniel, 406
Hayes, Rutherford B., 496, 497, 499
Hayne, Robert Y., 346
Headright system, 21–22
Helper, Hinton Rowan, 456
Henry, Patrick: biography of, 184–189; and Constitution, 188–189, 220; in First Continental Congress, 122, 187; as governor of Virginia, 188; as Patriot, 187–188; and Stamp

Act, 186–187; and Two Penny Act, 185–186
Henry, Prince of Portugal, 79
Henry VIII, King of England, 23
Herkimer, Nicholas, 148
Hessians, 139, 147
Heth, Joice, 530, 532
Hewes, Joseph, 166
Holland: colony of, 9, 31, 34; in Revolutionary War, 149
Hooker, Thomas, 29
Hooper, William, 166
Hopkins, Stephen, 166
House of Burgesses, 41, 70
House of Representatives, 218
Houston, Sam: biography of, 407–411; and Cherokees, 407, 408, 409; as governor of Tennessee, 408; and independence of Texas, 380, 409–411; and Jackson, 407, 408, 409; as president of Texas, 380, 411; as senator, 411
Howe, Elias, 362
Howe, William, 147, 148, 151, 156
Hudson, Henry, 9, 84, 86
Huguenots, 36
Hull, John, 72
Hungary, 174
Hunters, 319
Hutchinson, Anne, 27, 91
Hutchinson, Thomas, 114, 121

Immigrants: in 1700s, 35–36; in 1800s, 366–367
Impressment, 277–278
Incas, 9
Income tax, 467
Indentured servants: contracts of, 22, 33, 73; in English colonies, 65–66; in middle colonies, 32, 46–47; on plantations, 45
Indian Territory, 329–330
Indians, American: Columbus and, 5; as discoverers of America, 8; in English colonies, 57–61; in Florida, 330; in French and Indian War, 111; in North America, 57; in Northwest Territory, 280–281, 302–306, 329; in Portuguese colonies, 57; prejudice toward, 61; removed to Indian Territory, 329–330; in Revolutionary War, 139, 152; as slaves, 57, 59; in Spanish colonies, 57; in War of 1812, 281, 310; west of Appalachians, 280–281, 329
Indigo, 35, 45, 94–96
Industrial Revolution, 359–360
Industrialism, working conditions under, 370–374
Industry: in English colonies,

48–49; growth of, 359–367. *See also* Manufacturing; names of industries.
Inevitability theory of history, 110
Insane, care for, 413–414
Interchangeable parts, 363
Internal improvements, 287, 336, 339, 347
International Red Cross, 528–529
Intolerable Acts, 122
Inventions, manufacturing and, 361–362
Iowa, 331
Iron industry, 366
Irving, Washington, 405–406
Isabella, Queen of Spain, 80–82

Jackson, Andrew: at battle of New Orleans, 282; elected President, 332, 341; and election of 1824, 338–339; and Florida, 288; and Indians, 329, 331; and internal improvements, 347; and nullification, 347–348; as President, 342–345, 352; reelected President, 353; and Second Bank of U.S., 352–353; and Specie Circular, 353–354
Jackson, "Stonewall," 471, 472
James I, King of England, 15, 23
Jamestown colony, 19–23, 85–86
Jay, John, 220, 221, 260, 299
Jay's Treaty, 260, 262
Jefferson, Martha, 196, 199
Jefferson, Thomas: biography of, 195–199; death of, 288; and Declaration of Independence, 133, 139, 196–197; and Democratic-Republican party, 260, 262; elected President, 265; elected Vice President, 262; and Embargo Act, 278–279; and French Revolution, 259; on government, 207; as governor of Virginia, 188, 198; and Kentucky and Virginia Resolutions, 265; among leaders of American Revolution, 167; and Louisiana Purchase, 271–273; policies of, 253–258; as President, 269–279, 287; reelected President, 277; and scientific farming, 198; in Second Continental Congress, 196; on slavery, 198, 422, 423, 426; in Virginia legislature, 196, 197–198
Jews in Rhode Island, 92
Jim Crow laws, 500
John II, King of Portugal, 80
Johnson, Andrew: and congres-

566

2 3 4 5 6 7 8 9 10 · VH · 89 88 87 86 85 84 83